Paul winced. Months ago, he made a commitment to trust the Lord alone. Out of desperation, he had reneged on his commitment. Where did it get him? To a night of despair and humiliation! In a few minutes, he will be humiliated before his parents, his dear friends, and acquaintances. What worst fate could befall a man?

THE VAN CLYDENS'

FAMILY FORTUNE

SECOND EDITION

I J E Okello

Begin With a Word, LLC. Grand Prairie   2025

Scripture taken from the New King James Version ®. Copyright © 1982 by Thomas Nelson. Used by permission. All rights reserved.

This book is a work of fiction. In order to give a sense of the times, some real places, events and people appear in the book, but the characters and events depicted in this book are imaginary and all the names and events are the product of the author's imagination, or are used fictitiously.

The Van Clydens' Family Fortune – 2nd edition.
Begin With a Word, LLC
Grand Prairie, Texas 75054

Copyright © 2022, 2025, I J E Okello

All rights reserved. No part of this book may be reproduced or used in any form or by any means whatsoever, printed, electronic or mechanical, including photo-copying, recording or by any information storage and retrieval system, without the written permission of the Author. Inquiries should be sent to Begin With a Word, LLC, P. O. Box 540457, Grand Prairie, TX 75054–0457.

Library of Congress Cataloging-in-Publication Data

ISBN 979-8-9856167-4-3

Printed in the United States of America

Cover image: TJBavosi/Getty Images

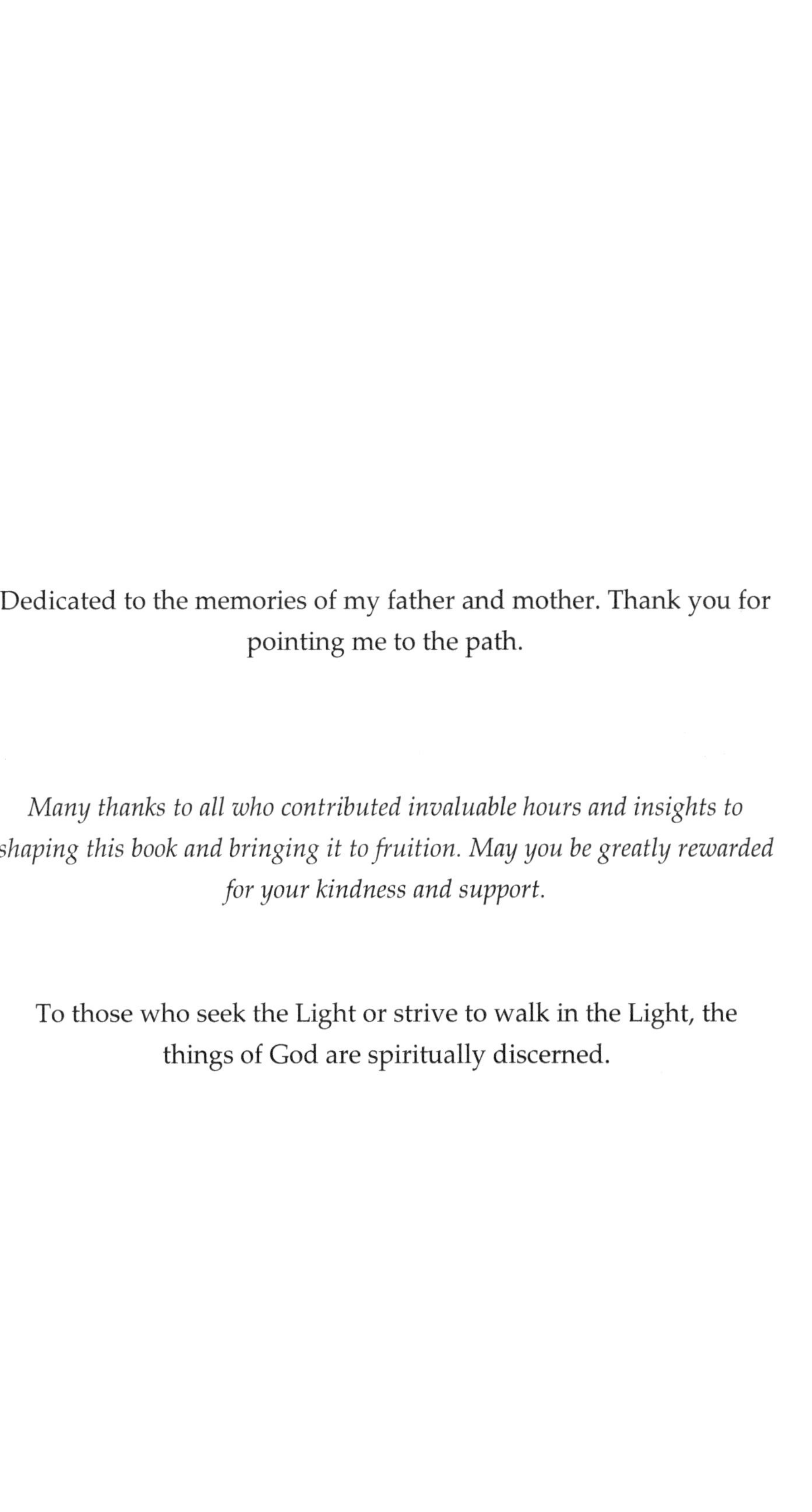

Dedicated to the memories of my father and mother. Thank you for pointing me to the path.

Many thanks to all who contributed invaluable hours and insights to shaping this book and bringing it to fruition. May you be greatly rewarded for your kindness and support.

To those who seek the Light or strive to walk in the Light, the things of God are spiritually discerned.

AUTHOR'S NOTE

The Van Clydens' Family Fortune is a novel set in Southern California in the 1990s. The book which was completed in 1999, paints a picture of the period during the last decade, through the eyes of a fictitiously closely-knit community of Southern California through their struggles and triumphs, as the world approaches the New Millennium.

THE VAN CLYDENS' FAMILY FORTUNE
PART I

1

In the distant hills, a lone coyote howled like a lone wolf; not a single nightingale to dispel his forlorn cry. Paul leaned over the balcony——a solitary lion, lost in a world of his own, but the incessant ringing of his mobile phone persisted, disrupting his thoughts.

He dashed back to his bedroom, grabbed the phone, and listened for a while, impassive, then he said, "You're kidding!"

"Nopes," Stanislaus replied.

"It's over?"

"Same condo; separate rooms."

"Really?"

"Mhmm. Yup. Stanislaus and Karen are no more."

"No going back?" Paul asked.

"Don't think so, barring a miracle," Stanislaus replied.

"You were perfect!"

"In the Yearbook. Take it from me Paul, only one Lamb was sacrificed over nineteen hundred years ago. I'm not that Lamb. I gotta go."

Paul returned to the balcony. The city lights winked at him in mocked succession——hope competing with the darkness that threatened to shroud it. He resisted the temptation to throw a rock at something. Few made it to his short list of people whom he admired. Stanislaus was one of them.

He returned to his bedroom again, shoved on his jogging suit and ran around the block at six minutes a mile, a lone jogger along the fluorescent lit streets of manicured, choreographed neighborhood, that tempted citizens to sleep with their doors unlocked and their keys in the ignition.

2

"I object," a voice yelled.

Paul jumped out of bed straight to the bathroom to brush his teeth. Not one for bad dreams, this one counted as one. He finished his morning routine and dressed for the outdoors.

Downstairs, his cousin Jonathan was seated at the piano with his headset on, music scores strewn all over the floor.

He wished him a good morning and asked, "Have we ever had a Japanese in the family?"

Jonathan blinked several times, thought for a moment, and shook his head. "No. Not to the best of my knowledge."

"Not ever!" he muttered. "Not even business partners?"

Jonathan replied, "Probably. Your dad would know."

"Knowing the Van Clydens, probably not; but then again, business is business." He eyed the scores. "Let me guess——you burned the midnight candle?"

"Sure did." Jonathan rubbed his eyes.

"When is it due?"

"Yesterday."

"Oh!"

He went to the garage, rubbing his chin, looking every inch his father's son, mulling over a major puzzle.

The ship of his life had left harbor, sailing to the deep seas, taking him along like a trapped deer thrashing around, looking for a way to escape.

♦ ♦ ♦

Paul kicked another stone, and trudged up the woodsy hill. His dark-blond hair crowned his brow in disheveled array. Strands blew in the wind, following the early morning breeze, seeking flight to the distant lands.

Miles away, the summer smog gathered. Without the breeze, the clear valley would soon be shrouded. He trudged on, ignoring the looming smog. Firm footprints of hiking boots trailed his progress up the hill in assured steps of a seasoned mountaineer searching for home, unsure.

He would sooner rake his brains deciphering a financial report, than spend a day in the hills sorting out his life.

On a clear day, the undulating hills of the San Gabriel and San Bernardino Mountains cradled the valley to the east, providing a layered tapestry of peaceful green and bluish gray background to the cities lined in array from north to south to west; and the sprawling foothills that annexed the northeast, merged into flawless harmony; but not today. The blurred mountains, and almost muddy air, did not provide much of an inspiration for meditation and clarity of thought for this weary searcher.

Despite a slight breeze, he felt hot. Saturday promised to be another drawn-out day with unanswered questions burning in his heart, seeking freedom to be released, discussed, formulated into a living, breathing soul.

Getting married to a commendable girl was number three on his five-year plan. How could his heart betray him at such a critical time in his life?

Not since his first traffic ticket had he prayed so hard that his problem would amount to nothing but a dream that would melt away without his parents finding out. His parents' status, his father's ambition for global expansion, and the impact of a careless decision on that vision, weighed on him. On the other hand, if this was nothing but a dream, he did not want it to end.

He raised his head; he had reached the apex of the hill. On an adjacent hill, a rider trudged along a horse trail with his dog trotting along.

Below, the demarcated blocks of cities laid in deceptive harmony. Despite their appearance of peace and calm, he knew that in some of them, there had to be at least one person whose heart was as heavy as his own. Had he a sibling, he would throw all caution to the wind.

With one last sweep of the valley, he roared at the top of his lungs, "I'm a sensible, intelligent, spirit-filled man. I'm not supposed to walk in the flesh. Urrrrrrrgh!" and fled the hills.

Back home, Jonathan was in the living room, pushing the wall with both hands, warming-up for his morning jog, his legs stretched to their utmost. Now clad in gym clothes, Paul went around him, selected orange juice from the fridge and filled a glass halfway.

"Well?" Jonathan raised his eyebrows.

"Well, what?" he replied.

"Did you call them?"

"Are you done with your orchestration? The last one did quite well in the charts."

"You're avoiding them."

"You should try writing a full symphony. I think you're ready."

Jonathan nodded. "Whatever it is, Paul, you know, sooner or later, you have to seek their counsel. Uncle Igor and Aunt Charlotte are very astute."

"I know." He emptied his glass, grabbed his gym bag, and said over his shoulders as he was walking out, "By the way, Stanislaus called last night."

"And?"

"Keep him and Karen in your prayers."

Soon after, he pulled out of the driveway, wheels screaming.

◆ ◆ ◆

A cacophony of noise between spoken words, booming drums and clanging cymbals, rattled the windows. Lily thumped a pillow over her head, muttering, "Lord help Lamar get his life together. He has brains. He should know better than to squander his life away!"

The noise persisted. Fed up, she stuck her legs out of bed——a whole forty-two-inches of them that complimented her five-foot-nine inches body. Given a choice, she would much rather be snoozing in some quiet condo, surrounded by singing crickets and swaying pine trees, than be trying to sleep through the noise below. She tightened her cream lace gown around her, bowed her head on her knees, then she finished her morning routine.

After a quick breakfast of toast and marmalade, she changed into modest exercise shorts and a t-shirt, and grabbed her water bottles.

When she hopped down the last step of her small apartment, hot air from the tarmac rose to hug her as a long-lost favorite relative would.

Saturday promised to be another hot, muggy day. Should she cover ten or twelve miles? Ten? With her head held high, hands gripping the water bottles, she marched on, a woman hurrying to meet her destiny.

After she had covered about one and half miles out of her neighborhood, heading towards the more middle-class red-roofs, a black Porsche zoomed past her. The driver slammed on the breaks and stopped.

Determined not to slow down, she moved farther into the grassy area of the sidewalk, and continued marching forward; but the driver reversed to her side and stuck his head out.

She found herself staring into Paul's piercing blue eyes and feeling as though she was swimming in the Aegean Sea.

Paul drawled, "Well, well, well! Look who we've got here!"

"Good morning. What a surprise meeting you here!" she said, hoping to ooze calm; but squawked like a duck instead.

He wished her the same and asked, "Why is it surprising?"

"Well, I don't normally run into you, I mean, what are you doing in our neck of the woods?" She sounded more gauche than ever.

"Can't a nice guy go for a drive in a nice neighborhood and run into a nice girl taking a nice walk, one nice, breezy, Saturday morning?"

"Five nices in one sentence, Mr. Van Clyden. Flattery! Flattery! Flattery! Beware of a man who enchants with five nices in one sentence!"

He gave her a heart-wrenching smile and sped away.

She elongated her swings and marched forward. "Paul Truen Van Clyden! Blue eyes, not my type. Moreover, his cup runneth over with plenty of dates, thank you! Though he does have some qualities, I concede."

Resisting the urge to sit on the grassy curb, she bent over, her knees wobbly, then with another surge of spirit, she moved forward toward the Park Reserve. But half a mile later, she faltered, bent down, and peered at the remaining distance.

Her golden dark skin glistened with muggy sweat from the summer heat of the valley.

♦ ♦ ♦

Still shaking from his encounter with Lily, and kicking himself for driving out of his way, Paul looped his way back to the freeway.

Why had he been frequenting Lily's neighborhood? What good would it do? As understanding as his parents were, he could just imagine their reaction to him frequenting such a neighborhood, not to think of his friends.

He pushed the gas pedal to the floor and the engine moaned and groaned through Hollenvine Hills back to the 10 Freeway. Was his encounter with Lily wistful thinking or providence? Could it be providence? Hadn't Abraham's servant met Rebekah as he was standing at a village well in Aram-naharaim on a mission for Isaac?

He had seen Lily exercising around Be Still Lake in the past six months; yet, he had not expected her to be heading there that time of the morning. Not exactly. Of course, he had prayed he would run into her.

He maneuvered his car, darting from lane to lane onto the 57, then the 60 Freeways and came within a few feet of a Land Rover perched on gigantic wheels, moving at fifty-miles per hour, slammed on the breaks and slowed down. The Lord had humorous ways of catching his attention.

Soon, he exited on the Brea Canyon off-rump, his knuckles white from gripping the steering wheel. A few turns more, brought him to Country Club Terrace Drive. He stopped in front of a condo nestled in the wooded corner of a deluxe complex, slammed the car door, and strode into the living room.

Jonathan was back from jogging, having a late breakfast.

Normally, he would grab a muffin or a banana, and thank Jonathan half-way upstairs. Instead, he bolted for his suite.

"There's plenty. The Lord's generous. Go ahead, help yourself," Jonathan yelled after him.

He took a quick shower, changed into a clean T-shirt and blue jeans, and returned downstairs, his hair still damp.

Jonathan had left him the remnant of orange juice. He filled his glass halfway, one ice cube at a time, then he topped it with the juice.

Jonathan watched him from the dinette.

The phone rang. He planted his backside on his favorite couch, crossed his legs, and drank slowly from the glass, in silent mutiny.

Jonathan took the hint and picked up the living room line.

"Hello. This is Jonathan. Can I help you?"

"I was hoping you'd pick up the phone," Sharon said.

"Great! Are we still on for this afternoon?"

"Yes. Is two o'clock ok? I'm running late."

Jonathan glanced at Paul. "Sure. I'm having a late start too."

"See you then."

Jonathan hang up, a silly, smitten look on his face.

That did it. Paul splashed his glass of orange juice on the counter and strode to the garage.

Soon the sound of "Thump, thump, thump," filled the room.

He heard Jonathan enter and from the corners of his eyes, saw him standing——his hands stuffed in his faded jeans' pockets——watching him.

"Paul?" Jonathan finally asked.

He hit the dummy a few more times, stopped and said, "Yeah."

Jonathan appeared to be praying silently.

"What's up?" Jonathan asked again.

He resumed hitting the dummy, taciturn.

Jonathan shifted his eyes. "Last time you punched a dummy was two years ago, when BF&S promoted that impostor amidst protests. Everybody knew he'd fudged on his résumé and CV."

He shook his head.

"Latest?"

He stopped, and wiped his brow with a towel from the rack.

"Didn't work out?"

He glanced at him and shook his head again.

Jonathan blushed. "You didn't. . ."

He raised his eyebrows in wounded protest.

"Phew. Then what? Playing hard?" Jonathan persisted.

This time, he moved his lips in a silent, "No."

He saw in Jonathan's eyes the unspoken remark he often used to tease him when he complained about how hard it was to get decent dates, "As virtuous as you are, Paul, no girl has ever resisted dating you, never mind you insist on going platonic!"

"Is she – – married?" Jonathan asked.

Again, he raised his eyebrows, crossed his arms in front of his chest and mumbled, somewhat bemused, "You really have a lot of confidence in my ability to make sound judgment, don't you?"

Jonathan threw up his hands. "She's not a believer. Uh? Witness to her! You're a mess."

"Sorry to disappoint you," he replied in a stronger voice, then in a softer voice, as though he was in a dream, he added, "Is a rose less sweet just because its blooms are dark, brown-red?"

Jonathan started at his Shakespearean tone, camouflaged his shock and said, "No!" then, "Why not? This is California. The twenty-first century's around the corner."

He stared at Jonathan, hoping for assurance that all would be well.

Jonathan scratched his head. "How can something that's so predictable, be so unpredictable?"

"Exactly! With a five-year plan of my spiritual, corporate, and personal vision filed away, I never saw this one coming."

Jonathan blew his cheeks and sat on the bench. For the first time he noticed dark circles under Paul's eyes, meaning Paul had not slept in days. He also noticed a fresh pimple, a sign that Paul was under extreme stress. With all the modern skin care products, the pimple would disappear soon enough, but the condition of Paul's soul worried him.

The two cousins stared at each other. In Paul's eyes Jonathan saw the answer. Even if this was the seventeenth century, Paul was not the kind of man whose moral rectitude would permit him to visit the servants' quarters, even if he was their master. He was too virtuous to take advantage of a girl and compromise his principles for a moment of selfish pleasure, not to consider the fact that the woman——whoever she was——may also be virtuous.

"Real virtuous men must treat all women with respect without a double standard, or lose their reputation," Paul once drilled into him, when he had been tempted to embrace fire in his bosom.

Realizing the intricacy of the problem, he walked over to Paul, patted his shoulder, and said, "Cheer up! It'll work out. Let's pray about it," knowing he was clueless as to how to help him.

He realized he had never had to deal seriously with the subject. All his previous pastors and mentors had also skirted the issue or glazed over it. Whether they taught with integrity or not, he would soon find out.

Paul thanked him and went upstairs again.

He called Sharon, and postponed their date to early evening, with a request for her to pray, in confidence, for Paul.

Paul leaned against his balcony, facing Hollenvine City, wondering what time Lily got home and how far she had walked. He envied her confidence, striding along the road, swinging her arms, her head held high.

True, he too was free, but that freedom also held him captive to himself and to societal expectations. He was free to fall in love with the woman who met his Proverbs 31 dream, but the fortress of his skin constrained him from pursuing his heart, regardless of how much his intentions remained grounded on honoring the LORD alone with all his life's choices.

◆ ◆ ◆

Perspiration drenched Lily's body as rain-drops drip off a leaf on a wet forlorn April day. Her clammy shorts grabbed her legs with every stride. Finally, she made it to her apartment, dumped her water bottles on the kitchen counter with a thud, and dashed to her bedroom.

She tossed her shoes into the closet, as though they were the problem, but when the phone rang, she grabbed it at the first ring and said, "Hello," in a warm voice that camouflaged her inner tumult.

"Morning, did I wake you up?" Laurel Morningsun asked, hopeful.

"No. You did not. I was out walking. How can I help you?"

"We need someone to help with the fourth graders tomorrow. The Berrys are quarantined. Little Coby has the measles."

"He does not."

"Measles in the mid-nineteen nineties? Yes. They do happen."

"I hope they caught them in good time?"

"By grace they sure did, or we'd all be in a pickle."

"Poor Coby! I will pray that he gets well soon."

Laurel thanked her.

"I would love to help. What's the theme?"

"Well, you have a choice. We're finishing up on God's beauty as displayed in nature. You could also start on the Shepherd and the Sheep——our theme for next semester. We've some nifty crafts to go with each theme. You know . . . beautiful sunshine and flowers, or little sheep and shepherd pictures, and a story guideline to help you. I'll leave the guidebook on the table in the Sunday school room. Perhaps you could come a bit early and review it? Sorry for the short notice."

Trying to retain highly paid workers without giving them frequent pay raises was challenging enough, but motivating a team of volunteers? Laurel's plate must be full. She promised Laurel she would come early.

She took a shower to freshen up. The warm water relaxed her taut muscles; but without a cool breeze, she broke out in sweat almost immediately, despite a ceiling fan. An old fan a friend had given her for her first Christmas in America came in handy.

A white pair of summer shorts and a yellow blouse of Indian muslin that she wore only indoors, caught her eye. She threw them on.

Restless, she took her diary, a Bible and a concordance to the living room and fetched a cold glass of pure guava juice from the kitchen. She had less than twenty-four hours to get a grip of herself.

After devotion, she reviewed her accounting books and financial journals, then she called two of her mentors and chatted with them about her frustrations, trying to finish her program, while bogged down with work. They encouraged her to prioritize her goals and return on course as soon as possible, or confide in her boss and let him know the challenges she was facing.

In her drawer was a sealed envelope, containing a prayer, with specifications of her perfect man——he must be at least six foot tall, with strong milk-white teeth, a full head of hair, and deep, dark-brown, dove-like eyes——from East Africa, of course. He must also be a teetotaler and a non-smoker, a college graduate, with good manners and one who would blend well with her family. And oh, must pray at least one hour a day. Absolutely no blonds!

3

The patio noise grew louder as the noise of a rushing waterfall would. Paul searched the sea of faces sipping coffee and eating donuts and pastries. Children darted in and out, their heads bobbed with colorful ribbons flying in the wind and shirttails trailing, announcing Sunday school was over.

"Children. Children! Walk, don't run!" a female voice called from the middle of the crowd. Donna, Pastor Tim's wife, bent over to tie somebody's shoelaces.

Finally, Paul spotted Lily. He veiled his eyes, ambled closer to continue observing her, while shielded by a group deep in conversation.

Lily stood perched on the highest step of the church hall, surveying the crowd. She perked up and cut through the crowd to Sharon. "Morning. How was Sunday school?"

"Morning. We missed you. I've the outline for the class."

"I was helping out with the fourth graders."

"Ooh! That's why I felt compelled to pray for you this morning!" Sharon teased. "How's Marc?"

"Very marcish!" She smiled.

Sharon cracked up, then said, "I hear the Berrys have the measles."

"Yes. I was subbing for them."

"Too bad. We'll pray for a quick recovery. Here, let's go grab some pastries. I espied them the moment I got to the patio."

"Naughty! Naughty! Naughty!" She waved her finger at Sharon.

"Shhhh!" Sharon bee-lined for the refreshment tables.

Paul rubbed his nose to hide a smile and skirted the crowd, his eyes riveted on Lily's movement, studying her, appraising her.

She got half a plain donut and a cup of tea. Sharon got a cream-filled pastry and a cup of coffee, then the two of them disappeared into the crowd.

She reappeared again, on the lookout for wallflowers. Every time she saw someone hanging back——old friends or visitors——her eyes would light up, she would go over, chat for a little while, and move on.

Lily gravitated toward the Jonesons, even as he spotted Matt, Jr at the outskirts, chatting with a group of teenage girls, among them, a Calderon.

Marjorie glanced at the group frequently. Did she look a bit anxious?

Lily gave three-year old Melanie a hug, then she turned to talk to a couple who appeared to be in their seventies or early eighties.

He joined the group next to them, turned at an angle and feigned interest in the group's conversation; but his ears remained cocked to the conversation next to him. Occasionally, he stole a glance at Lily's group.

The man introduced himself and his wife.

"You don't look familiar. Is this your first time at ENC?" Lily asked, after welcoming them.

"Yes," Mr. McGaelic replied. "We just moved here from Toledo."

"Toledo?" She sounded mystified.

"Ohio."

"Of course!"

"We lived forty miles from Toledo, but moved here to be near our grandchildren. Quite a remarkable church. What's the seating?"

"We can seat at least seven hundred, comfortably."

Again Mr. McGaelic spoke for his wife, "Seven hundred is a good size. Ours was only about one hundred." They studied the crowd. "So many young people! Your nursery seems to be bursting at the seams."

"We're doing all right. The Lord has been gracious."

"It seems over eighty percent is young. Look at you. You couldn't be a day above twenty-one. We've been standing here, hoping we don't step on any of the young-uns. Every time we turn around, there's a little one playing peek-a-boo."

"Emmett's a retired accountant. Ran his own business! Paid for all our four children's colleges too!" Mrs. McGaelic glowed.

"How wonderful! I'm an accountant too. I would say about twenty percent are over fifty-five, and thirty percent are between thirty-five and fifty-five. The rest are below thirty-five. So you see, it is a good mix," Lily seemed elated to be talking to another accountant. "It is a growing church, as Pastor Tim says, but with a good demographic ratio. I hope you can make this your home-church? We would love to have you come back."

"My wife and I thank you. A church of accountants is a good church," Mr. McGaelic joked. "Just kidding! It's what's on the inside that counts."

In one sentence, the McGaelics became part of the family. Paul's chest swelled at how Lily had handled herself. What's the quality of a CEO's wife?

"We love this church——a real beacon on a hill. Its lighted steeple stands out, a contrast to the dark night. My children love the avant-garde building with its modern architecture that rivals any city's," Mrs. McGaelic added proudly as though this was part of her family's inheritance.

Lily stared at the unusual roof design and angular glass windows. "Yes. It is lovely. Isn't it? Have you been inside?"

"No. Today will be our first. We drove by a couple of times. We hear it's beautiful, with all sorts of modern paraphernalia."

"Yes. It is. It has a state-of-the-art sound system for a full orchestra and choir, and power-point teaching and video specials." Lily surveyed the church steeple. "But, the pastors are informal——more concerned with inner transformation as Mr. McGaelic just said, than the outside. We're strong on the Word, but informal on appearance. I think you will like it."

"I think we shall. And you can call me Emmett," Mr. McGaelic said.

"And I am Abigail." Mrs. McGaelic also introduced her son's family who had arrived, "Lily, this is my son, Emmett Jr. and his wife. . .."

Soon after, Lily withdrew, tactfully.

In one corner, Lily spotted Jonathan and Sharon and two other girls. One in particular made her take a deep breath and walk taller. Sharon kept her warm, brown eyes on Jonathan's face, with a radiant smile. Only one phrase summed her up, 'Genuine, truly genuine.'

Kelly, the first girl, was apparently an old friend——talked a lot about, "When Jonathan and Paul and I were little." Jonathan and Sharon's circle of friends was expanding at the speed of the increasing competition for Paul. Paul seemed oblivious. But surely, how could he not know the magnetic power he had, as he looked in the mirror each morning?

Lily spotted Paul edging in her direction. He stopped to talk to a middle-aged couple, but from the top of their heads, his eyes locked with hers before he shifted his position to give the couple his full attention.

Feeling confused, she bolted for the sanctuary. Halfway down the aisle, she sank down on a seat closer to the wall, grateful for its soft, red cushions. She kept her head lowered, yet wished she could shift her position, but she could not brave locking eyes with Paul again.

However, she sensed Paul enter the sanctuary and his eyes rest on her for a moment, then he sat in the pew across from her. When she believed it was safe, she peeked at him. He was sitting erect, staring at the cross.

Sharon and Kelly soon joined him. He appeared not to mind Kelly's possessive clinging.

Jonathan entered. Again, Lily noticed him looking at her, then he sat next to Sharon. En masse, the group faced the front, where the pastoral team was already seated.

In the background, the pianist played a medley of "Holy Ground" combining lyrics written by Christopher Beatty and Geron Davis, yet the chorus blended so well. His curls bobbed with the rhythm of the music.

In the midst of the modern architecture, with its warm, discreet carpet tapestry and rows of interlocked red pews sloping to the podium, its high white ceiling, and an altar crowned with glass-stained windows——rays of light, echoes of heavenly design——amidst this display of splendor, with a backdrop of an empty cross, the congregation sat ready for the morning service to begin.

Now, as though sensing the unfolding drama, the pianist and the orchestra struck the chords for the call to worship and the drama of two worlds begun——two worlds coexisting at the feet of one cross. Two worlds based on two doctrines——the doctrine of those who repented as a prerequisite to forgiveness, and the doctrine of those who believed they were entitled to forgiveness without repentance.

It was a world of those who had humbled themselves and fallen on the Rock and a world of those on whom the Rock would fall.

4

At a corner office, Paul surveyed the city, distracted. He had been standing there for minutes on end, when the noise of secretaries across the hall, whacking away at their typewriters, unaware, penetrated his thoughts.

"I can't wait for them to install the new computers. As soon as our budget's approved, I'm gonna march in there and tell my boss this dinosaur has got to go! I demand a new computer," a secretary snapped.

"I dare you to!" another secretary replied.

"I will too!" the first secretary retorted.

Voices murmured, ribbing her.

Paul coughed softly, then he returned to his seat, and surfed Internet sites to compare computer prices. From the top shelf, he pulled out a navy–blue file; turned to the 1994 Fiscal Year and added five thousand dollars next to the line account item titled 'Computer Equipment'. In brackets he wrote, 'new computer terminals,' and replaced the file on the shelf.

But instead of working, he sat in silence, the only sound, a soft thud-thud of a pen, as it hit the top of his leather desk. Finally, he took a Manila envelope and reviewed the financial reports again. A thought that had nagged him for months, persisted, as he lynxed numbers from one particular department. He re-calculated the numbers and dialed a number.

"Give me five to ten minutes," a voice said.

He checked another report. Ten minutes later, he left, clutching a file, stopped at a door marked, 'Bill Daelvin, Director of Finance,' and entered.

A man with a hint of thinning hair toward the top, was sitting at the desk, his tie askew, frowning over a report. He raised his eyes and said, "Have a seat," then continued frowning at the report.

He closed the door, took a seat, and waited.

Bill threw the report across the desk, and said, "Don't ask me."

"I won't." He grinned.

"What's up?" Bill combed his hair and smoothed it back.

He pushed the file he had brought across the desk to him.

Bill flipped through the reports, then said, "And . . .?"

"And nothing," he replied.

"But . . .?"

"But may be."

"The night's still young. No smoke without fire."

He nodded and got up.

"How are things?" Bill asked.

He gave Bill a crooked smile and said, "Off limits. BF&S' policy."

With back slapping, Bill said, "Sheila and I think it's time, you know. . ."

"Tell me about it. Mum and Dad are hinting louder."

"Your problem Paul's not having too few choices, but too many."

"Thanks for the encouraging words."

"Hey! No problem! What're friends for? Don't forget, Sheila and I, are praying for you." Bill opened the door.

He thanked him and left.

A junior executive with Briden, Farrel and Seymour Financial Firm, or BF&S as they called the firm, Paul had used his 2-2-2-5 formula, to stay on target. The last summer before his senior year, he had interned with BF&S, positioning him for a permanent job with them after graduating with a degree in finance. Two years of saving for graduate school and two years of part-time grad school, had armed him with his MBA, that had positioned him to vie for the only financial management vacancy that had opened up and placed him on track two years later, at twenty-six years old, to becoming an heir-apparent for a vice presidency and more.

Somehow, his 2-2-2-5 formula had omitted a woman like Lily. Marriage, yes . . . but more like California or down south or even Europe.

He returned to his office pondering Bill's comment only briefly, then his thoughts took a different tangent. If Bill could read his mind now, what would he say? He massaged his brow.

5

Lily arrived at Denton & Terrell Accounting Firm with five minutes to spare for her morning cup of tea. She joined the seven o'clock staff standing around chatting, drinking their morning coffee, then she searched for a file from her shelf. She remembered discussing it with her boss, Zebediah Chancey. Sure enough, he had it. He informed her that he had touched base with his boss and there were a few other items they needed to iron-out on the file. Could she return in about ten to fifteen minutes?

Back at her desk, a familiar tap–tap–tap approached. Bernice entered, chewing gum, her red hair permed and cajoled to curly submission, her shoes glittered from polishing, and a pair of blinking rhinestone clips. She threw her arms out and announced, "Tadah! I'm here! Good morning. So how was our weekend? I called your apartment about eleven o'clockish on Saturday; you didn't pick up your phone. So, what did we do Friday even-ning? Huh?"

She grabbed a duster from her desk drawer and started dusting. "It was rather hot on Saturday. How was it in San Fernando Valley?"

Bernice gave her 'the look.' "Now, now, now, don't change the subject. And aren't we dusting rather hard? I thought you dusted Friday? I know the crews weren't here over the weekend. They would've told us to cover our stuff. Let's go back to Friday and work our way s-t-e-p by s-t-e-p to Mon-n-d-a-y m-o-r-n-i-n-g!"

She dug deeper. "Really nothing much. I just went for a walk Saturday morning, as usual, then church on Sunday."

Bernice popped a bubble in the air. "Mhmm. I see we're nervous about our, 'went for a walk Saturday morning.' I called, thinking you were back. So, how was your walk?"

She continued working her desk.

"Come on, you can tell me," Bernice coaxed.

"I would not change a thing. How was your weekend?"

Bernice swayed back and forth, with a discerning smile. "I can see we're not going to talk about the weekend. Okay, you win, for now. Guess what?"

"What?" She tried to mimic Bernice's exuberance.

"I went shopping and bought this gorgeous green dress . . . perfect for an evening."

"Bernice, that's wonderful! I hope you will get your wish soon."

"I'm hoping for more."

"Wouldn't that be nice?" she croaked. The last topic she wished to discuss with anybody, including her best friend, was their imminent engagement.

She sent a silent SOS prayer, asking for a diversion, as she always did in emergencies, expecting to get a quick response.

Right on cue, Brad, the office gascon, stuck his head in her cubicle. "There you are, Lily! I'd been wondering if you'd come in yet."

"Brad! How was your week-end?" She displayed more enthusiasm than she would wish, talking to Brad. He was not her type; but, as a colleague, she remained cordial with him.

"Great! Um, did you check on that question I asked you Friday?"

"Yes. I did, but I have a meeting. I will come over as soon as I can."

Ever the arbiter of fashion, Brad swaggered off, towering over the cubicles, his shoulder-length curls bobbing in rhythm to his springy steps. Occasionally, he snapped his red suspenders, making his presence known. Despite Denton & Terrell's dress code, which all employees endeavored to observe, nobody said a word about his hair or manner. Lily marveled that the firm could get away with a double standard while still expecting the rest of its employees to respect the company's code of conduct.

With his cat-like green eyes, Brad's genes dictated his place. Denton & Terrell knew it, so did the world. He had the languid insouciance of a man born with a silver spoon in his mouth. He took long breaks between chatting with whoever accommodated him. Instead of losing his job, or getting demoted, the company had promoted him twice in the short time that she had known him. Some eyebrows had hit the ceiling. Other employees had left the company in protest. She had suffered through it with grace.

Right now, Brad was her knight-in-suspenders.

Bernice watched his progress, her arms akimbo, popped another bubble. "Brad Benz Bentley! What do you know! Insufferable! Supercilious! Hubristic! Blankie-blank!" she mumbled, calling Brad by the nickname his colleagues had given him. "I can't stand some people."

She shushed her.

"Well, they spend as much time wandering the corridors of Denton & Terrell as they spend at their desk. If it wasn't for connections, I bet you some people would be out in the streets, begging."

"Bernice, be nice. He isn't that bad. A bit spoiled may be."

"If you say so. Well, I'd better be going. Talk to you later." Bernice shuffled out, but not before tossing over her shoulders, "Remember, we never did finish our discussion about 'The Weekend!'"

She laughed a clear, infectious laugh that made others smile and shooed Bernice off, "Get back to work."

Some people found Bernice's direct manner disconcerting; but she liked her and knew underneath Bernice's hard façade, she had a kind heart.

A familiar face flashed through her mind. She took a deep breath, and exhaled slowly. Her lips moved, but no sound came out, as she prayed.

With a thud, she remembered midweek activities at church. Should she quit, though the fellowship was for her spiritual good?

She snapped to——she had been sitting at her desk shuffling paper. Also, Brad was still waiting, but first, her meeting with Zebediah Chancey.

"Please help, Lord, before this thing devours me," she mouthed.

The phone rang. It was Mr. Chancey.

She grabbed her files and walked through the maze of cubicles, mulling over Paul's behavior over the weekend. The difference between Paul and Brad was that the former was a principled gentleman; while the latter drove parents, who raised their daughters well, to their knees——from what she had gathered through the grapevine, so far.

6

Paul brushed his teeth wondering whether Lily was up yet. What would it feel like phoning her each morning, acting as her alarm clock, a chore he would compete for with pleasure?

She took the 57 Freeway in the morning as he did; they could race each other to work . . . or rather, drive side by side to work, observing the speed limit. He smiled, remembering his close calls with traffic tickets while he was a teenager, and a few that not even his Dad's influence could stop; on the other hand, he would have probably landed more, without Dad's influence.

So engrossed was he in daydreaming about how he and Lily could have lunch together or go to shows, that he cut himself. Sheepish, he bandaged his face, praying no one, especially, Bill, would ask for an explanation.

He knelt down to pray, his mind in a jumble, but of one thing he was certain, he wanted Lily to have a great day. He mentioned it to God.

♦ ♦ ♦

Paul eyed a pile of reports due before the end of the week, pulled the thickest and placed it in front of him and doodled on a sheet of paper.

"Bother it!" He crumpled notes he had drafted and tossed them into the wastepaper basket. That brought him some relief, so he crumpled up a few more. They too followed their predecessors into the bottomless file.

"My, my, my, aren't we in a temper today?" Shane smirked at the door.

Shane was overlooked and would gladly take over in a blink.

"Morning, Shane. Did you need anything?" he asked calmly.

"Oh, no. Just happened to be passing by when I heard things whizzing in here. I thought I should investigate."

Nobody, but Shane, could hear paper whizzing through half-open door! The guy operated on sheer nosiness.

"So, what's all this? I know it's not my place, but are things getting a bit much, may be?" Shane eyed the neat stack of papers on the desk.

"No. But thank you for asking," he answered firmly.

"Think nothing of it. I'm having a great morning! Just a great day!"

He smiled.

Shane gave him a laconic tip of the hat and ambled out of the office.

That's all I need. Office gossip!

Promotional opportunities at BF&S for the executive track were very competitive. He worked hard to gain the respect of the partners but unlike Shane, he also networked and kept abreast of market trends and available opportunities. Right now, he needed to focus.

Normally, he mapped his financial project on paper first, then he transferred it to a computer. Often that was easy, except today. He gave up and went in search of a drink, breaking his habit of usually drinking plain, or mineral, water. A cluttered mind deserved a coffee break, he rationalized.

He spotted some vice presidents talking in the corridor, including the Senior VP and Chief Financial Officer. That did it. The whole situation——the financial reports, his secretaries clucking away about their social lives, Shane . . . everything, seemed to be crowding in on him. He headed for Bill's office.

Bill smiled, exposing a row of dental work as even as the day his dentist removed the braces. "There you are, Paul! Just the man I'm looking for. You look like you need a cappuccino!" Bill blurted out. "Missed you at the gym yesterday. What's up?" He closed the door, leaned against it for a moment, then he pulled two books from his shelf.

"Come on Bill, give me some space."

"Wow! Are we in a bad mood or what! Got stood up by your latest, huh?"

"I need a vacation. Can you spare me a week?"

"A whole week? Nopes. I'm generous, but not that generous."

He grinned and said, "You're tough."

Bill placed the books on his leather desk; thanked him and mentioned how they had motivated him to get deeper and apply the principles of servant leadership as an elder at church, in his daily life at home and at BF&S.

He recognized *The Pursuit of God* by A.W. Tozer and *Spiritual Leadership* by J. Oswald Sanders that he had lent him. "I'm glad you found them useful."

Among Bill's many qualities were: he returned books he borrowed; always to the right owner; within the timeframe he estimated; and in good condition. "Integrity's a virtue to covet in friends," Paul's father often said.

Bill swiveled his chair, his hands locked behind his head. "I've too many people out already. Why do you need a week's vacation?"

Bill's gray eyes bored into him. He shifted his eyes.

"Didn't you just have a long weekend, Mr. Van Clyden? Well . . .?"

He loosened his tie and cleared his throat. "About the vacation."

"Bull's eye! Come for dinner. Sheila makes the best lasagna, ever!"

"I know you and Sheila are like family. But, it's complicated."

"What's the problem? We trust your judgment."

He threw his hands up. "You needn't worry. She's a believer."

"But. . ."

"Just when you think you know the Lord's mind; He proves He will not share His throne. Nothing like the sin of presumption."

They locked eyes.

Bill ran his hands through his hair. "I understand. You'll let us know if there's anything Sheila and I can do, won't you?"

He knew Bill respected him. Had they lived in close proximity earlier, they would have been attending the same church, but that would have in no way interfered with their working relationship.

Bill opened the door and asked, somber, "When would you like to leave?"

"Friday would be my last day, if that's okay with you? I'll have the reports ready by then." He took the books and walked to the door.

"Friday's fine. Do I've a choice? Just kidding." Bill grinned. "I hope things work out. Sheila and I have you in our thoughts. You're like a brother."

He raised his eyes to the ceiling, blinked, and said, "Thank you," and continued to the coffee room through the now deserted corridor.

Enforcing a closed-door policy for the rest of the day was a no brainer. Nothing Bill said could alleviate his guilt of knowing that by being caught off guard, he risked disappointing generations of an established dynasty.

♦ ♦ ♦

Jonathan noticed Paul's books lying on the table as he rushed out to Bible Study. "Paul, I'm gone. It's my turn to give Mrs. O'Mallery a ride."

There was no answer.

"Paul?" Jonathan waited for a moment, and then as he left, he heard Paul chuckle and say, "Have fun!"

He assumed Paul would follow soon. They seldom rode together anyway. Besides, he didn't wish to make Mrs. O'Mallery late for the over fifties church night. She could afford a chauffeur, but she preferred to get her ride from the church——said it was less pretentious than showing up in a limousine. Barring doctor's orders, she would most likely barrel around town behind the wheel herself!

A puckish lady in her eighties, she loved to tease. On arriving at church, she would step out of the car, full of energy. If she spotted the pastor, she would announce, "Pastor Tim, I got the ride of my life this morning," then she would say to whoever gave her the ride, "Love getting rides from you and that cousin of yours. See you next Sunday. Bless you!"

One Sunday, she arrived at church flustered, cornered Pastor Tim and the other pastors and said, "My son——you know, the one we've been praying for––is here from New York with his wife. Makes a lot of money, but no sense . . . spent all night at some party . . . networking he says. Told him to come to church . . . says he's having late breakfast and going golfing. Keep praying for him. Anyways, when Paul walked up my steps, he choked on his coffee. He says, 'Mum, what are you doing? He's barely out of the crib!' Told him, 'Serves you right!' Then I told him if I remarried, I'd leave all money to my new husband! Oh, did he hyperventilate! Now he and that wife of his are thinking of moving closer." She had the pastors in stitches.

Jonathan grinned and started his engine, better not be late, or Mrs. O'Mallery would sure poke him with her cane.

Paul continued brooding, closeted in his room, praying it would not become a habit. He was looking forward to the weekend. Perhaps he could go to the beach, meditating and snorkeling. That should do it . . . a quiet week meditating.

◆ ◆ ◆

Lily fussed with her face and her books, as she prepared for the Singles' Bible study. No need to worry about the seating arrangement. Paul always sat with Jonathan and Sharon, and whichever girl was favored.

She warmed the left-over curried chicken and Chapatti and ate as she reviewed their next topic——How to Know God's Will for Your Life: Trust . . . Delight . . . Commit . . . Rest . . .——short, pithy directives.

At church, Paul's car was missing. Interesting! Not once had he missed midweek church, except when he was on vacation and, he was never late.

Around the corner, Sharon was chatting with four girls on the steps.

"There you are. We've a good crowd today," Sharon said.

"Yes. It is probably the topic. I could use some help with waiting," she replied.

"Couldn't we all? Patience's not my thing," Sharon said.

"You could have fooled me."

The girls smiled politely. She excused herself.

Sharon said, "I think we'll join you. We won't wait. The boys can fend for themselves. It's Jonathan's turn to pick up Mrs. O'Mallery."

"Oh, Mrs. O'Mallery! The life of ENC!" The girls chorused.

"She likes the boys! Treats them like her grandsons."

"Uh-huh!" the girls smirked.

"She's a respectful woman. She's full of life, that's all. I wish my grandma will be just as perky at her age." In playful, dignified protest, Sharon tossed her hair and accompanied her to the prayer rooms.

The girls lingered behind.

May be Paul and Jonathan reminded Mrs. O'Mallery of the grandsons she wished she had? Despite her chirpiness, she displayed a certain wistfulness when she watched children playing. Her son and daughter-in-law had no interest in having children, just money——lots of money——she said. Paul, on the contrary, attended to her needs like a grandson should.

7

A steamer blew a horn, a speedboat sailed past, sea gulls moaned overhead, a little girl picked up a sea-shell and brought it back to an elderly couple walking along the shore. Paul threw a pebble at a wave and watched the ripple melt into a bigger wave. To an onlooker, he resembled a beach-bum.

Occasionally, a sleek yacht passed by; he substituted himself for the captain, Lily by his side. The game worked, until another steamer, blowing a horn, brought him back to earth.

Apart from serving the homeless, he had seldom socialized outside his crowd; however, Lily was middle–class, like other girls whom he had dated.

Except for the year in South America, his closest brush with other cultures had been in school. Even then, he had kept to his group, but remained cordial with everybody——a "Good morning" here, a smile there and a few jokes, qualified him as the friendliest guy on campus——but he had never disguised his dating preferences, until love blew in unannounced. So here he sat at the beach, trying to inject meaning into his future, scared, yet trusting in the Sovereign Power.

The sun receded into the horizon. On a nearby blanket, a guitar leaned on a backpack. His efforts at writing a song had mounted to little more than a few school-boy scribbles. Perhaps, his emotions were still too raw to write a mature love song. He opened his mouth and crooned, cowboy style,

"Love's like a field of chocolates,
For the lonely who dare to dream.
Take a trip to the open fields,
Make your one choice with fervor.
You get to pick your own flavor
to put in your own holder . . . .

Live your life by faith and not by sight.
Let love and the Good Lord lead
you to the woman of your dream!"

The first time he saw Lily sitting as regal as Nefertiti in the red pews of Evangelical Neighborhood Church, she had hit him between the eyes like a cup of double cappuccino. He realized that he had seen her in Hollenvine Hills.

He had a sudden longing to touch her. Pastor Tim announced greeting time. Playing cool, he had shot out of his seat to shake hands and worked his way, until he had reached her and introduced himself.

She had smiled and said, "I am Lily."

"Are you new to ENC?"

"Yes."

He had said, "Welcome! ENC's a wonderful church. We've fellowship for everybody——families, students, singles, and more——I hope you can stay?"

"Thank you. Do you have midweek prayer meetings?"

"Yes. On Wednesdays." He had listed other midweek programs and returned to his seat playing cool, but praising the very Good Lord who made the heavens and the earth and created female as an afterthought to be a help-meet to man, because man was sure lonely without a companion, except for the animals that don't speak man's language. Right there, he should have known, time to bolt. Why hadn't he? And why was he praying for her?

Nothing wrong with admiring a stranger, occasionally——no man is born blind; even the blind can see, when it comes to love.

Lily stayed. He should have prayed for her to find another church. On second thoughts, she might just do that!

Realizing he had no control over her decision, should she decide to change churches, he stuffed his beach gear in his backpack and dumped them in the trunk, as though he had the enemy on his tail, then he changed into his jogging gear and took off at a brisk pace along the beach.

In the far horizon, where the skies married the sea, silhouettes of boats escorted the setting sun, like a bride, as she rushed to rise again in another continent, before the morning was due.

8

Three weeks running from Evangelical Neighborhood Church had done Paul as much good as it did an ostrich to bury his head in the sand. Life at the beach had left him dry and listless. Watching the ships sail had stirred in him the very emotion from which he was fleeing, his only solace, reading stories of virtuous men who had also faced temptation. Unable to resist the lure of the mountains, he had also gone up there searching his heart, with the same result.

As he prepared for work, he grabbed three crisps white shirts of pure cotton, selected one; then spread five neckties on his bed, stood back and studied them with the precision of a surgeon; and returned four to the closet. Careful not to cut himself this time, he shaved until his face shone.

When he emerged from his room, he was whistling softly.

Jonathan's door was ajar. He smiled, grateful that Jonathan did not snore, or he would surely test his cousinly devotion. Jonathan must have returned late from his show. Finally, his income was improving——he was right to stick with performance and composition, if he succeeded, he would not need to go into full time teaching, after all.

♦ ♦ ♦

Paul turned the corner and narrowly missed bumping into Bill at his door.

Bill dead-panned, "Drop by my office, after you've settled down."

He instructed his secretary on a letter that must be mailed by end of the day and treated himself to half a cup of coffee, first, bracing himself.

Bill's door was open. "Come on in. Close the door," Bill yawned.

He complied and asked, "What's up?"

Bill came to the point, "As you've heard, BF&S is exploring expanding to emerging markets. A project team has been convened. Bret's the lead, of course."

"Of course."

"Sharp guy—next to you I can't think of another. They'd like us to help with the financials. Beyond that, we won't be expected to travel. I'd like to nominate you." He pushed a thick file across the desk. "Take your time."

It was the file he had found Bill reading three weeks earlier, when he dropped by his office. "By when would you like an answer?"

"Oh, about a couple of days." Bill grinned to cushion the short notice.

He nodded and took the file.

As he was leaving, Bill asked, "How was the beach?"

"Lots of boats . . . lots of sand . . . lots of waves; then again, more boats, more sand and more waves. You get the picture," he replied.

Bill chuckled, "That bad, eh? I'm beginning to savor the novelty of Paul smitten. Never thought I'd live to see the day!"

He gave his boss a backward grin, and returned to his office.

◆ ◆ ◆

As Lily prepared for work, she did not cut her finger or something, but she thought about Paul more than she believed she should. She had no right to ask, but she needed a sign. Was Paul toying with her? It had been three weeks!

She pulled up Denton and Terrell, as Bernice's car squealed to a stop.

Bernice bounced out, chewing gum. "Hi, Lily! There you're, looking as cool as the morning breeze."

She wished her a good morning. "When you get poetical so early, I can't help but wonder what you had for breakfast. You look very nice, too."

Perched on stilettos like a giraffe, Bernice tried to coax her hemline down. She thanked her and said, "Really? You don't think it's too much?"

"You look perfect and as flat as a reed!"

Bernice whispered, "I don't believe in face-lifts, but trust me, I would sooner your looks than a tummy-tuck any day. You have it all!" and tugged at her hemline again, "You really think this isn't too much? Alex and I are going to a party afterwards."

Lily circled her. "It seems within the dress code. Even with the Chief in town."

Bernice darted her eyes, more scared than a kitten. "Chief's in town? I need my job! I should've listened to Mum."

"Bernice, you are a decent girl, but you do push the boundaries, sometimes."

"I like taking risks, but I can go on for weeks dressing proper, then the very day the Chief's in town is the day I wake up with the urge to wear something stylish." Bernice continued yanking her hemline down.

"That's why you are the entrepreneur. But, going on like that will only draw attention. I might have a solution." She led Bernice to the Ladies' room and pulled out an elegant scarf the size of a wrap.

"Oh my! That's a beautiful scarf. Are you sure you don't mind?"

"Positive." She opened the scarf. "Rumors have it that you carry huge purses to haul around devices for self-defense. I carry huge bags to stock extra scarves so I don't stress out watching you stress out when the Chief is in town."

Bernice laughed hilariously, and said, "I'm not confirming anything."

She showed Bernice how to wrap the scarf around her skirt, leaving just a peep of her hemline, like a very stylish design, then secured it with another elegant scarf. When she pulled out a brooch, Bernice said, "No, you don't!"

"Hanging around you has taught me. With this, no one would think you were headed to the beach. You look as elegant as a picture out of Vogue."

Bernice swirled around. "I dare the Chief to raise his eyebrows. My Mum says you're my guardian angel at D&T. This calls for lunch."

"As good accountants, should we stick to our burger place? Five max."

"Don't you go putting down the long-suffering accountants. Without us, where would the world of numbers be? And I'll have you know some of us are considered very rich by the world's standard." Bernice stuck her nose in the air.

"Pardon moi. I would not dream of denigrating accountants. I was just stating facts. We do love our numbers," she teased back, confident their favorite burger place was a safe haven to escape for lunch away from the office. Not a chance she would run into anybody there.

◆ ◆ ◆

At noon sharp, Lily left Denton & Terrell amid Bernice's chatter, drove her Honda through the crisscrossing streets of the L.A. Business District, straight to their hide-away restaurant, sandwiched between high-rise office buildings.

The Burger Place, with its limited seating, offered free parking, a luxury for customers on limited lunch time; one more reason she liked the place. The restaurant was about halfway full by the time they arrived.

They put in their orders: a barbecued chicken sandwich, well-done, and French fries for her, and a juicy hamburger, medium-done and a side order of onion rings for Bernice, and they took a window seat.

Between taking the first bite of her sandwich and French fry, she looked up and froze. A group of five young men in starched shirts and business suits entered. They ordered their lunch, then one in particular steered the group to a table along the opposite wall to hers, but closer to the door. He manipulated the seating to give him a full view of her table. For a moment, he held her gaze, and then turned to talk to one of his associates.

Of all the burger places in the whole of L.A.! There must be a kazillion. Who would have thought young executives lunched in a hole-in-the-wall?

She remembered! One day, at a singles' party, Paul had asked her about her favorite restaurant. At that time, she had dismissed it, attributing his marked interest to a cursory politeness he accorded everyone. If only her answer had been noncommittal! She continued nibbling her French fries, wishing she could slide under the table or switch seats with Bernice.

Bernice stopped babbling, turned around, and examined the corner she was boycotting. Bernice's jaw dropped and her eyes just about popped out. She put her burger down, blushed, and started playing with her hair.

"Oh my! That's the most perfect statuesque of human embodiment I've ever seen. Ever!" Bernice whispered and inspected the room again. "I'm glad I'm not the only one in the room with real blood in my veins."

Lily took another bite of her French fries. Unable to resist another peek at Paul, she checked his corner again. He was sitting at the edge of his seat, and appeared ambivalent.

"Aye yai yai!" Bernice muttered. "If he was looking at me, Alex would be history. I hope he's a believer, Lily."

"Don't look. He is a member of my church."

"He is! I knew I should've moved to San Gabriel Valley a long time ago. Why did I think you go to a predominantly black church? Or is it the other way around? Does he go to an African-American church?" Bernice mouthed.

She mouthed back, "No. It is eighty-five percent Caucasian and fifteen percent African American, Latino, and other groups. Their worship style is like back home." Not that Bernice needed any statistics at that moment, but she had to appear preoccupied and engrossed in conversation with her.

Bernice whispered back, "I think he's getting up."

She shielded her forehead with her hand. "I said don't look. Act busy. Bite your hamburger or something."

"Too late! He's up and he's headed straight for our table!"

Paul crossed the threshold in determined strides and stopped at their table, grinning from ear to ear. "Hi, Lily? Fancy meeting you here."

She was about to remind him this was her hideout, but bit her tongue, instead. "Hello, Paul. I haven't seen you for a while," she quacked. She had meant to sound formal, professional . . . cordial, but not too cordial, kind of warm in a not-too-warm a manner.

"Oh, yes, not since we ran into each other," he replied.

Bernice's eyes gleamed.

"I don't think you two have met. Bernice this is Mr. Paul Van Clyden. Miss Bernice O'Konnell." She slipped into her formal manners to play it safe.

"How do you do, Mr. Van Clyden?" Bernice too slipped back to her formal manners.

"Pleased to meet you, Miss O'Konnell," Paul said.

"You can call me Bernice."

"Thank you, Bernice. Same here——Paul."

"Okay, Paul."

"So, what's happening in church?" Paul addressed her; but included Bernice in the conversation.

"The usual——Vacation Bible School is next week. Some people are on vacation. How was yours?"

Paul loosened his tie. "How did you know?"

"I just surmised. You were gone for three weeks, right?"

"You noticed. Actually, I was on vacation for one week, then I'd some things I needed to do." He patted his tie.

She noticed Bernice lynxing Paul's hand movement.

"Well, you were missed at church," she repeated.

"Only at church? I mean, there're other possibilities too."

"True. But a good congregation notices when part of the body is missing."

"We? Church? Congregation? I suppose I should be thankful. I was hoping some of its members also missed me?" He held her gaze.

"Mr. Van Clyden, what is a congregation composed of?"

"Sheep," he quipped.

"Which are otherwise known as . . .?"

"Lambs."

"Lambs, or members."

"Yes. Members too. Well members, is a good start."

"Hope, they say, keeps us waking up in the morning, Mr. Van Clyden."

"On that positive note, I beg to be excused, ladies." He backed out, tightening his tie. "Nice meeting you, Bernice," he said to Bernice then he turned to her and said, "I'll see you at church, ma'am."

While Paul was talking to Lily, his back was blocking his table.

"Well, I can see someone's quite pleased with himself," a colleague said.

"Fancy running into that at a burger place! I see why we've been eating a lot of burgers lately. Paul must have the inside scoop on all the hot places. So, did you get her number?" Rod, another associate asked.

"Whose number?" he asked.

"Her phone number. Cute redhead. They don't make them like that anymore." Rod took a swig from his glass and licked his lips.

Ignoring Rod's comment, he glanced in Lily's direction and said calmly,——too calmly perhaps——"Oh, the redhead? She's a friend of hers."

Silence greeted his response. One by one, each man took a good look at the table and his jaw dropped. He had skillfully manipulated their seating so that they would not have the full view of the room. Now, they stared at Lily, unabashed.

"Exquisite," another associate whispered leaning into the table, as a man who discovers a precious treasure and decides to guard it.

"Ooo-ee!" Rod loudly. "My apologies! Correction, the redhead is cute, but the day they put that number together, they must've celebrated in heaven for seven solid days. Go for it, Paul! You got her number, right?"

Rod was a Casanova, a lawsuit waiting to happen. His associates knew it; BF&S knew it; everybody hoped for the best.

Phil, another colleague, leaned into the group with a tight smile, his eyes shooting daggers, and mouthed, "Lower your voice, Rod. I'm sure the whole restaurant can hear you. I'm absolutely positive she heard you!"

"I was hoping she would. Listen Paul, if you strike out, pass her number, eh?" Rod pointed to himself.

He smiled wryly. "Rod, it's not my nature to throw a lady to a wolf."

"What's the problem? A guy like you, ought to sow a few oats," Rod simpered.

With restraint, he glowered at him.

Rod baulked. "Okay. I'll back off. I just thought since you took the steps, you were interested in . . .?" He boxed the air with his fists. "I'm sure your dad must be anxious. Quite a bit of empire the Van Clydens have built, eh?"

"Rod, I don't think that's very professional. You couldn't make a commitment to any woman for all the diamonds in South Africa. You wouldn't recognize the word, if you saw it in the dictionary." Phil's tone stunned him. Always calm, this was the closest he had seen him come to wringing Rod's neck.

"Way to go, Phil. Tell him," one of the other boys said.

Good old Phil, always the diplomat. He threw him a grateful look, turned around, and held Rod's gaze long enough to unnerve him, then he measured his words, "I don't have her phone number. I don't need it. We attend the same church. Also, I'm a gentleman. You should know the difference."

"Okay. I'll back off. I didn't know she's religious."

Paul's tone dropped another degree Fahrenheit and his eyes turned ice blue. "She's not religious. She's a believer. There's a great difference!"

Phil glanced at him.

Paul composed himself, trying to camouflage the hidden hurt and pain of being misunderstood. He had discussed it with Phil and Bill on many occasions during their lunches. Phil knew the root-cause of that pain——the constant bashing and ridiculing of believers by the media enamored by the post-Founding Father's America, the pluralistic, anything-goes gods and humanists' capriciousness.

He had also admitted to Phil how much he disliked being called religious. Religion was something he could put on and off, as he would change shirts——on the same level with no moral absolutes. Calling Lily religious, when he knew otherwise, was equivalent to slapping her on the cheeks, while he stood by and did nothing. It challenged his commitment to civility.

"Wow," was all Rod could say.

Phil whistled under his breath. "Quit, Rod! You're over your head."

Rod shrugged. "What's the fuss? This is L.A. Have a life!"

"Quit, Rod!" three angry male voices roared.

Blushing, Rod looked around and took a big bite of his burger.

The other men resumed chatting quietly. Paul said little. Several minutes later, from the corner of his eye, he saw Lily get up, bringing her long legs to their full height, then he heard Phil whistle under his breath. The rest of the table gawked.

He dropped his gaze. Tiny drops of perspiration graced his brow, prompting him to loosen his tie again. Apparently unaware of the havoc she was creating, Lily took the only exit out, past his table, Bernice in tow.

Elusive whiff of her perfume again hovered in the air, then escaped—— Madame Rochas, a favorite of his mother's. If his source was reliable, the famous Marcel Rochas had the perfume created for his wife.

Rod groaned. "Nefertiti, eat your heart out."

"Thud," a sound came from under the table. Did someone bang their toes?

"Ouch," Rod yelped. "Phil, I know that's you. Adam was made of real flesh, okay. How's that for religiosity?"

The other men laughed sheepishly.

Paul stared at the now empty doorway, where Lily had just exited, took a big swig of his ice tea, and dabbed his brow.

$$9$$

Exhausted from his crammed schedule, Paul reclined in his car, listening to the evening news on low volume, the windows rolled down a tad. He could hear conversations around him, but he preferred to spend a moment of peace, waiting, hoping. Just then, Lily appeared.

Lily parked in her favorite spot. She was early. In about ten minutes, she could go in. Just then, the Calderons pulled up.

Miguel jumped out of the van and dashed across the parking lot. "Hi, Lily, are you going to teach our class this Sunday?" he yelled.

"I'm not sure, yet. I was subbing last week."

"I like it when you teach our class. You and Paul," he tossed over his shoulders and dashed off to the AWANA Youth Club. His family followed at a slower pace.

Lily clapped her mouth. Between Miguel Calderon and Marc Joneson, she was never sure what next would spew out of their mouths.

Of all the five Calderon children, Miguel was the most comfortable with her. She had taught his class.

Just before she got out, she spotted a black Porsche she had missed when she pulled up, probably because it was concealed by a van that had just left——a father who had dropped off his son. Her heart skipped a beat. The car seemed empty.

She slid back in her seat. "Would it convince You, Lord, for me to say I had really come here to pray, as izzzz my custom?" she prayed out loud, then paused, as if expecting an answer to fall from the skies. "Okay. You are not convinced. All right, so we go in. You lead the way, Lord; I'm right behind You."

She revered the Lord, but she also enjoyed talking to Him as she would to a friend or a father, not to dishonor Him, but to be real. After all, didn't He create everything, including humor?

She powdered her nose once more, determined to continue attending the midweek activities.

Twigs crackling put her presumption that she was alone to flight. She raised her head in time to look into a pair of sparkling blue eyes.

First you ruin my lunch and my afternoon, now this!

Paul approached her as wary as a lion. "Good evening," he said.

"Good evening, Paul. Were you waiting to go in or for someone?" She ran her words together.

"Probably someone." He continued to stare at her.

She started. "Me?"

He grinned.

Remembering his parting words at lunch, she asked "Was I supposed to be here at any particular time?"

"No. But you're usually here about, mmm, ten or fifteen to, right?"

"More, or less. You have been keeping a tab on me?"

"No. I just happened to notice."

She raised her eyebrows. "Look who is talking."

"So, may be some things go unnoticed, but others don't."

"Such as lambs and sheep?"

"Such as lambs and sheep."

"Then I guess we should go in and join the rest of the flock."

"Absolutely." He stepped aside and opened her door.

Jonathan lifted his eyes and tensed. Sharon followed his gaze. Paul and Lily were strolling down the parking lot toward them. Paul looked radiant. So, this was what had been going on! Being a practical girl and having been raised a missionary kid——MK as she was called——she grasped the situation immediately.

Evangelical Neighborhood Church was mature, but she had also seen some members squirming in their seats, when Lily sat next to them. A few church members had complained as much to her about Orientals, as they called everybody who didn't come from Europe. They behaved no better than some restaurants did. She had been a witness on occasions when her table was served last, until she realized it was on account of Lily. Beautiful as Lily was, there were those who only saw what they wished to see.

The last time she checked, statistics for marriage placed the ratio of landing a husband around two women to one man and in some cases, three women to one eligible bachelor.

Lily had been a popular girl until now. For how much longer would she remain so, with Paul hanging on to her every word? After all, wasn't Paul a mother's dream, not just at ENC; but in the community? Quite a few mothers would love to see one of their daughters catch him.

Looking at Paul striding through the parking lot, chatting with Lily, she straightened her back, tossed her hair, and held her head high. That instant, she decided to be Lily's friend. But for Jonathan coming into her life, it could have been her coming down that path, hanging onto the arm of a dark-haired Argentinian, or some dark-brown Hausa.

She lifted her chin, batted her eyelids at Jonathan, and said in her husky voice, "This is the first time I've seen Paul happy in weeks."

"Mhmm."

"Well, we'll go with the flow," she said softly.

"Mhmm."

"Hi, Paul! Hi, Lily!" they said in chorus, as Paul and Lily entered the foyer.

Jonathan stepped forward with a lot of backslapping. "You've been holding up traffic. Now, we can begin."

Lily smiled at them, guileless.

The prayer meeting flew by. Young adults and the college groups headed to the Fellowship Hall first, where Gary and Francine, the couple on duty, had served refreshments. The other groups followed.

On entering the hall, Paul watched as Lily was edged out from his inner circle. Whether by design or accident, female after female and some couples clamored for his attention. He had never felt more popular and more alone.

On the way to the hall, he had noticed a few enigmatic, yet pregnant glances cast their way. Evangelical Neighborhood Church never having given him cause before; he had dismissed all warning signs. His nostrils dilated a little, but he kept on smiling.

Edged out, Lily moved to a corner of the room.

Standing alone in a corner, Lily smiled bravely. With one special smile from Paul, and a short stroll down the path to the sanctuary, she had gone from being a popular girl to an émigré. She tried joining a group near her; one of the girls froze her out with a smile, and continued talking, ignoring her.

Did she exist or was she invisible?

She sat down in a corner, clutching her glass of punch, and took a deep breath. A member of the congregation, who had hinted that she should find a church closer to her home, gave her a saccharine smile. She couldn't really be sneering, could she? Nah. She was too spiritual for such venom.

How well did Lily know Evangelical Neighborhood Church, anyway?

The mid-summer breeze had turned into a chilly late autumn, winter-like weather. Perhaps it was the air conditioner. She was incredulous that about two hours before, she and Paul had enjoyed the cool summer breeze while strolling to the sanctuary. Should she leave early? That would be tantamount to admitting defeat. She fired off one of her SOS prayers.

Within moments, she noticed a few people looking at her with compassion. She sensed others may also be praying.

Sharon appeared. "There you are. I was wondering where you were." Sharon sat next to her and engaged her in an animated conversation.

Jonathan too appeared and flanked her. Two others joined them, along with the Calderons and the Jonesons. And another surprise, Emmett and Abigail McGaelic, who had moved from the Toledo area, also joined them.

Paul studied friends huddled around Lily and then his own group——their rapt attention and their body language that closed out the rest of the hall. In Lily's group he saw the freedom he longed for. In his group, people with whom he would have once loved to associate, but from whom now he longed to escape. The people resembled an octopus with tentacles——clammy hands clinging to him.

On another day, his popularity would have been comical, but not tonight, he thought. If he botched this evening, he could regress six months. How many more vacations could he afford? He had depleted his vacation time. He cleared his throat.

"Excuse me?" a female, hanging on his words, asked.

"A lot of people showed up today. We should mingle. I see a lot of new faces I haven't met yet," he hemmed and hawed.

Everybody laughed nervously.

"I didn't notice," another lady said. "I always enjoy talking to you, Paul. You're so knowledgeable."

"Thanks, Stephanie. I think I'm spoiled. It's so comfortable hanging out with friends." He craned his neck. "I see a couple over there; they look a bit lost." He excused himself and wandered around the room, working his way toward Lily's group, aware of curious eyes following his progress.

Lily was chatting with her group, now more relaxed.

"Hello everybody!" He pulled up a chair and sat down.

Everybody waved back.

"So nice of you to join us," Jonathan said with a touch of sarcasm.

He opened his arms wide and reciprocated. "The pleasure's always mine."

"It's hard to believe you two are cousins. You sound like brothers," Sharon said.

"That's another way of saying be nice, we have ladies around," Matt added.

Everybody laughed.

"See, we've a reputation to live down, Jonathan." Paul glanced at Lily.

"Yeah? Speak for yourself. For starters, what were you ladies having? Paul and I'll do the honors." Jonathan's eyes addressed Lily.

"Punch. Thank you." Lily smiled.

"Yes. Get us fruit punch, ice tea and cookies. No, grapes, and cookies. Oh, bring everything," Marjorie waved her hands.

"My wife knows my taste," Matt added.

"You're blessed. My wife has me on a diet," Norland said.

"That's what I mean. I'm on a see-food diet." Matt patted his stomach.

"You sound just like Emmett," Abigail said.

"You too, honey!" Emmett nudged his wife playfully.

Paul, Jonathan and a new friend headed to the refreshments stand, while the group resumed their jovial, quiet conversation.

When they returned, Paul handed Lily her punch, brushing his fingers with hers, then, he plonked down beside her, totally at home.

The irony, now it was the click–group who glanced often at Lily's group cracking jokes and laughing hilariously.

The clock was past nine o'clock, when Marjorie checked her watch and announced. "Time to get Melanie."

Paul took the cue. "The evening's young. Anybody for pizza?" He addressed everybody, his eyes searched Lily's face.

"Yeah, pizza sounds great!" somebody shouted from the back.

"Let's go for pizza," Jonathan and Sharon echoed.

Lily smiled.

"You young ones go on. Good night." Emmett helped Abigail out of her chair.

"I'll second that." Matt wished everybody goodnight, and followed Marjorie.

"I think we will join you. Norland has to drop off Miguel and the girls tomorrow." Maricela and her husband also wished the group goodnight.

"Gourmet Pizza or Original?" Jonathan left with the rest of the group.

"Original," the group chorused.

"Original Pizza place it is," Jonathan announced.

10

Lily snoozed, wrapped up in memories of the evening. She had laughed so hard that she could not remember what she ate. In a way, it marked what she suspected would always be the pattern. Some people would stretch out their hands to her in friendship and others would shun her.

"Thank you for those who are willing to love me like the Jonesons and the Calderons and the McGaelics. Give me the grace to manage the others who are not so kind, in a manner that honors You, Lord. Keep my spirit up I pray, and help me remain gracious to all," she prayed.

With one kick, she hit the ground, and went to the bathroom.

So reluctant was Paul to let her drive herself home that one would have thought she had never driven home alone at night. She had driven her car to church and to the restaurant, so he had no choice but to let her drive home, otherwise, how would she get to work that morning?

The sound of the phone ringing broke into her thoughts. Apart from her family, who could be calling her at six in the morning? The caller ID indicated the number was blocked. Puzzled, she grabbed the phone, her eyes on the clock. She had a few minutes left to beat the morning traffic.

"Good morning. Did you sleep well last night?"

Her heart skipped a bit. "Morning, Paul. You haven't left for work yet?" She said, breathless, instead of sounding nonchalant. Treacherous voice!

"Are you ready for another Californian heat wave, smog and all?"

"Don't know about the smog, but I will soon be on my way."

"Then, I won't keep you. Drive safely!"

"You too. Thank you for checking on me."

"My pleasure! I'll talk to you soon." Click. Paul hanged up.

♦ ♦ ♦

Lily floated from Denton and Terrell's parking lot to her cubicle. Espying her, Bernice came and leaned over her cubicle looking like a puppy waiting for a bone.

She smiled, and told her, "You are not getting any."

"I'm not leaving until I get my daily gossip," Bernice insisted.

"There is nothing to gossip about. Besides, gossiping is forbidden."

"Not if it's true. You've on a new dress, new hairdo, new shoes——new everything——I'm gonna get to the bottom of all that radiance by end of day."

"Time to go to work or your boss will be breathing down my neck."

"And you'd deserve it, keeping me in suspense! We'll talk at lunch."

"Sorry, I brought my lunch. I have a backlog. How about next week?"

Bernice was disappointed, "I'm gone, but I haven't left Denton and Terrell yet!" she mouthed over the cubicle, and retreated.

As Bernice's footsteps faded, she piled tax files and books on her desk to block out traffic and went to work. If she kept her mouth zipped, she could keep her secret longer. Bernice was a friend, but she had no wish to start a rumor.

At noon she found a quiet corner at the campus park to eat her lunch. When she got back, Bernice leaned over her cubicle again, making puppy faces at her.

"No gossiping. And I think I see your supervisor heading our way."

Bernice returned to her cubicle, playing wounded.

At the end of the day, she was congratulating herself as she pulled out of the parking lot, when she espied Bernice who appeared to be searching for someone. She stepped on the gas pedal and sped away.

♦ ♦ ♦

Paul closed his bedroom door, threw his jacket across the bed, and loosened his tie. He had dialed Lily's number and her answering machine had come on. Five minutes later, he dialed the number again. She answered, this time.

He took a deep breath. "You're home."

"Paul?" She sounded breathless as though she had been running.

"Where were you? It's almost six o'clock!"

"Good evening to you too," Lily said.

"What took you so long?"

"I was in traffic. Why?"

"Well, you should've told your friendly patrol to clear the freeway. You've an appointment."

"I could just see his face." She stopped and digested what he had said, "An appointment, with whom?"

"I thought you may wish to go to the movies or something. The new releases are out. They've been getting rave reviews."

"That sounds interesting . . ."

"But, what? You sound guarded." Steady! Your first formal date and you blow it. "Help, Lord!" he mouthed to the side.

"It's . . . um, what are the ratings?" She sounded cautious.

"PG. I thought you might enjoy it. Is that okay?"

"Ye-e-es and no-o-o. It depends on what the PG is for."

He coughed. "I'm not sure. Why? Would it bother you?"

"Well, I prefer family movies. I know those are rare now, but I keep hoping."

He coughed again. "Strict and conservative. Mmm. I'll make a note of that."

"Paul Van Clyden, are you taking notes on me?"

"Profusely, and loving it."

"Paul!"

"A pretty lady told me recently that hope's the last thing to die."

"Well . . ."

He should have guessed. Kicking himself, he made a mental note to do his homework next time. "If I promise to check on the content of the movie for later, would you consider dinner?"

"You don't give up, do you?"

"I'm the ultimate optimist."

"All right. I would be delighted."

She was not available that evening, but the next day would work. He promised to arrive by seven thirty. "Looking forward to tomorrow."

"Until tomorrow?"

"Until tomorrow." He hung up, skipped to his wardrobe, and grabbed his gym clothes, crooning, "Can't Help Falling in Love."

Lily flew to her wardrobe, combed through layers of clothes and tossed a few selections of formal dinner wear, cocktails and the likes on her bed. She always shopped ahead to avoid buying dresses that she would wear only once and then abandon to her closet. She had enough collection for any surprise occasion.

One dress in particular, jumped at her. She selected it and changed into her exercise clothes, glad that she had put her foot down about the movies. Training Paul to expect her to compromise on her values, was wrong—better to start right. Not a movie fan, she restricted herself to 'G' rated movies, mostly. Would she date Paul at any cost? She prayed not.

As she was about to leave for her walkercise, the phone rang again. She hesitated, wishing to beat the fading sun, then she grabbed it. Frances from church came on the line with an urgent prayer request. Ten–year–old Wes was just admitted to the hospital for an emergency appendectomy. Since Sharon was not reachable, could she please call the Jonesons to keep the prayer line moving?

She hung up, said a quick prayer, and phoned the Jonesons' house.

11

Marjorie played musical chairs with the pots on the stove to make more room, her mind focused on Wes, praying that the infection was caught in good time, or barring that, a miracle.

She lifted a huge pot of pasta off the heat and drained it in a colander. Steam rose, embracing her face, giving it a motherly glow, of a seasoned cook.

An aroma of fresh Italian herbs filled the kitchen from a thick sauce simmering on the stove. Marc sniffed the air, following the aroma to the kitchen; shuffled close to Marjorie and stared into her eyes with the confidence of one who knew he was loved. "I can smell it all the way down the street, Mum," he blinked.

Marjorie tossed the pasta in the air, biting her lips to suppress a smile and said, "In a moment . . . in a moment."

From the corner, Matt lowered his newspaper. He had the best seat in the house to listen in to the family conversation, and keep abreast of the challenges his family faced, in a world hurtling to oblivion——better than watching the games. Half empty bowl of blanched, salted peanuts and a can of soda sat at his elbow.

Marc dipped his hand in the bowl; up came a fistful of nuts.

"Ever heard of the word share?" Matt stared at Marc over the rim of his reading glasses.

"Yes."

"And . . .?"

"I'm hungry."

"As Mum says, leave room for dinner."

"Yes, sir." Marc popped the peanuts into his mouth, licked his fingers and dipped his hands into the bowl again, ignoring his dad.

"Why don't you just chew the bowl? It's only made of plastic."

"Oh, Dad!" Marc licked his hands again and returned to his Mum's side to inspect the salad bowl. "Melody," he yelled loud enough to be heard upstairs. "How many olives did you put in the salad?"

"How would I know? How many do you think there are in a can? Mum said to use a whole can."

"No. She didn't."

"Yes. She did, during family free time, remember?"

"Well, there won't be enough for dinner." Marc sounded as though he had mothballs in his mouth.

"Not if you stop eating them."

"That's not what Mum said."

"Yes. She did!"

"Marc, I mean MJ, no Marc, where's Melanie?" Marjorie asked.

Marc cracked up. "See Mum, you get tongue-tied calling our names. Why did you and Dad name us like that? My friends complain all the time, too many Ms in your family, they say."

"Because we're the M family. How else would people know we're a loving family? Families that rhyme their names stay together."

"I thought it was families that pray together?" Marc scratched his head.

"Pray together, rhyme their names, stay together." Marjorie emptied the pasta into a huge pot and added the sauce.

"Oh Mum! But it kind of gets confusing."

"Well, tell your friends that Mum and Dad like it. It's supposed to stimulate their brains. We need more thinkers in this country."

"How's that for profundity?" Matt asked.

Marc turned to the wall and crossed his eyes, then he said, "Dad, you really don't think you and Mum were being profound, do you?" He inched closer to the bowl and picked the remnants of the nuts.

"Okay, listen up! Here it is——five good reasons Mum and I named our children Matt Junior, Melody, Marc and Melanie——so the first letter of their names would rhyme with M for Matt Senior and Marjorie Joneson, who rhymed with M for Grandpa Melvin and Grandma Marcia Joneson, who

rhymed with great Grandpa Matthew and great Grandma Mary Jean Joneson–
—you remember great Grandpa Matt, never missed a deer half a mile away."

"That's three."

"And then there was great, great Grandpa Myles and great, great Grandma Macayle, they were preachers; and the great, great, great Maxwell Junior and Malissa and the great, great, great, great Maxwell Senior and Mabel . . . they were the ones who used to park their self-defense outside the church and walk to the sanctuary clutching their Bibles, till the preacher weaned them of it, then they just showed up clutching their Bibles; and finally, the great, great, great, great, great Milton and Madelyn Joneson . . . they were the real pioneers, without them, the Jonesons would be a myth."

Marc counted his fingers, his face knotted. "That's seven good reasons."

"Jewish seven's perfect. What's good for the Jonesons should be good for your friends."

"No, Dad. Five's the Jewish perfect number, and thirteen's the number if you're talking bar mitzvah."

"But Jesus was twelve," Matt challenged Marc.

"That's because He was special, born of the Virgin and the Holy Spirit," Marc shot back.

"Are we going to look for Melanie or not?" Marjorie yelled.

"Yes, Ma'am!" Matt and Marc yelled back.

Marc wiped his mouth on his sleeves and left, returning shortly with Melanie in tow, carrying her favorite doll with screaming red hair.

"Marc, there's something soothing about belonging to a household where names rhyme. Some African tribes also name their children with rhyming first letters such as A, or N, or M, or O. The Ugandan Luo——the Lango, for example——name their girls Akao, Alaba, Ateng or Awino. That's how they know from where they originated, just like the Europeans or Asians . . . why not us?" Marjorie combed Melanie's hair with her fingers.

"Imagine if we had twelve Jonesons with rhyming first letters, we could play soccer!" Marc's eyes grew bigger than a soccer ball.

"If you want to remain our favorite third M, better think of another sport," Marjorie frowned at him.

Matt rubbed his nose. "I knew this conversation was over, the moment you mentioned the magic number twelve."

Marjorie frowned at him and gave Melanie a big smooch on the cheeks. "Come on, pet. You're mum's favorite number four M and the last one. Two boys, two girls, perfect. Here, have a Cheerio! Table or bowl?"

"Table Mummy, and I wanth my bowl," Melanie lisped.

Marjorie placed Melanie in her arm chair, poured out cheerio on the table, and placed an empty bowl next to it.

Melanie thanked her and moved one cheerio at a time from the table to the bowl and then into her mouth and ate it, before going to the next.

"All boys good." Melanie smiled and clapped her hands.

"What on earth are you talking about?" Marjorie asked.

"MJ, good boy? Marc . . . good boy? Boys good, Mummy? Two boys, good boys." She laughed and pointed to Marc, then she went back to her cheerios, "One, two, three, four, five boys. Two girls, five boys, six boys, seven boys, eight boys, nine boys, ten boys. Basketball. Yeah!" She clapped.

"Those had better be cheerios you're counting, Melanie!" Marjorie growled.

Matt collapsed in his chair, while Marc rolled on the ground, clutching his stomach, "Oh Dad, I knew Melanie would come to the rescue."

"You're banned! If you boys are determined to be mean, you're banished, forever! No men in my kitchen!" Marjorie yelled.

"Bad boys! Mummy says, bad boys, go away! Yeah." Melanie pointed to her Dad and Marc, and clapped again.

Upstairs, Melody preened, while mulling over her discussion with MJ and Marc earlier that evening and what should be the next level before they approached Mum and Dad——that required another meeting.

She glanced in the mirror, tucked in her stomach and went downstairs. At the China cabinet, she swung around in front of the mirror, sucked in her breath some more and leaned forward to examine her chin and the deep pupils of her greenish blue eyes, but she only saw Melody staring back at her, not her mesmerizing eyes that could launch a world war. Then she walked regally to the kitchen and stopped within an inch of Marjorie's face.

"Mum . . .," she said.

"You know, you could move closer." Marjorie stepped back. "Why am I always so popular around dinner time?"

"Because you're Mum. Can I ask you something?"

"Yes?"

"How do I look?"

"How do you look?" Marjorie examined her dress.

"Yes. How do I look? It's my new dress." She lifted her chin, completed a pirouette, and posed, imitating a model with a long neck.

"Quite pretty. That's a lovely dress."

Her eyes lit up. "You think so?" She whirled around again.

"Yes. I do. When did you get that?" Marjorie stirred her sauce.

"Last weekend, when I went shopping with Alisa and her mum."

Marjorie raised her eyebrows. "You went with who?"

"You said I could go. Remember?"

"I remember. You said you were going window-shopping."

"Do I look elegant?" She ignored her mother's last comment.

"Yes. You look very pretty. Now, about Alisa."

"Do you think I look as elegant as Lily, for instance?"

Marjorie gave her a strange look. "Lily? Why?"

"I'm not comparing myself or anything . . . but, she's kind of tall. She's smart, elegant and very lady-like. I like her fingers a lot. They're as slim as a princess'. Mum, do you think she might be an African princess?"

"She's quite beautiful, isn't she? But, no matter how beautiful other girls may be, honey, remember, God made you special too. Every girl is a princess in her own way."

"I know."

"Well, there you are. You're special, too, and I think you're very pretty and not because I'm your mother. So that makes you a princess."

"Thanks, Mum." She stepped back, narrowly missing bumping Mark.

Marc slid a carrot between his teeth; his eyes studied Melody; his jaws worked the carrot. "Oh, Melody!" he said, after swallowing.

"Oh, Melody," Melanie repeated, first to Marc and then to their mother. "Did God make me th-pethial too, Mummy?" She selected the tiniest Cheerio, placed it in the bowl, then put it in her mouth.

"Yes, honey. God made you very, very special."

"See, Mum? Girls only think about themselves all the time." Marc's eyes twinkled.

"Not all the time, only sometimes. Stop exaggerating! Go make yourself useful. Go feed the dog!" Melody said.

Marjorie checked her sauce, as though she was alone on another planet, far from the Jonesons' kitchen and all the bantering. She could see the children's lips moving, but she blocked out their noises, a trick she had learned early when she became a mother. Then in a flash, she leveled her eyes at Marc and asked, "Marc, did you finish your homework?"

"Sort of."

"Which one didn't you finish?"

Marc backed into a stool and crossed his legs. "I guess Math."

"You know the rules."

Marc crunched the last stump of carrot and swallowed, then he sighed and said, "But it's not due until Friday after lunch."

"Another way of saying it's due tomorrow?"

Marc rolled his eyes. "Well, yes."

Marjorie raised her eyebrows. "I saw that young man! Just as I said, you know the rules. Go upstairs and finish your homework."

"But I'm hungry."

"Take a slice and I mean a slice. Dinner's almost ready."

"Do I have to?" Marc took a slice of bread from the fridge, planted his bottom on the wooden stool and crossed his legs.

"Afraid so. We pay the bills; you go to school," Marjorie asserted.

"Why do boys have to do their homework before dinner? How comes girls have all the fun?"

"Marc! Do as your mother says!" Matt boomed.

Marc hit the floor running, "Yes sir." He dashed out through the kitchen door; a slice of bread stuck between his teeth.

Marjorie shook her head. "Praise the Lord for Fathers. Melody?"

"Yes, Mum."

"Are you busy?"

"No, Ma'am."

"If you've finished your homework, please help Marc."

"Yes, Ma'am."

Marjorie thanked her, took out a pound of cheddar cheese and half a pound of mozzarella from the fridge. In rhythm, her hands worked, grating them into a wooden bowl, as she had watched her mother's slim hands and her grandmother's gnarled hands grate cheese for years in their wooden bowls passed down from generation to generation.

Melanie slid off her stool, pouting and resumed playing with her toy.

Matt sighed. "I don't know about my son. Will he ever grow up?"

Marjorie concentrated on the cheese strips as they folded into the bowl, then she said to the raised newspaper, "Don't exaggerate, you know they all grow up, sooner or later. Look at MJ!"

"Yeah! That's my boy."

"So, Marc will be like that too. The Lord's good."

"I sure pray so, honey. I sure pray so."

"That's all we can do. Set the table, honey. We're almost there."

Meekly, Matt fetched plates and cutlery from the cabinet and set the table. Melanie dogged his footsteps, sucking her thumb.

"Honey?" Marjorie called out.

"Yes?"

"Do you sense something's going on at church?"

Matt paused, a fork mid-air. "You're referring to the incident at yesterday's fellowship?"

"I don't want to start rumors, but you could say that. Lily's a decent girl. I expected better of ENC."

"So did I. The prayer list gets longer."

"Mhmm."

Lily's face as she sat alone in a corner, suddenly ignored by the very people who once treated her as royalty, still bothered her. And for what? Because Paul had smiled at her? Would they have been as jaundiced, had he smiled at one of their daughters?

On the other hand, the same people weren't bothered by Kelly clinging to Paul. She liked Kelly, but something about that girl did not add up. As glamorous as Kelly was, she did not consider her a good match for Paul. Perhaps time would prove her wrong. She prayed so.

12

Paul stepped up to the threshold, rang the doorbell, and waited, one hand in his pocket and the other holding a spray of bouquet.

Footsteps approached; he straightened his tie again and stood tall in his summer suit. As he was selecting his attire for that evening, a gut feeling made him choose a suit and tie. He could hear his Dad's voice saying, "A gentleman does not show up in jeans to pick up a lady for a first date."

The door opened. Lily smiled——a bit shy.

A whiff of Rochas escaped through the door and sailed past him.

One glance at her and he sent up silent praises for his father's wisdom. Faded blue jeans was the last attire any man would wear to accompany a girl dressed in a cool yellow, mid-length tank dress with a high square neck and modest white sequined straps, white stiletto shoes adorned with discreet gold ornament and a pair of pierced gold earrings. Not even for a fashion statement should a man in his right mind attempt search a faux pas!

A single gold chain——of what appeared to be twenty-four carats—— completed her look. On the couch were a matching evening purse, with gold rims and a yellowish gold shawl. She had combed her hair down.

He had dated girls of different shapes and sizes, some rich and glamorous, and some of modest income; some, beautiful, and some, pretty; but Lily, wow! She reminded him of fresh spring . . . exuding confidence in her gentle poise, yet he suspected she had a stubborn streak in her.

True, he priced most the inner beauty of a woman. He liked what he knew about her——her mystique was the result of her inner grooming——but he was also aware that as in Abraham's Sara, she had real physical beauty. Exquisite!

He adjusted his tie and said, "Charming!"

She thanked him and invited him in. It seemed her foreign accent was more pronounced in her humble place than he had noticed before.

He continued to stand transfixed at the threshold.

"Do come in. Please," she repeated louder and invited him to take a seat with an elegant hand gesture.

He unglued himself from the entrance, adjusted his tie once more, and followed her inside.

When he gave her the flowers, she thanked him, inhaled the fragrance, then she arranged them in a tall vase and placed them on her coffee table, next to a copy of a family Bible.

"Would you care for a soft drink, or perhaps, a cup of tea?"

Wonderful, in one sentence, she had spared him the discomfort of declining a glass of wine. "Soft drink, thank you," he replied.

"Apple juice? Sparkling cider, soda?"

"Sparkling cider sounds perfect."

She returned to the kitchen.

He exhaled to slow down his pulse racing faster than his Porsche on a freeway and finally noticed his surroundings——a coffee table of dark ebony wood stood in the middle of the living room and a zebra skin straddled the couch. The couch itself appeared to be hand-carved . . . perhaps, of ebony wood also. A life-size statue of a Maasai warrior stood at the corner, on the floor, a pure Arabian carpet. Exotic African shields surrounded by exotic paintings, pastoral landscapes, covered one wall and on another wall, a mix of western art——all skillfully arranged to blend the two worlds.

Few pictures——one family picture, probably her parents and their young family, then a smattering of others people——graced the room.

Why had someone who could afford such a living room settled for such a neighborhood? A fleeting thought crossed his mind, but he dismissed it. Sure, he had heard murmurs and news coverage of potential tenants who could not get apartments of their choices——all that was so far removed from his world that it was hard for him to understand it.

No, a girl as lovely as Lily should be free to live in any neighborhood she desired. Besides, this evening was special. This was neither the place, nor the time . . . in conclusion, the room was unobtrusively elegant.

His lips twitched as he remembered how she had invited him to be seated with the same elegant gesture as his mother's.

She re-appeared carrying a silver tray and placed it on the coffee table, next to the flowers, turning the whole setting, into an elegant formal living room. "Would you care to see the geography of my apartment?"

"Would love to. Thank you," he replied, amused. Such etiquette had long been phased out by many of his friends. The only time he ever saw any geography of a house was when he asked to use the restroom.

She showed him the kitchen and the adjacent dinette and the guest bathroom to the left, plus other amenities, as they crossed the living room.

Down the small hall, she started to say, "At the corner is the guest room . . .," then she stopped and appeared embarrassed.

Right ahead was what appeared to be the main bedroom. In keeping with the summer mood, the room was bathed in a cheerful theme of soft pastel. A bedcover which appeared to be of pure Egyptian cotton and silk motif draped the bed, with matching pillow shams, all arranged neatly. A dresser drawer that completed the set stood in one corner. On her night table, a Bible and devotional book stacked neatly.

As they stared at the room, she embarrassed; he ambivalent; but rooted at his spot, another whiff of Rochas floated down the small corridor, until it hugged the air between them. He leaned against the door and studied the room, his hands, shoved into his pockets.

From a nearby restaurant, live band music drifted in.

"And that's the master, or the main bedroom." She closed the door firmly, and retreated hastily to the living room. Since the other doors were closed, he surmised that in her hurry to open the front door when he rang the bell, she had rushed out of her bedroom, living the door ajar, unintentionally.

He woke up from his reverie, unglued himself from the door-frame, and followed her to the living room.

"Well, this is it! My humble apartment," she said apologetic, having regained her composure.

"I wouldn't call it humble. It's exquisite."

"It's very kind of you. Thank you."

"Seriously, it's very pretty."

She thanked him again and served the soft drink.

He raised his glass to her.

In the silence that followed, he tried to hold her gaze. She looked down, shy——that amused him.

He drained his glass, glanced at his watch and said, "We should probably be going; the freeway traffic should be light by now."

As they went downstairs, a neighbor opened his door a crack.

"Evening Lamar," Lily greeted him.

"Evening," Lamar replied, and closed the door quickly.

"The neighborhood watch," she said, softly.

He laughed. "I figured as much."

He took great care seating her, then he drove toward the beach, turning up the CD a notch.

Rolling hills, retreating sun, distant red skies . . . cool sea breeze, night lights——moments of natural beauty were not out of reach in Southern California.

Lily inhaled deeply. The breeze played with her lustrous thick, dark curls that betrayed some Arabian blood in her roots.

Paul studied her face furtively, then refocused on maneuvering around a driver shopping the lanes.

Lily smiled and resumed studying the landscape, hoping he would assume she was studying the sunset.

She had noticed his furtive looks and wondered what he was thinking. Did he have the courage to go steady with a woman like her? What about his parents and his friends, could they live with his decision? She dismissed the thought and this time, studied the sunset in earnest.

After another twenty-some minutes, they pulled up at the valet parking in front of La Vie Restaurant secluded in the offshore waters of Newport Beach, with waves lapping gently at its foundations.

The maître d'hôtel smiled——enigmatically——at Paul and guided them to a very private booth——more of a room, than a booth. Old friends, Lily guessed, while wondering how many times Paul had brought his dates here. As quickly as the thought came, she dismissed it and committed to make every effort in the future to avoid entertaining such thoughts.

The maître d' came in. Again, there was that silent dialogue. Soon after, a clean, starched waiter came in. He offered them a list, not of their house wines, but of their soft drinks. They had everything, from sparkling cider, cold duck grape juice, to exotic iced tea and juices.

She ordered sparkling white grape juice. Paul did the same and ordered assortment of appetizers.

The waiter served their soft drinks and appetizers in reasonable time. She selected the lightest appetizers from the platter and nibbled on them.

Paul watched, selected a cracker loaded with crabmeat, and placed it on her plate, then followed with selections of more mouth-watering appetizers.

"Do I have a choice?" she asked.

"Nopes." He grinned.

She smiled and took a bite.

He opened the menu, and asked, "Do you have any preference?"

"Not at all. Please," she replied, relieved that he was a true gentleman. The same Paul at church was the same Paul on a date.

If she had her way, she would sooner an old-fashioned gentleman than a modern man. Haggling over bills with her dates was forbidden and beyond her nature. If forewarned, she would choose straight arrangements where she paid her share of the bill, then, she would most likely not date that man again. On this first date with Paul, she sensed he would probably be offended if she offered to pay.

"All right. How does chilled cucumber soup, followed by grilled sole, veal medallions, and light strawberry mousse sound?"

"Great!" she replied.

"Sure?"

"Positive. I prefer my veal well done," she assured him.

"I prefer mine medium rare." He smiled one of his crooked smiles designed to jolt her heart.

On cue, the waiter appeared and took their order.

More relaxed, she studied the city lights through the window.

Paul watched her, riveted. "So, what do you think?"

"Pardon?"

"What do you think of the city?"

"It's lovely. Very lovely."

He kept on a string of conversation about surrounding cities.

"You know a lot about beach cities."

"I comb them."

"Between working hard at Briden, Farrel and Seymour?"

"Yup. Work hard and play hard."

"I should have guessed. No wonder you have such a great tan."

He thanked her. "You're not bad yourself." He seemed to realize what he had said and blushed.

"That is okay. Let's say, the Lord took care of it," she rescued him.

"Amen. I like it. It's um, natural——no need to spend hours in the sun. Beautiful."

She thanked him, looked down, and shifted her plate.

"Now I've made you blush." He took a sip of his grape juice. "You've settled well in ENC and you help with Sunday school. How do you like it?"

"Quite a lot. The kids keep me growing. I learn more from them, than I teach them, I think."

"Same here. Have you run into Marc?" He grinned.

"Marc! He is one of my best students and funniest. I've learnt a lot about patience with him in class."

"Marc's a gift to ENC. I believe every teacher would agree."

"I think so. I'm never sure whether he is paying attention. But, as long as Marc is in class, I never have to wonder what the other students are thinking. Sometimes I serve cookies and drinks just to make it through story time without too much interruption. May the Lord forgive me!"

He chuckled. "I know what you mean. I'm tempted to slap a duct tape on his mouth for the duration of Sunday school."

"Lately I have seen some positive change in him. He is maturing. I think he knows a lot more about the Bible than he reveals."

He seemed taken aback that she had noticed, then he veiled his eyes. "Yes, he's grown a lot. I've noticed too."

The waiter served their first course in reasonable time.

During the main course, Paul made light conversation interspersed with jokes; but became more serious after they had finished the course.

"I noticed you've a few reservations; one can't help but wonder where they stem from." He used a more formal business tone.

"Mum and Dad."

"You were raised in church?"

"Pretty much. But it was not until my early teens that I turned the corner. I'm thankful for my parents' guidance and support."

He smiled. "It's interesting that you should mention that. A common fallacy that some of us churched people make, is to assume that we become followers automatically by virtue of our associations."

"That is true."

"That's a risk. It makes it difficult to realize that we fall short of the mark, unless, as you said, our parents or other role models, guide us."

"Yes, our parents . . . even more so, the Holy Spirit." Her face glowed.

He gazed at her with admiration. "You're right. Without the prayer and support of family and friends, I don't know where I would be." He grinned. "I was pretty wild. I didn't do drugs or anything, but I did push the boundaries—–harmless antics . . . crazy teenage stuff, but painful enough for my parents."

She dabbed her lips. "Did you get grounded?"

"Lots of times, until my cousin and I were bundled off to camp."

"Was it an instant decision or a process?"

"It was a process that brought me to that watershed moment."

"I guess we all go through a process. But at some point, we know."

"Yes. For me, it was at camp. My Cousin Jonathan."

"Mhmm." She nodded.

"We grew up together and got in trouble together." He chuckled again. "We'd some pretty wild times back then. Well, our parents bundled us off to camp one summer and it was there that we turned the corner. Not a moment too soon——their best decision."

"The Lord's timing is always perfect," she said.

The Maître d' entered and seemed to notice the electricity between them. "Everything going all right?" His eyes smiled at Lily, then rested on Paul.

"Yes, Emillien. You have excelled yourself, as always," Paul replied.

Emillien tipped his head and asked. "Ready for dessert?"

Paul rested his eyes briefly on Lily, then he replied, "Yes. I think we're ready," turned back to her and asked, "Tea or coffee?"

"Tea, please. Thank you," she replied.

Again, she sensed a silent dialogue, as though everything was scripted. The dessert must have been held back on purpose.

The waiter walked in with irresistible strawberry mousse. The strawberries were so fresh, they must have come straight from the garden, minutes before they were arranged artistically on the mousse.

"Yes. They were."

"I beg your pardon?" she asked, startled.

"I said, yes the strawberries were picked fresh today. Emillien Anton is the owner of this restaurant. As part of his excellent service, he keeps a hot house that allows him to keep serving fresh fruits, salads and vegetables, throughout the year——including some exotic selections from other parts of the world. He immigrated from Mauritius via France and has a degree in agriculture and botany. He's very knowledgeable about gardening."

"I am speechless, how did you know?"

"Are you surprised?"

"Well, we have known each other briefly. I mean, we have been going to the same church but . . . we haven't really become better acquainted. I mean, um . . . usually, only people who um . . . who have known each other for a long time can read each other's mind." She stopped, confused.

Paul seemed amused by her confusion. "I like it when you blush."

"How do you know?"

"Your accent becomes more British."

"Oh dear!"

"I like it. It's cute. So, should I take it as a good sign?"

"I don't know. Or may be a sign that I should be cautious."

"About what?"

"Everything——the pace … life."

"What aspect of life?"

"I don't know."

"Now you're being obscure."

"Good, then I will hold on to that." She took a sip of her tea.

"On the contrary, I believe we need to continue this conversation and clarify that last comment, before this evening's over."

The waiter returned with the bill.

Paul settled the bill and steered Lily out, straight to their valet. This time, the clock-like precision of the valet's arrival did not surprise her. She would have been disappointed had he kept them waiting long.

As they sped past scenes of night-lights, weaving in and out of dark rolling hills, she wished their drive could last forever.

"It would be a perfect ending to a perfect evening," Paul said.

"There you go again, reading my mind."

"Which reminds me, why would you need to take precaution against the harmony of our spirit?"

"Spirit? It's too early to be talking about our souls."

"But I beg to disagree. Our souls have been united for some time now."

"Explain yourself."

"Very well. When two people are in the Lord and their lives are in harmony, then I believe the Holy Spirit unites them. So it's not unusual that the Spirit of God in the heart of one would commune with the Spirit of God in the other, making it unnecessary for them to put into words what they feel. I sense that, when I'm with you," he sought her face.

She sensed he was not expecting a response and studied the night, instead.

At her apartment, he escorted her to her door, but he did not enter. "It's late, I mustn't keep you. Thank you for a very pleasant evening."

She replied, "It was a great pleasure. I had a great time."

"The pleasure was all mine. I'll see you in church? Perhaps, we could go for a drive later? Does Saturday work better for you?"

"Yes. Thank you."

"Good night. See you Sunday."

"Good night."

In a flash, he was gone. She heard his Porsche pick up speed in the distance, as it escaped and took Paul away from her and her neighborhood, back to his own. When the last sound of the roaring engine had faded, a heavy feeling——more of an ache, as one who had just said goodbye to a loved one––settled in her heart. She walked slowly to her bedroom, deposited her shawl and purse, then she prepared a strong cup of tea.

13

To all who knew Igor, he was the best of husbands, a father among fathers, a highly respected leader in the community, the very epitome of what a man should be. And from all accounts, he deserved that reputation.

At the third ring, Jonathan grabbed the phone. "Hello, this is Jonathan."

"Good evening, Jonathan. What have you boys been up to lately?"

"Good evening, Uncle Igor. Nothing much." For reasons Jonathan would find out later, he had a sense of foreboding. Uncle Igor normally called Paul's mobile phone, and seldom did he call the house phone in the middle of the week, even less so did he ever start a call with, "What have you boys been up to lately?"

"Have you been keeping out of trouble?"

Jonathan chuckled. "Yes sir. No speeding tickets. We've been walking the straight and narrow."

"Gospel truth?"

"Yes, sir."

"I'll let your mothers know. How's your band coming?"

"Great! A major label has just selected a couple of my latest songs. I made five grand a piece, plus retained the royalty."

"Congratulations! We're proud of you. We should have you come back for a concert at the beach."

"That would be great, Uncle Igor."

"Good. Then we'll arrange for it. Is Paul around?"

"Yes. Just a moment." Jonathan covered the mouthpiece and yelled upstairs, "Paul! Pick up the phone! Your Dad."

Paul's heart hit the ground with a thud. "Hi Dad. What's up?" he said, trying to sound calm.

"Your mother and I haven't seen you for a while. How's everything?"

"Fine. How's Mum?"

"Okay. She'll do better after seeing you." His father paused, then added, "Sometime soon?"

"Sure."

"How's your schedule this week-end?"

He scratched his head. "This week-end? Um . . . I've a commitment. How about next week-end?"

"We were hoping sooner."

He recognized a command. "Do I have a choice?" He chuckled.

"Yes. You do," his father replied in a firm low voice, but with a chuckle also. "Let's say between this week and this coming week-end."

"Okay. I guess I could drop by Friday evening after work."

"Still won't give up your week-end. Eh?"

He sensed they were matching wits. "Well, Friday's still within the time limit and I could spend the night, right?"

"All right. I'll tell your mother to expect you for an evening. She was kind of hoping for something longer than that."

"I'll make it up to her," he replied and wished him a good night.

He sat still for a few minutes, then he went to the balcony and stared in the direction of Hollenvine. Up until now he had never discussed his social life with his parents beyond the qualities of a good woman. He had assumed that if he adhered to choosing only reputable girls, his parents would be pleased with his choice. He now realized that what he had considered socializing, had been homogeneous——may be a German here and there, perhaps French, Polish or Swedish——but generally, he had stuck with the staple. His parents assumed he would, so did he.

A chill gripped his heart. Apart from vetting his friends when he was younger, his father had never interfered with his social life.

14

Friday evening galloped in like a warrior going to battle. Paul had planned no meetings for the day, to give him enough time to scrutinize some of the financial reports and leave earlier, or at worse, by four o'clock.

As if the day was not tight enough, Shane dropped by his office, citing a problem with some of the financial reports. He traced it and unearthed nothing in his department, but he ran across something interesting. He sensed Shane's complaint was a smoke-screen, and took it all in stride, with the professional grace that had earned him his position as a junior executive, but he had to stop by Bill's office.

"I got a call from. . .," Bill tipped his head, and closed the door.

He understood Bill was alluding to the Senior Vice President and Chief Financial Officer. "I know. Shane mentioned something. I did some research."

"And?"

"My team seems fine."

"But?"

He shifted his eyes.

"Something I should know?" Bill asked.

Should he or should he not disclose his discovery? As a manager it was his duty to protect BF&S and morally right, but, some of the employees could accuse him of tattling. "Um, I also researched some project invoices. Um . . . a couple did not meet BF&S' procurement guidelines." He rubbed his neck, wishing he could be anywhere else but in Bill's office at that moment.

"Let me guess."

He nodded.

"How much are we talking?"

"A hundred grand."

Bill whistled. "That should require some disciplinary action."

"Not quite. The signature came from higher up . . . Ethics and Risk Management." He pushed a file across the desk to Bill.

Bill reviewed the invoices. "Did you talk to anyone about this?"

"Yes. The um . . . Chief. I hope I'm not misquoting anyone—according to the powers that be, BF&S' policies only apply to the lower ranks, senior management should be in a position to make sound judgment, and, BF&S' Balance Sheet is ten billion dollars strong. The amount in question's not considered material."

"By whose standard? I defy you to pick up a hundred grand on the street!" Bill snapped out of his chair and stared out of the window. "Your opinion?"

"A hundred grand here, a hundred grand there, pretty soon we'll be talking some considerable materiality." He rubbed his nose.

Bill abandoned the window, locked the door and with a flick of his wrist, motioned him to his conference table.

With their heads huddled together, Bill asked, "How bad is it?"

He pulled out more files and said, "Some of the services provided may've been negligible or nonexistent. I couldn't verify them."

By the time Bill had finished reviewing the files, he had turned pale. Someone had been authorizing payments of contracts obtained under the radii of BF&S' policy for years. BF&S' policy required that all contracts above two hundred and fifty thousand be obtained through competitive bidding, after an extensive comparative market research. To circumvent this policy, none of the individual invoices was large enough to draw attention; but after several years of this game, the combined total was in millions.

Moreover, BF&S' regular auditors were not as savvy; belying the seven-figure fees that BF&S paid them. Whoever handled the payments spread them to different ledger accounts, under different cost items, thumbing their noses at the company. To avoid scrutiny, the offenders had selected an employee outside his department to process and pay the invoices. That employee was rewarded with a promotion and several company awards for outstanding service.

Bill asked him to leave the file with him. "Don't worry about it. Do the best you can. In due time, the Lord will take care of things. And by the way, thank you for taking the financial lead on the project." Bill paused; his eyes smiled at him. "Not to pry, how're things?"

"A week ago, I'd have said great, but now, I'm not so sure."

"Getting second thoughts?"

"No. It's my Dad I may have to contend with." He squared his shoulders.

"Mmm." Bill's gray eyes softened with understanding. He came around the table. "Don't forget, Sheila and I are with you."

"Thank you." He returned to his office, ruffling through his hair, tense.

Despite Bill's comforting promise and a brief quiet time alone in his office, by the time he pulled out of BF&S, he was drumming his dashboard.

Once he was on his way to Orchards City, he slammed the gear, revved the engine, stepped on the gas, shopped lanes, and shot ahead of the speeding pack. He gripped the steering wheel so tightly throughout the thirty-some miles to his condo that his knuckles turned white. On arrival, he slammed on the breaks, inches from his garage door and went inside. The door vibrated in protest.

He gulped down a glass of orange juice and ran upstairs to take a shower. Jonathan was rummaging in the garage.

With the blow dryer running, he eyed his wardrobe, calculating how best to present himself for the evening. A silk summer shirt, matching linen slacks, and loafers, his mother's favorite, won.

Unconscious of how striking he looked, he ran downstairs with a male vanity bag dangling from his arm. Keeping extra wardrobe at his parents' home enabled him to travel light whenever he visited them.

Jonathan was back in the living room, packing his electric piano. He glanced at him. He shifted his eyes. Jonathan must have noticed, and said, empathetic, "Off to the beach?"

"Yup. Pray for me," he replied.

"I am. Don't forget, His grace is sufficient. Chin up! Uncle Igor and Aunt Charlotte are the best set of uncle and aunt anyone could wish for."

"I couldn't ask for better parents. Where's your gig?"

"At some new restaurant in Orange County. Salt and Light?"

He shook his head. "Never heard of it."

"Neither had I until a couple of weeks ago. They take gospel groups. It's supposed to be a pretty hot spot for now." Jonathan moved a drum set.

"Sounds like where you guys should be. May be Lily and I should visit it sometime," he said with a crooked smile.

"There you go!" Jonathan cheered.

◆ ◆ ◆

Two hours after leaving Orchards City, Paul drove through the gates of a well-lit mansion straight to the garage and parked his Porsche alongside his Mum's silver blue sports Mercedes Benz and Dad's silver Jaguar.

He could hear Percy scratching the patio door as only a determined German Shepherd could. Percy abandoned scratching and started barking and trotting his dog-run, excited.

Ignoring him, he spent a moment enjoying the view, then he entered the house through the connecting door to the garage.

His mother came out with familiar lights dancing in her eyes. "You came for the weekend!" She clasped her hands.

In the background his father hovered, dressed in a navy–blue jumpsuit, jiggling coins in his pockets, as his keen eyes weighed him. He braced himself, exchanged a polite greeting with him, and took his bag upstairs. His old room smelled fresh with not a speck of dust in sight. Mum!

His mother soon served a menu, suitable for a diplomatic peace talk—veal medallion, his favorite, for the main course and very light lemon meringue, his father's favorite, for dessert.

His father said grace, haltingly.

Paul shuffled his veal around the plate. Not since he was a teenager had he felt so much blood pumping in his ears. He was sending SOS prayers to heaven for a peaceful ending to the weekend. His father was his mentor and he had never questioned his authority, he had no desire to spoil that record.

After dinner, he rinsed the dishes one by one and stacked them in the dishwasher, as he had done many times before, but he did it in deliberate, slow motion to buy time.

His mother warmed up slices of meringue pie in the microwave, and placed them on the serving tray, with the mugs. She wiped the counter, squeezed the dishrag in the sink, next, she wiped the stove, squeezed the rag in the sink, then she repeated the cycle.

He watched. If his father raised the issue, how would he respond?

"Would you like whipped cream with your pie?" she asked.

"Just a dab. Thanks Mum," he replied.

"You never did like whipped cream. You take after Grandpa, that's for sure. He's the all–American health nut, if I ever saw one."

"Good for Grandpa!"

"He's always been the meat and potato guy."

"How's he doing? I've been zooming in and out. I should go by and spend some quality time with him . . . a week, or so, would be nice."

"He worries about you. He wants all his grandsons to congregate at his house for male-bonding, and then the granddaughters the summer after."

"Not this summer."

"Don't wait too long now."

"The boys and I'll work out something, the Lord willing. Surprise him."

"Ho-ho. He would love that."

She served coffee in the den in heavy mugs and helped him catch up with family news, bridging the awkward moments.

Occasionally, his father murmured something, more often, he watched them from under his brows, between sipping his coffee. After draining the last drop, his father cleared his throat and said, "So what's this I hear?"

"What's what, Dad?" he shot back——playfully, he hoped.

"There's a rumor going around." His father's lips twitched.

"What rumor, Dad?" He braced for the evening, wishing his father would postpone the heavy matter until the morning.

"I think he's being stubborn. Do you remember how he'd wrinkle his face and rub his nose, and give you the most deadpan look, which was his way of saying, 'You aren't getting anything out of me?'" his mother jumped in.

"Yes. I remember," his father replied.

"You might be getting one of those. I don't think he's ready to talk, honey."

"Ready to talk about what, Mum?"

She sighed. "Paul, we're your parents. The door is always open."

"Mum, there's nothing to worry about."

"That's not what I hear."

"I don't understand."

"Well, as your mother, I want you to think," she said.

His father shifted and crossed his leg. "I guess I'll jump in at the deep end. What your mother means is . . . certain friends have expressed concerns to us. You've been seen around town in recent weeks."

He smiled. "I'm always around town."

"I know. But not the way I hear lately."

They laughed.

"I can assure you Dad, I don't have a heavy metal jacket hidden in my closet. I thought about getting a motorcycle, but that's as far as that went and I've never been a fan of green hair——you can rest assured."

"Well, I don't know, son . . ." His father rubbed his chin, as though feeling for stubs of new growth he had missed. "Is um, Kelly still at ENC?"

"Yes." He leaned back and crossed his legs. Both hands gripped his chair.

"You mean the one who hangs out with Sharon?" his mother asked.

He wondered why she needed clarification since the Shinebonds were family friends, unless they had conspired.

"Yes. That's the one," his father answered.

"Isn't she adorable? She's such a well-groomed girl . . . the most charming manners . . . such a pleasant girl . . . excellent tastes . . . and those adorable blue eyes! It's a miracle she hasn't been snapped up yet."

"Yes. She's a nice girl. Comes from a solid family. We go back along ways. Come to think of it, our families always end up in the same neighborhood."

Not by design I hope.

"That's true. But while Jeremy and Angela are unaffected, the Shinebonds are kind of aloof. Of course, their daughter's charming," his mother said.

"It's true that they may be on the high side. It's understandable, but I don't think they mean any harm, honey. We've known them a long time. They command a lot of respect in the community. Quite an influential family."

Steel blue locked into Aegean Sea steel blue.

The decision was already made. Why try to reason with them? Paul turned on the TV, cupped his hands behind his head and let his legs slide forward, until his body stretch out to its full length, and stared at the program on the television, but he did not really see the program.

Mum and Dad run their household almost as a royal palace. They avoided shouting matches and vulgar exchanges. It would be disrespectful to start a family argument now. He exhaled.

In the silence that followed, persistent scratching and whimpering and sneezing and whining from the patio continued to pester the intended audience. Unable to ignore Percy any longer, his mother let him in.

Percy whizzed past her to his side, crawled on his knees for a pat, and nuzzled behind his feet.

His Dad and Mum stared at each other, nonplussed.

"Well, would anybody like another cup of coffee?" His mother's eyes pleaded with him.

In her eyes, he saw turmoil. She seemed torn between her love and respect for his father and her love for him, and something else——fear. He wished he could assure her that everything would be all right——that God was in control, no matter what.

"I'd love some more coffee," his father replied.

"Paul?"

He collected himself. "No thanks, Mum. Perhaps later."

"All right." She retreated to the kitchen.

His father watched him try to cheer up Percy, then he said, "Perhaps I came across too harshly, son, but your mother and I don't want to see you hurt. Take your time. Shop around, as they say. You understand?"

"Yes sir," he replied, even as exhaustion sailed down his body.

Percy twitched his ears and kept alert for any signal from him.

On the one hand Paul determined to block out Lily from his mind; on the other hand, could he disobey his parents and still be counted among the faithful sons who respected their parents?

In Apostle Paul's letter to the Ephesians, he instructed children to obey their parents in the Lord, so did the fifth commandment in Exodus.

He had memorized those verses in Sunday school. If only there was another way! As dedicated believers, surely, his parents must have weighed their decision to favor Kelly, before summoning him home?

15

At a red light stop, Paul dialed a number on his mobile phone and waited.

"Hello?"

"It's me. I'm sorry, I won't be able to make it this evening," he said.

"Of course. I understand." A pregnant silence followed, as Lily waited.

Finally, he stammered, "Um, see you at church and um, have a . . . pleasant, day." He gripped the steering wheel, as he waited for the light and drove on like a robot, gnawing his lips, oblivious of the scenic course through gated estates, hiding behind mature garden-scapes.

Lily's trustful voice, with just a hint of a question, tested his resolve to obey his father. He cringed——he hadn't the nerve to break up with her face-to-face, after six months of pursuing her publicly. She would figure it out soon enough, especially, when she saw Kelly hanging on his arm.

♦ ♦ ♦

Paul walked into Jonathan sitting at the breakfast counter, wolfing down scrambled eggs dripping with tomato ketchup, strips of bacon and a stack of toasts, on the side plate, a muffin and slices of apples.

"Let me guess, you guys didn't eat last night."

Jonathan stuffed his mouth and asked, "What do you think?"

"How did it go?" He tried to distract him from prying.

Jonathan downed the bacon bits, licked his fingers, and said, "Better than I thought, but never mind how mine went. How did yours go?"

"Just as I thought."

Jonathan whistled. "That's unlike Uncle Igor."

"Try both."

"You're joking. Right?" Jonathan seemed taken aback, as if he had truly believed his uncle and aunt would be reasonable.

"Nopes." He threw his car keys on the coffee table, flopped onto a couch, and combed his hair with both hands, his face grim.

Jonathan abandoned his breakfast. "What's next?"

"Kelly again."

"They do not!"

"They do too."

Jonathan groaned. "What about the other girls?"

"Within limits, I could and I will, but I think Kelly's top of the list."

Jonathan started pacing the floor. "Have you told her yet?"

He blew his cheeks. "Yes. I did."

"And . . .?"

Through the window, he watched a humming bird hover over a trellis of bright orange trumpet creepers, looked at Jonathan——calm, deep, then he went upstairs, whistling, 'Can't Help Falling in Love with You.'

Jonathan bowed his head and prayed, unsure——long interludes, followed by select words. When he opened his eyes, Paul was sitting at the top of the carpeted stairs, holding his Bible. How long had he been sitting there?

Paul left at noon and returned early evening, laden with shopping bags.

Jonathan abandoned his music scrolls momentarily.

"What?" Paul asked.

"You went . . .," Jonathan threw his hands out, "shopping?"

"Yes. I did," Paul dropped the bags on the floor. "Knock yourself out."

Gingerly, he inspected a bag, reluctant to intrude into Paul's private life and whistled. "Bed and Bath?"

Paul nodded.

He held up a comforter set made of pure Egyptian cotton with silk motif. "You must've spent a fortune on these——last time I checked this comforter alone was at least three hundred dollars."

"They were worth it."

He examined two paintings from the second bag. "Are these real?"

"May be."

"I didn't know you were into art. Uncle Igor and Aunt Charlotte, of course! But, you?"

"I am, now. Sucked it from my mother's breasts!"

He lifted up a rug from a huge bag and said, "A moose skin rug, that's pretty cool. Where did you get it?"

Paul took the rug, shook it in the air, and threw it on the largest couch. "At the mall. The only one left. I couldn't find zebra rugs."

"Excuse me?"

"I said, I couldn't find any African zebra rug."

Jonathan stared at the bags, his arms akimbo, shaking his head. "What's with the shopping spree? It's unlike you, Paul, to shop on impulse."

"Who said I bought them on impulse? I have it on the highest authority, male and female created He them. A man shall leave his father and mother and cling to his wife. Some things are worth fighting for. I should've bought an Egyptian quilt months ago." He grabbed his bags and went upstairs.

Frowning, he watched Paul retreat, then a light dawned. "Did she have a Monet?" he shouted. "You didn't do anything stupid, did you? You never step out of line and she doesn't strike me as that kind of girl."

Paul gave him a haughty, quelling, but amused look. "I'm a gentleman. And if I were not, I'm pretty sure she'd have broken my leg, but, she showed me the geography of her house. It was like seeing a glimpse of heaven. Since a glimpse's all I have left, I thought I should hang on to it." He turned and shut the door behind him.

Jonathan whooped, "Paul's got the bug. Who would've thought!" Paused, a light dawned. "Why not? Moses and others did."

16

Paul rubbed his eyes, turned to the sixth chapter of Ephesians, a reference to Exodus' fifth commandment and read,

> "Children, obey your parents in the LORD, for this is right. *'Honor your father and mother'*; which is the first commandment with promise: *'That it may be well with you, and you may live long on the earth.'*"

He went and leaned over the balcony, wishing he could rewind the clock. How could a person know whether his parents' advice was given in the Lord? Pray? But lately it seemed all he heard was silence. Shouldn't any counsel given in the Name agree with the Word?

How long could he hang in there? As a dutiful son, he had been dating Kelly for two very long, painful months. Only his reverence for the Lord and love for his parents prevented him from rebelling.

The brief moment of happiness that he had with Lily continued to sustain him. Avoiding her at church had been easy, since she refused to claim her place by his side, but the memory of their dinner lingered.

Had it been Kelly, would she have been as compliant?

The last time he broke up with Kelly, she had gone on a merry-go-round about town, probably just to show him what a fan-base she had! And was she in society pages! How could anyone have missed.

He frowned. Kelly was a sweet girl, but he found her possessive assurance tiresome. More important, he found it hard to hold any deep discussion with her. Had she learnt anything in her twenty-six years of spiritual pursuit?

Not looking forward to the evening, he dragged his feet back into the room to dress for a fund–raising party at the home of family friends in Bel

Air. The fact that their host and hostess were in their early forties, and not his parents' contemporaries did little to help.

He seldom attended the same party as his parents now, but being the heir apparent to the Van Clyden Enterprise often called him to duty, even though he worked for BF&S. On this particular occasion, duty called.

At Kelly's condo, he ambled to her door and rung the bell. She opened the door, glowing from head to toe——a mix of hangover and mouthwash hit his nose. Her eyes looked a bit glazed, though her speech was still lucid.

She must have had a manicure and pedicure and massage and the works. To boot, she was wearing a new perfume, very much a twin of Fabrice Étrange's La Mystique de Mademoiselle Musk——her current favorite.

♦ ♦ ♦

The party was in full swing when Paul and Kelly arrived and the music louder than Paul preferred. He spotted his parents chatting with their contemporaries at one end; and at the other end, close to the bar, the Shinebonds standing with two other couples.

Stanislaus and some old friends had cornered a spot in the room. Leaving Kelly to catch up with her girl-friends, he circulated around the rooms, engaging people in the usual polite conversation that good manners required, then he joined Stanislaus' group in their corner.

The crowd grew louder as the evening progressed. He studied each face. *What am I doing here, anyway? Will my life be like this in a few years——accompany my wife to a party, watch her get inebriated, then chauffeur her home? Dad and I need to talk.*

Stanislaus said something, bringing him back to earth. He shook off the morbid thought and refocused on his group. So engrossed was he in their discussion that it took him a while to hear Kelly's voice raised above the crowd. Empty bottles and half empty bottles covered their coffee table.

Excusing himself from his group, he strolled over, thankful for the soft lights that camouflaged his beet-red face.

A stunning blonde took tottering steps toward him, leaned forward at a dangerous tilt to the left, and said, "Ladies prefer marriageable dark-blond gentlemen. What's your preference?"

"I hate to break up the party, we need to go." He grinned, embarrassed.

"What's the hurry? We just got here," Kelly slurred.

It's been two hours at least. "I've a commitment," he said.

"Oh, come off it! Commitment! Commitment! You're a wet blanket!"

"I know. We need to go." He restrained himself.

"If you insist! I'll say goodnight to Mum and Dad," she tossed over her shoulders and walked in regal steps, her head held high. Along the way, if she tottered, she disguised it by landing naturally on the arm of the nearest guest, engaged the guest in a charming conversation for a minute or two, and then continued on until she reached her parents.

Paul eyed her progress. He should have accompanied her to wish his future parents-in-law goodnight. Resisting the temptation to emote, he searched for his parents in the adjoining room. Before he reached them, he caught his dad's eye from a distance and blushed. His father must have observed the whole scene.

Mortified, he ambushed a lone guest standing nearby and engaged her in a conversation, briefly, to compose himself, then he continued.

Kelly's cackling and her group's raucous conversation had caught Igor's ears, all right. Getting red around the gills, he watched the content of the bottles on their table get lower in proportion to the number of times each girl refilled her glass. In his eagerness to preserve his dynasty, he had not bargained for that package in his future daughter-in-law.

Since voicing his preference for Kelly, he had finally noticed what others must have known all along? Tom and Trish were a lot like their daughter——or should he say Kelly was a chip off of the old block?

He glanced over in Paul's direction. Paul was nervously playing with his tie. He dared not look at his wife.

True, the Word did not condemn alcohol outright, but it cautioned those who would be leaders to have self-control. As a father and a leader, he had counseled his family and friends often, concerning this controversial matter——the gray area. Some believed that Christ drank wine too and others argued that Christ did not drink fermented, potent wine, but a special type of grape juice commonly used during that period. Whatever Christ drank, He never made a cake of Himself.

Moreover, he believed he was his brother's keeper. His brothers could be recovering alcoholics who sought refuge in the place of hope. If they could not depend on him, then who could they trust?

He sensed that his friends and acquaintances scrutinized his life and venerated him. For some, he could be their last hope. And as the laws closed in, he dared not get pulled over with a blood level in excess of the limit. For him and his wife, their watershed came about twelve years earlier, when Paul was a sophomore in high school and showed signs of growing up.

And the clincher? After Paul started driving, he evaded to tell them about a traffic ticket by going to traffic school. Imagine what could have happened, had Paul added imbibing to his list of rebellion?

How does as a parent tell a child to behave? In a snap, he and Charlotte became teetotalers and not a moment too soon.

"Whenever dealing with a gray area, go for the straight and narrow," he had counseled his family. Could he live up to his own advice now?

How did Kelly measure on the scale of the straight and narrow? The rate at which she and her friends had emptied the cellar, betrayed no evidence that Kelly understood her future role as Paul's wife and his daughter-in-law. How could she be so insensitive! Her behavior portrayed some sort of entitlement and a lack of restraint. She appeared to enjoy basking in the sunbeams of revelry.

For a fleeting moment, he wondered how Paul spent his time on a date with the unknown young woman——probably out in some exotic restaurant in the inner city, eating with his fingers and dancing to loud rap music—— with pellets flying every half an hour, and police sirens whizzing past, though Paul rarely danced? He sighed and refocused on the other guests.

Why was he in this party, anyway? With what type of crowd did he socialize? Diamonds and emeralds all around, each trying to out-shine the other.

He and his wife and the Kaarlyles were teetotalers, yet liquor flowed freely in the parties they attended. It was good for business, he rationalized.

As if on cue, Paul appeared. He wasn't smiling. It was only nine o'clock.

Kelly chatted with her parents, returned to her friends and her glass again.

Paul came over, murmured, "We should be going," and guided her gently by the elbow through the crowd.

"Take your hands off me!" Kelly lunged at him with her clutch.

He broke her lunge and said, ice cold, "That was uncalled for!"

Just then, he caught Stanislaus' eyes, grabbed Kelly, walked over to him and said, gently, "Take her home!"

Stanislaus nodded.

He thanked him and walked out. Kelly called him a name he wouldn't want his parents to hear. He kept on walking.

Considering all that Kelly had put him through, her behavior was unjustified. He felt no remorse at abandoning her at the party. Organizing a ride for her was more than sufficient. She had the whole Shinebond clan and fans to keep her company. No Shinebond was ever in need of a ride!

But before he reached his car, he felt, rather than heard a voice say, "Take Kelly home." He turned and bee-lined for Stanislaus.

"I knew you would do the right thing. Hang in there, buddy. It'll be all right. We're all praying!" Stan whispered in his ear and patted his shoulder. "Miracles happen. Believe it!"

"Pull over. I think I'm gonna puke." Kelly clapped her mouth, retching.

As soon as it was safe, Paul slammed on the breaks, pulled over to the side of the freeway and turned on the hazard lights.

Kelly opened the door and stuck her head out, just in time.

Once the retching had stopped, he asked, aloof, "Ready?"

She slammed the door, wiped her mouth, and closed her eyes.

Without a word, he drove all the way to Kelly's condo. Without a word, he held her hands to the door, more out of habit, than good breeding. Without a word, he settled her in her living room, made a strong cup of coffee and watched her drink it, as he flipped through TV channels. Without a word, he took a cashmere shawl and covered her with it. Then without a word, he bolted the door behind him and returned to his car.

The Van Clydens don't leave their dates at parties. No Van Clyden had ever knowingly endangered the life of a woman regardless of who she was, or her social standing. Also, the Van Clydens did not risk the reputation of their friends. Stanislaus was trustworthy, but Kelly was capable of jeopardizing the reputation of anybody. He could not impose that kind of responsibility on Stanislaus, especially.

If Kelly ever accused him of anything, let it be that he was too much of a gentleman for her taste.

Back home, he knelt at his bedside for a long time, numb.

♦ ♦ ♦

Half an hour after Paul left, Igor steered his wife out of the party and drove in silence to the Pacific Coast Highway. "Honey, about this evening——"

"I was kind of surprised too." Charlotte interrupted him.

"I guess that was something we didn't consider."

"Mhmm."

He took a deep breath, "Well, I don't mean to be hard-nosed, but Paul's happiness is my concern. After all, he is our son."

"Mhmm."

"I'm sure if he discusses his sentiment with her, she'll understand."

"Yes. She dots on him. But, she has a mind of her own." Charlotte hesitated, "She's charming; but I find it hard to communicate with her sometimes. I noticed it takes her a while to see things from a spiritual perspective."

"Mmm."

"Sometimes I feel as though I'm talking to a wall."

"Funny you feel like that. The Shinebonds have been with our crowd for as long as we've known them. Twenty years, perhaps longer."

"At least twenty years. Kelly had just started kindergarten when our families first got together. Though I'm not sure that time is always an indicator of true character. We haven't spent as much quality time with them as we have with our other friends."

"I agree." He mulled over Charlotte's comment, then asserted, "It'll work out. I'm convinced it will. Kelly comes from a solid stock."

"Our Paul's a good catch. I don't believe he'll have any trouble at all. Kelly's a charming girl . . .," Charlotte's voice wavered.

17

Paul parked on the side of a quaint breakfast place in Orange County and walked a step behind Kelly, instead of holding her hand.

The waiter took their orders. Paul ordered fruits, toast, and coffee, hoping Kelly would do the same. She ordered slabs of sausages and bacon and eggs and hash brown, muffled with onions and as an afterthought, as if to portray some redemptive quality in her, a small bowl of fruit.

After the waiter had served them, Paul watched her down her plate of sausages and bacon and eggs and hash brown, muffled with onions and ketch up, sucking her bright-red, claw-like fingers in between crunching bacon strips with her sharp, orthodontic teeth, as he nibbled his toast, her putrid smell of hangover from the night before now replaced with the smell of onions, garlic and bacon.

Occasionally, he studied the Saturday morning customers picking through their breakfast——some more bored than him.

If he persisted on honoring the arrangement, perhaps he too would become as bored in one or two, or perhaps . . . three years? That was about as long as he thought he could pretend to be happy in his marriage with the woman that now sat across the table from him; but he would have to remain committed to her for life. What would he do during the rest of that time, if she didn't toss him aside? Tread waters . . . or work late . . . unless, she became miraculously transformed, and he fell in love with her, after all?

How long he could remain committed was not his nightmare. If he allowed her to drag him to the altar, creating a survival routine during their first year, was daunting——perhaps breakfast Saturday mornings, or a night to the movies on Friday, and of course drag themselves to church with plastic smiles on Sundays, and pray no one noticed. What about the rest of the week? Would she agree to go to midweek prayer meetings, or would she abandon her pretext the moment he slapped a ring on her finger?

Her perfume kept hitting him in the face. It had greeted him when he picked her up this morning; he had endured it along with the putrid smell of her hangover during their ride.

He settled the bill and steered her out of the restaurant.

As they sped along the freeway, he dove in. The drive home the night before had been silent. Breakfast was strained. Why not keep up the trend?

He shifted gears and stepped on the gas. "Kelly, could you refrain from, eh . . . certain behavior in public?" He measured his words carefully.

"How do you mean?" Kelly replied.

"Yesterday, for instance."

"I still don't get you." She played dumb.

"Well, your group was having quite an uninhibited time."

"So, you don't want me to party?"

"That's not what I said."

"You implied it. You want me to just sit there and stare at people? That's not very social."

He threw her a look——his nostrils dilated, slammed the gears and revved the engine. "Let's stop playing games. Okay? Last night was uncalled for. There're better options to be sociable."

"Hon, you know who I am. Do you want me to be a hypocrite?"

"That's not what we're talking about. I want nothing of the sort. But we should be good examples. For crying out loud, I'm a youth mentor!"

"So you mean Jesus doesn't like us to have fun?"

"Stop twisting my words. Why wouldn't the Creator want you to have responsible fun? But He *is* also Holy. We should mind the gray areas."

"I don't get you."

"Oh come on Kelly! Don't give me that! You're a smart girl! You know that the laws have tightened. As a believer, I'm convinced we should strive to help one another by avoiding the gray areas that could ultimately lead to dishonoring the Lord. As things are, I believe we should abstain."

"You're mad about last night, aren't you?" she whispered raspy, frail.

He disliked it when she pulled one of her whispery vocal tactics on him. He pinned his eyes on the road ahead, his jaws set, as he counted to ten, and tried to think of a suitable kind word to say to her.

If only she showed remorse or admitted she needed help. He did not buy that bit about disease or ingrained in the DNA. This was one disease the victim could avoid by steering away from the environment or staying away from bad company, especially, with supportive, loving family and friends.

He had done his best to introduce Kelly to suitable friends with similar interests, but who would never re-enforce her bad habits. He had gone to functions simply to please her and protect her, to what avail?

"I appreciate that you abstain, honey. But what's that got to do with me? We're adults. I do what I want. We're free to do what's best for ourselves," Kelly continued.

"We're our brother's keeper."

"Excuse me?"

He blew his cheeks. "I was thinking out loud."

"You haven't answered. What has my preferences got to do with yours?"

"I thought I just did."

"Oh."

He slammed the engine again and did two jerky lane changes. "Okay. Let's say I was recovering, how would you help me resist the temptation?"

Kelly shrugged. "I don't know. Perhaps I wouldn't offer you——"

"And . . .?"

"And would inform my friends to do the same."

"As a believer, Kelly, what should you do?"

"If you're insinuating that I should abstain, I've a problem with that. You're free, so am I. We're all different."

"You got that right." He restrained himself from sounding sarcastic. "But on the contrary, I think we should be considerate and responsible. Look, you know as well as I do, that we live under constant scrutiny more than any other group. Almost everyone judges us by a different standard. The press is always waiting for us to make one mistake——to nail us."

Kelly turned to the window and crossed her eyes.

Paul continued, "Other people can get away with almost anything. It's one thing when we stumble; it's another when we blow it deliberately. Kelly, you hang out with people whose judgment I find questionable. What if one day you were pulled over? Then what? What would it do to your parents?"

"I don't see where this conversation's going. My parents are none of your business. You're getting preachy, you know that?"

"I, preachy? If you intend this relationship to work, I suggest that you weigh your options . . . and your parents' happiness should be my concern. I'd hate to spend the rest of my life defending my inconsistency on the subject. More so, I'd hate to be a stumbling block to other people."

"I get it. You're upset at my friends. Right? What's a little bit of fun?"

"Is that what you call it?" he snapped. "I'm glad you clarified that."

"So am I!" Kelly retorted.

"Ships that pass in the night," he muttered.

"What did you say?" Kelly spat out.

"I said, two ships passing in the night."

"Paul! California's thirty-one million strong, each free!"

"I suppose we're into stats now," he muttered.

"What's that supposed to mean? Are you insinuating that I'm not smart enough or as enlightened as your friends?" she snapped.

"You're jumping to conclusions. You graduated with honors——it's engraved in my mind . . . We were talking about freedom, yours, or mine?"

"Smart mouth! Mr. Van Clyden, I'll have you know I can do as I——"

He pulled over, slammed on the breaks, and turned on the hazard lights. "Don't you dare! I won't have you cuss or swear in my car! I put up with enough as it is. Kelly, you're unrepentant. You make no effort to even try. If you wish to continue compromising to fit in with your so-called progressive . . . liberated circle, it's your prerogative; but a man's car is his sanctuary." He dropped his head on the steering wheel, in despair.

Kelly turned her face again to the window.

He raised his head. "If you think virtue's wrong, you're entitled to your opinion, but respect me! You humiliate me Kelly——in front of my family and friends! Is this the way it will be? You disgrace me; I swallow my pride, and you act as if it's no big deal?"

Kelly opened and shut her mouth without a sound. They had had similar discussions before. This was the first time he had blown a fuse with her. Profanity and cussing repulsed him. His own friends respected him and appreciated his stance, but she made little effort.

Knowing she was his parents' preferred choice, assured of his hand, Kelly was acting as one who had leverage over him, most likely abiding her time, hoping she could tempt him with a glass here . . . a glass there, and after she had conquered him, have him eating out of her hands, as tame as her lap poodle, as she had with all her past suitors——before she got tired of them.

But was she in for a surprise! He had developed a survival plan. Right now, it was obvious she would not apologize——she rubbed her ear, tossed her head, tweaked her loose curls, and raised her chin.

He signaled and joined the traffic. "Is this your idea of walking in the Light——swearing . . . running your mouth? No right and wrong, anything goes——one moment praising the Lord, the next, blowing with the wind?"

"As I said, this is California. I have rights and I'm free to date whomever I please. It isn't like we're already married," Kelly said, subdued.

"You said it. I think we should start seeing other people," he tried to bring the unpleasant conversation to a firm conclusion.

"I don't believe I am hearing this," she mumbled.

For the duration of their ride back, he stared straight ahead, except for checking the rear–view mirror or changing lanes.

Kelly stared out of the window.

He did not despise her; he disliked her effrontery in believing they were destined to be together for life, while failing to understand his world and the responsibility he bore to his family and his family name.

At her condo, he opened the car for her and held her hands to her porch, reticent. The moment she turned the key in her door, he escaped back to his car.

Later, when Jonathan brought the grocery, he was downstairs, whistling, doing laundry, after a sweaty work-out, punching the dummy in the garage.

To dodge Jonathan's questions, he caught up with his Sunday school work, reviewed the financial news and finally, watched a family comedy.

What about seeking other wise counsel, besides Jonathan's? He was losing all objectivity toward Kelly and worse, he feared, all compassion for her. Was it premature to consult with Pastor Tim or maybe not?

18

Pastor Tim studied Lily, then he turned to talk to a couple who had been waiting to catch his attention. His conversation with Paul had revealed to him a depth that he hadn't fathomed in him and challenged his own assumptions. Without mentioning any names, Paul had given him enough to persuade him to change his perspectives on other members of ENC.

"Which class were you teaching today?"

Lily turned around. Sharon was standing behind her.

"Third graders. Fun group . . . so willing to please." Her eyes twinkled.

Sharon agreed. "You haven't run into Marc lately?"

"Oh Marc! The joy of my life. Marc, be still! Marc, stop squirming! Marc, don't disturb the class! Marc, give Maryann back her pink crayon——she likes to use colors that match her dress. Marc! Come over here and help me distribute the crafts. Good job. I call him my lesson in patience. As a friend of mine is fond of saying——strips the religiosity out of one and exposes the real Christian."

Sharon laughed so hard, she turned red and fanned herself with her hand.

Lily placed the Sunday school materials in her car and strolled with her to the coffee stand. After chatting briefly with her, she circulated, greeting a few people, in between scanning the crowd for wall hangers.

Paul worked the outskirts of the crowd, talking for a minute here and there, then moving on, his hands in his pockets. Kelly was nowhere in sight. Lily thought Kelly might be out of town or sick, otherwise, he would be holding Kelly's hand or rather, Kelly would be clinging to him.

Paul lifted his eyes and looked at her, a steady look that burned through her skin, straight to her heart. She turned hastily, confused and embarrassed, ashamed for being caught staring. She excused herself and headed for the sanctuary. Even with her back turned, she could still feel Paul's eyes burning through her spine, as she walked. She sat in her favorite seat, assuming he would sit with his friends. However, she sensed him behind her when he entered the sanctuary.

She took one look and froze, then she turned and stared at the cross, biting her lips. Paul had sat a row behind her pew, at an angle designed to give her the fullness of his eyes.

She refused to speculate what had happened between him and Kelly. It was none of her business. When he called her that Saturday morning, she had hit the streets at less than ten minutes a mile afterwards, numb. No need to spell it out. It was over between her and Paul. What now? Change churches?

Two weeks basking in Paul's favor did not entitle her to him. Her parents had raised her to be sensible, what had possessed her to let down her guard?

◆ ◆ ◆

Mid-afternoon, Paul was in his room, staring at the ceiling, tracing subtle patterns from one corner to the other, having abandoned the adventure novel he was reading. For a free Sunday afternoon, he should have been resting, as his parents had drilled into him. Hadn't it been a Sunday, he would have been out hiking in the hills or working out his frustrations in the gym.

The phone rang. By instinct, he knew it was Kelly. Jonathan had taken Sharon to lunch, so it was useless wishing Jonathan would answer.

He turned his head to the wall, ignoring the ringing, hoping the caller would leave a message. After seven rings, it stopped.

Five minutes later, the phone rang again. He shifted to his back and cradled his head. No relief, ten minutes later, another round started. He grabbed the receiver, and snapped, "Hello."

"It's me. I just wanted to say sorry," Kelly whispered, in her sultry voice.

He kept quiet.

"Paul, I know you're angry and you've every right to be. I shouldn't have said all those nasty things and I'm sorry . . . the whole weekend . . . everything."

He said nothing. He felt trapped. He should forgive her. It must have been hard for her to admit that she was wrong. But, knowing Kelly, he suspected she would want more. She sounded like it. In forgiving her, he risked raising her hope that they would pick up from where they had left off. He had no intention of letting her do that to him; but forgive her he must, for his sake.

"Paul?"

"Yes?"

Kelly sighed. "Look, all I want to say is I'm sorry. Okay?"

He took a deep breath, "Apology accepted. I'm sorry too."

Kelly waited. He knew she was expecting him to say more. He too waited. Finally, he heard the phone click.

He replaced the receiver and returned to entertaining himself staring at the ceiling, moving his eyes from one corner to the next, then back. He lay in that state, until he drifted off to sleep.

As he dozed off, he replayed Lily's face that morning, tracing his progress above the crowd. Perhaps he could reconnect with her at the Burger Place.

19

Paul dazed his way through the morning, wishing he had done his graduate work out of state——would the change of environment have increased his chances of meeting other girls?

Shane nipped at his heels, dropped by, pretending to consult a colleague in his department about an invoice——no doubt to have another quick glance at his leather chair. Later, Shane cornered him in the corridor and asked, exuding confidence, "How're things going?"

He raised his head, surprised. "Quite fine. Thank you. How's your project coming along?"

"Great! Just great! Listen, we haven't been out to lunch in a long time, how about sometime this week?"

"Lunch sounds great. But I'm kind of tied up this week. Perhaps sometime in the future?" he answered.

"Sounds good. Let's keep in touch." Shane sauntered off.

We've never been out to lunch, period. He watched Shane's swaggering back disappear. It was only Monday; would the rest of the week improve? And Thanksgiving?

Despite Kelly's apology, he had no intention of keeping any of their dates for the week. Now Shane!

Feeling stifled, he longed to escape to the hills, as far away from voraciously ambitious people as he could. Was it the hills he longed for or a complete change of environment, such as do an international stint——with a diplomatic twist to it——to broaden his horizon and acquire more multi-cultural executive grooming?

He had lived abroad before; would another international stint be escaping? What was wrong with escaping? *A wise man sees trouble and flees.*

A fool falls in. He shook his head and rebuked himself. Lily was not the trouble, his attitude was, so was his approach.

To ensure that Shane did not corner him again and he did not have to lie, he rounded up his lunch buddies for lunch on Wednesday, but not to the Burger Place. The thought of returning to the Burger Place made him break out in cold sweat, but the idea of spending time away from California was becoming increasingly palatable.

♦ ♦ ♦

Lily walked to her cubicle, clutching her files in one arm and rubbing her temple with the other hand. She had just finished a meeting with Mr. Chancey. "Your work's excellent," he had said. He was even hinting at a promotion, but that could have been another ploy to appease her and get her to take on more projects.

It was no secret that she was one of Denton & Terrell's workhorses. She trained the new recruits and raw managers, and they and Brad got the promotion. To protect herself, she had learnt to bridle her hopes, even as she continued to pray that all that would change, one day. She would do the work and get the promotion also, or better yet, she would start her own accounting firm and leave the company.

A Certified Public Accountant (CPA), if she remained frugal and saved, she could start her own accounting firm within ten years.

Out of the corner of her eye, she espied Brad standing at a T-junction, chatting with a brunette——a new assistant office manager, been with the firm for just two months——name was Crystal or Tamara or something. Not in the mood for pleasantries, she made a left detour to avoid him.

Unbeknown to her, when she had turned the corner, Brad raised his eyes and studied her back, as a window shopper would long for an expensive diamond in a jeweler's store.

Bernice watched Brad from her angle with razor sharp eyes. She had been searching for Lily, when she caught sight of him.

Lily settled down at her desk and massaged her temples again.

"You know, sooner or later, you have to confide in someone," Bernice's voice came over the cubicle. She mouthed, "Who's he?"

"How do you know it's a he?" she mouthed back.

"Experience. It's Paul. Right?"

Loathed to lie, she nodded in agreement.

"Would you care to talk about it? This really calls for dinner, but I know you've mid-week prayers tonight. How about lunch?"

"Lunch sounds fine. Thank you."

"Then we could go out for dinner this Friday, if you're free? Alex and I would love to treat you to dinner."

Bernice pulled out of Denton & Terrell and drove to a local Deli. Not feeling hungry, Lily ordered a salad; Bernice ordered a Tuna Melt Sandwich and potato chips, with a side order of salad. The orders were served timely.

The moment Lily finished saying grace, Bernice snapped a big chunk of her Tuna Melt with her teeth.

To postpone Bernice's questions, she chatted about the difficulty she was having, trying to love her rap neighbor——she even played her classical symphonies louder than she preferred to, but he didn't take the hint, "So, I am determined to find a new place, may be even buy," she concluded.

"I heard that one judge makes them go to the opera," Bernice chuckled.

"That should do it."

"What type of house are you looking for?"

"I think I'll try a condo. My income qualifies, but . . ."

"But what?"

"Try walking up a real estate office and asking for a nice condo! You would think things have changed."

Bernice licked her fingers and stared at her, comprehending. "Oh, I see. Consider it done."

"Excuse me?"

"I'm dedicating my Saturdays house-hunting. If anyone turns you down, they'll hear about it from the press! I've a friend who knows what to do."

"Thank you; but I'm leaning on grace. The Lord will come through. He has never let me down, as long as I allowed Him to guide my steps."

"My Mum says, the Lord can use people He puts in our lives. Don't you worry about a thing," Bernice said, stuffed a lettuce in her mouth and asked, "Now, where would you like to start?"

She dimpled at Bernice's direct approach, so typical of her. "I don't know where to start. I don't have a story."

"What do you mean? We all have a story. But, can you trust me? Yes. You can. I'm your friend, remember?"

She debated Bernice's face. At what angle should she approach her non-existing relationship with Paul? "To begin with, the whole thing was over before it started. I think from start I was deluding myself."

Bernice waved a potato chip at her. "I don't believe that for one moment. What the two of you had that day was more than an illusion. Any woman in her right mind would die to have that much power over a man."

"I don't think I am his type, Bernice."

Bernice took a big bite of her sandwich, chewed while waving a fork at her, sucked her fingers, and swallowed, elongating her neck, then she said, "No, no. Don't go putting yourself down, Lily. Some of us may be obtuse about a situation like yours, but what I saw in his eyes was real. If a guy ever looked at me like that, I'd whisk him up that altar so fast he wouldn't know what hit him! And what more, he'd love it."

Forgetting her manners, she stared at Bernice, her fork poised mid-air. "Bernice, thank you for encouraging me, but he is dating someone else. From the looks of it, they are practically engaged."

"Practically engaged isn't the same as engaged."

"It is almost the same."

"No. It's not. Is he happy?"

"What do you mean? Isn't happiness a choice?"

"He doesn't strike me as the type of man who makes up his mind in a hurry. Or who flip-flops once he's made up his mind."

"How do you know? You just met him that one time."

"He had a square jaw, yet his eyes turned soft——vulnerable——when he looked at you, as though he dared not hope, yet, dared to hope."

"You got all that from that brief meeting?"

"I know these things. To prove it, you've invited me to church numerous times. I've taken rain-checks. I'm coming to church with you this Sunday."

Surprised, she blurted out, "Why?" Then she hastened to correct herself, "No. I didn't mean it that way. I would love for you to attend church with me any time. It would be a great honor."

"Great! I need to evaluate him myself."

Her jaw dropped. "Bernice. What about the Lord's will?"

"That's what I'm going to find out. It may take a while for others to come around. But as long as you both honor the Lord, I believe He will bless you."

She tried to cut in, but Bernice put up her hand, "Yes. I know, we can impose our own will, claiming it's God's will and end up hurting everybody in the process; but, we can also deny His will if we insist on having it our way."

Struggling to hide her shock, she stammered, "If I did not know——or at least think I knew you well——I would swear you were a believer."

"Thank you," Bernice replied, one hand across her chest, flapping her eyelashes, in a show of holiness.

Despite her pain, she laughed, a happy sound that made other customers smile. After the difficult past months, she needed that.

She studied Bernice, seeing another angle of her spunkiness. "You're something else, you know," she finally said, shaking her head.

"I'd like to think of myself as your friend."

"And you are, Bernice."

Had Bernice left it to her, she would have clammed up about Paul. The lunch had proven more cathartic than she had expected.

She declined Bernice's dinner invitation for Friday night, citing another commitment, but would she and Alex like to go to a concert with her on Saturday, instead?

Bernice replied that if Alex was not free on Saturday, she could go, after helping her find a good condo.

Back at the office, Lily spotted Brad again in the corridor, talking to the same woman who had been hanging on to every word that fell from his lips. Didn't the man ever do an honest day's work in his life?

But, as Lily passed, if she had eyes on the back of her head, she would have seen Brad shift his position and follow her progress to her cubicle. The assistant office manager tossed her hair and huffed back to her cubicle.

Brad returned to his cubicle, frustrated that his attempt at making Lily jealous had fallen on blind eyes. He cradled his head, until he heard his boss' voice——that prompted him to grab some files from his shelf and slam them on his desk. It felt good, so he collected another set; they too suffered the same fate.

"Hey, keep it down there, will ya!" Bernice yelled.

"Mind your own beeswax!" Brad snapped back.

"I'm minding my own beeswax. It's the noise that's bothering me."

Several people chorused, "Peace. Order! Order! Com'on!"

For the rest of the afternoon, Brad stayed at his desk shuffling papers and paging through files noisily. At the end of the day, he drove to his favorite hang-out.

An hour later, the bartender said, "Tomorrow's a work day, man. Do you want me to get on the wrong side of your old man?"

Why did he bother to come? He could have gone straight home to the privacy of his house; but he hated the silence of his own company. With a hand that was still steady, he pointed to the door and told the bartender, "I'll see myself out," then he swaggered out in measured, dignified steps of silent despair.

◆ ◆ ◆

Talking to Bernice had cleared Lily's brain. She was not the type of woman who would allow a man to dictate her happiness indefinitely. Without confiding in Bernice, she met with Mr. Chancey as her mentors had advised her earlier on, disclosed to him the challenges she was having completing her PhD and asked for half a day off the Tuesday after, to register at UCLA. This was something she had to do for herself.

Lord, "If I should remain single, at least let it be as one who can manage her own affairs well and honorably," she prayed.

When she arrived home, she researched other Bible-oriented local churches again through the yellow pages. She had grown fond of friends at church, but it had become evident that Paul's imminent marriage left her only one choice.

20

For weeks Marc and Miguel had been poking around looking for answers to a puzzle. Not satisfied with the way the adults were behaving, Marc tried another angle——why not put it on the topics for the family debate? With a proper approach, he, Melody and MJ could lobby their parents to reveal their position on the delicate matter.

Melody planned her strategy with MJ; they had more than one reason to pursue the subject. If they tackled the problem the wrong way, their parents could revoke all their privileges.

Monday evening was a good time to start a serious discussion—— pastor's sermon still fresh on everybody's mind and everybody was relaxed after the weekend. And, wasn't it also the Thanksgiving season when everybody was kind and happy?

Melody called a mini family meeting before supper. Calling the meeting was easy; getting the meeting going required the skills of an arbitrator.

Marc entered and bee-lined for Melanie.

"Marc. Leave my hair alone!" Melanie yelled.

"Marc! Don't upset Melanie. She's not your toy," Melody ordered, trying to sound grown up and in charge.

Marc sighed. "All right! I was just trying to straighten her ribbon."

"She doesn't like it, okay? You know she won't let anybody comb her hair, except Mum."

"And you?" Marc shot back.

"Yeah. And me. Anyway, that's not why we're here."

Marc picked up Melanie's shaggy doll——limp on one hand, with screaming red hair——and squirmed from side to side, making faces at it.

"Marc! Stop squirming and get serious!" Melody ordered again.

"I am serious. I'm here, aren't I?" He shook the doll in the air. "I don't like dolls. Why do girls like dolls, anyway? I could never figure that one."

"Marc! Settle down," MJ ordered. "In another three to five years, I bet you'd have a different perspective." He coughed.

Marc dropped the doll and plopped on to Melody's bed. "I will! Okay?"

"How comes he only listens to you?" Melody asked MJ.

"Because he's my brother," Marc shot back.

"Oh yeah? He's my brother too."

"Okay, okay. Let's get the meeting going." MJ tried desperately to stop his lips from twitching.

Melanie pouted at Marc and scrambled up next to Melody, rubbing her hair. She handed over the beleaguered ribbon to Melody, "Put it back on my hair." She sat still, her hands folded in her lap, and her head bowed.

MJ found a place to sit and gave Melody a steady look, their secret signal. "Okay Melody, you have the floor." Between him and Melody, they had already decided how the meeting would end.

Melody took a comb from her night table, and brushed Melanie's hair into a pony tail, while surveying the room. "All right. We have to do something about the situation. There's no other way. I just feel we need to do something." She fluffed the pony tail just the way Melanie liked it.

MJ nodded. "You're right. I've kind of been wondering whether nothing could be done. I understand where everybody's coming from, but I still think from Christ's point of view, the whole thing is farcical."

"What's farcical?" Marc asked.

"Ridiculous. Irrational is a better word," MJ ruffled his hair. "I don't know what Jesus would do. But I don't think He would side with everybody."

"Yeah. They're not dishonoring God. When they teach our class, they emphasize that we should not play games, 'cause God sees our hearts and knows when we're rebelling," Marc said, sounding rather grown up.

"You're right, buddy. I've assisted in both their classes. They're fun, but also very humble. It's not wrong to want to do the right thing. Besides," MJ blushed, embarrassed, "there're other reasons."

"Well, some of my friends and I've also been thinking, but we don't have the answer either. Miguel says he thinks it's the media and the trend––to accept everything, even some questionable stuff, except . . . you know . . . people like Paul and Lily. Nothing's changed even after two centuries. Well, everything's changed, but again, everything's the same." Marc seemed shy, but pleased to be elevated to the level of an adult.

"Plus, it could all come to nothing, anyway," MJ observed. "Nothing wrong in getting better acquainted."

"Okay. We'll go through with the usual plan." Melody turned to Marc, "Marc, you know what to do."

"Kind of."

She gave Marc one of her charming smiles she reserved to coax others to do her wish. "Yes. You do. You've seen MJ and I do this before. Just follow our example."

"Why not ask Melanie?"

"Melanie's too young. She can barely string a sentence together. Her turn will come. So, you're next in line."

"I don't know how. I don't think I can pull it off."

"Yes. You can."

"What if Mum and Dad get on my case?"

"No, they won't. Just tell them . . . no, we'll all tell them that we need some clarification. They can't get mad. They're the ones who're always telling us to be kind. Remember?"

Marc brightened up. "Then you do it, Melody. If Mum and Dad won't get mad, you do it!"

Melody tossed her hair back, "Marc, don't be chicken. Of course I can do it, but it's your turn. Sooner or later, you have to do it. MJ and I've already had our turn. And we did it for all of us. Besides, you're still at that age where Mum and Dad won't get upset at you for speaking up."

"All you've to do is be polite," MJ added. "Remember the rule."

"Yes. And you can start from any topic and end with any topic, as long as you honor God. Okay? Keep in mind we're not trying to manipulate Mum and Dad, or change the Word. We're only trying to make sure we understand it correctly," Melody said.

"Okay." Marc looked a bit fazed.

"And I'll tackle it from another angle. You know how Mum loves to take me on." She paused, looked around, making sure she still had everyone's attention. "Then we'll work our way slowly to the point. And don't forget, we'll all be praying. Okay?"

"You'll do fine. I'm counting on you, buddy." MJ ruffled Marc's hair, again playfully.

"Okay," Marc grinned. He loved it when MJ ruffled his hair.

"But it won't be right away. We'll build up to it over the next few days. And we have to make it look real." Melody said, with a stern look.

"What do you mean 'make it look real?'" Marc asked, suspicious.

"I mean not staged. It has to be like any normal family debate otherwise, they might think we planned it. Which we did of course, but we had to start somewhere."

Marc's face lit up. "That's cool. That's real cool."

MJ clapped his thigh. "Watch out Melody, he's gonna cream you."

"Don't worry MJ, I'll return the favor." Melody assured him. She paused and surveyed the room. Everybody's eyes were still on her. "Okay. That's settled."

"I'm glad something's finally getting done," Marc said, gleeful.

"So am I. But we definitely need help. We'll all take turns praying and MJ, can you please close for us?"

"What're we praying about?" Marc asked.

"That everybody will be humble and choose to do what is right. We're not asking anybody to impose their own will. Rather, if we define what God doesn't like, can we find out what's okay or what He doesn't mind for His children to do? And, feel free to pray as you wish."

They made a circle and held hands. Melanie gripped Melody's hand on her right, grabbed MJ's on the left, and squeezed her eyes shut. She didn't understand everything, but she knew it was so important that everybody had to pray real hard.

A few minutes later, loud footsteps descended the stairs as if a troop was approaching the kitchen. At the thundering sound, Matt raised his head. "Here comes the Lord's army. Hope dinner's ready."

Marjorie replied, "Lord have mercy!" placed a macaroni casserole into the microwave and fluffed a large bowl of chopped lettuce. Small dishes of chopped tomatoes and garbanzo beans, already drained stood by on the counter, in the sink, a colander of peeled carrots.

"Dinner's almost ready. Everybody, make yourself useful——grab a plate, a knife or a pot. Marc, make sure Shaggy's fed and I hope you've finished your homework!" she yelled.

The last plate was in the dishwasher and sealed dishes of leftovers were stacked away in the fridge, brimming with fresh produce.

Matt flopped down, grabbed his western fiction, and dove in.

Marjorie wiped her brow, then started on the counter. Every now and then, she glanced at the grandfather clock in the corner.

Marc entered, but hesitated at the door, scratching his arms, while following his mother's progress with his eyes, then he took a deep breath and stepped forward. "Mum, can I ask you something?"

"What?"

"If Jesus is love and we should all confess our sins, then why don't Christians always get along?"

Melody peeked at Marc from behind their mother, and nodded.

"Is that what you think?" Marjorie asked, taken aback, but trying hard to mask her face. After all, this was Marc talking.

"No. That's not what I think; that's what I know," Marc replied.

"Well, believers are not perfect. They're in the process, honey."

"So does that mean until Jesus returns, we won't get along, ever?"

"Marc, don't exaggerate," Melody cut in.

"Well, almost. Otherwise we wouldn't have all the different denominations. Right? We'd all sort of be able to worship in any church and belong anywhere, as long as we understand the language. Right?"

"Right." Marjorie nodded.

"Then, if we could all worship in any church, we'd all kind of belong together, as in the early church. Right?"

"Right."

"So then we wouldn't make each other miserable because of some sil——I mean, man-made rules. Right?" Marc caught himself in time.

"Marc! Watch your language!" Marjorie paused, rag in hand. Was there more to the conversation? "What man-made rules are you talking about?"

"Well, all kinds of man-made rules. You know, rules that make people not act like Jesus."

"Really? Name one."

Marc thought for a little while. "Well, Jesus left only His disciples, but now we have all kinds of denominations——Catholic, Presbyterian, Evangelical, liberal, conservative——you name it. But I thought being a believer means becoming a disciple of Jesus?"

"You're right. Jesus left only one type of believer——His follower. And yes, loving us is important, but, He's also holy. Some of us seem to forget that very important detail."

"But He's loving all the time. That's the most important."

"Well, Dad and I love you all, but we also have a standard that sets us apart as the Jonesons. And," she leaned forward and rubbed noses with him, "though we're not blind to your faults, we expect better of you. God expects us to abandon things that don't honor Him and do things that honor Him, because we're His children."

"That's what Pastor Tim and the other pastors say."

"That's right. So, yes, I agree with you. If everybody was simply Jesus' disciple, emulating Him, there would be no denominations, and we wouldn't cherry pick or argue over definitions. We'd all allow our lives to be molded by His standard and . . . we would be very different from the world." Marjorie finished wiping the counter and worked on the stove top.

"That's what I said——I believe we've to think about what pleases God first, instead of what pleases us and then do what's right instead of just talking about it."

Matt coughed loudly; Marjorie gave him a warning look. He pulled his Western up to his face to hide a smile. After a brief moment, he put it down and took Melanie upstairs to read to her and tuck her in bed.

Soft whining came from the patio, followed by loud barking and scratching on the door.

"Shaggy, be quiet," Melody commanded.

"Marc, did you feed the dog?" Marjorie asked.

"What dog?"

"Is that a no?"

"Yes. No, Ma'am. I mean, right away." Marc bolted for the exit.

Melody sighed and shook her head. "Oh Marc! When will he ever remember to feed that dog on time? Mum, will Marc ever grow up?"

"Yes. He will. Some people I know used to be just like that."

Melody batted her eyelids. "Not anybody I know, I hope."

Marjorie chuckled. "No comment." Marc was the one child who had been puzzling them. It was hard to get him to focus, but now, out of the blue . . . she smiled. It could have been Pastor Tim in the pulpit.

She stashed away the last of the pots in the lower cabinet, next to rows of baking trays and asked Melody, "Where's MJ?"

"Tinkering with his truck."

"Tell him no fixing trucks in the driveway. Neighborhood policy."

"Relax, Mum. He's in the garage." Melody squeezed the wet dishcloth she had used for drying the pots and pans, collected the rest of the dishrags from the kitchen counter, and went to the laundry room.

Marjorie heaved a sigh of relief and said, "Praise be for sons!" While Marc was maturing well, MJ was becoming a mystery.

Why had MJ been spending so much time working on his truck, lately? He seemed preoccupied. Was he getting into bad company? She didn't think so. He was popular enough at school——seemed to be turning into another Paul Van Clyden, what with his dark, angular looks——otherwise, he always came straight home after football practice, unless he was hanging out with his church group.

There was nothing about him, or his room, that suggested he was hiding anything, yet, he had become so quiet, always pensive.

"Lord, I sure hope all's well," she prayed. Too early to confide in Matt Sr and it was definitely not her place to get Paul involved, though he was MJ's mentor. No decent mother should cross that line, no matter how tempted to. When MJ was ready, he would most likely confide in him.

21

BF&S buzzed from the corridors to the coffee rooms with news about global projects and refining future corporate vision. As a finance manager, Paul was swamped with requests for financial forecasting, painting different scenarios and most likely outcomes. He and Bill worked overtime, sometimes, to meet executive demands.

True to his commitment, Paul squeezed out enough time to go out for lunch with his buddies. Boycotting Lily's restaurant, he steered his group to Italian Sicilian Ristorante, but remained taciturn the entire way, and concentrated harder on his driving than usual.

The restaurant was half-way full and catching steam mostly with white-collar type professionals. Seating took about five minutes. Not bad.

Paul ordered ice tea; Phil ordered a Sprite. Rod and Julian, the other associate, disregarded company policy.

The waiter returned with their drinks and took their lunch orders.

Rod jumped right in, tipping his glass frequently, breaking BF&S' policy of no alcohol while on duty. Some employees observed it; others—including some managers, ignored it. Paul always insisted on driving.

Rod took another gulp of his drink. "So, how's our dating life coming?" he addressed Paul, rubbing his hands together.

Phil cut in, "Rod, let's stick to the rules——no personal questions, no raunchy jokes and absolutely no profanity or cussing!"

"That's right," Julian, agreed.

Paul wondered why he bothered to network with Rod, who was more of a colleague, than a friend.

Of the three, Phil was the closest to him. Julian had become a friend on account of Phil. Rod had managed to become a friend by ingratiating himself to his inner circle. There was a time he thought Rod had some redemptive qualities in him. Now he wondered. That God could help any man who asked for help, he did not doubt; but that he would be the instrument to help Rod change, he was not so sure now.

He sketched a smile that started from one corner of his mouth to the next, and no more, then he switched to sports.

Rod played along, in between letting his eyes rove the restaurant, but returned to his favorite topic at the earliest opportunity.

Paul had had enough. "Rod," he said in a calm voice, too calm for Phil who knew him better than any of the men at the table, "You're aware of course, of the changing times?"

"If you mean am I cutting it close? I would say yes——"

"Then let's stop while we're ahead," Phil cut in.

Rod laughed, nervous. "Folks, lighten up. It's lunch time. Relax. Let nature take its course."

"Rod, you're a wild mustang," Julian added in a low voice.

Rod guffawed loudly. "Hey, I try not to disappoint."

"It wasn't meant to be a compliment."

"Julian, lighten up. Everything . . . is . . . under . . . con – trr-owl. Cheers everybody." He emptied his glass and refilled it.

Once again, Paul steered the conversation back to business, and engaged the group in a heated debate over the market. Where was the Nasdaq Stock Market headed by end of the year? What about the Russell 2000 Index? Would the upward trend continue?

Rod searched the restaurant bored, sporadically, locking eyes with a female trapped in his gaze, then raising his glass, and without warning, jumping back into the conversation, before resuming shopping the room with his eyes again. He tossed his second glass down.

Paul counted. For Rod's two glasses, Julian had sipped his first glass only twice. "Rod, we've a meeting this afternoon," he cautioned him.

"Don't worry. Everything's cool."

"I know."

Everybody chuckled, uneasy.

Paul, Phil and Julian resumed discussing the market. Paul assured them the analysts were betting on small stocks and steering off large techs.

Finally, the waiter brought their orders.

Midway through the meal, Rod siphoned the last drop of liquid from his glass and emptied the content of the bottle into it, covering only about an inch of the bottom. Signaling to the waiter, who walked over, wary, he said, "Another bottle please."

"We had intended to order some orange juice. Is it too late?" Paul asked, genially.

The waiter took the hint. "Not at all. I'll get some right away."

"What's your problem?" Rod scowled.

"Could you excuse us for a moment?" Paul said to the waiter. After the waiter had gone, he turned to Rod and said, "Let's step out."

Rod shrugged and followed him out to the corner of the parking lot, away from customers' view.

He eyeballed Rod and said with a smile, "Rod, we'd love for you to remain our lunch buddy, however, we understand you have choices."

"You're the designated driver," Rod tossed out.

"That's where I draw the line. If you object, take it with upper management this afternoon." He kept his voice low, but his ire was clear.

"You controlling freak!"

"I have responsibility to my employees and to BF&S. If you don't like it, find other lunch-time buddies. But I will not have you ruin the careers of stellar employees and my friends who've worked their heads off to gain BF&S' trust to get where they are . . . nor mine. Got it!"

Rod remained taciturn.

"You can leave now and find your way back to the office or we can go back in, be civil, and finish lunch. What will it be?"

Rod took a deep breath, extended his hand and said, "Got it."

"Thank you." He shook Rod's hand. "If you need help, Rod, you can talk to me. I'm here to help. I'd like you to have a successful career with BF&S."

"I know," Rod nodded.

They returned to the restaurant. When the waiter glanced over, he signaled him to come over. "Can we have the orange juice, please?"

"And milk?" Julian asked.

"I would say coffee," Phil added.

The waiter nodded.

Paul wished he could help Rod——if Rod was willing——but he must also protect his friends. How long would Rod remain at the firm?

He wondered about Shane too. Avoiding lunch with Shane had driven him to organize lunch with his group. Had he not run into Shane on Monday, he would be seated at his desk, working through his lunch.

While Rod's philandering and inebriation were potential lawsuits——DUI or sexual harassment——that could enrage BF&S; Shane was a thorn in the flesh——a thorn he wished he could extract permanently. Everyone deserved a job, but must Shane be such a nuisance?

Shane tested his resolve to love people; Rod crystallized his need to walk the straight and narrow. Watching Rod sapped his energy. The more he networked with Rod, the more he wished to find the right woman, marry her, and never let her go.

What if he found a suitable girl and his parents refused to yield? He dismissed the thought. "Faith is believing; believing is faith."

22

Lily believed that God designed her body and soul to function together. As in the Garden of Eden, one day of rest a week was as important to her as a day of hard work. Scrubbing and cleaning on Friday evenings and going for her hard work-out on Saturday mornings, liberated her Saturday evenings to attend concerts, if she wished and her Sundays to dedicate to the Lord and relax. On days she did not attend concerts, she curled up with a book, a bowl of fresh fruits by her side.

Before she and Bernice, and hopefully Alex, could attend the Los Angeles Philharmonic concert, she had a tight schedule for that day.

For her exercise, as always, she escaped into the hills after a light breakfast, away from the city into quiet solitude. Once out there, she popped in and out of sepia woods, enjoyed the view of the valleys and listened to the sound of birds singing and the gurgling brooks, all joining their praises in adoration of Him——God's tapestry, spread before her.

In the background, the low humming of traffic on the Freeway reminded her that Southern California's population was swelling. Her neighborhood had not escaped. But in the sheltered park reserve, surrounded by trees, she escaped to another world, a world like her youth. Years ago, she and her sisters would trek out into virgin woods around her grandparents' home, to collect wild fruits, when they were too tired to weed the field. During school break, they always helped their grandma weed millet and ground nuts and maize fields. But, in the late afternoon, tired from bending over, they would abandon her parents in the field with grandma and grandpa and escape into the woods.

The thought of spending hours up in the hills lighted up her eyes.

The phone rang, interrupting her thoughts.

"Morning." She sounded cheerful, as though expecting that call.

"Morning! What time this afternoon? Are you working with a realtor? Do you have anything lined up?" Bernice asked, excited.

"Yes, to both. But I wanted to go out alone first. I like low-key sales."

"I found two places you might like."

"Great. Let's meet at two o'clock," she said.

"Do you mind if we change at your house for the symphony?" Bernice added. "Alex would love to come."

She said she would be delighted. That would give them three hours of house hunting, before dinner and the concert.

On second thoughts, it was kind of Bernice to show her the ropes of buying a house in America. She had done extensive research on the real estate market and she was capable of making good deals, but she was also aware that some realtors were more motivated about making commissions than serving their customers.

She prayed for a condo in a quiet neighborhood. A two-bedroom condo——with the bedrooms upstairs and the living room and kitchen downstairs——would be the best for family visits.

She patted her cheeks, cleaned her face and dressed for the road. She didn't wear headsets while out exercising. According to researchers, it was risky on busy streets. She did not believe in careless living, but preferred using common sense and faith, instead. Or did she? Setting herself up for a broken heart——though a gentleman Paul be——was not wise.

No longer nervous about running into Paul again as she did when he had a crush on her, she swung her arms with confidence.

If only this weekend would bring her closer to a better understanding of her future, she wished, while half her mind debated what to wear to the symphony——business casual pants and a more formal blouse, definitely.

Alex and Bernice arrived before two p.m. "Lily, this is Alex," Bernice, introduced a slightly stocky built man of about five foot, eight inches tall, with a pleasant face that cancelled the severity of his twirled mustache. His eyes spoke volumes when he saw Lily.

"How do you do, Alex?" Lily greeted him.

"Please to meet you, Lily. It's nice to finally meet you. I've heard a lot of good things about you," Alex answered, still struggling to keep cool.

"Same here. I have heard a lot about you too."

"Good things, I hope?" He grinned.

"Of course! Bernice only says nice things about you."

"Well, I'll leave you girls to it. Is four-thirty good?" he asked Lily.

"Four-thirty is good. We should be back by then," Lily replied.

Berlioz and Debussy, Bernice's chirpy presence and Alex's quips, relaxed Lily. After the intermission, she was preparing to enjoy the second half, when she froze. No mistaking it. Across the aisle was Paul sitting erect and alone, no sign of Kelly. She turned her head quickly, and stared at the orchestra, tuning up.

Bernice and Alex seemed to think she had become quiet, mesmerized by the musicians.

"It's amazing that after all the cacophony, the same group will actually produce sweet music in a few minutes," Alex joked.

She joined in the laughter, praying hard that Bernice would not notice Paul. How long had he been sitting there? How did she miss him before the intermission? He must have changed seats. But why was he alone at the concert? Or may be Kelly was in the ladies' room?

She checked the crowd, discreetly, but she did not see Kelly. One woman looked like her, but nah! The other lady was sitting with another man——probably her date or husband? And on second looks, didn't resemble Kelly that much, just her hair style.

At the end of the concert, Lily hurried to the side exit, after the second curtain call, knowing Bernice and Alex would follow, even though the audience was still applauding for an encore.

At the exit, she glanced back in time to lock eyes with Paul; he seemed uncertain.

23

Paul walked the outskirts of the crowd, thinking about the concert the night before, with Kelly clinging to his arm as a stick of glue would.

A week ago, Saturday, his father had called and hemmed and hawed about the virtue of maturity and commitment and seeing things from adults' perspective and how love was not always what it was cracked out to be and how when you get older, things that seemed so important when you were young, did not seem so important anymore. His father ended the call by inquiring after Kelly.

He had suffered in silence and accorded his father the respect he deserved as the man who had fathered him and raised him. Until that call, he had dodged all dates with Kelly.

As soon as his father had hung up, he had zoomed to the gym and spent an hour pumping iron, and reciting verses under his breath. Out of his sweat came a conclusion, a risky one, but nevertheless, a conclusion—lunch was the longest he could remain polite on a date with Kelly.

Assured that he would most unlikely dishonor his parents' wishes, lunch was the only excuse Kelly needed to pose again as his intended. So here he was, once more drawn into the web.

A redhead popped into his view. He recognized Bernice and stiffened, wondering how he could extricate himself from Kelly, before he went over to say hello to her. In no way would he throw Kelly in Lily's face, with Bernice as a witness. One day, Bernice could become his most useful ally.

From above the crowd, Jonathan spotted him. He signaled. Jonathan followed the direction of his eyes to Lily and back. Casually, Jonathan guided Sharon through the crowd, heading toward him. Kelly, unaware, continued to jabber away, with her renewed confidence at her ability to outwit him.

At the other end, Bernice was also on a mission. She popped another grape in her mouth. Her jaws moved from side to side as a cow chews curd. Then she alternated sipping her coffee and resting her lips on the rim of the cup smudged with red lipstick, as she watched Paul chatting with his group.

Every time Paul glanced in their direction, she lowered her eyes and took another sip, letting the warm liquid slide down her throat.

Lily stood with her back to the crowd. "Bernice, you are something else, you know that?"

"As I said, leave it to me. Keep standing as you are. Don't block my view."

"I feel like an eel, letting you do this."

"This is America, girl. You've got to be smart. Somebody's gotta watch your back. If I don't, who will?"

"The Lord does, Bernice. He watches over me."

"That's why I'm here. The Lord works in mysterious ways, His wonders to perform."

Lily burst out laughing. "And what does her ladyship say?"

"Abide your time. He's yours! If he lets himself get swayed, he's a fool and doesn't deserve you!" Bernice said from the side of her mouth.

"Bernice, how can you be so sure?"

"The body language! His body language is so tense; it's a miracle he continues to be civil. His jaw's set, his face is frozen. I don't think he likes the way she's hanging on to him. There's no way a man can be so tense without cause. Another couple just joined them. The lady's giving her a hug. See, he used that excuse to move away from her. Look, he keeps on looking your way and he's got his hands in his pockets in the most interesting way."

"He is looking my way because you are looking his way. And men always put their hands in their pockets, as a habit, when they are standing, talking." She resisted the temptation to take a peek.

"A-a. Not the way he's doing it."

"Maybe they disagreed again."

"No. I know that look and time will prove me right," Bernice whispered, a cunning look on her face.

She shook her head. "Bernice, you make my day. You know what we're doing, don't you?"

"What?"

"Coveting——plain coveting——that's what it is."

"No, no. Coveting's when you long for something that doesn't belong to you. Hoping's when you wait for something that's yours to come to you."

"You sound like a believer. What's keeping you?" she said louder.

Bernice laughed, showing a row of fine teeth. "That's good. You're good. By the way, what're you doing for Thanksgiving?"

"Don't know yet——may be moving. Why?"

"I'd like to invite you to spend Thanksgiving with Mum, me and my brother . . . I mean, Mum, my brother and me . . . and I think you should definitely buy a condo."

She promised to think about it seriously.

"Were you thinking of going home?" Bernice asked as an afterthought.

She admitted that she had considered it, but she would need at least two to three weeks to make the trip worth-while.

"Then I'd like you to come home. Think about it." Bernice lowered her face into her cup. "Psss. Don't look!"

"Why?"

Bernice locked her jaw as a ventriloquist would and said, "He's moving. I think he's coming this way."

She opened her eyes wide, panic-stricken. "Bernice, you have done it! If he makes an excuse to talk to us, you are in trouble!"

"Au contraire, I love it. I hope he comes straight here. Yes. He's coming straight here. Yes . . . he . . . is."

"I'm going to get you for this!"

"Hi Paul! So good to see you again," Bernice flashed her two-thousand-dollar smile.

"Bernice! Good to see you, too. Have you ever visited ENC? I don't remember seeing you here before," Paul greeted Bernice warmly.

"No. I thought I might surprise you."

"I'm pleasantly surprised. You must come back. I could use a few more friends around here." Paul turned and bore into her eyes from under his eyelashes, and drawled, "Hello Lily."

He might as well had kissed her hand.

"Hello." She flashed her teeth, wishing she could crawl into a hole. Treacherous heart! When would it ever learn?

After he had left, she turned her back and ventriloquized, "I am not swimming in the Aegean Sea. I'm standing on the ENC patio, waiting for the service. I'm a woman with a balanced head and I can and will to keep my feet on solid ground. I've done it before; I can do it again."

Bernice stifled her laugh. "Is the Aegean Sea really as blue as I hear?"

"Sparkling clear, sea green——but, I'm not going there."

"As I said, abide your time. Someone up there's looking out for ya!"

She threw a glance over her shoulders at Paul's retreating back; then she walked with Bernice to the lawn, away from the crowd.

"I wish life was as simple as you think, Bernice. I believe in Paul's world, I don't matter. I'm this face he sees at church——an ephemeral curiosity that's been cured. He seems to treat me as a passing fancy, his toy to conquer, then abandon."

She did not confess that she had seen Paul alone at the concert the night before, instead, she studied Bernice's earnest face, then continued, "When I was a teenager, I used to pray that God would change the world just for me. What I really meant was, Lord, please twist arms to fulfill my wish. Now that I'm older, I realize that I would not want the Lord to force someone to love me, any more than I would want Him to force me to love. Also, we are waiting for Paul's engagement to be announced any time now. The least I can do, is respect his wishes and conduct myself with dignity."

In like tone, Bernice said, "No. I think you're misreading him, Lily. You're beautiful inside and out. It's that combination that attracts good men. Don't under-rate yourself. I'd give a lot to have half of what you have. Come on, chin up! It'll work out. Trust me, it will!"

She smiled a sad smile, as one who humors an obstinate child. "Thanks Bernice. Let us go in. After church, we will go for lunch. It is my treat."

♦ ♦ ♦

Restaurant Street in West City offered a nice selection of restaurants, so, to Restaurant Street Lily took Bernice, for steak, where Bernice continued to quiz her about Paul. She would have preferred to discuss the matter of faith further, but Bernice was rather blasé about it. She prayed that Bernice would become more serious about the state of her soul. Until then, just being her friend, was enough.

On her way back from lunch, she mulled over what she and Bernice had discussed. Was it wise to fight for a relationship that did not exist? Supposing she got Paul, for how long would it last? Why didn't Paul talk to her the night before, even if only to say, "Hello?"

Among her friends and acquaintances, she could not remember a single happily divorced couple, even when the decision was mutual. She had spent hours wrestling in prayer, alone or with a group, supporting couples through their transitions from marital bliss to nightmare, to life alone—near calloused knees her reward for those hours.

She saw their pain, their deep humiliation, and their struggle to hold up their heads with dignity as they adjusted to living alone. Some of those divorces she believed could have been avoided, if at least one of the spouses had heeded that still, small voice, before they wedded.

Since arriving in America, she had kept a tally on couples that used two familiar phrases while announcing their rushed engagements, "We're adults" and "We know what we're doing."

If someone had paid her a thousand dollars for every intended couple who had said that, she would have a decent sum added to her savings. Invariably at least sixty percent of them ended in divorce within less than five years, compared to zero percent for the couples whom she knew had waited and heeded good counsel and their intuition. With this backdrop, would it hurt to leave her future in the Lord's capable hands, even if that meant losing Paul to Kelly?

On a positive note, the thought of buying a condo with an excellent sound insulation against loud music and other disturbances, buoyed her.

24

Paul maintained his public charade with Kelly. At crossroads at minimal described the magnitude of his turmoil as he tossed about like a trapped animal, watching the sun come up on Saturday morning. He felt duty-bound to continue honoring his parents, but he could foresee himself heading for an unhappy life, barring a miracle, if Kelly remained his only choice.

"Love is a commitment," upright teachers had taught through the years. But for him to commit, he must want to commit for life. Kelly did not fit the quality of the woman he desired. He was puzzled that his parents had missed the obvious. A failed marriage would destroy so many innocent lives and contradict the very values he had defended for so many years——values they and Grandpa had instilled in him.

On the occasions he had vacationed with Grandpa, the wise man had drilled into him, "Son, you can be the most powerful, sought-after billionaire, with the world eating at your feet, but if you can't keep your family together, you'll wake up one day and find yourself talking to your dog, alone. Dogs make good pets, but they can't bury you. Always keep the big picture in mind. Don't work late and help your wife read to the children in bed."

Since he already knew he could not devote himself to Kelly, who would he blame if his marriage failed?

Supposing he obeyed his parents, would his love for them compensate for the tedious hours with Kelly? Moreover, what did Kelly mean by 'she could date whomever she pleased'? Why her tone of defiance?

After twenty years growing up in the same neighborhoods, the Kelly he thought he knew was a myth of the Kelly he was beginning to know.

And regarding his parents, he did not question the integrity of their faith, but how much did they understand regeneration?

Did he want his parents to be perfect? No. Neither he, nor they, had reached the level of perfection of the One and Only. He wanted them to continue growing, upward bound, just as he wished for himself. He had memorized such verses at camp as a teenager.

Had his parents submitted to the lordship of the One? What about him? Had he? On the other hand, could he be attempting to remove the speck from his parents' eyes, while ignoring the log in his own? Was this as much a test of his humility, as a test of their faith?

His parents were mature in many areas of their lives; but they appeared to be struggling with relinquishing him into the Lord's hands.

"If I can't love believers I see, how can I love God whom I've not seen? There, I've said it," he paraphrased the First Epistle of John, chapter four, verse twenty and blushed at the thought of supposing his parents were anything but loving. Still, he vacillated on calling them. He used to give them his Christmas schedule at least a month in advance. Convinced that they were waiting for him to make the first move, he lifted the phone from his bedside table, chickened out, then replaced the receiver down.

In one swoop, he rolled out of bed and went to the bathroom.

When he got downstairs, Jonathan was gone, but there were two twenty-dollar bills, with a note on the fridge that read:

Low on grocery. Schedule yesterday was tight——same today, band has another concert gig. Sorry. Sharon will pick up oranges and apples and drop them off later. Plse pick up the other refills. Go easy on the beans. Be generous with the beef, bacon and eggs. Pasta, tomatoes, and pasta sauce are fine. Lettuce, beets, and cucumbers are tolerable and pick up some extra cereals. No oatmeal, unless you're prepared to eat it. Hot pockets——cherry or apple fillings——are fine, and any items I missed.

Typical Jonathan list. He grinned, put the bills in his wallet, and the note in his jeans' back-pocket. "Try milk, OJ and Grape Juice; carrots, celeries and any of my favorites. I should tease him and get loads of Brussel sprouts, broccoli and lima beans," he muttered. "Glad Sharon will soon be taking over."

Aunt Angela had asked him to let her know if she should encourage Jonathan to take on more private piano students, but since Jonathan's career had taken off——studio work, new compositions, etc.——his financial situation had improved tremendously.

◆ ◆ ◆

Paul trudged uphill, a jacket over his shoulder. Occasionally, he paused to observe white tailed squirrels as they dashed back and forth, collecting nuts. He stood still and watched a bold one, chomping away at a pinecone, envious of the little fellow's freedom.

From the side, he heard rattling in the tall shrubs, not a welcome sound for his last trip into the hills perhaps for some time. Only one more Saturday remained to the week of Thanksgiving. If California's winter weather proved capricious, he might not return before early spring and spend more weekends skiing, instead.

He continued trudging up the trail, heading to the top where there was a cleared patch safe enough to sit, undistracted. Every now and then, he peered up at the sun. The warm weather did not feel like autumn.

Lily huffed and puffed up the last leg of the hill to the apex, thinking about two promising condos she had found, with the help of Bernice and Alex, and praying about making an offer.

Breathless, she paused and stared at the traffic flow below, and the undulating hills around her. Two joggers raced along a trail on the side of the next hill. A horseman and his dog took their time on a crisscrossing trail. They made it look so much fun, that she was tempted to trek along the same trails, minus the dog.

She turned in the direction of the mountains and saw the head of a man bobbing uphill toward her. The figure looked familiar, but she didn't recognize him, until he was closer. Hoping to escape before he saw her, she pulled her cap closer to her face and turned to head down. Her left foot slipped on the dry grass and she started a downhill spiral. A firm hand gripped her from behind.

"Steady," Paul's familiar voice said.

"Thank you." She tried to keep her eyes averted.

"Lily? Lily! Of course, it's you! Who else combs these hills?" He grinned.

"Hello, Paul." She sounded like a school girl.

"What're you doing here alone? Is it safe?"

"I come here all the time. There are plenty of people around——bikers . . . hikers," she mumbled and stepped out of his way. A sharp pain shot through her left foot.

"Are you okay?" Without waiting for her answer, he examined her foot.

The hills are Yours. You created them for everybody to enjoy. Why not Paul? But, if he has to help me down, I'm done for. Please help me walk down without limping. She prayed in her heart.

"Did you walk all the way up here from your apartment?"

"Mhmm." She nodded.

"Come on. I'll give you a ride home."

"No, no! That's very kind of you, but I'm all right. Really."

"Sure?"

"Yes." She moved and felt another sharp pain on her left foot, then she put more weight on her right foot and tried to walk down again with dignity, while trying to maintain her balance.

"Are you sure you're all right?" Paul called after her. "I can give you a ride. It won't be any trouble at all. It's a long way back."

"I'm fine. Thank you." She continued hobbling down. Soon she heard footsteps and felt a firm grip around her upper shoulders.

Ignoring her protest, Paul guided her to the Park-N-Ride lot where he had parked, took great care to seat her, then he drove her to her apartment.

She need not have worried about chitchatting. All the way, he focused on his driving and asked only once if she was okay.

"Yes. Thank you," she answered.

Several topics came to her mind, such as the concert or his call the night before, but silence won. She felt like an impostor, sitting in Kelly's seat. What would Pastor Tim say, if he saw her sitting in Kelly's seat?

"I'd soak it in ice water and alternate warm and hot compress for a few days. It might be a good idea to see a doctor, if the swelling persists," he said, escorting her to her apartment, with Lamar and a few curious neighbors staring.

He settled her on the couch, fetched her a glass of water and placed the phone on the side table near her, then he left. The fading sound of the Porsche as it gained distance told her once more, he had escaped her neighborhood, as he had done after their first and only date.

Half an hour later, the phone rang. It was Sharon, offering to take her to the emergency room, or run errands for her. She assured her that the injury was minor——nothing that two days of rest could not solve.

After Sharon hung up, she wondered why Paul had told her——perhaps because they were all members of the Singles' Group? *Oh Lord, I hope he did not start the prayer line going.* "But then again, thank you for praying friends."

♦ ♦ ♦

Paul parked and hiked up hill again, kicking himself for not milking the scene more, yet worried about Lily's foot. Hopefully, Sharon would check on her. He had a good excuse to carry her downhill and he blew it! She couldn't weigh more than a hundred and thirty pounds. At this rate, how long before he gained her trust again? Would he ever get another chance?

His life had come full circle. Only this time, he had the opportunity to get acquainted with Lily better and he had blown it. Had he known, he would have taken his time——a cup of coffee or tea, here and there, may be a group date to the games——making it less formal, until he had gained her trust and gauged his parents' sentiments toward such alliance. Would she ever trust him?

So, who could he blame for the gaffe he committed several months ago——four months ago, to be exact? His parents? Society? Perhaps, society had something to do with it. It had been over a hundred years since emancipation, yet it appeared little progress had been made. True, there were now more educated people than at the turn of the century, but socially?

Conversely, it was easy to blame society. What about the individual? Isn't society composed of individuals responsible for their own actions?

Was he in danger of rationalizing as Kelly would? Perhaps, and again, perhaps not. What was he saying? That he, not his parents, nor society, was responsible for the choices he made, in light of the Truth he knew and his commitment to holy living, as he understood it.

God gave a free gift of life that anyone could accept simply by allowing that free gift to transform them. Would God set two standards to judge the world——one standard for the ostensibly privileged and another for everybody else? No!

He had lived a privileged life, but, his ancestors——noble as they were——plundered, destroyed and stripped others of their dignities. Would his genes be a plausible defense for him on judgment day?

One Lord, one faith, one baptism; one God and Father. Without the shedding of blood, there's no remission of sins; without repentance, there's no forgiveness——and thus, no heaven. Grace is free, but I can only benefit from it, by living the life of one who's truly repentant.

He mulled over scriptures he had memorized. When he raised his head, he had reached the apex. He surveyed the valleys, wishing he could rewind the reel to four months back.

The thought of Lily flying downhill to escape him——no doubt——made him grin.

After a while, he collected twigs and made a small heap at the center of the patch. There was little grass surrounding the patch, but he took extra precaution nevertheless. Using his pocketknife, he scratched a rudimentary ring of sand to clear the edges next to the shrubs, before lighting the twigs. The smoke was so thin that he was sure it would not raise a false alarm.

He could still hear the rattlesnakes in the shrubs, but at a greater distance. Nature was good for the environment, but it had its limits. He sprayed repellent around the edges to keep away critters.

Once the fire was steady, he got his pocket Bible and sat down facing the valley, but thoughts kept on distracting him. How did Abraham succeed in spending a whole day in quiet reflection concerning his future?

He put the Bible down, fished his coat pockets for the small flashlight he had brought and slipped it into his jeans' pocket. The jacket made a comfortable pillow.

At first, he sat there, listless, then, he slumped back, rested his head on the jacket, and continued staring at the smoky blue skies above.

How many people really understood the full impact of the suffering, death and the resurrection of the Lord? How many understood the significance of the veil being torn in two and the real freedom Christ bought with His blood? Did he?

Tired of the empty blue skies, he closed his eyes.

Memories of his fruitless phone call the night before flooded his mind. After seeing Lily with Bernice, his hopes were kindled, so he had mustered enough courage to try to patch things up with her. He got what he deserved——she had answered her phone in a formal tone that reminded him of ice on a fresh wound.

He had tried to chat. Finally, he had stammered out an invitation. She had thanked him and said she was already committed for the week, then as an afterthought, had thanked him for greeting Bernice on Sunday; but she did not mention Saturday night, even though she must have seen him at the concert.

She had hung up so decisively that he had said goodnight to the wind. Just in case he was mistaken, the silent ride home this morning dashed any morsel of hope he still had. Clearly, she was expecting nothing more from him.

Never having suffered gut-wrenching rejection, this was a first for him. The night before had exposed the magnitude of what Lily thought about him. What had possessed him to walk away from her without a molecule of reasoning with his Dad?

He had never used any woman ill, nor did he admire men who were guilty of such an act. Yet he realized that a man who did not touch a woman, but treated her with little respect, was little more than the men whom he disliked for their wanton treatment of women.

Up until Lily, he must have thought that some people were species from another planet. How else could he have set himself up to accept advice that implied she was not good enough for him?

Had he considered Lily his equal, he would have persuaded his father to permit him to get better acquainted with her first, before deciding if he and Lily were compatible. He had lived as an exchange student in Brazil, with his parents' permission, would convincing them this time have been any harder?

He suspected his father's greatest fear was not so much of mixing pedigree, as that the woman whom he married might impact the market share of the Van Clyden Enterprise negatively. But since wealth spanned the globe and the stratosphere, how could his family's good fortune be tied to a single person?

His father and other entrepreneurs desired doing business in Africa. He was considering expanding his steel business, or exploring textile manufacturing, or better yet, diversifying into fiber optics. For centuries, diamonds, copper and other raw goods flowed out of the continent——was his Dad implying that while Africa's wealth was good enough for the Van Clydens, Africa's children were not?

On the other hand, was it entirely his father's fault? Not really.

He took full responsibility for setting himself up for his current pain. He had allowed himself to see Lily as an object, with no feelings, or, whatever feeling she had, not as important as Kelly's heart. Though he knew Kelly was heartless——collected men for toys——he had considered Lily's broken heart of no consequence.

Yes, in his subconscious mind, he must have believed that he could admire Lily secretly, perhaps date her, but not commit to her for life.

What did he really think? That the LORD would allow him to mislead one of His own precious daughters and get away with it?

He sighed. No. Castigating himself for societal stance——the society he knew, served little more than self-flaying.

True, at first, he was curious; but months before he took Lily out, he knew her bright smile and soft voice and the way she prayed, more than attracted him. He reacted to her as he would to any girl. He could never take her for granted. Knowing that, what in the world possessed him to be so inconsiderate?

He added more sticks on the fire, then resumed his meditation.

It was paramount that he obeyed and served the Lord wherever He sent him, but he had fantasized over settling down, one day, on a four-acre piece of property in a quiet suburb. He had envisioned his house on a peaceful hill, shrouded by palm trees and every exotic tree he could get——approached through a winding private driveway——all that would have been for her.

He sighed. Perhaps it was best that he went away for a while, refocused his attention on the Lord.

"Lily may be lost forever, but You promised You'd never leave me, nor forsake me," he prayed to the skies.

Should he contact Pastor Tim for advice on short-term missionary work? Of course! His parents? He had reached an impasse with them.

If ever was a time to help someone else in need, it was now . . .

The fire had died down; he watched the glowing embers, with no desire to rekindle it. Lassitude set in. A warm feeling engulfed him.

A baby was cooing, his eyes fixed on him. He was the cutest little thing——kind of exotic. He fumbled with the baby's diaper, his mouth full of pins. In the background, a familiar voice cheered him on.

The baby gurgled, kicking his legs, and grabbed his shirt in a firm grip. His wedding ring pressed against the baby's soft skin, leaving a small mark.

"Sorry buddy," he apologized and opened his eyes, startled. No, he was not changing diapers. It was nothing but a dream. He must have dozed off.

Beside him a small heap of ashes and a few stubs of un-burnt twigs lay cold. The warm summer air had retreated into chilly autumn weather, in keeping with the season. Red skies marked the place where the sun had been just hours before. By his wrist watch, it was after four thirty.

Below, city lights had begun to waken. Nearby, there was no more rattling. He muttered praises, rose up from the ground, and shrugged into his jacket, mulling over the dream.

He had already made a commitment to serve in the missionary field. The dream could be just a ploy to sidetrack him——just wistful thinking. He dismissed it, stored away his Bible, and started downhill to his car.

The last rays gave him just enough light to see the beaten path, without a flashlight, as he emerged from the hills, a new man.

25

Last bags——Paul kicked the door shut behind him, as the phone started ringing. Thinking it was Lily, he dumped his bags on the kitchen counter and ran upstairs, two steps at a time, to the privacy of his bedroom.

"Hello?"

"Hi, Darling. You've been quiet. Are they working you too hard?"

He was disappointed it was not Lily, but pleased it was his mother. Since the night at the party, he had not talked to her. "Not, really." He tousled his hair.

"Well, are you coming for Thanksgiving?"

"How's Percy?"

"You can ask him yourself when you come."

He kept quiet.

"Well?"

"He should love it in the mountains," he said.

"Yes. He loves the snow. We could spend a couple of days up in the cabin Thanksgiving weekend. Leave Friday and return Sunday. That should work. You know what? We could have the whole gang up there."

"I'm going skiing this year, Mum," he said.

"Of course! There should be plenty of snow by then. But you will be coming home first, right?"

"Mum, it's difficult to get reservations this time of the year."

"Reservations! Did Dad rent out the cabin? I didn't know." She sounded confused.

"It's beautiful in Lake Tahoe this time of the year, but I'm going farther."

"How farther afield are we talking?"

"Lionridge."

"Colorado! Oh."

Her disappointment sailed through the wire and hit him in the face, but he offered her no further explanation.

"Um. Well, if you've got to go then I guess I understand," she said.

"Thanks, Mum." A weight lifted off his shoulders.

"What about Christmas?"

"Mum, Christmas is just around the corner."

"I know, but you could come the weekend after Thanksgiving. If you came straight from work, you could spend the night."

He shifted a vintage toy on the dresser.

"Paul?"

"I guess it should be fine." He loathed for her to beg.

She wished him a great Thanksgiving.

He thanked her and wished her the same.

"And Darling?"

"Yes, Mum."

"Don't go breaking your leg now."

He chuckled. "No. I won't, Mum."

He hung up with a heavy heart. His mother had avoided mentioning Kelly's name, yet she might as well have shouted it.

Whatever his Mum thought, he was growing into a strong son, respectful as always, but steadfast in his goal. He was responsible for finding a suitable wife for himself, yet mindful of the wisdom of his elders.

After years of their tutelage, he was confident that he had accumulated enough sense to make the right choice. The same principles he had learnt, he now used to mentor teens——young men like MJ——who venerated him and sought his counsel frequently. He prayed that his parents would understand in due course.

Thinking about mentoring, recently he sensed that MJ was struggling with something, but it would be wrong to discuss his concerns with Matt and Marjorie before talking to MJ, first. As a mentor, he must walk the tight line between respecting parents' roles and gaining the trust of the young men.

He stored away the grocery, then he phoned the Jonesons, as he rehearsed how he would get to the truth, diplomatically.

◆ ◆ ◆

"Jonesons' residence. This is Marjorie."

"This is Paul." Paul chatted with Marjorie briefly, asking after her family. She sounded cheerful enough and said they were about to leave for their family Saturday night out. If MJ was in trouble, wouldn't she have mentioned something to him, as a friend of the family and MJ's other mentor?

He asked to speak to Matt Sr.

Matt came on the line. He mentioned to Matt a ski trip he was organizing for ENC's youths. Would he mind if MJ came along as a volunteer counselor?

"Not at all. Going skiing with you? No hail, no storm would stop him!" Matt handed the phone to MJ.

◆ ◆ ◆

Matt and Marjorie shepherded their family back to the family van after their dinner and a movie. Melanie and Marc clung to their medium size hot-fudge sundae; Melody and MJ carried a banana split each.

As Matt was pulling out of the parking lot, Marjorie checked; everybody was buckled up. "I hear you're going skiing?" she asked MJ.

"Oh, yeah. Paul's looking for youth–counselors," MJ went into a lengthy chat, the first he had been excited about anything in a while.

After a lull, she asked, "So what did you think of the movie?"

"I think it was okay, Mum," Melody answered, distracted.

"What about you Marc?"

"I sort of enjoyed it. I thought it was funny, not all the time, but it had funny parts. The cartoons were great, they looked real."

"I'm worried I'll be singing the theme song for the rest of my life," Melody said.

Everybody laughed.

"Mum, we haven't seen the Professor for some time, did he move?" Marc changed the subject, "He said he was thinking about moving back east to be closer to his children."

"I think he's still around," Marjorie replied, wishing they would continue discussing the movie, but she sensed the children were bored with the topic. May be later on, after they had settled down for the evening, they might respond better. "You know how he is——he usually comes around, almost becomes a permanent fixture around the house, then he disappears for months. He's probably recharging, mulling over some theological discourse, before he shows up again."

"I like it when he comes around, as long he doesn't stay too long. He forces me to think. I don't always agree with him, but he makes me think and work hard for my position," Marc said.

MJ chortled. "He does go on, doesn't he? I wonder what else he does with his life, besides think?"

Melody nudged MJ. "Do you remember the day he showed up in the garden? He'd disappeared for six months with no calls and no surprise visits, then we opened the door that Saturday morning, and there he was, observing a hummingbird hovering over the flowers."

"Yeah, then he stayed for breakfast and lunch, and spent the whole day with us, comfortable, like a long–lost uncle," MJ replied.

"He's a dear old man. I think he misses his wife," Matt added.

Marjorie brushed stray hair from her brow, turned, and noticed Melanie's neck was tilted uncomfortably to one side. She propped her up and shifted her neck to a more comfortable position, causing Melanie to open her eyes and sit up.

"I'm sure he does. They were very close. Well, now that you mentioned his name, I'm sure, one day we'll open the door and voila! He'll be standing there, rocking back and forth on his heels," she said.

"Yeah, then he'd probably stay for dinner," Melody sounded bored, until she started debating Marc.

Matt studied the four through the rearview mirror; occasionally, he rubbed his nose to hide a smile.

Melody started harping on women issues; Marc took the opposing view. MJ served as a referee. At first, Melanie watched them, then her eyelids began to droop again. Soon, she was sound asleep.

Marjorie listened to the heated debate. "Melody," she finally said, "you're a pretty smart girl, but the impression I get is that you're against intellectually inclined women. Well?"

"No, Mum. That's not true."

"Then what is?"

"Well, it's not really intellectual sophistication I'm against. I wish I could be smart all the time."

"Oh really." Marjorie's lips twitched. "But do go on."

"I said I'm not against intellectualism, as long as it's not empty."

"Why? I'm sure others may not see it your way," Marjorie prodded.

"Because Mum, no matter how smart we are, if we try to run the world in a spiritual vacuum, we create more problems——isn't it written somewhere that even when God appears foolish, He is still smarter than men and when He appears weak, He is still stronger than men?"

"Something of the sort. First chapter of First Corinthians, probably."

"And maybe in Psalms, I think, that to fear the Lord is to be wise?"

"Psalm one hundred and eleven, verse ten, I think."

"See, Mum? So, no matter how smart or powerful we think we are, we could never outsmart God, or become more powerful than Him."

Marjorie glanced at Matt.

"If God is really wisdom, and I believe He is, then anyone who tries to go it alone without Him is really being arrogant," Melody concluded.

"Some people listening to you might consider you arrogant. I fear they may think it presumptuous of you to perceive them as arrogant, because they don't believe as you do."

"Mum, anyone who thinks the universe is a mere cosmic explosion, has got to be determined to ignore all the evidence around. They really have to be some very determined anarchistic skeptic."

"Mum, what's anarchistic skeptic?" Marc asked.

"An anarchist is someone who rebels against the law——but I think here it means someone who refuses to consider the possibility that God exists." Marjorie turned to Melody and said, "Is that what you meant, honey?"

"Sort of," Melody answered.

"Oh, I like that! Anarchistic." Marc's eyes gleamed in the dark. He turned his head at an angle to take a better look at Melody.

"Don't even think of it!" Melody said.

"What?"

"I know what you're thinking. Don't go there. I'm not an anarchist! I respect the law," Melody repeated.

"I didn't say a word. I just looked that's all."

"Oh, yeah?"

"Oh, yeah."

"Peace. Peace, everybody. Calm down." MJ coughed loudly to muffle his laughing.

Marjorie turned and stared down the two, as though they could see her face in the dark. "Apologize to each other. Marc, your remark to Melody is not right. First, there's no one in this car who's an anarchist and none of you, my children, especially Melody, doubts that God exists. So your application is totally inappropriate. Second, Melody, we need to be loving and kind to all sorts of people, including those who do not believe that God exists. Remember at times you too struggle when the Lord doesn't answer your prayers right away, yet He still loves you anyway? And how do you know? May be one day they too will believe."

"I'm sorry Melody, for teasing you," Marc apologized.

"I'm sorry for raising my voice at you and I'm sorry Mum, I didn't mean to sound that way," Melody countered.

"Okay. As you were saying?" Marjorie prompted.

"As I was saying a person really has to be determined to ignore all the evidence that Someone greater is in charge of this universe."

"Yeah, that's true. God's beauty's all around us, if we choose to open our eyes and really see. He displays His beauty through nature——the verdure of spring . . . the pastoral hills . . . the trees . . . the beautiful flowers . . . the music of the birds and the matchless timing of the seasons——that's what Lily taught us," Marc observed, back on Melody's team.

The van swerved.

"Honey, watch the road!" Marjorie cautioned.

"Did I just die and go to heaven or did I hear my son speak up?"

"Your son has been speaking up lately. Where've you been?"

"So, Marc, how does one stay close to the Lord?" Matt glanced in the rearview mirror.

"By talking to Him, reading the Word, and helping people, and stuff, and acknowledging that we need His help, instead of trying to do it all by ourselves," Marc replied.

"You're coming along, son. You're coming along!"

Marc beamed.

MJ pumped his arm, and roughed up his hair. That elated him more. Two of his favorite men had just paid him the best compliments.

Marjorie shook her head in disbelief. Of all her children Marc! To think Marc might become the pastor in the family. Each day revealed a new side of him that astounded them.

Matt turned the last corner; rows of manicured lawns came into view. A few neighbors were out taking a late evening walk. He pulled up the driveway of a split-stucco in a cul-de-sac and stopped. MJ, Melody, and Marc trooped inside the house through a well-lit porch.

Matt removed Melanie from her seat and carried her into the house. As soon as he stepped inside, Melanie popped up, bright eyed and chirpy.

He patted her playfully, "Come on pet, time for bed."

"No. I wanth to watch TV," Melanie replied.

"No pet. Not tonight. Daddy will read to you. Okay?"

"I wanth rabbit," Melanie said, her thumb stuck in her mouth.

"Don't suck your thumb, honey. You're a big girl now. I will read a story about rabbits."

"No, I wanth David and Golith——big, bad giant gone, gone."

"Okay. Daddy will read you David and Goliath."

"I wanth the whole story."

"Okay. I'll read the whole story."

"Promith?"

"I promise."

"Okay." Mollified, Melanie stuck her thumb back in her mouth and laid her head on his shoulders.

He carried her upstairs. After helping her change into her pajamas, he watched her brush her teeth, tucked her in bed, then he read to her.

Downstairs, Marc was kneeling, watching TV, inches from the screen.

Marjorie prepared snacks in the kitchen and returned, carrying a tray. "Turn that TV off, Marc. You know the rules."

Marc complied. "What game are we playing tonight?"

"Mum, can we play Scrabble, please?" Melody cut in.

Marc stepped in front of Melody and said in his mother's face, "I want to play Monopoly."

"I want to play Scrabble and I asked Mum first," Melody said.

"How comes you always get your way? I want Monopoly."

"Calm down everybody, we will toss a coin," MJ interceded. "Heads or tail, Melody?"

"Heads."

MJ flipped a coin in the air, "Monopoly it is."

Marc slid to the ground, hands in the air. "I wo-o-n!" he exclaimed.

"We'll play Scrabble tomorrow, honey," Marjorie consoled Melody.

As if on cue, Shaggy started barking.

"Shaggy's b-a-a-r-king, someone forgot to feed the d-o-o-g," Melody yelled.

Marjorie removed her glasses and glared at Marc. "Marc, did you feed Shaggy before we left?"

Marc's face went blank. He turned to MJ and pleaded, "MJ, could you feed the dog for me, please?"

"No, buddy. That's your responsibility. I'd help you, if you were sick. But as it is, you feed the dog, I mow the lawn and Melody helps with the laundry and we all help clean the house."

"Oh shucks——"

"Watch your language, Marc!" Marjorie rebuked him.

"Sorry, Ma'am."

"Come here, son." Matt's voice announced he was back.

Marc shuffled toward his father.

Matt squatted to the ground, at eye-level with him. "Son, in this house, we don't cuss or swear or use profanity," he said gently.

"I didn't, Dad. All I said was——"

"Today that word, tomorrow what else?" Matt interrupted. "Where did you learn that word?"

"In school. My teacher sometimes reads books with modern stuff and Mr. DuNothing, doesn't seem to mind."

"You mean the Principal, Mr. Weissentunchen?"

"All the kids call him Mr. DuNothing."

Melody clapped her hands on her mouth; MJ coughed loudly.

"Well, when the kids complain, he doesn't do anything. The teacher says it's modern literature."

"Son, a lot of these benign words are often substitutes for some unpalatable words. Your teacher should know better!" He turned to Marjorie and said, "Honey, I think we should have a conference with Mr. DuNothing——I mean Weissentunchen."

Marjorie nodded in agreement.

Back to Marc, he said, "Your Mum and I spend hours working on your manners. I can't speak for other families, son, but in this house, we honor the Lord with our speech and action. It wounds His heart when we use our tongues carelessly. We don't want to restrict any of you from having fun and being free to say what you want, as long as you honor the LORD, and respect other people. That's all we ask."

Marc kept his head lowered. "I'm sorry sir."

Matt talked to Marc, until Marc had understood him and then he gathered his family together for what he called moments of learning in humility——moments that he snatched at the end of correcting a child. "Lord, I'm sorry for any shortcoming on our part. Mum and I want to be examples to our children. Teach us to let our speech be gracious and to honor you with our tongue. Please forgive us where we've failed you . . . Amen."

 MJ's eyes softened as he saw remorse on Marc's face. "We'll wait while you feed Shaggy."

Marc's face lit up. "Coming, Shaggy! Coming!" He grabbed a bag of Good Eat Dog Food from the pantry, and hauled it out to Shaggy.

During family devotional time, MJ, Melody and Marc circled the subject of friendship and love, kissed their parents goodnight, then they retreated upstairs to their bedrooms. Soon, it was quiet around the house.

Marjorie tidied the living room, and went upstairs.

Matt turned on the dishwasher, took out the last trash bags, and followed her. She was at the sink, brushing her teeth when he entered. He changed into his pajamas and joined her.

She rinsed off and worked on her hair in front of the armoire. Midway through untangling a strand, she paused and looked at him through the mirror, "So what's it going to be?"

He nodded and said, "You mean transfer him to a Christian school, or continue to take a chance, and hope he'll be none the worse? MJ and Melody seem to be managing fine."

"Each child's different."

"I'll drop by Christian Academy on Monday. Then we'll discuss it with him."

Marjorie put the brush aside, took a generous scoop of night cream, and asked, "Do you get the impression the children are wrestling with something?"

"Kind of."

She massaged the cream on her face and neck. "So do I. For some mysterious reason, I'm convinced there's a close connection between our family and the Van Clydens'. We should get to the bottom of whatever it is. In fact, if things keep going the way they are, I think we should call a family-meeting soon. What do you think?"

"Okay. I'll back you."

"What do you mean you'll back me? I think you should call the meeting and I'll back you. They're your children."

He looked at her and twinkled, but said nothing.

"Good! That's settled." She finished brushing her hair, then she slipped to her knees at the foot of the bed.

He followed, knowing that she would ultimately call the meeting, but as his loving wife, let him lead and she would ferret out the truth from the children by the end of the meeting.

A wise man is one who leads his family gently. There's a time to be firm, and there's a time to let the wife take the initiative. Why spoil it? His mused.

26

In Paul's last effort to tell his parents he had tried and to appease his conscience, he drove to Kelly's gated condo complex the Saturday before Thanksgiving, climbed up the short steps to her semi-detached duplex and rang the doorbell.

A whiff of Fabrice Étrange's La Mystique de Mademoiselle Musk Perfume mixed with fresh mouthwash preceded Kelly out of the door. Paul rued the day the nascent perfumer entered the field and wished Étrange had waited——perhaps another five years?——before creating his masterpiece. By then surely he would have selected a bride for the Van Clyden Enterprise?

Thank heavens he had stuck to his prior commitment while at the gym to go for a late lunch, and a movie, instead of dinner and a late show.

Taciturn, he drove to West City's Restaurant Street, more worried about Lily's foot than the woman occupying Lily's seat. He had called once more to check on her. She had assured him that the swelling had gone down and she was on the mend——which seemed true when he saw her midweek.

Their eyes had met during refreshment time in the Fellowship Hall. She had smiled at him and looked down, embarrassed. That was all the encouragement he had needed to walk over to inquire after her foot and that was as far as he had got before Kelly had planted herself between them, overpowering them with La Mystique de Mademoiselle Musk.

So here sat Kelly now, confident, feeling entitled to him, in a seat reserved exclusively for Lily.

For the duration of their time, he went through the motions of chivalry, parked in auto mode, making little effort to talk.

By the time the movie ended, the sun was setting. In better days, he would have driven her to Newport Beach for a walk along the beach, if the weather permitted.

On their way back to her condo, it seemed like a good idea to take Grand Avenue, instead of the freeway. He tried holding a civil conversation with her; he would have been better off focusing on the road, instead. "Jonathan and Sharon were thinking about going to Mexicali with PHLU. Wouldn't it be great if we joined them?" he said.

Kelly smiled and bit out, "That would be fu-u-un. Pursue Holy Life has been doing so many neat things with the community."

He glanced at her.

She rubbed his shoulder. "Isn't it great we've been going steady for over four months now? Our six months' anniversary is around the corner. Everybody was so thrilled for us a year ago. They said we make a great couple. We should've been celebrating our second anniversary." She snuggled closer to him.

He sketched a smile and resisted the temptation to pull his arm away. "We were too young."

"Nonsense! Lots of couples our age have settled down."

He drove on, his face inscrutable, then out of the blue he said, "I was thinking of spending more time in ministry."

Kelly recoiled and flipped her hair. "What area of ministry?"

"I don't know. Depends on where the Lord leads."

At first, she was silent, then she drew out, "Africa has its share of missionaries. Don't you have to go to a seminary for that sort of thing?"

"Not necessarily. Ultimately, if one envisions a long–term commitment, it helps to get additional training. But no. I don't see the need. Besides, who's talking about Africa? The Lord could call us anywhere."

"Us?" Her nostrils dilated a little.

"Well, yes. Would it bother you?"

"Don't you kind of have to be a missionary to be a missionary?"

He suppressed a smile, then he said, "Meaning some people are more called to be missionaries than others? I suppose you've a point. Yet that wouldn't excuse me from obeying the call to help in some way."

"I'll tell you what big boy, being a great daddy is ministry enough." She patted his stomach playfully.

"Missionaries make great dads too," he murmured, uncomfortable, wishing Kelly would stick to her side of the car. He realized he was pushing her to the limit of her commitment to a higher cause.

She yawned. "It's tiresome talking about so many needs. It gets overwhelming sometimes."

He concentrated on watching tail-lights for a forbiddingly long time, then he asked her, "You remember Stanislaus and Karen?"

"Yes," Kelly deadpanned and seemed surprised at his switching topics.

"I think their marriage might be in trouble."

"Impossible. They were the perfect couple."

"Perfect couples can deceive, sometimes."

Kelly yawned again, "Oh well, I'm sure it's nothing but rumors anyway. Things happen, honey——a stray diversion here and there, a few inconveniences——I'm sure they'll work it out, whatever it is. They just have to be adult about it." She patted his hand.

"Meaning?"

"Oh c'mon Paul, things do happen. You know that!"

Was that impatience or a little display of temper he detected in her voice? Apart from the spat they had when they were returning from breakfast the morning after the beach party, he had been all politeness to her. He felt the urge to push on——after all, Kelly had started it. "Is that a hint or are you just expressing your opinion?"

"I've always been a straight shooter. I think couples should give each other some space. So we make mistakes——a bad decision here, and there . . . relationships that we shouldn't have started . . . the aftermath . . . a few interruptions that we take care of . . . that's what liberation's all about. A woman should have control over her body, don't you think?" She challenged him with her eyes.

He gripped his steering wheel, avoided a group of cyclists, and shot forward. "Is that what you think? At any rate, I don't think that's the case with them. I don't have the details. Stanislaus is a decent chap."

He resisted despairing at Kelly's revelation. She had as good as admitted she would go into marriage with the back door open. That was not his vision. He had prayed that regardless of his potential bride's spiritual status, by the time he proposed, she would be committed to life with him, his God, and all that it entailed. That Kelly was not yet at that point, was obvious. Since he was ready to settle down, if Kelly was to be his intended bride, how much time did he have to hope for a miracle?

Out loud he said, "So, how would you treat First Corinthians, seven?"

"What about First Corinthians?"

"A healthy relation between a husband and wife."

"You don't really believe in the literal interpretation, do you?" she scoffed. "I think it's more of a guideline, subject to opinion."

"As a matter of fact, I do——especially, if the husband and wife have deep respect for each other." He pulled into the guest parking lot and opened the door for her, then he stood back.

She raised her eyebrows. He always parked in front of her condo. He stared back, impassive. Apparently expecting him to catch up with her, she started walking ahead, then she glanced back. He was standing with the passenger door still open, watching her tap her heels to her condo, alone.

"Aren't you coming in for a cup of coffee?" she asked in her charming, sultry voice.

"No thanks. I have to prepare for Sunday school." He closed the passenger door firmly, got into his seat, accelerated out of the parking lot from zero to fifty miles per hour in seconds and drove away from her neighborhood of middle-class condos, without looking back.

He ignored the freeway and drove past Lily's apartment, noted with satisfaction that the lights were on in her living room, then he zoomed to her neighborhood's grocery store and bought a box of plain black tea.

By the time he arrived home, it was past seven o'clock. After a quick shower, he prepared a nice, hot cup of tea and spent half an hour completing his Sunday school prep work, savoring every drop of liquid he could extract from his cup. He was becoming an expert at making a good cup of tea, if he may say so. Sharon and Jonathan agreed.

Finally, he confirmed his flight to Colorado.

27

Paul merged onto the Interstate 5 Golden State Freeway, from the Pasadena 110 Freeway, exited, and parked in a nice corner of the long-parking lot, congratulating himself for leaving early and for getting an early flight through Denver International——which was unusual, considering regular flights to the ski resort only left twice a day from Burbank Airport.

Four hours after leaving Burbank, his plane taxied to the arrival terminal——not too bad, despite a jabbering passenger next to him with flight jitters. He accommodated him, even discussing with him why he was a believer——in response to the passenger's question——then he loaned the chatterbox his magazine and closed his eyes, until he heard the scared fellow snoring.

After landing, Paul drove his rented land cruiser from Eagle County Regional Airport and headed to Lionridge Resort through the I-70 East, Denver and the 201 Frisco/Breckenridge Exit.

Despite Thanksgiving week, the city was awake with families bundled up for the mountain weather. The happy laughter of children riding sleds lifted up his spirit. Finally, he arrived at the Castleridge Lodge, lit up, warm and inviting——a welcome sight after his long, lonely drive.

The memory of Kelly had long since vanished with the dust of his Porsche as he cruised along Freeway 110 to Burbank Airport.

He checked in, had a quick shower and went downstairs for supper.

A youngish looking waiter asked, "How many in your company, sir?"

"One. Thank you," he replied.

"This way, sir."

He followed the waiter, his head erect, barely acknowledging the waitress who smiled at him, and ignoring a few curious glances.

The waiter seated him at a window with a view of the night. Festive lights twinkled on the mountainside, awakening in him nostalgia. The empty chair at his table glared at his aloneness. A soft pulse drummed at his temple, reminding him of sleepless nights gone.

Soon, the waiter took his orders and served him a light meal of sole, rice and vegetables, as he continued to stare at the city lights, disinterested.

"Careful with that, sir, the plate is hot," the waiter warned him. "Would you be needing anything more, sir?"

"No thank you."

"Enjoy." The waiter retreated.

Two mouthfuls of flaky sole and Paul noticed a couple that appeared to be in their early forties, sitting two tables away from him, engrossed in each other, reminding him of what could have been. His heart skipped a beat.

With a quaint little nose, and rich copper skin that radiated in contrast to her thick, curly hair, he concluded the lady must be exotic. Of note, the man's dark-brown hair blended with her exotic looks. If there was anything unusual about the two, nobody seemed to notice. Discreetly, he noticed the huge diamond marquise set on her left ring finger. Her companion also wore a gold band on his left ring finger.

Just then, the lady caught him staring and smiled. He blushed. He seemed to have struck a kindred spirit. Her companion followed her gaze. Strangely, he exhibited no evidence of jealousy or anger.

Paul finished his supper, then he checked the schedule. Back in his room, he flipped through magazines, in the background, classical music, as he pondered the reason for his flight from California. His father had drilled him to treat girls with respect. Why didn't he heed him when he broke up with Lily? How could he get back into her good graces? By flaunting Kelly in Lily's face in front of Evangelical Neighborhood Church, after jilting her without cause, he had humiliated her and thrown her to the mercy of gossipers and may have blown it with her. As hard as he was praying to get her back, he sensed she was praying harder to resist him.

28

A scruffy looking man with short stubs——resembling a cross between a rugged mountain man in a jeep commercial and an outback logger——stared back at Paul in the mirror.

Only for a moment did he toy with the idea of not shaving, then he went to work. Twenty minutes later, he emerged from the bathroom, scrubbed and clean-shaven, in time for his breakfast and morning papers.

He examined the content of the tray——croissant, fruits, and scrambled eggs——a pile fit for a hungry man soon disappeared.

The thought of calling his parents occurred to him just briefly, then it fled. They would most likely still be in bed, anyway. He used the extra time to pray longer.

The sun was up when he emerged from the hotel, dressed for the ski slopes. He was an avid skier, but not a dumb risk-taker. It was his first trip for the ski season so he took a lift to one of the easier trails, to begin with.

Midway through the morning, for reasons he could not fathom, he returned to the bunny slopes. As he approached, a family caught his eye.

The man had light golden hair; his wife could have been from anywhere——Islander, Jamaican, East African or Ethiopian?——he couldn't tell. But she had the high cheekbones and the regal look he had come to associate with some immigrants from Africa.

Two small children played nearby. The girl couldn't have been more than ten years old and the boy was probably about five or six. Their rich, shiny, golden copper faces stood out like tropical islanders amidst the snow-peaks of Colorado. A chord tugged at his heart. He slowed down and studied them unobtrusively, he hoped.

The boy scooped snow and handed it to his mother, his face knit in serious concentration. His mother placed it on the snowman. A small hat capped his face, but there was no mistaking the innocence of a young boy.

Adjacent to them, his sister worked on a smaller snowman. Her heart-shaped face glowed in the snow. She caught his eyes and dropped hers, shy.

The boy saw him and waved. "Hi!" He grinned, toothless.

"Hi!" He waved back. Was he that friendly when he was little? He remembered being more reserved, may be curious, and he preferred to study people, more than talk to them.

He halted close to him and asked, "What's your name?"

"Landon Braden."

"Hi Landon Brandon?"

"No. Braden. B-r-a-d-e-n," he said.

"Braden."

"Yes. What's your name?" Landon Braden asked.

"Paul."

"Nice to meet you, Paul," Landon sounded rather grown up.

He responded likewise.

The mother smiled; her hands continued to work the snowman.

By now the girl had stopped building her snowman and had moved closer to her mother, all the while biting her gloved fingers.

"Nice day for skiing," the mother said.

"Beautiful day. You've lovely children, if you don't mind my saying so."

She thanked him and added, "We get a lot of compliments about them. We're thankful."

"I didn't mean to intrude. My name's Paul."

"That's okay. I'm Deirdre and this is my husband, Jonah." She indicated her husband who had joined them by now. "My daughter, Candace—she's the shy one in the family." She gave Candace a tiny hug, "and my son, Landon Braden, the outgoing one."

He said he was pleased to meet them.

Jonah answered for the whole family, and said, "You too decided to break away from it all, eh?"

"Yup. Sometimes it's the best thing this time of the year."

"I agree."

"Well, enjoy the weather. It might snow this evening," he said.

"That's what I hear," Jonah replied.

He wished them a pleasant day, twirled around and skied off into the horizon, satisfied he was headed in the right direction. If Jonah and Deidre could achieve their dream to be just a normal family, chitchatting with strangers on the bunny slopes, why couldn't he?

Landon Braden watched the tall man ski into the horizon, then he placed his arm around his mother's shoulder, bent close to her ear and said, "Mummy, he's nice. He resembles a movie star."

Jonah lifted his eyes. "He does, doesn't he?"

Landon threw a pack of snow as far as his arm could throw and asked, "What movie is he in, Dad?"

"I don't know, Braden. But, sooner or later, we'll find out."

"Yes. He's nice, isn't he, honey?" Deirdre agreed.

"There're some very nice people out there. It's refreshing to run into them," Jonah said, thinking about the times when certain people had not be so nice and boycotted them in a crowd.

"Yes," Deirdre agreed, in a soft, still voice, full of memories.

"I'll race you, Candace. Let's go!" Jonah took off, Candace at his heels.

Deirdre continued to stare after Paul's now faint, retreating figure, as her hands worked the snowman. Her lips moved in silent prayer, even as she hoped Braden would not ask her to disclose what she was praying about.

Her family did not seem to be in any danger. On the contrary, she knew that look. She had seen it before in the likes of Paul confronted with the fear of falling in love with a woman like her. Without knowing him, she felt that Paul was running from something, or more specifically, someone.

When Jonah realized that he was in love with her, he had fled so far, no fishnet could have drawn him back from Beijing. The pain she endured—the many times she fell to her knees, devastated—no one would ever know. And it was only after she had given up, nursed her broken heart, and started dating her countryman that Jonah had returned and fought for her. By grace, he had overcome his fear. His love for her could not keep him away.

Whoever this girl was, who had put Paul to flight, Deirdre prayed that the Lord would protect her from getting a broken heart.

♦ ♦ ♦

Late afternoon, Paul returned to the hotel, his stomach growling, reminding him he had skipped lunch. He ordered a cup of hot chocolate and a banana, and went up to his room. With classical music his companion, he mulled over the couple he had met on the bunny slopes, while flipping through magazines. If he could get Lily to take him seriously, could he do it? Would theirs be as happy and as stable a life? Would he one day race his daughter down the slopes of Colorado, as his wife and son built a snowman?

In one swoop, prepared for an evening out. His option was sensible—— a quiet dinner, no bars and no entertainment centers.

An hour later, a handsome cowboy look-alike in black, with a tawny jacket, got into a cruiser, and drove away. A few minutes later, Paul pulled up at the Warmheart Restaurant for a hearty regional American meal.

He held himself erect, the epitome of dignity, as he walked alone past couples already seated tête-à-tête.

♦ ♦ ♦

The Shinebonds spread themselves on one pew for the Thanksgiving eve service. Kelly checked the door frequently, as though expecting someone.

On seeing the Shinebonds, Igor and Charlotte stared at each other, baffled. Charlotte had assumed that Paul wished to spend more time with Kelly, away from family intrusion. Didn't he go skiing, after all?

Charlotte whispered to Igor, "You think he went home to change? His work clothes would've been fine."

Igor shook his head. "I don't know. Maybe he needed to freshen up," he said from the side of his mouth.

They, too, expected Paul to walk in any moment. He had only missed Thanksgiving Eve's service twice: when he was an exchange student in Brazil, and when he went skiing with his European cousins. Jonathan might know more, but he was in the back, somewhere, sitting with his old friends.

29

Bernice buttered half a slice of plain, toasted bagel, took a bite, contemplating Jake's face, the smell of turkey sizzling in the oven gracing the O'Konnell's breakfast table. "Jake, there's something I've been meaning to tell you."

As the Thanksgiving weekend drew near, she had been struggling with how she would broach the subject of Lily's visit.

"Yeah?" Jake cut a thick slice of butter, and slathered it on his toast.

"About this weekend——"

"Oh, yeah, I remember. You said you've invited a guest." He grinned.

"Get serious, Jake. For your info, my guest is a girl. If we were not at breakfast, I might be tempted to do something I'd regret, though you're an adult now."

"That, I know you would. I don't mind getting wet——saves me a trip to the shower!" He bit a chunk of his toast, leaving teeth marks at the edge.

"It's hard to believe you just celebrated your twenty-fourth birthday and consider yourself a graduate student."

"I am a graduate student and I did just celebrate my twenty-fourth birthday." He slurped his coffee and snapped off another chunk of his toast.

"My friend will soon be here."

"Which one? The one with the name like a flower from . . . Guyana?"

"Not Guyana. Uganda, Kenya, East Africa! Where's your sense of geography? I just wanted to warn you. Behave yourself! She's as good as taken, though she doesn't know it yet."

"Bernice, you know me, I play it by the rule."

Bernice dug into him with her eyes. "Jake, roses come in different shades. Some petals are red, some are peach, some are burgundy; and I once saw a rose, it was so dark-red, it looked almost brown——sort of . . . chocolate red, but it was beautiful."

"So poetical." Jake paused, a dreamy look on his face, then snapped out of it. "Nah. Not me! I stick to the rules——blondes, red-heads and maybe, dark-brunettes." He slurped his coffee again.

"You wanna bet?"

"Bernice, I may not know where I'm going, but one thing I do know, my taste, they've been the same ever since I could say, 'Duck, duck, goose.' I'm an O'Konnell. Remember? I stick with the staple. What's been good for all the O'Konnells, is good for me——moi, Jake Roy O'Konnell."

Their mother batted her eyelids playfully.

Bernice dabbed her lips and went to the kitchen to refill the flask. "Okay, have it your way. But as I said, roses come in different shades."

Jake was her brother. She loved him but not his cocksure attitude. If only he could change. Not if he continued associating with the same group. Perhaps if Jake changed, he would settle down. Right now, he was sounding more like an obstinate teenager, than a computer graduate student.

Lily had said she would arrive in the early afternoon. By midday, Bernice was checking the window frequently at the sound of cars approaching. The motorists either headed to their neighbors,' or zoomed past.

◆ ◆ ◆

At noon, Lily headed for San Fernando Valley, grateful that her left foot had healed enough not to call attention to itself. She was back taking short walks, howbeit, avoiding steep hills.

After a long year, ENC's traditional Thanksgiving's Eve service the night before——celebrating the Holy Communion combined with a feast of roast turkey——was just the touch she needed to begin the festive season.

Apart from the poor turkeys, a commercial free Thanksgiving, with no other ulterior motive, satisfied her spiritual thirst for a wholesome holiday. She prayed it would remain so in the coming years.

Every three years, she re-read the history of America and the first Thanksgiving——before the bloody land-grabbing that followed.

She also used the long holiday weekend to review goals she had achieved during the year and to start making new ones for the coming year. As 1993 closed, she had no achievement to celebrate and two incomplete goals——her PhD program and house-hunting. She had sapped her energy mooning away. Would she fare better in the new year?

At what point did one become an expert on love, or was love something to contend with for life——hoping for quiet interludes, until the next time?

When is it too old to fall in love or suffer the pangs of love?

If she reached over ninety years old and was still a spinster, would she still be vulnerable to love, and if so, would she toss and turn all night, if she fell in love with some dashing old man? Her lips twitched. The more reason to get married as soon as possible. What was God thinking when He created the love between a man and a woman? Could a marriage be as powerful without it? What about cultures that arranged marriages?

At times she wished she had a beeper designed to go off just once, when she met the right man. Then she would never have to experience the pain of rejection and the arduous task of screening for the right companion.

Paul was not at the Thanksgiving service. He and Kelly were gone, as were some families; but other students were home for the long weekend——so the church was full, although it still felt empty.

Did Paul take Kelly to meet his parents? What better time of the year to bring home the good news of an impending nuptial?

Just where about did they live? In California or out of state, for example: Connecticut, Vermont, or did they live in the south——Georgia, for instance? Paul had not mentioned where he grew up; she allowed her imagination to run wild.

Pasadena's modest high-rise buildings loomed ahead, pricking her conscience. Since the autumn session begun, she had only attended their Thursday night's symphonies four times and given the rest of her tickets to colleagues. It was nice to be generous, but careless of her to throw away money, when she should be saving to start her own business.

As she left the city, the landscape changed from clusters of buildings to rugged raw land and hills, a bit like a drive up the mountains.

"Definitely, a southern gentleman," she muttered. "If Californian, he is very genteel——his parents must have worked hard on his manners. Except for breaking up with me on the phone, his manners are impeccable." She stepped on the gas-pedal and the Honda shot forward.

Twenty-six miles into her drive, she exited on Lowell Avenue and followed Bernice's directions towards the hills. About forty minutes after she had left her apartment, thanks to the light traffic, she drove up the driveway of a sprawling ranch style single family home, with a generous, well-manicured lawn and luscious happy gardens, on Hiddengate Street.

♦ ♦ ♦

At the approaching sound of a car, Jake stuck his nose to his windowpane, in a most ungentlemanly fashion. A lime green Honda pulled up and the female driver got out. His eyes grew to the size of soccer balls, as he watched every detail of her magnificent physique walk to the trunk and unload weekend bags. Who else could it be but the golden, dark-red rose Bernice had described at breakfast?

In a jiffy, he ripped off his ragged jeans, hopped into a clean pair of new ones and stuffed his head through a decent long-sleeved sweater. "I'm not given to praying, but HELP! Of course, I love roses, who doesn't? Long stems, short stems, peach, red, burgundy . . . specially the red ones, the darker the better——chocolate red's my fa-vo-rite. When the Good Lord created the chocolate red roses, He must've had redheads like me in mind. Mysterious, dark-red roses with l-o-o-o-ng stems blend very well with redheads, bringing out the rich b-r-o-w-n in them-m-m. You can make them real dark any time, Lord. And I don't mind going to church at all. I've always thought church's a cool place to be. It wouldn't hurt at all. No Sir-ree!"

He stuck his eyeballs to the mirror and tousled his hair, giving it a more roguish look, then he licked his fingers, polished his eyebrows, and shot out as though he had the law on his tail; but Bernice had beaten him to the door.

"There you are! I was so worried you might get lost," Bernice beamed. "Did you have any problems following my directions? You know Hiddengate's not the easiest street to find. So how did you do?"

"I did okay. Thank you," Lily replied. "You give great directions!" She looked around. "Lovely gardens!"

"Thanks. My Mum would be tickled to hear that. She works hard in that garden. It's her other baby. Come meet my family."

Bernice took the suitcase and Lily followed with her weekend bag.

A young male version of Bernice, but taller, rushed to their rescue. Lily suspected he was Jake.

"Here, let me help you with that." He grabbed the big bag from Bernice, and Bernice took the vanity bag.

Bernice said, "It's so nice to have you here. I'm so excited. Oh Mum, this is Lily!"

A calm woman with salt-and-pepper hair, about Bernice's height, and a slightly fuller curve——but just as trim——walked out of the kitchen.

Mrs. O'Konnell said she was pleased to meet her and added that she had heard such wonderful things about her.

She reciprocated and thanked her for inviting her for Thanksgiving.

"I'm glad you could come." Mrs. O'Konnell straightened her sweater. "Please make yourself at home and call me Gloria. We're very informal."

She hesitated. "May I call you Mama Bernice?" she asked.

"Is that what you would call me back in your country?"

"Yes."

"Then Mama Bernice it is."

"And this is my brother Jake," Bernice said.

She extended her hand to Jake. "How do you do, Jake?"

Jake stood transfixed, staring at her.

"Jake. Jake? Ja-a-ke! This is my friend, Lily. The one I told you about," Bernice repeated, trying hard to keep a straight face.

She held out her hand again, smiling warmly.

Jake woke up, grabbed her hand, and just about dislocated her shoulder. "Nice to meet you. I'm Jake O'Konnell, Bernice's *younger* brother."

Mrs. O'Konnell smiled and turned toward the kitchen, "Lunch is almost ready, please make yourself comfortable. We'll visit this afternoon. I'm anxious to hear about your country."

Bernice rubbed her upper lip, trying hard to hide a very broad smile. "Come on, let me show you to your room." She took her to the guest bedroom.

Jake followed at a much slower pace, contemplative.

"Jake looks so much like you," she said in a low voice.

"Yes. We resemble a lot," Bernice replied, then mouthed, "except right now I think he's trying to get his bearing. I hope you don't mind?"

"No," she deadpanned.

Back in the living room, all kinds of nose-tingling aromas assembled, accentuating the feeling of home and love. Lily gave Mrs. O'Konnell a small gift she had brought for her. Mrs. O'Konnell was pleasantly surprised.

Bernice indicated a seat opposite a moose head.

Lily stared at the stuffed animal. "That was one big moose."

"Father-son's last trip into the wild country. Dad had it stuffed for Jake," Bernice replied.

She smiled at Jake. "You must be a very good shot."

Jake blushed. "Been hunting since I was eight years old."

"Don't get him started. I don't want him spoiling your appetite," Bernice cut in.

They all laughed, then she said, "My grandparents own a farm."

"There you go!" Jake said.

She surveyed the room, taking in the décor——cowboy gears, a saddle, leather antiques and cowboy paintings among others, stood out. "You didn't tell me you love country?"

"My dad was an aspiring country singer at one time. He did all right for a while, then he went out and got a regular job," Bernice said.

"Any recordings?"

"A few. I think he still gets royalty from them. We don't get to see a penny." Bernice sounded a bit melancholy. "Mum," she yelled.

"What?" Mrs. O'Konnell yelled back.

"Does Dad still get royalty from his stuff?"

"Sure do. Last I heard, he's doing all right. He was smart enough to sign up with some savvy organization that tracks down royalty."

"That's because you took care of it, Mum." Bernice turned to her, "Mum's the accountant in the family. As long as she was in charge of managing the business-end of things, Dad did very well. If they had stayed together, I think Dad would've made it to the top of the charts. While Mum was around, he raked in the dollars, even managing to hit top twenties. His second wife gorged herself on Mum's sweat, then dumped him. It was Mum who helped him pick up the pieces again."

"You should be proud of her. She did a good job with you and Jake."

"Thank you. We think so too. She'd love to hear you say that."

Jake focused on the television set, in appearance only; frequently, stealing glances at Lily, when he thought she wasn't looking.

The mouth-watering aroma that waltzed into the family room announced the turkey was ready.

Mrs. O'Konnell garnished the salad, amused. Jake's gawking face was worth a mother pearl stuffed with diamonds! She loved the O'Konnell men, but not their cockiness. Few of them would succeed without a good woman, but you wouldn't know it listening to them talk. Short of losing Jake, nothing would hurt her more than him becoming like his father—thoughtless, taking a good woman for granted, until he met his match, then letting the virago lead him by the nose.

For years she had prayed so hard that Jake would turn around, that she was seriously contemplating joining a local Baptist church. Praying at home alone and watching televangelists were no longer enough.

Jake needed a good praying woman. She had heard such good reports about Lily, as proof, Bernice had changed a lot. Without Lily's influence, Bernice would probably not be going steady with Alex. Alex was a good man. She did not doubt their marriage would work, if Bernice took that final step. True, not everybody who went around praising the Lord had a praise the Lord marriage, but she would sooner a Christian marriage than none.

Bernice suspected Lily's quiet strength came from hours she spent in secret on her knees. Lily didn't discuss it, but Bernice had deduced it from her comments. Oh, for another prayer warrior in the O'Konnell clan!

Bernice had hinted about the Van Clydens' boy. May the Van Clydens' name not get in Paul's way! She prayed. *Nothing beats getting a good woman.*

"Okay. Lunch's ready," she announced.

On the table were all kinds of scrumptious dishes and the centerpiece, a huge golden turkey that could win an award, given a chance. The sight was enough to make even the most resistant hungry.

The O'Konnells' unassuming style made a guest feel welcomed at the table. After the late lunch, Mrs. O'Konnell sat in her rocker, with a cup of coffee, threw an afghan shawl on her lap, and bombarded Lily with questions about her homeland and how did she like it in America? How often did she see her family? That Lily had helped her wash the dishes and clean up after lunch, seemed to have raised Lily up a notch in her esteem. Lily displayed initiative, with an unaffected attitude——attributes Mrs. O'Konnell admired in a good woman and had drilled in Bernice.

"Lily's looking for a condo, Mum. She wants to move," Bernice announced after her mother paused to take a breath.

"What type of condo?" Mrs. O'Konnell asked.

"Two bedrooms, two-story, and attached two-car garage," Lily replied.

Mrs. O'Konnell assured her that a gated community was the best choice and explained the advantages in detail.

Lily was not thrilled about gated communities——too many restrictions——though she liked their landscape maintenance service; but she held her counsel and thanked Mrs. O'Konnell for her kind advice.

"I know you don't like raunchy movies. Would old classics work for you?" Bernice asked late afternoon.

"Yes. I love old classics. What do you have?" she replied.

Bernice listed the 'G' rated movies in their library. She selected three.

"Okay, Jake, you're in charge of snacks," Bernice announced.

Jake shot up and disappeared into the kitchen, returning a few minutes later with hot drinks, popcorn buttered to their eyebrows and finger-food with homemade dips and relishes.

Mrs. O'Konnell lounged back in her rocker, cradling a bowl of popcorn in her lap; Lily and Bernice sat on the rug, eating their snacks and watching old movies. Jake pretended to be focusing on the screen. Did he owe Bernice an apology, perhaps?

Lily was glad she had come. For a fleeting moment, she wondered how everybody else from church was spending their Thanksgiving. Paul overshadowed them all. Quickly, she refocused on the sidesplitting comedy on the screen, until she remembered the night at the pizza place when Paul and Jonathan competed to outshine each other, cracking jokes.

30

Paul stretched his muscular body to the ceiling, then he sat back on his bed. His face resembled that of a little boy who had just woken up in a bad mood and would love a hug from his mama. However, the last thought that lulled him to sleep the night before and the first thought that woke him up that morning was not about his parents. If this continued, he was done for.

Without missing a beat, he followed his routine from the morning before, then skied non-stop until one o'clock.

More relaxed, with a free afternoon to spend as he pleased, he ate tuna melt and vegetable soup at a slower pace at a corner deli, watching a few hungry skiers wolf down theirs, praying no one choked.

Lionridge had other amusements. He had driven horse sleighs before; never having ventured to the North Pole, dog-sledding seemed adventurous enough. So, with the help of a local guide, he spent the rest of the afternoon learning the art of it.

At sunset, with enough dog-sledding to last him a life time, he returned to his room for a quiet dinner, alone.

A favorite of Lily's was plain French fries, cooked in peanut oil; so one hour later, when Room Service knocked on his door, gourmet French fries and a medium burger was the dinner on his tray.

Something about the last bite that drives a man to face his life. When that last bite of French fries disappeared; it was time for spiritual surgery. How long? He had no idea. Skiing and adventure were the excuses that got him to Lionridge, but sedulous scrutiny, the truth that would set him free.

Armed with his Bible, a diary and a pen, he settled at the desk, and researched verses to help him grasp his life at crossroads.

What were his options? Should he continue pursuing his instincts? It was pointless mulling over Kelly. He did not miss her, instead, he was relieved their charade was over. Once more, he could make his plan to serve the Lord, without worrying about how his future wife would react to his decision.

He did not need a PhD to recognize he was through with Kelly, but he felt compelled to revisit his reasons again. Also, breaking up with her would not absolve him from the need to forgive her. However, if his instinct was right about Kelly's insinuations, could he ever forgive her? Did he have a choice?

God did not give him the luxury of holding grudges against those who had hurt him. As he had known all his spiritual life, it was incongruous to submit to the Lord, while latching on to unforgiveness.

"'But if you do not forgive, neither will your Father in heaven forgive your trespasses,'" he quoted Mark, chapter eleven, verse twenty-six, the tail end of the Lord's answer on the matter of faith and getting prayers answered.

If Kelly's hint was an attempt at confession, for his own sake, he must ask the Lord to help him forgive her. However, her betrayal had hurt and disappointed him. In dating Kelly, hadn't he sacrificed his own need? Then again, he should give her the opportunity to explain herself, before jumping to conclusions.

In x-raying his soul, he was also preparing himself for starting a healthy relationship with another woman——having set himself free of grudges against Kelly. But, if his father insisted, what reasons would compel him to marry Kelly?

Paul halted his study momentarily. Three things came to his mind for considering Kelly as a candidate:

1. his respect for his father——his father meant well.
2. he did not wish to hurt her feelings.
3. she was one of them and to use her own words, "came from the same class."

Apart from loving his father and trying to reason with him, the other reasons sounded hollow to him. What about Kelly's feelings? What feelings? Kelly was a survivor who considered men her toys, up there with her lap poodles. Correction, at least she gave her lap poodles a chance——

when she got bored, she dumped them on her parents, to return them to the dog-pound.

Even if he sacrificed his future to please his father, would Kelly be faithful to him for life? What was the point of marrying homogeneous and divorcing and repeating the cycle over and over, when love waited across the seas? Would the Lord object to such a union, across the seas?

In Nehemiah, God forbade the children of Israel to mix, because their children would speak mixed languages. But what was the language of Ashdod? Was God concerned about earthly languages? If so, he too could be sinning by speaking English. His father was Dutch-Swedish and his mother, English. As a believer, should he be speaking Dutch, Swedish, or Hebrew?

What was God really concerned about? Children speaking mixed languages, or children worshiping other gods that would be a snare to them?

"You shall have no other gods before me . . ..," his lips moved, reciting the first commandment.

So, if his children had brown eyes, would God care? According to Nehemiah, no——provided the whole family worshipped the one and only true God. Solomon became apostate by collecting many wives and their foreign gods under his roof, an abomination to the LORD.

Supposing Kelly was Lily, would he still love her despite everything? Was Lily capable of behaving like Kelly?

His lips curved into a gentle smile. "Nah." But how well did he really know her? Instinct. By instinct, he sensed she would not betray him. If she did, could he stop loving her?

Mulling over what Kelly did, aroused his anger at her; but pondering on whether Lily could do the same, provoked in him primitive jealousy and a desire to wring somebody's neck——the man who could lure her away from him. Never had he felt such an intense reaction against a competitor——some jealousy, may be, but nothing so aggressive. The feeling was so primordial, that he fled to the window.

So that was it! Whatever surface attraction Kelly had, was insufficient to overcome her fault, he concluded, trying to shake off the raw, ferocious, jealousy that thinking about Lily inflamed in him.

Supposing Kelly was not the problem?

Since love's a commitment, is my real problem the inability to commit to one woman——making excuses . . . looking for an exit, as Bill had cautioned me?

He stared at the beautiful mountain lights displayed before him. It was imperative that he got to the bottom of his problem. He came to Colorado not to baby himself, but to be honest with himself before the Lord.

He blew his cheeks. No. Fear of commitment was not his problem. If that was true, then could he overlook Kelly's faults?

Yes and no. Why? As a believer, he must forgive her, but, as a man who respected marriage, he did not wish to commit to Kelly as his future wife because in his knowledge of her since their youth, she lacked the qualities he desired in a wife.

If he married Kelly at his father's behest, could they hold off or would Kelly trick him? If she did, could he commit his children's future to a mother who teetered on the edge, had no qualms about fickleness, and thought it was her prerogative to be forgiven?

Knowing everything he knew now about her, with perhaps a few more unsavory truths, would it be wise to persist on going forward?

True, God could change anybody, but could Kelly ultimately become the kind of godly companion he had longed for, searched for, and waited for all his life, without sapping the life out of his future? How long would it take? At what cost?

The Lord could answer a prayer in an instant as He had done many times before, but, what about the human will? Didn't God give each person the freedom to choose? It was not his place to presume on Kelly's willingness to become his dedicated wife. Didn't Apostle Paul warn against such presumptions?

Supposing he took the risk, but Kelly persisted in her own ways? Did he have the right to predestinate his children to a life of an unrepentant and may be ruthless woman who had no scruple about extinguishing a delicate life——her own flesh——though she be blonde and blue-eyed?

Did unconditional love cover premeditated destruction of the innocent, with no remorse?

His parents loved Kelly, believed in her and saw no flaw in her. Her orchestrated charm continued to beguile them. Which parent had never fallen prey to her lure? The Kelly he knew, however, mistook the purpose of God's forgiving grace——believing it gave her a carte blanche to indulge herself. To Kelly, repentance was a sign of weakness; entitlement her right to exist for her utmost pleasure.

Kelly took him for granted. He disliked it. Without some rude awakening that shocked her into realizing that he wouldn't always be there for her, she would most likely persist in presuming on his love, until she got bored with him. So, it was prudent for him to relinquish the master plan for Kelly's soul into the Lord's capable hands and move on.

If he persevered and married her, despite all the warning signs, he would be guilty of premeditated sin four-fold: first, against their children; second, against her——having known he could not commit to her for life, nor she him; third, against his second wife, if he remarried; finally and above all, against the LORD.

Where unrepentant sin abounds, should grace abound more, though it ruins the lives of so many innocent people?

He shook his head. He was getting it wrong. Forgiveness was not about what Kelly did; but about doing right in God's eyes, and eschewing bitterness, despite what Kelly chose to do. His freedom and growth depended on it. Bitterness would not be a virtue, but an albatross around his neck.

In short, Kelly was the right woman, but not for him. One day, some guy might crow over marrying her. Whoever he was, he wished him well.

Why was something which could be so simple, so complicated? Given any other circumstance, would he be sitting here arguing over the obvious?

"Is love less sweet or less deep, because it comes wrapped in chocolate brown paper?" he asked the empty room.

He returned to his writing desk and placed a Gideon's fleece. "Lord," he prayed, "let the girl who will connect into my vision for serving you, the girl who can read my mind with little explanation, let her be the one. I'm prepared to accept your guidance. Please let Mum and Dad see the qualities that I see in her."

◆ ◆ ◆

Lily was sitting, her long legs stretched out in the O'Konnells' family room, alongside Bernice, mellowing out, after a scrumptious breakfast of pancakes, fresh fruits, and other delectable food that Mrs. O'Konnell had prepared to grace her table, when the doorbell rang.

Bernice jumped up to answer.

Lily heard voices in the foyer. Soon after, Alex entered, his brown hair gleaming. He had a new hair cut that gave him the finished look of a man well-groomed. He smiled, exposing a set of small, even, white teeth and when his hazel eyes lit up, his whole visage belied the severity of his mustache and betrayed his true age of thirty-two and the reason Bernice was hoping for a proposal soon.

"Alex! It is good to see you again."

"Lily! Good to see you too." Alex kissed her cheeks. "How was Thanksgiving?"

"Wonderful! Mama Bernice has been spoiling me."

Alex chuckled. "You deserve to be spoiled."

Again, Alex kept his emotions in check. Bernice had warned him about Jake's reaction the day before. "Whatever you do Alex, remember to act normal as you did at the concert. I would appreciate it; I believe so would Lily."

Waiting for Mrs. O'Konnell to finish packing lunch, while resisting gawking, he was grateful for Bernice's warning. Praise be for the generous God who created beautiful women in every continent.

Mrs. O'Konnell brought in two picnic baskets and two flasks. "Make sure the coffee and hot chocolate are upright," she handed him the flasks.

He packed the picnic baskets and the winter jackets in his four-wheeler, seated Mrs. O'Konnell first and waited to seat Lily, as Jake slid to the back, and finally, seated Bernice in the front, then he headed to the mountains. Born in Wisconsin, but having spent as much time in the San Fernando Valley as in that dairy state, he knew the hidden treasures of the Valley as much as anyone born in it.

Lily smiled at how Alex had demonstrated his gentlemanly character as he seated the women. He grew a notch in her book of real gentlemen.

Up in the peaks, Jake persuaded Lily to build a snowman. As they chitchatted, he mentioned that he was in between relationships. The spring before, he had returned to school for a Masters of Science Degree in Computers and had broken off with his girlfriend. He preferred to complete the two-year program before settling down, but she wanted to get married right away. Then he slid to home base, mentioning that in his opinion, two years was the ideal length of time for getting better acquainted before taking the big plunge.

To dodge the direction the conversation was taking, Lily asked him about his other hobbies, beside hunting.

He replied, "The University of San Diego suits me fine——hang out with friends in between studying . . . surf on Saturdays or make a trip to the border. Occasionally, some of my friends drag me to church, but I never let out a tweet to Mum——not good for my tough image." He grinned.

◆ ◆ ◆

As the Thanksgiving weekend ended, Jake brooded about his predicament——he had considered himself free, until Lily walked in. A good thing, he would be returning to examinations' week to end the semester——that should keep him busy.

Bernice had a secret ball, tickled that the Lord was as generous to men from other continents as He was generous to the American men, contrary to Jake's initial cocky attitude——never mind Lily was practically off the market. For if the only beautiful women in the world were peach–cream, how would men from other continents enjoy marital bliss as the Good Lord had intended? Alex had admitted, not to offend her, but to be honest.

◆ ◆ ◆

At the beach, Kelly spent the Thanksgiving weekend mooning around, trying even the patience of her dotting parents, while the Van Clydens tried to soothe a whining, distressed Percy. Thanksgiving had always been his very special time with Paul, whither was he gone?

31

Paul adjusted his tie, yanked it off, and threw it on the bed, then he selected another one. It suffered the same fate. He took a navy blue one with the most discreet patterns. That too ended on the bed.

How informal should informal be? He scratched his head. How about a casual business attire? After two such experiences with serious contenders, one would think he would know the drill for dignified casual by now——a suit with a handkerchief, but eschew the neck-tie or cravat.

To the wardrobe he returned and selected a muted colored jacket to match the season, then he rearranged his ties in the drawer.

Next, he combed every strand of hair, until the highlights shone, stepped back and stared at his reflection in the mirror, then he slipped a white pocket square handkerchief into his breast pocket.

A fresh smell of light after-shave lotion hung in the air. The task before him required dignity, style, and grace. The moment he turned sixteen, old enough for group dating——by his parents' estimation——his father had drummed into him, "Whatever your feelings, son, show respect. Once you've made up your mind, confront the task head on. Don't prevaricate. Above all, conduct yourself with dignity."

Much good did his father's advice do him five months ago! Would his insensitive behavior cost him forever? Lily's extra formal attitude toward him and her politeness was worse than a slap on the face.

To have someone he held in high esteem treat him with the utmost decorum, devoid of any morsel of warmth he once enjoyed, sent a chill down his spine and left him trembling with much trepidation. He put on a brave face for public appearance only. What heavier price would he pay?

He deliberately arrived late to the Tuesday Bible study. Kelly tried to make eye contact; but he avoided her. A few other people also did a double turn. It was obvious he was either going to a function or had come from one.

Kelly had never bothered much with singles' Bible study——interfered with her other commitments——but she had become a regular, hanging out with Jonathan and Sharon, as she did in church.

He passed the empty seat next to her, and sat as far away as possible, next to another couple who had been dating for several months. Yet when Bible study ended at a quarter past eight, he fell in step with her before they reached Fellowship Hall, and asked, quietly, "Did you get my message?"

Kelly smiled, uncertain and replied in the same tone, "Yes. I did."

"Well, shall we?"

"Now?" She stepped into the Hall.

"Mhmm."

Kelly was extra charming chatting with a few friends; he followed suit, then they left. To all appearances, they were going to a function.

Was it insensitive to pull her how out of fellowship? No. He could have chosen a weekend or some other time, but Kelly had played hard to get, probably as a revenge for the weeks he had avoided her and his behavior at the end of their last date——though he had displayed utmost decorum.

Always a confident girl, Kelly seemed uneasy, more so, when Paul suggested that they should drive in separate cars to a favorite steakhouse. In separate cars they drove and parked next to each other at the restaurant.

As the waiter led them to the most secluded table, Paul walked taller. He had always been a confident man, but this evening, he seemed more assertive, as though he had become his own man . . . could no longer be manipulated easily.

Thanks to the midweek and late evening, there were only two couples, sitting at the other extreme end. The empty tables between them created an atoll of privacy that would prove very useful to Paul and Kelly as the evening progressed.

The waiter brought their order of soft drink——Ginger Ale for both of them. By Kelly also ordering the same drink, she seemed to be making an overture at a compromise.

Disinclined to drag the evening, Paul plunged in as soon as the waiter had served their orders of steak. "Kelly, I don't want to take up your time. I just wanted to let you know————"

"I saw your parents at the club last Friday. Your Mum's always so regal. I wish I'd half of her deportment," Kelly interrupted him.

"We tried——"

"Your Mum had thought it would be a great idea to go shopping to Europe. What do you think of Milan or London? Or perhaps a cruise?"

"I believe it's time to move on," he continued.

"So many couples bond and refresh on cruises. You work too hard."

"Kelly, please!"

"You're absolutely right," she said, calmer. "There're so many opportunities out there. But, um . . . we've been friends for a long time."

"I believe we've some common grounds, but launching from different platforms. Is the Lord in it?"

"I don't follow you. Shouldn't two people look at their common grounds in deciding the will of the Lord?" She sounded cautious.

"Yes, if their meeting of minds is *in* the Lord," he shot back.

"We've been friends since childhood. We're of the same faith."

He winced. "Kelly, should the Lord call us to a foreign country, would you be willing——if it is an emerging economy, with less material comfort?"

"Don't be ridiculous, of course not everybody's called to be a missionary. What's wrong with serving the Lord right here?"

"Very well. Would you be willing to move to an urban area, if we felt called to say . . . the inner city?"

"The majority of people now commute, so what difference would it make? Nobody lives in the city anymore."

"But, if the Lord called us to live there?" he persisted.

She frowned. "Paul, honey, what's the matter? What's come over you? God gives different people different callings. There're people who're gifted to minister to the inner city. They're much better equipped for that kind of work."

She almost sounds spiritual. He was struggling not to be cynical. "And we, of course, don't have that special gift?"

"I personally don't feel called to serve on Skid Road."

"I appreciate your candidness."

"Besides, I wouldn't feel safe raising our family in such an environment."

"And children from the inner city are a lot different, aren't they? They wouldn't need the same type of security as our children would, would they?" he mocked, wishing he could remain kind and respectful to her, despite the difficult task before him.

She fumbled with her glass and tossed her hair back.

"Okay, so what else do we have in common?"

"All kinds of things . . . the community. They need the Lord too, you know." She ignored his sarcasm.

"Yes. They do," he agreed, gentler. "Do you feel called to share the Lord with the community?"

She hesitated. "Well, I would, but my friends really have their hands full with all kinds of commitments." She laughed, hoping to get support from him. He remained aloof. "They don't like too much of the religious stuff."

He winced again. If there was a word he disliked, it was religious. Kelly couldn't have struck a rawer nerve at such a critical moment! How many times had they discussed this before? The last one, as they were driving back from Stanislaus and Karen's house. He had told her, "Religious, is something a person wears on and off as they would a shirt. It encompasses a multitude of beliefs——the all-inclusive, where all roads lead to heaven."

"Well, we should be more broad-minded," Kelly had said.

"To what? Why do you think we stand on one cross, one resurrection? Religious is a terminology some use to avoid all personal responsibility. A word I've heard used to wrap up the 'he' god, and the 'she' god and the 'it' god and the sun god, and the moon god into one. Where there's no right, or wrong . . . where you're right and I'm right and we're one big happy family, as long as we all agree to compromise and stand up for nothing, except pleasing everybody else and letting them stand up for what makes them happy, no matter how wrong it is and how far it takes us away from our own principles and from the Truth." He disliked the word, with a passion.

He snapped back, she was saying, "Oh, once in a while, a friend shows some interest. Also, Mum and Dad think we shouldn't impose on other people."

"Even when they're searching for the meaning of life and they appeal to you for help, because they admire what you have, do you just blow them off and let them wallow in their pain?"

"Well . . .," Kelly searched for the right words. "I mean, I could invite them to church and stuff."

"Very well then, I guess that brings us to church." He fixed his eyes on her. The kindness was there, but devoid of warmth, more of a steady look of a stranger listening to her, politely.

She shifted. "Really Paul, I feel I'm in an inquisition or something."

"No, Kelly. We're trying to establish a mutual bond between us."

"Um, I do help, occasionally, but it requires commitment."

"And that of course is pretty time consuming." He sighed, weary.

She turned on her charm. "Yes. It does consume a lot of time. You know Paul, sometimes I get so busy, I don't know where to begin."

He leaned back, wishing he could get as far away from her as possible. "You're right. Sacrifice is what it takes."

"Oh, I'm so glad you understand," she beamed. "But you know, honey, there're so many people out there who're equipped to serve. As long as we do our best, I don't think God would be upset with us. After all, we tried, right?"

"Right. But I also believe, in fact I know, God looks at our heart," he paused lending weight to his next words, "and our motives."

"I think it's time we worked on a project, as you suggested."

Finally, she was acknowledging that he was more than her lap-poodle.

"To borrow from you, I need to explore other opportunities."

Whatever she chose to do, this was one toy she would not get. But the moment he mentioned the phrase, 'other opportunities,' Kelly's face became contorted with animal-like rage.

"It's her isn't it? You cheat!" she spat out.

He recoiled. "I don't know what you mean." He had never mentioned any other female interest to Kelly. It had not been necessary. He felt hurt that she should hurl such accusation at him and of all times, at that moment.

"I have my sources. I rarely fail in my mission."

"Kelly, you're not making sense. I've treated you with the utmost respect and put you first, only after the Lord, it's unfair of you to accuse me of such an act. You're one to speak." He struggled to hide his disdain.

Apparently Kelly realized she had betrayed her true sentiment. She retreated. "What do you mean? Paul, have you been listening to gossip? Whatever you heard, it was over."

He frowned. "I don't get you."

For a moment, she looked trapped, then she raised her chin, defiant, "Paul, wake up, smell the roses. Move with the times. You're still living in the Victorian era, the rest of the world has moved on. At no time did I ever lie to you. I'm comfortable sticking to my own, are you? I admit I got a little carried away. Anyway, it's behind me now." She held her head up high, a woman in command.

With a thud, he knew his suspicions about Kelly's earlier allusions before he flew to Lionridge were right. He leaned forward as he would, approaching a rattle snake. "What's behind you, Kelly?"

"I suppose, a little bit of confession's good for the soul."

"What are you getting at, Kelly?"

"Just a minor faux pas. I wasn't really serious. And, you seemed distant. I needed some reassurance. He was there. But then . . ." She started wringing her hands. "Everything's fine now. Don't worry," she said, in a soothing voice, as though she was speaking to herself.

He watched.

She placed her hands on the table and raised her chin again. "I'd my career . . . and us to think about. Besides, it wasn't serious. We both knew that. His girlfriend was acting up and you were . . . cold. Paul, you've always been special . . . and . . . I couldn't bring that kind of responsibility into our relationship. I just couldn't."

He narrowed his eyes. "What happened to the Kelly I thought I knew?"

Her face hardened again. "I told you months ago, I'm free."

"Kelly, you're contradicting yourself. On the one hand, our relationship's important, on the other hand, you're free. Which Kelly do you want me to believe?"

"You don't own me." She flipped back stray strands of hair from her face. "I'm an adult. You're supposed to forgive. Isn't that what the Word says?"

He stared at her, stunned. Kelly was well versed with the biblical mandate to forgive, but blind and deaf to the same book's mandate to repent. He had never treated her as anything, but a fine lady, yet this was how she rewarded him! He felt a growing revulsion to her, though he had never touched her.

He composed himself and said, "Kelly Shinebond, I hate to tell you this, your freedom to choose bellows up and down California. Every time you indulge yourself and fail to take responsibility, some innocent person pays a hefty price."

"You're not being very charitable."

He burrowed his face into hers. "Is that your idea of charity? To push the limit, defy the Holy God, spit in the face of all that's proper, and demand the right to be forgiven? Is that your definition of a common bond that will propel us to a stable home?" He struggled to keep his voice low.

"Who are you to judge me? You make it sound as though God discriminates against people. He is loving, and kind, and forgiving. I am who I am. Why would He create me and not love me? Don't paint Him as some hard-nosed, uncaring being."

"As you just said, God's loving; but He is also holy." He cupped her hands in his hands. "I forgive you, but can I count on you? Are you sorry? Can you look me in the eye and assure me that I have no reason to doubt you? If I made the same commitment to you, would you commit to a future with me and close all the exit doors?"

Kelly pulled her hands away, fumbled with her gold chain and took a sip of her drink. She tried to meet his eyes, but she couldn't. "Well, it's true that faith is very similar," she said in a gentler voice, "but I believe that unless two people have the same status, any relationship they develop would be on shaky grounds," she finished, recalcitrant.

"I agree that areas of similarities foster a stronger bond. But, I also believe that no other foundation can we lay than Jesus Christ. I believe that He alone is the solid base for an enduring relationship between any two believers, heaven-bound," he paraphrased from First Corinthians, three, his voice trembling with conviction. "Kelly, can we be a team?"

"All I hear's Jesus, Jesus all day, when you hang out with your born-again friends," Kelly spat out.

He leaned back. "Don't exaggerate! We don't talk about Jesus all the time. You've been involved in our discussions on global affairs, sports, music, etc. And we rarely hang out all day, and you know it. And as you've known for years, I'm a believer, but not all my friends are. Do you now want to control my friends, too?"

"It's all about moderation——that's hard for you to understand."

"Moderation! Look who's talking! Tell me, what moderation was there when Jesus' back was ripped open thirty-nine times and the crown of thorns pressed on His head, with blood running down His brow, or when his hands and feet were hammered to the cross and His side pierced? Or do you consider that just another fable? If I cannot share my passion with you, then with whom can I be myself? Kelly, my hand was yours for the taking. We could've been planning our wedding by now. You worked so hard at pushing me away, you succeeded. Congratulations!"

Kelly rubbed her neck.

He continued, "I'd given you all the liberty any decent woman could desire, provided you respected my friends and me. Relationship's about making the effort to compromise on things that don't infringe on our un-negotiable values. You did nothing to meet me halfway. Your friends ridiculed my values. From the very beginning, it was obvious you meant to mold me into your lap-poodle. I do all the compromising, and you do all the taking."

"Stop preaching at me," she snarled in her whispery voice.

"You're right. I've no right to preach at you." He placed a wad of dollar bills on the table, helped her into her jacket and followed her out, their plates still full.

He had a light spring to his steps that had not been there for months, but his heart was heavy. Almost spiritual was not the same as spiritual, almost a believer, not the same as a believer.

That he owed Kelly his compassion as she struggled to find her way, was indisputable; but, no one could make decisions for Kelly. She must learn to trust the Lord. If Kelly refused to accept God's help, none could force her to change.

He escorted her to her sports BMW, followed her to the freeway and drove behind her towards the Foothills City.

Knowing he had shocked Kelly or whatever depth of feeling she was capable of, and loathed to spend the night worrying about whether or not she had arrived home safely, Paul escorted her all the way, brooding.

At the beginning of the evening, he had thought he would spend some time praying about his own future later, but all he wanted to do was to get home and lay his head on the Bible.

Kelly had as good as confessed what he had suspected all along——she reveled in a life of irresponsible freedom. If she had designed to hurt him, she had succeeded. She did not consider infidelity wrong or despising life a sin worth grieving over. Her commitment owed no loyalty to any other universe than the world of Kelly.

Her cold, reckless behavior had endangered her life in more ways than one and could have impacted his health and that of their future family, had they married.

To Kelly, morality was drifting with whatever predominant belief governed the moment. To him, morality was adhering to one standard——a standard that did not shift with the culture, but acted as a lighthouse, protecting him from getting shipwrecked.

Another thought occurred to Paul, almost making him pull off the freeway. Had Kelly acted responsibly, would her passing fling have cooperated? If the man was a louse, and had abandoned her, would she have appealed to him for help, instead? Worse, would she have lied, like Potiphar's wife had, embarrassing him before Evangelical Neighborhood Church, his family and friends? That she was no Mary when he started dating her, of that he was now sure.

A cold chill ran down his spine. Kelly was capable of anything. If Kelly had manipulated the truth, would the church have seen through her deceptions? If they had bought into her lies, it could have shattered the confidence of the youths whom he had mentored to respect women, unless those young men had continued to cling onto grace to remain strong and not become discouraged. For surely, he would have had to resign his many positions of moral trust!

How could he have defended himself to his parents? Grandpa? He had promised them he would strive to uphold the Van Clydens' name. That they would have forgiven him in time——due to their love and kindness——he was certain, but would they have believed in his innocence?

What Kelly had confessed to him was so preposterous for someone who was supposed to be besotted with him, that he did not trust himself to delve into the meaning of it, while still on the road. She had wounded his trust, more than she had hurt his pride.

He turned on the radio to a classical music station, but the music aroused memories. He flipped it off.

After about half an hour, Kelly signaled and turned on Glendora Avenue, a few miles later, two more turns brought her to Privilege Lane.

He followed her car all the way to her gate, watched her enter and the gate close behind her, then he sped back to the freeway.

Would he ever forgive her? He should. He must. He had promised.

The moment he arrived home, he dashed out of the car. A minute later and he would not have made it.

Jonathan was downstairs, studying a music score, baton in hand, when Paul zoomed past. Soon, he heard retching coming from Paul's room.

The last time he saw Paul was at the fellowship hall when Paul was slipping out with Kelly. Alarmed, he ran upstairs, two steps at a time.

"Paul! Paul!" he shouted, "What's going on?"

There was silence, then a fresh bout of retching followed.

"Paul!"

Another brief silence, then Paul stuck out his head through the door, looking ashen.

"Where's Kelly?"

"It's over." He blushed.

"What happened? Where were you?"

"We're not suited."

Jonathan, more urgent, "Where were you when you broke up?"

"In a restaurant. Nothing happened. Okay? From the restaurant, I escorted her to her condo, turned around, and came home. That's all."

"You drove in separate cars?"

"Yes."

"All the way to Privilege Lane?"

"Yes. She entered, the gate closed, I came home."

Jonathan sat down on the stairs. "Thank heavens!"

"It's all right. Nothing happened——just stuff that caught me off guard. Oil and water don't mix. Dad will just have to accept it."

"That woman's capable of anything. If she'd ruined your life, I'd have found it hard to forgive myself." Jonathan plodded back downstairs——nothing scarier than marrying the wrong woman, for all the wrong reasons.

Praise the Lord for His grace. May Paul never date someone like her again! He also prayed that Uncle Igor would stop being in denial and accept the truth.

If Kelly was trying to change, he could be more supportive, but it was apparent that she was on a mission to conquer and destroy Paul. Why? What crime had Paul committed against her? He had been the consummate gentleman to her. Was it fair to sacrifice Paul's future, when there were so many great girls out there?

Jonathan flopped on the couch, remembering his own close call. For a brief moment he had foolishly thought that hanging out with the in-crowd, partying all night was better for his music career, after all, the industry expected it of him, as a rising star.

Though he had never confessed, it was Paul's strong commitment that had kept him from ending up in some dark alley. Every time he came home, there was Paul armed with a concordance, digging away——encouraging him to also buckle up.

The bad period had passed. He and Sharon had reconciled and he had Paul to thank for it. Had Paul been a friend, he would have still gained his devotion; but as his cousin and friend, Paul had earned his fierce loyalty.

He went to the kitchen, put two scoops of cappuccino into the percolator, and watched it percolate, as he boiled inside.

Paul took a shower and knelt beside his bed, struggling for words. "I find it hard to forgive her," he prayed, "I know I should, I want to . . . I told her I had, but I can't in my own strength. Please help me see her through Your eyes. Without Your grace, I risked losing all the ministries, for who would've believed in my innocence . . . that I'd treated Kelly as a virtuous woman? What would've become of MJ and all the youths who trust me, unless You had helped them overcome their disappointment——my supposed betrayal?"

He got off his knees and went to the balcony. The evening had been as unpleasant as he had suspected it would be. Kelly, like her parents, believed church was a duty that fitted in between convenience and diversion——good for networking. If the perception of good citizenship was all that mattered, the Shinebonds would be among the first at heaven's gate.

He prayed fervently that one day, Kelly would change. It was obvious that the Shinebonds were as different from the Van Clydens as night and day. Yet as old friends, he respected them and cared for them. So, what course should he take, given the turn of events? Besides continuing to pray for them, he could think of none. It was one thing to respect them; it was another thing to allow their lifestyle and capricious faith to influence him.

He had no idea how they would react if they discovered the truth——if they didn't know already——or why he took his stand and risked disappointing both families. But, he was also committed not to betray Kelly's trust, not even by dropping hints.

Regarding their split–up, it was up to Kelly to inform her parents. As to friendship, he would assure them that he was still their friend.

If only Kelly showed some remorse! God's mercy and grace, abundant as they were, should they be taken lightly or for granted? No.

He grimaced at the memory of their meeting. His estimation of any goodness in Kelly, or her ability to compromise for the sake of their future, had greatly surpassed her ability to rise to the occasion.

With one last longing look towards Hollenvine, he went downstairs and spent the rest of the evening drinking coffee and comparing notes with Jonathan——helpful tips from mistakes that Jonathan had never revealed before.

32

"Morning, Paul! This is due today." Paul's secretary placed two large intercom mails on his desk, stamped 'Confidential'.

"Thank you." He dropped his briefcase in a corner, hung up his jacket and appraised the two envelops, warily. Then he spent an hour and half responding to the content. By then, he was thirsting for a hot cup of tea, his new passion——a taste he had acquired by watching Lily at church.

First, he flipped the memos on top of his desk, but on second thoughts, locked them inside the desk. With Shane on the prowl, leaving the memos exposed was as risky as leaving a can of kerosene near an open flame.

He walked past Bill's office, turned and retraced his steps. Smart managers don't make the same mistake twice. He felt foolish bothering Bill again——lunch would have been a better venue.

"Hi Paul, what's up?" Bill greeted him.

"Same routine . . . slight variance . . . another year." He closed the door.

"How was Thanksgiving?"

"I went skiing. How was yours?"

"Great. We did the rounds with the grandparents. Sarah and Brittany enjoy it a lot. So, how're the reports coming? Think we'll close timely?"

"I'm pretty sure we will. Right now, we're validating our numbers."

"Good! That's what I like to hear. So, how's everything?"

"Love your painting. Haven't seen that before." He stared at a landscape painting on the wall above Bill's head.

"It's new. Classy. A bribe for something, no doubt." Bill swiveled his chair.

He turned and paced Bill's office. "Um," he ruffled his hair.

Bill stopped swiveling his chair, but continued watching him.

"What do you do when you've disappointed someone?" he asked.

"Gain her trust," Bill replied.

"How do you know it's a she?"

"Rumors get around."

"I can't believe this is happening. I'm a level-headed guy. Dad and I are at an impasse. Worse, I've betrayed the trust of someone I respect."

"Paul, are you sure this is really what you want? Is it about trust or because you've never been at the receiving end of rejection?"

He looked up, surprised. "I know what you mean."

"And?"

"It's not like that. I've suffered a couple of losses in my youth——mutual decision. Puppy love's still love. But this is different. I know what I'm doing, the more reason I'm kicking myself."

"If she's worth it, then regain her trust. But I warn you, if the rumors are true, you'll need to show her your vulnerable side."

"No kidding."

"Nopes. Hell may have no fury than a woman scorned, but heaven has no greater prayer warrior than a woman who believes she let her heart lead her and missed God's will. When you broke up with her, you made her question her ability to read the Lord's guidance correctly. She wouldn't want to make the same mistake twice. She'll fight you . . . on her knees."

"I sense she's already doing that."

"Take heart. If the Lord's hand's in it, He'll guide her back to you."

"I sure hope so. I do pray so."

"As always, Sheila and I are praying for you." Bill gave him a thumbs up.

"Thanks Bill." He dragged his feet back to the corridor and narrowly missed bumping into Shane. "Morning," he muttered.

Shane flashed his teeth, snarled, "Hi Paul," and scurried away.

Paul studied Shane's back, rubbing his chin. Perhaps if he prayed more for Shane, he would see some good in him. Surely the generous Lord, must have created at least one virtue in that man? He continued to the break room, mulling over the pros and cons of his options for the evening.

33

"Paul, your mother and I did not raise you to be inconsiderate. You're a gentleman!" Igor boomed in the phone. "The Shinebonds were not too pleased to see us last Sunday."

Paul dumped his briefcase in the back and hopped in the driver's seat, muttering, "A Labrador pup's going for seven hundred; ten to twenty grand, if you're going for a champ. But then again, poodles are à la mode."

"What?" his father yelled.

"Love you too, Dad!"

"Is that all you have to say? Think!"

"I've been doing nothing but thinking for a whole year." He chuckled.

"How long have you known Kelly?"

"Since we were children."

"And . . .?"

"Kelly's a nice girl, in her own way."

How can Dad miss the obvious? None of Kelly's friends have any qualms about who she is. She's in the social pages, the antithesis of who I am. How can he think the two of us could ever be happy together? We're living everybody's dream of what their own perfect life should be——I the mural to show off their vision, and they the painters to dream big.

"Dad, what is it about Kelly that you esteem so much?"

"Your mother and I were thinking of going on a ten-day cruise. A good time to get to know Kelly better," his father said.

"I have to work, Dad. Please tell Mum I'll drop by this weekend." Paul said goodbye to his father, turned on the ignition and took off.

◆ ◆ ◆

"Well I guess that's that," Charlotte yawned. "Serves you right for meddling!"

Igor scoffed and threw another log on the fire. "I, meddle? I was only trying to talk some sense into him."

"A twenty–six–year old should be able to make up his own mind." Charlotte paused, chewing her nails. Igor was twenty-two when he decided to go steady, twenty-four when he proposed. Should she remind him? Nah.

Igor looked at her with a gleam in his eyes. "I know what you're thinking."

"What?"

"We were much younger."

"You're right."

"Honey, things were different then. A thirty-year old today may be too young. How do you tell your son that you're concerned . . . scared for the future of your unborn grandchildren?" He lifted his eyes up. "I was not born to conquer frontiers, Lord. I'm only a simple businessman, following in the footsteps of my fathers. I'm no trailblazer. I'm a meat and potato guy. I haven't even taken to dumplings yet."

"Igor," Charlotte intervened.

"He's my sole heir. I don't like losing control!"

"Igor!" Charlotte said again.

"Yes, honey."

"Stop planning the answer. Let Him lead the way."

"I wish I'd your faith."

Charlotte's eyes softened. "My faith Igor? It's His faith. Why don't you ask Him? Whatever His will is, He will see us through. He has never let us down, why would He start now? His very nature is faithful and true."

34

Lily hoisted her leather briefcase over her shoulders, grabbed her winter jacket, and walked toward her apartment, but Lamar was sitting on the steps, looking despondent again. Too tired for a polite chitchat, she just wanted to get home and wash her hair and wished he was somewhere else. The parent companies she was assigned had so many shell companies, she didn't know where to begin——New York, London, Paris, Lausanne, the British Virgin Islands, Jersey, Liechtenstein, or the Cayman Islands? But her boss expected her to solve the puzzles!

"Hello," she greeted Lamar.

"Good evening, Lily. You lucky girl!" he replied.

"Why do you say that?" she asked, her voice as quiet as a mother bear, on the prowl. But Lamar was apparently clueless.

"You've your life together——a job to die for . . . a nice car. Your life's good, girl."

Not you too!

She said, frowning, "Lamar, I hate to disappoint you——few people are given beds of roses. Those I have known, ploughed a field to get theirs."

"At least you have a field," Lamar replied, still clueless.

"Lamar, I lean on God and like other people, I heeded my parents' counsel to finish school. So can you. Why did you drop out again?"

"Well, I have a lot of things going on."

"Like what?"

"Stuff. Me and my girlfriend broke up again." He hung his head.

"Which one, this time? At this rate, you won't have a girlfriend to brag about."

"Well she means a lot to me. I need some direction."

"Are you kidding? Were it every one of your girlfriends moved to Wisconsin and changed their phone numbers! I'm having a bad hair day. Excuse me."

Lamar recoiled. "Man, you're in a bad mood!"

"Lamar, I had a long day and I am tired. Every time I turn around, you are breaking up with one girl or another. I can't keep track of them. They exploit you and dump you. The only thing I appreciate about you is that you are clean——your head is straight, and you don't hang out with the wrong group——loud music aside. That is why you are still alive."

"I know."

"We had this conversation last summer. Remember? I had suggested that if your counselor couldn't help, then seek Cal Poly's help. Tell them you would like to transfer to a four-year college, but prefer to stay closer to home——are your classes acceptable? What else do you need to meet their standard? Did you?"

"Well, I had issues."

"What issues?"

"Me and my girlfriend broke up."

"What has that got to do with finishing school? Did she take your brain too? You were supposed to talk to your counselor or contact Cal Poly."

"I know."

"Then why are we having this conversation again? You are good at math and designing. There are so many good fields you can get into with those skills. You are six units shy of graduating. You should be graduating this summer. That was the plan, remember? You live in a country where you have financial aid to help you get ahead. Stick it out! Finish your AA degree, and transfer to a four-year college. Before you know it, you will be inspiring other people and cheering them on to stay focused. Once you have a steady life, you will meet the right girl."

Lamar got up and stepped aside. "I suppose you've a point."

"You know I do. You are twenty-one years old. By grace you should still have a lot of life ahead of you. Don't waste your life away. Keep your eyes on the Lord. Take advantage of financial help and stay focused and achieve your goals."

"Well said. I'll go talk to my counselor," Lamar cheered up.

She continued upstairs. "You always say that, then you don't follow through——lion in the street . . . dog ate your shoes . . . broke up with your girlfriend! I had recommended you to Professor Moretov."

Lamar started, surprised. "You know Professor Moretov?"

"Business association network. But, don't change the subject. He waited——you never followed up. I'm embarrassed. Either you contact Cal Poly, or we are through with this conversation. I can't help you. Ask God. He's our help."

"I know. I'll follow through this time. You can count on me."

"Good evening." She reached her apartment, determined to stay focused on her goal to start her own business. "Lord, I'm tired. I need a break," she prayed, unlocked her door and pushed it open.

Woosh, plop, and thud, thud! Her jacket and briefcase made it to the bedroom, and her high-heels flew to the middle of her wardrobe. She padded stockinged feet to the kitchen muttering, "Please help Lamar. I'm tired of excuses. I can't fix other people's problems. I have enough of my own. Kelly's all over town again——red ribbon flying in the air . . . talking about her wedding and plans for her honeymoon cruise to the Mediterranean. Help! I feel so humiliated! I need a strong cup of tea and some peace and quiet." Clap, clang, and whack, the kettle landed on the stove.

She left the water heating and returned to the bedroom.

She was rinsing her hair, when the doorbell started ringing. She grabbed a towel, wishing she could finish working on her hair. Perhaps she should have washed it the day before, but she had to work on her dissertation.

The ringing persisted. Who could be at the door——Lamar again, trying to borrow sugar or tea or something? Her neighbor, Devonne, wasn't due for tea until later. She unlatched the door and threw it open.

Paul stood on the threshold his tie askew. She had ignored all his calls during the week and missed the singles' Bible study and the Wednesday midweek prayer meeting to boot, choosing to pray at home, alone, instead.

Paul took in her form at a glance. She looked slimmer in her white lounge robe. Even the red flowers spotting the gown made her look slimmer than when she opened the door for him the summer before, dressed in her riveting yellow cocktail dress. He had failed to notice that when he escorted her down from the hills, too busy milking the excuse to put his arm around her shoulders.

She stared at him. He fidgeted with his jacket. A soft train of Handel's Messiah filtered through the half-opened door.

She drew her robe tighter around her, embarrassed to see him. A chilly breeze blew in as it had the evening some members of Evangelical Neighborhood Church had shunned her. A shadow crossed her face, slicing through his chest like a knife.

Perhaps she saw her pain mirrored in his eyes. "Sorry. I thought you were my neighbor. She had promised to drop in for a cup of tea. Please come in."

He thanked her, ran his hand through his hair, and waited as she collected throw pillows scattered on the floor.

With a careless gesture, she indicated a chair, then she disappeared into her bedroom, leaving Handel's Messiah to keep him company.

Right away, he noticed her new décor——hanging on the wall was a large clock of gold trimming. If he remembered correctly, those models went for about five to ten thousand dollars. Something about her did not fit in the neighborhood.

She returned, dressed in a jade jump suit, her hair combed back, slumped down on a couch and faced the wall.

After a moment, she stirred herself and asked, "Would you care for a cup of tea or perhaps coffee?"

"A cup of tea would be great." He missed drinking anything with her.

"Milk?"

"Please. Thank you."

She made the best tea——boiled her water and her milk until piping hot, then she brewed the tea in a warmed teapot, before serving it.

Steam still escaped from the silver kettle she had just removed from the stove and milk was warming in a small pot. A Wedgewood English tea set of small, English rose, sat daintily on a no less pretty tray of matching pattern. She added another tea cup and carried the tray to the coffee table in the living room.

Paul smiled. The set reminded him of his mother's sets, which she bought while on vacation in England. Except his mother's sets were gold-rimmed. He had no doubt Lily's set must have also come from Harrods' or a comparable shop.

She served him a steaming cup of tea, topped it with hot milk, her face blank, and placed a silver bowl of sugar on the side table next to him, then she served herself a cup——black with no sugar.

On her way to her seat, she re-looped the Messiah CD.

He asked about her foot. She thanked him for asking and for giving her a ride back to her apartment and assured him that she had improved much, and had resumed taking short walks. After that, they ran out conversation and listened to the Oratorio, instead, as they drank their tea.

The soft train of the Messiah sailed from the deck and twined itself over their heads and rested between them. As the Overture died down, the recitative 'Comfort ye, comfort ye my people,' followed. How ironic.

Paul finished his tea, and cleared his throat. He glanced at Lily, as his father would, when he was uncertain of what his mother would do, combed his hair with his hand, and cleared his throat again. "I'm sorry, perhaps I shouldn't have come . . . I mean, I'd no right just dropping in."

"That's okay, I had no plans for the evening, anyway." She smiled, faintly, then reclined her head on the couch.

The clock on the wall seemed to tick the futility of time as it passed away——precious time that he wished he could roll back.

"Lily," he began, then stopped, confused, and uncertain of how to proceed. He lowered his eyes to the ground.

When he looked up, she was still sitting in the same position. "Lily . . . I've no excuse, except to say that I'm sorry for . . . everything."

She kept her eyes averted.

He tried again, "I mean, it was heartless, utterly irresponsible of me."

Silence.

"It was circumstances beyond my control," he pressed on.

She looked at him, her face distorted with pain, then she turned to the wall and rubbed the corners of her eyes.

Should he offer her his handkerchief?

Unsure, he remained rooted to his chair. In all his years, he had never begged a woman. Groveling had never been his style, but remembering

Bill's advice to permit himself to be vulnerable, he said, "I covet your understanding. We've a lot in common."

"We? I'm afraid I don't follow you. I guess my brain is tired. It's been a long week." She struggled to keep her voice low.

"It's just things . . . other factors . . . I would like to explain."

"That did not appear to be the case, five months ago."

Five months ago! That she had kept track was worse than if she had slapped him. He tried to detect patterns in the solid carpet as he considered how to come clean, without betraying his parents' role in his current predicament. "Lily, I was wrong. I'd no right . . .. There were so many things coming at me. For a while, I thought my duty lay elsewhere. Um. . .."

Lily stared at him, hurt. To her, he was mouthing platitudes. *Why did he bother to come, to appease his conscience?*

"Duty! Is that how you perceive me?" she moderated her voice.

Paul tossed up his hands, frustrated, but matched her low tone, "I'm saying it all wrong. My life's been in chaos——that's all."

"You don't say! So, you feel duty-bound to come to me to fix it?" She was hurting him; but should she care? "No, Mr. Van Clyden, you owe me no explanation."

Her spiritual side urged her to forgive him, her flesh craved raw revenge——to inflict on him the same pain and humiliation he had inflicted on her. Like a volcano ready to erupt, her anger mounted, making it difficult for her to focus on the correct thing to do.

The magnitude of her anger shocked her. Realizing she must conquer her raw emotions, she walked to the window and stared at the Christmas streetlights below, her back turned to him.

"My behavior was despicable," Paul said.

She stiffened her back, elongated her neck, and stood at her full height, her back straight and regal, as she continued to stare into the night, finding solace in her hurt. She did not realize she had so much suppressed anger against him, until she saw him on her threshold. After the way he had behaved, how could she ever trust him again?

Kelly was preparing for her honeymoon. Did they quarrel again? Could she win the competition over Kelly? If rumors were true, what future could she have with a man who dropped her at the slightest prompting of his father?

Having Paul on her doorstep set her heart in turmoil. She could trust him, yet she couldn't——he had been a gentleman and had helped her downhill . . . and braved gossip by checking on her a week afterwards during coffee break at church——that ought to count for something; but, he was engaged! What other choice did she have, except to insist on him honoring his commitment to Kelly?

She looked at his bowed head. Her heart melted somewhat, but the pain of his fickleness and Kelly's triumph, humiliating her in front of ENC still goaded her.

Why did he come? What about the engagement and the cruise! The two-timer! She resumed contemplating the night.

Paul continued cradling his head. "Paul, my friend, listen . . . listen very carefully. I am telling you this my friend. The woman doesn't always yell when she is angry," a Nigerian acquaintance once joked. "When she yells, but cooks, you're fine; but, when she stiffens her back, elongates her neck, and refuses to talk, drop to your knees, and pray like crazy!"

Lily had prepared tea, but for her guest. She probably offered it to him more out of politeness, as good hostesses do, than because she wanted to cook for him. He prayed silently for a small miracle, a glimpse into her heart.

Minutes later, she returned to her seat and averted her face again. "I don't know what your situation is, but I need space."

He raised his head, his eyes alight with hope. "I respect your position. When would you like us to continue this conversation?"

She glanced at him briefly. "I should forgive, as the Lord does; but I believe what happened is for the best."

"You can't mean that."

She looked at him with her gentle brown eyes. "Paul, at the risk of sounding like a movie script; you and I come from two different worlds." She drew out her next words, "Surviving and thriving in my world requires a lot more than feelings. For a very brief moment, I thought we had something deeper——a bond that transcends everything. Now, I'm convinced that you do not understand the depth of commitment that it would take to live in my world."

"With all due respect, I beg to disagree. I destroyed the seed of friendship that was planted. I stand chastised."

"Thank you. I know God gives second chances and much more. Where would I be without His grace? But quite honestly, I need some space."

"And you should have. You've every right to. But how can we move forward, if you shut me out?"

At Paul's comment, Lily snapped. It seemed to be the last straw——that Paul had dropped in, expecting to resume where he had left off, betrayed a sentiment that he considered her his back-up plan. She was not his back-up plan, had never been one, and had no intention of becoming one!

She gave him a long look, "I was under the impression your future lies elsewhere. One day, you will meet the woman who will bring you to your knees, and when that time comes, look up and pray like you have never prayed before." She opened the door. "Good evening," she said, then with her head facing the outside stairs down which he must walk, her back straight and her chin tilted in the air, she stood back and waited.

As he rescued his jacket from the couch, footsteps approached.

"Good evening, Ms. Devonne! Come in!" Lily smiled.

A middle-aged woman of about fifty, wearing a gray jumpsuit, appeared, carrying a plate of baked chocolate cookies covered with a transparent wrap. "Did I come at a bad time?" she asked, embarrassed.

"Not at all. Come in. Tea is ready," Lily replied.

An awkward silence followed. Lily remembered what polite people normally did, even when they were most displeased and said, "Devone, this is Mr. Paul Van Clyden." Her lips smiled, her eyes did not.

Paul mumbled a response and stumbled out into the dark, chilly night.

35

Another tissue flew across the room, followed by a stuffed sneeze. Paul pried open his eyes and sneezed again. He ambled to the mirror, his head throbbing. Puffed eyes stared back at him. After leaving Lily's apartment, he had wandered the streets in the chilly night, trying to clear his head. He would have done better going to the gym.

He took two caplets of pain medicine and called in sick.

"If you look as bad as you sound, I don't want you setting foot anywhere near BF&S till next year. And drink plenty of chicken soup!" Bill ordered.

He promised he would, pulled his new Egyptian quilt up to his nose and tried to go back to sleep. Groggily, he wondered whether he should keep his promise to visit his mother in the evening, or postpone it and risk her rushing over with a battalion of remedies.

Midmorning, he got up and spent the rest of the afternoon meditating on Bible scriptures, riding his bike, and drinking hot tea.

Late afternoon, he went to a quiet corner of the balcony, shrouded by autumn golden hills, and stared at early Christmas lights awakening all over Orchards City and beyond, as he wondered whether daybreak would ever come. He permitted his thoughts to wander in the direction of Hollenvine. A constricting tightness gripped his chest. To ease the pain, he inhaled deeply, before returning to his room to take a shower.

A few minutes later, he dressed in a pair of old jeans, a warm sweater, and a thick winter jacket, ignoring his head that was throbbing like the thundering rhythm of a native-drum beat.

He took two more caplets of pain medicine. Bouts of sneezing greeted them. Disregarding the sneezes, he grabbed his overnight bag, and lumbered downstairs. Jonathan was on the couch watching the evening news, relaxed and seemed in control. For a moment, he wished he had just a quarter of Jonathan's confidence, but dismissed it, loathed to dwell on self-pity.

Jonathan abandoned the news, measured him with his eyes, and said with conviction, "It'll be all right. It may take time, but remember He's always in control."

He thanked him, went to the garage, and soon pulled out into the thoroughfare, welcoming the solitude the long drive in the horrendously slow weekend traffic would accord him. Often, he was in a hurry to get home to his parents.

He did not hit gridlock, however, until downtown and then he got through it quickly. If only life's unknown proved as pleasant, he wished.

Jonathan said a quick prayer for Paul and resumed orchestrating his latest piece, wishing he could do more, or that Paul would circulate and perhaps meet other girls out there that would please his aunt and uncle. Still, Lily was not a bad girl.

But for grace, he too, could have been back on the market looking for a suitable mate, had Sharon not forgiven him his gaffe.

◆ ◆ ◆

At the sound of a car approaching the gate, Percy started barking. Paul entered a code and drove straight to the garage. Percy's welcome grew louder. He toyed with the idea of playing with him, but resisted the urge. Instead, he collected his overnight bag and went inside.

"He's here," his mother said, elated. He was already at the foot of the stairs when she came out of the kitchen.

His father emerged from the family room, dragging his feet or perhaps more unsure of seeing him, than less eager?

He watched him, wary.

"You came! I was beginning to wonder whether you'd make it this weekend." His mother offered him her cheeks.

He wished both of them a Merry Christmas and assured his mother that he had remembered his promise.

"Merry Christmas," his mother replied.

That triggered a bout of sneezing.

"Oh, you have a cold!" She touched his forehead.

"Just a slight one, Mum."

"You're burning. Did you take anything for it?"

"A couple of Tylenols. Don't worry, Mum, I'll be all right."

"I'll get you a hot drink."

"Good to see you, son," his father said. "They must be working you hard. I suppose you must be closing the books?"

"Yes. We've been trying to wind up everything."

"Good."

His father returned to the living room. He went upstairs, unpacked and came down shortly, to find a cup of hot chocolate waiting for him on the side table.

Tired of hearing Percy scratching on the patio door, he finished his hot chocolate, fished out an old ball from a box in the toolshed and played catch-ball with the dog.

"I know Percy misses you, but do you think you should be out there with that cold?" his mother asked through the patio door.

"I won't be long, Mum. I just need to quiet him down."

"You've plenty of jackets in the closet."

"I know. I'm almost done."

He continued to play catch-ball a moment longer, then he coaxed Percy back into his warm kennel.

Percy yawned and flattened his nose against his mat, a sign that he was pleased with his brief attention, for the moment. "You manipulative dog!" he teased him and ran upstairs to wash up.

The fresh air had done him a bit of good.

When he came down, his mother said, "There's more hot milk on the stove, if you need a refill. Dinner's almost ready."

He thanked her and refilled his cup with steaming chocolate. Since she had already set the table, there was nothing for him to do, so he rejoined his father in the family room, more relaxed, but still guarded.

At dinner, when his father said grace, he stumbled over familiar words he had prayed so many times before.

"Our annual Christmas party's just two weeks away. Will you be coming?" His mother chatted about everything and nothing to bridge the awkward moments.

"Which one, Mum?" he asked, sidestepping the issue.

"Family of course. I like church Christmas potluck, but you know we've never expected you to attend, unless you're home."

"I'm not sure, Mum. We'll see."

She picked up an asparagus spear. "I would like you to come. We saw you only once this past summer."

"Sorry, Mum."

"Oh, the men of this family!" She shook her head.

His father concentrated rather hard on cutting his steak, then stole a glance at her from under his bushy eyebrows. He knew better than to answer her. They labored through dinner with long bouts of silence, except for their utensils scraping their plates.

After serving coffee, crumbly slices of blueberry and pumpkin pies left over from Thanksgiving, his mother retreated to the kitchen to finish planning her party and to start baking the desserts.

He flipped through offerings on the TV, occasionally catching his father watching him.

Finally, his father cleared his throat twice between a bite of his pie and a sip of his coffee, a sign he was getting ready for an unpleasant conversation.

"How was summer?"

"Okay."

"You and Jonathan minding your reputation?" his father joked.

"Yes. We try." He put the remote control down.

"How was Colorado? It was Colorado you went to, right?"

"Yes. Nothing to brag about. Just the usual holiday crowd."

"What resort did you go to?"

"Lionridge."

"Lionridge. Mmm. Nice resort."

"It's all right."

His father took another bite of his pie and gulped his coffee. "Lots of people I'd assume. One would think more people would stay home for Thanksgiving. What's become of tradition?"

He scratched his chin. Dad had never interfered with his life, since he became an adult, except for giving advice when asked. "I guess the world's changing," he mumbled.

His father scoffed. "Never heard of anybody changing their mind about pumpkin pie and ice cream. Your Mum and I ran into the Shinebonds the other day."

He grinned, and stabbed a chunk of blueberry with his fork.

"Is Kelly still working for that company? What's the name?" His Dad clicked his fingers to jog his memory.

"Premier Public Relations," he came to his aid.

"Yes, that's the one. Premier Public Relations."

"I suppose so. At least, last I heard of it."

"Uh-huh." His father crossed his legs and rubbed his elbows.

Paul was sure he had already been briefed by the grapevine and the gatekeepers of genes. Placing his fork down, he stared at flickering figures on the screen, without registering the characters——statues in business suits, obeying orders from one man.

His father had been nothing but loving and kind to him. How much of his father's persistence was due to fear from not knowing Lily, and how much was due to his love for him? Did his parents really know Kelly? The Kelly of public relations could very well be the only Kelly they had ever been allowed to know.

"They say Kelly's planning a trip to Europe." His father pushed his plate away.

"Good for her. Europe should be pleasant this time of the year. A bit chilly, but not too touristy." He flipped to the sports page of the Los Angeles Times.

"Oh? We were under the impression you were going together?"

"That's news to me."

"Are you implying someone told your mother and me less than the truth?"

"No. I'm not. All I know is I'm not going to Europe."

To his father's raised eyebrows, he smiled and returned to the sports page, then he resumed flipping channels again, as his coffee grew cold.

After a forbidding silence, his father said, "Kelly's unhappy."

"Dad, what's your vision?" He shoved the remote control on to the coffee table. It slid to a stop with a soft clatter.

"What do you mean?"

"What future do you envision for me, vis-à-vis shopping around?"

"Kelly's nice. I'm not saying she's perfect, but she's a nice girl."

He got a fresh bout of sneezing.

His father waited, then said, "I did not rule out other options. Kelly's nice."

He sketched a smile, bitter. "It sounds like the same thing."

"Son, as I recall, God commanded the daughters of Zelophehad to marry only within their tribe."

"Numbers thirty-six, verse six?"

"Probably. Sounds about right."

"Within context, I believe the verse refers to inheritance. Joseph's descendants did not wish to lose their inheritance to the other tribes of Israel."

"Good for them!"

"Exactly, Dad." He grinned.

"Their husbands, their children . . . Nehemiah makes other references."

"I beg to disagree, Dad. Male heirs were excluded. Moreover, we're adopted Israelites, under grace, though still bound to honor the Holy One."

"The new Israel, the old Israel. Israel had twelve tribes and God's command was very clear——each to his own!"

"Let me try to understand, had you a daughter who honored you and the LORD, would it matter? We're bonded through the shed blood."

His father raised his hand in protest. "Don't preach at me!"

He was shocked. His father had seldom been brusque, and never since he became an adult. "Dad, with all due respect, you introduced the subject. I'm trying to understand your perspective. I'm not saying Kelly's not a nice girl. I'm sure she'll make some man very happy."

"Kelly comes from a solid stock, worthy of attention."

"And I suppose other girls aren't?" he addressed the carpet, took a deep breath, and said, "Dad, what's your greatest concern?"

His father stared straight ahead.

Had I a sibling, would that have lifted my burden of being sole heir? Since I've always held a job from my teenage years, and walked the straight and narrow, I'm hardly a prodigal. I could start my own business, if it becomes necessary.

"Look, if it will help, I'll strike out on my own."

"So that's it! You'll walk away from what your mother and I built?"

"Dad, I respect you and Mum. You've always been my role-model, and will always be, but I also want to give myself a shot at keeping the covenant."

"Life can be very long. Of all the women in California . . . in America? You know, I wouldn't mind if you brought home one of those tongue-twisted Europeans with an accent thicker than a double ketchup." His father tossed his hands in the air. "A life time is a life time."

"I know."

"Mhmm."

"I'm not saying other options are perfect, nor that I'd succeed. All I'm saying is, I believe I stand a better chance at remaining committed——"

"Exotic. You're mesmerized. That's it, you're fascinated with the foreign . . . the exotic." His father shook his fingers at him.

On the side-table was a picture of his beautiful, regal grandma, a Dutch-Swede. He rubbed his nose to hide a smile. Dad seemed to have forgotten that Grandma migrated from Holland and still had her Dutch accent.

"It's her accent, isn't it? I know you young people are fascinated with foreign accents. Kelly's a fine girl. Got into some bad company no doubt, but with a little bit of effort, she'll come around."

"I don't mind helping Kelly as a friend."

His father's face turned grim. "Kelly's a fine girl."

He stared at his father, his head pounding. "Dad, I respect you and always will. True, the Shinebonds are a good business asset, but how much do you know them——what impact they could have on our lives?"

"I don't deserve that!"

"Neither do I, Dad," he muttered and ran upstairs to his bedroom, stuffed his things back into the overnight bag, and walked out.

A few minutes after Paul ran downstairs, Charlotte heard a car engine roar to life, followed by squealing wheels. She rushed to the front door.

"Paul? Paul? Paul!" she called to the taillights disappearing into the night, amidst Percy's wild barking, then she stormed into the family room, where Igor was standing, staring at the empty door in a stupor, her eyes spitting fire.

"I knew it! When you stammered through grace at dinner, I knew you were struggling again——being stubborn! What did you do to him?"

Her husband transferred his blank eyes on her.

"Igor, I asked you, what did you do to him?"

He continued staring at her, dumb.

"Igor Emmanuel Van Clyden, why did my son drive out into the night with a fresh cold and a burning fever?" Her executive voice rocked the rooftops, her blue eyes flashed red and her hair blazed fire.

Igor lowered his head.

"I cleaned and scrubbed all week and I had the maid come in and clean and scrub. I cooked and baked all his favorite pies and cakes and roast, thinking my son was coming home at last after a long, lonely summer. And you chased him into the cold night with a fresh cold. You stubborn, sorry excuse of a . . . a . . . a hard-head! You chased out my only child into the night with a burning fever. Why? Your mother can hardly string together a sentence in English and you're concerned about accents and sole heirs! If anything happens to my son, Igor Emmanuel Van Clyden, you will experience what it means to go through twenty-four hours of solid, raw child-labor, without a pain-killer!"

◆ ◆ ◆

Paul shopped the lanes on the freeway, at a speed not wise to document on paper, numb. By grace, a traffic officer did not stop him. Around ten o'clock, he drove straight through to his garage, in one piece.

Upstairs in his bedroom, he changed into his pajamas, took more medication, climbed into bed and pulled the covers over his head, too stunned to pray. For the first time in his life, he had exchanged angry words with his father and walked out on him in the middle of a discussion! Not even in his wildest youth had he ever been so disrespectful! Worse, he remembered he did not say goodnight to his mother. Never before had he been so thoughtless and discourteous.

36

Bill and Sheila were in the family room, sorting gifts for family members.

"I feel we need to stop and pray," Bill said.

Sheila agreed. Together with Sarah and Brittany, they formed a circle on the floor, held hands, and started praying. At first, they prayed around the world, then they started focusing more and more at home, until Paul's name resurfaced again and again. They prayed for him earnestly, not knowing what they should pray for, but pray they did, covering all the bases, and most importantly, his safety.

♦ ♦ ♦

At ten o'clock, Lily rose up from her prayer cushion and washed her face. For the first time, she noticed she was hungry and had not eaten since morning. She prepared a bowl of fruit salad and peanut butter sandwiches, her mind on Paul.

That same morning, she had woken up feeling blah and reluctant to face the world. Unsure of Paul's real motive in trying to return to her, she struggled with trusting him again. In the past, she never gave a second chance to a suitor who used another woman to entice her or make her jealous. If he did not hesitate to use another woman, how could she trust him not to do the same with her? But, if he was serious about her, what about the other woman, didn't she also deserve to be treated with dignity? Were her feelings of lesser import?

If Paul had ended his relationship with Kelly permanently this time, it was up to him to persuade her to trust him, besides trusting the Holy One.

She had called in sick to Mr. Chancey. Bernice had called her back soon after, and threatened to come over, after hearing her voice.

Throughout the day, Lily's emotions had alternated between anger, pain and a need to forgive. At about a quarter to nine in the evening, she had felt a heavy burden to pray for Paul. She was lying on the couch, trying to prevent her cold from turning into a fever. The heater was going full blast; the room bordered on hot. A warm towel lay on top of her plugged nose.

She had debated calling Sharon. But after chasing Paul out, she believed she had lost any vestige of privilege that she might have still had to phone him or his friends, so who else could she call to verify what was going on?

Abandoning her self-pity for a moment, she had knelt down and started praying for him, with all her mind and soul. She prayed that other prayer intercessors would also feel the call to pray for him.

So intense had she prayed that she could not remember lying down on the floor, with her hands stretched out——the ultimate form of intercession she only used in extreme circumstances——until just now, when she felt the burden lift.

She finished preparing her snack, still worried about Paul.

As an intercessor, she labored to remain neutral. She wanted the best for Paul, even if that meant losing him to another woman. Why was it so urgent to pray for him that evening? Was he in danger? How could she find out?

It was at moments like this that she felt frustrated at not being part of Paul's inner circle. Despite his half-hearted attempt at reconciling with her, she felt she was still an outsider, intruding in his life.

She deduced she was experiencing four hundred years of American history, though the battle had shifted somewhat to psychological abuse. Not that it mattered. The shackles were as heavy, perhaps even heavier, in some cases, than any physical chain——for one who entrapped the mind, ultimately entrapped the whole body, if allowed. It was an insidious trap that would capture every aspect of one's life, if permitted, a constant reminder for her to choose to be free.

When she had just arrived in America, she believed she could conquer the world, as she had been raised to think. Covertly, her environment had tried to redefine for her what the perimeter of her success should be—— trying to suck her into a ravine of superimposed limitations that had nothing to do with who she was, nor who she was capable of becoming through God's power.

The monster she had been battling was the constricting power of ingrained expectations——not so much through physical, as through psychological repression——that questioned her existence as a human being endowed with full emotion, cognitive abilities, talents, and the same privileged access to the throne of grace as other human beings. Societal expectations, the subtle questioning and sometimes blatant disregard of her abilities, the constant scrutinizing and downgrading of her achievements, attributing them to mere coincidences, a series of good luck.

While she had been obliged to deal with the continual battle of proving herself, on the one hand, on the other extreme, she felt a new pressure to remain true to her roots——intimations that unless she lived by the unwritten code of what was considered a true native child, she was a traitor to her own people——a demand that had not been placed on her when she was in East Africa, perhaps because, as a native child, she did not have to prove her allegiance to her root.

Some of her worst competitors were the very ones whom she had assumed would be on her side. The clawing, the vicious competition——the malice and petty jealousies ad nauseam——over career advancement down to potential dates, had driven her to restrict her circle of friends. She was not prone to elbowing her way anyway. The very idea of being malicious churned her stomach. So she limited her choice of friends to people with whom she shared some common value.

What would the Lord say to the artificial barriers designed to shackle her if she permitted them? Definitive word was 'if.' Praise be!

Had she refused to acknowledge that she needed God's help, that she could not measure up to His standard on her own merit, that would have been arrogant. But she had submitted herself to the transforming power of the Great One and continued to do so.

The Lord had empowered her to be strong. But, any deep friendship with Paul could be so manacled with societal expectations that, barring a miracle, she must accept that his world was different, despite it being the last decade of the twentieth century.

Raised sheltered, did Paul understand? Was he mature enough to weather the level of commitment that such a friendship required? In some ways he was mature, but she was still ambivalent. The night before, was that enough evidence that he was ready to carve a new life? Even if he could, she would hate to separate him from his parents and friends.

What about Kelly? Until now, she had assumed that Kelly was her rival, for good reasons, supposing Kelly was no longer a threat, then what? Would she always hold up her head and conduct herself with the dignity that Paul's status required——create a secure environment that would undergird him, and earn him respect in the eyes of his peers? To push against barriers that might be raised against them if he proposed?

Even without a racial divide, the demand of fitting into Paul's family would still be challenging enough. How much was she depending on herself to succeed? How deeply did she trust the Lord?

"'I can do all things through Christ who strengthens me' as long as I steadfastly honor God," she cited Philippians chapter four, verse thirteen. This verse had meant a lot to her as she arrived on American soil.

She sighed. The verse had not changed; neither had she. She would continue to trust in the One who steered her across the seas and continued to watch over her. Her strength lay in resisting the temptation to love any man more than she loved the Lord! To be happy, she must put God first.

Though she had not met Bill and was unaware of his counsel to Paul, she was fulfilling his prophesy. She promised to battle Paul on her knees.

Once more, she prayed that the Lord would allow her to get married to a man who inspired in her the best of both worlds——the desire to be the best woman that He had created her to be and the desire to be committed to serving Him——a man who would never compete with God for her love.

She took her light supper to the living room without much of an appetite.

37

"Waiting is the 'W' word that many dread. It can be their downfall, or a ground for maturing——stretching their patience, their imaginations, their emotions, or taking them to the brink——making them dig deeper, until they're emptied of all and brought to a place of total surrender to God. That's the key. When God keeps you waiting, it's because He wants to mold you into His masterpiece. Let Him be God. Honor Him with your life.

"And again, some Christians approach God as if it's their way or the highway. They love to dictate to God. They manipulate the Word or reject it altogether; then they wonder why this world's gone crazy. But God wants to help you, if you'll let Him lead you. Stop having an attitude with God, just because He hasn't answered your prayers yet, or He has, but in His own way. Don't fight the LORD. Keep your eyes on Him. Humble yourself and let the Lord be God!"

Paul tossed the covers aside. No, he was not in church; he was in bed. His subconscious mind must have locked up——verbatim——Pastor Tim's introduction to his Sunday sermon. What was he afraid of? Failing God or his parents or just plain failing?

He completed his morning routine and changed into a fresh long-sleeved tee-shirt, a pair of jeans, and a pair of mountain boots.

If the Lord was stretching him, he should not throw jabs at Him but listen, humbly. He would go into the mountains and seek Him.

He read Psalm 126, verse five and six and searched his soul. May be, he was consumed with his own desire. When was the last time he sought God's Kingdom first? Was his regard for Lily coming between him and his relationship with the Lord? Or was the Lord testing the depth of his commitment to Him? How could he know the difference?

His nose still felt stuffed; but his sneezes were sporadic, so he resolved to go to Alegria Peak in the San Gabriel Mountains.

Beside him lay his mountain ensemble and a backpack loaded with a flask of hot coffee, his lunch bag, and loads of tissue paper. As a precaution, he had also packed his mountain survival kit.

Soon, the snowy peaks of Alegria loomed into view. Being Christmas, the number of family vans, jeeps, Cherokees, and all manner of cars parading up the mountain, surprised him——some determined mountaineers no doubt, he mused, trying hard not to focus on his crumbling life. One Christmas gift he had bought in hope . . . perhaps another Christmas.

About two miles from the peak, he pulled up at a campsite and parked. Little bundles of children darted in and out of clusters of adults. He observed them for a moment, then he turned his face to the mountains.

Grim-faced, he shrugged into his tawny jacket, slapped his black felt cap on his head, shoved his gloves on and hoisted his backpack over his shoulders. His eyes appraised the mountain peaks; his feet started up the trail with the sure footing of a mountain goat, with no set goal of distance or time, except to conquer himself. Years of mountaineering bulged out of his jeans.

Half a mile up the trail, he relaxed, and began pondering his earlier commitment for volunteer missionary work. He had not yet discussed his plans with his parents. Needless to say, he may have blown that chance.

An appointment with Pastor Tim would be easy and thanks to BF&S' policy, he could go on a sabbatical for a year, if he proved that the sabbatical was for self-development or volunteer service. But, where would he go? To an international country or should he research a need within the country? Wherever the Lord guided him, he would go, he concluded.

Next, what would he be doing? On the international scene, he could volunteer to teach English or business, but within the country, what could he do? Help build a school at a Native American reservation? That missionary places needed volunteers for building projects, he was sure. The work would be backbreaking, but it would do him a bit of good.

For the first time in days, his entire face lit up. Yes, volunteering for real grunt-work, should put him back in shape. Moreover, there were as many building projects within the country as without and summer was the best time to go.

"I'll go to the first part of the world that needs an intern for a two and half months' building project——whether Guadalajara or Timbuktu or a Navaho community," he prayed and quickened his steps up the mountain.

Next, research the cost of the trip. The majority of missionaries raised their own support. If his trip was confirmed, Evangelical Neighborhood Church would finance part of it out of its missionary fund. Raising the rest should not be a problem. He had many reliable friends who could help.

He could also ask his parents, in order to free the church funds for other missionaries, but he would rather be independent——perhaps, self-sponsor.

Finally, his share of the mortgage. If he lived frugally, financing the three months away should not be a problem. Conversely, could he provide accommodation to a struggling student for the summer? Better yet, could he persuade his other two cousins——still undergrads——to stay the summer and drive Jonathan crazy? Jonathan might flee and marry Sharon speedily, just to stay sane. He grinned.

Buoyed, he continued trailing up the snow-covered peaks. His feet trekked upwards; his thoughts turned to Lily. What was she doing today, shopping, perhaps? Yup, she was probably pushing through the crowds to get that one last gift.

No. His eyes softened. He doubted that Lily was the type of girl who would push through the crowd to grab a designer bag.

♦ ♦ ♦

Not a fan of Christmas shopping, Lily lay on the couch, the heater leveled at near maximum, an afghan shawl wrapped around her up to her chin. Cradled in her lap, a book on the discipline of the Christian life——just the therapy she needed for a weekend that promised to be dreary.

Earlier, she had driven to Be Still Lake's park and ride, then disappeared into the hills to sort out Paul, the puzzle, being careful this time to scrutinize all hikers for any sign of him, from a safe distance.

She achieved some semblance of conversation with the Lord in between fits of sneezing, as she marched inside the hills, to the rhythm of her prayers.

Semblance of conversation was the understatement. "Lord, I am not angry," she had started her prayer conversation. "I'm just having a pity-party.

Thank you for Paul. Thank you that he is a gentleman and godly——and serious about his commitment to You . . . and I can trust him to treat me with respect, except when he broke off with me on the phone. But I don't understand him. He favored me briefly, then he threw Kelly in my face. Then he wants me to date him again! I don't understand the American way, Lord. I don't care for men who try to make a woman jealous. I thought as a believer, he would date one girl at a time. What about Kelly?" A fit of sneezing interrupted her.

"Is she and Paul still dating? Will Paul keep waltzing in and out of my life? I am not his back-up plan and have no desire of becoming one." She sneezed again and persevered, "I need Your help, please show me the way. Yes. I want to get married, but not to a man who vacillates. I respect myself and I honor my relationship with You. James' letter says if anyone lacks wisdom, they should ask You for guidance. Psalm 37 says to trust in You, delight in You, commit my way to You and rest in You. Lord, I trust you and I do commit everything to You. You are not a god of confusion. Please straighten things out, and show me the way. I need to move on. Give me strength to finish my PhD and move on. I trust You with my future. You have never let me down and You promised You will never fail me. Give me Your joy and peace, and show me the way ...."

Onward, she marched. "And about yesterday Lord, did something happen to Paul? Please show me. I do care about his well-being . . .."

By the time she returned home, she felt motivated to call Sharon.

"Lily, how nice of you to call!" Sharon had said.

That was a good sign. If something was wrong, Sharon would sound subdued. She chitchatted, then she said, "I guess I'll just come to the point. Um, last night, I almost started the prayer chain going."

"You too!"

Praise be, I'm not making a fool of myself. "You also felt something?"

"Yes! I was in the kitchen baking, when I felt the burden to pray."

"For Paul?"

"Yes! Jonathan and a bunch of other people I talked to, also said the same thing, that they felt compelled to drop whatever they were doing and pray around the world, until Paul stuck to their minds."

Her heart lurched. "But he is all right? I mean, nothing serious happened, right?" Her voice was very quiet.

"Oh no, no, no! Everything's fine. Mercy prevailed. Paul had a spat with his Dad and left in a huff," Sharon seemed to be making light of matters.

"A spat?"

So his parents live close by. Was the spat about Thursday evening? I pray not. Or was this an old family feud?

"Whatever it was, the Lord protected him and the other drivers," Sharon said in a more subdued voice. "If Paul had done something grossly wrong, he may have had to face the consequences of his actions. He had a lot on his mind yesterday. I'm sure he'd not meant to leave like that."

"Praise be for grace and mercy," she said relieved.

Sharon said, chirpier, "You know how parents are. Paul's parents are the sweetest people. They love him to pieces. But just like other parents, they too sometimes struggle communicating. You know how that goes. I'm sure it'll be fine. Paul respects his parents very much and they know that."

She realized Sharon was hem-hawing; but she had no wish to bait her into betraying family secrets either.

She hung up relieved that Paul was okay, plugged a medley of contemporary Christian Christmas tape in the player, turned up the heat and cuddled up with Dr Chuck Swindoll's *Killing Giants and Pulling Thorns.*

Now lost in the book, she allowed words of wisdom to sink into her heart. Knowing other believers also went through experiences similar to hers, boosted her faith in believing that the God who worked in the lives of ordinary people through thousands of years, was the same God who was alive and relevant in her life and the lives of ordinary people in the late autumn of 1993.

Seldom given to napping, a fresh bath, the warm room, and the soft music lulled her. Her hands relaxed, the book slipped to her bosom and she drifted off. Two hours later, the jarring sound of the phone woke her up.

38

Marjorie put the phone down relieved after Lily's assurance that nothing serious had happened and Paul was all right. She too had been thinking about Paul. In a lighter mood, she refocused on organizing her house.

Between stirring the chilly beans and chasing Melanie playing with a glass of water, she glanced out of the family room window and broke into a broad smile. Who, but the Professor was walking up the driveway, his hands folded behind his back, his head bowed reverently to the ground? He walked with a slight bounce to his steps, rang the doorbell, stepped back, with his hands in his pockets, and kept bouncing in place, his eyes lifted to the skies, a sign that he was mulling over some exegesis.

She fluffed her hair, adjusted her sweater, and yelled, "Melody, call Dad, he's in his office, and get the door," then she pulled out a serving tray.

A moment later, she heard low murmurs, followed by loud talking and laughter, coming from the living room.

Melody came to the kitchen, her eyes atwinkle. "Mum, the Professor is here!" she said.

"I know." She drained her cup and refilled it to the brim. "Ask him if he would like a cup of coffee. I'll be there in a moment." She started setting the tray without waiting for the Professor's response.

Melody popped right back. "He said, 'black with one teaspoon, thank you,'" she mimicked the Professor's deep voice.

She gave Melody a warning look, put a teaspoon of sugar in a large mug, filled it to the brim, then she filled another mug halfway for Matt.

On her way to the living room, she passed boxes of Christmas tinsels. Strewn in the corner of the room were pieces from the nativity scene. Her stomach fluttered. They should have started their tree decoration on Thanksgiving weekend. Already a week late and feeling pressure over the to-do-list for the Christmas season, she radiated extra sunshine as she greeted the Professor, to hide her anxiety.

He loved to drop by for a visit when he wanted to sharpen his intellectual mind and expound on some theological point. A strong believer in the historical Jesus, he questioned the tenets. It was a marvel he still considered himself a believer and not without cause, he had earned the reputation of being liberal. However, convinced of his superior intellectual prowess, he seemed to believe his special visits brought her family up to snuff on the modern trends in theology.

She and Matt believed in the un-negotiable truths——the holy birth, the death and the bodily resurrection, integrity of true miracles, along with the infallible Word and the second coming. Having taught their children to also embrace the tenets of the Faith, they thought otherwise of the Professor's visits, but held their counsel, convinced their support and love would help him one day.

Matt was on his recliner, his legs stretched out, and his arms folded on his lap, languid——prepared for a long evening. She sat on the couch closest to him, prim and proper, becoming of her station as his loving, docile wife.

MJ sat in the dining room, and, as the oldest child, listened politely to set an example for the young ones, as they had taught him.

Melody sat beside him.

Melanie entertained herself, sliding down anybody's knees she chose, except the Professor's. Finally, she patted her chair and Melanie sat by her.

When the Professor started expounding on the historical Jesus, Melody winked at MJ. Marc stifled a sigh and tried hard not to roll his eyes, then he slid out. He returned soon, sneaking in Shaggy and started tickling him. That solicited a small whimper from the dog.

She raised her motherly eyebrows at Marc. Her first instinct was to ask him to take Shaggy out; then she realized that it may not be such a bad idea to keep him in after all. She signaled Marc and mouthed, "Get his toy!"

Marc slipped out again and returned with Shaggy's favorite toy.

The Professor coughed out long theological jabber to his seemingly captive audience. He made no secret that he was opposed to the Holy Spirit and did not believe in the deity of Christ. But he was puzzled why young, earnest seminarians had fled en masse and transferred to stable seminaries that remained planted on the Rock.

As he pontificated, Marc turned his face to Shaggy. From habit, Marjorie knew he was counting one, and two, and three, and four, up to twenty. She was convinced of it when she caught him glancing at the clock and stifling another sigh. Again, he studied the Professor briefly, and repeated the cycle.

Cognizant that Marc was capable of committing a diplomatic faux pas with a careless jab at the Professor, she had tolerated him bringing Shaggy in. Better to have a Shaggy distracting the room, than a loose-lipped Marc expressing his opinions.

At timed intervals, she shifted her glasses to her nose and gave him a stern glare, designed to send a maternal chill down his spine.

Finally, the Professor took his leave looking satisfied with the evening, and apparently unaware of any shortcomings on his part.

As his car rolled down the driveway, Marc said gleefully, "He was only here less than an hour. I don't think I could've lasted much longer."

"We know," chorused the family.

"I'm not that bad!"

"Yes. You are," they all chorused again.

Matt Sr. put his arms around him and said, "Son, it will get better. Soon, you'll grow up and make us all proud."

"Yes, he will," Marjorie agreed. "But first, dinner."

Marjorie asked Marc to take Shaggy out and watched, as Shaggy protested. Then she shepherded the family back to the kitchen, set on preparing supper on time.

Melanie tagged along with Matt Sr. Once he had settled down in his favorite stool, she climbed up to his lap, wriggled her little body into a comfortable position to watch the scene from behind his newspaper and sucked her thumb, waiting.

Melody placed the rinsed salad ingredients and a salad bowl on the counter, perched herself on a stool and chopped carrots.

The smell of boiling corn mixed with the aromas of roast beef, filled the kitchen, giving it a warm cozy feeling of love and comfort.

Marc returned, bee-lined for the sink and splashed his hands. His eyes ravenously shortened the distance between his teeth and the salad bowl.

MJ watched amused for a moment, and returned to the garage.

Melanie slipped off her father's lap and trotted over to the sink. "Marc, what wath he talkin' about?" She pointed toward the living room——alluding to their guest.

Without missing a beat, Marc answered, "Theology."

"Why?"

"Because he's a theologian."

"Wath a lologian?" Melanie scratched her head, her hopes pinned on Marc to explain the mystery of the last half hour, which reminded her of church, when she was the only one allowed to play, while everybody else was required to sit still.

"Theologian. Who's a theologian, not what's a lologian." Marc corrected.

"Whath a lologian?" Melanie persisted.

"A theologian is someone who spends a lot of time studying and looking for a lot of difficult words and ways to explain God."

"Why?"

"Because it makes him feel important and knowledgeable."

"Why?"

"'cause he can appear to be closer to God than everybody else."

"Marc, what nonsense are you teaching Melanie?" Marjorie paused, a chopping knife mid-air.

"Well, it's true, Mum. The only One who really understands them is God, because He knows everything, but nobody else does. Even theologians themselves spend a lot of time arguing among themselves and writing contradicting stuff."

"Really Marc!"

"It's true, Mum. It really is. My friend Miguel was telling me that his brother went to a cemetery to study——"

"You mean seminary?" Marjorie interrupted.

"That's what I mean. My friend Miguel said his brother, Maurice, went to the semi . . ., well he went to that college. Anyway, when he went in there, they buried him in all kinds of books and he came out more confused than when he went in. Do you think he's dead, Mum?"

Matt coughed, trying hard to keep his newspaper still.

Marjorie chuckled. "Really Marc! You did say he's still around, right?"

"Well, kind of. I mean, he walked out on his two flat feet, and he's dating this girl——probably engaged——but he's kind of very erudite and all over the place."

"In what way?"

"Well, Maurice said they don't teach like Jesus did. They're like the Professor. They tear the Bible apart. And some of them get real upset if anyone talks about the Holy Spirit. They don't even believe in miracles! Imagine how they would've reacted when Jesus healed people and stuff!" Marc seemed distressed.

"Marc, not everybody believes in healing."

"Uhuh-ah, but Jesus healed people all the time and He taught His disciples to do the same. So why can't we be like Him?"

"I like it that you're mindful of Jesus' teachings, but you boys seem to think too much. I think there're a lot of good theologians out there, who try very hard to stick to the Truth." Marjorie tried to be impartial.

Melanie trotted over to her father and scrambled on to his knees, pushing aside his newspaper to make room for herself again.

Matt lifted his paper, skirting her small form and continued reading. With the view of the room cleared, Melanie laid her head back on his chest, and continued sucking her thumb again, as she surveyed the room from under his newspaper.

Wasn't it her idea to start the conversation in the first place?

"I think what Marc means, Mum, is that some theologians are like people who try to solve women problems," Melody said.

"This is getting interesting," Marjorie murmured. "By that I assume you mean the feminists, don't you?"

"No. Not necessarily. Just anybody," Melody said, then she paused, thought for a while, "Yeah, I mean the feminists, not all the feminists, extreme feminists, post-feminists, may be, but not all the feminists."

"And pray young lady, in what way are theologians like them?" Marjorie pulled her glasses over her nose, to see her better.

"Not all, just the extreme liberals," Melody emphasized.

"Okay. In what way are the very liberal similar?"

"Well it's like this," Melody said, using both hands for emphasis.

"Like what?" Marjorie teased.

"Mum, be quiet! I'm trying to talk," Melody said.

"Young lady, I'll have you know I'm your mother!"

"Sorry Mum. I didn't mean it that way."

"Apology accepted."

"Thank you." Melody gave her mother a small peck on the cheeks. "Anyway, the liberals spend a lot of time studying about God, trying to undermine the Truth. On the surface, it appears they're doing good——writing books and stuff."

"So do the orthodox, but do go on," Marjorie murmured.

"Well the liberals belabor their point," Melody said firmly, "But the more you try to understand them, the more confusing everything becomes. In the end, it's all emptiness and a chasing after the wind."

"You mean vanity and a chasing after the wind," Marjorie said.

"Yes, vanity——thank you——leaving the gullible more confused. Perhaps if they don't believe in Jesus, they should not call themselves believers at all."

"Oh? Melody, that's hard-nosed."

"No. I'm not hard-nosed, Mum. I think someone should be honest with them. People just pamper them, Mum. Nobody forces them to believe. Why associate with someone they don't believe in? Only one cross——no liberal, no conservative——just one very painful cross and one triumphant resurrection."

"You're right, but allow them some grace, honey. That's what it's all about. If you were God, you would give up too soon on so many people."

"Should we continue sinning that grace may abound?"

Matt glanced at Melody and coughed.

Marjorie stifled a smile. "So the post-feminists are like liberal theologians, you think?"

"Well, they're kind of like that too. Mum." She held the salad bowl under Marjorie's nose, "Are these enough olives?"

Marjorie eyed the bowl, "Put more green ones. I like the green ones. Open another can. There're plenty in the pantry."

Melody complied and slid back on her stool. "On the surface, they seem to be doing good and appear to be very smart——well educated and well informed——but, the more you look into them, the more confusing everything becomes."

"Melody!"

"I know. Women from many parts of the world still suffer a lot and are abused and need a better life, without destroying the best of their cultures; but I don't think that in our case, everything the movement's doing is above question, Mum or for our good."

Marjorie murmured, "Melody, honey, I don't want you to get in trouble."

"But I want her to think and say what she believes with confidence. It's free speech country," Matt interjected from behind his newspaper.

Melody blew him a kiss, "Love you, Dad."

"Love you too!" Matt replied.

"Mum, Melody's practicing her free speech behind closed doors. Just make sure the doors are bolted." Marc inched toward the salad bowl, selected a slice of tomato and dropped it down his throat.

"Yeah, it's free speech. It's kind of like all the roles are now mixed." Melody paused, watched Marc and shouted, "Marc, stop eating all the tomatoes!"

"Marc, leave some room for dinner," Marjorie added.

"Yes, Ma'ams," Marc replied and inhaled another slice of tomato.

Melody shook the bowl to make room for the carrots. "Anyways, as I was saying, everybody's getting all confused now."

"That's a sweeping statement," Marjorie said.

Marc jumped up. "Phone's ringing. Maybe it's the Professor——left his glasses or something," he said and dashed to the living room to answer.

Marc listened intently and said, "Just a moment," covered the mouthpiece, then yelled, "MJ, telephone! One of your girl-friends——name starts with an M . . . Makayla, Marisol or something. At least, you're on the right track."

"My girl-friends don't call me. I call them." MJ appeared, grabbed the cordless phone, and punched Marc's arm playfully.

Marc returned to the kitchen.

"Was that really MJ's girlfriend?" Melody asked him.

"'ourse not! Some snake-oil sales rep." Marc solicited a round of laughter.

MJ ducked his head in the kitchen. "I'm gonna get you, buddy!"

Marc dove for cover. MJ returned to the garage, carrying the phone.

Marjorie removed the roast from the oven and placed it on the counter to rest. The chilly beans and the roast should be enough to feed the Jonesons' army for some time, if Marc curbed his snacking to bread, carrots and fruits. "Are the post-feminists responsible for all the confusion in the world today?" she asked.

Melody frowned. "No. Of course not. That's not what I said."

"That's what I heard you say."

"No, Mum. Just some of the confusion, not all——the important ones——like they should not denigrate the role of traditional women. Despite the trend, some girls prefer to marry and stay home, if it is financially viable."

Marjorie stifled a laugh. "Some feminists are also married."

"But they're hard on girls who don't agree with them. I think it's nice to come home to a mother. I know you're smart and have a college degree and could be a corporate executive and everything."

Marjorie beamed and thanked her.

"You're welcome," she replied. "But I like it when I find you home. Some feminists themselves don't seem to know what they want."

"Honey, they seem pretty intelligent and goal-oriented to me."

"Intelligent but not always right. Some sound confused. One moment, they want equal treatment, the next moment, they want to be all woman."

Marjorie laughed outright. "Say it again, girl!"

"Yeah, the girls meddle into everything." Marc crunched a carrot.

"Marc, stop exaggerating. Girls don't really meddle into everything."

"Well, we were talking about theology to begin with," Marc selected another carrot and snapped it between his teeth again.

"Marc! Mum said to leave some room for dinner."

"U-uh, but she didn't say not to eat any carrot."

"Marc, mind Melody," Marjorie interceded.

"Yes, Ma'am," the fire-eater answered.

"As I was saying," Melody resumed, "you've all kinds of activists . . . cultural, radical, ecofeminists, ..." Melody ticked off her fingers, her knife abandoned for the moment. "My friend's mum says some of them who made it up the corporate ladder say they found it empty up there. Now they wish they'd lived a more traditional life."

A tremor ran through Marjorie's body. She mouthed a "Thank you" up for their foresight in having family free time, for how else would they know the worldly influences that intruded in their lives? "Melody," she said, "I shudder to ask what those titles mean. Where did you learn them?"

"Through research."

"Where?"

"Books——the library and the Internet."

"Not in this house. Who allowed you on such websites?"

"We can get into lots of websites at the library, as long as it's for education."

"Oh really? That's it. You're grounded! No more research, no more Internet, and I need to drop by our local library to file a complaint."

"I'll handle it, honey. Will discuss with Pastor Tim, the elders and the other church leaders in the community then we'll act en masse," Matt Sr. assured his wife.

Marjorie blew him a kiss. "Keep the mothers in the loop."

"Will most certainly do!"

"Mum, how'll I get my homework done? Besides, I like to be ready to debate other people. They laugh at us and say believers are soft-brained and narrow-minded and walk around praising the Lord all day. I love to praise the Lord, but I also like countering their arguments with in-depth research——within reason of course——and knowledge of the Word. For example, I'm not a goddess. I am Melody! I am real, with all my flaws, knowing the Lord expects me to be real with Him, so He can help me. I'm strong, but I know I don't have to be perfect. I would hate the burden of someone praying to me, expecting me to answer their problems. I love the freedom to be me and bring my problems to God and know it is okay."

Matt threw his newspaper in the air, drummed his feet on the floor and shouted, "Praise the Lord! That's my girl!"

"Alleluia!" Marjorie cradled her head, relieved. Of course Melody had a noble cause in mind! "I applaud your effort to defend the faith, but check with me or Dad, first. And your computer's coming down into the living room. And don't forget beyond books, the Holy Spirit will help you debate anybody, at the very moment you need wisdom. Reverence for the Lord unlocks the door to wisdom."

"True, but the Holy Spirit doesn't work in a vacuum, Mum. Plus, there's no room down here."

"Yes, there's plenty of room or there'll be, as soon as you know who, moves some things around?" Marjorie yelled over her shoulder.

"Consider it done, honey," Matt yelled back.

"Mum, I assure you I don't surf forbidden sites, not even for research."

"I know. Love you too! Don't forget your Dad's very smart. He'll give you important pointers on how to debate tough people." She cupped her hands and yelled again, "After all, he graduated magna cum laude."

"Dad graduated magna cum laude! Cool. I've always known you were smart, Dad," Melody dashed over and gave her father a peck on the cheeks.

Matt cupped his hands and yelled back, "And your Mum graduated summa cum laude, but chose to dedicate herself to raising her family."

Melody's eyes popped out. "Mum! You're a genius? Wow! I've smart parents!" She sat down and stared at her mother in awe.

Marjorie blushed. "Well. Let's say, the Lord's good. Anyway, you were beating on the post——oops, I mean preparing yourself to debate with poise and grace and intelligence. So, as you were saying, the feminists are not responsible for all the confusion in the world, but the world's confused, right?"

"Right."

"So, how do you explain that?"

Melody thought. "Well . . .," paused to observe Marc attacking the bowl.

"Marc, that's enough olives," she said.

Marc licked his fingers, and continued stalking the rest of the olives.

"What I've been trying to say . . .," she resumed her thought.

This time, Marc selected a plump, green olive, and demolished it.

"Marc, I said no – – more – – olives! If you stick your hand in that bowl again, you're going to be in real big trouble!" she yelled.

"I'm hungry, Mum. Can I have some bread please?" Marc addressed his mother, ignoring Melody.

"Marc, you ate two whole peanut butter sandwiches since you got home, you can't be that hungry," Melody cut in.

Marjorie assured him dinner was almost ready.

"Thanks, Mum," he said, then as an afterthought, "Almost ready as in five minutes, ten, fifteen minutes?"

Marjorie chortled. "Just a few more minutes."

Marc glanced at the clock. "I wish the Professor wouldn't come so late. Why does he always come near dinner time, anyway?"

"Most likely because that's when Dad's home," Marjorie replied.

"But he could come after dinner."

"He's probably busy——maybe he has to teach a late class."

"On a Saturday? Maybe you should invite him for dinner more often, Mum. He says he gets tired of eating out. His wife was the cook."

"Right, honey."

"What I've been trying to say is," Melody said, firmly, "No matter how smart we think we are, without God in the center of that smartness, we'll end up with a confused world that thinks it's getting smarter and better all the time, when in fact it's becoming self-annihilating." Melody took a deep breath.

"Mum," Marc stepped into his mother's face and asked, "what's self-annihilating? Melody, why do you always use such big words?"

"So do you," Melody retorted.

"No, I don't."

"Yes, you do."

"All right! Let's have some peace and quiet in here," Marjorie shouted.

"Yes, Ma'am," Melody and Marc chorused.

"Thank you." She turned to Marc, "Self-annihilating is like self-destroying, as in the world is destroying itself." She turned to Melody, "Melody, if men listened to women more and respected them more, perhaps the movement would not have been necessary in the first place. I love it when men respect me."

"But Mum, some women dislike being treated as ladies. Also, I read somewhere that a godly woman, who wanted more quality life for her family, started the original movement."

"Is that so? It doesn't look like it now, does it? And for those who prefer wrestling with men over being treated as genteel ladies, it's their loss." Marjorie examined the salad bowl. "Perhaps some associate being a lady with negative experiences in their lives or they just don't like being restricted."

"Life's full of restrictions," Melody observed.

"The Victorian lady was of a certain class and presumably high moral values. She did not indulge in unrefined speech and the likes."

Melody tilted her head to absorb this piece of news. "You mean they didn't swear, cuss, or crack bad jokes and stuff?"

"Mhmm. No cussing and no profanity."

"So, those who wish to do their own thing, join the post-movement?"

"Something of the sort."

Melody smiled. "I prefer to be a lady. Lily doesn't cuss. She's the same, no matter where she is, even when she's upset. I heard some people complain that Kelly cusses a lot. I like being consistent. I think it's better and more real to be myself and do what I know's right, than try to fit in."

Matt lowered his newspaper and looked at his wife. Marjorie returned his gave briefly, then lowered her eyes on her task.

"Don't be hard. I'm sure they're not all extremists. Some may love the Lord, but as in any movement, it opens the door for all sorts, including those with hidden agendas."

"That's what I've been trying to say," Melody perked up, "Whenever we exclude God in solving problems, we complicate things. He sees the big picture."

"Indeed?"

"Mhmm. As I said before, First Corinthians says, 'The foolishness of God is wiser than men, and the weakness of God is stronger than men.' So even when God appears foolish and weak, He's still smarter than us and stronger than us."

"The battle for the sexes is the battle for the ages. Only the Good Lord will have the last word. I pray and hope my family will always choose to be on the Lord's side, regardless of the trend," Matt Sr. said.

"And on that note, we better eat." Marjorie pulled out a serving dish.

"Mum, I'm not finished," Melody protested.

"We'll have plenty of time later. I've a decoration project for everybody. First, dinner. Okay table set-up team, you're on."

"Right away." Matt placed Melanie down, dropped his newspaper in the newspaper bin, and washed his hands.

"As usual, you let me take all the heat," Marjorie flirted with him.

"Yeah," a pouting little voice answered.

Marc clapped his cheeks. "Melanie, we forgot about you. You were the one who asked about a lologian. Did we answer your question?"

Melanie pointed at him and said, "No. Bad boy!"

"Yeah, tell him. He owes you an apology," Matt cheered.

"Com'on Melanie, don't be angry at me. Give me a big hug," Marc tickled her.

Marjorie watched for a while, then she sent Melody to fetch MJ.

Melody was not associating with the wrong group. What a relief! She had always been more mature than her age. Knowing that Melody invested time in preparing to debate others who looked down on her faith, warmed her mother's heart and boosted her courage not to fret about the future of each child in a world running amok with the freedom to self-indulge.

After years of toiling away at evening lessons to instill some value in each child, no better compliment could she ask from a daughter. All that worrying for nothing. If only she could relinquish all her worries to the Lord and trust Him!

"What Mum?" MJ asked from the door, cutting into her thoughts.

"What type of a question's that? Where did you learn your manners?" she teased him. "What were you doing in the garage anyway? You treat that truck like a Lamborghini. Did someone scratch the silver paint or something?"

MJ blushed. "I was on the phone talking to Paul. He invited me to go surfing with him and a bunch of other guys from the single's group——when the weather permits——but we're still on for skiing."

"Oh. Of course! Go wash up. Dinner's ready." She blushed and busied herself, covering for interrupting MJ's call with of all people, Paul, his mentor!

39

Paul hoisted the Sunday school materials in his arms and slammed the car door shut. What had possessed him to volunteer to sub for the fourth and fifth graders' Sunday school teacher, after so many years of teaching High Schoolers? On second thoughts, the missionary field demanded any skill, if he was serious about volunteering as a missionary, what better place to start, than at home? His conversation with MJ the night before was proof he should stay the course of helping young people.

The good news was Laurel Morningsun, the Director of Sunday School, had promised an experienced person to co-teach with him.

He prayed that he and his co-teacher would bless the children.

Between moving a table and a chair, a faint whiff of Madame Rochas floated in with the morning breeze of late autumn——enough for him to know he was in trouble. Pretending to be dusting the table, he glanced casually in the direction of the breeze. Lily was standing at the door, looking as cool as the wind that had just blown her in. He inhaled in deeply, hoping for another whiff.

That Lily would be in the same room, on a joint mission so soon——was a miracle. "Morning. Did you need something?"

She stepped into the room. Her limp was gone. "Morning. I think I am supposed to team-teach this class?" She looked puzzled.

"Well, if it's the fifth and sixth graders, you've come to the right place." He adjusted his tie. Bother it! Lately, he had been having problems selecting ties. And what was Laurel thinking, making such a guffaw by pairing them? Was she so blind that she couldn't see, or deaf that she couldn't hear?

"I'm sorry about this," he gestured with his hand. "This wasn't my idea. I guess I should've asked. Um, I mean, I never thought to ask . . .."

"No need to apologize. I'm sure the Dillingtons did not plan on being snowed in. Emergencies do happen. I am glad it was nothing worse."

"Amen." He ruffled his hair with a silly grin.

"If it will make you more comfortable, I would be glad to switch, though I cannot guarantee that Laurel will find a replacement at such short notice."

"I was only concerned for your sake. I hope you don't mind?"

Time stood still and the months rolled away.

"Oh boy! Oh boy! Oh boy! It's Paul and Lily teaching today. All right! Are we going to have fun or what!" Marc ran in.

Maryann, a diligent student, tiptoed in at Marc's heels, dressed in a proper pink and sky-blue dress, her shiny ringlets bobbed around her face. "Hi Paul! Hi Lily! Are we having craft today?" she asked in a sweet voice.

"Yes," Lily smiled. "And we will have some other fun stuff too."

"All right! See, I told you they're fun," Marc declared.

"I know they are," Maryann answered primly.

"Hey Paul! Are you guys friends again?" Marc stared at Paul.

Paul reached for his tie.

"You know what Paul? You know what my friend Miguel told me?"

"What?" Paul twinkled and braced himself.

"My friend Miguel was telling me his brother said if you buy really large ties, they won't choke you. That's what he said."

"Is that so?" Paul chuckled.

"Yup and he wears his real large too. So, are you friends again?" Again, Marc locked eyes with Paul.

"Sh-sh-sh, Marc, be nice," Maryann whispered.

"I am being nice," Marc whispered back, loudly.

"But you're not being very polite!" Maryann whispered louder.

"I'm polite too! I like them and I think everybody's ungrown up."

"Marc, be quiet!" Maryann ordered, her eyes ready to pop out.

"All right. I'll be nice okay?"

Paul lifted his lesson book to his face.

Lily suddenly became very busy straightening chairs around the room and distributing Sunday school materials.

Maryann selected pink and blue crayons to match her pink and blue dress and her pink and blue hair ribbons and her pink socks with blue laces and her pink and blue shoes. She placed her drawing paper in the dead center and lined the crayons around it. From every angle, she studied her arrangement, leaning in to gauge the lines. They made a perfect rectangle. Gently, she arranged her pretty frock to drape the sides of her small chair, then she sat up straight, placed her hands on her lap, and waited for Sunday school to begin.

Paul appraised Maryann. Was it just his imagination or did Maryann need help? Her penchant for controlling her environment pointed to more.

On cue, the rest of the Sunday school class trooped in. He glanced at Lily and heaved a sigh of relief. Briefly, they permitted the class to chitchat, uninterrupted.

He observed Lily as she listened——on the lookout for students who needed help. She seemed to pay subtle attention to Maryann, perhaps she too had noticed?

"Who would like to open in prayer?" He surveyed the room.

Maryann's hand shot up first.

He thanked her, bowed his head, and the class followed suit, as Maryann prayed, insightfully mature for her age, surprising him.

First, he led them in a discussion about sheep and sheep's habit, then he showed them a short documentary of a sheep farm, and sheep-dogs and finally tied it to the Bible verse from John chapter ten, verse fourteen.

For the remainder of the class, he and Lily circulated around the room, helping small groups with their crafts and praying for each student silently.

To his delight, soon, rudimentary papier-mâché of sheep and shepherds covered the little tables, amidst laughter and chatter.

Before closing, he and Lily took prayer requests and encouraged the children to pray for one another's needs. Marc prayed for Maryann's mum and dad, revealing a deep understanding of Maryann's hidden needs and an amazing side to him. Lily reminded them to continue praying for the Professor, as Marc had suggested. Miguel volunteered to pray.

Finally, the students trooped out in search of their parents, leaving him and Lily to clean up and restore the room to its original setup.

He fidgeted with his tie, cleared his throat and said, "Thank you for stepping in to help at such short notice."

"No problem. I enjoyed it." Lily smiled.

"I'm sorry about Thursday evening," he said quietly.

She accepted and added, "I'm sorry too, if I said anything out of hand."

He sensed her reserve. No one was responsible for slamming the door on his face, but himself. "One of the reasons I'd come, among many, um, I'd hoped . . .." He started to say, lost his confidence and groped around for words, "I'd hoped . . . I've been polling friends on an important decision I need to make. May I ask for your opinion?"

Lily paused with a box of pencil and answered, "Sure. What is it?"

"Um, I was thinking about going on a short-term mission trip this summer. What do you think?"

"That should be okay." She continued walking to the storage closet. "May I know why you asked?"

He blushed. "I need your opinion."

She gave him a backward smile that raised the temperature in the room a notch and said, "I'm flattered to hear that."

"Well, I'm serious," he said.

Lily continued straightening the chairs silently. He waited, wondering why her hesitancy? She gave him a measured look.

"You haven't answered," Paul persisted.

"I really don't think it is my place. Mission work is a noble commitment."

"But you don't think I should go or I'd be a good candidate?"

She thought for a while. "I think you should be okay, if that is what the Lord wants. You are already involved in a lot of ministries here. It is a bit different going to another country, but with the Lord's help, you will be okay. It would be a good experience."

"I'm convinced I should be involved in some kind of ministry, but I'm not sure whether it should be missionary work or something else."

"So committing to a short-term missionary work would help?"

Paul lighted up. "Yes. It would certainly help me find out whether I'm cut out for the job," he replied.

"Then, I think it is a great idea. A trip to another country would definitely give you a feel for your calling." She sounded more enthusiastic.

"You really think so?"

"Mhmm."

"Thank you."

With that temporary truce, they returned their Sunday school materials to their cars and walked over to join the fellowship on the patio.

Paul walked taller; but Kelly appeared out of nowhere. To his chagrin, Lily retreated to the sanctuary in a dignified sway, reminding him that he had not yet regained her trust. Before he could stop himself, he sighed.

"What's the matter, honey? You tired?" Kelly asked, petulant.

"Kind of." He chuckled, to hide the revulsion he suddenly felt.

"You work too hard. You were gone all day yesterday."

"I'd some commitment."

"Oh?"

He offered no more explanation.

Kelly pouted. "Of course, if you don't want to talk about it! Anyway, Mum was asking about you?"

Doesn't the woman take a 'no' for an answer?

Had Kelly not told her parents that their presumed engagement was off, permanently? What game was she playing now? Attempting to make Lily jealous or saving face for herself?

"Do I hear a lovers' quarrel or something?" a friend joked.

He smiled, without responding.

As confident as one who had a life-claim on him, Kelly nudged his shoulder and said, "Not a chance."

A strong whiff of La Mystique de Mademoiselle hit him between the eyes. Casually, he moved, placing another girl between him and her.

Kelly glanced at him, uncertain.

He sketched a smile. "We should be going in." But as Kelly accompanied him, he excused himself to talk to the pastor and left her to trek it alone.

From the background, Jonathan raised his glass of punch to Sharon in a silent toast and downed it in one gulp, then in quiet concert, they both walked to the sanctuary. From the back, they searched for the victor's face.

Lily was perusing through the bulletin.

Jonathan and Sharon found their seats at the exact angle they had desired. Did they hate Kelly as a person? No, but they also did not believe that Kelly had Paul's spiritual health at heart. Like Paul, they believed that marriage was not a missionary field. Marriage did not guarantee that the unbelieving spouse would eventually choose to honor the Lord.

They loved Paul and wished him the best choice, regardless of who the girl might be, provided she was godly. Should she be in the top echelon of beauty queens, the more power to him! In courting Lily, Paul was making such a statement about his preference——a woman who was beautiful on the inside and on the outside.

Several minutes later, Paul appeared. The sanctuary was almost full, including the balcony. One empty seat was pointedly next to Kelly, sitting with two of her friends, who were rooting for her. Somehow, she could not squeeze herself into Jonathan's pew, this time. Jonathan and Sharon had reserved only one seat, in between them, within clear view of Lily.

For a brief moment, Paul paused at the entrance, then holding himself erect, he walked past a few curious glances, sunk into his reserved seat, unbuttoned his jacket, and exhaled discreetly.

At a glance he was sitting aloof and stiff, but on closer observation, he slanted his eyes occasionally, stretching them to the utmost periphery, as he tried to study Lily's face, without moving his head.

This service was crucial to him. He yearned for confirmation from above that he was on the right path. Up in the mountains, he had made a commitment to volunteer, even so, he wished for an altar call, to ensure that he was not just on an emotional trip.

Yet even this surrender, he was to learn, was only one more step toward surrendering the total command of his life. As he was to discover, seeking guidance and obeying the Lord's higher authority was a life-long process. He could only surrender that which he knew he was holding back and he could only surrender them as God revealed each area to him.

Pastor Tim served as a missionary to Africa and Asia, before he returned home to pastoral calling. Since becoming the Senior Pastor of Evangelical Neighborhood Church, one of his passions was encouraging missionaries on the field. He understood when a call tugged at a heart. He did not give altar call every Sunday, however, this particular Sunday, he felt compelled to invite those who needed the Lord's special touch to come forward.

In a flash, Paul stood up.

His eyes lit up. Midweek, Paul had consulted with him. It gave him joy to see such a promising young man, so dedicated. Smiling broadly, he stepped forward and took his hands in a firm grip.

After Paul knelt at the altar, two gentle hands touched his shoulders——no need to check that Jonathan and Sharon were behind him——then a few more hands were laid on him. Only when he turned around at the end did he see the Jonesons, the Calderons and Mrs. O'Mallery among them.

Wishing she could join them, Lily watched from the pew and prayed for the Lord's will to be done in Paul's life——whatever that will may prove to be.

Had Paul a window to her heart, he would have understood her earlier hesitation, when he asked for her opinion. His apologies still left the question of Kelly dangling. Since they had never discussed her, she felt uncomfortable initiating the conversation.

The world was abuzz with rumors of his imminent engagement. How could any woman compete with the sanction of not just one clan, but two, and a crowd of friends? Could Bernice's positive disposition change that?

Paul's surprise appearance at her door on Thursday raised a hope that she had no right to nurture. No matter how popular he was, she had no desire of permitting him to weave in and out of her life at his pleasure. If he and Kelly had quarreled, then he should resolve it with Kelly, like a gentleman.

She was right all along, what business did she have hoping to win the heart of a man who was engaged? Wasn't there a name for it? In the Jewish biblical times, an engaged couple was as good as married. When did hoping to date someone who was already engaged cross the line?

Virtue has been my pursuit; virtue shall remain my pursuit, as the Lord is my strength. Lily lowered her head and continued praying.

Of one thing she was certain, Christmas promised to be the loneliest, since she came to America. The thought of leaving town was becoming increasingly attractive.

40

Boxes of decoration piled in the middle of the family room, and near the window, a seven–foot high Christmas tree waited to be decorated. On the mantel and around the fireplace stood the completed set of the nativity scene, including Matt's train, their effort from the evening before.

Marjorie wiped her brow.

Little globes, stars and tinsels of white and gold themes, exchanged hands, as each person attacked an angle of the tree.

Marc lifted up Melanie. "Here, Melanie. Put a gold globe up here," he pointed to a spot on the tree.

Melanie hung the globe and clapped. "Pwetty, that'th pwetty."

"Yes. Very pretty," Marc agreed. "Put another one up on this side." He moved Melanie to another angle of the tree.

Melody watched their progress. "I like the stars."

"I like the gold globes," Marc shot back.

"You just said that to contradict me. You can't make me mad——it's Christmas!"

"No. I really like the gold. They're easy to place," Marc insisted.

"So are the stars. They've the same type of hooks."

MJ tried not to laugh. Melody and Marc, never missed livening up the Jonesons' tree trimming. "'Peace on earth. Good will toward men,'" he said.

"Amen," Matt answered.

Melody stepped back again and studied the tree. "Can you imagine, there're people who don't like Christmas trees?"

Marc placed Melanie down and walked over to Matt lining up more indoor lights. "Is that true, Dad?" he spoke into his face.

"Feel free to step on my toes any time, Marc. The closer you get, the better I can hear."

"Sorry Dad." Marc stepped back.

"Is what true?"

"That some people don't like Christmas trees? How can they not like something so beautiful and so fun to make?"

"For many reasons."

"Name one."

"Christmas trees are not in the Bible. And if you think about it, they could be a contradiction, unless one takes it as just . . . decorating, in the party spirit." Matt straightened a string of lights.

"But doesn't it represent life and stuff, like Him?"

"That's one theory. It's a free world. Everyone's entitled to their opinion. I know Jesus' cross was rudimentary, like the crosses of that period."

"That's depressing!" Marc wrinkled his nose. "But where else could we put our gifts? It's boring putting them by the fireplace. I like fun."

"Try the manger, in a humble animal shelter, a cave. If we wanted to emulate God's gift to us, then we should tone things down quite a bit and focus on giving to those who're unable to reciprocate."

"Yeah. And may be we should give gifts to Him, not to ourselves," Melody said.

"I like getting Christmas gifts." Marc moved a gift from an uncle to a more prominent place.

"Don't we all? But we get birthday gifts on our birthdays, then we get more birthday gifts on His birthday. And if the commercial world could pull it off, we would be giving each other gifts on every major holiday. How would you feel, if everybody gave each other gifts on your birthday, except to you?"

"Honey, is that what we should be discussing now? I'm having fun." Marjorie adjusted her glasses and gave her husband a stern look.

"Why not? Seems as good a time as any," Matt replied.

"Well, I like Christmas and Christmas trees," Marjorie said, firmly.

"Dad's right, Mum. The other day I was listening to the radio, this female commentator——Jewish, I think——anyway, she said what she disliked about Christmas are Christmas trees and Santa Claus," Melody interjected.

"Yeah. That's what stops some people from believing," Marc added.

"And Easter Bunnies don't represent the Resurrection," Melody added.

Marjorie paused, and studied the tree or appeared to be studying the tree, then she nodded. "You've a point. I've never thought of it that way. I wonder how other people celebrate Christmas?"

"Let's ask the Calderons," Marc said.

Marjorie shook her head. "The Calderons are Americans. Norland and Maricela have been here forever."

"I know who we could ask," Melody perked up.

"Who?" the family chorused, all eyes on her.

"Lily."

At the mention of Lily's name, Marc inched closer to Melody. "Yeah. She and Paul might teach us again next Sunday, then I'll ask her."

Melody stood straight, her arms akimbo. "Lily and Paul taught your Sunday school class today?"

Marc nodded. "Ye-e-s. They d-i-i-d!"

"Wow! I wish I'd been there."

Marjorie dropped a set of silver globes back into the box. "What're you two getting at?" She took off her glasses.

"Nothing," the two chorused, perhaps too fast.

"Blue lights or white lights?" MJ climbed up a stool, holding two choices of Christmas lights in his hands, his face impassive.

Melody glanced at him. "White and yellow. Let's match everything with gold," she also dead-panned. "Is that okay, Mum?"

"Yes. I think it'll look very pretty," Marjorie said, still pensive.

MJ returned the blue lights and twirled the white lights around the tree.

Marjorie stood back and examined the tree from every angle. "It's coming along. I like it. It looks . . . classy . . . elegant. I like it a lot."

Melody stepped behind Marjorie and nodded at Marc.

Marc moved over to Marjorie's side, rubbing his neck, his eyes guarded. "Mum, can I ask you something?"

"What?"

"Is it true that Paul likes some people better than he likes other people?"

"What type of a question is that?" Marjorie's voice was very quiet——a mother reading her children.

"He's miserable. I don't think he likes the people he hangs out with."

"Yes. It's true, Mum," Melody agreed. "I think he's happier when he's hanging out with those who're really nice and approachable, and conversant too, and more sincere in their faith." Melody tiptoed around names.

Marjorie looked from one to the other. So that's it! "You two have been listening to gossip. You know how Dad and I feel about that!"

Melody returned a red globe to the box. "It's not gossip. He looks miserable, but I don't think he wants to disappoint his mum and dad."

"Yeah. Miguel told me that they think Paul's dad doesn't want him to hang out with some people anymore, so he started hanging out with other people, because his parents like the other people better," Marc said.

"That, Marc, is what *is* called gossiping," Marjorie rebuked him. "And I say good for Paul! It's good when children obey their parents."

"What if the parents have a blind spot?" Melody asked. "I don't think Paul likes their choice. There're lots of nice girls out there. He could do much, much better, Mum. And I'm not the only one who thinks that."

"The Van Clydens are very caring people. They're our friends and I've heard nothing but good reports about how they raised Paul. We should not be repeating rumors about them." Marjorie snapped a trinket box shut.

Matt looked at his wife and placed a red globe at a high point, next to a silver globe. Marjorie placed a yellow globe next to it.

"Mum, I don't think they're being reasonable," Melody insisted.

"What do you mean? Explain yourself."

"Well, if parents love their children and raised them well to honor and obey God, and if they have open communication with them, then they should really listen to their children's point of view, since their children observe the same holy standard," Melody paused and took a deep breath.

"That seems fair enough. But some things haven't changed much."

"Like what, Mum?" Marc asked.

"Like in this case. I think Paul's right in obeying his parents."

"Uhuh-ah. But he's not happy, Mum. I know he's not."

"Life's not always about being happy, Marc," Marjorie replied.

"You and Dad are. We're a happy family. Jesus said we're to rejoice and He gave us abundant life. Also, my teacher, Mrs. Kuwolsky said God created us to honor Him and sent Jesus to help us achieve that, so we don't have to depend on our own strength."

Marjorie's jaw dropped.

Matt threw himself on the sofa and kicked his legs, beating the air with his fists. "Glory, alleluia! Praise the Lord!" he hooted.

Was this the same son who spent his time fidgeting during Sunday service? Finally, the resources they were pouring into his education were paying off.

"Okay, Marc, I agree with you," Marjorie said, after getting her breath back, "I agree we should be tolerant of one another."

"Uhuh-ah! Not tolerant, Mum. I think that's what Melody was talking about the whole evening. I wish we could find another adjective."

"I'm not sure if I should dare ask any of you to explain yourself. MJ, do you know what they're talking about?"

"Yellow or white?" MJ held up the globes. "We're on home stretch."

"MJ, are you stonewalling?" Marjorie replaced her glasses and adjusted them to the tip of her nose to stare better at him.

"What, Mum? About the white lights?"

"You know exactly what I mean."

"So, is it going to be white lights or yellow?" MJ asked straight-faced, as though he had not heard his mother.

"I think you should put more yellow to bring out the white and silver globes, MJ," Melody answered smoothly.

"Melody?" Marjorie adjusted her glasses again and bore into her.

"What, Mum?"

"Melody," Marjorie repeated, ominous, "Don't play games with me now. You know I'm going to dig it out of you. C'mon!"

"Oh, Mum!"

"Give up," Marjorie cajoled.

Melody sighed. "Well, if you insist, Mum. The way I see it, I think love's more Christ-like, than tolerance is, for example, how we treat people, within boundaries, of course. You and Dad love us, but you also set a clear standard that's acceptable in this house, because you want the best for us."

"You got that right."

"So, we should also model how to make choices that honor the Lord."

"Yes, Mum. Tolerance kind of contradicts itself. Mrs. Kuwolsky said tolerance's the best the world can do to imitate Christ's love, without really helping those who may need help. That's why it ends up silencing those who prefer to get help. Tolerance tries to make us feel good, but if what we're doing's wrong, then it's wrong, no matter what the trend is," Marc added.

Melody clapped her hands. "Yes, Mum. Yes! Scaring people into silence will not shut down our God-given conscience, you and Dad are always telling us. No matter how much other people rationalize to make us feel good, if what we're doing's wrong, it's wrong. They should not delude us into thinking it's okay. No one can save us from ourselves."

Marjorie moved a few ornaments around to more suitable places on the tree. Her hands worked, her mind mulled over what Marc and Melody had said. How much of this was Lily and Paul, and how much of it was MJ? The Calderon girls, where did they fit in? Why had she dismissed their presence, even though they spent more time with MJ than the other girls did? She could no longer ignore her maternal perception.

"I'm not saying you children don't have a point there, but you'll understand as you grow older," she addressed the four.

"You mean when we begin to think like adults?" Melody stammered.

"Not everything grown-ups do's wrong, Melody."

"So, are you saying, Mum, that if any of us wanted to move to Argentina, for example, you and Dad would not support us?"

MJ cautioned Melody with his eyes. She reciprocated with her eyebrows.

Like a soothing river, MJ opened his mouth and said, "It's true. Paul's a real gentleman and he'll honor his parents, as all children should. But in this case, I think they should reconsider. Paul's friends know he's averse to certain comportment. He believes the conduct of the party his parents recommended is scurrilous to all the values they espouse. Paul's friends believe the party is unsuitable. His parents may be surprised, if they knew the truth. I believe among qualities Paul's searching for is spiritual compatibility."

Marjorie bit her lips. Rarely did MJ speak up. "Honey," she turned to Matt, "feel free to jump in."

Matt cleared his throat and said, "Let me see if I follow you. You feel that Paul and Lily . . . it's Lily we're talking about, right?"

"Yes. Sort of." Melody blushed. "Or a girl who's more genuine——who understands his values."

"Okay. So you believe that Paul and Lily should find their own way, but with spiritual support from their parents . . . that when parents teach the right stuff, they should become more of mentors as their children become adults, because the children will remember and apply those morally acceptable principles that their parents taught them, as they make important decisions that impact their faith, and matter to their parents. Right?"

"Yes, Dad. Something of the sort," Melody answered. "I think in such cases the children need more of a prayer support than anything else. Alisa's Mum and Dad are kind of like you and Mum. But Briana says she tries to be nice to her parents, because they're really good to her, but at times when she insists on doing crazy stuff, at first her Mum reasons with her, then she lets her go, but then her Mum prays up a storm behind her."

"Briana's Mum is a woman after my own heart," Marjorie said.

"That she is. And Briana says she runs into the Lord big time when her Mum fasts and prays, so she knows better than to ask her for anything she knows is wrong. I know the Lord helps us make decisions, as long as our parents and friends keep praying. If we fail and cry to Him, He will rescue us. Mum, you and Dad can't go everywhere with us, but the Lord does."

"Yes Dad, could we pray for Paul and Lily and Paul's Mum and Dad during our prayer time, please?" Marc cut in.

Marjorie looked at Matt. He replied calmly, mindful of his wife's warning, "That sounds fair enough. That's a good suggestion, Marc."

"Thanks, Dad." Melody laid her head on her father's shoulder briefly.

Melanie followed suit and hugged her father's knees.

"Yes, thanks." Marc exhaled and chuckled, nervous.

MJ moved to the farthest corner of the room and said, exuberant. "All right, how do the lights look?"

"Ready for Melanie to put on the Star of Bethlehem," everybody shouted.

"Come here Melanie, go for it!" MJ lifted Melanie up.

Matt kissed his wife on the cheeks and whispered, "Good job, honey. I think we better move fast, before this thing gets out of control."

41

Charlotte punched a few throw pillows and arranged them at an angle on the sofa, then she moved a few decors, frequently stopping to admire her work.

Someone buzzed from the gate. She frowned. Her schedule was free, until Igor got home. Whoever was at the gate might have mixed up their days. Nice that she was still dressed in her elegant green lounge suit, not her sweat pants.

She rearranged her scarf around her shoulders, checked the security camera and asked, "Who is it?"

"Marjorie."

She buzzed her in. A familiar face, hidden behind a pair of large sunglasses, drove through the gate in a silver-blue Buick LeSabre.

A gatekeeper would help screen the guests, but she and Igor preferred to live simply, belying their opulent environment, though they used a cleaning lady and a gardener once a week and for special parties, caterers.

On her way to the door, she fluffed another throw pillow. "Marjorie! What a surprise! I didn't know you'd be coming over when I talked to you this morning." They greeted each other with a kiss.

"I wanted to surprise you."

"Well, I am pleasantly surprised. Moving from the Foothills has put distance between us. Look at you——so trim and proper. Love your hair."

Marjorie patted her hair and did an eighty–degree turn, right and left, imitating a model. "We're not going to go there. Can you say Lady Sh-h-h?"

She darted her eyes around in mock horror. "Sh-h-h!" she whispered. "Don't tell our secret. Come in before the word gets out!"

"Mum is the word. I hope I'm not interrupting your schedule?"

"Not at all. I'd just finished straightening up around the house. We had our weekly women's Bible study this morning."

She led Marjorie into her spacious kitchen, looking calm on the outside. This morning Marjorie said that she had called to chitchat. She must have been calling to check her schedule. She considered Marjorie her equal and enjoyed her occasional surprise brief visits.

Marjorie used her degree in psychology judiciously. She had thought she would have fun working in a human resource department for a while, after she and Matt got married straight from college. After all, didn't she love people and wouldn't she be helping them? Two years into her dream career, she was ready to quit corporate America. Matt suggested, tactfully, that she should stay home and prepare to start a family.

Her life as a full-time homemaker contributed to a certain air of diffidence when she was around career women, such as, her former college mates. God did not favor people based on their status——professionals or stay–at–home——she knew that, but her schoolmates' accomplishments, at least at the surface, made them appear more confident than she, despite her stellar academic records.

Unbeknown to her, the women she admired coveted her success as a full-time mother with a wonderful husband, four brilliant children, and a five-bedroom suburban home.

Charlotte was aware that Marjorie placed her, as a CEO's wife in demand with charity organizations and social functions, in the same category——that she was a graduate student, while Marjorie was an undergraduate did not help either. But Marjorie was much more capable than she gave herself credit, as her academic records testified. Matt loved to hear her take on the children and boasted, often, about her to his friends.

For this visit, Marjorie had an assemblage of wardrobe fit for a country club or an upscale restaurant any day——a periwinkle casual suit and a black car coat of pure wool, a flowered scarf draped around her neck, softened her look and an elegant purse and a single brooch gave her a casual, but elegant air of a well-nurtured homemaker, of some means. Her dark hair and slightly buxom looks added to her glamour.

Charlotte fluffed her curly, red hair and straightened her regal stature–—sculptured by years of playing tennis, golf, horseback riding, and more–

—the consummate corporate wife, who could do her husband proud, if he chose to run for office. Paul's remarkable blue eyes aroused one's curiosity, the mystery which was solved on encountering her. "You caught me in the middle of having a cup of coffee. Won't you join me?" she asked.

"Please. Thank you," Marjorie replied.

She served Marjorie a cup of coffee and a slice of blue-berry pie, left over from the women's meeting.

Marjorie thanked her again and added, "I came by briefly. I hope you don't mind. I'll need to beat the Friday afternoon traffic and make it home before the children; otherwise, Marc would've eaten down the house by the time I get back. That boy has razor blade teeth lined all the way down to his stomach."

"You've one of those?" She chuckled.

"Yes. We sure do. A couple of days ago, he practically worked his way through salad, before I could get dinner on the table."

"Paul didn't have too much of an appetite, but it didn't make any difference. He always had plenty of friends who made up for it."

"Boys!"

"Aren't they something?"

"Mhmm. Marc never ceases to amaze us. For a while Matt and I despaired whether he'll ever get it together."

"Sometimes, when they're that young, it's hard to tell. Paul gave us quite a few scares too, not to think of those speeding tickets."

Marjorie laughed. "Not Paul! I would never have guessed. He's so sweet."

"O-o-h, yes! He has his vices." She nodded vigorously.

"Not too serious I hope?"

"I can't complain. We had a couple of close calls, but when I hear the woes other parents go through, I count my blessings. The saving grace was our friends were always looking out for us. He didn't so much as blink out of line before a friend corralled him in. And, the Lord was there, from the moment we committed to Him," she said.

"Thank heavens for parents who're not ashamed of asking for help from Him." Marjorie pointed up.

"Mhmm. The best thing for us was when we sent him to camp with his cousin Jonathan, where they changed for real——not just another passing phase."

"Matt and I keep hoping Marc would straighten out too. Thank heavens, he doesn't have a driver's license, yet. To keep him still in church, we make him sit between us." Marjorie patted a chair.

"Oh, my."

"Even then, he keeps fidgeting. When he gets bored, he leans forward, with his hands on his chin, sighing periodically. But, occasionally, I catch him staring at the preacher as though he's really listening! Hello!"

She rocked from side to side, in stitches. Marjorie had a way of telling stories that made her forget the sleepless nights of raising a family.

"The puzzle was explained this weekend, when he and Melody got into a protracted discussion," Marjorie continued, "Then it turned out we'd nothing to worry about, after all. On the contrary, we may have a real preacher growing up right under our nose."

"Can you imagine all that worrying for nothing!"

In the ensuing silence, the droning noise of a lawn mower, followed by the fresh smell of cut grass, brought her to her feet. She closed the patio door that was slightly ajar and sat down again.

Marjorie cuddled her cup for a while, then she asked, "Are you ready for Christmas?"

She sighed. "Christmas does come around doesn't it?"

"As sure as Autumn and Winter," Marjorie replied.

"Well, I'm not sure how it'll turn out this year," she said.

"Will you be doing anything special?"

Her eyes darted to a picture of Paul in her kitchen office. "Well, we were thinking of having a few friends over the weekend before Christmas and we sometimes serve at the shelter. Otherwise, we were hoping for a quiet Christmas. We'll just have to pray about that one. How about your family?"

"We'll probably do the same thing. Usually, we also go downtown to minister at a shelter. Otherwise, we also try to keep it quiet."

"That's what Christmas should be."

When they had exhausted all polite conversation, Marjorie stirred. "Well, as I was saying, Melody and Marc had a heated discussion for two nights. Matt and I wondered why they were going on and on. Matt and I encourage family free time. It's really our excuse to get into their world to try to understand the challenges they face and the things that are important to them. You know how that goes."

"Tell me about it. All the opinions out there! It's all we parents can do to get a word in. What was the discussion about?" She steeled herself.

Marjorie took a sip of her coffee and placed her cup down, gingerly. "Marc went on and on about theology and the teaching of the Truth, especially, as the Lord taught. Melody was all consumed with God's plan for the world, through relationships between men and women. The whole discussion led to unconditional love. I concede they did qualify it within the context of the Holy God and His uncompromising Holy nature."

"My goodness, your family must've had some very interesting discourses."

"That we did. I think I learnt more about them in two days, than I've learnt in all my years as their mother. Melody was quite direct. I tried to pass everything off; she countered, but with a firm stand on the need to honor the Lord, which pleased us a lot." Marjorie glowed.

She topped her cup, mulling over the perspective of the Jonesons' children. "That's a word we all struggle with," she finally said.

"I agree. Matt and I had never really delved into it deeply either, until this past weekend. In the end we concluded that they were concerned about only one thing——the need to emulate Christ in all aspects of our lives."

Marjorie drained her cup and placed it gently on the counter.

"More coffee?" she asked her.

"I should be cutting down on caffeine, but just half a cup. Thank you."

She served Marjorie half a cup of coffee.

"It's so easy to think we're not so bad, as long as we avoid the crucible of character proofing," she spoke more to herself than to her.

"That's what we thought too. Perhaps that's what many people think, until they're forced to go beyond the surface," Marjorie observed.

"Even then, some of us are unprepared for rigorous truth. On the other hand, I think the young ones see the world through rose-colored glasses. How do we protect them from the world?"

"I tried that line last night; I was rebuked roundly. According to them, though God grieves over sin, He loves His children, hence His transforming power, provided we're willing to receive His help and honor Him."

"Oh my! What else did they say?"

"They challenged me to think. If we parents raise our children in the LORD, then we should trust them to make the right choices as adults. Through our consistent prayers and loving example, our Father is able to guide them back to Him, if they stray. I think implied is that much as it may hurt me as a mother to release them, when they become adults, they're accountable for their actions. After I've done my best, I must release them into the Lord's capable hands——that's a liberating thought."

"Oh dear, your children have done a lot of thinking, haven't they?"

Marjorie clasped her hands. "Charlotte, he's miserable."

"Oh Marjorie, he and his father disagreed last Friday. He left in a huff. We haven't heard from him since. It was Jonathan who told us he'd arrived home safely. I don't know what'll happen next." Her voice broke.

"I'm sorry Charlotte. So sorry."

They stared at each other for a long time. Marjorie finally turned and stared at the floor, as rims of water brimmed in Charlotte's eyes. In the silence, the kitchen clock, that had been there all along, could now be heard ticking away the precious seconds.

Marjorie waited; her mother's heart poured out for Charlotte to see. Perhaps she too was worried about her children? Had she to face the same dilemma in her family, how would she handle it? MJ was almost an adult. Had they addressed the issue with him?

"I should be leaving shortly," Marjorie said.

Charlotte stirred herself. "Thank you for coming. I sure appreciate every prayer I can get. Do you mind if we pray, before you go?"

Marjorie nodded. "I would love that."

They bowed their heads at the kitchen counter.

First, she thanked the Lord for guiding Marjorie to spring into action, then she asked that she and Igor would heed her good counsel. Finally, she blessed Matt and Marjorie's family for being such wonderful role models.

Marjorie closed, praying, "Dear Lord, thank you for being our Loving Father to whom we can freely come with our joys and our concerns. Thank you that You're merciful and willing to forgive us when we truly repentant. Please forgive Charlotte and me——we've failed to love perfectly. Cleanse us from our sins, and teach us to love as You love us through Your Son.

"Please give Igor and Charlotte Your wisdom in supporting Paul, as he seeks Your guidance concerning his future. Provide him a deeply Christ-centered woman for a wife, I pray and Father, please also help Matt and me know how to support our children in whatever decisions they make, as they grow up in the knowledge and nurture of Your Truth. Put a hedge of protection around them and protect them from the confusing doctrines of the world. No matter who they associate with, let the light of Christ always shine through them. Deepen their root in You, I pray. Amen."

Marjorie gathered her coat and purse and took her leave.

She escorted her to the door. "Thank you for coming over so quickly. It must have been hard. Nobody wants to be the bearer of bad news; but a true friend is one who cares and helps us take a good look in the mirror."

Marjorie thanked her. "I wasn't sure how you would react, yet, if any of my children was struggling, I'd appreciate it if a friend alerted me."

"Same here. You'll keep my family in your prayers, won't you? We sure could use a lot of that. I'm at the end of my tethers. I've been taking it one day at a time. My greatest joy is that whatever Paul decides, he will still be in the Lord's original plan in the Garden. He has never wandered from the path—always humbly seeking the Lord, and obedient."

"We've been praying and we'll continue. I admit Matt and I were a bit slow at first, but Melody and the team were ahead."

"Out of the mouth of babes and sucklings."

"Amen." Marjorie slid into the driver's seat.

She watched her pull out of the driveway and through the gate.

Isn't it amazing how the Lord works? It seemed only yesterday that Paul was MJ's junior high Sunday school teacher.

As a woman of faith, she believed her family's future was in good hands; but as a mother, it was good to know the Jonesons cared so much that they had become some sort of Paul's surrogate aunt and uncle. Having their support, boosted her to resolve the conflict between Paul and her husband.

At the thought of her husband, her nostrils dilated. She grabbed the remaining blue-berry pie and slammed it back into the fridge.

42

"Hey boy, missed me? Did you miss Daddy?" Igor patted Percy.

Percy wagged his tail and followed him into the study room, where he left his briefcase. Year-end——endless meetings, mounds of paperwork, last minute decisions, followed by endless signatures, before the inevitable midnight of December the thirty first.

By the end of the day, he was more than ready for the weekend. Perhaps he should have asked Charlotte out for dinner and a concert instead.

One look at his wife and he wished he had worked late. Paul's silence was turning into an icicle between them. He longed to reconcile with him before Christmas.

Since Charlotte said nothing, he also held his peace and patted Percy back out with a snack. Upstairs, he took a shower, praying whatever had upset his wife would be far removed from his impasse with Paul.

He returned to the living room; his hair glistened in the soft light; a small whiff of aftershave lotion trailed him. Soon after, he heard pots banging in the kitchen. He threw his newspaper aside, grabbed his Bible and read a chapter from the Book of Psalms, then he switched to Sports Illustrated.

When the aftershave lotion floated to the kitchen, Charlotte gritted her teeth and slammed a pot on the stove, splashing the gravy she had been working on all over the hot plate. No aftershave lotion tonight!

Normally she would chitchat with Igor about his day at the office, instead, she set the table, taciturn, and mumbled, "Dinner's ready."

Igor guessed what she had said more from habit than from her clarity of speech. He threw down his magazine and came to the dinette to face a dry table consisting of a simple roast, with just enough gravy to tantalize the roast and not a drop more. There was no sign of mashed potatoes anywhere on the table, but there was plenty of boiled white rice, which absorbed most of the gravy, as soon as the gravy hit the plate. She had also par-boiled fresh vegetables, so he had to coax the same reluctant supply of gravy to liven them up.

She had plenty of condiments piled away in the fridge, and the pantry, but he dared not ask, nor get up to fetch them himself. Instead, he gave thanks that she had allowed him to set foot in the house at all.

Muted dinner would be exaggerating the amount of happiness at the table that evening, he mused. After supper, he stacked the dishes in the dishwasher, before retiring to the den, where she served coffee.

Except for barbecues, or when guests were around, no matter what he might be accused of, a kitchen man was not one of them; but he tried to help her as best he could. However, he took over the kitchen on her birthday and Mother's Day and their wedding anniversary, if he elected to prepare an intimate dinner for two. He also enjoyed gardening with her——attending to her roses and exotic plants.

Selecting a book on technology, he settled down again to read.

Charlotte served coffee and sat in a corner, flipping through financial newspapers. Abruptly, she tossed the papers aside. "Marjorie was here."

"How's Matt and the children?" he asked.

"They're fine."

"MJ's turning into quite a man. He's promising to be a tall, handsome fellow, isn't he?"

"Yes. He is. But she didn't come about her family."

"Oh?"

"Would you like some more coffee?"

He glanced at her and replied, "No. Thank you."

"How's business? Did you finalize the contracts?" she switched gears.

"Two. Three postponed to next year," he replied.

Charlotte grabbed the Financial Times again and flipped a page. "He's perfectly miserable. You should give him his freedom."

He shifted. "He has his freedom."

"Is that what you call it?"

"He and Jonathan make their own financial decisions, even signed a contract when they invested in that condo of theirs, to avoid any conflict, should either of them marry first. How many young people do you know who've that kind of financial acumen? And he financed himself through graduate school. Last I heard, he's almost paid off his student loan. What more freedom does he need? We hardly see him anymore."

"And whose fault is it? A son can move out in name only."

"I, controlling? Is that what he said? What's a little bit of advice?"

"He's not calling it anything. Until last Friday, I'd not seen him since summer. When I called him about Thanksgiving, we didn't discuss the elephant in the room. All he said was he was going skiing. It's not him you have to worry about. ENC is seven hundred members strong. The Jonesons' children only repeat what they hear."

"What've they got to do with my family?" He threw the book aside.

"Try the theology of a holy, forgiving God who loves all those who honor Him. It was only at the end of the two-day debate that they realized the children may've been building more than a defense for Paul, but perhaps their own future as well? It seems MJ has been eyeing one of the Calderon girls . . . you know the construction guy." She eyed him.

"Yes."

"It could be just Marjorie's imagination. But our mothers' instincts are never far off."

He snapped up and went to the window. "It's all very well for children to tread where angels fear to tread."

"Don't bother with that line. Marjorie already tried it. They insisted Paul's intentions are aligned with the Lord's master plan. The girl loves the Lord, as much as your son does. I hear she's a lot of fun. The children adore her."

He gave his wife an inscrutable look, muttered to the window, "Christian duty's all very well," then he returned to his seat and said, "I think I should know what's good for my family."

"If your idea of what's good for our family's what you exhibited last weekend, think again. Are you sure you don't want another cup of coffee?"

She might as well had offered him another cup of beetroot juice.

"I know what's good for *my* family."

"Igor!" Her eyes blazed red sparks, then they softened. "I think I'll get you another cup of coffee. Do you want it with milk, honey?"

Igor gripped his chair. The only time his wife ever called him by his first name . . . he glanced at her feet and heaved a sigh of relief. She had on her winter booties. He remembered all too well, she could throw a shoe at him, if pushed far enough, as he discovered soon after their honeymoon. Though maturity had mellowed them, could she do it again?

He exhaled slowly and said, "Milk's fine. Thank you."

She refilled his cup and dumped it on his table. "I'm not with you on this one. You demanded obedience from him. You got it. Now the whole world knows what an obedient son we have! You've proved your point."

"Honey," he said, softly, "you don't understand. We may be at the brink of the twenty-first century, but society hasn't changed that much."

"Let society take care of its own. I've a son who has a heartbeat. His intentions are honorable. How many can make that claim today? You, of all people, should know better."

"Honey!"

"I don't understand you. For months, you've been trying to get your foot into the continent through the Abrafimqodesh's Company. You obviously have no problem doing business with them."

"That's different. Business is business."

"Oh really? Where building your empire's concerned, you've no problem tossing your principles out the window. Is that it?"

"I don't deserve that!" he gasped.

"And what do you deserve? You think the people whom you kowtow to now care a hoot what happens to . . .," she took a deep breath, "your family? Your son spent a lot of time up in the hills seeking the Lord. I know my son. We trained him. And what do these people know?"

"Honey!"

"All they care about is their hide!" she spat out.

"Honey!"

"Some of the very people you're trying to please are nothing but a bunch of phooeys that would sell you down the river for a good price. Are they the kind of people you wish to emulate?"

"Honey, you're asking for what's out of my control."

Charlotte shook her head. "I can't believe I'm hearing this! I got married to you, Igor, because I saw in you something better. You'd a kind of mature quality. Somehow, I knew deep in my heart you were the right man. Yes, we made mistakes, but we matured when we acknowledged our faults. I knew you would be a good leader and father to Paul. I believed in you, Igor. You, not the world. You!" She dabbed her eyes and continued, "Had the Lord given me dark, curly hair——for instance——would you've married someone else?"

Igor buried his head in his hands. Through his twenty-six years of parenting Paul, he had never experienced the fury of a mother to this level.

She pressed on, "Honey, he respects you. You've been his mentor from birth. Just think what this is doing to him! Be grateful she's from Timbuktu."

"East Africa," he retorted.

"At least you know your geography."

"What's that supposed to mean?" he growled.

"What do you mean?"

"I was never smart enough for your father. You should've married that doctor of yours."

"I don't deserve that, neither does father. You know he changed his mind a long time ago. He's been nothing but loving and supportive to you. Feeling as you do, you, of all people, should understand. Let the Lord have His way. If it was meant to be, it will be; if it wasn't, it won't. I want my son back!"

She grabbed a tissue paper and blew her nose, then slumped back her head on the couch. The silence was deafening.

He raised his eyes and groaned. If only there was a better solution to his dilemma! "I'm tired. It's been a long day," he said.

Even as the words escaped him, he knew he was buying time. On their wedding night, they had promised each other that they would never go to bed angry at each other. By the clock on the wall, he had less than two hours.

Determined to have his way, and concurrently reconcile with his wife, he went to fetch his overcoat to escape for a brisk walk in the chilly night.

Igor shrugged into a sports jacket, his face grim, ignoring the persistent shrill phone. But only silence came from the den. Wondering who was calling, he grabbed the phone in his study room and snapped, "Hello!"

"Hey Igor! Are we on for tomorrow?" Jeremy asked.

"Of course! I'd almost forgotten," he faked Jeremy's cheerful tone.

Jeremy fumbled, "The boys should be home in a few more days."

"Yes."

"Paul's quite a fellow, so's Jonathan. I wish he'd commit to teaching. On the other hand, I shouldn't complain. Thirty grand for playing piano and doodling dots on paper's all right. That's as good as some teachers take home a year."

"You could say that. Jonathan's a fine boy."

"Now if he could sell a few more CDs and get some royalties lined up, my life's complete. That condo of theirs is building up equity too. That's a good nest egg right there. A deluxe condo's as good as a single, family home any day. Quite enterprising of them to start investing so early!"

"I was pleasantly surprised," he commented in a flat voice, knowing Jeremy needed little encouragement to continue.

"When he and Paul split up the equity, if either decides to sell or marry, as they contracted so smartly——nothing breaks up a family faster than money——that should give them plenty of down-payment for a real house. Now, if he and that nice girl marries, they should be able to scrape together enough for mortgage and start building a little nest egg. The Lord's good I shouldn't complain."

He cleared his voice, but said nothing.

"Igor, you know I have your back," Jeremy came to the point.

"I know."

"Not only are we in-laws, but we've been friends for a long time."

"Yes. We have. I appreciate your support. You and Angela are pillars of strength to Charlotte and me. Same here, you can count on us."

He hesitated. Should he, or should he not? They had agreed in their couples' support group to holler for help if they needed it. Jeremy could have called earlier on during the week to confirm their game, but why the timing? Was it a mere coincidence or divine prompting?

In the silence that followed, he knew Jeremy was holding his tongue, and would not speak again, until he opened up. How many times had they counseled each other to do the same for others?

"Well, as you may know, Paul and I've not been communicating very well." He hesitated, then continued, "Boys will be boys."

"I know," Jeremy agreed. "Have you, eh, talked to him lately?"

"Well he was here Friday. His mother and I were just discussing it."

"Mmm."

He could hear Jeremy breathing, doing a great job holding his tongue.

Finally, Jeremy said, "And before that?"

"I spoke with him briefly about a week ago."

"Mmm. And his mother?"

"Charlotte called him around Thanksgiving. She arranged for the visit."

"He didn't just drop by?"

"No."

"Did he mention Christmas?"

"Not quite. Eh . . . we had, um . . . a slight disagreement."

"I see. And he hasn't called?"

"No."

"Have you called him?"

"No." Igor wished the inquisition would end. As a father, he had never felt such a failure as he was feeling, sitting there, listening to the echo of his own voice.

Jeremy digested Igor's responses. He cleared his throat again. So did Igor.

"Igor, how long have we known each other?" he asked.

Igor replied, "Close to thirty years. At least thirty years, I'd say."

"Thirty years. You may not know, my father and I had a fall-out, when I was, oh . . . some six, seven years younger than Paul is now. That's how I ended up in California."

"Oh?"

Jeremy took a deep breath. "Igor, Jonathan and I butt heads occasionally, but I've learnt to pull back and let him seek my counsel, when he needs it. After all, our sound advice is always a phone call away, or tucked away at the back of their minds. Ultimatum's sure a way to lose them, faster than you can say, 'Piccadilly'."

Why Piccadilly? It was the underground connection to Heathrow Airport, the hub of international flights to the world, for anyone who wished to start over elsewhere. But why did Jeremy mention it?

"Well, it may be too late to close the barn."

"No. Not all's lost. At least, he hasn't left the country yet," Jeremy joked, in his normal, jovial mood again.

A chill ran down his spine. "I hope you're right, Jeremy."

Before hanging up, Jeremy prayed with him.

He coaxed his body from the chair and forced himself to take one step toward the door and the next, back to the room from where he had just fled. Before he had reached the family room, his hands began to sweat.

His wife was still in the same chair, her hair disheveled. He hovered around the entrance again, mustering courage to say something . . . anything, but the silence.

"No need to cry, honey," he stammered. "I get carried away, sometimes. Don't mind your old man. I know I've been less than a perfect father to my boy. You're right, with the Lord's guidance and support from friends like the Jonesons, we will do what's right for our family."

Charlotte blew her nose. "I knew you'd understand. He respects you a lot."

"After the way I behaved, I hope he'll find it within himself to forgive. Well, no point calling him home. Christmas's just around the corner. I'll have a talk with him then. Last Christmas he was home for a week, right?"

"About a week . . . no, a week and half."

"That should give us plenty of time."

She stopped sniffling and gazed at him with her heart-wrenching blue eyes. He sent up a silent prayer to heaven. Never again!

"Would you mind if we pray?" He cupped her chin.

"Not at all," she smiled, "I could use some right now."

Without another word, they slipped down to their knees.

Coming to a resolution on the surface was a lot easier than relinquishing power. Igor tossed and turned all night. As a responsible father, he should have phoned Paul that evening, but as the older man, he was avoiding locking horns with him again and perhaps holding on to his pride?

If Paul got his way, what would become of the Van Clydens' future? He loved him too much to give all his wealth to charity; but he also baulked at the alternative.

Worse, if he continued to insist on his way, Paul might leave the country, as Jeremy had hinted. Could he afford to lose him?

He wanted to obey God without sacrificing Paul and he wanted Paul to know that he still loved him, without succumbing to his desire. Above all, he wanted to retain the reputation of being an upright man——a pillar of his community, a warm, loving husband and father, a dedicated servant to the cause of Christ——without embracing fully his fellow believers who had the same quest for achieving a holy life. He wanted to be regenerated, without being transformed.

Were regeneration and transformation the same, or was transformation the evidence of regeneration? If a man claimed to be regenerated, but resisted transformation, could he be truly regenerated? He mulled over scriptures, mouthing the first verse of Romans chapter twelve, so as not to wake up his wife.

Obeying, he could probably do, but surrendering Paul would force him to move from the realm of phileo love to agapao love. Could the Lord accept his obedience without asking him to surrender his son? On the other hand, when Abraham offered up Isaac, God had a ram already waiting; though Abraham did not know it, until he had obeyed. Since the LORD forbade the sacrifice of children, what did He really want? Most likely, He desired Abraham's full devotion to Him. Dared he follow Abraham's example, as his wife had?

He studied his wife's soft breathing form, and her tranquil face, envying her, her faith. Still restless, he shrugged into his robe and went to the balcony.

A few minutes later, he heard the balcony door open from behind him, then he felt his wife's arms wrap around his shoulders.

"Come inside, before you catch a cold," she said.

43

Buried behind her morning papers, Charlotte crunched a slice of wheat toast. Across the table, Igor was also hiding behind his papers. He peeked at his wife. This was the longest argument they had ever had, as a couple. The chilly silence was deafening, reminding him of a day he thought he was lost in a blizzard——as the winds howled for miles and miles of white silence——only to hear his parents calling a breath away from him. He prayed he would never again reach that level of despair with his wife, as long as he lived.

He refilled his cup and cleared his throat. "Jeremy and I have a game."

"Whose turn is it?" she asked in a monotone, knowing that had it been his turn to host, it would have been her turn to prepare refreshments.

"Jeremy's."

"Did they repaint the court?"

"Mhmm. A couple of weeks ago. It looks nice."

"My love to him and Angela," she said, then resumed her reading.

Igor studied the back of the newspaper for a while, walked around and kissed his wife on the forehead, on his way to the garage.

At the door, he turned and looked at her. She flipped to the next page of her newspaper, and continued reading, her face impassive.

◆ ◆ ◆

The maid opened the door. Angela was reading and sipping coffee.

"Good morning, Igor! You look so glum, as though you've been through a tornado," she teased him, unaware how closely she had hit home.

Igor chuckled, trying to appear cheerful. "Tornadoes in California? I would sooner a minor rumbling of no consequence."

"Sh-sh, don't say it too loudly!"

Jeremy entered, dressed in a tennis outfit. "Morning, Igor! Perfect timing, and was that a shushing I heard?"

"We were talking about choices——to have a tornado or a mild earth movement? Take your pick," Igor explained.

"Oh no, no, no! We'll have a good game. No tornadoes, no earthquakes. Agreed?" Jeremy fetched his tennis gear and led the way to the courts.

"Agreed." Igor hoisted his tennis bag over his shoulder.

At the sports arena nestled in the south corner of the estate, they cantered around the court like prized stallions, stretched and started the game.

"That's two loves, Igor! Hello?" Jeremy shouted ten minutes later.

Igor tried to concentrate, but his serves floundered all over the court.

An hour into the game, Jeremy shouted, "Game up! You know, I like to beat a man who's all here, not miles away."

He went to the gazebo and ordered brunch through the intercom and added more logs to the stove.

Angela appeared. Behind her, the maid, dressed in navy blue and white, pushing a trolley containing refreshments of coffee, fresh fruits and pastries. Angela seemed to be scrutinizing Igor's face while pretending to be re-arranging the décor. She returned to the house and phone Charlotte.

Jeremy refilled his cup and asked, "So, how's Charlotte this morning?"

"Not so good. We barely spoke at breakfast."

"Mmm. But you broke through to her last night?"

"I think so."

"Mmm."

Igor pushed his cup and plate aside. "Jeremy, you spend your life, everything going smoothly——company doing great, business growing, profit margin positive . . . wife's fabulous . . . son out of college, moving up in the world——just as you're beginning to look forward to the grandchildren, then boom, everything changes."

Jeremy leaned forward in rapt attention.

"One moment I had a loving family, and the next moment, I feel like a character out of a soap-opera, for want of a better word."

From Jeremy's past, a face flashed. "Jeremy, after you've suffered for a little while, the God of grace, who called you to His eternal glory, will Himself perfect, strengthen and restore you. And when He has strengthened you, Jeremy, strengthen your brethren, strengthen your brethren, strengthen your brethren!"

"Igor, entrust to the Lord those you value most. Nobody guaranteed us a bed of diamonds," He mixed his metaphors deliberately. "After praying as best you can, face your challenge, and remember the Lord will never let you down! You can either let this thing destroy your family, or turn it into victory. Should Paul follow through, I challenge you to choose to become the best father-in-law, ever."

"I'd actually hoped English or even Swede, barring American, of course."

"Perhaps it'll all go away——just a phase. You know how the young ones are. If not, would you rather be alone?"

"No. It won't come to that." Igor picked up his cup.

"Won't it? You just said it——we plan and trust, but unless we're willing to surrender all, no one guarantees us the result. Only the Lord can show you why, after you've surrendered. Don't flex your muscles Igor. Trust Him."

Igor stared at Jeremy over the rim of his cup, then he took a sip.

Jeremy continued, "In the past the immoral master made trips to the servants' quarters, while continuing to be considered a model of virtue. But God knew. Times have changed. And Paul's not the kind of man who would exploit a woman. We taught our boys to scrub behind their ears and straighten their collars and . . . and tuck in their shirts . . . and seat the ladies and treat all women with dignity . . . and say their prayers before bed."

He dabbed his lips with a handkerchief, stirred the fire, then sat down again. "You know I was once married?" he asked, his face still, too still.

"Yes."

"So does Angela. I told her before we started dating. What I didn't disclose——not even to her——is that my situation was similar to Paul's."

Igor placed his cup down with a clatter.

He paced around the gazebo, relating parts of his story. Igor watched.

"Jeremy, I'd no idea. And the divorce?" Igor asked, strangely.

"Dad took care of everything. He was that powerful——old money, and so forth. I was a mess. His attorney tracked me down to sign the papers, but in the eyes of Heaven, my marriage was still legit. After leaving home, I kept hoping I would honor my commitment, like a man. Two years later, I gave up, then I buried myself in work and school."

He stirred the fire. "I was taking night classes when I met Angela. In hindsight, I should've tried harder . . .." He sighed. "I should've gone back in person; but I needed my job. May the LORD forgive me," he spoke the words as a catharsis, then he jumped up and added, hastily, "Don't get me wrong, Angela's my life now. I've never been unfaithful to her."

"What was her name?" Igor asked, quietly, as if in another world.

"Desiree. My Desiree."

"De-si-ree," Igor drew out each syllable.

Jeremy sunk onto the Raftan chair; the fire crackled in the silence.

"I'd no idea," Igor repeated, shaking his head, "Absolutely no idea!"

In a flash, Igo comprehended so much of Jeremy that had never made sense before. What other surprises lurked around the corner? In the vastness of America, Jeremy could have married any woman from among the millions of women, but Angela. Perhaps it was for such a time as this, but again, it could be mere coincidence. If Paul matured, his case could ultimately be just a passing phase——two people momentarily attracted to each other, before moving on. Only time would tell.

While Igor sensed that divine providence had brought Jeremy into his life, he wished he could discuss the divorce further, but held his peace. Paul's pain had reopened Jeremy's old wound, leaving him——a virtuous man—— bleeding profusely.

Igor and Charlotte watched the door in vain. Paul did not come home for Christmas. Embarrassed, they avoided mentioning his name, but they never ceased gleaning news of him at every opportunity. Often, Charlotte swallowed her pride and lifted the phone, only to lose heart.

Igor mulled over Jeremy's counsel, careful not to create further rift between him and Charlotte. He also recalled his own father's advice about raising a child——the wisdom of praying first, especially when tempted to speak out of turn——the wisdom which he had tossed aside when he had tried to have his way.

44

Paul checked his ticket again, found his seat by the window, and stored his carry-on luggage and guitar in the overhead bin. He took out a magazine from his backpack and a cassette player, slipped on his headphone, and turned on the music he had queued.

Beside him, his very capable assistant project manager also settled down for the long flight. At his insistence, BF&S had bought his other team members business class tickets, instead of the economy. For the project, the company had selected very capable employees——three males – – one manager, two analysts; and two females – – one senior analyst and one office administrator——whom he was confident would pull off the monumental job they had been assigned.

Soon after, the nose of the Boeing 707 soared up, the wings slicing the air above the Los Angeles Airport right through to his heart. He closed his eyes for a moment, steeling himself for the many months he would be spending thousands of miles away from California. In his ear, the singer crooned the popular country song, "Always on My Mind." He prayed in his heart that he would fulfill his missions to East Africa.

Yes, he was on his way to the mission field, but not as he had planned. He had always known that doors opened miraculously to those who relinquished their dreams to a life of faith and obedience. But this time, the miracle had happened so fast that his head was still reeling from the triple blessings of three missions in one package that had required him to leave earlier than he had planned.

On learning about his plan for short-term summer missionary work, BF&S had piggybacked their project to his trip. They were ready to launch their project. All the numbers were in, the team members were already selected, but at the last moment, Brett, the star project manager, had resigned, citing a better job offer. The truth? He did not relish the idea of a branch office in East Africa. He had been lobbying for Europe or Asia.

The first week of January, as he was closing the last of the books, Bill asked him to drop by for a chat. After five years of working with his boss, he had come to recognize his different tones, enough for him to be wary.

"Hey, Van Clyden, it's been a while!" Bill had said, with a lot of backslapping. "Consider yourself blessed among men."

"That sounds like a Christmas greeting straight from the Gospel of Luke. The only problem is, the Messiah has already come and whatever I might be mistaken for, mother Mary's not one of them."

Bill bellowed. "Very promising! He's in a good mood. That's my boy."

"Correction, cautious good mood. Why do I get the impression I'm not going to like what I'm about to hear?"

"Paul, have I ever told you anything you disliked?" Bill flashed a smile.

"There's always a first time."

"How could a free lunch be anything but a good thing?"

"Depends on what else is on the menu. If it's important enough for you to offer me a free lunch, Bill, the more reason to be concerned."

"Humor Van Clyden, is why I like you as my Finance Manager. Have faith. Come on, before the barbecue ribs get cold."

True to his promise, Bill drove to a barbecue grill.

After the waiter had served their lunch, Bill waltzed around issues, while he sat on pins and needles, wondering why he was having lunch with his boss in the middle of the busiest week.

Bill took a bite of his burger, worked it, and said, "Paul, consider this a blessing. You've been singled from among all the rising stars. This is a great growth opportunity." Bill gulped his diet coke, eyeing him.

More suspicious now, he said, "Then why do I have an inkling, Bill? Okay, let's start with the but . . .." As also a friend, Bill was the only boss with whom he dared to be so bold.

"Bad news? What bad news? Nothing but good news Mr. Van Clyden, where you're concerned, nothing but good news." Bill wiped his mouth again. "The good news is, BF&S offered to finance your entire trip to East Africa and you can leave slightly earlier than you'd planned." Bill eyed him and took another swig of his coke.

He selected a French fry and nibbled on it, as he would at a food-testing facility. "How slightly earlier are we talking?"

Bill shifted. "Just a tad earlier. You get to spend the rest of winter in a warm and much more pleasurable weather. Only two more weeks of California Mr. Van Clyden, then the next thing you know, you'll be sunbathing at Mombasa Beach or . . . occasional weekend in Zanzibar——first class all the way——the best tan any man could get, and, you won't have to pay a dime for it! Think of that!"

He raised his hands in protest. "In two weeks! Out of the question! You know my situation."

"The more reason you should take time off. Besides, we need you to lead the team. You know Brett backed out."

"I heard something of the sort. The guy is a primo uomo."

"I'll settle for prima donna any day——a real divo!" Bill paused.

Paul realized the situation was more serious than he had fathomed.

Bill continued, "Well, you're the next logical choice. In fact, the company now regrets not giving you the project in the first place. You should feel good about this. We've confidence in you."

"Thanks, but this'll set me back a whole year. You know how it is."

"I know. Sheila and I've been praying. But think of this, you were already planning on your trip anyway."

"For three months not almost a year, and in six months, not yesterday!"

"Same thing. You'd have still been taking a leap of faith. BF&S needs you to lead this team. It's a growth opportunity I highly recommend for a young executive like you. I wouldn't say this just to anybody——everybody was very impressed with the support you provided to the team. It's unfortunate that Brett waited until the last moment to back out. It's been duly noted. You're the most logical choice."

He pondered Bill's request, his lunch abandoned for now, but he continued playing with his French fries.

Bill watched him, as a crouching lion watched his young make a tough decision to conquer a prey, wishing to help, yet daring him to launch out and try his wings.

Paul recognized an order. Of course, he too could refuse to take the offer and quit; but, would leaving BF&S in a lurch be honorable? Would that be the best way to reward his boss and friend?

Moreover, he had known Bill long enough to guess that Bill disliked forcing him to take on such a daunting task at such short notice, just because BF&S had chosen the wrong project manager. Sometimes, the best lesson was to let the company swallow its pill and learn from it.

As though Bill had read his thoughts, he said, "Of course, if this'll really upset your plans, I understand."

Yes. Bill was reluctant to pressure Paul at such short notice. East Africa being thousands of miles across the waters, he himself would have balked at flying so far away into the unknown, with only days left to get immunized.

Moreover, he disliked exploiting his friendship with Paul to rescue BF&S from a pickle. Paul was very capable, but he also cared more for him, than for company politicking. Instead of playing politics, BF&S should have prepared a solid back-up plan from the onset——simple project management common sense.

Worse, the assistant project manager who should have taken over was incompetent——came from the list of the executives' pets, and not from the list of heavy lifters, renowned for getting the job done.

As Paul's superior and mentor, he remained calm on the surface; inside, he was livid at the firm. Before calling Paul, he had had a row with the executives and told them if they messed up again, he would quit, than abuse his friendship with Paul.

Though he thought about all these things, he kept his counsel to himself. Paramount was the need to support Paul, regardless of Paul's decision.

Paul asked, "Could I have a day to think about it?"

"Of course. Take your time."

In addition to mentoring the team, Paul had traveled widely on vacations since his childhood. To seal it, he had completed a one-year stint as an exchange student in Brazil, an experience that would be useful for the assignment. But, unlike his colleagues, if he accepted the offer, he would have exactly two weeks to prepare.

After lunch that day, Paul had missed bumping into Shane barreling down the corridor. Usually ingratiating, Shane had stared straight ahead, his face stony. The grapevine must have moved at the speed of lightning, Paul had surmised.

He had continued down the corridor wondering about him. Regardless of Shane's attitude, he had neither asked for, nor coveted the assignment. His intention for going to East Africa was to serve the Lord. That could be what triggered BF&S to entrust him with more responsibility. If so, so be it.

As a believer, extending to Shane the same civility as he accorded the other people should have been easy, but not so. Determined to exert himself more in the future, he prayed for a kind word to say to the older man. Perhaps he should invite him to lunch or better, a game or two.

How his extended trip would affect any chance he had of reconciling with Lily, was another matter. What would the ultra-conservative BF&S do, if they discovered the truth? Would his purportedly rising star sunset before noon? Would he need to rush to another job?

With headhunters knocking at his door often, he was fully cognizant of his marketability, or he could start his own company. Not many men he knew would sacrifice their careers for a woman; but to him, a regenerated man, Lily was no ordinary woman and worth everything a man could sacrifice, short of his relationship with the Lord.

Just then, he had noticed a perennially cheerful director approach from his left side. Hanging onto his arm was a lady whom he could mistake for anything, but a brunette. The Director had stopped and introduced the lady as Prudence, his wife!

Two very fast weeks had reeled by since his lunch with Bill. Paul adjusted the volume of his headphone and reclined his head, prepared for the long flight to London Heathrow and the twelve–hour layover before his evening flight with British Airways. He drifted off to sleep midway through the flight.

On arrival, he freshened up and had a late breakfast. In lieu of touring the city, he and his associates strolled through the airport, then they ate a late lunch. Finally, eight o'clock rolled around. As he boarded the Boeing 707 plane, he braced himself for a land he had never visited before and again drifted off to sleep, after reading for about two hours.

"Welcome to Nairobi. We'll be landing in thirty minutes. For those of you visiting, please fill your visitor landing card . . .."

Paul woke up. He must have been more tired than he had thought. On the table was the visitor card. He completed it and lent his pen to the German passenger next to him.

Soon, the plane taxied to the gate. For the first time, he saw the land that would become his home for ten months . . . ENC and all who mattered to him, oceans away, but not the searing pain buried deep beneath his Ralph Lauren shirt. A good thing, he had the whole weekend to adjust.

◆ ◆ ◆

Lily tossed her corporate finance book aside. Only one chapter in four hours! At that rate, completing her dissertation in a year as she had proposed, would take a miracle.

Even the short Christmas break she spent in New York, visiting with her former schoolmates from East Africa, had done little to alleviate her mood. They had suggested that she should apply for a job with international organizations, such as the World Bank or other large financial institutions. She had complied, lukewarmly. Still, she would much rather start her own CPA company as soon as possible.

At church, Kelly's fans were gloating over Kelly's apparent success—a good reason to move to another church, but Paul would be gone for ten months, so the pressure was off. If she nurtured a habit of retreating from the likes of Kelly, then when would she develop a thick skin to survive life's disappointments? There were also other reasons, such as: she had yet to buy a condo and she hated losing her friends and starting all over in the middle of such an intense schedule.

But, if Paul returned earlier and Kelly announced her engagement, would it be wise to stick around——given all the other choices she had——just to condition herself against pain, or to stay close to friends? Absolutely not!

45

Perched on a stool, Melody buffed her middle fingernail with a nail file, her face creased in a puzzle. She raised her fingers to the light, blew on them, then spread them back on the counter and continued buffing, then she examined them again. Satisfied, she inspected her mother's work—chocolate chips covered the top of the dough. She selected the plumiest ones, then she plopped back on the stool. Her jaws worked the chips; her eyes watched her mother mixing the dough.

MJ would soon be in college. Mum and Dad had been dodging family discussions. Marc would not tackle this one. When she negotiated with MJ, he promised to talk to them, but he also told her to take the initiative. "Mum? When MJ goes to college, will he commute from home?"

Her mother frowned. "I don't know. That's up to him."

"What if he decides to go farther afield?"

"Did he say that?" Her mother sounded as quiet as a mother hen over her chick.

"I don't know. I mean, you know, he's applying to several colleges, some out of state . . . Mum, are you all right?" she interrupted herself.

Her mother had turned pale and seemed panicked. It couldn't be on account of MJ going off to college, could it? They had always known that he would and had been very supportive, making it clear that all their children would graduate from college.

Her Mum dug into the dough. "Fine. I'm sure the Lord will work it out."

"That's what I say."

"Get me another bag of chocolate chips from the pantry."

She complied and her mother thanked her.

"Mum," she said.

"Yes, honey."

"When MJ goes to college, who'll give us rides?"

"What do you mean by who would give you rides?"

"Well, MJ kind of helps us with rides."

She measured her with her eyes. "Melody, are you asking for a car?"

She turned red. "No. But it's kind of nice to have rides and stuff."

"Melody, according to the Jonesons' calendar, you're still a bit young. We'll cross that bridge when we get there."

She sighed. "It was worth a try." She reckoned it would be a lot harder to get her way than she had thought. For weeks she had built her strategy, hoping her parents would relent. She was willing to work for the down-payment, in fact, she had fifteen hundred dollars squirreled away from her allowance, baby-sitting jobs and gifts from her grandparents.

Her mother chuckled, as if she knew she was beginning to test them, so she switched gears. "Mum, can I ask you something?"

"What?" her mother replied, without lifting her head.

"We're a pretty caring family, right?"

"I want to say yes, but knowing you, I know more's coming. What's it?"

"Nothing."

"Well, let's start with, 'nothing'."

"Oh Mum!"

Her mother emptied some chips into the bowl and gave her the bag. "You might as well come out and say it——whatever's eating you," she said.

She popped a few chips into her mouth. "Well, it's not really that at all."

"Then what is it?"

"I've been wondering."

"What?"

She disliked it when her mother said that. What was she supposed to do? "How comes ENC's so clickish?" she asked.

"You think ENC's clickish?" her mother echoed her.

"Yes."

"How did you reach that conclusion?"

"We hang out with a lot of people, but they're kind of the same."

"Everybody's the same sort of people. What else could they be?"

"We're nice to people, but I feel . . . the church's not really comfortable."

"I still don't get you. I think we're a pretty nice church——very warm and welcoming——that's why we chose ENC. I like our fellowship, a lot."

Melody sighed. Sometimes trying to reach her mother was like trying to drill through steel walls. Mum could be very astute, when she chose to be; except when she was determined to be obstinate. How could she miss the obvious?

"Don't get me wrong, Mum, we're very middle-class, no doubt about it."

"Middle-class! Is that what you think of ENC? Some sort of a social club? Honey!"

"Well, we're proper and polite and professional, but . . .," she hesitated.

"But, what?"

"We're not really very comfortable."

"Speak for yourself. I'm comfortable, so are a lot of people who love ENC. That's why the church's growing." Her mother greased another cookie pan.

"True, Mum. But in click groups."

"So does it bother you that people prefer to choose their friends?" She studied her. "Melody, no one person can like everybody. That's unrealistic!"

"I'm not saying we should like everybody. Love's an action, Mum."

"But some people want it all, even as they persist on rebelling. Melody, if we allow them to influence us——may they never succeed——we would be separated from heaven! And if the church became just another social club, where anything goes, it would be like crucifying the Lord all over——so what's the point? Shouldn't we be contrite? Didn't free grace come with a price . . . His blood? Should we abuse grace?"

"Now you're beginning to sound like me."

"Let me finish. Paul says in Romans absolutely not! Unconditional love does not mean we should sacrifice eternal life. Jesus said some will choose the narrow gate, and others, the broad way. We should love and serve as commanded, but not at the cost of eternity. If we permitted the world to lure us, I shudder to think of the consequences. That's where I draw the line!"

Melody stared, stunned, then she fidgeted, shy. "Mum, I agree with you absolutely. You're right. We're in the world, but not of the world and we should walk humbly with the Lord and honor Him in all our ways."

Marjorie bit her lips. Melody had seldom been shy about expressing her opinion. Therein lay the problem——the danger of mistaking her candidness for maturity and missing her yearnings. And yes, she was sounding like her daughter.

Just then, she heard a sound coming from upstairs. She asked Melody to check. Melody tiptoed upstairs, in case Melanie had dozed off again.

Melody returned downstairs, her father right behind her. She announced that Melanie had rolled over and gone back to sleep, then she plopped herself on her stool again.

Marjorie thanked her.

Matt Sr. sidled across the kitchen, his eyes agleam, placed his hands on his wife's shoulders, and inspected a cookie tray ready to bake. "How long do those take?" he asked.

"According to the Jonesons' tradition, eight and half minutes," Marjorie mimicked the British accent, reducing her audience to stitches.

"I think I could survive that long." Matt grabbed a vintage auto magazine and retreated to his corner.

"No game today?" Marjorie asked.

"It can wait," he answered.

"Dad, I need your opinion," Melody said. "Mum and I were argu——oops, I mean, having a civilized discussion about ENC's clickishness."

"Mhmm. Who was win——oops, how far did the discussion go?"

His wife fluttered her eyelashes at him.

"I take it my daughter doesn't like clickishness?" he said to her, then turned to Melody, "What about your friends, Melody? Alisa, Briana, Dan and Jumaine——aren't they part of Melody's elite?"

"Oh Dad!" Melody blushed.

"That's what I've been trying to tell her," Marjorie said. "Melody, you know better than to appeal to your dad. I want to understand. What would you like ENC to do? In any crowd, you're bound to find a few people standing alone. That's just part of human nature."

"It's not what I'd like to see happen, Mum. It's what I don't see happening."

Marjorie continued scooping the dough on to the second cookie sheet. "I don't get you?"

"Well, take our family. How comes we don't go to some people's homes when they invite us, though you allow them to come here, sometimes?"

"Melody, we always go to other people's homes."

"Uhu-ha. Not really. Only you, or Dad, go, but not us. Is it because you don't want us to mingle? Actually, I don't blame you. I don't like mingling with just anybody, Mum, though God loves everybody. Are you afraid something might happen to us?"

"Honey, that's not fair. Your Dad and I try very hard to be loving to everybody."

"Yes. We do," Matt echoed.

"Then you'll allow us to visit our friends' homes when we're invited?" Melody pressed on.

Marjorie stretched out her hand to Melody and Melody gave her the half empty bag of chocolate chips. She poured some in her hand, counted five chips, and replaced the rest in the bag, then she handed the bag to her husband. One by one, she dropped each of the five chips in her mouth, chewed slowly and swallowed, then she asked Melody, "You mean certain particulars of your friends?"

"Yes," Melody replied.

"Well, why don't we talk about it, when you're invited? Remember, your Dad and I are still obligated to shield you from any imminent danger, whether you like it or not. Not everybody who pretends to be a friend is your friend, Melody, and not everybody's good for you, no matter how nice and loving they may be. That's where we come in, as your parents."

"Absolutely," Matt agreed.

Melody sighed. Her mother's answer was the best she would get.

She launched from another angle. "Mum?"

"Yes." Marjorie glanced at the kitchen clock and speeded up scooping the cookie dough on the last tray.

"Do you think it's possible to mistake middle-class behavior for Christian?"

Marjorie stopped working. "Melody, what are you getting at? I don't see anything wrong with being middle-class, do you?"

"Mum, everyone's welcomed to church, as long as they understand that they must honor God with their lives and be a godly example to others. Of course, if they just go through the motions, then what's the point? Besides, as Revelation warns and as you just pointed out, if they don't walk the walk and they keep messing around, the Lord will reject them." Melody paused to take a breath.

"Melody, honey, learn to breathe in between sentences. I'm afraid one day you might choke cramming so many words in one breath."

"I do breathe, Mum, except when I have important things to say."

"Breathe even when you've important things to say," Marjorie coaxed. "Learn to talk like a lady."

"You mean learn to smile and say nothing, while appearing to say a lot?"

"Melody, a lot of ladies say a lot of important things, lady-like."

"You mean, without rocking the boat?"

Marjorie flipped a stray strand behind her ears. "Honey, a while back didn't some girl I know say she wanted to be a lady?"

"Yes."

"Then you've got to learn to speak slowly. Ladies articulate."

Melody resisted rolling her eyes. "But Mum, if I slow down, it'll take forever for me to say what I have to say."

"But you'll be more eloquent and poised . . . and have a command of your audience. Honey, you need to learn to use the velvet touch."

"Oh Mum, can't I start after I've turned sixteen?"

"You're almost sixteen," Matt reminded her.

Marjorie blew him a kiss. "The earlier you start, Melody, the easier it'll get. As long as that's what you want, I support you one hundred percent. I think it's a good idea that you want to be a lady. One of these days, you'll be getting your own wooden bowl."

Melody wrinkled her nose. "Wooden bowl? You and grandma are always talking about the wooden bowl as though it was some secret code. Should I know?"

"You sure should," Matt teased her.

Marjorie threw her head back and laughed, as Grandma laughed when talking girl-talk with the women. "Melody, Melody, Melody."

"Well, Mother?" Melody said sternly.

"All right. If you insist. Each girl gets an old wooden bowl when she comes off age, a sign that she's now an adult, able to manage her own house and get married. In another six, seven, or ten years . . . who knows? With the slim pick of qualified suitors today, what's a mother to do? I pray you won't take forever. When I was young my Mum advised me to get a decent man who treats a woman right and is not afraid of family responsibility."

Melody dropped her eyes and turned tomato red.

"Now you made your daughter blush." Matt grinned.

Marjorie said, "Tell you what? How about going to ENC's first Valentine's tea party together next week? You would like that, won't you? I'll pick up the tickets at church. Tomorrow's the last day."

Melody gave her mother a strange look. "Is that the Mother-Daughter thing?"

Marjorie chuckled. "Yes. It is."

"I guess so."

"Is that a yes?"

"Yes, Mum, I'd love to go, but my dresses are passé. Alisa's Mum just got her some new clothes."

"Honey, you've a wardrobe full of clothes! Didn't we buy you a whole set of new clothes last summer, come autumn?" Marjorie protested.

"Yes. We sure did, hundreds of dollars' worth of debutante clothes," Matt chimed in.

"Yes. But not for a Valentine tea party."

"Melody, don't exaggerate. I'm sure you've more than enough suitable dresses for any party——even dinner at the . . . White House. Tell you what? We'll go through your wardrobe, if we don't find anything suitable, I promise, we'll go to the mall and find something better. Okay?"

Melody gave her mother a big hug. "Love you, Mum!"

"Good! That's settled. Now, about the middle-class, I still don't get you."

"Mum, I think it's possible to be very middle-class, but not be changed at all. I believe our action's a reflection of what's inside and tradition."

"Melody, everybody holds on to tradition. Show me one person who doesn't hold on to some tradition and I'll show you a hypocrite. Even the so-called modernists or post-modernists, will hang on to their traditions——call them history or scientific theories or relativity, if you will——and revere them and commemorate anniversaries, just like the rest of us. So please, don't tell me that tradition that allows me to stand for what I value is bad!"

Once again, Melody was rendered speechless.

Matt chuckled at the look on her face. "Told you, don't get your mamma going on about modernists and post-modernists."

"Wow, Mum! I'm not a modernist or post-modernist, and I agree with you one hundred percent, about everything. I was only talking about Lily. Do you think some people——Lily, for example——may see more than they reveal?" Melody explained after recovering her breath.

Ah, Lily! Of course! Why didn't she dig deeper, first? Of course, it had to be Lily!

She kicked herself, lowered her head, and asked in a flat voice. "Why would you think that?"

"Because Lily's a very smart girl. I don't think anybody fools her. I think she sees through people. She may hide her feelings, but I think she understands everything and she sees a lot more than she reveals."

Marjorie stared at Melody. "Melody, do you ever stop thinking? You amaze me." She paused, cocked her ears, and said, "I'm sure this time Melanie's awake. I can hear her calling. Go and check."

Melody twirled around on the stool, laughing. "Okay, Mum. I take it you're not going to answer my question?"

"Later!" She placed the cookie trays in the oven.

Melody headed for the door, sliding her feet on the floor, her bottom planted firmly on the stool. "Melanie! Melanie!" she yelled.

"Shout louder. Pastor Tim needs fresh ideas for his sermon."

"Oh Mum." Melody slipped off her stool, selected two more fat chocolate chips from the bag, and munched them, as she worked her way upstairs, on foot.

Marjorie stared at the empty door, shaking her head. "Lord, You've given us some daughter! I guess we needed to keep growing, that's why you gave her to us."

"Yes. Indeed," her husband agreed from his corner.

46

Marjorie studied faces in the crowd. For the first time she saw them——a motley crowd congregated, sipping coffee and tea. Familiar people stood in small clusters, chattering like a flock of yellow-rumped warblers. Spotting the clusters of happy click-groups were individuals and couples who looked lost. Was this what Christ had in mind when He said, "'By this all will know that you are My disciples, if you have love for one another'?" she cited John, chapter thirteen, verse thirty-five, under her breath.

Lily attended the single's class, helped with Sunday school, appeared in plays and more, but now, she was an outcast, unlike a few months ago.

Few smiled at her, stiffly. Others walked right by her, a miracle they didn't walk through her. Of all people, Lily, ignored? Why had she become an outsider? Why were they treating her as though she was invisible?

Were they blaming her for Paul and Kelly's break-up? Or were they angry because Paul had favored her? Wasn't Paul entitled to seek happiness just like their own sons? Who forces their child to marry into a life of misery?

Based on Marjorie's observance, not once did Lily try to warm her way into Paul's favor, on the contrary. Kelly had her chance and blew it.

If any of them bothered to know the Kelly her children had exposed, they would be delighted that Paul saw through her in time, or did they not care about Paul's future happiness, as long as his progeny had pink cheeks?

And how did they know that Paul and Lily would marry, anyway? Wasn't it up to them to decide, after they had become better acquainted?

Sharon also studied Lily from the outskirts. Bless her heart! Then she and a new lady approached Lily and engaged her in conversation.

The experience educated Marjorie. These were seemingly mature believers——was this how they behaved when consumed by jealousy? How did Melody see so much? She marveled again at what a blessing their daughter was to so many.

Not one to let things roll by, during the Midweek adult Bible study class, when Thad, their leader, asked for prayer requests, she whispered to her husband, "I think we should say something, don't you?"

 Matt nodded and hemmed and hawed. "Thad, Marjorie and I've been concerned about a minor trend——probably just a hiccup——that could impact our fellowship. ENC's a great church. We love it a lot, so do our children. But, um, sometimes I feel we get carried away and neglect our other brothers and sisters. I think we should be more conscientious. Let's pray that the Lord will let ENC exhibit more maturity during fellowship. If ENC is a beacon on a hill, then we should start acting as one."

A pregnant silence followed, then a male voice from the back said, "Matt's right. I think we do need to be more aware and caring."

The Leader nodded, "Thanks, Matt. I'd noticed something along that line. It's been on my heart and thanks for bringing it up. We need to reach out to our brothers and sisters. We can never over-emphasize that and I trust that all of us will commit to lifting up this special need to the Lord during the week." He jotted Matt's request down on his master prayer list.

His wife interjected, "Yes. Marjorie and I will also bring it up in our ladies' fellowship. We do need to remain vigilant."

Matt patted Marjorie's hand and held on to it. But for the grace of the Lord, he too could have fallen in love with another girl, and ended up with a different combination of four little Jonesons, or none——a thought he preferred to push to the furthest corner of his mind, and keep that door bolted. Would Melody be Melody, with a different mother?

Well, no point worrying about the might have beens that never was anyway. He refocused on the prayer requests.

47

Melody stifled a yawn——around her, mothers and daughters, primed in their Sunday best, nails manicured, gnawing on cucumber sandwiches, and all sorts of delicacies, amidst themes of pink, red and spring.

She tried to stay out of the conversations, but she was pleasantly surprised that when she spoke, others listened, making her feel rather mature. What more, she was impressed that everybody shared good news about their families with each other. If they had problems, for once, they left them behind.

Among the guests were wives——mothers and working girls——with career fields as varied as full-time homemakers to secretaries, teachers, lawyers, and doctors. Mothers who juggled their multifaceted roles with faith and prayer.

So varied were their professions that a mother on their table was an engineer. Nothing about her shouted, "I climb poles and bridges." She was the most lady-like engineer Melody had ever met, yet, her Mum said the engineer headed multi–million–dollar projects, working all day with her brawny male associates——designing bridges——then she went home, a regular wife and mother.

The highlight of the tea-party was spending a Saturday afternoon with her mum, Alisa and her mother. She and Alisa had dressed up like debutantes or guests in a rather formal wedding. To top it, her hair held up with a gold and pearl comb, made her neck resemble a swan's, kind of like Lily's neck, and to finish it off, a touch of blush and make-up, that deepened her hue to tan and golden. Perhaps with a bit of effort, she might turn out to be quite pretty, after all——not as tall as Lily, but with a more svelte form, and high heels, she could almost look tall. What would Jumaine think of her in her new outfit? He and MJ would soon be going to college.

She struck a conversation with Alisa, until game-time was announced.

"That was nice." Melody stored away the center piece she had won.

Marjorie hugged her. "Wasn't it? Love ya! We should do it again."

Melody bit her lips, loathed to disappoint her mother. Yet she realized, as a future wife and mother, she must acclimatize herself to attending women's functions and collaborating with them as suitable, without losing her God-given identity or ceding her purpose in life, just like the guests she had met—none seemed to have any problem being leaders in their own right, while still collaborating with their husbands, and deferring to them, as necessary.

In hindsight, the older ladies had motivated her by treating her as an adult. She may never again be just another teenager searching for where she fit. She belonged among the women of faith——the faith that had carried her grandmother and ancestors, as her father had recounted so aptly.

Without a word, she understood that one day, she too would bring her daughter to the mother-daughter thing and feel just as proud as her mother was at the wheel, while her husband took care of their little one at home.

No doubt one day, she too would get married. She might not yet know to whom, but certainly, she would marry. And she was certain, as long as she trusted the Lord, her husband would be just as committed to her and their family as her Dad and Mum were committed, and the Jonesons before them had been to theirs. A community of well-grounded families, who were not afraid to talk God, was where she belonged. It had been good for her mother and grandmothers; it should be good for her.

Her mother had accomplished what she would not have, had she lectured her on the merits of growing up godly with a Bible in one hand, waving a spoon with the other, in a business suit draped with her favorite apron, and a brief case slung over her shoulder. She glanced at her Mum.

Marjorie caught that look. "What?"

"Nothing." She took a deep breath. "It was really very, very nice. I hope the pictures turn out. I want to show Jumaine," she said with an enigmatic smile and added quickly, "And MJ, of course."

"Glory! Alleluia!" Marjorie stepped on the gas pedal.

48

Southern California struggled through a broody winter——one moment warm, the next moment, the chill factor near freezing. Finally, Lily found a condo——made to order——in a secluded neighborhood, with a private porch, overlooking the hills. Another attraction, the condo was seven miles closer to her work, shaving off fifteen minutes of commute time——one way.

Escrow closed the week of Valentine. She moved in soon after her new carpet was installed, to the delight of her friends who finally vocalized their sentiment about her former neighborhood. Sharon and Jonathan rounded up friends from church, including MJ. Along with Bernice and Alex, they couldn't get her into her new place fast enough.

They showed up armed with dozens and dozens of boxes and were delightfully surprised to find everything packed, sealed, and labeled and her clothes standing in the middle of the room in a portable mobile closet.

Even Lamar——now more confident——having negotiated to graduate with an AA degree by summer, had lent a hand. His prospects to transfer to the Polytechnic University looked very promising. He had consulted with Professor Moretov to ensure that all his classes were acceptable. With that new confidence, he had already found a job that promised more hours during summer break and was walking on air——gone were his woes about girlfriends. No doubt, the new Lamar would succeed.

She straightened a picture frame. Lamar! He was always borrowing stuff . . . some tea or sugar . . . or a pencil. Listening to his woes had helped her stop pining after Paul and get on with her life. That Lamar was back on track for a four-year college degree! Miracles never ceased!

She now spent some of her free time, planning her interior decoration with all the fervor of owning her first home.

◆ ◆ ◆

Evangelical Neighborhood Church had moved on to preparing for The Passion week. Several people had auditioned for parts in the Passion enactment, including some organizers of the Mother-Daughter party.

Lily did not attend the party, of course.

"We missed you at the tea-party," Marjorie said.

Surprised, she said, "I understand it was a great success. I think it is a great idea to help mothers bond with their daughters."

"Don't you worry about that! It was a misunderstanding. Some singles attended. Next year, we'll clarify that all women are welcome. And you must sit with us. Melody will be thrilled."

She thanked her, hoping she would go home to visit her parents, or have some other commitment, so that she would not offend the women who felt that the party should be restricted to mothers with daughters only.

"And congratulations. I heard you got a narrative part in the enactment of the Resurrection." Marjorie seemed truly delighted——unlike some people.

She thanked her again and reciprocated, congratulating her on MJ who got the part of the Apostle John.

"It's his first major role," Marjorie confided, "He's thrilled. He always plays cool, but I can see he's excited. It's a great honor for him. And the church hired a professional director from the industry, not to think of the Lead——is a professional actor too. I forget the name of the movie he appeared in, but I know he's a believer."

"Isn't that great!" She, and Nigel——a Brit who was studying theology at Biola University——would narrate. Nigel would narrate the men's scenes and she, the women's scenes, and they would share the mixed scenes.

A leading mezzo soprano with a rich timbre——which could be one moment light and playful, as Mary, the young mother, watching her son grow, and the next moment dark and somber as the grieving mother at the feet of the cross——got the part of Mary, the Mother of Jesus.

Another, with a three octave range from lower F to the F above upper F, got the part of Mary Magdalene, also believed by some scholars——though debatable——to be Mary, the sister of Lazarus.

Too young to play Peter and too docile to play a son of Thunder,

Jonathan got the part of Philip, more suitable for his friendly nature.

Only the actors and actresses attended the first four weeks of rehearsals, but as the Resurrection week drew near, all cast members and crew came on board. Not a fan of enacting the cross, Lily approached her role prayerfully. How could anyone enact Christ's suffering? *How could we crucify Him all over? Who could possibly simulate the Resurrection? Should we?*

"Only one cross and one resurrection; then the judgment," she argued.

With a deep understanding of Biblical times, the director lived up to his reputation and captured the heart of the message, without getting gruesome. Loathed to trivialize the ghastly sight as the soldiers hammered nails into Jesus' hands and feet, he staged this scene off-stage. The audience heard hammering, but in the foreground, they saw a darkened stage.

Even so, Lily felt every blow of the simulation, welling up emotions she had squashed, and forcing her to put them in perspective. No amount of humiliation at Kelly's hands could ever match the agony that Christ suffered for the world. Subordinating her emotions to her duty, she delivered her part in concert with Nigel, lifting their audience to a higher ground.

The 1994 presentation of Christ's Resurrection was among the best presentations that Evangelical Neighborhood Church had ever staged. Many were moved to walk to the altar for the first time——a clear illustration of Apostle Paul's claim that God's strength is perfected in our weakness.

That verse bolstered her, as she approached the first anniversary of her first and only date with Paul, before he dumped her unceremoniously.

Kelly, too, must have remembered. She arrived at church bedecked in diamonds, sporting a new dress and hair style and referred often to how well Paul was doing and how she missed him so much. That he had already been to Mambasa Beach, meaning "Mombasa Beach" and was having a great time.

She withdrew, leaving the stage to Kelly and her friends, convinced that Paul's overture to her before he left for East Africa, was to make Kelly jealous.

When she arrived home, she poured herself in her books, more determined than ever to complete her paper and get on with her life.

49

The mild spring weather galloped towards summer and Southern California braced for drought and smog. If the shortfall continued, rumors circulated that Los Angeles County might ration water.

As though the smog wasn't enough, Kelly continued with her charade——or truth——frequently drawing attention to how much she was wasting away and how difficult it was to have Paul so far away and hinted that her parents would have preferred to have announced their engagement before he left for East Africa.

To Lily, the year could not move fast enough. By late winter, she had driven into the mountains for solitude twice. Occasionally, she attended concerts with friends or alone, but it was the trips to the melting late snowy peaks that gave her real solace.

Whenever she drove to the mountains, she parked at the best view of the valleys. As the snow melted, she went up to admire the beautiful, peaceful, rolling green hills, bursting with blooms of spring.

After the weather had warmed-up, she took three one-day vacations to Balboa——a quieter beach, compared to the other beaches with their attractions of the eclectic——lugging her academic work along. Midweek was the best, when the residents abandoned their playground for their city jobs. She loved to cruise down Balboa streets, past souvenir shops, to the quiet ocean beach-front, lined with bungalows.

Armed with a flask of tea, and her reading material, she would lie on the beach and read, or watch birds fly over, or study ships as they passed by.

At church, more people were nicer to her than when Paul first favored her.

From Paul, she had heard nothing, except for bits and pieces of news that Jonathan seldom volunteered, and, Kelly's pining. Perhaps she had dreamt it all. Could it be that for just one moment, she and Paul had been more than cursory, polite friends, or that he had apologized to her before leaving for East Africa?

While at an impasse with Paul, she could not say the same about Sharon and Jonathan. Was it her imagination, or were they dogging her steps? They were popular, yet they preferred to socialize with her group. Why? What was propelling them to make time for her?

Twice they had attended concerts with her——first, a contemporary gospel, then a symphony. She had planned on going to the symphony with Bernice and Alex; the evening turned out into a group outing, complete with dinner.

"I love symphonies. Thank you so much for inviting us," Sharon had said, cutting a piece of chicken.

"My pleasure. It's more fun coming with friends. Did you enjoy the evening with Steve Green?" she had asked.

"We loved it! He's the greatest," Sharon had replied.

"He's the best. What vocal prowess!" Jonathan agreed.

"He's wonderful! I believe he could have just as easily succeeded, had he chosen opera. Our gain that he chose ministry."

"I agree," Jonathan said.

She dabbed her mouth. "Have you attended a Larnelle Harris' concert?"

"Jonathan has, but I was out of town," Sharon replied. "We've got to attend one of those. I've seen him on TV with Sandi Patti, he's wonderful!"

She had then asked Jonathan how his music business was coming. How difficult was it to get into the industry? Did a music degree help? And had he collaborated with some of the big names?

That got Jonathan excited. He kicked off a lively conversation about the latest top Gospel artists and who among them had toured Southern California in recent years and who he had met.

She was not putting herself down. She appreciated friends, but she sensed the coincidence of running into Jonathan and Sharon, happened more often since Paul left, than before. The thought that her two friends might be feeling sorry for her, irked her.

If she had her druthers, she would much rather spend her evenings at home, catching up with her work, than be out socializing even at the mildest functions, except for her favorite concerts.

But, she also had no desire of mooning over Paul! So, once in a while she stirred herself to meet other nice young men. Her effort amounted to little, though, for with a lot of backslapping and fast talk, two of her potential dates had ended up on front row seats at the baseball game with Jonathan, while she and Sharon took another trip to Nordstrom Rack, shopping.

Between Bernice, Sharon and Jonathan, she did not know whether she was standing on her head or her feet.

As she was closing escrow on Valentine's week, she had continued juggling her schedule. Burdened with overtime and the long commute to work, she had taken a semester off, interrupting her PhD at UCLA shy of writing her dissertation. That was a mistake which she had remedied. Also, she had not taken a break from her literary review and research, had co-authored a research paper which was published in an accounting journal and had remained abreast of her profession——that had placed her on target of her schedule, when she finally resumed school.

If she continued to apply herself, she could complete her dissertation by Autumn, and walk in the spring commencement.

50

In a secluded corner of the quadrangle, Lily cradled in her lap a copy of the Decision Magazine she had been reading, as she tried to guess the tune Bernice was tapping with the pointed tip of her right shoe.

"Brad Benz Bentley," Bernice muttered Brad's nickname, watching his progress across the grass. Her forest-green silk scarf floated in the mid-day breeze, softening her razor-sharp gaze.

"You two really don't have any love lost," she said.

"We have our moments," Bernice replied. "To think that at one time I was actually mad enough to give him a blinking chance!"

"Really!"

"Uh-huh. Just one tiny moment, then I grew up real fast and I met Alex and was Mum glad! He's not my type. If he'd so much as stepped out of line, he'd have wished he'd met another O'Konnell. Ne-ver again!" Bernice rolled every word.

She chuckled, when she realized what Bernice had just said. "Is it true that you carry large handbags for a reason?"

"Let's say, the O'Konnells are a unique clan. My Dad stuffs moose heads in his spare time." Bernice flipped a stray strand off her face and watched Brad chatting with a group of employees, her eyes veiled, then she smiled at her.

"What are you smiling at?"

"It's decided," Bernice announced.

"What is?"

"We're going to Palm Springs to redesign the city."

She placed her magazine on the bench. "Bernice, what mischief are you cooking up that brain of yours, this time?"

"No mischief——just good old-fashioned fun."

"I beg to disagree. The last time you persuaded me to go to your version of good old-fashioned fun, Alex chased us up and down Hollywood Boulevard. Absolutely not again!"

"The nerve of that man! Can you imagine he'd the gall to follow us? And he'd told me he'd some business to attend to. How was I supposed to know he was trailing us?" Bernice seemed truly indignant, but unrepentant.

"Bernice, he is almost your fiancé."

Bernice shrugged. "So? Unless I missed it, he's yet to propose."

"He won't propose at this rate." She sensed Bernice was more serious about Alex than she cared to admit.

"Are you coming to Palm Springs or not?"

"Not if you plan on repainting the city."

"If I promise to behave myself, will you come?"

Despite Bernice's attempt to sound somber, her naughtiness seeped through. "By the way, how's Juan doing? Has his English improved?"

Bernice started to say, "You mean Benito? Oh, he's doing great. His English is so much better. He found a better job and he . . ." caught herself, then with her arms akimbo, said, "You're good! You know, you're real good. It's over. There's absolutely nothing between Benito and me. We stopped dating over a year ago. And you know it was purely platonic."

"Bernice, two-timing is two-timing, even if it's platonic."

"Are you going to let me beg, Lily? Look, I've been on the straight and narrow. You can trust me. Cross my heart." Bernice placed her right hand on her chest and seemed sincere.

"As you know, I am a low-key person. I enjoy quite a few things, but not big parties." She drew the line.

"Who said we're going to party?" Bernice continued to be evasive.

"And what exactly are you planning on doing while you are there?"

"Can you say shop till you drop?"

"Help! I should have guessed."

"All I want is for you to get away and take a break. Celebrate your new condo. You've done nothing, and been nowhere, since last year. Spring's here——what have you to show for it?"

"The beautiful mountains, bursting into spring?" She opened her arms toward the hills.

"Very funny! You wouldn't even come to my Valentine party. I was hurt. I know, you were moving and you needed to pack; but you could've taken just one evening off. Alex was hurt and you know Alex's as old school as you are. Like a broken record, he kept telling me, 'Make sure the party's tame . . . make sure the party's tame.' I said, 'Okay, will do.' And he said, 'And no booze.' I said, 'No booze.' So, I got rid of all the liquor, bought wine, tonic water, and soft drinks, and reserved for you the best sparkling, non-alcoholic apple cider ever. I was telling everybody, don't touch that bottle, my best friend's a teetotaler, I want her to feel at home, and you didn't come!" Bernice's face turned red, speaking volumes of how she must have felt.

"Oh Bernice! I'm so sorry. I hope you still had a good time." She was mortified at embarrassing Bernice.

"Not as we would have, with you there." Bernice laid on more guilt.

"I'm sorry I ruined your party. I know nothing I do could ever make it up to you, but would you and Alex care to come to dinner and a concert with me?" She felt guilty, though Bernice had issued a casual invitation and never betrayed how much she had wished her to attend the party.

"Apology accepted, but it's my turn——I insist. I think you should get out more . . . get some fresh air into your lungs once in a while."

"I get plenty of fresh air when I go out for walks."

"Smog's more like it." Bernice scoffed.

"According to the weather forecasters, Palm Springs is as smoggy, as any part of Southern California, except San Diego, perhaps."

"So, you'll come to San Diego, then?"

"No. Thank you. I am quite comfortable with my boring life."

Bernice scoffed again. "Look, it's decided. I've already made two reservations at a very nice family-friendly hotel. I'll drive. It's my treat. We leave on Thursday afternoon and return on Sunday."

"I appreciate your thoughtfulness, but I have to be in church. And, I have to study."

Bernice paused, taken a back. "Study for what? You've already got your CPA. And we don't need to take refreshers this year. I'm not going near any book, unless it's a required course."

"I like to continue challenging myself," she replied, without disclosing that she was completing her PhD.

Bernice seemed wistful, "I wish I'd your brains." She perked up. "Look, they've churches there, you know."

"I know."

"And you can bring your books?"

"Ha, ha, ha. Very funny! And so I will, so you can hang out alone."

"I promise, I'll not blink at so much as a priest." Bernice batted her eyelids. "I'll think of Alex first in the morning and last thing at night. I'll not only bring my manners; I'll mind my best manners. I'll be so Victorian; I'll make that old-fashioned queen look like a modern teenager."

She laughed so hard, she almost split her sides. "Bernice, you make my day. And how do you plan on nabbing——oops, I mean, taking a day-and-half off work in the middle of a busy season?"

"I don't nab. I just take off." Bernice pretended to be indignant.

"Excuse me. I can't think of any other verb that would be more suitable. How do you plan on getting it past the bosses?"

"Watch me!" Bernice turned on her heels and headed straight to the office, her scarf floating in the wind in regal indignation.

She shook her head. Spending a long weekend in Palm Springs was not her idea of celebrating the arrival of spring.

After Bernice had disappeared into the building, Lily resumed her reading briefly, before her break-time was over.

Half-way through a file, she heard Bernice's familiar tap, tap, tap.

"It's a done deal," Bernice announced cheerfully. "We're off for Le Weekend. All the bosses are on board."

Disappointed that their bosses had not cited an excuse such as backlog––to deny their time off——she camouflaged her emotions. "How did you manage to pull that off?"

"My usual charming self," Bernice purred, showing a set of fluoride–soaked teeth, the result of her last dental appointment.

"Good job. But I still need to discuss with Mr. Chancey. I'm on a special project."

"Understood. Let me know."

"Great!" an intruder announced. "I hear we're going to Palm Springs."

Lily did not need to investigate who was behind her. She grimaced. But when she turned around, she had on a placid smile.

"Brad, I hate to burst your bubble. We're going to Palm Springs while you will be at work, catching up on tax codes." Bernice softened her tone with a clenched smile.

"Bernice, if I didn't know you, I'd think you didn't like me." Brad stood toe to toe with her.

"Brad, if I didn't know me, I'd think I didn't like you either," Bernice spat into his pupils.

"Oh, she's cool . . . way cool. So what time are we leaving?"

"Brad, we're leaving; you're staying. The tax codes chant your name with sighs of deep longing."

"Sounds so lyrical——almost persuades me. But who needs to memorize, when we've two brilliant females at Denton & Terrell's?"

"The two brilliant ladies say, s-tu-dy the tax codes. Comprendo?" Bernice tapped every syllable with her index finger pointed at his chest.

Brad's shoulders sagged. "And you, Lily?"

She returned Brad's gaze, unflinching. "Do you really want my opinion?"

Brad's face fell. "I get the impression I'm not welcomed?"

Before she could reply, Bernice retorted, "How did you figure that out?" Bernice's teeth smiled; her eyes spat out fire.

"Very well, I can take a hint." Brad slinked away, feigning being wounded, but with a canny look on his face.

They watched his swaggering back, disquieted.

After his head had disappeared, she signaled for Bernice to follow her to the small conference room. "Bernice," she closed the door, "I don't care for that look on Brad's face. I know he is professional, but he is spoilt and used to getting his way." She inhaled deeply. "As long as he tows the line, it won't be necessary for us to have a chat."

Bernice did a double turn at her firmness. "'Love your British upper stiff lip! I didn't know you could be so tough."

"We all have our moments. I always hope I never have to resort to any unpleasantry. It is so much better to be nice."

"I knew there was some fire underneath that cool exterior. Rest assured Brad knows when he's pushing it. If that creep shows up in Palm Springs, I'm gonna break his legs," Bernice whispered, in menacing voice.

"You think he will? I hope he is smarter than that." She could take care of herself, but she despised confrontations, especially, with company employees. More so, she did not wish to put herself in any situation that may appear compromising.

Bernice narrowed her eyes. "I don't know. There's something about him that tells me he's capable of doing just that."

"May be we should stay in town——go to a movie or something."

"We'll be all right. Even if he shows up, I think he'll behave himself. He may be pampered, but I don't think he's dumb. He knows his limits, especially, if he wants to continue working at Denton & Terrell. He may come from a powerful family, but I doubt 'specializes in harassment' is what he wants on his resume."

"We pray."

"Amen."

"As a precaution, I will ask some of my friends to pray for us."

"That would be nice. I'll also tell Alex. Though he may make a fuss about it, I think he'll be fine, if he knows I'm with you."

They returned to their cubicles, Lily mulling over the plan. Was it wise to insist on going to Palm Springs? On the other hand, should she allow the Brads of this world to dictate her life?

She turned her back to the corridor. "Lord," her lips moved in prayer, "I neither wish to live rashly nor do I want to become a recluse. Help me live responsibly. Thank you for letting Bernice invite me for a shopping trip to Palm Springs. Please watch over us and keep us safe. Throughout the weekend, let Bernice see You in me. On the other hand, if we should not take this trip, please make Your will also very clear and I will accept it gladly; then provide us a better alternative for a relaxed weekend, I pray . . . Amen."

She made a one-hour appointment with Mr. Chancey, for a complex case.

51

Lily eyed a thick file, wishing she could dump it in the trash. How some Denton & Terrell's clients operated their businesses!——jet-flying multi-millionaires with private beaches and islands and yachts and mountain chalets to boot, yet without a penny to rub together! Her parents would frown on such complex business structures. Understood, someone had to handle those cases. As usual, Mr. Chancey had volunteered her.

Working on her dissertation was helping her grapple with that world—a world she had skimmed through during her undergraduate studies; and was still wary about getting involved in. What would her father say? "It always pays to walk the straight and narrow, children. You never have to rehearse what to say," he had drilled into them as they were growing up.

Mollified that Zebediah promised to discuss the case with upper management, she took the file to his office, then she locked up the rest of her classified assignments and dusted her desk.

Brad was toiling at his desk, for a change. Whether this was a sign that he would not go to Palm Springs or the opposite, she was uncertain. Should it become necessary, she would confront him, but so far, Brad had been evasive.

Soon, she heard the soft thud-thud-thud of heels vibrating through the corridors. She guessed only Bernice could rock the floor that way, even as Bernice ducked her head in her cubicle and asked, "Ready?"

"Just about. Two more minutes."

Bernice followed her hand movements from side to side. "I'll pop home to pick up my car. I borrowed my mum's this morning. My mechanic's servicing my little sporty. Mum insisted on it. Every time I go outside San Fernando Valley, she has that poor thing turned inside out."

"Your Mum is a great mother." She re-shelved the last file.

"That she is. I told her about——," she pointed backwards, and lowered her voice, "she insisted, if he so much as blinks at Palm Springs, we should call the police. I assured her he's not a bad guy, just a terrible flirt, who apparently, is looking to settle down——that would be something to behold. But Mum has Jake on stand-by in San Diego, in case we need him and she insisted Alex should know."

She organized her desk, took her briefcase, and strode to the door, in case her boss remembered a last-minute rush, which would not be the first time.

Bernice kept pace and promised to be at her condo by two thirty p.m.

♦ ♦ ♦

Lily zipped her weekend bags and took one more glance at the mirror. She looked all right, except for her hair, perhaps. She tousled it, debating whether she should comb it or wait until Palm Springs.

A loud honk announced Bernice had arrived. She parted the curtains. There, in her driveway, its hood rolled down, was a red Miata Mazda. Inside sat a woman with a scarf draped around her head, wearing classy looking sun glasses. From the rest of Bernice's appearance, she guessed that Bernice had coordinated her wardrobe to resemble that of a seasoned movie star on her way to Palm Springs. She dimpled, wondering whether her casual linen travel outfit, with a touch of a Spanish design would do.

The weather was warm enough for her to adorn a pair of sandals she had bought, also while on a trip to Mexico and though it was a bit early for straw hats, she slapped one on her head and dashed out.

The moment she had stored her bags away, Bernice rotated the Miata at a hundred and eighty degrees into the street, then she sped on to the freeway, wheels screeching, tires smoking, amidst a myriad of chatter.

She tightened her hat's strings, thankful for friends praying for them.

To distract her mind from Bernice's driving, at first, she counted the sports cars on the freeway, then she engaged her in light conversation.

"How's Jake doing?" she asked, after Bernice had quieted down.

"Still nursing a wounded heart. You know, he has a crush on you."

"I'm sure some fine girl out there will snatch him up in a blink."

"He swears he won't date again and spends all his spare time surfing, with a picture of you and him building the snowman, sealed in his wallet."

"The ocean air should do him good," she murmured.

"I'm still gloating. You know, up until he met you, he used to be so cock-sure no woman could sway him, unless she was blonde, auburn, or maybe, dark-brunette. He used to drive me nuts, now it's a different story.'"

"He will be all right. I will pray that some really nice girl will come his way. He exhibits the qualities of a strong man."

"Don't let him hear you say that or I'll never hear the end of it."

She smiled and resumed studying the landscape. Except for two trips to San Diego, she had never traveled past the City of Ontario. Long ago she learned about California's arid climate, the Andreas Fault and the Cascade Mountains. She noted the dry, desert terrain with its semi-arid vegetation.

Her avid love of nature, kept her staring, at seventy miles per hour, at the near dusty terrain, wondering why she had not taken keener interest in California's myriads of landscapes——the lofty mountains, the rolling seas. By seven o'clock, they pulled up at the La Villa Familia Spa & Resort.

"I hope you don't mind that we're not staying in Palm Springs proper. I thought the outskirts would be more relaxing," Bernice said.

"How far away are we?" she asked.

"About thirty minutes? But I think you'll like it."

"Just what I needed. Thank you for your thoughtfulness." She paused, then said, "By the way, I'll pay for my portion, if you don't mind?"

"As a matter of fact, I do. It's my treat!" Bernice insisted.

"We are both accountants, scraping the barrel, hoping for a bright future."

That earned her a chuckle, then Bernice said, "If you insist, but I'm still treating you to the spa and dinner—my belated birthday gift."

She thanked her.

Parents and children milled around in the lobby. It appeared some guests had just returned from golfing or were on their way. She wished the rest of the weekend would be as relaxed as her first impressions promised.

52

The sounds of dawn trickled into the room, like the beginning of the early morning rain. Soon the first lone car, then the second and the third buzzed by, followed by silence, then the cycle repeated itself.

Lily remembered the day's schedule. "Crazy Bernice——five-thirty gym on her weekend off——she's got to be out of her mind," she muttered. An early riser she was, but not at five thirty on her day off.

Her phone rang. "Good morning! Are we ready yet?" Bernice chirped.

"Morning. Did you seriously say five-thirty?" she asked, groggy.

"Cheerful and bushy tailed."

"Don't talk to me," she croaked.

"Is she in a good mood or what! Lord help!"

She laughed, more alert. "May be I should be grumpy more often—— would make a believer out of you."

Bernice chortled. "I'm getting there. Meet at the elevator in fifteen minutes."

She hung up, said a quick prayer, and prepared for the gym.

A quarter of an hour later, she stepped to the elevator, and almost collided with Bernice, a picture of perfection in her dark green, gym suit.

At the gym entrance, they froze. On the bike, working out, looking as placid as a dove, sat Brad. How in the world did he know which hotel to book? Bernice remembered that in her excitement, she had told her boss.

"Good morning ladies. Come join the party!" Brad said.

Bernice walked forward, her face set and whispered something in Brad's ear that made him blush every shade of the Lord's glorious world.

"I'm hurt, Bernice," he said.

"No, Brad. Hurt's what you'll be, if you so much as blink! I've watched you at Denton & Terrell. I have one piece of advice for you, get over it!" she said softly, menacingly.

They glared at each other.

Lily watched their exchange from a bench. "What was that all about?" she asked, after Bernice had returned.

"Nothing. We were just having a good morning chat."

"It looked pretty intense to me."

"The early birds usually fight over the crème de la crème."

Lily turned her face to the wall and clapped her mouth shut, so Brad wouldn't see her expression. "I'm not going to ask you to explain that one."

Bernice's lips twitched. "Come on, let's work out." She glared back at Brad, her head tilted in the air.

Starting with the stationary bike warm-up, followed by bench press, they worked on their gym routines, boycotting Brad's corner.

Lily withdrew into her own world, a headset strapped to her waist playing gospel music. Though grateful that Bernice had handled Brad adeptly, she was peeved that Brad had showed up, uninvited. As an adult, Brad was free to go wherever he chose, but it was obvious he came to Palm Springs after eavesdropping——that was tantamount to intruding.

Recalling how she had reprimanded Lamar, she elected to be civil to Brad, for now, praying that she would avoid a nasty confrontation with him, where she might be tempted to censure him and regret later. Instead of dwelling on his shortcomings, she prayed that he would sort out his life soon.

Brad pumped iron harder, sweat glistening on his biceps. Seeing the glint in Bernice's fiery eyes, Brad knew he had met his match. According to rumors, Bernice put herself through college after working as a hairdresser, in a tough neighborhood in which many women would not have fared well. He had a brush with that toughness when they dated briefly. For all her contradictions, she preferred Lily's company, because Lily adhered to her moral principles. It was also rumored that for the same reason, Bernice had chosen Alex, a man who respected her and refused to make ungentlemanly demands on her. When Bernice chose Alex over him, more than his ego was bruised.

Brad had more than one reason to be wary of Bernice. He had overheard a colleague hint that she had taken classes at a shooting range to improve her aim, that was, after her unconventional father had schooled her in the art of hunting deer when she was barely a teenager. He exhaled slowly.

After gym, Lily showered, changed into a two-piece white embroidered cotton slacks and blouse and came down for breakfast. Ravenous from her work-out, she ate toast, scrambled eggs, bacon, fruits and yoghurt and drank almost her entire pot of tea, while Bernice chatted away over a plate of pancakes, sausages and a bowl of fruits served with cottage cheese washed down with a cup of coffee, a picture of crystal brilliance.

Before they left for their sight-seeing and shopping, Lily meditated on a passage about moderation and living responsibly. Since Bernice had kept the rest of the weekend a surprise——apart from dinner plans——she welcomed that caution, then she spent an hour reading her Corporate Finance textbook.

◆ ◆ ◆

As Palm Springs' sun pounded the earth, the early shoppers meandered around, trying to get ahead of noonday. Lily and Bernice mingled with them, weaving in and out of the shops.

They were about to cross the main street, when Lily heard a familiar husky voice behind them say, "Lily! Is that you?"

She searched the crowd with her eyes. "Sharon! Jonathan! What are you doing here?"

"Hi Lily," Jonathan hailed with cheerful innocence.

"What are you doing here?" she repeated.

"Taking a short break." Sharon had the same bland face.

By now, they had caught up with them. Jonathan introduced two young men who were with them as his cousins, Aaron and Michael.

"How do you do?" She shook their hands.

Bernice followed suit.

"We usually call them the 'Two Cousins'," Jonathan said.

"Like you and Paul?" She smiled.

"Yup," Jonathan replied.

Aaron and Michael exchanged looks and Aaron raised his eyebrows, playfully.

"Well, well, well, a Palm Springs gathering!" a voice announced from the side.

"Brad! How delightful to run into you!" Bernice bit out.

"Bernice, what a surprise." Brad oozed charm.

He stopped before the group and introduced himself. They reciprocated.

"Well, where were you ladies headed?" Sharon asked.

"Just hanging around, shopping," Lily replied.

"Nice! May be I should join you. Let the boys fend for themselves."

"Great idea." Bernice beamed.

"Tell you what, how about if we all meet later on for dinner? Where're you girls staying?" Sharon asked Lily.

"At The Spa & Resort, about half an hour's drive," Lily replied.

"La Villa Familia Spa & Resort——the Family Villa?" Sharon's voice rose up a notch.

"Yes."

"We're on the fifth floor," Bernice added and mentioned their room numbers, straight-faced.

"How wonderful! So are we. I'm two doors from you; Jonathan's across from Lily's and Aaron's and Michael's are just around the corner. So, how about if we all meet downstairs at La Villa Familia after seven o'clock?"

"That's a great idea! But where are we going?"

"Well, may be I should've asked. What were you ladies planning on doing this evening?"

Lily said quietly, "Go for dinner," as her mind came awake at the coincidence of their rendezvous.

"To . . .?" Jonathan prompted.

"We were thinking, Le Cretien? A bit pricey, but we thought it'd be fun and more proper." Bernice said to Lily, "Eating well's part of the fun. Right?"

"Le Cretien it is," Sharon spoke for everybody.

"I think we've to make reservations," Jonathan said.

"That's where you come in, honey," Sharon purred.

"Will do." Jonathan turned to Brad. "Brad, you'll be joining us?"

Brad seemed relieved. "Sure you don't mind?" He glanced at Lily.

"Not at all. Unless you had other plans?" Lily kept her eyes leveled just above Brad's chin and avoided looking at Bernice, knowing she would burst out laughing if she did.

"No. I'd love to join you. Thanks," Brad replied.

"All right. See you later," Sharon.

The boys departed to explore the city on their own.

Lily's mind plunged into the logistics of the coincidences. Since Paul left for East Africa, a certain feeling had been nagging her——too many coincidences nipping at her heels. Just how did Sharon and Jonathan end up in Palm Springs the same weekend as she did? She remembered asking her Sunday school to pray for a safe trip, but, she had not disclosed where she would be staying. So, was it a coincidence that Sharon and Jonathan selected La Villa Familia Spa & Resort in particular?

For crying out loud, Jonathan's room was just across the hall from hers, Sharon's was two doors from Bernice's and the boys' rooms were just around the corner, all hedging her in! Why didn't they say something to her if they were planning on coming to Palm Springs the same weekend?

Even more mystifying was why Aaron and Michael had trotted along. The obvious answer was that they were cousins, therein lay the puzzle. Whatever fleeting relationship she and Paul might have had, surely, he must have informed Jonathan and Sharon that he had stopped dating her and they must have considered how awkward it would be for her to hang out with his cousins, given the circumstances? Wasn't it Kelly who needed bodyguards? Shouldn't they be shielding her?

If they were being solicitous because they felt guilty, then they should know that they were under no obligation and she would harbor no resentment against them, if they resumed their normal lives.

◆ ◆ ◆

Lily lay still on her bed, her eyes closed, a symphonic piece floated in the air from her bedside radio. Despite her athletic ability, spending a whole day at the mall, meandering in and out of the crowds, often gave her tight muscles. A half an hour at the spa was helpful, but she still had a mild headache when she returned to her room.

Given a choice, she would have preferred a quiet dinner, catching up with her reading, to being out on the town. Her goal was to read three chapters a day; so far, she had plodded through only two chapters.

More relaxed, she selected a hip-hugging rust red dress. Forty-five minutes later, she emerged from her room and ducked in time to avoid Bernice knocking on her nose, as a whiff of Rose Mist Perfume floated in.

"Well, you do look sharp, if I may say so. If only Paul could see you now." Bernice stopped, clapped her hands on her mouth, "Oops! Sorry, I shouldn't have."

"That's okay. So do you. I like that spring look, so vibrant and . . . cheerful."

"You don't think it's too much?"

"No. You liven up the place."

"Oh, thank you. Allons!"

They took the elevator to the lobby.

"You are really French?" Lily asked.

"Only my Mum's part French. My Grandmother used to speak French to us when we were young, but I never mastered it."

"You speak it with a beautiful accent."

"Thank you. How did you know? I only spoke one word."

"I like how you pronounce Le Cretien."

"You've a good ear for languages."

Downstairs, they spotted the others congregated in a corner.

Jonathan greeted their arrival with a bow; his eyes harbored a secret joke. "All right! You ladies look ready for the evening," he addressed them both; but his eyes swept over Lily from the tip of her black pumps to a pair of black onyx earrings cascading from her ears.

The in-vogue dress was a one piece, straight to the hem, with pastoral sleeves, tapered at the wrists. A silk scarf with small prints of black and red, softened its solid rust red color, and crowned her face, emphasizing her deep, dark eyes, and long eyelashes. She had tousled her curls to give her a windswept look——making her unconsciously resemble a model.

"Yes, you both look very elegant," Sharon said.

Jonathan looked dapper——very much the artist, in cocktail black, complemented by Sharon in an off-white outfit.

Brad strutted in soft, gray slacks and a crew neck sweater, with matching dinner jacket, designed to knock a healthy lady off her feet. Apart from a cursory politeness, the girls however, ignored him.

He devoured Lily with his eyes, until Bernice gave him the eye, then he cornered Aaron and Michael in a spirited discussion on sports.

Aaron and Michael took him on. In their casual woolen slacks, and open-neck shirts, showing a bit of their hairy chests, they were prepared to handle anybody. Just in case anyone doubted, their leather jackets dismissed all doubt.

"How will we handle the short trip?" Sharon surveyed the group.

"How about if the ladies rode with one of us?" Jonathan suggested.

"I don't mind driving," Bernice cut in.

"It's a bit late. The boys should ride with you ladies, and we'll give Brad a ride. Will that work?" Sharon slid to home-base.

"I don't mind driving. How about I give someone a ride?" Brad tried to conceal his disappointment.

"Oh, no, no no! No problem at all. Jonathan and I don't mind giving you a ride." Sharon emphasized the "you."

"Not at all. We'd love it," Jonathan echoed.

Outnumbered, Brad accepted the ride, kicking him. Nothing was working out as he had planned——first Bernice, now Sharon and Jonathan. He had hoped to impress Lily on this trip. His intentions were good. Who were these people? Why had they hijacked his weekend?

I finally meet a woman I wish to know for the right reasons and a bunch of busybodies interfere!

He brooded, forgetting he was trespassing on their weekend.

Would he ever settle down? His reputation had tarnished any crumb of decency he still had. If only he could rewind the clock and erase the years of bad choices that seemed so much fun back then! Too late now to discover that his past may have sealed his future forever. Not even his family wealth could help him bribe his way into the life he coveted. None of the women who jockeyed for his attention fitted the bill for the type of woman he was vying for, beautiful as they were.

Underneath his flamboyant lifestyle, he wanted peace and love in his home. He wanted to know that the woman he selected would love him for himself, not the wild parties or the family power or the opulent lifestyle. He wanted the assurance that he could grow old with her. But he also loved the privileges his family connections accorded him.

♦ ♦ ♦

Unaware of Brad's turmoil, Lily welcomed the excuse to withdraw into another world, and abandon her books, if only momentarily. Le Cretien, nestled in the hills of the San Joaquin Mountains, granted her that evening.

Jonathan had reserved a premium table for eight o'clock.

Lily found herself seated between him and Aaron. Bernice sat between Aaron on her right and Michael on her left. Sharon sat on Jonathan's right, sandwiching Brad between her and Michael.

To talk to Lily, Brad had to lean across the table and every time he attempted that feat, the whole table stopped and listened.

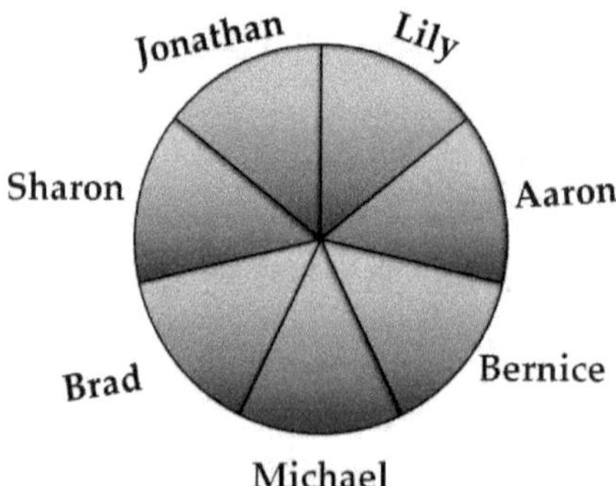

The waiter took their orders for appetizers and soft drinks.

"So, are you two undergrads or grads?" Lily asked.

Aaron drummed the table, as he replied, "Undergrads——USC."

"Nice. I have heard good things about USC."

"How exciting! When do you graduate?" Bernice turned on her charm.

"Last year this Fall," Michael replied.

"Good! You'll soon be joining us. I'm curious. Which side of the cousins are you?" Bernice asked.

"Maternal," Jonathan jumped in, "Aaron's mum comes after my Mum and Michael's mum is the youngest in the family. Paul's mum is the oldest of the four girls, though Paul's a year younger than me."

"How exciting!" Bernice beamed.

"And what are you all studying?" Lily asked.

"Accounting," Aaron replied, "and Michael is——"

"Civil engineering," Michael said.

"Good courses. The market's good for those two professions," Brad interjected.

"Actually, you guys are looking for summer jobs. Right?" Sharon asked.

"Yes," Michael and Aaron chorused.

"I could lobby for something with Uncle Jeremy," Michael added.

"Uncle Jeremy?" Brad looked puzzled.

"My Dad runs an environmentally friendly construction company. He might have something suitable for Michael," Jonathan explained.

"Eco-friendly company——that's a switch," Bernice commented.

Jonathan coughed. "It's the wave of the future. In theory they're supposed to use biodegradable materials."

"In theory," Lily repeated with loaded meaning.

Jonathan's lips twitched. "I know. They mean well."

Lily smiled back. "With a lot of environmentally friendly products, it takes a concerted effort of all employees, suppliers and subsidiaries to ensure company policies are enforced consistently."

Sharon looked surprised by Lily's remark, though at this stage, she should be used to Lily's shrewdness. She murmured, "That's very true."

"They say it's usually not a good idea to build a resume based on a job with family. Better to prove yourself first." Brad smirked.

"You don't say?" Bernice cut in, sarcastic.

"You bet! Best thing's to establish oneself first, before joining family business." Brad's chest swelled.

"Bridge Eco-Friendly Corporation is private only in that it's non-governmental. I would hardly call it a family business. It's a publicly traded company——owned by a bunch of stockholders——with at least ten thousand employees globally," Jonathan said in a restrained voice.

Lily studied Jonathan——he was always cool, never out of sorts.

"I could probably look around for something else," Michael said. "My girlfriend's here, so it makes sense to spend summer here."

"Yes. Something in the city civil engineering department——perhaps? I hear they sometimes hire interns for the summer," Bernice said.

"There you go!" Sharon agreed.

"Yes. Dig ditches, starting from six a.m., that should get you going, Michael!" Jonathan teased.

Bernice patted Michael's hand, while everybody laughed.

Lily turned to Aaron, "And how about you, Aaron?"

"My girlfriend wanted me to go back east, but I think I'll stick around. I'd prefer an internship with an accounting firm." Aaron turned tomato red.

"Seriously? I'm sure something could be arranged."

Not one to miss opportunity to shine, Brad sidled his chair closer to Michael and spent the rest of dinner trying to impress him and Aaron with his regiment of connections. Neither one of them seemed to mind, nor apparently did anybody else, as they carried on with their own conversation. The seating arrangement was working perfectly.

Lily studied each face furtively. Was it a coincidence? Why did Aaron blush? What were the odds that he would work at Denton & Terrell for the summer? Brad had invited himself to Palm Springs, but it was obvious Sharon and Jonathan had invited Michael and Aaron and Bernice seemed to be hiding something.

Lily took a sip of her sprite and smiled at Jonathan. He gave her his undivided attention for the rest of the evening, while Sharon and Bernice listened and made comments occasionally.

At the back of her mind, Lily mentally rehearsed the next day, willing it to be quiet——out sightseeing, but away from the crowd.

53

Work-out started at six thirty a.m. Would Brad be there? What if it became necessary to confront him? Should she or should she simply downplay his attitude? Anxious, Lily rolled out of bed, knelt by her bedside, and asked the Lord to guide her day and minimize encounters with Brad, if any.

She ordered room service for breakfast, spread a towel on the floor, warmed up, then phoned Bernice to meet her at the gym.

At the gym, Lily darted her eyes from corner to corner. A middle-aged man was already up, working on his arms in one corner; in the middle, a teenage-looking boy was bench-pressing; and to the side, a woman was riding a gym bike and reading a magazine——probably a family, she surmised.

Brad was nowhere in sight.

She mouthed a silent, "Thank you."

"I saw that," Bernice said.

"Pardon me?"

"I saw you giving thanks. I know why. I'll say it out loud. Thank you! Thank you! Thank you!"

"On that note, I will start with the bench." Lily got the free forty-pound Olympic bar——similar to the scanty gym equipment she permitted in her condo——and bench-pressed.

Bernice cycled on the other gym-bike until perspiration ran down her brow.

After gym, Lily showered, had breakfast and read for an hour. When she emerged from her room, she was dressed in jeans and a light blouse, wearing sunglasses and a sun shade. Bernice was already in the lobby.

On arriving in the city, she tried to steer Bernice to the quiet streets, looking for spots where they could sit and relax, but, wherever they went, inevitably Jonathan's group popped up. They surrendered to an hour with them, sipping soft drinks, while Lily continued to hope for a mild evening.

"What're you doing this evening?" Sharon asked, as they were leaving.

Bernice mentioned some nightspot.

Lily caught Jonathan throwing Sharon a glance.

"That's a great place," he said. "It has a pretty good reputation. Cool place——we played there a while back."

"That's good to know," Lily replied, with some enthusiasm. She could trust Bernice's commitment to steer away from unseemly places, but it was good to have a second opinion. To avoid unwanted surprises, she had also researched reviews of popular places.

After the many months, she had come to trust Bernice as someone who was careful in selecting her friends. Despite the joking and teasing, Bernice enjoyed her friendship because she had helped ground her and free her from the need to apologize for being virtuous.

Friends at Denton & Terrell had accused Bernice of being a goody-goody. Bernice's reaction? To avoid them. When Bernice dropped by her cubicle to welcome her to Denton & Terrell, her eyes had lighted on the *Billy Graham Evangelistic Decision Magazine* sitting on her desk. Bernice was elated. Here was an associate who was not ashamed of her values.

Also, the trust that she had earned from Mrs. O'Konnell and Alex, had put more pressure on her to be a model and hold Bernice accountable, without being a wet blanket.

For this evening, they chose to make it an early night. They would arrive at about seven o'clock and leave by ten o'clock at the latest.

Moreover, she had persuaded Bernice to attend the early Sunday service with her, before they left for home.

Walking into a reputable place should not be a chore, but try telling that to two decent, single women about town. Making sure they brooked no misunderstanding as to what type of women they were, Lily and Bernice adorned on very proper business pant suits. Lily's suit was of soft grayish deep blue; Bernice's of soft cream and rust brown color.

They arrive at the restaurant and Lily froze at the entrance. Sitting in the middle of the restaurant, where no one could miss them, were Sharon, Jonathan, Aaron and Michael, sipping soft drinks, totally relaxed, as though there was no better place for them to be, than right there.

The nerve! Lily thought, while flashing her teeth.

"I'm beginning to like this," Bernice mimicked a ventriloquist.

"It is not funny, Bernice. You know they're dogging our steps."

"But I like it. I like little puppies nipping at my heels. I love drama—— the more, the better."

"At least, Brad isn't among them."

"Alleluia," Bernice mouthed.

She shook her head amused. Was Bernice finally coming around to living her concealed faith in public?

"Ladies," Jonathan stood up, "We've been saving your seats. You know this place fills up pretty fast on Saturday nights."

What's with Jonathan? Why are they following us around? Is there something I should know? What should I be focusing on? Lily flashed a radiant smile at Aaron as he seated her. Did she spot a gleam in his eyes too? He and Bernice should sit together.

Bernice glowed with mischief as Michael seated her. She too appeared to be nursing a secret joke.

Lily appraised her quietly, wondering how she could extract the truth from her. Whatever was going on, she had no desire of hearing it through Marc or the other Jonesons' children, or the church grapevine.

To top it all, half an hour later, Jonathan went to the Gent's room and re-appeared on stage with his band, simultaneously as the Jonesons walked in with MJ, explaining the mystery of the three empty seats at their table.

Marjorie announced that the trip was an early treat for MJ's graduation and added that they planned on leaving soon after the end of the school year for a much-needed cross-country family vacation.

Matt Sr grinned.

54

Marjorie searched the crowd with her eyes. Finally, she spotted Melody waving from the front center. Melody pointed to empty seats around her.

"Let's move to the center." She led the way to the seats.

Twenty people stood up en masse from all over and followed her. Melody, Alisa and their friends had reserved the best seats for the two Jonesons' clans.

On the warm morning of June the 18, Marjorie sat proud on the bleachers surrounded by the Jonesons' and the MaClouds' clans. She could not believe it was over two decades ago that she was at the front, waiting to receive her diploma.

She craned her neck, trying to spot MJ again from among the graduates. For once she did not mind that earlier on, she had spotted him talking to Viviana Calderon and her senior group. She was so proud of him today; he could do no wrong.

From the side of her eyes, she sensed Matt's eyes on her and turned to look at him. Buckets of love flowed from his eyes. His camera lay poised in his lap, waiting for the moment when MJ walked out.

He cleared his voice. "Okay?" he asked.

She patted his hands. "Yes, honey," she said, remembering the family prayer time they had had in the morning with the two clans gathered at breakfast. She had never felt so proud of him.

That fleeting look was all the time they had, then the graduates began to march to the front.

With MJ graduating summa cum laude, she dismissed all thoughts, determined to enjoy her day of glory as a mother. Today was not the day to reminisce about her children's social lives or last week's family discussions. "Mum. Can I go to Jumaine's house? His party's on Saturday?" Melody had asked.

She had anticipated what was coming. They had been down that road so many times before that one would think Melody had finally got the message. "I thought you were hanging out with Alisa?"

"Yes. But we want to go to Jumaine's party."

"You know the rules."

"You allow him to come here and you say you like him. You invited him to my sixteenth birthday party."

"Well, have him come over here then."

Melody resisted rolling her eyes, took a deep breath, and said as patiently as her new level of maturity would allow, "Mum, he's having a party at his house. It's his graduation party. Do you expect him to move his party to our house?"

She frowned. "I thought you said you were going to give him his present at school?"

"That's beside the point, Mum. He's a friend and he comes to my parties and MJ's. It doesn't make sense for me not to go to his party."

"Melody, don't be tiresome. You know the rules. And, he's MJ's age."

"Six months younger. Mum, he lives only a couple of miles away from here. His neighborhood's just as nice——no overnight parking in the streets. They mow their lawns twice a month and their yard always looks manicured, just like ours. The whole neighborhood does. And he's kind of a friend and very smart. He plays basketball and he and his family go to church every Sunday."

"What's his score?" Matt asked.

Melody appealed to MJ. "Eighteen?"

"Eighteen to twenty," MJ came to her rescue.

"Eighteen to twenty!" Matt whistled. "Not bad."

"But he doesn't want to play basketball in college. He wants to be a doctor or a lawyer. His dad won't hear anything about sports. He butted heads with the coach. His dad was like, 'My son's going to college to study medicine or law. We have enough sports stars. I want him to contribute in some other positive way to his community.' Coach knew he had met a match."

"When will he graduate?"

"With MJ. So it's his last year and everything. And he's going to Princeton," Melody replied.

"Better and better," Matt mumbled.

She and Matt had locked eyes for five seconds, then she had said, "Melody, I feel more comfortable if you don't go into certain neighborhoods."

"Mum, it's just a neighborhood. Children there run and play like children in any other neighborhood and nobody parks on the streets——everybody parks in their driveway or their garage. And the street lights work all the time. Street sweepers come every other week, and their neighborhood's Christmas decorations are one of the best and the most synchronized in the whole of the L.A county, if not Southern Cal."

"Melody Lou Ann, have you been disobeying my orders behind my back?" She struggled to keep her voice calm.

"No."

"Then how do you know children there run and play like in other neighborhoods and they mow their lawns twice a month and their Christmas lights are better than everybody else's?"

Melody dropped her eyes. "We passed there."

"We? You and who?"

"Um, some of my friends——Dan and Alisa and others——and I, one day dropped off Jumaine and his sister, that was before Jumaine's parents got him a car."

At the mention of a car, Matt raised his eyebrows. She lowered her head momentarily, then asked, "You went to his house?"

"Just to drop him off. We didn't get out or anything."

"You're grounded. No more Dan and Alisa."

Melody raised her chin. "Mum, you're side-stepping the issue. I feel you sometimes talk with two-sides of your mouth."

"Melody!"

Melody blushed and apologized.

"Let her speak," Matt intervened. "Why do you feel your mother sometimes talks with two sides of her mouth?"

Melody hung her head.

"Melody, you can speak your mind, as long as you respect your mother."

Melody threw her Dad a grateful look. "I feel that Mum's over-reacting. Dan, Alisa and Jumaine are clean kids. I'm sorry Dan's dad doesn't go to church——though Dan loves him——but his mum does, you know that, Mum. And we're praying that one day his dad will also understand why it's important for him to model spiritual value to his family, not just how to make lots of money. You've met all of them. You know they're good kids. Mother, has it ever occurred to you that Jumaine's parents care for him as much as you and Dad care for us? They screen his friends. He has curfew hours. He's not allowed to roam around like some wild kid."

She rubbed her eyebrows, all of a sudden tired. "Melody, I'm glad his parents care about him; but this is not the time to talk about it. I need to prepare dinner."

"Mum, you've already prepared dinner."

"It's probably okay to let her go, honey," Matt appeased her.

She implored her husband with her eyes. "I just don't want what happens at other parties to happen to them."

"You mean that incident at the border towards the Foothills last year?" Matt nodded in understanding.

"No. It wasn't the Foothills. That's one of the safest cities. I think it was in another city." She tried to remember, "Palomares or La Palmina or La Puerta or something. It slips my mind."

A light dawned on Melody; she came over and squeezed her. "Mum that was an unfortunate incident. I'm glad it wasn't serious and the boy's back in school, and is walking normally, and the doctors say he'll be perfectly normal. You taught us to cover ourselves with a lot of prayer. You and Dad also pray for us all the time."

"I just want you to be safe," she pleaded with Melody.

"Mum, I'll not try to do anything daring or stupid. But I also want to be free to choose my friends. Otherwise, when will I ever learn——if not now? Don't worry Mum, I'll still ask for your opinion and pray for wisdom."

"That's my girl." Matt got up, and patted his stomach. "She should be all right, honey. After all, we have it on the highest authority that the lawns in Jumaine's neighborhood are mowed twice a month and the shrubs are trimmed neatly just as frequently——no cars parked on the streets——street sweepers never miss and the Christmas lights are the best in the State. He's six months younger than MJ, and to cap it, his parents just gave him a gift of nothing less than a car. What model?"

"A Corvette." Melody seemed surprised by the question.

"Arctic Blast?"

MJ nodded. "'94 C4, V8, three hundred horse power."

Matt whistled again. "Now you see? Nothing like a roaring Corvette to wake up the neighborhood! How many parents do you know who would go the extra mile for their kids? He's probably spoiled too. Don't forget, he wants to be a doctor or a lawyer and he's very smart. Learning to mingle will prepare Melody for the real world. That's how it's in the job market now. You've to get along, while never losing your focus. The Lord's good. Well, what's for dinner?"

"Pot roast," Marjorie replied.

"That's my girl." Matt gave her a peck on the cheeks and went to the living room, where Melanie was playing under Marc's supervision.

MJ went to the dining room.

Marjorie glanced at Melody and threw up her hand, disgusted. At times she loved her men with a passion; at times they reminded her they were boys. "I can always count on boys to talk shop in the middle of an important family discussion."

For all her complaining, she was relieved. Matt liked Jumaine, so did MJ. That was the best she could hope for in a world changing. For one guilty moment, she had remembered Paul Van Clyden. Perhaps Marc and Melanie, yet again Melody, might surprise them.

That was last week. Today——Marjorie fanned herself with her program——*Today, I celebrate a boy——my son——becoming a young man. Soon, it will be his turn to crane his neck to catch a glimpse of youth fading to give way all too soon to adulthood in a world that he may struggle to comprehend, while never forgetting that the same Lord, who had guided his ancestors through the years, would guide him.*

55

A tan RV with a blue trim swayed in gentle rhythm, as Marjorie handed the last suitcase to Matt, who handed it to MJ, who tucked it away inside the camper. Melody, Marc and Melanie watched.

Finally, the last of the guests had departed, leaving them five days of scurrying around, packing, and checking off the must-do-list. Marjorie felt like a mother-hen, pecking and prodding her brood to move it. For two days she had scrubbed and cleaned, turning every room inside out.

In turn, Matt whistled a lot, fussed over his toys, and insisted it was time the Jonesons moved to Oklahoma or Colorado or New Jersey or . . ..

After over twenty years of marriage, Marjorie did not bother to ask, instead, she threatened to pack all his toys and dump them in the garage.

Then MJ promised that if a local university offered him a scholarship or financial aid, he would stay in California and would come home on vacations and long weekends, and any time he could spare.

Marjorie packed her scrubs away and threw back the curtains.

Matt returned his electric train to its spot and the pilgrims' ship back to the mantel. The toys were fine and the house had never looked cleaner and the neighborhood was the best——they could not have selected a better neighborhood to raise their children.

So here they stood now, in the bright morning sun, loading up their vacation camper. Drops of water dripped from Marjorie's brow and Matt's t-shirt clamped to his body, as smog and heat circled the air.

Matt peered at the air. "I love California. It's the smog that'll get ya!"

"The more reason we should be gone before it gets too hot." Marjorie placed her carry-on bag on the front seat.

Marc shifted the Monopoly box to one arm, hoisted up his pants, switched the box back, and said, "I got my eyes on you Melody."

Melody made faces at him and placed her backpack in her seat.

Melanie stood by hugging her collection of toys, her face set.

Marjorie noticed; her eyes softened. "Melanie honey, you're not going to take all those toys, are you?"

"Yes. I am," Melanie replied. Her chin rose up a notch.

"Sweetie, remember what Mummy said last night? Just one toy for the trip——we've limited room."

"No!"

"Melanie, you promised, remember?"

"No!"

"Melanie, you don't want Mummy getting upset, do you? Then you won't take any toy at all."

"No!"

"Me-la-nie!"

Melanie squared her shoulders and brought her chin up all the way. "No. I want to take all my toys!"

Marc hoisted his pants up again and jumped, landing close to Melanie's feet. "Melanie can speak full sentences now, especially, when it comes to her toys," he said, rubbing his forehead with Melanie's.

"You bet you," Matt joined in the teasing. "Melanie, give me some of your toys. I'll keep them safe for you. Promise."

"No. I don't want to."

"Come on, sweetie pie. Daddy loves you."

Melanie's face puckered.

"Give them to Daddy. Daddy will keep them in a very safe place. Nobody will touch them and Shaggy won't eat them."

"Promise?"

"Yes. I promise."

Melanie handed her toys to her father, leaving only her favorite teddy bear, watched him go inside the house and return, empty handed.

MJ patted her hair. Strands escaped from her ribbon and blew in the warm wind. "Come on, Melanie, come up here. Come sit with me." He scooped her up in his arms and tickled her. She squirmed, delighted.

The rest of the family boarded into their favorite seats.

Matt clapped his hands, buckled up and turned on the engine, "Okay. Prayed up. All aboard, man and dog!"

Slowly, the camper rolled down the drive way. In a panic, Melody looked around. "Shaggy! Where's Shaggy?"

Matt slammed on the breaks.

"Oops." Marjorie stuck her head out of the car and cupped her hands. "Sha – – ggy! Shaggy come here."

Silence echoed back.

She turned and rested her eyes on Marc, a slow stare that started out as cold ice and turned into smoldering coal, hot enough to roast an elephant. "Marc, did you tie up Shaggy this morning?"

Marc looked at her blankly, lowered his eyes, and dug into the back of the front seat with his feet. "I was packing," he muttered.

"I told you to finish packing yesterday." Marjorie sighed and got out of the car. "Okay, everybody out. Nobody's leaving until Shaggy's found. I sure pray he didn't take off down the road."

Marc headed for the shrubs; MJ ran to the pool area; Melody went around the corner; Melanie tagged along. Matt stepped off into the street and peered down the road, scrutinizing the avenue of trees.

Echoes of "Sha-a-ggy! Sha-a-a-ggy!" filled the air.

"He disappeared into the fences an hour ago. I wondered why he was so upset, chasing birds. I should've known you. They never like change, do they? I give mine tranquilizers, but they always know when I'm off on a trip and they don't like it," a neighbor said.

"Edith. What a relief! I pray that's where he went." Marjorie sighed with relief.

Edith tugged on two red-ribboned, white poodles——shampooed to their eyeballs——and peered at Marjorie. "How long will you be gone?"

"Three weeks."

"Three weeks! That's a long time for a family vacation."

"MJ's gift. He's starting college in Fall." Marjorie beamed.

"They do grow up fast, don't they? I remember him as a little lad, when my girls baby–sat him. Well, don't worry about your house, we'll keep an eye on it. You just enjoy your trip. Enjoy your family while you can. Next thing you know, they'll have a family of their own."

Marjorie thanked her. Marc bolted for the fences.

Loud barking came from the shrubberies. Shaggy raced for the camper, leaped into the air and landed like a ball in Matt's outstretched arms, amidst cheers, and a spray of mud, and something that looked like——

"A dead bird!" Marc yelled at the remains of a carcass sticking on Shaggy's beard. "Shaggy, there are three hundred and sixty–five days in a year, and of all the days to find a dead bird, it had to be today! And where did you get all that mud? You miserable dog!"

"Whose fault is it?" Melody snapped, "You should've tied him up."

"I know. I'm sorry. I didn't mean to spoil everybody's vacation."

Matt shook mud off his clothes. "That's okay, son. We'll give him a shower and we'll all be set. Somebody will have to blow-dry him en route."

Marjorie's eyes softened again. "I'm sorry I snapped at you, Marc. It's been a long week. Come on, get a hose and we'll be done in no time."

Relieved, Marc dashed for the water hose.

Matt washed, changed into a crisp t-shirt and rinsed off the soiled one.

Finally, at eleven o'clock, the camper rolled down the driveway, amidst lively chatter, en route to their family vacation back east, set on their goal to cover as much ground as possible during that time.

Shaggy stuck his nose to the window, wrapped, waiting to be blow-dried.

◆ ◆ ◆

Matt and Marjorie relished every moment of their three weeks, taking endless family pictures . . . MJ playing with Melanie . . . MJ tussling Marc's hair . . . MJ chatting with Melody . . . MJ snoozing . . . MJ driving the family camper . . . MJ playing ball at the park with Shaggy . . . MJ waking up in the morning . . . . For once, thoughts of ENC and all their friends pushed to the back of their minds, except when they prayed for them at family altar time.

56

The late summer sun blazed, though with softer intensity. Matt reclined on a lounge chair, enjoying the cool shade, Shaggy nearby, licking his slippers. Melody floated on the opposite side of the pool, reading. A lazy barbecue sizzled on the patio.

With the family trip behind them, Matt was adjusting to a house without MJ working on his truck, or walking through the door, his book-bag slung over his shoulders, smelling of sweaty workout.

He watched his wife floating close by, with a twinkle. Encased in a five feet six-inch frame, a thirty-inch waistline, a neck reminiscent of bangles piled atop each other, crowned with a full head of dark hair that fell in textured ringlets around her shoulders and sea-blue eyes that jumped at you out of a clear fresh pink skin, Marjorie was an absolute delight to watch. He grinned at her, roguish.

"You wretch! What're you looking at?" His wife splashed him with water, slid out of the pool, and covered herself with a beach-wrap.

He dried himself; his eyes still twinkling.

A postcard in a pile of mail on the table caught his attention. He skimmed it and broke into a broad smile, "Someone pinch me! I feel I'm floating on air. Honey, guess who just popped out of the blue?" He held up the card to her.

"Who?" Marjorie flicked a strand of hair off her forehead.

"Guess."

"Great Grandpa Joneson."

"Seriously."

Marjorie wrinkled her nose for a moment. "The Greenes? I've been thinking about them lately. We ought to call them."

"Yes. We should. But no, much closer to home." Matt see-sawed the postcard in front of Marjorie's face.

"The Professor?"

"Yup! Professor Ray K. L. Grothe. He took a year's sabbatical to explore into greater depth the possibility of the bodily resurrection of the Lord. And for that he intends to take a trip to Israel and some of the world's museums that might hold the key."

"Yippie! So many blessings in one summer. I could get used to this. To think our prayers might be answered much sooner than we'd thought!" Marjorie dabbed her eyes.

"You have not, because you ask not. I'm glad we asked others to pray. Thank heavens for all the saints who've never given up on him. You ask, and do not receive because you ask amiss. In this case we were not asking amiss. We asked because we cared. Lily made it her mission to remind us to keep praying for the Professor. She's persuaded me, as long as we ask with a clean heart and according to the Lord's purpose, He'll hear us. Remember how she would pray?"

In chorus, they recited, "LORD, our Father, nothing is impossible with you, please help Professor Ray Grothe, and those whom he has influenced, hunger for your Truth. Let them use their intellectual talent to research into greater depth the bodily resurrection, and then let the Holy Spirit open their eyes to see and their hearts to believe that Jesus is beyond question the Messiah. Move them beyond their skepticism to believe that Christ came, lived, and sacrificed His life for our sins and is alive and now at your right hand. Finally, LORD, please help them understand that you will one day judge each of us based on the choices we made while we were still here on earth. And help them understand that you love them, and desire them to come into your Kingdom. Father, I pray. . . .."

Marc bust through the patio door, "The Professor got saved?"

"Not yet, but he's going to the Holy Land to do some research on the resurrection." Matt held up the postcard to Marc.

Marc's eyes darted back and forth, scanning the postcard. "Cool. I know we prayed for him at home, but after I told Lily in our Sunday school, she asked us to pray for him every day. She said the Lord would answer, if we don't give up. Oh, are they going to be happy! I'm gonna tell Miguel, then we'll go and tell Maryann. Come on Shaggy," he grabbed Shaggy by the collar and dashed off to get his bike.

"B-B-Q's almost ready. Don't be late for dinner. The Jonesons' train doesn't wait," Matt yelled to the wind.

Marjorie read the card again, stunned. "Now if only the Lord would answer our other prayers. Have the Van Clydens heard from Paul yet?"

Matt shook his head. "They know he's in Nairobi, on a mission trip that doubled as a project trip for BF&S. Jonathan keeps them posted."

"Any hope of reconciliation?"

Matt gazed at her steadily. "The older I grow, the more I'm convinced the Lord will bless me a lot faster, the sooner I surrender."

Marjorie fluffed Melanie's hair and straightened her swimsuit. "My mother's heart goes out to Charlotte."

"I often wonder what we would do in their shoes? She's not a bad girl. I like her and I know she would be a solid spiritual mate for Paul, if he settles on her. Uppermost in my mind as we approach the twenty-first century is for my children to be happy, have a fulfilled life and honor the Lord in all their choices, as we taught them. If they achieve that, I'll be happy." Matt seemed to be thinking out loud.

Marjorie removed her wrap, and slid back into the swimming pool. "Here Melanie, come swim with Mummy."

57

Like a wary cat, Paul pulled out a box from the bottom drawer, opened it, and placed it on the red faux Siberian tiger skin blanket which cradled the dark gray king-size bedframe. He did not feel like the tiger that stared back at him. He turned and faced a pedestal fan adjacent to the chest of drawers and watched his frame silhouetted through a gold trimmed full-length wardrobe mirror, as the fan played with his hair.

On one knee, he knelt on a solid cream and dark-gray Persian rug that cushioned the hard floor and lined the letters and post-cards on the bed. A small fan atop the nightstand purred softly, adding little to the air. He stared at the un-mailed letters, his enviable bedroom décor—courtesy of BF&S—doing nothing to calm his nerves, then with sweaty palms, he dialed a number.

"Hello," a groggy female voice answered.

The soft cotton at his breast kicked in mock rhythm to the commotion going on behind his thin t-shirt. He hung up.

Since the middle of January, he had been down this road enough times to rehearse the scene in his sleep, but that was the first time he had braved phoning Lily. He gave himself an 'A' for effort and a 'D' for courage. His attempts at e-mailing had suffered the same fate. He stepped out to the balcony and watched the last of the beautiful tropical sunset, caressing every drop of the receding golden red skies with his Grecian sea blue eyes.

♦ ♦ ♦

Lily thumped her pillow. Callers who never apologized for dialing the wrong number, irritated her, yet based on her instinct, this caller was different. She should contact her phone company and re-subscribe to caller-identification system.

In another hour, she should be up preparing for church. What church was Paul attending in Nairobi? She wondered. It seemed a whole year had passed since he left and not just eight months. But what difference did it make?

Kelly was spotted at some function, again. The reporter had mentioned that "Her secret fiancé was rumored to be in Africa, on a long business trip and not expected back until Fall" and had commiserated with Kelly on how difficult it must be for her to be managing under such difficult circumstances and how bravely she was holding on. Wasn't the sight of Kelly smiling like a Cheshire cat enough screaming sign for her to move on? Not without cause did the Word say, "The heart is deceitful."

Resolute, Lily had been burning the midnight candle on her dissertation. Nothing was keeping her in California, except her friends and the condo. Modern technology shortened the distance to friends and she could rent out the condo. Still groggy, she prayed for strength to keep pushing forward.

She got up, had breakfast, and dressed for church, then she pulled out her curriculum vitae, promising to sacrifice an evening working on it. By Friday, she would send out her first batch of job applications to Arizona, Colorado, and New Jersey. She had received a promising nod from the World Bank, thanks no doubt to her connections. They would like her to contact them again after she had completed her program.

If she could not land a job shortly after completing her PhD, she would move to another church nearby. Of course, she could move farther afield to Europe——England, for instance, or return home to East Africa.

Elated that she finally had a vision for her future, she drove to church and floated up the steps of Evangelical Neighborhood Church——a woman free to obey the Lord and go wherever He led her.

◆ ◆ ◆

Paul shoved the box of un-mailed letters back to the drawer and phoned Jonathan. Working on the mission field had cleared his head. What more, doing a favor for BF&S had given him leverage in negotiating his next move——BF&S welcomed aspiring young executives interested in honing their skills abroad. After returning to California, he would express his desire to work in Europe, especially, England. That move would also help him get better acquainted with his maternal relatives from the old country.

"Are you sure?" Jonathan's voice relayed his doubt.

"Positive," he assured him.

"You're not just running?"

"The thought crossed my mind; but no. I know what I'm doing. Nothing like hauling bricks and wielding a mallet to clear one's brains."

"You've already been at the site?"

"Yes, for the last month, but I'm still available. I was back this past week to sort out a few things and write my report. I don't plan on doing anything for a year. If no progress in the other front, definitely, Europe it will be."

"And Uncle and Aunt? I'm not touching them. No sirree!"

He chuckled. "Don't worry. As soon as I patch things up, I'll let them know. By the way, how are things at the front?"

"Relax. Everything's covered." Jonathan became more excited, once he understood that Paul would not rush his plan.

Paul prayed that after returning home, he would remain focused, short of a clear vision directing him to go elsewhere, or to remain in the Sunshine state, or . . . he sighed and kicked a golf ball.

On his desk was an executive summary on the status of the pilot project for a new BF&S branch in East Africa. He would have that mailed to the company, confidentially, in the morning.

Pleased that he had a plan for his future, he packed his backpack to rejoin the other church volunteers at the construction site for building a new school at the orphanage——the main reason he had come to East Africa.

In the crucible of rejection and facing the truth that not every woman found him irresistible, he had been forced to evaluate his life——to reach for a higher purpose——and in so doing, conclude that true strength did not depend on him or his family's wealth, but on his level of commitment to the one true God——the One who had the secret to strength, the One who held the key to the future. In his weakness, he had become strong.

THE VAN CLYDENS' FAMILY FORTUNE
PART II

58

"This is the Captain requesting all passengers to take their seats and buckle up. We'll be landing in about thirty minutes," the captain said.

High-rise buildings, freeways, parks, rectangular roads crisscrossed like airport runways, demarcating blocks of homes, and private estates that were still visible in the late afternoon of Friday October 14th; then blinking lights signaled the Los Angeles Airport runway.

As Paul's plane taxied to the gate, he peered through the window, wondering whether Jonathan and Sharon were already there, waiting for him? He was glad to be home, yet wistful of leaving East Africa. Why? He did not know.

He collected his carry-on bag and guitar and exited to the arrival lounge. As he emerged, he saw a long banner with a row of legs protruding from the bottom of it and a row of heads just visible above it. On the banner were words written in huge letters "WELCOME HOME PAUL, WE MISSED YOU!"

Projecting from the mouths of the heads that protruded above the banner were loud words, voices, shouting his name as loudly as the big letters that spelled it on the banner. "Love you Paul! We miss you! Love your sun tan! Welcome home!"

Some whistled and some whooped.

He blushed.

When he had overcome his embarrassment, he recognized many from the singles' group, and from his office, Phil and the other associates. In vain he searched for the other missing faces.

To compound his pain, he noticed a couple——former members of the singles' group who had married over the summer——now extensions of each other.

Not that he was ungrateful for all the people who had come, but their presence intensified his loneliness, reminding him that when all the excitement was over, he would be left holding on to his aloneness, alone. Scarcely one hour after landing, he was convinced Europe was his next destination and perhaps, destiny?

How would he tackle his relationship with his parents? Not before getting over the jetlag.

The rapturous group dragged him to eat his first real juicy, fat-dripping, mouth-watering, hamburger in Los Angeles in nine months.

59

Paul cruised along the avenue of well-lit, landscaped architectures that reminded him of a drive he had taken, while in East Africa. The invitation was for seven o'clock. Given the circumstances, he had driven from Orchards City, ready to be surprised by the guests' list. Had he never been to the Kaarlyles' home, he would have found it, for there, in bold letters, was another welcoming banner and balloons at the gate.

He collected the gifts he had brought and stepped up to the front porch. Ingrid welcomed him with open arms. "Paul, we missed you! Jonathan was becoming like a bear——counting the hours and the seconds," she shouted, a sign that she was excited to see him.

"I heard that!" Jonathan appeared.

"Here he comes, tanned like a seafaring captain," Uncle Jeremy boomed. "Welcome home, Paul!"

Aunt Angela appeared, arms outstretched. "Paul!" she wrapped her arms around him, making up for the hug he had wished from his own mother.

He kissed her cheeks and drawled, "I'm glad ye'all missed me."

After his eyes had become accustomed to the room, he recognized many familiar faces. In the background, standing unsure, were his parents. In a way he was not surprised——he had sensed they would be there.

But, not everybody was there! Masking his disappointment, he circulated around the rooms greeting guests, while he rehearsed what he would say to his parents——a dull pain from their last encounter pulsed beneath his shirt, along the artery that tied him to his mother.

His father stood with his hands in his pockets, unsure, while his mother clasped her hands together, a faint smile on her lips.

She stepped forward first, and offered him her cheeks. "You're home! So good to see you." Her eyes misted.

He swallowed hard and gave her a big hug. "Hi Mum."

"You look perfectly tanned, almost brown." She turned to his father, "Doesn't he, honey?"

"Oh yes, a couple of months more and he'd have definitely turned into a real native. Well, good to see you, son." His father placed his hands firmly on his shoulders and searched his face, trying to extract from him the answer for the many months of his silence and exile.

He scrutinized his father too. In his face, he saw a man torn with questions, such as how long would he be home before he took off again? So much time wasted, and so much to be said.

From behind, his cousins ribbed him. "Hey Paul! Where're the lion cubs? They'd make great Christmas gifts! Did you go hunting with the Maasais?"

"Not this hero. I stuck to my cameras——shooting at a distance."

"That's why you were on our prayer list," Ingrid added.

"It appears the gang missed me," he said to his parents.

His parents chuckled, more at ease, as he rejoined his cousins' group.

Occasionally, he raised his head, hopeful, as late guests arrived.

"I bet you took a lot of pictures," a guest said.

He thanked her for reminding him. "I brought one album tonight. I'll be putting together the videos shortly." He fetched the album that contained snapshots of Nairobi, Mombasa, Nakuru, and other places he had visited.

Once the other guests were engrossed in the album, he returned to his parents, chatting with his Uncle and Aunt and some friends.

"It's so good to have you home, Darling." His mother rubbed her eyes. "You'll come home soon, won't you?"

"I'll try, Mum."

"We need to talk," she mouthed into his eyes.

"Son," his Dad said in a low voice, "Come home."

"I'll be on vacation, then I'll be giving a report of my trip to the church. I should be free after that," he replied.

"You're speaking in church?" His mother looked surprised.

"Yes. The Sunday after my vacation."

"Good." She turned to his father, "We can spend the day with him."

His heart lifted. She had never missed an opportunity to support him.

"Then you could drop by before Thanksgiving? I'd like to have you home before Thanksgiving," she finished confident.

"Friday November the eleventh is Veterans' Day."

"Good. And don't worry about us, we'll meet you at church on Sunday morning." She stood taller.

"Yes. We should be there by coffee break," his father added, stronger too. "If I remember correctly, you've only one service." He grinned.

"Yes. It should be a full service." He followed his Dad's drift, all the while praying Lily would not go church-visiting that Sunday, of all Sundays.

♦ ♦ ♦

Figures flickered on and off the screen, casting shadows across the room, a droning noise in the background. Lily shifted around for a comfortable position on the couch. Ignoring the Saturday special on Christian Television, she flipped back to the page she was reading. On the side table, a plate of lemon ginger cookies and a cup of tea waited.

Restless, she had bought two Christian novels from Faith Christian Bookstore. In her current mood, it would have been pointless trying to toil at her dissertation anyway. After her power walk, she had spent two fruitless hours studying, given up, then left for her hair appointment. Having invested four hours per evening grinding away all week, and into the early dawn on Friday, she deserved a short break, she rationalized.

Sharon had tried to persuade her to attend Paul's party at the Kaarlyles'. She had excused herself. When she made her hair appointment for Saturday, she had no notion it would clash with Paul's party. Concerned that if she attended the party, Paul's family might think she was intruding, she refused to move her appointment and prayed the Lord would forgive her.

Kelly's behavior since Paul returned, led her to believe that Kelly would be at the party. What more, Sharon said that Paul's parents would be there. In no way would she expose herself to such public humiliation in front of them! Competition had never been her style; she was not about to start now.

She liberated a cookie from its waiting misery and crunched it between her teeth, just as the phone rang. Of course, it had to be in the kitchen!

She flopped back, resumed her position and crossed her legs. "Hello?"

"Why aren't you at the Beach?" Bernice scolded.

"You know why. I have accepted the Lord's will."

"You mean you've given up. Lily, I think you're misjudging him."

"Facts don't lie." She wished Bernice would leave well alone.

"And the facts are?"

"He has not permitted me to drop in on his parties. What more, some people have been very vocal. As far as I can see, it is a done deal. We are waiting for the engagement to be announced any time. I respect that."

"Kelly?"

"Mhmm."

"It could be tactics. I told you to watch out for those tactics. Short of the royal crown, no one's entitled to anything. Grandma says God honors those who're humble. He hates being manipulated. Did Paul respond?"

She bit her lips. What else was Bernice not saying? "No. I have not bothered to substantiate anything. He has not been back to ENC yet."

"See? You're jumping to conclusions." Bernice sounded confident.

"I don't think so. Why should I humiliate myself? I know the Lord can change hearts; but I also believe Paul can choose whoever. I respect that."

"He made overtures to you before he left. Over half of your single's group met him at the airport. You weren't there. I've a sneaky suspicion he was hurt. Sharon and Jonathan seemed to think so. I trust their judgment."

"How do you know? Where are you calling from?"

"The Beach."

She sat up. "What beach? Are you at the party?"

"Yes. We sure are. Me and Alex . . . I mean, Alex and I, accepted the invitation only because we thought you'd be here."

"Alex? Who else?" Sharon did not mention Bernice and Alex.

"Everybody——his parents, cousins . . . other friends I don't know . . . everybody . . . the Jonesons. Aaron and Michael were looking for you."

"Bernice, what else aren't you telling me?"

"Nothing. Just that . . . why did he choose East Africa? Think about that. People change, you know. I gotta go. See you Monday." Bernice hung up.

Lily sat at the edge of the couch, pondering what Bernice said. Why did Paul choose East Africa for his mission trip? On second thoughts, why not?

The weather's good, the people are open to the practical demonstration of the Gospel as are other parts the world, so why not East Africa any more than East Asia or South America or Northern Europe?

Then there was his family. Paul's dad was his hero. She had no intention of coming between a father and his son. While love may conquer all, could love conquer a father's specific preferences? Was it so wrong for a father to wish the best for his son? How long would it take for her prayers to be answered to change such a mindset and would it be right to focus only on her need, never mind the Van Clydens' dreams for Paul?

Her parents, too, had expectations for her. They were loving people, but they were still her parents. She should also prepare them. She took a great risk in presuming that she could predict how they would react. Paul's love for his parents and the realization that she loved and respected her own parents as much as Paul loved his parents, had galvanized her to pray even harder for her future than she had before, when she thought she could predict to what type of man she would get married.

In trying to contain her parents' expectations, she had gained a better insight of the challenges Paul faced with his own parents and had thus concluded that the road to freedom for those who seek to live for a higher purpose, are peppered with corpses of relinquished love. Bernice would probably consider her point of view fatalistic, but from her personal experiences through the years, she could testify with certainty, that the Lord never failed those who surrendered to His will. Without self-denial, there is no maturing in the Lord. Only in subjugating her wish, could she realize the higher purpose and blessings that the Lord had reserved for her.

She was confident that if she relaxed and trusted the Lord more, sooner, or later, He would fulfill her heart's desires, His way. Waiting was not a bad thing, as long as the results honored the Lord.

She raised her hands up in the air and prayed, "Father, it is all in your hands. I will carry on with my plans to move out of state. Please guide my feet. I trust you. Your will be done . . .. Amen."

60

One last tug at his tie, and a slap of light aftershave lotion to finish, Paul grimaced at his face in the mirror trying to ignore the thumping below his starched, smoky blue shirt. His face stared back at him, grim. Unable to postpone the torture any longer, he grabbed his car keys from the dresser.

For one who had recently returned from the missionary field, his first Sunday back at Evangelical Neighborhood Church was giving him unusually sweaty palms, belying the cool weather.

The meeting with Pastor Tim early on in the week had been a blast. Having been a missionary, the Pastor reminisced about his own experiences, mishaps and all. He prayed his short video flip would go just as well.

He was not sure why he was nervous. Should he brave the single's meeting or miss one more week? Would Lily wear her favorite perfume or a new one? She did not seem the type to wear La Mystique de Mademoiselle.

Whatever she does, I pray she doesn't choose this Sunday to switch perfumes or if she does, please let it not be Fabrice Étrange's La Mystique!

As if the one hour he had prayed at dawn wasn't enough, he knelt by his bedside again clutching his car keys. Humbly, he prayed that he would remain focused, and that the congregation would enjoy the video.

A final glance in the mirror, then he ran downstairs, whistling the old Gregorian chant, *"Be thou my vision"*——a favorite of Lily's that she asked often, when members of the congregation made their selections.

Outside, autumn leaves covered the ground in shades of gold and brown and red, heralding the first week of November, and reminding him of happier days——even Southern California had its moments of fall colors.

"You look all set and ready." Jonathan gulped down his coffee.

"Sort of, but as nervous as a first date."

Jonathan almost choked on his coffee. He wiped his mouth and said, with a crooked smile, "You'll be all right."

"Think so?"

"Mhmm. Cheer up. Sharon and I had everything covered." Jonathan gathered the Sunday morning papers and cleared his breakfast plates.

He downed a glass of orange juice. "I'll take your word for it."

Jonathan stared back at him and patted his shoulders. Months of silence passed unspoken.

"And Mrs. O'Mallery?" he asked.

"Will she be glad to see you! Sharon mentioned she needs cheering up. She gets melancholy around this time of the year."

"Her birthday's coming up. Can Sharon spy out her favorite restaurant?"

"That she'll do."

He left first. About fifteen minutes later, he pulled up at the church parking lot, with Jonathan following close behind him.

Taking a deep breath, he hurried to the general Sunday school classes, careful to avoid the singles' Sunday school class.

The first corner he turned brought him into view of three senior citizens. One of them bent over to the other and whispered loud enough for him to hear, "Leona, look who the wind just blew in!"

The other woman turned around; her eyes grew rounder than a saucer. "He's back! Pastor Tim, look who I found?" Mrs. O'Mallery's voice quivered. "I can get the ride of my life again. Not that your cousin's not good. But I get to have the double honor." She tilted her head and waited.

Paul kissed her on the cheeks.

"Oh, if heaven smells anything like this! Oh! Now I can go in peace."

"Not so fast, Mrs. O'Mallery. You're as sprightly as a spring chicken."

"He called me a spring chicken. You noticed. See? I don't have my cane. I took your advice and I've been exercising and I don't need to use a cane anymore!" She craned her neck and said, "I heard you're a very good dancer. I can do a whole waltz now! I'm determined to stay young for as long as possible. The Good Lord has given me only one life to live and I intend to enjoy every moment of it!"

That earned her an all-around applause.

He finally untangled himself from the ladies and continued to his class. Despite dodging Lily, and the happy encounter with Mrs. O'Mallery, Sunday school was a blur. All he could hear was the blood drumming in his ears.

Finally, he joined the crowd in the patio and was immediately surrounded by friends, eager to know every tiny detail of his trip. Over their heads, he watched Lily conversing with some new people.

At one point, she passed close enough for him to get a whiff of what he was positive was her perfume. Phew, not La Mystique de Mademoiselle Musk Perfume! Praise be! Her new perfume was so pleasing, he wished he could get another gulp; but she eluded him yet again.

About ten minutes before the service, she worked her way towards the sanctuary, greeting others along the way.

Pastor Tim came into view. She stopped and said to him, "Autumn is in full swing Pastor Tim and you have a full house."

"A delightful dilemma," Pastor Tim gave him a loaded look that shortened the distance between him and Lily, then he smiled at Lily.

With sweat crowning his brow, he smiled his way through the crowd, and floated towards the sanctuary.

Why didn't Lily welcome him back? Didn't she see him or didn't she know he was back? He squared his shoulders and started walking into the sanctuary. Just then, he heard his parents behind him and turned to see a distinguished couple——made any son proud——walking towards him.

His dad's conservative dark gray suit and a tie speckled with tiny rust-colored motifs, complemented his Mum's rust colored business suit of pure wool, a soft cream blouse and a lovely gold brooch. He had forgotten what a fine set of parents the Lord had given him.

He steered them to seats near the front, partly not to spook Lily. As he struggled to resist the temptation to glance in her direction, he prayed again in his heart that he would remain focused on recounting his trip.

When Paul entered the sanctuary with a distinguished looking couple, Lily shifted and averted her face, glad that she had sat closer to the side. They must be his parents, she guessed——one could not miss the resemblance.

Jonathan and Sharon glanced at her and came over. After chatting briefly in low tones respectful of the sanctuary, Jonathan excused himself and went to his aunt and uncle.

Sharon whispered that Jonathan thought his uncle and aunt might appreciate some company.

Two more friends bolstered her——what with Paul's parents so close, and yet so far. Linda had become increasingly warm, perhaps because she was Sharon's friend and Raya, a first-generation immigrant, with whom she had become acquainted at graduate school through working together on a project. Among the whole project team, she and Raya got the most ribbing over their distinct accents, though Raya's Hungarian was more marked.

At the end of the service, Lily gathered her purse and Bible. "Ladies, thanks for keeping me company, I truly appreciate it. By grace, I will see you mid-week." She bolted for the exit.

Her friends exchanged glances.

"She's one slippery fish, isn't she?" Linda said.

"You can say that again." Sharon nodded.

"One step forward; three steps back." Raya shook her head.

"Mhmm," Sharon and Linda agreed.

"Let's go over and greet Paul's parents." Sharon rallied her friends.

The Van Clydens, preoccupied with Paul, had missed Lily sitting closer to the side aisle, in the back. Only two other women came close to the description. One was tall, but bigger-boned and was wearing what resembled an engagement ring on her finger; the other was shorter and plump and walked in with her husband and children. The two had American accent; Jonathan had said that the girl had a distinct British accent, and was easy to spot.

Charlotte swept the mingling, exiting crowd, with her eyes; none of them resembled the girl she had hoped to see. According to rumors, she was tall, elegant and beautiful. But, pretty as the other women were, none fitted that description, except for one tall, slim woman with dark, curly hair she had spotted striding out. The young woman moved so fast, Charlotte thought she had imagined her. From the little that she saw, she had long legs and golden-brown skin. Could she be the one? She wished she had spotted her earlier.

Paul loosened his tie. Lily must have bolted for the exit the moment the service was over. Throughout his report while he was up at the pulpit, he had tried so hard not to look in her direction. Bad idea!

He grinned and ruffled his hair.

His Mum glanced at the exit. "I suppose not everybody came today."

"Or some probably left early."

"The bird flew the coop?" his Dad side-mouthed.

"So it would appear," he replied.

Sharon and her friends appeared. Paul locked eyes with her and raised his eyebrows.

Sharon spread out her hands, as if to say, "Don't ask me. I know nothing."

Wishing he could rewind the clock back two hours, he devoured the exit with his eyes, then he turned his attention back to his company.

After he had introduced his parents to Sharon's friends, Raya excused herself.

"Hi Igor! Hi Charlotte! So good to see you," a saccharine voice said.

Paul resisted flinching.

Charlotte smiled. Kelly was standing inches behind her, decked from head to toe in all her finery. La Mystique de Mademoiselle oozed from her pores.

Kelly kissed her cheeks.

"Kelly, how delightful to see you," she said.

"Yes. It's nice to see you, Kelly," Igor echoed, less enthusiastic than on the previous occasions.

"Hello Kelly," Paul sketched a smile and steered the group out. He and his Dad flanked his Mum in the middle; Jonathan, Sharon and Linda followed immediately. Kelly trailed them, bringing up the rear, alone.

♦ ♦ ♦

Lily slammed on the breaks, inches from her garage door. The moment she entered the house, her purse dropped on the side table, her Bible landed on the coffee table, and her back flopped on the couch.

"Finish your dissertation and get on with it! Get a grip!"

If Paul Van Clyden thought she was going to make a fool of herself in front of his parents, he had better think again!

She remained motionless in that position for half an hour. In the quiet of her mind, one verse after another streamed through. But on the outside, the only evidence that she was still alive was her soft breathing.

She had prayed for Paul as his plane took off and had prayed for him every day of the nine months he was gone. She had prayed until the very air that she breathed sung of Paul. She had invested so much time praying for him that she had teetered on the brink of neglecting all the other prayer needs.

On the day that his plane landed, she felt it, though she was some fifty miles away from the Airport. Where was it all leading? How would it end? How could she know?

She fetched her dissertation paper, propped her head with a cushion, then she covered her face with the paper and permitted her mind to review the events of the last eighteen months. Was is sane to remain at ENC?

About an hour later, the phone rang. She ignored it. It continued ringing, until her answering machine came on.

"Hi Lily. This is Sharon . . .," Sharon's voice came on the line.

She grabbed the receiver. "Sharon! Thank you for keeping me company this morning. That was very kind of you."

"What was that all about?"

"What was what?"

"Come on! Why didn't you come over to greet Paul's parents?"

"Are you kidding?"

"Not at all. Sooner or later!"

She raised her eyebrows, as though Sharon could see them. "Me? I don't think so. I hardly know Paul."

"That's what you think." Sharon paused and said, "Listen, we were thinking of doing something special for him soon, to welcome him home."

"That would be nice." She tried to sound enthusiastic.

"You don't sound too excited." Sharon had noticed.

"Sometimes I feel like I'm imposing."

"Whatever gave you such an idea? We can't always go by our feelings, Lily. So, should I count you in?"

She hesitated, not from a lack of confidence, but from a desire to give Paul his space. "Yes. I suppose you can."

"All right! Since it's Thanksgiving month, I was thinking the sooner, the better, how about this Friday?" Sharon sounded elated.

"Friday sounds good."

"Okay. I'll have it announced at the six o'clock service. That's also the best time, since Paul will be out with his parents. You know how he gets embarrassed and all. His parents won't be able to attend . . . prior commitment." Sharon paused to let her comment sink in, she guessed. "I'll call those who don't show up this evening."

"That's a good idea. Can I help?"

"You most certainly can." Sharon sounded pleased. "I'll give you the list later this evening. We also need help with room set-up and decoration."

She promised to be there. Sharon thanked her and hung up.

She placed the receiver down and cradled her head. Determination sailed down her body——she must complete her doctorate and get on with her life. Moving out of the San Gabriel Valley was a done deal.

She jumped up and surfed the Internet in her small office in the nook.

"I will not be embarrassed again, if I'm the last spinster standing! I've got to pull myself together!" She whacked the keyboard, remembering Kelly oozing with diamonds.

61

Sharing the same room with the one who makes the heart pump faster has never been the pursuit of those in flight.

The Bible study leader had set up the room in a semi-circle of two rows, with fewer chairs in the second row. Raya, another lady and two men were sitting in the back row.

Lily pulled a chair and with a charming smile, asked Raya and the other lady, "May I squeeze myself here?" making sure that there was no space between them and her. The two ladies shifted their chairs. Right then, Paul appeared.

In her naivety, she had thought that if she squeezed herself in, Paul would take the hint or the others would stand their ground. Instead, Paul placed his chair at his desired spot, smiled and the room parted like the Red Sea, leaving a gigantic space for more chairs than she had wished.

Paul drawled, "Well, well, well! There's Miss Elusive!"

In attempt to sound nonchalant, she tripped over her words, "Hi Paul! So nice to see you. How was your trip? Did you enjoy East Africa?"

"Wonderful! It was great. I had a wonderful time." He gave her an enigmatic look. "Looks like some people have been training for Olympics. So, are we on the Olympics team or something?"

Sharon appeared. "I've wondered too." She pulled up a chair, plopped down, and patted the empty space next to her, hinting loudly to Jonathan.

"Yup." Jonathan placed his chair at the spot Sharon indicated, his eyes alight. "There was so much dust on Sunday I thought we were having a dust storm." He grinned, crooked.

"Oh. Wouldn't it be awful if we'd a tornado in California?" a girl who was sitting within earshot, remarked. She seemed to have missed the group's mood.

"That would be awful." Sharon rubbed her nose.

Lily tried to compose herself as she accommodated Sharon and the men, while acknowledging the other woman's comment with a dignified smile. "We wouldn't want a tornado in California, we pray!" A few uncharitable thoughts crossed her mind. It was obvious Sharon was in cahoots with the boys.

The Leader entered, apologizing for being late. He welcomed Paul back and gave him a smile that swept the room, rested on him for a few seconds, then settled on her, as though she too had gone on the trip!

During the meeting, she caught Paul's glances on her a few times. He had the same naughty twinkle as when he entered the room, though he remained decorous. She had this strong urge to unzip his brain and examine the content, if she couldn't fathom him, perhaps miss the Singles' Bible Study, until she had grasped what was going on with Kelly.

She braced herself for how her opponents at ENC would react, if word got out, though Kelly was absent from the meeting. Did Paul wish for a repeat of the previous year? Should she confront him? His popularity never waned, but that did not justify his toying with her.

62

Lily scrambled for the meeting room. Thanks to a last-minute conference with Mr. Chancey, she had left the office late, to top it, freeway traffic was backed-up.

She spotted Paul hovering on the steps, talking to two people, in appearance. In reality, he appeared to be waiting for someone. When she walked up, he excused himself and fell in step with her towards the meeting rooms. "Traffic must've been jammed up."

"I had a last-minute assignment." She hid her surprise——it was obvious he had been waiting for her.

"That explains it." He guided her lightly by the elbow to the prayer room.

When they entered, Jonathan heaved a sigh of relief. "About time. We were getting concerned."

Sharon patted the chair next to her; Paul seated her and then he sat next to her, very comfortable, as though he had been playing the happy groom all his life.

So much fuss over one girl, she thought.

Kelly was sitting in the front seat. Surprise! On seeing her enter with Paul, Kelly turned and chatted animatedly to a group behind her, until the Leader had entered.

After the last "Amen," Paul escorted her to the Fellowship Hall, leaving Kelly's group behind and this time, he stuck by her. This was balm for the humiliation of the previous summer——come autumn——when she had suffered so.

The sudden change in his behavior baffled her. Was he really trying to come back or two-timing?

Judging by Kelly's behavior that night, she and Paul must have disagreed again. Rumors had it that Kelly shopped around, but Paul apparently did not care. Some men preferred to fight for girls that gave them headaches and a lot of engaged couples reconciled after breaking up. But whatever the truth might be, two-timing a man had never been her style and she was not about to start.

By all accounts, Kelly was Paul's choice for a bride. Blonde, blue-eyed and from an affluent family, she was Mr. Van Clyden's first and only choice. Was Paul trying to make Kelly jealous? If so, that was mean. She had no intention of allowing him to use her as bait for luring Kelly back to him. Not to think, the Lord hated the sin of presumption.

It was not presumptuous to assume that Kelly had won Paul; it was foolish to assume that Paul would now renege on his commitment to Kelly, because she wished Paul would prefer her over Kelly. Paul had a lot of good qualities, but did he think the same about her, apart from seeing her as a tool to make Miss Shinebond jealous, perhaps?

If Kelly had found favor in Paul's sight, would the Lord change that? On the other hand, was it possible that in choosing Kelly, Paul might have listened to ungodly counsel?

If Kelly was not the one, who else could measure up to Paul's high expectations, not to think of his parents'?

She wished she could speed up her relocation process. One potential employer had given her a tentative response. They too had requested her to contact them again after she had completed her doctorate. That left her in limbo.

Determined not to get too excited about the potential employers or to let Paul distract her from her goal, when she arrived home that evening, she listed five more potential companies to query before the end of the week and drafted individualized query letters to their business specialties.

63

The sound of scraping on wood floor filled the hall. Men dashed back and forth, moving heavy furniture; women scrambled to set up the food.

Lily checked a few more dishes, including her curried chicken dish. Since five thirty, the women had turned the kitchen into a steam-room of sweet aromas so thick it drew a smile from every man who ventured in.

Sharon ducked her head in to check on the ovens and microwaves.

"We have enough. We should manage," Laurel replied.

Sensing Sharon's concern, Lily asked, "What still needs warming?"

"We have enchilada, lasagna, curried chicken, fried chicken, egg rolls, rice and a few other hot dishes," Laurel ticked off her fingers.

"Great! Why don't we leave those until the last moment, then we can warm them up as Paul is closing his presentation?" she suggested.

"Good idea. Okay, team, let's carry the cold dishes out and set them up on the tables." Laurel led her team to the dining room.

"Linda and I will set out the desserts." She also explained that Raya, the other team member, was still stuck in traffic.

She checked ice cream flavors packed inside the freezer, then she pulled out bowls of fruit salads, leaving the ice creams till later.

"We'll handle the salads. We still need to chop up a few things. It should go pretty fast." Marjorie stepped up to the salad section.

In a blink, the dishes and desserts covered the harvest decorated tables.

Soon, cars rolled in, as streams flow into the sea. Did they come because they loved to see what God was doing in East Africa, or because Paul was the one presenting the video? Probably both. Paul's popularity had not waned, though he was favoring her now, if only for a moment.

It was a given that Pastor Tim and his wife would come, but that all the associate pastors and their wives also came, spoke volumes about Paul.

What's a video, without work friends? Bill, Sheila, Phil and a few of Paul's other associates whom Sharon had invited, sat toward the middle.

Lily waited for Bernice and Alex to park, glad that they came.

To open the evening, Pastor Tim introduced Paul and gave him the floor. Like a natural, Paul stepped to the podium. First, as an icebreaker, he cracked jokes about gaffes he had made when he arrived in Kenya, gaffes such as showing up at a dinner invitation of new friends——wife Ugandan and husband Kenyan——whom he had met at church——attired in jeans——only to walk into a semi-formal business dinner party.

To everybody's delight, he showed a fifteen-minute video of the missionary school and a Christian center that the Kenyan believers had set up to help orphaned children. He did not forget interesting people whom he had met——village pastors with few worldly possessions, but lots of contagious joy; young children with hope shining out of their eyes——each with a dream of becoming a doctor, a nurse, a teacher, or a business man or woman, one day. Finally, a short, but very appropriate video of the newly created BF&S office in a high-rise building in Nairobi.

The congregation, "Oohed" and "Wowed," watching a professionally made video of Serengeti and other game parks he had visited——lions curled up with their cubs, herds of the wildebeest and the wild trekking along the plains, with their young ones jumping and prancing around—— demonstrating another career Paul could easily add to his résumé.

To close, he asked the guests for a free-will offering, the money which would be earmarked for the East African special projects.

Kelly had sat close to the podium, bedecked in her version of "Friday casual," cheered on by her friends, but often during the presentation, Lily felt Paul was talking to her. She had sat in the back, yet his eyes pierced through the crowd, into her soul. She tried to keep her expectations in check.

All too soon, the organizers had to leave to warm up the dishes.

The last dish——enchilada——had made its way to a spot between fried chicken and lasagna, when the first group of guests entered the hall.

Paul finally entered. He and Jonathan sat at Pastor Tim's table along with an unfamiliar couple, who sat with their backs to Lily's table.

To complicate matters, a new girl sat between him and Jonathan. Lily had never seen him so relaxed with a woman before. Was she another Kelly he had been hiding or a new rival? How could she ever compete with that?

For a brief moment, she felt jealous; but then she remembered how kind Paul had been to her lately. Moreover, would Sharon and Linda be sitting at her table, if the new girl meant more to Paul?

Her two friends, however, seemed unaware of anything amiss. Bernice and Alex too, were relaxed and enjoying the evening.

She didn't know how it happened, but sometime during the evening, Sharon said in a low tone, "I'd like to introduce you to some people, Lily."

She looked up surprised, "Who?"

"Come." Sharon side-stepped her question.

She followed Sharon, her mind a whirl of speculation. To her dismay, Sharon approached the Pastor's table. The mysterious couple turned around.

Sharon smiled, arcane. "This is Lily Nyaber, the lady I've been talking about. She's from East Africa. Mr. and Mrs. Kaarlyle, Jonathan's parents."

At the realization that she was meeting Paul's uncle and aunt, Lily's heart skipped a beat. She averted her eyes from Paul.

"I'm delighted to meet you," Mrs. Kaarlyle said.

Mr. Kaarlyle got up. She returned his gaze steadily. She was looking at the older version of Jonathan——that careless, laughing eyes, that gave the impression that a hilarious joke was seconds away.

Jeremy's face too was unfathomable. "Sharon definitely did not do full justice to all the details. A pleasure to meet you." He veiled his face, mindful of the Van Clydens' warning that she had eluded them after Paul's video presentation. Too bad, they did not see the girl. If he was not married and older, he would resolve this matter very quickly. He coughed to hide his emotions.

"Yes. Lily's a treasure to ENC——always ready to help," Pastor Tim said.

"I can imagine. She looks like a responsible young lady," he replied.

"And this is Ingrid, Jonathan's sister," Sharon introduced the new girl.

64

Paul buttoned his cuffs, nervously checking his watch, as though it would disappear into thin air. East African Time Zone was becoming a memory. He had spent the first week after he returned alternating between riding his stationary bike and jogging on the treadmill in the middle of the night.

He made a quick job of his morning routine, selected a pin stripe gray business suit to match his white shirt and red tie of discreet patterns. With a three-day Veterans' weekend coming up, he had back-to-back meetings before he left for the weekend——hopefully, by three o'clock.

As was Martin Luther's habit, the busier he got, the more he longed to pray for two hours before starting his day; but by the time he had dressed up, he had ten minutes to spare——better than nothing.

On his way out, he grabbed his overnight bag.

◆ ◆ ◆

At BF&S, Paul reverse-parked in the space closest to the exit and strode to his office, the epitome of an executive with a full day before him.

Strategy-building sessions with the East African team, including two people BF&S finally appointed to head the East African office and a local associate from East Africa, kicked off at nine o'clock, the CEO and the other executives in attendance. They all spoke highly of Paul's outstanding leadership during the nine months he headed the project.

Around eleven o'clock, as he was on his way to meet with the finance group, he encountered Shane. Shane turned the corner at the speed of a race course, staring straight ahead. No doubt, Shane was avoiding him and not without cause. Before leaving for his trip, he had made a commitment to be more amicable to him. He prayed for the chance to keep his word.

When the last team meeting was over, he returned to his office, then went in search of a strong cup of tea. He was stirring his tea when Shane walked in. *Not now!* When he prayed for the opportunity to talk to Shane, he had not expected the answer to arrive so soon. He was too busy to spare even a minute to anybody, that moment.

He nodded to him, and headed for the exit. Just then, The Imperials' gospel song started playing in his mind, *"You're the only Jesus some will ever see . . ."* He rummaged within himself——if not now, then when? He may not like Shane, but at least Shane invited him out to lunch. When had he ever invited him for a cup of coffee or baseball or a Super Bowl game?

Already in the corridor, he retraced his steps to the coffee room. "Shane, I owe you an apology. Things have been crazy this year. With the last-minute switch in the project team, I'd barely enough time to get my immunizations. Look, I haven't forgotten. Can I cash that rain check?"

Shane raised his head, sugar spoon midway, his mouth agape.

"I mean, your lunch invitation?" he explained.

"Oh, yes." Shane laughed, uncertain. "Oh yes. Yes! Of course!"

"Well, some of the guys and I will be going to the game the weekend of December the eleven. I have an extra ticket. Of course, if you've other commitments, lunch would be fine. Wednesdays work for me."

"No, no! I wouldn't miss the games for anything. Better than a trip for a burger. Far superior! On a scale of one to ten, a perfect ten!" Shane gushed.

In a whoosh, Paul's heavy burden lifted. Perhaps he had misunderstood Shane. On the other hand, he was not so naïve as to suppose Shane had become a saint overnight——the man would have eliminated him, given the opportunity. But, could Shane's acerbic outlook on life be the result of his experiences? Were his friends ever kind to him, without asking for a favor?

On his way back to his office, he hesitated by Bill's office. They had both been busy, except for occasional quick chat. Hoping he was not interrupting Bill's schedule, he stuck his head in.

Bill was seated at his desk, jacketless. He beamed, as a proud father who had witnessed his son score the winning goal. "Hey! Good job!"

"Hey! Same to you too. I hear you did an excellent job holding down the fort." He sat down and crossed his legs.

Bill waved off his hand. "No problem. It was a pleasure. You'd run such a tight ship, all I'd to do was mark time. Your staff were very well prepped and up to speed on all the critical issues."

"I'd a good teacher. Listen, I need some catching up on office gossip——oops, I mean . . . news. Of course we don't gossip, we just update each other on relevant local and world news." He rubbed his nose. Bill chuckled. "We got a bit of it on the field, but obviously a lot went on."

Bill motioned for him to close the door, then he started swiveling his chair, and snapping his red suspenders. "Consider what I'm about to tell you classified news. Well, where would you like me to start?"

"Let's start with Rod."

"Unfortunate situation, but we all saw it coming."

"So, BF&S finally took a stand?"

"BF&S took a stand. Phil told us you tried to help. The executives appreciate your effort. Without your intervention, we'd have been hit at some point. Rod had no clue of the risks——the potential for lawsuits that could cripple a company . . . thought he was above the law. So, we'd to let him go."

"Sorry to hear that, but it was for the best. How's he doing? Has anybody kept in touch?"

"Phil has. Apparently he got another job. Of course, due to personnel policies, we usually don't disclose why an employee was released. With his charm, it wasn't difficult for him to land another job."

"All's well that ends well."

"Amen. The rest you heard——a possible grand jury and so forth."

"No!" Paul pulled his chair forward, stunned.

A pregnant silence followed. Then pacing the floor, Bill updated him. In the months after he had turned over the files containing evidence of his discovery and during his absence, Bill and some powerful allies had been busy. A major shuffling of upper management culminated in a few hasty exits. Since his discovery was all in the line of duty, Bill shielded him from publicity, knowing he would appreciate that. For all purposes, those employees who had some inkling were told that the financial irregularities were discovered through an external audit. "You know about the hasty exits, of course."

"Of course."

"There'll be a grand jury, since several people are suspected."

"How much are we talking about?"

"Ten or more years of loot. They cruised under the radar, using a well-oiled process that circumvented BF&S' system. Naturally, Shane was on the take, probably more from misguided ambition——promise of promotions and so forth. He made a deal with the authorities. I shudder to think where it would've all ended, hadn't you intervened——our heads most likely on the chopping block or worse . . . bankruptcy, ultimately."

He whistled. "I just invited him to the ball game."

"On the contrary, we'd appreciate all the appearance of normalcy. Few know what's going on. No better illusion of business as usual than an evening at the ball game. Once more, you've come to BF&S' rescue."

He shook his head, in disbelief.

"By the way, he was hospitalized during summer——some sort of infection."

"Really?"

"Mhmm. Close call." Bill brushed his hair with his hands. "So, tell me about East Africa——the game parks, the Nile, the great lakes, Mt. Kilimanjaro——all the major attractions. Great videos last Sunday! Those were some of the best videos I've ever seen of Africa, bar none. Sarah and Brittany can't wait to see more pictures of the game reserves. Sheila and I would love to have you over for dinner. How does first Friday of December sound?"

He accepted. Relieved that BF&S would shield his name, he recounted his trip again——providing more details about the new office.

Bill briefed him on all the other important news about the firm that occurred during his absence. BF&S was thinking about opening up another office back east, though they had not yet decided which city . . . Chicago, Philadelphia or some other more relaxed city?

By mid-afternoon, Paul left the office looking forward, guardedly, to a weekend with his parents. He queued a piano classics CD and Duke Ellington's Newport Festival Suite 1956 for the long drive and hit the road. The holiday traffic was already flowing like streams out of the city. As he guessed Pacific Coast Highway was also another nail-biting treat, adding to his anxiety.

65

Paul pulled up and parked in front of the house. Like a wary cat, he eyed the front door and plodded up the front steps, ambivalent, wishing to get upstairs without bumping into his parents, yet hopeful that his parents were downstairs. He opened the front door and walked straight into his mother's outstretched arms.

She clung to him. Her slim body trembled so much that he could feel the tremor through her sweater. After a year of anguish, she seemed incredulous that she was holding him in her arms, even though he knew she must have remained on her knees many nights, praying, as she used to do when he was a teenager.

Tears flowed down her cheeks. "Thank you! Thank you! Thank you, Lord!" She untangled her arms from around him, and dabbed her eyes, then she held on to his arm with one hand and traced every contour on his face with her other hand.

He swallowed hard. In the silence, Percy could be heard scratching the patio door.

"Honey, he's here," his mother finally announced to his father.

He shifted. Seeing her in tears wrenched his heart, but much still remained to be patched up with his father. He prayed it would not be a heavy weekend. Above all, he did not want his mother upset anymore, nor did he wish for another round with his father. More freedom in making important decision concerning his future was all he wanted.

If he had to give up Lily, he would, but not without first reasoning with his father and this time, he would explain everything to Lily in person, beg her to remain friends, then he would probably never marry.

A whiff of his father's aftershave lotion floated downstairs. He lifted his eyes and saw him standing at the top of the stairs, his semi-damp hair glistened in the chandelier lights. Remorse, anxiety and something that resembled hope, emanated from his soul. His father came down slowly, hesitated at the foot of the stairs and appealed to his eyes.

His mother freed the space between them and he took the first step toward the man who had fathered him and been his primary mentor all his life.

In one big stride, his father clasped him firmly around the shoulders and said, "Good to see you, son. I assume you've settled in. Is everything finally getting back to normal?"

"Yes. We're preparing to close the books."

A moment of awkward silence followed. He waited for his father to say something; he in turn struggled for words.

"Well, would you prefer to take a shower before dinner?" his mother broke the silence.

"Yes. I think I'll do that. Thanks, Mum."

"You're skin and bones. They must've starved you in East Africa."

"Hardly, Mum. They've some pretty neat food there."

She patted his chest. "It's chicken cordon bleu. I hope you're hungry."

He went upstairs, unpacked, and took a quick shower. He viewed the ocean from his balcony, reminiscing about his teenage years, and wishing he could linger in his room, but it was impolite to avoid his father. He returned downstairs dressed in jeans and a forest green sweater that dated back to his college days.

The morning papers were on the side table where his father had always placed them every morning for years. He grabbed them and joined him before the family fire, but on second thoughts, he went out to inspect the gardens in the remaining evening sun. About a year had passed since he had seen them.

Minutes afterwards, he heard footsteps behind him. Another faint wisp of cologne announced his father.

"Mum's baby's breath are coming along." He squatted on the ground to observe them at close quarters.

"*Gypsophila*," his father said.

"Give me a Latin name and I couldn't tell a rose from a daisy."

"You should've seen them during the summer. Beautiful white blooms, lighted the place up." His father swept the gardens with his eyes. "This home's missing something."

He too examined the four corners. "Mhmm. May be another shrub. But where would it go?"

"Sure, we could use another shrub in that spot." His father pointed to a bare spot at the south east corner of the garden. "Takes away the austerity. I'll check with your Mum and talk to the gardener. But no," he shook his head, "I don't think that's the problem." His eyes lit up. "Daffodils and . . . children . . . little children playing. That's what daffodils remind me of."

He rubbed his neck. "They certainly would add some life around here." It was at the tip of his tongue to suggest that they could invite his second cousins over for the summer, but he bit his tongue instead.

His father turned and looked at him. "Well?"

He sketched half a grin, but said nothing.

"You know what to do about it. The Van Clydens' clock's ticking."

He wished his father would surrender his dream. Dashing his father's hopes had never been his ambition; neither had prolonging the inevitable.

"Kelly did not work out." He braced himself for a long lecture.

His father snapped off the head of a dead rose that the gardener had missed and examined it from all angles, then he threw it to the ground, and dusted his hands. "I see. Well, at least you tried."

"Thanks, Dad." He wished he could say more, but that was neither the time, nor the place. "About the shrub. What's Mum's favorite? She's got just about everything from London to the Himalayas."

"Lord, please help Igor and Paul get along. I love them both——they're your gifts to me." Charlotte whispered over the chicken cordon bleu.

After months of trepidation, Igor had finally agreed also to surrender. She was praying things would remain jovial throughout the three-day weekend. Igor was determined to resolve all issues before Sunday evening. Without pushing Paul too much, he wanted a united family by Christmas, the old Paul, the son he knew.

Paul was the apple of her eyes, he in turn loved and respected her. The last thing she wanted was a chasm between them. She understood the issues at stake. As a parent, she related to Igor's fear of the unknown girl, but, as a woman, she empathized with her.

In Paul leaving her and Igor and clinging to his wife, what principle would he be breaking? Male and female God had created them. Yet she couldn't ignore her motherly angst. What were her foundations for such anxiety? Marjorie's opinion? According to Marjorie, the girl had a solid character. The better Marjorie got acquainted with her, the more she proved to be a woman of deep faith, much more than many of the other girls Paul had dated. If Marjorie was right, why had she assumed the worst without even knowing her?

She wished they had arrived earlier at ENC that Sunday. Embarrassed, she realized she did not know the young woman's name. She had avoided discussing her with Paul. Marjorie volunteered much information, but she, too, did not mention her by name.

Angela had referred to the video presentation evening by saying, "Sharon introduced us," without mentioning names. The Kaarlyles had hinted that they should reconsider their position and have more faith. Jeremy coughed a lot and kept on mumbling about how "The Lord works in mysterious ways . . .."

As Paul's mother, she had taught him everything a mother could. She was confident that Paul would heed her counsel, regardless of who his bride might be. It was up to Igor now.

By intuition, she knew that weekend would be the watershed for them to define their commitment to *the Living God who demands faith before seeing; obedience before the evidence; sacrifice before the sacrificial lamb——drawing, stretching, molding, shaping, until those who obey find themselves on a new level——deeper, richer, wiser——a tower of strength, faith and encouragement to others.*

"Mum, can I help?"

She turned. Paul was leaning against the door, watching her.

"I'm almost there. The table's already set——perhaps, a carafe of water. I think I forgot to take it out."

Paul filled a crystal jug with filtered water and took it to the dinette.

She followed him around with her eyes, until the timer went off. While the chicken cordon bleu rested, she carried her other dishes to the dinette.

Once everybody was seated, she gripped the hands of both men and prayed, choking over every word, "Lord, I don't know where to begin—— thank you for bringing Paul home. I don't know what else to say, except thank you! Thank you! Thank you!"

Igor prayed, more subdued, but he too expressed his gratitude for having his family back together and asked that whatever happened over the weekend, would be according to the Lord's will and to His glory. "Lord, please bless us as we partake this food to the nourishment of our bodies. Bless our home and bless this evening and the rest of this weekend . . . Amen."

For his mother's sake, Paul took a more generous helping than the knots in his stomach permitted.

His father cut a chunk of chicken, pondered it in his mouth for a while, then swallowed. "Bill's girls are grown up now."

"Where does time go? They promise to be quite beautiful, just like Sheila," his mother added.

"They're pretty neat girls. Bill's very proud of them," he said.

"He should be," his father agreed.

They labored through supper. He and his father skated with their words, as would two high-ranking diplomats on the last leg of a peace talk, with their war tanks standing by, waiting to be deployed, in case of an impasse.

His mother chased chicken around her plate, occasionally joining in the conversation with some light chatter.

At last, the long dinner drew to an end. Most of the chicken cordon bleu remained in the serving dish or lay on the plate, diced to pieces. The rest of his mother's gourmet dishes suffered the same fate.

His mother started clearing the table.

"Mum, you work too hard. I'll take care of that." He cleared the table and stacked the dishes in the dishwasher.

"All right. I'll get the coffee." She fussed with the cupboards, looking for his favorite mug. It was in the last cabinet.

A plate of his favorite chocolate chip cookies landed in the middle of the family silver heirloom, surrounded by personalized coffee mugs.

His father had been hovering by. Before she could lift the tray, he stuck out his hands. "Here, honey, I'll take that."

"Thanks, honey. I think I'm getting spoiled here."

His father grinned, took the tray to the den and added another log in the firegrid.

After serving coffee, his mother backed into her rocker, her eyes on his father. His father seemed to understand.

Igor had understood, all right. If he blew it, Charlotte would break his leg! During the months that Paul was in East Africa, he had woken up in the middle of the night and heard her blowing her nose, hiding her tears. If Paul dashed out again into the night as he did the year before, as sure as he sat in his Lazy-Boy, he would end up in the hospital emergency room, hobbling on one leg, clutching ice over his head, thanks to his lovely, docile, godly wife!

Paul ran upstairs with light steps as he used to, arousing hope in him that the old Paul was back. Soon, Paul returned with gift bags, filled with artifacts from East Africa, including small carvings of game-park animals and batik paintings. One fascinating painting, in particular, he explained was made from the bark of a special Ugandan tree, called "mutuba."

He lifted a set of animals seated at a roundtable, playing chess, and examined it from every angle. "Where did you get this?"

"Uganda. They've stands of crafts all over the city, but I visited this tourist row at the Uganda Theatre. They've some pretty neat things there. I thought the prices were decent, but the Ugandans said the price were fixed for the tourists."

"I can imagine. I'll take this to my office."

"Oh no, you won't. That's for the den," Charlotte protested.

"I guessed as much. It was worth a try." He surrendered it.

"Here Dad, you can take the Maasai warrior. With that little fella standing guard at the corner of your desk, no one will mess with you." Paul handed him a one–foot high statue.

"That should do it." He grabbed the statue. "Here, put it in my brief case, before Mum changes her mind."

Paul strolled to the study room and left him and his mother haggling over what else should or should not end up in his office.

When Paul returned, they peppered him with questions about East Africa——the people, the food, the climate, tourism——then came a full minute of silence.

Finally, he locked eyes with his wife again for a moment. She excused herself to work on her Christmas holidays plans.

Paul added another log on the fire, which was already burning bright.

Out of the patio, Percy's moans persisted.

"I suppose you could let him in," his mother said from the kitchen. "He missed you a lot."

Paul opened the patio door. Percy slinked in with a wounded look, dumping all the guilt he could on him, for refusing to go out and play ball before dinner.

"I get the point. Sorry." Paul coaxed him down at his feet.

Percy complied.

Paul flipped through channels, seemingly disinterested. Igor watched him, his hands cupped behind his head.

Percy lifted his head, then flattened it on the ground and stuck out his nose. Occasionally he flapped his ears——one eye shut, the other, scrutinizing their faces——as if waiting for something to happen.

Finally, Igor cleared his throat.

Percy stopped flapping his ears, stretched his legs in front of him and opened both eyes.

Paul also stopped fidgeting with the remote control, crossed his arms and slid back, letting his legs spread out in front of him.

Igor sensed Paul had closed the door or was getting ready to shut him out. "You indicated that BF&S practically ordered you to go to East Africa, but I understand even before that, you'd decided to go on a summer mission?" he asked.

"Something of the sort," Paul replied.

"Is that an overture to something else?"

"No."

"But you're considering it?"

"I'm open."

"Mmm." He stared at Paul's forbidding profile, rubbing his chin. "Even if that means working abroad?"

"Mhmm."

He rubbed his chin again. He wanted to heed his wife's advice and let Paul be the adult he had become; but he also wanted to know what lay ahead——would Paul stay or would he leave? Did he still have a son or had he already lost him?

"Would this be about what we, um, discussed last fall?"

Paul sketched a chuckle and flipped channels again. Finally, he said, "Not necessarily," and replaced the remote control on the side table.

"Mmm."

Percy rolled over to his side, closed his eyes and stretched himself to his full length. At his master's feet, he lay docile, feigning sleep. He seemed to be enjoying participating in the discussion.

A dog never really gets consulted on important family discussions; normally, he figures it out for himself later and sometimes, at a great cost.

Percy grunted, imitating him, opened his eyes just a squint and shut them again.

"But you would definitely go abroad, given the opportunity?" Igor asked, after another long pause.

Paul ruffled Percy's fur.

Percy rewarded him with a one-eye peek, flicked his ears, then flattened them back again.

"Well?" Igor asked.

"There's nothing to discuss, sir," Paul replied.

Igor stretched out his legs. "You're right, but I beg to disagree."

"I'm sorry, I don't understand."

Igor crossed and uncrossed his legs, looking for a more comfortable position. "I know from the grapevine and from what you mentioned this evening that you did your best, for which I'm grateful. But I also know that you're not your usual self. Now that concerns me."

Paul appeared to be studying the mosaic patterns on the carpet.

Igor would sooner bang his head against a steel wall than talk to Paul in this mood. Not since childhood, had Paul offered such a square chin. He shifted again and crossed his legs. "Is there something you'd like to discuss?"

Paul kept his eyes fixed on one spot, and alternated scratching Percy's ears and rubbing his back.

Igor sighed, angry with himself. If he could roll back the clock, he would zip his mouth and pray more. Why didn't he heed Charlotte's warning? Months ago, when rumors started circulating, Charlotte had warned him to wait and spend more time praying about it. He had to be the man. He rued his Nordic blood.

He had worked hard to provide for his family. Paul was his sole heir. All the hopes he had invested in him, and the grandchildren . . .

Throughout his adult life, he had tried to put his faith first and sought guidance to lead his family as best he could. Often, he had prayed for grace to love his family and other people. Was this a test? What if he won the battle and lost Paul, as Jeremy had warned him? What type of an example would that be?

He selected his words carefully, "I know that things haven't been very open between us lately, but I want you to understand. . ."

Paul's veins stood out.

Percy shifted until his nozzle rested across his shoes.

Igor shoved his hands in his pockets, tense. "Paul, son, I can't live your life. But some things make more sense as we mature." He left his chair and stared out of the window into the night, as if to ferret out the truth. "Son, I don't want you to get hurt."

Paul took a deep breath and jutted his chin.

Igor tossed his hands in the air and refocused his eyes on a lighted statue supposed to mimic the likeness of the Arch-Angel Gabriel towering in the air, surrounded by water fountains of four kneeling horses——facing the four corners of the earth——spewing water out of their nozzles. He had designed the water fountain to be the focal point from the window.

"You can lead a horse to the river," he muttered.

Paul glanced at him and grinned, then he lowered his eyes again. A silver coin that the cleaning lady had missed, glittered in the light. He flipped it in the air and caught it in the palm of his hand.

The Lord had given him a son all right, as stubborn as a mule——a Van Clyden to the core. "I regret that Sunday didn't turn out as your mother and I'd hoped."

Paul adjusted his collar the way a man straightens his tie when he sees a beautiful woman and knows he's in trouble.

A memory of over thirty years ago stirred in his mind. With a light twinkle, he said, "Mmm. That bad. Eh?"

Paul looked at him and for the first time, he saw a ray of hope. He had no idea what would become of his family, or how he would hold up his head among his peers. On the other hand, he had experienced what life would be like, without Paul.

Remembering Jeremy's advice, he ploughed on. No turning back——to live by faith was to gain his son.

"I do appreciate your trying with Kelly." He returned to his chair. "You'd said you wanted to strike out on your own? I've no objection to your trying your wings; but I want you to know, your mother and I love you very much."

At last Paul opened his mouth and began speaking, cautiously, "Dad, I respect you, but I also covet your understanding."

"Paul, you don't know what you're getting into," he started to protest then caught himself.

"Oh, I think I do, Dad. I think I'm beginning to get a pretty good grip of how things really are."

"Then why, son?"

Compared to all the other girls, this girl had hit Paul hard. If he succeeded, it would end only one way——in marriage.

Despite the uncertainty, Paul had also made it clear that he would prefer to get their blessings first. As a parent, that gave him some leverage, but not the kind of power he would like to have over a son whom he loved.

"Besides the LORD, you and Mum, there's nobody I hold in higher esteem. Dad, I see no reason for concern. She's totally dedicated, well mannered, highly educated and articulate. It's wrong to make comparisons, but, in my opinion, I believe she has the better qualities. Given other scenarios, she would top the list."

"There're so many good girls out there and feelings change." Igor took another risk, knowing Paul could slam the door in his face forever.

"You mean snap out of it? I agree she's rather attractive——beautiful in fact. So was Abraham's Sarah. Are beauty and godliness incompatible? Dad, with someone like her, I believe I could do anything . . . go into any line of ministry . . . answer the LORD's call at a moment's notice and she would be my most devoted cheerleader. In striving to serve, what matters most to me is strength and support from those who're important to me. Dad, you taught me life's about commitment."

Igor scratched his throat, worried that Paul had underestimated what it would entail to marry out of class.

From the kitchen, Charlotte cocked her ears for three very long minutes. Nothing but silence emanated from the family room, yet she sensed it would be too soon to return to the den. As she was standing up, she heard Igor murmur again. She refilled her coffee mug and continued perusing through her home-keeping magazine, in between checking on her baking and praying for better days to come.

"You're still young. Socialize more, before, um, making the most important decision of your life," Igor said.

Paul leveled his eyes on his father. "Dad, how old were you when you and Mum got married?"

Igor chuckled. "I knew you'd ask. Twenty-four. I was twenty-four when your mother and I got engaged and just under twenty-six when we married."

"And, have you ever regretted it?"

"Of course not!"

Paul's lips twitched. "I had good mentors."

Igor grinned, and rubbed his nose.

"Great as the other opportunities are," Paul continued, "I . . . um . . . don't feel the same. I don't doubt that they are just as good for other men, but I, . . ." he rubbed his neck. "Dad, I'm not a cash cow!"

"I didn't realize that's how you feel, son. Naturally, some people may treat you with deference. It comes with the territory," Igor said, surprised.

"I'm not saying she's perfect. Neither am I. And I know quite a few men prefer the girl next door. But she appears to have many of the qualities I'm searching for. The scary thing's I know she's independent, as she has demonstrated. I wouldn't blame her, if she has moved on, given how I treated her."

"Son, I'm having a hard time understanding your point of view." Igor started down the same path that had caused the impasse before. "Nehemiah states that such alliances were forbidden."

"Chapter and verse, Dad." Paul shifted to the edge of his chair.

"How about chapter thirteen?"

"Context matters."

"And?"

"That wasn't the intention of the chapter."

"Oh? Explain yourself."

"In Nehemiah, God's concerned with the spiritual condition that would've resulted from such alliances. I don't believe He'd have cared who the Israelites allied themselves with, if they all worshipped Him, Adonai."

"But Nehemiah said their children were bilingual," he parried.

"I see it differently. These were pagan women and they caused the Jews to sin——case in point, King Solomon." Paul sounded confident of his footing.

"That doesn't explain Nehemiah's objection."

"Dad, I believe he was referring to mixed worship. The language of Ashdod was probably the practice of worshipping the Philistines' idol and so forth. In other references, the Lord makes His position clear."

"Chapter and verse, son. Chapter and verse." He straightened up, preparing to debate Paul as in the old times.

"Deuteronomy seven, verse three; Joshua twenty-three, verse twelve; Ezra nine, verses twelve to fourteen, especially verse fourteen; Judges, Second Kings, and more, specifically, Malachi two, verse eleven," Paul ticked off his fingers.

Percy lifted his head and wagged his tail, as if to say, "At last, some action!"

"All right. All right." Igor put up his hands. "Give me a quote."

Percy put his head back on the carpet.

Paul thought for a moment and said, "Let's take Deuteronomy. God told the children of Israel not to ally themselves with the Canaanites, lest the Canaanites turned their sons away from following Him."

"Okay. Give me another."

"Joshua's a reminder of God's warning. Ezra's the consequence the Israelites experienced after centuries of ignoring the Lord's warnings."

"Uh-huh. Uh-huh."

"In the same vein, passages in Kings and Chronicles testify to the apostasy and abominations that ensued, when the Israelites adopted the foreign idols of the surrounding nations."

Igor nodded.

Paul pressed on. "Then in Malachi, the Lord rebuked Judah for profaning His holy temple. At no point, Dad, did He mention the outside of the vessel. He was always concerned about the heart or what could become the state of our soul, and hence, our relationship with Him."

"I see."

"Consider, Dad, that English's not the original languages. So, if I pursue your point of view, then all of us who worship in English would be sinning in the Lord's sight, regardless of our convictions."

Igor stared at Paul. Enlightened as he was, he had always assumed that English was universal and by tacit agreement, approved by heaven.

Paul smiled. "Relax, Dad."

"Galatians?"

"Yes. Three, twenty-six to twenty-nine."

"All right, but that still doesn't explain Ham." Igor prompted Paul softly, wishing to prolong the discussion.

"What about Ham, Dad?"

"Noah cursed him. I believe that curse still stands."

"I beg to disagree. Despite theories and speculations, I don't believe anybody knows beyond a shadow of doubt, where all of Ham's descendants are located today. We can only speculate."

"But you don't deny they exist, like the descendants of Shem and Japheth?"

Paul nodded. "I don't. But, even if we could pinpoint their location, all believers are free under the new covenant, and, there's been so many intermarriages through the centuries. So, if a descendant of Ham married a descendant of Japheth, and they have a son, would the Lord punish the poor boy for Ham's sake or bless him for Japheth's sake?"

"Aha," Igor cried, "don't slip that one by me. Chapter and verse!"

Percy jumped up, sat on his hind legs and wiggled his tail.

Paul grinned. "Galatians three . . . thirteen and fourteen."

"Go on. Go on," Igor could not conceal his excitement. For twelve months, he had coveted and prayed for this day.

"Don't you see? Christ is either able to liberate every tribe and kindred or none. He came to set all human beings free——as many as are willing to ask for His help——not just parts of the human race."

Igor saw Paul's soul for the first time. But for the surroundings, Paul could have been a pastoral candidate, giving his trial preaching, where every word and every gesture, counted. Despite their frequent debates, never having attended Paul's classes, he was amazed at how much he had grown from the new convert who returned from camp years ago to the mature young man who now sat before him.

Paul pressed on, "Think Dad. What type of a god would create a world full of beautiful men and women, sacrifice his own son to give them opportunity to choose eternal life, then turn around and deny them the freedom to fulfill his first mission——the Genesis mission?"

Igor stared at the Arabian rug beneath his feet.

"We live in temporal bodies, Dad. I pray that I would not dishonor the LORD. Besides my duty to serve, I can't think of a better way to honor Him than by living His original plan for mankind."

"I find some parts of Corinthians ambiguous——who has the gift, and who has not. Apostle Paul can be convoluted sometimes." He threw Paul a curve.

Paul grinned. "How about Hebrews thirteen, four? Paul also makes it clear that living holy is as critical. Does God contradict Himself?"

Igor nodded. "No. You're right. You've a point. But I still think there should be a clear line of demarcation in certain areas." He grasped at straw, afraid to bring up the subject of inheritance again. "Yes, we should embrace holy lifestyles, but why are there tribes and kindreds?"

"Why, sir? What was the point of all your teachings? You and Mum taught me to honor God and choose my friends wisely. Had I violated those principles, I'd understand. Knowing what I know, how can I continue to defend boundaries torn down when the veil was split in two? How could I live with myself? Dad, I believe in every broken heart of a Lily is the bleeding heart of the Lord. Never forget that, Dad!"

In total agreement, Percy barked out loud.

Igor gasped. "Paul! Son! Percy! Quiet down!"

Percy grunted and fixed one eye back on Paul.

Paul came to himself, sat down again, and cradled his head. Percy snuggled close to him.

In her kitchen office, Charlotte bowed her head and pleaded that her husband and son would remain calm, but kept to her seat.

The grandpa clock at the corner ticked away the minutes.

Paul restrained his frustration. "I'm sorry sir. I didn't mean to raise my voice. I just wish I could communicate better." He hesitated. "I'm convinced that when I consider foreigners as less than I am——speak with an accent, have less possessions, or may the Lord forgive me, assume because they don't speak Queen's English, they must be dumb——I become an obstacle to the Way, not a beacon on a hill. Dad, you taught me to be real. When I was in East Africa, I learnt that other people can see through a phony just like that." He snapped his fingers. "They may receive my charity, but deep down, they know it's just that——charity!"

Igor rubbed his arms. How many hours had he poured out his heart, praying that Paul would grow up to be a man of principles? "So, you believe that how we conduct ourselves tie into the Great Commission?"

"Yes, sir. I fear if we continue to differentiate against other believers, we might discourage them. I am not saying we should turn a blind eye to their vices, nor am I saying we should pursue an all-inclusive trend——where no one's held accountable; ——I'm referring to the true followers."

"Where're we now? John?"

"Yes."

"Twelve?"

"Yes!"

"He promised that if He is lifted up, He will draw all people to Himself, as He was talking about His imminent resurrection." Igor murmured.

"Yes, Dad. 'By this shall they know that you're my disciples. . .,' the emphasis is on disciples——those sold out on Truth——"

"The New Commandment, John, thirteen."

"Yes Dad! Yes!" Paul exclaimed, "Don't you see? Am I making any sense at all, sir? I wish I could communicate better."

"I believe you have, son."

Paul raised his eyes, a bit surprised. "You do sir?"

"I am not saying I'm completely there, but I do see your point."

During the early years of Paul's conversion, he and Charlotte had toiled to help him mature——driving him to vacation Bible schools, paying for

Christian camps and going on family retreats. After all their efforts, he should have been proud to reap the fruits of their labor, instead, he was amazed at how much Paul had matured. Why? Perhaps in his subconscious mind, he had expected him to become little more than a good citizen, thus, under-estimating the power of the Holy One.

Behind their back, the Almighty had been working on Paul——chipping away at the rough edges——perfecting, revealing a masterpiece in progress.

He slumped back in his chair. A light went on. Paul was a gift entrusted to him and Charlotte to nurture; but the gift belonged to God to be shared with the world. But why him? Why should he, Igor, sacrifice his son?

He remembered the months when he fretted instead of trusted. Those same thoughts still hounded him during nights when he worried about Paul, until he relinquished them all to the Most High.

"The Lord God who gave us a son, demands total submission——an unwavering, singular love that can only be demonstrated by relinquishing he whom we love. And only in that total surrender can we unlock the bottomless chest of His bountiful treasure——the Giver who can never be out-given," he had encouraged himself on nights, when he thought his wife was asleep.

Always an eloquent man, generously endowed with equanimity, he fumbled with what to way. "I'm sorry, son, for causing you so much grief. Marriage has its moments——even the most suited still depend on grace and hard work. I'm confident that you'll make the right choice through His guidance and remain committed as your mother and I have through the years. I know we raised a good and sensible son."

"Then I have your blessings, sir?"

"Yes. You have my full support," he stammered.

"Thank you, Dad!" Paul's voice cracked. He took a step and another toward his father.

Igor felt good hugging Paul again, without reserve.

A car headlight flashed through the curtains, as Paul started on his way to the kitchen to tell his mother the good news.

66

The four occupants of the jeep were unusually quiet and had been for the greater part of their short trip to the Van Clydens' home.

"For heaven's sake, I don't think it'll be that bad," Angela said.

Jeremy turned the wheel, but said nothing.

"Oh, come off it, honey! What happened between you and your father's not necessarily a precursor to how other people resolve conflicts with their children. Igor loves Paul too much to let this fester for years. If you walk through that door with that long face, it could make things worse."

Jeremy rubbed his cheek, always jovial, seldom did he use that gesture. "I suppose, I'm not so much concerned about Igor's ability to bridge the chasm, than about Paul. When he left home last autumn, he was hurting. We could've lost him on the freeway, but for grace. A child alienated is sometimes harder to win than an army. We need the grace to intervene."

"Dad, Paul's more resilient than you think. He's one of the most sensible and humble men I know," Jonathan said. "If Uncle Igor meets him half way, I think he'll rally around. If not, I believe he's also prepared to accept Uncle Igor's position and move on into full time missionary work."

Ingrid agreed. "And, we've already prayed, Dad. It will be alright."

"May the Lord grant it!" Jeremy pulled up at the Van Clydens' gate.

♦ ♦ ♦

Paul was in the dinette when doorbell rang. Before he could get there, he heard voices——Uncle Jeremy, Aunt Angela and his father's and two other voices. Ingrid and Jonathan had mentioned nothing about dropping in!

Uncle Jeremy breezed in. "Merry Christmas everybody," he boomed.

"Happy Thanksgiving to you too," Igor replied.

"Well? Are we good?" Jeremy searched Igor's face.

"We're good," he said.

"Alleluia!"

"Praise indeed. All I needed was to surrender."

"There you go. Easy does it! We're all learning."

"I'll say amen to that."

"So, does that mean we can invite ourselves to coffee?"

"Honey!" Angela said in mock horror.

"I came here expecting to look for the exit——turns out I can stay and have some of that delicious cheese cake my sister-in-law always prepares when she knows I'm coming."

"You took the words out of my mouth. Coffee's percolating and the pie's warming." Charlotte re-organized the throw-pillows for her guests.

"See, honey. That's what I call the Van Clyden hospitality. I told you they'd be delighted to see us. And if we're extra nice, we may even get a piece of that pumpkin pie Charlotte's baking for Thanksgiving."

Igor threw his head back and guffawed.

"That's Jeremy for you!" Angela squeezed her husband's arm.

"I'm on a roll——giving thanks, till the New Year," Jeremy said.

"And so you should," Igor agreed.

The two men gazed at each other gravely.

Without further ado, Jeremy sat down in his favorite chair and the leather cushion adjusted to his weight with a swish.

Igor took the adjacent chair.

Jonathan sat with Paul, cognizant that from childhood, Paul hated anyone feeling sorry for him. At any rate, the worst appeared to be over, but to what extent? He assumed a jovial demeanor, as his family had agreed and waited for his Aunt's pie. She had always been the best cook in the family.

In the kitchen, the women prepared the coffee and desserts.

Entertaining used to curl Angela's hair, having spent her youth hammering the keyboard. The second in the family, she felt especially close to Charlotte, her older sibling, for more reasons than one. Oberlin Conservatory of Music offered a Masters degree, so after completing her undergraduate work in music, off to Oberlin she went, determined to become a nationally renowned pianist——as far away from housekeeping as possible.

The lonely hours at Oberlin gave her a jolt. After two years away, she promised herself never again to live so far away from at least one of her siblings. California offered so many opportunities and Charlotte. The decision of where to move after her postgraduate was simple.

The arrival of Jonathan just added one more title to her growing list of wife, mother, teacher and performer. She juggled her duties, until Charlotte chose to stay home after Paul's birth and volunteered to be Jonathan's babysitter. Then along came Ingrid and finally, she got her life's calling. She threw out her busy schedule, except for occasional guest appearances. Her streakish gray hair returned to a natural silky brunette.

After abandoning her dream, she mastered the art of cooking and entertaining, thanks to Charlotte.

Between her and Charlotte, they made a team, driving the little cousins back and forth from soccer games to ballet lessons to judo classes and whatever they fancied. She provided the music lessons and Charlotte tutored. The three children inevitably grew up more like siblings than cousins.

Now here they were playful again——like girls, over plates of apple pies and pumpkin pies and Danish pastries——mothers, looking forward to bright futures for their children.

After serving the room, they settled on the loveseat and continued chatting. Ingrid joined the boys in their corner.

During a lull, Jeremy addressed the room, "You all know our families have been through a lot together, but the Lord's been faithful. He's brought us through every one of them."

"True. I see His hands at work, every day." Igor's eyes rested on Paul.

"Whatever the outcome, my family and I'd like you to know that we're one hundred percent behind you. Not only are we family, but we're here for you, whatever you need." He addressed Paul, "You're a fine young man. We all look up to you. There're many who admire you."

Paul thanked his uncle. After so many difficult months when he thought he had few friends left, it was touching to have their support.

"May we, the faithful, mature beyond this, please, Lord," Angela said.

"Amen," Charlotte affirmed.

"And on that note, time for pie," Igor said.

"I'll second that," Jeremy cheered.

The ladies served the refreshments.

Angela handed a plate to Paul. "We should have an evening when we can quiz you about East Africa. It was a bit crowded at our house and we didn't really get to spend much time with you at all. We enjoyed the event at church, but I feel there's still so much more you've not shared."

Charlotte glowed with pride. "Oh, yes, we were thinking we should do something around Christmas. But you're right, we should have a special for the family. What do you think, Paul?"

"I think it would be nice, Mum." Paul beamed.

Jeremy slid to the edge of his chair. "That would be great. It'd help you decide, Igor, whether East Africa's ready for you."

"Yes. I'd hoped that I would assess the region aggressively, in the near future. Even with emerging e-commerce, I think it's still prudent——common sense really——for one to do a feasibility study of a new business frontier. If I can't work a deal with Abrafimqodesh, I'll look into other alternatives."

"He's very personable. Busy, but not impossible to reach," Paul said.

Twelve eyes stared at him. Jeremy spoke first. "You met Abrafimqodesh?"

"Yes. I did." He mumbled, "My third mission," and then louder, "I called on him in May; he wasn't in the office, so I met with one of his directors. Just before I left, he invited me to a cocktail party at his house. Listen to this, an alcohol–free cocktail party! Can you believe that?"

"You attended a daiquiri-free cocktail party?" Jeremy boomed.

Paul nodded. "Uh-huh. Not a drop."

"At Abrafimqodeshes' house?"

"Uh-huh."

"He's one of us?" Jeremy's eyes popped.

"He appears to be."

"Upon my word! What do you know? Igor, he beat you to it."

Igor's jaw dropped. He realized he had not lost his son——goofed up, yes, but even before he had apologized, Paul had already forgiven him. Fear gripped him——the fear that had he ignored all the wise counsels, he would have alienated Paul and might have lost him forever, when all along, Paul wished for a father who understood him and reciprocated his love.

He shook his head. "The Lord never ceases to amaze me."

Paul radiated with the joy of a son who had done his father proud.

Igor kept staring at him, even as he asked, "Talking about business, how're things at the headquarters?" He turned to Jeremy.

Jeremy gave him a warning look.

Sensing some tension, Angela asked, "What's going on?"

"Nothing to worry about, honey." Jeremy licked his finger.

"Sounds to me that it's a little bit more than nothing to worry about," Angela stared at her husband with her lovely eyes.

"Just the usual stuff," Igor cut in, rubbing his neck.

"What usual stuff?" she persisted, now really intrigued.

Charlotte stared at her husband and Jeremy. "Sounds like you two are hiding something. Whatever it is, you know we'll ferret it out of you."

"Nothing more than some benign process," Jeremy hemmed-hawed.

Angela put her plate down. "How benign are we talking here?"

Jeremy looked at Igor and threw his hands up, "Something to do with NAFTA——just routine stuff."

"NAFTA is about trade agreement, right? What's that got to do with Bridge Eco? Recently, I heard rumors, was that about NAFTA?"

The men fidgeted.

"Not necessarily unless it can be connected to SARA and CERCLA." Igor bridged the awkward silence.

"Right, SARA and CERCLA. That makes a good marriage," Paul joked.

The men chuckled, trying to ease off tension in the room.

"Sara? Who are Sara and Cercla, and why should their marriage cause any concern to anyone? What's going on, Jeremy?" Angela frowned.

"Nothing important, honey, just environmental games companies play. Often it amounts to nothing——the parent company is usually local, and the subsidiary's international or vice versa."

"I get it! SARA——the Superfund Amendments and Reauthorization Act and the Comprehensive——," Jonathan caught his father's eyes and coughed. Though a musician, he was not totally ignorant of his father's business.

The Superfund Amendments and Reauthorization Act (SARA) and the Comprehensive Environmental Response Compensation, and Liability Act (CERCLA), both enacted by Congress, were intertwined by design. If Bridge

Eco-Friendly Corporation was involved in litigation that involved SARA and CERCLA, it could spell trouble, especially, if the offense included violating community safety and health.

"It happens all the time." Paul slid to home base, also trying to rescue his uncle. He poured a cup of coffee slowly——not to drink it, but to appear busy and nonchalant. The problem seemed a lot more serious than his father and uncle were disclosing. "Some processes are really business strategies," he continued, "For example, the pharmaceutical industry——the brand names and generics sue each other to stall and amass market share. Occasionally, the lawsuits are legit. But the environmental arena's young."

"Yes. The environmental arena, especially the NAFTA agreement, is very young. They're making the rules as they go. So, if the parent company is international, then why go to a local court? How much jurisdiction do international courts have anyway?" Ingrid was not sure she understood, or whether her argument was valid, but it was worth a shot to calm her mother.

"So, it's a game companies play to garner market share?" Angela heaved a sigh of relief.

Paul grinned. "Something of the sort. A few may have grounds, but ultimately, someone takes home the dough or case is dismissed. And whoever cries foul in their backyard, could be violating the same laws in someone else's backyard. In the meantime, competitors are tied up."

Charlotte patted Angela's hands. "So much frivolous lawsuits, it's just daunting. I wish there was some way of curtailing them."

Jonathan nodded. "A deterrent like make the losing parties foot the bill."

"That would do it. And on that note, I'll have another pie." Jeremy cut another chunk of pie and threw Paul, Jonathan and Ingrid a grateful glance.

Being the CEO of Bridge Eco-Friendly Corporation and its global subsidiaries gave him many perquisites and a good dose of responsibility. The eco-friendly corporation——a cutting–edge construction company that used high-level technology in the futuristic design and construction of both commercial and residential buildings——had garnered enough market share to solicit unwelcomed attention, though the company used materials compatible with the environment. Another way of saying it operated in the milieu of aggressive competition fueled by political whims, environmentalists' scrutiny, legal rigmarole and morass and survival of the fittest.

Despite the pressure of running such a company, his moral values made him a just taskmaster. It was those values that had bonded his family with Igor's, drawing them closer beyond the bond of being in-laws alone.

He snapped a chunk of his pie.

His wife chuckled. "Last I heard we were doing well on our diet."

"Oh, honey, it's just a little piece——nothing that a turn around the court and a couple of push–ups couldn't handle." He patted his stomach.

"I believe you."

Igor examined his mid-rib. He followed Igor's eyes. His tall athletic build and big bones hid the visible result of the pie from inquiring eyes.

He got up, flexed his muscles, pivoting around. "Not too bad, eh? Five pounds less and I could qualify for the iron man championship. I'll bet you a free golf club, by Valentine, this will be gone." He patted his stomach, sat down, and stuffed another generous chunk of pie in his mouth.

"You're on!" Igor rose to the bet. "Talking about golf, are we still on for tennis this weekend?"

"I wouldn't miss it for anything," he answered, crumbs escaping from his mouth, soliciting an uproar from everybody.

In the midst of the low murmur that followed, the phone rang. Igor answered, "Hello Matt," and stepped out of the room to his study, smiling.

After a polite chat, Matt came to the point. "Well, Marjorie, I and my team just wanted to let you know that we admire Paul deeply. You raised one very fine young man. You've every reason to be proud of him as we all are."

"Thank you. It's good to hear you say that. Charlotte and I've always treasured your support, more so now. We appreciate everything your family's done for us. I'm most grateful for Marjorie's self-less act of taking the lead and of course your children. Thank them on behalf of Charlotte and me. Sometime soon, we plan on visiting with you. In the meantime, we covet your prayers."

"You can count on us." Matt wished him goodnight and sent his regards to Charlotte, apparently unaware that Paul was also at home.

When Igor hung up, the phone rang again. Aaron and Michael came on the line, for a three-way conference call, just to chitchat, they said.

67

The phone rang on and off on Saturday, helping Igor and Charlotte gain a better understanding of grace and love. Friends they had never considered capable of supporting them, extended their hands of friendship, in their own quiet way.

None of their trusted friends gossiped; so, who prompted those who phoned to call them? The only possible answer was grace at work.

Two camps of friends were developing——the camp of those who were regenerated and the camp of those who focused on the outside vessel. Igor was surprised by who was on each list.

Sacrifice? No, he would not be losing Paul, but gaining new friends who understood agapao——holy love——as the Mighty one defined it. Friends who would challenge him to grow, while supporting him and his family through the journey.

Realizing that the true believers did not consider him a failure—— imperfect father though he be——he felt a new sense of freedom.

Whatever doubt he had about Paul's decision, vanished.

He and Charlotte consumed Paul. They went shopping again, even though they had already bought their Christmas gifts. After shopping, they decided to go for a walk along the beach.

"Miracles happen." Charlotte stared at her image in the mirror and tied a tan wool cardigan around her shoulders to complement her chocolate cotton twill jeans and a soft yellow jewel-neck, pullover.

Igor buttoned his t-shirt. "I think we'll be all right." He selected a matching jacket suitable for a walk on the beach and dinner out.

She gave him a long look and a peck on the lips. "The Van Clydens have always had solid heads over their shoulders. More importantly, the Lord is faithful. Don't you forget that."

"I know."

They joined Paul and Percy in the driveway. Percy jumped up to greet them, and took off playing with Igor.

Charlotte seized the moment. Under the pretext of dusting lint from Paul's jacket and straightening his collar, she whispered, "Why don't you invite her to Thanksgiving?"

"Mum! I'm starting from scratch!" Paul replied, shocked. He hadn't secured a steady date with Lily, let alone proposed to her yet.

"I bet you'll get a lot more questions answered faster! Don't worry about him." She pointed over her shoulders in Igor's direction. "I'll handle him."

Paul studied his mother's face for a moment, then tipped his head in consent.

Together, they joined Igor and headed for the beachfront.

Exhilarated at having Paul back, Igor strutted, tall.

Charlotte walked in the middle, leaning on his arm as they strolled along the beach——the epitome of middle–class gentility. She gazed often at Paul, confident and as proud as any mother could be.

Percy ran ahead of them or lagged behind chasing sea gulls——now playful, now racing and jumping in the air——showing off his athletic prowess. Occasionally, he squeezed himself between them to have a better look at Paul and get a nice pat on the back, before taking off again.

Hungry from the fresh ocean air, they took Percy home, fed him, and had a leisurely dinner at a popular family café.

In the grid, the fire crackled. A soft light highlighted a Van Gough strategically centered in the den to add ambience of muted elegance.

Igor and Charlotte were reclining on their rockers, drinking coffee, watching a rerun on a sports channel. Paul's cousins had hijacked him for the evening. The phone rang.

There was nothing unique about the telephone ring, yet, its sense of urgency jarred their peaceful, languid evening.

In a flash, they both jumped up for the nearest phone on the coffee table. Charlotte beat Igor to it.

"Hello! Van Clydens' residence."

"May I speak to Charlotte?" a watery voice asked.

"This is she."

"This is Trish."

"Trish, you sound muffled. Are you coming down with a cold? I was about to call you about lunch next week," Charlotte said, her face impassive; her voice moderated.

"Is Paul there? Kelly can't reach him." Trish sniffled.

"He went to a concert."

"Oh," Trish replied, then she said to someone in the background, "He went to a concert. I suppose I could drive."

"Drive where?" Charlotte asked her.

Trish continued to chomp her speech, "You drive. You're her father!"

"I'll sleep in the back," the male voice slurred.

"Fine! I'll drive. You put on the breaks."

"What about the lights?" the voice yelled.

"I'll shift the gears. You figure it out!" Trish yelled back to him.

"It's automatic. You should know. Always want a brand-new car. The old's not good enough for you!" the voice yelled back.

"Don't yell! It's you who likes new cars. I put up with it!" Trish snapped, then back on the phone, she asked, in a mellow voice, "Where did you say Paul went again?"

"To a Gospel concert . . . with his cousins."

"Of course. It's a pleasant time of the year to go to a concert, what with all the festivities and all. When do you expect him back?"

"I don't know. May be, about ten. We've church tomorrow. What's going on?"

"Never mind. We'll figure it out." Trish turned to the man and said, "You *will* drive! You are *her* father!"

Charlotte heard glasses splintering.

"Stop it!" Trish yelled. "You always do that when you want to shun your duty. Get the key and drive! Your daughter's in trouble. Oh Lord!"

In a deep contralto voice, Trish crooned, "Jesus, Jesus, Jesus, sweetest Name I know. Fills my every longing, keeps me singing as I go . . . "

"Stop it! You're giving me a headache!" the voice yelled.

"You give me a headache!"

"Why did you have to call them?"

"You told me to get Paul, 'cause you won't take responsibility. I'm proud of your so-called success, but diamonds are not a girl's father—real, or . . . fake! Get your priorities right! All you do is chase deals and . . . happy hours!" Trish yelled back, then said to herself, "I should've divorced him a long time ago; I guess I must love him!" She stopped. "Oh fiddle! The phone is still on!" and in the phone, she said, mellow, "Charlotte, are you still there?"

"Yes. I am."

"Sorry about that. Where did Paul go again?"

"To the concert. Is Tom there?" she asked.

"That's one way of putting it," Trish replied.

"Put him on."

She heard Trish talking to the same male voice in the background. Then she heard her give the phone to him.

"Hello. Tom?"

Silence.

"Tom, this is Charlotte."

"Is Igor there?" Tom sounded strained.

"Just a moment."

Igor was on his feet hanging on to her side of the conversation. She handed the phone to him.

"Tom, what's going on?" he asked.

"Where did we go wrong?" Tom answered.

"What happened?"

Another silence.

"Is Kelly in trouble?" Igor continued probing.

"Where did we fail? We tried to be good parents," Tom moaned.

"Tom, calm down. Start from the beginning."

"I got a call. Kelly's in custody for . . . um . . . driving . . . um . . . she and a bunch of her friends . . . partying somewhere in L.A., next thing . . . Igor, what're we going to do? If her name gets in the papers . . ."

"First things first. You're right. We need to keep this out of the papers. We'll pray that the heavy-weights will cooperate. They're parents, just like us. I'll make a few calls and get back."

Knowing that Tom was too incoherent to make sense, Igor made quick calls to reinforce Tom's pleas to spare his family from public angst. Not even the Shinebonds' elevated position, or Kelly's public relations career could spare them. On the contrary. Worse, Tom sounded inebriated.

By grace, the key people were reachable by phone. With some negotiation, he reached an agreement with them to either not disclose the names of those involved, or to refrain from making the story front-page news. Assured, he called Tom and arranged to take them to the station, praying they would snooze in the back and leave the driving to him.

Charlotte packed a flask of strong black coffee and two plastic cups for hot liquid. They pulled out of the garage by eight thirty.

Paul entered the house expecting his parents to be in the den, instead, only one light was on in the corridor. His eyes lighted on a note on the kitchen counter from his mother——they had gone out, and would explain later, but to pray for Kelly.

He prayed for Kelly as best he could, then he rummaged around the kitchen and found a box of Bigelow Black Tea——a favorite of Lily's. A moment later he was back in the den with a steaming cup of hot tea and a plate of chocolate chip cookies.

He rekindled the fire and watched the flame. The concert had distracted his mind and he had a blast with Jonathan and his other cousins, but he was back reviewing the events of the weekend and added to it, worrying about his parents.

It was getting late, yet wait up he must, though his parents were adults, so he selected an investment magazine from the library to keep him company.

Sometime along the evening, he must have dozed off. Voices in the corridor woke him up. The clock on the mantel pointed to after midnight. In the background, the TV droned on.

"You're still up!" His mother asked, surprised.

He stretched and yawned. "What happened?"

His parents looked at each other, then his mother recounted the events of the evening briefly. "Let's say, it was good you were at the concert. The Lord works in mysterious ways." Her voice spoke volumes.

One step, then another, brought his father toe to toe with him, his face contorted. "Son, is this what you've been trying to tell us?"

He returned his father's gaze, then averted his eyes. "Kelly's a nice girl, in some ways. She has her good points."

"But not the points we're looking for. It's inconceivable that we almost wrecked your life! What type of a mother am I? I missed all the cues!" His mother looked dazed.

His father held his mother in his arms for a moment, "There's plenty of blame to go around, honey." He turned and gave him a manly hug.

Holding both their hands and with the compassion of a man who had experienced the pain of almost losing his son, he prayed for Tom's family and for the first time since he and his father disagreed, his father broke down. In praying for the Shinebonds, his father prayed the prayer he should have prayed for his family a year before and concluded by saying, "Father, I know we should forgive and I do, but how can I predict how long it will take for Kelly to change? What right do I have, to sacrifice my son and all my future generations? Only You can help Kelly and her parents in Your own time. Show us how to support them, I pray. . ."

68

Paul blinked and reviewed the events of the previous evening, numb. He had expected to be exonerated sooner, or later, but not so soon. While he felt sorry for any pain Kelly was capable of feeling, he felt no remorse for breaking up with her.

Had he loved Kelly a little, he too might have tried like other men, who endured a lot for the sake of any redemptive quality they saw in their mates.

Kelly had been a fixture in his life. During those years, he had never had cause to suspect that he loved her beyond the platonic, consequently, he felt very comfortable with not thinking of her as his future wife.

In hindsight, he realized Kelly conducted herself as one who had a right to him. Did Kelly feel entitled to him because of her family lineage, or because others presumed her to be entitled to him because of her ancestry?

He conjectured further that the unspoken creed of entitlement assumed a normal man like him could in no way suffer any enduring pain over the loss of a love like Lily, or that Lily could in anyway be his compatible mate. In that respect, he had become a victim of the very privilege to which he was born.

"An Asian's assumed happy only with another Asian, and may be, a white spouse——the Asians consider that marrying up," he paraphrased a friend who recently complained to him about the challenges he was facing searching for a wife, snapped to his feet and landed on the floor, ready to start his Sunday morning.

By the time he went downstairs, he was dressed in a gray suit, with a smoky blue shirt and an excellent choice of a tie. His mother was at the kitchen counter, also ready for church in a charming one piece.

When he entered, the smell of warm muffins greeted him.

She offered him her cheeks. Her delicate arms hugged him tightly, as she had on Friday evening. She looked thinner than he remembered. Her eyes searched his face. In them he saw the heart of a remorseful mother.

In the background, the coffee pot gurgled. She served him a cup, hesitated, then asked, with an arcane smile. "Would you rather have a cup of tea?"

"Coffee's fine. Thank you, Mum." He grinned.

"Dad will soon be down." She handed him the Sunday papers.

"Thank you." He grabbed a stool and perused the sports pages.

When his father came down, they transferred their quiet rapport to the dinette table, each focused on their papers, interspersed with a comment or two, or a joke, until it was time to leave for church.

◆ ◆ ◆

Paul watched from the entrance, as his parents searched faces in the sanctuary, until they spotted Trish and Tom sitting erect in their pew with two of their children——Alison, and Justin. Kelly was missing.

They walked over to sit with them. At no time did they mention Kelly's name——no judgment and no condemnation. For all appearances, Kelly was back at her condo in the Foothills City.

Out of the Kelly episode, and due to how Igor and Charlotte had protected the Shinebonds' dignity, Trish and Tom responded timidly and acknowledged that they needed help. Without equivocating, they accepted that Kelly had blown her chances with Paul.

Kelly was still too stunned to fathom the full ramifications of her behavior. However, she rationalized that because the Van Clydens rescued her family from the embarrassing ordeal, and continued to support them, she must still be their preferred choice for a future daughter-in-law; but she dared not show her face in public, yet. True, there were many good catches out there, who were enamored with her, but, as long as there was a glimmer of hope, trapping Paul to marry her was like conquering the Commanding General of virtue. For now, she hastened her plans for a two-weeks' cruise with an aunt and uncle who dotted on her quite a bit.

♦ ♦ ♦

Sunday evening, the sun——now softened——retreated behind arrays of clouds into the horizon. In the sunroom, Paul was on the couch, picking his guitar; Percy lay at his feet, content.

Three hours before Paul left for Orchards City, Christmas lights started popping up like stars as darkness crept over the city.

Igor was reclining in his chair, occasionally studying him, while Charlotte continued to flip through her fashion magazine.

"Well, I believe we've come a long way," Igor said.

"That's true," Paul replied.

He took a deep breath. "So, how are things?"

As a father, he felt uncomfortable prying into Paul's affairs, now that things were back to normal. He believed it was no longer proper to discuss Paul's social life; yet, he could not resist asking Paul once more, to purge his guilt for the misery he had caused him.

"I've a lot of fence-mending to do," Paul admitted.

"Mmm. We really put our foot in this one, didn't we? Remember son, if it was meant to be, it will be. Also, don't forget your mother and I are praying for you, not to think of good friends like Matt and Marjorie."

Paul thanked his dad.

"I love you, son." Igor clasped Paul around the shoulders.

"I love you too, Dad."

Without a word, Charlotte put her arms around both her men, her eyes misty. "I'll prepare a quick bite, before you leave." She dabbed her eyes and left Igor and Paul to enjoy the last of the sunset.

69

Except for the formalities, Jonathan felt practically engaged. He should have proposed already, so what was holding him back? It wasn't that he loved Sharon less, on the contrary. He switched the phone to the other ear.

A woman of action, Sharon said she hated to stand by and watch Paul in pain, especially when he was one of the most eligible bachelors on the US soil. "I'd hoped Paul's one year as an exchange student in Brazil would count. True, I found Argentinian culture different from West African's."

"And West Africa is different from East Africa?"

"It would appear so. After we left South America, my parents served only in Ghana and Nigeria, then we came home. I find their manners slightly different. Overall, I think they may be more accepting than we are. All the same, Paul needs to circulate and meet more people. Time flies, and he could miss other opportunities. Good picks don't mark time waiting for the undecided," Sharon said.

"I agree." He sounded doubtful.

"We need to do something."

"Like what? I've my reservations. Paul has never needed help. There's still a slew of candidates standing in the wings."

Sharon talked. He listened.

After Sharon had related her plan, he said, "I like that. Linda might work. He'll probably break our legs. He dislikes being set up."

He heard the droning of a car engine approaching the condo. "He's here! Gotta go." He dropped the receiver, grabbed a blank sheet of paper and slid back into his working chair.

Paul noticed Jonathan seated at his desk, but an unfinished music score lay on the coffee table, evidence that Jonathan had not been at his desk a minute before. Why was he pretending to be busy, with an empty piece of paper?

"There you are Paul." Jonathan grinned. "How was church?"

"Okay. Great teaching. Thanks for the concert. I had a blast!"

"No problem. By the way, Sharon's looking for you." Jonathan scratched his head.

"She was here?"

"She called."

"Any message?"

"She's throwing a party. Can you make it?"

"When and what's the occasion?" he quizzed Jonathan.

"This Friday. She has a lot to be thankful for this year."

"Party, eh? She's turning into a party girl."

"Yes. Something about a formal dinner. You know how the girls are."

"Mmm. She's going all out."

"I guess. She's practicing hosting parties," Jonathan deadpanned.

"Watch out Jonathan, your days are numbered." He appraised Jonathan for a moment. "She isn't planning a blind date, is she?"

"Why?" Again, Jonathan tried to sound indifferent.

"Because she's Sharon."

"Look, all I was told was to relay a message."

"Who else is invited?" he continued to grill him.

"Friends. Supposing she was arranging a date, would it bother you?" Jonathan blinked and removed an invisible hair from his eyelashes.

"So she's arranging a blind date?"

"About the time, she's shooting for seven thirty. We could ride together," Jonathan said, knowing they drove in separate cars, anyway.

"We could do that." He rubbed his nose.

"Well? The invitation cards are on their way, but they may be late. She needs an RSVP, ASAP."

He studied Jonathan's face. "You and Sharon are up to something."

"Hey, look, I am only the messenger, okay?"

"Mhmm. You know, you look so guilty; but, unlike Sharon, there's nowhere to hide. Feel free to confess any time you're ready."

"So, you'll come? Good. As it happens, I'm on my way to a gig. See you later." Jonathan grabbed his car keys and bolted for the door.

He continued staring at the door through which Jonathan had just escaped, shaking his head, as his brain reeled through all the possible blind dates Sharon might be arranging and came up blank. Jonathan and Sharon had been his best allies, were they having second thoughts?

A blind date could relaunch his dating life, but he had no wish to feel like a cash cow again and, he had already made his decision. Also, Stanislaus had warned him about girls who attended grooming schools to trap men like him. It would be foolish to ignore his best friend's advice.

The notion of leaving himself so vulnerable and risking his future happiness was so abhorrent, that he fled upstairs and ripped into his gym clothes for a serious work-out.

70

Paul's Porsche roared up the driveway to the front of the garage. The car door slammed shut behind him as he was halfway into the house. His briefcase landed into a corner to the echo of his footsteps running upstairs.

He ducked to avoid colliding with Jonathan, dashing downstairs tying his tie, looking as sharp and rugged as only he could. Jonathan mentioned change of plan——Sharon needed help setting up. Did he mind driving? Then Jonathan dashed out.

Paul paused and with his eyes, quizzed the empty door where Jonathan had just exited. No clue there. Chuckling, he shrugged off his day clothes and dashed in and out of the shower in a blink of an eye. Nothing like a fashionably late gentleman to make a bad impression on a blind date.

In the five days leading to the party, he had prayed a lot. He felt ambivalent about the evening. No matter what happened, he dared himself to trust in the Lord as he used to, soon after he had become a believer.

He had always resisted being paired up, even when the matchmakers were trusted relatives. Had Sharon not been his trusted ally, he would have declined her invitation with no remorse. More critical, if Lily found out . . .! But then again, Lily was resisting him. What a muddle!

A part of him was standing on the sideline watching the drama unfold. When was the last time anybody set him up with a blind date? What did one say? Discuss the football scores? Talk about the latest movie? The weather? Besides California fog, what was there to discuss about the weather? On the other hand, he had no problem deriving topics to discuss with Lily. If he really tried, could he learn to forge ahead, by grace?

On second thoughts, was it right to cling to hope or was he just being stubborn because Lily was out of reach? He didn't think so. Until Lily came along, at no time did he think someone like her would high-jack his attention and consume his energy, except for his dedication to the Lord. Lily had caught him by surprise and before he could rescue himself, he was submerged to his head.

He gave his tie one last tug. Jonathan had already set the standard, so he selected a dark gray suit and a French-blue shirt and finished with a slap of a light aftershave lotion, then he knelt down and prayed, "Please help me not raise any hopes this evening. If Lily's firm, I'll go to Europe or return to East Africa, unless You will otherwise. I'm committed to serving You for life, even if it means staying single. Not my will, but Thine be done. Amen."

◆ ◆ ◆

Paul adjusted his tie and rang Sharon's doorbell. Jonathan answered, looking carelessly debonair as only he could. When Sharon emerged in a mid-length, straight, jade green dress, they made a striking couple. Her gold accessories reflected the yellow in Jonathan's jade and yellow tie.

Paul stood back to admire her. "Well, well, well."

"You know one thing I like about you, Paul, among many, is how you flatter me without a word!" Sharon said in her husky voice.

"Where you're concerned, I don't need to flatter you at all," Paul drawled, mimicking a Texan accent.

"Watch that Texan!" Jonathan teased.

"And you buddy——we need to talk."

"Trouble?" Sharon looked mystified.

"Mhmm!"

"Hey, I know of no trouble. In fact, if Jonathan could get us some more soft drinks, we would be set. More people showed up than I'd expected. But I'm glad, especially being the Christmas season and all, I wasn't sure anybody would come," she explained.

Jonathan grabbed his coat on his way out. As he reached the door, she called after him, "Do hurry up, dear."

Paul found himself maneuvered into her spacious living room. Unlike him and Jonathan, Sharon was still renting a condo, thanks to her modest earnings. Thirty thousand dollars a year, as a junior manager with Stretch A Dollar——a Christian non-profit organization——was barely enough for her to scrape by and pay off her college debt.

After graduating, she ate tuna fish sandwiches and at less than fifty-cents a cup, a lot of noodles: vegetable, chicken and beef, all for less than three dollars a week, to save enough money for a down-payment to purchase a red-roofed three-bedroom condo, within three to four years after graduating. That had been her goal. Jonathan changed all that.

Now, she and Jonathan were saving to buy their first house when they got married. As a financial manager, he applauded their plan, though that meant Sharon would not have her own equity built. But he believed that Jonathan would remain steadfast, once married.

He recognized familiar faces around the room, grateful that Sharon had invited friends. "Matt! Marjorie!" he greeted the Jonesons.

Matt was equally exuberant. "It's been a while since we last visited with you. Church goes by too fast."

"Thank you for calling Dad last Thursday." He kissed Marjorie's cheeks. "I sure appreciate that."

"No problem. Marjorie and I are with you, whichever way the Lord leads. And don't forget, the Jonesons' gang thinks tons of you."

"Yes. Keep looking up!" Marjorie looked elegant in a baby-blue gown.

He thanked them. "How does MJ like his school?"

"O-o-oh, we can't tear him away. In a way, we're glad he's taken to college life; on the other hand, I feel jealous. It's all we can do to get him to visit once in a while." Marjorie glowed with the pride of a mother who had finally got one successfully out of the nest, to college.

"Pursue Holy Life is a good school."

"Yes. It was such a blessing that they offered him a full sports scholarship at the last minute. Initially, he thought it would be either UCLA, or Cal State. His heart was really set on PHLU," Matt said.

"The clincher was Viviana," Marjorie added.

"Viviana?" Paul whistled. MJ had dropped hints during the mentoring time.

"Mhmm. Of course, he hasn't made it official, yet, but Matt and I have our suspicions. We found out through her parents she's also attending PHLU. We parents are always the last to know."

"Blind as a bat. But what a relief! For a while we thought he was into some forbidden stuff. He'd become too quiet for our comfort." Matt patted his wife's arm.

"Always fiddling with his truck after school——only talked to Melody and Mark——and, those endless whisperings! Matt and I were praying up a storm. Then it turned out it was the same old story."

"Love will do that to ya!" Matt chuckled.

"I'm happy for them. What a relief it was nothing worse. I hope things will work out, as the Lord wills." Paul encouraged them. "My best to the rest of the gang. Every time I see Melanie, she's a bit taller, with a bit more of her sense of identity showing."

Marjorie laughed. "We call it the terrible three, going on to five!"

Paul made a mental note to check on MJ, then he moved on. Everybody seemed paired, except for one or two. Just then he spotted Bill and Sheila.

Bill gave him a firm hand-shake and a pat on the back.

He reciprocated, then greeted Sheila with a kiss. "Sheila, I owe both of you a trip to the movies or the games."

"We'd love it!" Sheila's eyes danced.

"We'll hold him to that——remind him every time we see him, until he delivers——just kidding." Bill chuckled.

"Your lucky day Paul, he's just around the corner," Sheila teased.

"I remind myself every day," Paul groaned, in mock horror.

"That's why I have you on my prayer list," Sheila whispered loud enough for her husband to hear.

"'Can't fool my wife." Bill replied.

"No——just kidding," Paul held up his hands. "He's the best boss I've ever had. I thank the Lord every day for him. To have a brother in such an environment, I can't say enough. It would take more than an evening for me to recount the many times I've leaned on him."

For a moment, Bill rested his hand on his shoulder, six years of working together, pulling for each other, flew by in the unspoken silence.

With another backslap, Paul continued circulating around the room, searching for his blind date, certain Sharon had arranged for one. It would be unlike her not to live up to her reputation as an ardent matchmaker. At least his options would be among friends and acquaintances, he mused.

Just then, Sharon steered him to Linda from Evangelical Neighborhood Church. She was a nice girl. Her close-cropped brunette hair was quite becoming. But that was the extent of his admiration for her.

Sharon introduced them and asked whether they had met already?

"Yes. We have——briefly, during coffee break," Linda replied.

He agreed. "So how do you like ENC, so far?"

"I love it. The people are warm. I especially appreciate new friends like Jonathan. Sharon and I go back to college. She was a very good friend of mine. We kept in touch. It's good to be living so close again."

"I'm thrilled to have you around too. We'd so much fun in college. We didn't really get in trouble, did we?" Sharon batted her eyelashes.

Linda chuckled.

"You, got in trouble?" Paul interrupted, "Nah!"

"I'm not gonna answer that!" Sharon flicked her hair, then said to Linda, "I was excited to know you'd be settling at ENC. It's so good to have you near again." She chatted briefly and excused herself to welcome another couple who had just arrived.

Not too bad, he thought. May be a social friend to avoid awkward moments, but not for too long. Now that he had met her, the excitement he had drummed up the whole week waned. The idea of returning to East Africa as a full-time missionary——and as far away from blind dates as possible——or transferring to Europe, was a sealed deal.

He noticed some spilled over guests standing in clusters in the balcony, under the canopy, shielded from the chilly winds.

Linda's voice——inquiring about good diversions in California—— brought him back to earth. He had missed the rest of her conversation. Always a good listener, he turned tomato red. Sharon had gone to great lengths to get him back into circulation. Moreover, Linda made a good conversation partner. It was impolite to be inattentive to her.

If he befriended her for social functions, he must be forthright from the onset about his intentions. But the very thought repulsed him. If he encouraged her, he would be cheating and untrue to himself. He longed for solitude. The trip to East Africa had given him a sense of purpose, he would hate to lose momentum.

Tactfully, he delivered Linda to two other guests, excused himself and continued circulating. As he was turning to talk to the newly-wed couple who had met in the singles' group, he heard Jonathan's voice in the hallway.

The door to the living room opened. The lively conversation went on, but a bit subdued, with smiles directed towards the door. Curious, he checked the root–cause. His eyes came to rest on the doorway, where Jonathan and Sharon were standing; but he did not see them.

There she stood in a straight crew neck dress. The royal-blue bodice hugged her waist to her hip, and merged seamlessly into a black straight skirt to her knees. Her pretty ankles peeked from a pair of no less elegant black evening pumps. A black single pair of onyx earrings fell in cascades from her ears, accentuating her long neck——no need for a necklace.

The tie! He had forgotten to take Marc's advice to wear one of those large, loud ties that Miguel's brother had recommended.

Looking as innocent as a pair of doves, Jonathan and Sharon introduced new guests to Lily, until they reached Bill and Sheila. Instead of greeting them and moving on, they shepherded the group toward his group.

Soon after they had joined his group, and chatted briefly, Sharon announced, "Everybody, dinner's served."

Midway through the party, Paul surveyed the room and counted at least twenty people invited to the buffet dinner. Linda had a date all along.

Startled, he realized Bernice and Alex were also in the group. If he had not been so preoccupied trying to guess with whom Sharon had paired him, he would have noticed them. On second thoughts, was Bernice around before Jonathan returned? How could he have missed her?

He shot a glance at Sharon. She looked as innocent as a dove!

Later, Bernice and Alex assured him that his instincts were right. They were in Lily's entourage and had been waiting for Jonathan's cue.

Linda also cornered him. "I knew I didn't stand a chance!"

He blushed and confessed, "I owe you an apology."

"It's okay. What are friends for? Sharon and Jonathan, what can I say?"

"I know. I give thanks every day for them."

"I hope you can consider me a friend too?"

He thanked her. "I look forward to having you as a friend." He glanced at Lily talking to the Jonesons and the Daelvins.

The guests started dispersing after ten thirty, merry and full of Christmas good cheer from Sharon's alcohol-free punch, and sparkling cider, plenty of good ribbing and the joy of sharing an evening with friends.

Forgetting that this party was a plot to reunite Paul and Lily, some guests expressed how much they were looking forward to the second annual gathering the following year, and would reserve their schedules for about November, seventeen——did that sound about right?

One guest complained that the trend had become so casual, that she was afraid of being conspicuous in a formal attire, unless she and her husband purchased exorbitant tickets for the opening night at the opera——which they couldn't afford, what with saving for college tuition and all. She welcomed the excuse to dress up and enjoy an evening with friends. Sharon took it in stride, with a charming smile.

Paul and Lily lingered briefly, then they too left.

Lily said, "Jonathan and Sharon may have told you that I moved?"

He was genuinely surprised.

♦ ♦ ♦

The ride to Lily's condo was quiet, except for a classical CD——two people on a journey of rediscovery.

After a long silence, Paul said, "I'm sorry about everything."

Lily kept quiet, unsure. This was the second time he had apologized, but it gave her no elation and little satisfaction. After a very forbidding silence, she replied, "I'm sorry too."

She said it not so much because she felt she had any reason to apologize, but because it seemed it was the correct response to his apology. She sensed he expected her to say something, so she did. She was still wrestling with his betrayal. Though their friendship remained platonic, and she welcomed that, she was not his back-up plan.

Could she trust a man who dumped a woman at the drop of a hat? What if his father gave him an ultimatum later on, after they had bonded, would he reject her again? Could she handle the pain? What would it do to her faith?

Perhaps due to changes in the weather, she sneezed and grabbed a tissue paper from her purse. A soft cloth touched her face and a small whiff of aftershave lotion escaped in the air. Her stomach fluttered. She thanked him.

At her condo, Paul sat still, then he touched her face gently, before he opened her door. "I like your new place."

She thanked him and led the way. At the threshold, she unlocked the door, and turned on the light, but she did not enter.

Without tempting her, he held both her hands, and drank in her beauty, her questioning eyes——gentle, yet resilient.

"Tomorrow?"

She almost blurted out that she had to study, but replied, "Tomorrow."

"We could go to the mountains, say about ten o'clock?"

"Ten o'clock should be okay."

"Good night." He released her hands reluctantly, then he escaped.

She closed the door behind her and stood transfixed at the threshold, staring at nothing. The smell of his aftershave lotion brought her back to earth. Reminding herself to return his handkerchief in the morning, she washed it and threw it in the dryer.

Her eyes lighted on her computer and a pile of books waiting for her. She had a long night before her to make up for the lost evening.

Finally, her advisor had approved her panel. Still nobody——not even her family, except Zebediah Chancey——knew she was about to complete her doctorate. But, as soon as the college accepted her application to graduate, she would inform her parents.

Had the course not required her supervisor's recommendation, she would not have told Mr. Chancey——he had agreed to keep her secret.

Bernice still believed that she was completing a few classes to expand her horizon as a CPA.

Slowly, she walked to the kitchen to make a very strong cup of tea.

71

A plate of half-eaten omelet, toast and a cold cup of tea yawned at Lily. In a short while, Paul would arrive. After settling down, she had invested three hours in her papers, before retiring, then she had counted brown sheep and white sheep and spotted sheep, to float down from the excitement of the evening. She caught only two hours of sleep, before the sun rose up in the sky, and the dawn escaped.

Since waking up, she had put toothpaste on her face, burnt a toast and watched her milk boil over.

She stacked the dish washer and washed and chopped the ingredients for the dish she would prepare for Thanksgiving dinner the next day.

It had started snowing in the mountains; she dressed appropriately in a warm olive green, polo neck shirt and matching jeans. Paul loved the outdoors and lots of it, so she selected thick brown boots and leather gloves in-padded with sheep's skin. Her dark brown leather jacket could cope with any mountain snow.

When Paul rang the doorbell, she was in the living room, waiting. Gone were the books, academic journals and dissertation papers. In their places were copies of the Wall Street Journal, local newspapers and Christian Magazines.

Her heart flipped at the sight of Paul in a cowboy outfit. She fussed with throw pillows to hide her confusion. "Um, would you like a tour of my condo?"

He tipped his head and let her lead the way. He seemed very pleased, but said nothing until the end. "Very nice. I like it a lot."

At a restaurant on the way towards Alegria Peaks, he ordered two cups of hot chocolate, then nosed the Porsche up the mountain at a morning ride's pace. Occasionally, they stopped to admire the view of the rolling, hazy mountains and the valleys.

Higher up the altitudes, trickles of streams still struggled through partially snow-covered ravines——typical of a Southern California's late autumn.

Lily inhaled deeply, thankful that Paul shared her love of the outdoors. Long drives between undulating hills reminded her of her student days, when her family drove through the countryside to return her to boarding school. She would stare at rolling hills and streams with smatterings of fishermen rowing their boats, lost in thought, or she would read teenage novels to break the monotony of flat plains.

The sound of the engine slowing down woke her up from her daydreaming. They had arrived at a restaurant perched on top of the mountains. A few cars were already in the parking lot. Above them, the ski lifts glided up the slopes, into the horizon.

From the familiar smiles and "Hi," Lily concluded Paul came frequently. His bulging muscles were evidence enough.

Some people appeared unhappy, perhaps? She chose to ignore them.

Paul requested and got a table by the window.

She ordered a burger——well-done, fresh fruits and a cup of hot tea. Paul ordered the same, but with medium well-done burger——no blood.

The cheerful waitress brought their orders in a decent time. Lily thought that either the waitress was really nice or afraid of Paul, for surely, she would have delayed serving them an extra fifteen minutes, as some did?

A variety of holiday music filled the air. Outside, families playing in the snow and a few skiers on the steep slopes added to the festive mood.

Lily felt Paul's eyes burning through her. To cover her confusion, she said, "I enjoyed your video presentation at the church very much."

He thanked her.

She felt awkward. It had been over a year; they were starting from scratch. Unlike their first date, her fantasy of a sublime future had been shattered by the reality of the last twelve months.

He fumbled with his invisible tie and took another sip of his hot tea, then placed his cup down very slowly, as though in deep thought.

His eyes appealed to her. "I know things have been kind of crazy this last year. I don't want to make the same mistake again." He paused and took a deep breath. "Your opinion means a lot to me."

She sipped her tea to keep busy, while she pondered where he was leading, grateful for the music that filled the silence between them.

Paul seemed pensive. Much later, he would confess that among other things, he longed to know more about her family. He knew she had siblings and both parents were still alive, but she had not been very forthcoming about them.

She measured him with her eyes. "Is anything the matter?"

"Nothing." He fidgeted. "Well, I've been wondering," he smiled sheepish.

"What is it?"

"Um, have you thought about missionary work?"

"Who? Me?"

"Yes. You."

She dropped her eyes. "What a strange question!"

"No. Really. Seriously."

"What do you mean? Do you mean international work or serving in another state or locally? Any of them could be a venue for missionary work."

"Absolutely," he agreed, excited. "Well, I mean all the above."

"I've thought about it occasionally." She hesitated.

"And . . .?"

"I've always thought if I ever did, I would probably return home."

"Of course. What about if you felt called to another country?"

She was surprised. "To be honest, I have never thought of it that way. I don't consider myself missionary material . . . at least, not in my definition of a missionary. I consider myself more of a facilitator . . . I try to be wherever I'm needed for the Lord's work. I suppose God can use anybody who is willing, and He could call anybody He chooses, to any country. He has done it before. He could do it again."

"Well?" His piercing blue eyes bored into her.

"Well, I suppose, since He can call anybody, He could call me. Nothing is impossible with Him." A tremor ran through her body. She shifted her eyes.

"Mhmm." He changed gears. "What do you think of partners in ministry?"

"How do you mean?"

"Friends of mine say it's hard to serve on the field without support."

She pondered his question, her face in knots, but refused to speculate what he meant. "I believe it is always good to seek guidance for such endeavors. Group trips are popular. A lot of churches now partner with local Christian organizations for trips to places like Mexico, for instance."

"So, you would go then . . . on a joint mission, I mean?"

"If I believed it was the Lord's will, yes. I would."

"And, um, urban ministry?"

She gave him the full benefit of her brown eyes. "You mean inner city?"

"Right."

"Again, explain. Do you mean live in the inner city or commute some evenings for voluntary work——at a soup kitchen, for instance?"

"Both, I guess," he chuckled, surprised. Unbeknown to her, he was trying not to compare her to Kelly. Lily's qualities were more precious than rubies and diamonds.

"Same thing. It would all depend on the direction the Lord is leading. If living in the inner city is the best option, then so be it. I believe people in ministry should always understand and follow the Lord's calling."

Paul's broad smile said how much he was satisfied with their conversation. "That's nice to know."

"How did we get to me? I thought we were talking about your trip."

"And so we were." He laughed heartily.

At that moment, a group walked in, among them, a popular member of Evangelical Neighborhood Church who seemed to dislike Lily, though they were only on greeting terms. Several times, the woman had made her the brunt of her veiled resentment, while maintaining her angelic aura. The others also looked vaguely familiar, may be, new members of Evangelical Neighborhood Church? The waitress seated them.

The woman shifted her weight around, patted her rounded bosom with satisfaction, then sat up erect. "I guess young people are doing things differently nowadays," she said loudly, "isn't that Paul Van Clyden? I could've sworn," she leaned over and whispered to a woman in the group.

The other woman nodded and replied softly, "I think so," while glancing at Lily, with the serious look of a delegate in deep consultation to protect her country's territory at a United Nations' conference.

"Well, isn't he and Kelly Shinebond engaged? Trish and Tom would not like this at all, if word gets back to them," the first woman boomed.

Gloating, she gave Lily a smile bordering on a sneer, then turned on her most dazzling smile at the waitress. "I'll have one of those bacon cheese burgers on toasted rye, a side order of onion rings, salad, and some coffee." She twirled her strings of faux pearls and leaned back with the feline look of a cat that had just swallowed a canary.

Every vein on Paul's forehead snapped to. But, when he spoke, his voice sounded as tranquil as a quiet brook, flowing down a flat valley. "We should be heading back. It'll be dusk soon."

Taking the cue from him, Lily replied, "Of course." Her face smiled; her hands gripped her purse.

Paul left a generous tip on the table, and guided her out by the elbow, holding himself erect, as he passed near the table with the offending guests.

After settling her in the car, he mumbled about checking the ski season with Dale. Dale, she gathered, was the owner of the restaurant. When she and Paul walked in, he was one of those who had chatted with Paul.

She waited; her view of the restaurant obstructed.

Had she sat within reach, she would have seen Paul beeline for the offending woman's table and murmur to them, smiling charmingly, "I overheard your comments. I hate to disappoint y'all, but Kelly and I are no longer seeing each other. We've both moved on. I believe . . . so can you."

The woman fumbled with her beads, staring at him, nonplussed. The other women fussed with their purses and the men looked sheepish.

With one last charming smile, Paul walked out, a man in command.

Dale studied Paul's progress to the exit, then he studied the group, then he stared again at the now empty door and shook his head.

Rumors had it that Paul, though always charming, did not suffer fools. Dale had never seen this side of him. He shook his head again, even as he wondered how Paul's father would react. He was not acquainted with the old man; he just knew that he carried a lot of clout in high places.

He stared at the now empty door, again, then he resumed his chore.

Paul pulled out of the resort after three o'clock. He negotiated the angular snow-frosted curves, down towards the valley, uncommunicative.

Lily closed her eyes, and only opened them again when she heard the sound of the city approaching. Before them were the merry lights of the valley, behind them, the blurry silhouettes of the sleeping mountains they had just left.

A few houses in the neighborhood were already bedecked with Christmas lights and Mountain Avenue shops were beginning to show signs of the holidays.

On the 10 Freeway, they hit red taillights——the last straw! Lily slumped back on her seat. Before she could catch herself, a sigh escaped her and a tear trickled down her face. Paul squeezed her hand and handed her a handkerchief.

A few minutes later, they exited on Grand Avenue off-ramp and headed towards Orchards City, but then he drove towards the hills and stopped at a peak. Around them was a forest; and ahead, a lighted residential area.

She recognized the newly built area of Hollenvine Hills. The houses were barely ten years old. Not a while back, those hills were cow meadows by day and coyotes' play ground by night. But the coyotes had been pushed farther into the hills.

She could see Paul's profile from the soft glow of the street lights.

He turned and gazed into the silhouette of her face, as he held her hand. There was nothing sensual about the touch——just a gentle, serene touch.

"I learnt a lot last year," he said. "I learnt that some people derive their happiness out of misery or by trying to make others unhappy. But you know?"

Again, he did not wait for her answer, but continued on, reaching deep down to her hurt, as though he wished to pull it out by the roots. "I'm becoming increasingly convinced we've choices. We can choose to curve a life of our own and focus on honoring Him. He, the Holy Lord, is our strength."

He placed his right hand around her shoulders, again, with no suggestion of any impropriety. His left hand clasped both her hands.

"If more of us who claim to follow Christ, would emulate Him, our fellowship would be so much stronger." He blew his cheeks, then he kissed her hands.

Why would anybody want to hurt someone who didn't hit back? Hadn't she been through enough? She had carried herself with dignity throughout the whole ordeal. Why would anybody want to go to war with an enemy who didn't exist?

He continued to hold her hands and watch the city lights. Finally, he released them, and pulled off the curb.

Lily held her emotions in check, uncertain of how to respond to the new Paul who was emerging before her eyes. Could she trust him to be resilient this time, in the wake of people like the woman they had just left up Mount Alegria?

On the other hand, she was falling in love with him all over. "Lord, please help!" she prayed, even as she worried about meeting the asinine woman at Thanksgiving potluck dinner the next day. She had yet to prepare her dish. Fortunately, she had already assembled the ingredients.

After seeing Lily safely to her condo, Paul drove away at twenty-five miles per hour in a thirty-five-mile zone, and thirty-miles per hour in a forty-mile zone, frequently looking back in the rear-view mirror——a man towing an invisible condo delicately, to annex it to his house, to make them one.

72

Lily glided downstairs, her night gown sweeping behind her. The smell of the East African sumbusas she had prepared the evening before, still lingered in the air, reminding her of those mornings when a basket-full of her mum's sumbusas waited for them at the breakfast table. She eyed them, debating. The Thanksgiving potluck service was not until the evening. If she resisted gratifying her appetite, they would survive until then.

She had breakfast and drove to church wondering how Paul would behave, not for too long. After Sunday school, as the congregation mingled in coffee fellowship, Paul sought her out and stuck by her.

The unpleasant woman in the mountains fussed with her purse, or pretended to be occupied, whenever they crossed paths.

Paul, on the contrary, gave her his rapt attention, only chatting occasionally with other members of the congregation, out of politeness.

Shortly before the service began, Jonathan and Sharon joined them and they entered the sanctuary together.

Externally, Paul looked calm, but goosebumps, were what he had, as the choir and the congregation belted a mix of favorites from both modern choruses and old hymns. To top it, the choir sung a special selection from the sacred classical choruses accompanied by a full orchestra.

Having come full circle, he prayed in his heart not to blow it, this time.

Jonathan must have noticed. He especially sought him out during greeting time, though they were sitting shoulder to shoulder.

A wonderful service deserved a wonderful meal. Restaurant Street in West City had the best restaurants within reasonable driving distance.

Four people driving four cars never made for a romantic Sunday afternoon drive out to lunch. Paul followed Lily to her condo; Jonathan followed Sharon to hers and then there were two cars and two couples.

Potluck dinner was at six p.m., giving them ample time for lunch and a leisurely afternoon. What more, cool breezes interspersed with bouts of warmth, as the sun smiled through the thin layer of gathering clouds, made the late autumn weather beautiful for an after-lunch stroll.

Paul seated Lily in his car, his face impassive. Lily raised her eyebrows. He grinned, pulled out of the parking lot and headed straight for the 55 Freeway, with no explanation.

"Newport Beach?" Lily asked.

"Balboa."

"You love the beach?"

"Mhmm." He glanced at her.

Her eyes danced merrily. "Do you own a pair of cutoffs?"

"Two."

"Really?"

"No, kidding. Three."

"Guitar?"

"Mhmm. A Yamaha."

"And . . .?"

"A Fender."

"And . . .?"

He chuckled. "You're getting to know me."

"Well, . . .?"

"A Gibson."

She raised her eyebrows.

"Bought the Yamaha and the Fender. Gibson was a birthday gift. Jonathan also got one. Our parents bought them to bribe us to stay away from the wrong crowd. Uncle Jeremy also got a high-end violin for my cousin, Ingrid. Not that they need've worried——my closest affinity to life in the fast lane is fast cars, but none of that other stuff."

"Paul, drives fast cars? Nah!" she teased him.

"When I started driving, all I heard was Mum yelling, 'Paul slow down.' Then, 'Have mercy on that boy!' I can still hear her voice today, when I step on the pedal."

"That's exactly how I pray, when I see you zooming around!"

"There you go. Nothing like having my name on the prayer lists of two of my favorite women!" He grinned.

"You are really a beach fan?"

"In good weather, on my day off, and, depending on other things." He gave her a veiled look from under his eyebrows.

"What's that supposed to mean?"

"Nothing." He grinned again, mischievous.

She let his comment pass and stared out of the window, trying to calm her racing nerves, then she switched gears. "How's work? Is the corporate culture accommodating? For instance, do you find it easy to manage people, apart from the obvious leadership challenges?"

He gave her a loaded look. "If I keep my mouth shut."

"That's an oxymoron," she murmured.

He burst out laughing. "You bet you. It's always about the bottom-line. Bill, my friend and boss, lends me his ear. You met him at the party."

She nodded.

"I can depend on him to back me up with prayer."

"There is no better friend than a praying friend."

He threw her a grateful look. "Yes. It really helps to know there are people we can trust. I know that when I ask you to pray, you take it seriously."

"It takes grace," she said, then she realized his comments were leading somewhere. "Is there something you would like me to pray about?"

He took a deep breath. "An associate who's a thorn in my side. I've reached the end of my rope with him. I need wisdom. What I really need is to show him some Christian love. I'm afraid I've been avoiding him."

"Thank you for sharing. What is his first name, if you don't mind?"

"Shane."

"Shane. Ok. I will pray for him." It felt so natural that they would be sharing their faith, in the same breath as they discussed the corporate world. She wanted to know more, but resisted the temptation to probe further.

He thanked her and continued to glance at her on and off, as they speeded along. He had prayed for a woman who would understand his work——the stress, and how he handled it. That Lily would take the time to draw him out, exhilarated him. He prayed that she would heal from his betrayal and trust him enough one day, to let him into her world.

No doubt, she also faced similar obstacles, living her faith in a world more excited over Wall Street and the Broadway, than straight street and the narrow way.

Beethoven's *Fifth Symphony*——playing in the background——bridged the comfortable silence between them, as they cruised along.

About forty minutes later, the scenery turned to beach houses, a sign that they were approaching the end of Newport Beach Boulevard. But, instead of heading toward the crowded Newport Beach, Paul took a left turn to the Balboa Peninsula, her favorite beach——more peaceful and suitable for a quiet stroll.

He parallel-parked along the curb of a quiet street near the beach, and was beside her in one stride, before she got out of the car. A cool breeze blew by. She grabbed her shawl.

First, he led her through the sand, to the nearest jetty, guiding her as close to the end of the jetty as was sensible, and they watched the sailboats and occasional ships pass by.

Overhead, Mew Gulls and the Heerman's Gulls coasted; echoes of their semi moan-full songs filled the air. Below, Red-necked Phalarope floated in the gentle waves, serene, ignoring the boats and humans bustling around them.

Paul turned to her, "Ready?"

She nodded, wrapping her shawl around her neck.

They retraced their steps to the sandy beach and headed back toward Newport Beach, waves flirting with their heels. Occasionally, he raised his head to watch the boats speeding past.

Around them, Western Sand Pipers pecked at the sand, darting in and out of the waves, between the legs of Californian Marbled Godwits and American Avocets.

Lily stared at the birds, registering each one in turn, only with her eyes. Her mind continued to mull over a puzzle.

Paul slowed down, kicked the sand beneath his feet and looked at her. "So, how did your spring and summer go?"

"Average over eighty degrees and smoggy, except for the breezy days," she dead-panned.

He chuckled. "Did you go anywhere?"

"The mountains."

"And . . .?"

"More mountains and the beach," she continued toying with him.

"The mountains are great. Love the mountains. I could build a cabin there. Did you . . . go anywhere, special?" He locked eyes with hers.

"Mhmm. Palm Springs, if one could call it special."

"How was the weather there?"

Was that a smirk at the corners of his lips? Was he toying with her or being polite or perhaps curious?

"Palm Spring's weather varies——even in spring, it can get high. Jonathan probably told you. You know, Jonathan and Sharon were there," she said straight-faced again.

"Oh yes. I remember vaguely. He mentioned something about it." He rubbed the back of his neck.

She scrutinized his face again. It had gone blank. She had probably imagined the smirk after all.

"Met any nice people?"

"Nice is as nice does."

"True. Any one special?"

Lily examined his face, as she tried to find the right words. "Of course there are always nice people to meet."

"Mhmm."

"What would you like me to say?"

"How about, yes, Paul, I met some very nice people and yes, I met someone very special?" he said.

"All right. Yes Paul, I met some very nice people and yes, I met someone very special," she mimicked him.

He stopped, bringing his full weight on to her path. His eyes traced the contour of her face, the hint of a not-so-amused smile on his lips. Slowly, he resumed walking in the same direction as before. She kept pace with him.

From time to time, he glanced at her from under his long eye lashes. Then he walked at an angle until he was blocking her path and they were forehead to forehead. "Did you think about East Africa once in a while?"

"Of course. I was raised there."

"And . . .?"

"Nice weather too. No snow, praise be! Lots of rain during the rainy season." She adjusted her scarf.

"Who cares about the weather."

"I do. I don't like getting wet. Do you?"

Paul sighed. She didn't have to tell him that he was beyond skating on thin ice. He could see patches of dark spots where the ice had melted already. One false move could land him at the bottom of the lake, freezing, with no hope but to resume hiking into the mountains alone again.

"Well?" he asked.

"What?" she shot back.

Paul took a full half a minute exhaling, took in a deep breath and then took both her hands and bore into her soul. "Lily," he caressed her name, "last Christmas I laid bare my soul. A man does not make himself vulnerable for a trifle."

She stared back at him without flinching, slipped her hands away from his, and continued walking.

He lengthened his stride to catch up with her.

She half-turned. "Paul, sometimes I feel like I'm living in a fog."

"You'd mentioned that you needed to work things out."

"Yes."

"That was before I went to East Africa, um . . ."

"It's too soon."

She sensed his frustration rise. He had waited for two years, and "Too soon" was the best he could extract from her?

"A day can be like a thousand years," he murmured.

"Paul, you own three cutoffs and three guitars, and occasionally, you hung out at the beach to unwind, that's about as far as I have come to knowing you better, besides your deep love for the Lord. What else do you own in triplets? Gold cuff links . . . horses, and . . .?" she said facetiously.

He coughed and tweaked his ears. "Um, diamond cuff links——birthday gifts from my parents."

"Understandably. And horses? Thoroughbreds, Arabians or Lipizzaners?" she teased him again.

He did a double-turn when she mentioned Lipizzaners, rubbed his nose again. "Arabian——a gift from my parents; a Thoroughbred——courtesy of my maternal grandparents; and a Lipizzaner——courtesy of my European cousins who're very fond of me."

"Nice. Why three? Why not two or five or four?"

"Three cords' stronger than two. I believe in things that are strong and enduring. I also believe in the Three in One."

"That's commendable." She pondered that for a moment, then said, "Paul, I know we share the love of the LORD, but what do I have in common with the world of Fenders and Gibsons and Stradivariuses or Thoroughbreds and Lipizzaners?"

He replied, quietly, "Lily, nothing's lonelier than a Gibson over alone fire and a Thoroughbred, though tall and proud cannot stand alone, forever." He gazed steadily at her. "The very fact that you know Thoroughbreds and Lipizzaners are two separate breeds, not some . . . vintage wine, says a lot more about you than you'll ever know."

"I too believe in endurance——things that last; things that don't break. The Lord doesn't make mistakes. If I listen to Him more, I believe He will guide my steps. I want what pleases Him. So should you."

He leaned back and traced her long neck with his eyes——the contour of her cheeks, her full lips, her exquisite nose, her long eyelashes and her eyes that gazed back at him solemnly.

"Was it what happened yesterday?" he asked.

The ugly scene up Mount Alegria flashed before her. She averted her face.

"Okay, we'll be just friends. How about dinner tomorrow night?"

"I have a prior commitment."

"Tuesday meetings are over by eight or eight thirty."

"I'm an early riser. I prefer to beat the morning commute."

"Would ten o'clock curfew work?"

She considered it——she must finish her paper. "That might work."

He smiled. "ENC's Thanksgiving Eve service is usually well attended."

"Yes. But I am afraid I will miss it this year."

With so many choices of beautiful, affluent women out there, the Van Clydens' pride would have moved on a long time ago, but Paul wanted more. Ultimately, he must humble himself, if he wished to marry the right kind of girl. No amount of affluence could fill the void of spiritual companionship for which he yearned. He wanted to be true to himself and he had also promised himself that he would undo the damage he had inflicted on Lily and gain her trust.

Her parting words to him over a year ago, flashed through his mind. "One day, you will meet the woman who will bring you to your knees." *Sooner, or later, every man does.*

"I hear ENC has put together a great Christmas concert this year, that is, if you don't have a prior engagement? I believe Jonathan and Sharon will be there."

She hesitated, then said, lackadaisically, "ENC stages great concerts."

"Well?"

"Yes. It will be an honor to attend the Christmas concert with you."

"Thank you. The honor's all mine." He started to say something, then he put his hands up in a truce. "Very well, we'll leave it at that, for now."

Her lips twitched.

He continued walking toward Newport Beach, clutching her hand.

She raised her eyebrows.

He glanced at their hands. "I know, we're just friends, so it's allowed."

She chuckled, like a muted bell. "Paul Van Clyden, don't you ever give up?"

"No," he said. He was not laughing.

Alarmed and surprised that Paul, with all his charm and freedom, would take the time to lock in a date with her, after so many months of taking her for granted, Lily went home, ready to fall to her knees. Just what was she supposed to learn from the change in his behavior? Was there hope with the same man, after he had shredded a woman's heart to pieces?

The men who broke her heart did so because she had insisted on honoring the Lord above their ungodly demands; yet, knowing she had made the right decision did not cushion her pain. Paul, on the contrary, had the qualities——spiritual and gentlemanly——that she sought in a potential husband, even so, she had never permitted the same man to break her heart twice.

Then there was the business of his making his back-up plans in triplets. She knew about Kelly, but who was the third woman? May be at work? Never again, would she permit herself to be so vulnerable.

73

Paul slammed the car door shut and strode into the condo. For some reason, Jonathan was on the floor——blocking the door——his music scores spread out before him, but watching a movie. He never worked on Sundays, unless he was invited to give a Sunday evening concert. That night was Thanksgiving dinner, so it was unlikely he had a concert later.

Jonathan apologized, flopped on the couch and stretched his legs out as though he had no intention of budging from there before the last trump.

"What's this?" Paul pointed to the music scroll.

"I fancied doing some work after I returned from a walk in the park with Sharon, but promptly resisted the temptation——my day of rest."

Paul fetched a glass of orange juice and siphoned the yellow liquid in stormy silence. Ever the gentleman, he slammed the glass on the table. Common decency prevented him from smashing it to smithereens.

"Okay. Out with it. Who is he?"

"Who's who?" Jonathan replied without looking up, but he lowered the volume of the movie.

"The man she's dating!"

Jonathan dropped the remote control and jumped up. "The who?"

"The man she's dating."

"She's what? Are you sure?"

"Positive. I can't get her out on dates."

"Can't be. Kelly, I can believe, but her? Sharon and I had all the bases covered. Bernice and Aaron covered the work front; Sharon and Linda worked the social scene; Michael dug ditches with the weekend crew and the night crew——even befriended Lamar from her former apartment and a couple from her new condo complex. Sharon, Linda and I covered the church." Jonathan checked off his fingers.

"Obviously, there was one base not covered!"

Jonathan paced the room, frowning. "She could be putting you on."

"Nah. Don't think so."

"She won't date at all?"

"Only on her days off."

"Okay. So she has commitments." Jonathan shrugged.

"What commitments? All the big days are gone——Thanksgiving's history, so's Christmas . . . I think she's buying time to brush me off. She's available only once a week and wants us 'to be platonic friends!' To be fair, I blew it."

"There was this one guy." Jonathan thought for a moment, then he shook his head, "No. Not the slightest chance."

"How can you be so sure?"

"He's not a believer. Knowing her, that eliminates him right there."

"But she did go to Palm Springs?"

"I doubt there was anything to it. Sharon and I sensed some hostility with the guy——Brad was the name. Loaded. Think I've seen him before."

"That Don Juan!" He snapped.

"You know him?" Jonathan asked surprised.

He nodded.

"I don't think he was welcomed. For whatever reason they went to Palm Springs, I'm positive it wasn't him. We discovered it was Bernice's idea."

He absorbed this piece of news, frowning. "She went with Bernice?"

"Not as you think. Bernice dragged her——what with you, gone."

He started, surprised.

"When Bernice's with her, she makes Bernice walk the straight and narrow. Bernice's mum is one of us——the reason for their strong friendship."

"Then why?" He threw his hands up and stared at the trellis outside.

Jonathan sat on the edge of the couch, his fists clasped tightly, in deep thought. Then up he jumped again, as though he had sat on hot coals. "But she agreed to go out with you, once a week?" His voice rose up a notch.

He turned. "Yes. She did."

"Good. There's hope. Don't panic. Never mind she may've slipped one by us. She's probably playing it safe. Once burnt, twice shy."

"You think so?"

"I know so."

"You, too?" He couldn't recall Jonathan being unhappy with Sharon.

"Me too!"

"You blew it?"

"Uh-uh. A couple of years ago Sharon threw me out of her life. Remember the time I used to mop around the house?"

"And I thought you were having a hard time shaking off Kathy!"

"Kathy was the foolish mistake I almost made."

He whistled. "How comes you didn't tell me?"

Jonathan punched two cushions into submission. "I felt stupid."

"Jonathan!"

"All right, I should've told you. I felt foolish. Okay? I'm older. Don't worry, you were there——kept things in order and kept me going. You're more than a cousin, Paul. You're the brother I've always wanted."

A new light dawned on Paul. Back then there were moments when he wanted to grill Jonathan, but he had kept his mouth shut believing it was more important to model the right behavior to him, than to berate him. Thank heavens for the grace that guided him.

"You'll make it through this. If it was meant to be, it'll be. If assurance's what she needs, then assurance's what you'll give her." Jonathan affirmed.

"I can't believe it's come to this."

"It happens, Paul. I doubt that any man who finds his dream girl ever feels one hundred percent confident all the time. It's probably healthy too."

"Always living on the brink?"

"Always keep alert. Never take her for granted! Even after you've secured her love, stay on your toes!"

Paul tugged at his collar. "In my blind pride, I never thought I would be reduced to this. But with the divorce rate so high, better humble now than later. You heard about Stanislaus and Karen?"

"No!" Jonathan's face paled. He shifted to the edge of his chair.

"Afraid so."

"They were the perfect couple——mentors to so many people . . . voted for two consecutive years as the most likely couple to succeed."

Paul shook his head. "Not according to Stan. A year ago, I heard rumors."

"I remember you mentioned something."

"Uh-huh. He called me last week. He'd seen it coming. To quote him, 'We lived everybody's dream of what we were supposed to be.'"

Jonathan gave a low whistle. "Scary, isn't it?"

"Humbling. He'd wished to be in the seat of power——hence Karen. He hinted had he abandoned his ambition; he'd have married another girl."

"Let me guess."

"Uh-uh."

"Ingrid would be happy to hear that, but she's happy with her current. They seem serious and we like him. I don't think I should apprise her yet."

Paul nodded. "Good idea. Stanislaus says, 'Humble yourself, pray like crazy. If you must go on your knees more than once, do.' And as you said, never take her for granted! No woman wants to be taken for granted. These are common sense advice. I should've used them a year ago."

Jonathan left the couch to organize his work table.

"And listen to this, when I told him about Lily, he was amazingly supportive. After what he and some of his friends have been through, he believes any virtuous woman can be a life-mate, if we put the Lord first."

"What's his plan?" Jonathan made room for his score on the piano.

"He's torn, but well versed with the Gospels' position and of course, Paul's letters. On the other hand, he doesn't think he has the gift of remaining single and chaste, that's why he sought my advice."

"Any hope of reconciliation?" Jonathan asked.

"No," he shook his head. "Karen has moved on, and, had probably been moving on long before the marriage was over. If he could justify another marriage, it would be his last trip to the altar, he says."

Jonathan dumped the scores into the drawer and slammed it shut. "Scary. Real scary," he repeated, as though marrying the two words was cathartic. "It's all about grace, and remaining humble, isn't it?"

To Paul, it was time to go to war, but his spiritual side also told him to pray. The Lord had been faithful to him. But, if He said, "No," then what? He remained firm on his commitment to the call to serve Him.

"I need to pray. I'm feeling too spread out right now." He tossed his jacket over his shoulders on to a chair and grabbed his Bible.

"So am I." Jonathan turned off the movie.

◆ ◆ ◆

Themes of brown and pumpkin and Autumn leaves greeted the guests as they entered the Fellowship Hall.

Paul's eyes x-rayed the single males in the hall, like a cowboy bent on routing out the bad guy. Jonathan assisted him.

Women bustled around laying out their special dishes on the tables that the set-up crew had organized after church.

Marjorie's head bobbed in rhythm to her counting the tables.

Melody popped into the hall, searched the crowd until she had spotted her, then she hurried over and whispered in her ear.

"Tell her to stop fussing. I'm coming," she said, and resumed counting.

Melody returned to the nursery.

MJ and group tossed chairs around, in between jostling——setting up chairs they called it . . . more like creating a raucous, if truth was told.

Matt cupped his hands and called to them, "Hey guys! Any chance we'll get done before dinner gets cold?"

"Yes, sir," MJ replied for the group.

In a blink, the additional chairs were neatly placed around tables with place settings. Matt might as well had announced a drill sergeant was coming to get their hide.

Marc dashed off to continue jostling with his group on the lawn.

MJ——home on Thanksgiving break——sidled his group in a certain direction, in pre-determined steps. After using this tactic so many times before, he had become a professional at it. He made half a circle move, the group shifted, paused and pretended to be in deep conversation, then he made another half a circle move, and on the game continued as they inched their way toward their goal.

Interrupting his on vigilance, Paul coughed. When MJ finally merged his group with Viviana's group; he burst out laughing. Slick! Like mentor.

Jonathan followed the direction of his eyes and chuckled also.

At the buffet table, Maricela Cecilia Calderon made room for her homemade enchiladas and reserved a seat for her husband at a corner table.

Paul veiled his face. So much, and yet again so little, had changed. The Calderons and their five children tried to mingle and should feel welcomed.

To the best of his knowledge, their children were well regarded——Miguel, their youngest son at eleven, a spirited young man; Norland Angel Maurice Jr., their eldest son——called Maurice, to avoid confusing him with Norland Valdez Calderon Sr.——at twenty-three, an aspiring evangelist who joined the Pentecostals with his girlfriend, Adriana.

Then in the middle, the girls——Felicia, a legal secretary with an AA degree; followed by Rosa Maria, a student at Citrus Community College, planning on transferring to a four-year college, and then Viviana Manolita, a freshman at PHLU——all decent young women.

Maricela Cecilia herself was no pushover and a model to her children. She too had earned her AA degree in Business Administration, which she utilized in managing her husband's business. An exacting woman, she ran her house; her husband cooperated in manly silence of a mariachi——the head of the house, the poster child for economy of words. But out in public, she kept her counsel, often looking for corners to watch the parade. Among her own, she could talk anybody under the table, with one side of her mouth.

Once again, Paul wished better for the Calderons. It occurred to him he could remedy that, perhaps invite Maurice to social events?

He watched Maricela wipe her mouth to hide a smile, when she noticed MJ talking to Viviana's group, then he resumed searching for Lily. Was she hiding in a corner like Maricela or out with her latest flame? "Careful now! You won't make any progress traveling down that road," he muttered.

"I heard that. Take it easy," Jonathan muttered back.

Like in a miracle, Lily appeared, placed her dish down, and beelined for Maricela.

Paul broke into a broad smile.

Lily stopped in front of Maricela. "There you are Maricela! What are you doing hiding here? I'm sure they could use another hand."

"Everything's done." Maricela folded her hands in her lap.

"No. Not quite. I think some tables lack water and juice."

Maricela reserved her seat with her shawl and accompanied her to a group of more friendly women. Soon after, Maricela teamed up with one of them, serving water and juice, chatting about where to get good Christmas deal.

Lily and another lady completed their section, before she slipped away to a discreet place. The festive atmosphere——children running around, people talking to each other——was more like the fellowship of believers among whom she grew up. She observed clusters of people humming. As bees hovered over flowers, their voices rose and ebbed across the hall. If only every day was like Thanksgiving and Christmas!

From the corner of her eye, she noticed Paul tracing her movement around the room. Believing that he and Jonathan would join Sharon, she reserved a quiet table for herself, Raya and another friend.

A new girl to the church——probably in her thirties——searched for a vacant table, with a tight smile. She watched her. Thrice, the lady failed to get a seat——all those tables were reserved.

"There is plenty of room over here," she called to her.

"What a relief." The lady introduced herself as Greta, new to ENC.

She welcomed her, and asked whether she had found any midweek group to join, and proceeded to tell her about all the options.

As the tables filled up fast, she leaned two chairs against the table for her friends. "Make that seven," Sharon's voice said from behind.

"Pardon?" she turned.

Sharon had her fingers up in the air, counting. "Yes. Seven. I bet you, you'll have more company than two."

"Are you sure? I don't want to tie up more chairs."

"Seven. Trust me," Sharon winked and melted into the crowd.

In disbelief, Lily leaned five more chairs against the table and observed the traffic flow. Over twelve months later and how far had she come? Seven chairs, instead of one. And of course, the McGaelic family who had reserved the adjacent table. Was this a sign that she should remain at Evangelical Neighborhood Church until she found a new job?

An acquaintance——Giovanni, ENC violinist——came over. She introduced him to Greta, then she gave him her rapt attention, while still including Greta in the conversation. Giovanni was a decent man.

So engrossed was she in their conversation that she failed to see Paul frowning. Giovanni finally left to chat with his other friends.

Another charming church member took over the vacated seat. A minute later, he felt a friendly pat on his shoulders.

"Hey, I don't think we've met before," Paul introduced himself.

The young man stared into steel blue eyes. Smiling as Paul's lips were, the rest of him was not. The man jumped up as though he had been stung by a yellow jacket and introduced himself.

She flashed a smile at him and resumed talking. The poor man relaxed a little and carried on bravely, but Paul stood his ground, prompting his comments with back-slaps. Jonathan joined in the conversation, a bit too loudly, perhaps. Never had roasting a turkey generated so much heated discussion. What made a turkey more delicious——marinated in cranberry sauce or buttered herbs or grandma's secret recipe? The young man looked back and forth from Paul to her, uncertain.

Sharon, observing the scene from a distance, came over, her face awash with laughter. "I see you're holding down the fort very well."

She sighed, relieved. "Another minute, and I would have had to release your seats. So many people showed up."

"The best way to know how many attend ENC is to hold a Thanksgiving dinner." Sharon shifted her chair to make room for Matt and Marjorie, just as Raya and the other friend also took their seats.

She nodded in agreement, but before she could reply, Pastor Tim stood up to welcome the guests and give a brief message. And to prove that he was a man of his word, he sat down after exactly five minutes.

"Pastor Tim's a seasoned pastor," Marjorie addressed the table. "He keeps it short and simple at Thanksgiving potlucks."

She joined in the laughter, surprised many friends had chosen her table.

As if on cue, Paul passed her a turkey tray and an asparagus platter. "My lady," he bowed his head.

She thanked him, somewhat embarrassed.

"That should do it Paul. Chivalry! We could use more of that," Matt joked.

She lowered her eyes. A glow of mist drifted down her brow. She sought Marjorie's face, looking for sympathy; instead, Marjorie gave her the biggest wink. What was going on? Did anybody care that she could get hurt again? Praise be, her vacation was coming up!

$$74$$

It was the norm in the information age of the late twentieth century, that anyone who desired more information could turn to the experts or the Internet. In fact, it was considered prudent that the wise would avail themselves of these global services. A man driven could just as easily mistake his jealousy for prudence. Throughout Monday, Paul made calls and crossed off names. His seventh sense urged him to have more faith; his sixth sense was beyond reason.

No doubt, had he been a man of less independent means, he might have spent more time weighing his dilemma. Though embarrassed, he pushed forward, galvanized by the jungle call "The Van Clydens never lose. They're winners!"

In the evening, he interviewed——separately in a restaurant——three of the candidates. The final candidate was the one a friend had recommended highly.

"What's your usual fee?" he asked.

"Five grand per project."

"How long?"

"About two months – – give, or take."

"But your fee is firm."

"Yes. You can count on me."

"Very well." He signed the contract, gave him a firm handshake, settled the bills for the refreshments and departed.

Even after his missionary trip, he was still learning the meaning of being committed to the One who promised to care for him. The process began after he answered the call, but, with every step forward, he was discovering areas where he should permit the Lord to be his absolute manager.

◆ ◆ ◆

Paul slammed the phone down, grabbed his coat and briefcase and stormed out of the office, frowning. To top it, Lily had missed the Tuesday evening singles' meeting. Sharon was just as surprised.

Still scowling, he maneuvered his car out of the city to Santa Monica Freeway and hit red tail-lights. Twenty-five miles per hour and drivers cutting in and out of traffic don't mix. By the time he drove through his family's gate, his executive blue eyes were darting red sparks.

Charlotte took one look at Paul and sent up a prayer, "For our sakes, let him not drive through that gate empty handed for Christmas or we'll all be a' coming home a lot sooner than we thought!"

That it would be one of the longest Thanksgivings the Van Clydens had ever had, she didn't need a Harvard graduate to elaborate it to her.

◆ ◆ ◆

The Ontario-New York plane taxied to a gate at La Guardia Airport. Off-boarding passengers rushed through the Thanksgiving Eve's crowd to the luggage terminal. Twenty minutes later, Lily emerged and approached a young man who appeared to be in his late twenties or early thirties, waiting at the arrival terminal. He was at least six feet two inches tall, handsome, distinguished and very confident, enough to make any competitor jaundice.

In the wings, a man in dark glasses watched the rendezvous, his carryon luggage slung over his shoulders.

Lily chatted with her companion, apparently unaware that she was being watched. At the taxi curb, the young man mentioned their destination to the supervisor. The boss yelled it to the driver and seated them in the cab, city-bound.

The man in dark glasses took the next taxi, and followed hard on their heels. He had hit gold when he overheard Lily's destination.

Lily's taxi drove to a five-star hotel near Fifth Avenue. The young man settled the fare and they checked in. From the chitchat with the concierge, it was obvious he was no stranger to the hotel.

The man in dark glasses' cab also pulled up; paid the driver in a hurry and rushed in, but Lily and her companion had disappeared. He had been lucky getting a seat on the plane——Lily's early flight and departure from the less busy Ontario Airport, had put him at an advantage. Would he be as lucky this time? As he was soon to find out, his luck had run out.

At the reception, he could not get out a peep from the attendants. No sob-story moved them. The hotel guest list was strictly private. No, the hotel had no vacancy and no, the attendants did not accept bribes. From the corners of his eyes, he spotted hotel security approaching and hurried to the exit.

Around the corner, he dictated his notes into his dictaphone, then he searched for a modest hotel. The pay was good, but he had a family to feed. However, since the per diem was included in the contract, he rented a car.

Thanksgiving Day he returned, but remained outside at the curb. There was no sign of Lily and her friend.

The day after Thanksgiving, he woke up earlier and again pulled up two blocks before the hotel, then he waited.

About ten o'clock, Lily and the young man appeared. They took a taxi and went shopping on Fifth Avenue. The man tagged along, without his dark glasses.

It was easy to see her companion was spending lavishly on her. She did not appear to mind, on the contrary, she was in high spirits.

Since he had seen enough and had hit a brick-wall with the hotel, he went on standby at the airport and finally boarded a plane for home. To compensate for missing Thanksgiving, he had promised his wife he would drive the children to the mountains on Saturday, to hunt for the largest Christmas tree ever.

75

In veiled anger, Marjorie dragged a box to the living room, and mopped her face with a giant handkerchief, the size of a hand towel. The whole day she had been scrubbing and cleaning. Matt and the children helped, in between getting in her way, or watching TV, or asking for snacks.

Matt was now rocking in his favorite chair, watching TV. At least, he had herded the boys to clean the yard and put up the outdoor Christmas lights——for that, she was grateful.

"What does a Joneson mother have to do to get some attention in this place?" she muttered, then she cupped her hands and yelled, "Whatever became of the gentlemen in this house? Used to be a lady could lounge back polishing her nails, while the men hauled boxes around the house!"

Matt popped out of his Lazy-Boy. Marc and MJ dashed downstairs like a troop responding to the bugle call.

"We'll get that," chorused three very intimidated male voices. Nothing like getting Mum upset at the start of the Christmas season!

Melody waltzed in with Melanie. "Are we ready yet?" she asked.

"As soon as you know 'who' get all the boxes down," Marjorie pointed backwards with her thumb.

"Last box down," MJ yelled. "Where do you want this, Mum?"

"In the center."

"Center it is." MJ placed the box in the center, turned and gave Melody and Marc a stern look. "We're all agreed, we're one year older, right?"

"Wow, Mum, MJ's beginning to sound like a college student. Yes. We promise." Marc saluted MJ.

MJ punched him playfully.

"Okay gang, time to line up." Marjorie adjusted her glasses.

"Mum, when will you help me finish Mrs. O'Mallery's afghan?" Melody asked.

"Oh dear!" Marjorie rubbed her forehead. "Could we do it next week?"

"But you said you've other commitments and I want to dry-clean it so it looks pretty and professional, like the ones in the shops."

Marjorie cradled her head for a moment. "Okay boys, help Dad. Melody and I'll finish the afghan."

Melody fetched her sewing box from upstairs and spread an afghan blanket on the dining room table.

Melanie grabbed two snowflakes. "I want to do it myself." She dangled the snowflakes in the air.

Marjorie moved out of her way. "Melanie, dear, stick to the lower part, until we get to the angel."

The boys sorted the decorations and went to work, while she demonstrated to Melody how to trim an afghan and make it look elegant.

An hour later, she threaded a ribbon through an eye in the afghan and raised her head. Matt had not let out a single sound since they started decorating and was nowhere near the tree. She studied him, curious.

Matt placed another wheel on.

She scowled. "Honey, what's that doing in here?"

"Getting ready to take its place at the nativity scene." He tightened the wheels. Small beads of perspiration clumped his salt pepper hair.

"What has a train got to do with the nativity scene?"

"It's the alternative transportation we would've used," he answered.

"Dad, there were no trains back then," Marc said.

Matt adjusted his glasses and combed through his hair with his hands, leaving it no less improved than before. "Use your imagination. If the Jonesons had paid their homage, we would have used a train."

"Why not a boat?" Melody measured more ribbons.

"There were no rivers in Nazareth or Bethlehem, Melody," Marc said.

"Are you sure? What about River Jordan? They used boats all the time." She cut the ribbons and handed them to her mother.

"In lakes, of course," Marc replied.

"Same with a river," she countered.

"How would we get to the manger?" Marc asked his father.

"Let's say it was too dark for the Jonesons' family to use a boat to the nativity scene." Matt grinned.

"As long as we're using our imagination, we could've used a bus or a family van or even a plane," Marjorie joined in.

"Folks, where's your sense of adventure? Electric train's the only mode of transportation that carries a lot of people and doesn't use gas."

Marjorie removed her glasses and stared at her husband for a full five seconds. "Or somebody's toy, who shall remain unnamed?"

Everybody laughed.

"Busted, Dad! Just say you're busted," MJ said.

Marc shifted decorations around. "I'll make room for Dad's train."

Marjorie handed the afghan to Melody and checked the Nativity scene. "I don't think that train will hang from any tree, unless we move the whole Nativity to the Sequoia Forest. As a long-suffering wife, I suppose I could find room for it. It's always been my lot to be the meek wife who accommodates her husband's need——like fitting a train in the Nativity scene, even though there were no trains back then," she sniffled and batted her eyelids.

"That's more like the Christmas spirit." Matt gave his wife a peck on the cheeks and went back to tidying the carpet, a sly look on his face.

Melody chuckled. "Yes, it comes around once a year and then hibernates for the rest of the year."

"That's what the homeless say——same place, same time, next year. That's kind of sad. They know the people who flock to feed them wouldn't go within a smiling distance the rest of the year. I guess they're expected to disappear into the wood–cracks, or something." Marc searched for another spot to place his gold globe.

"The more reason we should be consistent," Melody replied.

"Until then, let's spread some Christmas cheer around here." Matt popped out of the floor. "Another gold globe and snowflake up here and Melanie, you do the honors." He propped Melanie over his shoulders. "I guess this year, I'm not thinking so much about the homeless——important as they are——as I'm about the Van Clydens. I'm reminded of how easily we could lose what we treasure most."

"The most important thing, Dad, is that grace and mercy were watching out for Paul all the time." Melody said, happy about the turn of events.

"Paul and his parents," Marjorie added, admiring the tree. "Melody, you can finish. I'm sure Mrs. O'Mallery will be thrilled. It's beautiful."

Melody thanked her and straightened a light on the tree. "I hear Kelly's been doing better, well, sort of. I think the break-up was good; it made her take life more seriously. So, in the end, everything worked out."

MJ locked eyes with her for a moment.

"Sometimes parents don't have answers for everything. I think what I'm trying to say is, if Mum and I've disappointed you in any way this year, can you forgive us?" Matt swept the room with his eyes.

Marjorie squeezed his hand and handed the angel to Melanie. In silence, the family watched Melanie place the figurine gently atop the tree, then they held hands, as she prayed, "I wish that God and Jesus give everybody a wonderful Christmas everywhere and that everybody's happy 'cause we're remembering that. . . um," she hesitated and asked her father, "Dad, Jesus was born when shepherds watched their flocks?"

"Mhmm." Matt nodded.

"It was snowing?"

"No. It was earlier. Christmas is the official day we celebrate Jesus' birthday, but He was born earlier, when it was still warm enough for shepherds and their flocks to stay out in the field." Matt kissed her head.

Melanie nodded. "Okay. So, God, thank you that Jesus was born earlier, when shepherds were watching sheep and thank you for Christmas, His official birthday and thank you that . . . that, Paul and . . . his dad and mum and . . . what's their name, Daddy?"

"Van Clydens."

"And that Paul and his dad and mum and Van Clydens have a good Christmas and thank you for Jesus. Amen."

"Amen," chorused the family.

76

Coffee servers lined up cups in rhythm to the approaching feet of the first Sunday school class. Not a spare chair in Sunday school——the first Sunday of December promised to be a full church. Servers counted pastries and fresh fruits, willing them to multiply. Two ladies arrived with two full trays into outstretched arms of "More goodies! Alleluia! Put them over here."

Paul espied Lily over the crowd, mingling, Sharon and Linda close by her. She had no shame, no guilt and so much power over him.

He did appreciate all the efforts Sharon and Jonathan had invested in preserving his dignity. "Hold up your head like a man," was good advice to the adviser, not the advisee. He felt the pain, the shame and frustration she must have felt, when he had rubbed Kelly in her face with no concern for her dignity or pain. It was a miracle she had not switched churches.

Friday, he finally went to dinner at the Daelvins' house. After the girls and Sheila had stepped out into the kitchen, Bill had again reinforced his Dad's advice cautioning him to be certain that he was following the Lord's guidance and his motives were right. Now with both their words ringing in his ears, he approached Lily with his most charming smile.

Sharon excused herself, taking Linda with her, claiming she was going in search of Jonathan, though Jonathan was clearly in view, talking to a couple.

Lily smiled at him, in complete innocence.

"Well, hello," he crooned, "so, how was Thanksgiving?" He walked her away from the crowd to the lawn area.

"Snowy weather always makes a good excuse to cuddle up and drink hot chocolate. How was yours?" She flashed her white teeth.

"Long."

"Oh? You took more than a week?" Her question seemed innocent.

"No. You were gone for over a week, right?"

"No. I was not."

"Really?" He perked up. "When did you get back?"

"Wednesday."

"Oh? And what have you been doing?"

"Relaxing."

"Alone?" he blurted out. "I mean, you've been around?"

"Excuse me?"

"It seems you've been busy." He was back sliding through very thin ice and could soon be needing his water galoshes to finish this conversation. Another slip of the tongue, and he could be at the bottom of the lake, frozen out.

"No more than normal," she replied.

"Good, then perhaps we could go for a drive after church?"

Lily crinkled her nose. "I had plans for this afternoon."

"We'll make it brief——no more than a couple of hours."

"Thank you, but I really have to catch up with my work," she said.

Sharon had initiated their reconciliation, that should have been enough, but was Lily dragging her feet? She appeared determined to give him his space. She started walking to the sanctuary. He accompanied her.

No one beats a Van Clyde!

He was determined to celebrate Christmas with Lily. He applauded himself for locking in the Christmas concert, he hoped.

Back home, Paul wished he could roll back the reel. Remembering his promise the night of the party, he dialed MJ and chatted around issues such as MJ's first year and social life——had he met anyone nice?

MJ perked up. "There's someone I like a lot, but she's playing hard."

"Does she meet the standard we discussed?" he asked.

"Yeah. She goes to ENC and her middle name starts with an M, so I'm praying that will satisfy the Jonesons' tradition."

He chuckled. "Always stick with the Ms? Eh? As long as she's a believer, you're on the right track. As we discussed, try not to approach marriage as a missionary field. And never assume it's only a date——love can catch you unaware. Once you take that plunge, no guarantee she'll change her mind and embrace your faith. Do your homework."

"Yeah, but . . ." MJ hesitated.

"But what?" he asked.

"I've asked around and," MJ sighed. "Her family's very strict."

"Then ask for permission."

"What?"

"Ask her parents."

"I like her a lot, but I'm not there yet." MJ sounded embarrassed.

"I know, but it's the polite thing. I'm in the same quandary. There's someone I admire, but her parents are international. I regret that I didn't follow protocol, as my Dad taught me. I wish her parents lived closer."

"My Dad hinted along the same line," MJ concurred.

"He's right. That's how their generation did it before the laissez-faire culture. I know you're polite, but don't stand in the driveway and honk—introduce yourself. And it doesn't hurt to get a new haircut, as your Dad said."

"Wow. Thanks! I'll do that right away." MJ sounded relieved.

"I'll be praying for you. Let me know how it goes."

Paul became more cheerful. If MJ succeeded where he had failed, some good would have come out of his debacle with Lily. He liked the Calderons.

◆ ◆ ◆

In the ensuing weeks, Paul redefined courtship. He gave Lily her space, but had flowers delivered to her condo on Saturday mornings, braving her ire at being woken up so early. Extravagant as the flowers were, he rationalized that they compensated for the months he failed to take her out for dinner or symphonies. The Van Clydens never dated cheap. He was not about to start.

The cloud on his horizon was his promise to go to the games with Shane and the boys. Why should he be nice to a man who had been a thorn on his sides and sought to ruin his career? Nevertheless, he continued to pray for a kindness which he would not have otherwise extended to such a one.

But first, Mrs. O'Mallery was like his surrogate grandmother. He had noticed that she was not in her best element, though she was still sprightly.

77

Paul discussed how to cheer up Mrs. O'Mallery with Jonathan and Sharon. She always became melancholy on the anniversary of her husband's passing. They agreed that Christmas gifts and lunch should do the trick.

Sharon ferreted out her favorite restaurants and invited three of her friends. They were so elated, that they expanded the invitation. By the time Paul heard about it through the grapevine, the news was, "Leona's friends are taking her out to lunch at this wonderful five-star restaurant in Newport Beach. Can you make it? We would love for you to come. And of course, she prefers to get rides from you."

He assured them that he wouldn't miss it for anything and gave Mrs. O'Mallery a ride, prepared to foot the bill, as he had planned.

Mrs. O'Mallery decked herself in silk and diamonds, her husband's favorite, looking every bit a woman of substance——elated at the five-star venue they had selected and having her friends there all dressed up in their Sunday best.

After lunch, Jonathan and Sharon excused themselves, citing a prior commitment to shop for a very special birthday gift for Sharon's aunt. Did she mind very much if they stopped by later to visit with her?

Mrs. O'Mallery replied that she always loved Jonathan and Sharon stopping by to keep her company and to her delight, Paul invited her for a walk, while her other friends also went shopping. What better place than Balboa Beach, a quieter cove?

Gallantly, he offered her his arm and guided her, as they walked along the sandy shores. He had never seen her so happy.

"You remind me of my husband," she said.

Paul grinned.

"He sure knew how to treat a girl right. My son's nothing like him. I think we spoiled him. He just thinks of himself . . . hangs out with the nouveau riche——splashing his father's money around. We tried to interest him in the simple things, but he would have none of it. I pray he will mellow with the Lord's help."

"I'm sure he will," he agreed.

"Will you keep praying for him?" she pleaded.

He promised he would. She seemed satisfied with that.

She observed her setting, welcomed the fresh breeze, a contrast from the inland smog, and thanked him again for his kindness, then she became quiet.

After some hesitation, she said, "Paul?"

"Yes, Ma'am," he replied.

"We've been friends for a good time."

"Yes, Ma'am. We have."

"Some people think I'm just a silly old woman."

"No. You're not. We respect you, Leona."

"Then you don't mind my saying this?"

He tipped his head in consent.

"I was very happy with my husband. Had he been from Bolivia, I would have got married to him in a heartbeat." She gazed at him. "But as it happened, he was from Wisconsin. God's gift comes wrapped in a surprising package, sometimes. I've been praying for your happiness, as I'm sure so have your dear parents. There's nothing worse than getting stuck with the wrong choice."

He hesitated, unsure of where the conversation was going.

"I've searched the scriptures and never found a passage that forbids marriage that honors the Lord's master plan through Adam and Eve. So, had my husband been from Timbuktu, yet equally virtuous, I would not have hesitated in a blink."

He stopped and stared at her. A light dawned on him.

She touched his cheeks, "I've watched you waste away, pining for what's within your reach. Give yourself a chance to be happy, Paul. I want you to be happy!"

He swallowed hard and continued staring at her, numbed by her astuteness, then he kissed her cheek and croaked, "Thank you."

They walked on, enjoying their deeper friendship, as he marveled at the wisdom that had prompted him to befriend a woman his grandmother's age. As long as he honored the Lord, first, what more confirmation did he need? A lightning bolt?

♦ ♦ ♦

Lily opened the door and invited Paul in with an elegant gesture, unconscious of how charming she looked.

He selected the couch facing the kitchen, sunk down and unbuttoned his jacket, relieved that Lily had agreed to a date at such short notice. He attributed it to Mrs. O'Mallery. When he dropped her off that afternoon, she had prayed for him and asked him to be brave.

"Orange juice?" Lily asked. Without waiting for him to reply, she served him a glass of orange juice.

He gave her a silent toast. She lowered her eyes, bashful, then she fetched her winter coat from upstairs and came down clasping a small, evening velvet purse, trimmed with rhinestone.

In the evening light, her silver long-sleeved gown glittered, falling in free moving pleats to the floor. Dark, soft, shoulder-length curls accentuated her tall, slim height. He veiled his eyes and gulped down his orange juice in one long swig.

A man of independent means who owned at least three pairs of diamond cuff links——but seldom wore them——a pair now shone from his starched, white cotton shirt's cuffs. The determination in his face would set any healthy girl's heart fluttering. Ever since he returned from the mission field, without a doubt, it had become evident he had a square chin.

As they went to the parking lot, he floated on air, like at their first date.

When he took the 10 Freeway to 57 Orange County Freeway, Lily concluded that they were driving toward Newport Beach.

Paul glanced at her and smiled; a wistful look fleeted across his face——perhaps he too was remembering their first drive to the Beach.

He took the 55 Costa Mesa Freeway to the I-405 North and exited on Bristol Street, then he continued until he pulled up in front of Chez Germain on La Via De Paz, around the corner from Anton Boulevard.

Lily had heard about the restaurant. She searched her surroundings for a familiar landscape, but found none.

Paul handed over the keys to the valet and escorted her inside. Among the mix of guests from casual business to formal, Lily felt at home. Though a popular restaurant, they were seated within ten minutes.

The waiter brought them their house wine list. Paul declined, so the waiter switched to soft drinks and gave them the menu. They ordered non-alcoholic sparkling cider and Paul ordered appetizers.

The French provincial and American menu gave them a good selection. Lily ordered salmon sautéed in butter, well-done, for the main course, and Tiramisù for dessert and hot tea. Paul ordered the braised veal house specialty, medium-well done, and went Mediterranean all the way.

In contrast to their first date, he spent most of the evening looking at her, without saying much.

She could not ignore his tan that glowed above his dark, gray suit, reminding her of a tropical islander. Reluctantly, she admitted he meant more to her than she had cared to admit in the eighteen months of their sporadic romance. But where would it all lead? How could she determine the right path? Throw up more Gideon's fleece?

When they started on their dessert, she took a sip of her tea and asked, "So, how really was your trip?"

"Pretty good."

"Did it meet your expectations . . . did you accomplish your mission?"

Paul searched for the right words. "Much more. I completed all three missions. The business end went well, minor glitches——all resolved. I'd a good team. The local people cooperated, despite our initial misgivings. I couldn't have asked for a better set of people to work with. BF&S doesn't pretend to espouse my faith, but I believe they got blessed as a result of paying for my entire trip."

"We can never out-give God."

"That's true. The missionary part was a change of pace. We went deeper into the village, but the people had a great spirit. I met some very special people there and I hope to see them again. In particular, Mr. Odhiambo——gave of himself so willingly to ensure our comfort . . . ran errands . . . worked extra hours."

At the mention of Odhiambo, she played with her dessert, then she asked, calmly, "Were you able to, um, finish the project?"

"Almost. The locals and the long-term missionaries will complete the cosmetics. I'm confident they'll finish before the new school-year begins."

"I am glad. You spent your year well."

"Thank you."

"And the third?"

He seemed surprised and a bit embarrassed. "Oh. Um, I'd some stuff to take care of for my Dad——I thought it would be nice to take the initiative and surprise him with a potential business partner, and so forth."

She peeked at him from under her eyelashes and dabbed her mouth. "How did you like their chicken?"

"Oh, the chicken!" He held his head in mock horror. "You know, at first I found it too chewy, but it was quite tasty——had real natural taste and needed very little spices to bring out the flavor. Then I got used to it, and loved it. Now I'm having a hard time adjusting to our softer version."

She laughed. "What about the hen, doesn't it compare?"

"The hen's too soft, plus I think natural bred chicken is very tasty."

"Well, I am glad you got used to at least one food."

"More than one. I loved sumbusas and African sweet potatoes."

"Of course! How could anyone not like sumbusas? I love them for snack."

"Don't they make great snack?"

"I'm relieved things worked out." She paused. "You mentioned you would like to see some of the people again, does that mean you hope to return some time?"

"It depends. East Africa has great weather and excellent business opportunities. I ran into some internationals who went for a short visit, but stayed on. The place grows on one. I could see myself living there, if the political climate remains stable." He studied her above the rim of cup.

She followed suit, and drank slowly from her cup, her eyes locked with his, then she put her cup down, and dug into her Tiramisù.

He followed suit and settled the bill the moment they completed their dessert. Throughout their meal he was relaxed, but now he glanced often at his watch, as he drove up Bristol Street. A few minutes later, he slowed down.

She recognized The Performing Arts Center.

"Do you mind?" he asked.

"Not at all. Love it. What's on?"

"Their Christmas program. It was almost sold out, but we were blessed to get last minute tickets."

They arrived at their front row seats in the first tier just before curtain call.

Back at the condo, Paul escorted Lily to her door, but did not go in. Instead, he took her hands after unlocking the door and surprised her by kissing them.

"I'd a great night, thank you," he said.

"And thank you." She smiled, trying to steady herself.

"I'll see you Saturday?" he asked.

He had been keeping their appointments, but her heart still plunged at the familiar phrase, cautioning her to brace herself for the moment when Paul's dad may put an end to her fantasy.

She smiled bravely and said, "Saturday," expecting him to leave, but he continued to gaze at her. At last, he dragged out his final goodnight. Soon after, she heard his car engine roar and take flight from her neighborhood.

She stared at the taillights of the escaping car, steeling herself for what Saturday might bring, wondering whether she had been wise in letting Paul back into her life, but not for too long. When she entered her bedroom, her eyes lighted on the dissertation papers she had dumped on her bed, to hide them from him.

Paul arrived home, amazed at the power of a praying grandmother for a weary searcher. He kicked himself for not taking Mrs. O'Mallery into his confidence sooner. He was sailing along well, until he remembered the upcoming game. He did not relish the thought of keeping company with Shane, never mind his other friends would also attend. Could he renege on his commitment and shake Shane off? Would that be honorable?

78

Shane's private world had come to a fork in the road. During the summer, when he was hospitalized with a bad infection——blood poisoning——only his middle-aged neighbors, became his regular visitors. They also took care of his dog, the same dog that he used to allow to poop in their yard and pull up their new plants.

The only other surprise he got was from his ex-wife, whom he had not talked to for years. She called to check if he needed anything. An old mutual friend on his way to visit his father, happened to see him and stopped by briefly. Later, the friend had alerted her. He had assured her he was fine, but, she had still sent another mutual friend to check on him, for which he would forever remain grateful.

After he was discharged, his neighbors had checked on him regularly, until he had returned to work.

He regretted his earlier behavior and cringed at the recollection of how he used to respond to the lady's kind invitation, "I don't believe in that stuff. I go solo," he would say.

Her husband would grin and reply, "Well, all in the Lord's time."

As he resumed work, he dreaded things returning to normal——hoping they would remain friendly and invite him again.

Loathed to violate his privacy, neither his associates, nor members of his social organization, had visited him or telephoned. But for the couple, he would have been alone in the hospital.

His associates gave him a well-wish card after he had returned to work.

The club, on the contrary, did not know he was sick; they had assumed he was on vacation, and forgot to tell them. There was no guarantee they would have called anyway. When he finally showed up after three weeks' absence, apart from welcoming him back, they moved on with their meeting agenda as though he had just returned from vacation.

Had things taken a turn for the worse, what would they have done?

In his adult years, he had bought into caricatures of believers as a bunch of bigots and intellectual incompetents and had latched on to this view, until his neighbors' kindness had debunked his preconceptions.

Shocked at the brevity of life and the realization that true friends were not always who he thought, he went on a pilgrimage to re-examine his attitude toward his neighbors and his parents' faith.

Initially, he had thought networking with Paul would advance his career at Paul's expense; but now, adrift, he wished Paul could see a different side to him, as he searched for a place to anchor his life.

He had assumed BF&S would tap him for the lucrative project that Bret had quit, but when his executive ally leaked the firm's choice to him, he had turned moldy green. Whatever bleep he had had of rivaling Paul and surpassing him, had vanished from his radar screen. What more, Paul had not dropped the ball, as he had hoped Paul would.

And now, as a result of his health scare, he was also going through the metamorphosis that had forced him to question dogmas he had accepted. What was the implication of Paul asking him out to the ball game? Could he hope that BF&S' position towards him had changed?

There was another reason he was becoming increasingly convinced that his job security depended on how he treated Paul.

79

The Los Angeles Coliseum teemed with fans. Under his dad's watchful eyes, a young boy braved burly knees of seasoned attendants across the bleachers back to his seat, clutching a hot dog muffled with onions, ketchup and mustard, his face animated with unsuppressed excitement.

As he passed, Paul said, "Yeah. Now that's a hot dog! Buddy, you've captured the art and science of putting together one mean hotdog! You nailed it! Give me a five!"

Shane joined in the laughter, seemingly at ease, for once. He glanced around the packed Stadium and even risked a smile at a fortyish-looking girl across the bleachers. No one seemed to consider him an outsider.

His sandy hair had streaks of gray——a testament to his forty-some years on earth. At five feet ten and half inches tall, with pale skin and cloudy gray eyes, his deportment was that of a man who was slightly lost and he had the habit of reminding everybody that he was five feet, eleven inches, almost six feet tall.

He carried his five feet ten inches' frame in a five feet six inches' stature, but heaven helped anyone who hinted that he was less than six feet tall! So obsessed was he with his height that he had marked a ruler on his bedroom wall, to measure his height once a month, afraid that he might grow shorter as he aged.

"This is awesome. I've never sat so close at a game," he said.

Paul cupped his hands. "Looking for some real action!"

"Here, here." The other men chorused.

◆ ◆ ◆

To say that the noise level at the restaurant was decibels above normal, would be the understatement of the year.

"Twenty-three to thirteen, I could live with that any day." Paul pumped his fist in the air.

"The Broncos were licked!" Phil said.

"I wouldn't have missed it. Thanks again." Shane clapped his hands.

"I'd have to drag my girl to one of these," Julian complained.

"How can anybody miss football, man? What turns her on?" another guy asked.

"Ballet or symphony. Watching the other gals twirl around in their tutus with their necks elongated, or some penguin flap his wings. To think I actually got an A in Music Appreciation---miracles do happen!" Julian replied.

"Then try a ticket to the ballet," Phil said in a calm, droning voice, from the side of his mouth and took a bite of his hamburger.

"You're kidding. Right? I already accommodate her with operas! Jazz and country's my thing." He licked his finger and gulped his ice tea.

"Nopes. Not joking. A little honey goes a long way, unless she's the wrong one, then decide fast. If she's worth the keeping, she's worth the tickets."

Paul leaned over to Julian, "Trust Phil. He's the expert. Besides, who says you've to stay awake for the whole performance?"

"I've never been known to snore. Always tell her to wake me up if I start snoring too loudly. Rule number one, stay awake for the opening number; number two, be awake last number before the intermission and for the grand finale. And, be sure to clap loudly. Finally, hold your end of the conversation. It helps to read up before you go, failing that, attend the pre-show lectures."

"That's a boy, Phil!" Paul and the other boys cheered.

Shane seemed uncertain.

The other men resume chatting, but their ears remained cocked.

Paul turned to Shane, "How often do you come?"

"Seldom now . . . used to come when my wife and I were still together. I could've used a few tips back then."

"Sorry to hear that. Children?"

"Nopes. She never wanted any, back then. Interfered with her career."

"That happens. It's the times we live in."

"And you?" Shane asked.

"Working on it. There're some pretty nice girls out there."

"Tell me. In hind sight, I was to blame. I was confused——my wife noticed. She has two kids now with her second and last she says, adamant."

"She sounds like a stable girl," Paul observed.

"That she is. She tried – – I wanted out. Broke her heart. She returned to school, got her masters in Literature and Language Education, then she got a lectureship at a junior college and showed me what I'd missed."

"My Mum was a teacher before she stayed home full time."

"Really?" Shane lit up.

"Yup. Masters in Geography and Maths . . . undergrad minor in Literature."

"Small world. Wow!" Shane grew an inch.

"My Mum went into social studies," Phil said.

"Mine was Agriculture. Farming's in my blood," Julian joined in.

"Then what are you doing in finance?" Phil teased.

"Taking care of family books," Julian shot back.

"In the middle of L.A.?"

"I go home once a year and beat the auditors to the punch."

"Behold the auditor! Spoken like a true son of finance," they chorused.

"Thanks be. The man has some good in him," Paul ribbed him.

"But can you tell a cow from a moose?" Phil asked.

"Hey, I'm an excellent farmer. I get up at 5 and milk the cows," Julian protested.

"Where the cows?" Maurice Calderon asked.

"Two miles from his duplex, at the Taco Stand El Grande and the Burger Gourmet," the other boys chorused.

Julian shot back, "Come summer, you're all coming for a grueling week at my family farm in Central Valley. And that's an order! No excuses!"

"Bring some boots. And make sure they're Duluth," Paul yelled.

"You can be sure Phil will show up in a slick Oxford," Julian jabbed at Phil, eliciting chuckles. The other boys slapped themselves silly.

"Complete with a morning coat and a top hat," another man said.

"And when he gets there, the cows they look at him and they say, 'Who are you? Have we met before?'" Maurice quipped.

The boys roared with laughter.

Paul cupped his hands and said, "Guess who's treating?"

"As we were saying, Phil's the greatest, the best!" Julian patted Phil's back.

"Hurrah! Phil's the greatest!" the boys cheered.

Phil bowed. "I aim to please. And for your information, my great grandparents were farmers."

"So they were." Paul nodded. Phil's great grandparents had faced tough times during the depression and had created a private farmer's bank for survival, initially, before they grew to the many branches they now had.

Shane raised his hand and confessed timidly, "My parents were farmers."

"See, we're in farmland. Tread carefully," Julian said.

The men ribbed each other a while longer, then resumed their dinner, chatting in low voices, amidst the noises around them.

More relaxed now, Shane picked up his story, "For a while after my divorce, I did some dumb stuff and rationalized a lot, swept by the moment. Finally came to my senses. It's the straight and narrow all the way. In a way, working at BF&S has helped me. I've been trying to find a local church—visited a couple. I hear some of them provide spiritual resources."

"What city are you living?" Paul asked.

"Outskirts of Barren Trees City——in the vicinity of Hollywood, Beverly Hills, but I prefer something more suburban. I found a condo towards the San Gabriel Valley. Love my dog."

"What breed?" Paul asked.

"Collier, same breed as my parents' but I'm beginning to believe there's a big difference between man and dog. One pays taxes; the other consumes them. Too many rights——who's watching out for mine? I am the one who pays the big bucks!"

"Here, here!" the other men chorused.

"Well, if you're ever around the Valley, you're welcomed to visit my church. We've resources that span the gamut," Paul replied.

Shane thanked him and joined the conversation, more confident than he had been at the beginning of the evening.

With Paul's commitment to be kind to Shane fulfilled, he felt liberated to turn his attention to the rest of his Christmas season——parties to attend, special Christmas programs and above all, trying to crack the mystery of Lily.

◆ ◆ ◆

Paul threw his car keys in the basket. He ran upstairs, closed his bedroom door and fell to his knees. "Father, now I know why You insisted that I should reach out to Shane. I'm sorry it took me so long. Please tune my ears to Your voice better, as You lead me. Even when I find it hard to relate to the person, help me do the right thing I pray . . . Amen."

It was too soon to talk to Bill; but it was not wrong to find other ways to encourage Shane to continue improving as a person. Ultimately, he would do whatever he could to help advance his career, legally.

Praying for Shane was the easier part, but Paul was not sold yet. Ever since he invited Shane to the game, he had noticed that Shane had become mellow——going to the extent of ambushing Bill in the corridors to chat. This evening was another indicator of Shane's apparent transformation. Despite that, Paul still cautioned himself to tread softly and be wise, especially with the legal proceedings in progress as Bill had alerted him. After all, this was Shane!

80

Thinking "Strike while the iron is hot" Shane phoned his boss and asked for the day off, to finish moving to his new home.

Still absorbing his new status as part of Paul's circle, he drove to a remote part of Santa Clara River at midday, ripped open a Manila envelope and pulled out a document two hundred pages long. The title of the document was 'PTVC Toxic Mission'——the code word for Paul T. Van Clyden. He flipped through it, reviewing five years of lies and traps he had set for Paul——in vain——then he placed it in a metal container, and set it on fire.

He watched, as the document burned, until the last flickering flame had turned to ashes, then he scattered the ashes over the river.

While a member of BF&S' Diversity, Love, Tolerance Committee and the Considerate Social Group whose mission was to stop the advancement of believers, he had labored to block Paul's promotions to management. Paul's occasional expressions——such as "The Lord willing"——upset them; but then the same people were not offended by their own free expressions——profanity, cussing, and all.

His mentors had groomed him in the art of maintaining a positive, professional conduct, while committing the crime of blocking the advancement of his perceived opponents. The drill was over-laud the work of those whom he favored——no matter how substandard their work was; and down-play Paul's contribution to the firm——no matter how great. Yet once his candidates were promoted, their inexperience and incompetence, forced BF&S to depend on Paul and other capable employees to do their work.

He was succeeding, until his encounter. There were gods and gods, then there was the One. His lucky day, he had pitted himself against that One!

The more he tried to under-mind Paul, the more unfulfilled his life became and his successes tasted to him like gravel and sawdust.

"Shane," his mother had warned him, "if you oppress believers, you offend the Lord, as Saul learnt on his way to Damascus——sooner or later, you will encounter Him. You may appear to be winning for a while, but in the end, you will lose. Avoid malicious people. Stay away from them!"

His mother had explained to him that whatever love she and his father had for him, could not rival God's love, and though He was a loving Father, He could be as firm as any good parent would be, when it was necessary.

This was when the theology of an all-loving God who never held him accountable for his actions, fell apart. His parents had loved him, but they had also tried to mold him into a good citizen. Whenever he had strayed, their love had sometimes carried with it severe, but wise punishment. As a youth, he had hated it; in hindsight, he was grateful.

The saying that you can't serve too many masters must have come from the Good Book, if he was right. It came home to roost at a camp retreat when the leader proposed a theme to bond and commemorate the great strides they had made. The camaraderie spirit was great, higher than on the other days when sectarian groups vied for their rights——covertly or openly.

The group broke up into smaller groups to brainstorm, then they reconvened with suggestions: create a mug or pen, or how about a T-shirt or a plaque?

"Let's create a recipe, include everybody's favorite——you know, make it wholesome," an intellectual announced.

Everybody had cheered, "Yeah. That's a great idea!"

"Great idea, but I only eat fish, not beef," a female member said.

"Chicken's my preference, but vegetables are fine," a male member said in a pleasant voice designed to appease the rest of the group.

"And don't forget pork. It brings out the richness and character of any soup. Just pops in the mouth. Mmmmm!" a mystical, female poet said.

Several people nodded.

"Great idea, but I think it may offend some," a voice said.

"And so might beef," a member of Asian origin mumbled.

"Beef's what this country was built on," a man thumped the table.

"Simon, be sensitive," the mystical poet said.

"Oh com'on! Someone has to speak up," Simon snapped.

A young woman in her twenties jumped to her feet, "Yes. What about our feelings? Who cares about our feelings?"

"Cornelia!" a few voices cautioned.

"All weekend, all I've heard is vegetarian this and vegetarian that! I'm a rancher; so's my Dad," Cornelia snapped, "and so were my grandparents and great grandparents. Ranching runs in my blood."

"Nobody challenged your ancestry. You're over-reacting!" the fish eater said.

"Oh yeah? My Dad's paying our school fees because someone eats beef. What will become of my family and all them ranchers? I've watched my family toil to put food on the table, and pay our bills——beef is what keeps my family going. Are you saying that when you guys are in power that . . . you'll ban beef? Who'll care about our survival? If we can't feed our people, what will they eat? Grass? Or worse, depend on other countries, like . . . import our food from . . . Russia or China or wherever?" She threw up her hands. "This is not working for me. I need some reasonable, intelligent group to work with!" She grabbed her backpack and stormed out.

Shocked silence followed.

"Oh let her go!" some scoffed.

The mystical poet said, "I never thought of it that way. Um…"

The vegetarians stepped in, "Cornelia's right. Let's have two pots—— one for vegetarians, one for meat."

"Leave out the broccoli," a member cautioned.

"And corn, and tomatoes. Allergies," another member added.

"No bell peppers or any hot stuff," yet a third member added.

"I like the idea of separate pots, but we need more time to decide what the ingredients should be," another intellectual said.

"Well, pick the vegetables and leave the meat, or create a booklet of our favorite recipes," the beef eaters suggested.

"Use some common sense. Of course, you can't just pick the vegetables. Vegetarians are not carnivorous. Separate pots make sense. And who's talking about a booklet? We need to eat!" the intellectual argued.

"Are you saying the rest of us are carnivores and have no sense? I like my meat cooked," one woman who had been quiet, snapped.

"You're twisting my words."

"I, twisting your words?"

"Guys, let's remember the rules," the facilitator raised his voice. "Respect each other. Don't get personal."

"What's the point? You don't have to like everything," the leader snarled, caught himself and softened his comment with a tight professional grin.

"But for some people, it's a health issue," the allergic said.

"Yeah and other concerns," a couple murmured.

"Come on! Unite guys!" The leader shouted.

"You don't understand! You only want your way!" a fiery woman yelled.

"Guys, calm down!"

"No! You calm down!" the woman jumped up and shouted back.

Hours later, the united camp had broken down into a debate over rights. The leaders threatened that if the group could not come up with a compromise, they would make the final decisions and since meats offended so many, it would be prudent to be sensitive to the needs of the majority.

Shane had baulked. "The majority as in whose definition? I counted only five vegetarians——two real and three converts——among the one hundred members present." He had enjoyed growing up on his family farm and had loved his cattle ranching neighbors. He would not change a thing.

So deep were they in their debate, that when he had distanced himself to a slope to watch them from a far, they had not noticed. Convinced that he would never climb out of the hole that he had dug himself in, he had despaired, then the sight of Cornelia marching off had galvanized him. Perhaps he should pray, but not since his parents' tutelage had he prayed a sincere desire to turn the corner. The only prayer he had uttered in recent years was to try to twist God's arm.

The group permitted only the universal prayer——designed to appease every god human beings invented——which his parents considered sacrilegious. As a sign of respect for his parents, he started boycotting the offensive invocation by wandering the corridors during the invocation, or by leaving to get a cup of coffee. That small step had brought him so much relief that he had sought other ways to redirect his life and move on.

A line from a song of Ascent to Jerusalem, his mother used to recite, flashed through his mind, "I lift up my eyes . . .," he remembered, but then he jumbled the rest of the words. He lifted up his eyes and said, "I've gone solo for so long."

A moment later, he had remembered a common advice his father used to give him, "It's never too late, son, to throw in your lot with the Lord. If you mean business with Him, He will come through for you. Remember, no one else will plead your case on that Great Day, except Him!" That meant none of his friends or those who exploited him for their own gain, would qualify as his defense attorneys on that day. So why was he there?

The prayer his mother often prayed for him had come to mind, "Lord, please help my son; never let go off him."

He had returned to the group and scrutinized them——the professional, the influential, the revered——not one of them would have his mother or father considered a true friend——as spiritual, and friendly, and kind, and wonderful people, as the group considered themselves to be. A few considered themselves his cordial associates; but he could count on none to vouch for him, if he got in trouble. How did he know? He had tested them.

Everyone present would compromise their values for a better position, power or prestige, and some already had. And they would not hesitate to get ahead and blame others if they could and some already had.

Right then, he had known he wanted a better way——the courage to make a stand, as principled people like his parents and Paul had done through the centuries. Could the same LORD who had sustained them, help him? If Paul could commit to this Being, why not he?

He believed he was headed in the right direction. The sign? Just when he thought he was doomed to prison for his part in helping upper management manipulate BF&S' financial books, the authorities had worked out a deal with him. In exchange for testifying about his role in processing the purchase orders and other questionable contracts, BF&S would drop all proceedings against him. Some might call him a traitor, but would the upright judge him if they knew the truth? The perpetrators were unrepentant——only sorry that they were caught.

BF&S understood that his superiors had used deceitful tactics, some hard for him to have fully grasped at that time. But, he had to promise to remain on the straight and narrow. Short of a lightning bolt, this was the closest he had come to experiencing a miracle. Was it possible that Someone was looking out for him, though his parents were long gone?

Remorseful about the injustice of destroying other people's careers, afraid that one day the Lord might turn the table on him and let him drink from the cup of his own evil, and mindful of his parents' teachings, he started missing meetings until he had mustered enough courage to withdraw from the organization officially. Just as he had cut himself off from associating with other believers, he reversed his direction and distanced himself from the two organizations.

The final step? He had informed the Diversity, Love, Tolerance Committee and the Considerate Social Group that unless they offered the same opportunity to everybody,——including those who honor Adonai-Elohim——he would resign. Their defiant response? Two days later, the committee nominated a colleague——a heavy hitter for blocking promotions——to the top one percent achievers. He had resigned in protest. Then, Paul had surprised him.

After so many years of searching, his instinct told him that in Paul's group he may have found a place to belong without being exploited.

"I was wrong——so wrong." Shane stirred himself from the river bank where he had been sitting, reviewing his past. As his mother used to pray, he yelled, "Lord, help me never again allow myself to be confused over who I am! You created me for a purpose. Central to that purpose is to love You and honor You and serve You, with all of my being."

The Santa Clara River was cool, but manageable for a December weather. He changed into his wetsuit and immersed himself in the water, to cleanse himself from his ugly past and spiritual prodigaling——the best he could do, in lieu of the River Jordan. Purified, he emerged from the water a new man.

Now renewed, could he meet some nice girl and remarry? If not, he vowed to honor his body, single. Never again would he permit himself to be manipulated to believe that right was wrong and wrong was right.

Finally, he rinsed and dried the metal bin. He placed in the bin a sealed envelope containing the honest sweat of his brow to prove he had been transformed——he would not give anything tainted——and sealed the bin with a tape, then he watched it float down the river——the same river he used to revere——praying that someone who needed it more, would find it.

Immediately, he drove to the City of Barren Trees to finish moving, and contacted his boss to ask for a week off to attend to some family matter. To sweeten the deal, he offered to work during the Christmas week. His boss told him to report for half day the next day, then he could leave for the week.

◆ ◆ ◆

Upbeatson was downstream at the river, cleaning fish for his dinner. He was on his last bread. Upbeatson's career had tanked a long time ago and he had sold all his music gears to survive. Tired of drifting, wishing he could belong, the river was the farthest he had got on his desire to return home to Louisiana. Living on the river bank and fishing for his meals, had kept him going, until then. As things stood, he would most likely return to the streets of L.A.

He lifted his bowed head and noticed a floating object on the river, rowed his battered boat——a gift from a friend who had moved up in the world——and brought the bin ashore. Carefully, he broke the seal, examined the content and the note that read, "Enjoy. The Lord is good!"

Soon, a loud, "Hallelujah! Someone up there loves me!" filled the air. "Whoever this is, bless them! I can buy a one-way ticket back home to Lagniappe! Oh, thank you! Thank you! Bless them!"

The twenty-five crisp hundred-dollar bills were enough and some, for a train ticket to Lagniappe——a quiet fishing town where he was raised. Fed-up of city life, he had longed to return to the three-bedroom house his parents had bequeathed to him——a home of his own. And, he knew where to get a decent wardrobe and travel luggage for less than fifty dollars!

◆ ◆ ◆

Having worked half-day, Shane drove his Ford to his parents' farm in Idaho, now managed by his older brother and his family. He had not seen his niece and nephews——now teenagers and probably much taller——for years.

He had carried his resume to scout the field for a new job. The moment BF&S' fraud case was settled; he would resign and move to Idaho permanently. Until then, "It's San Gabriel Valley and church to you!" he muttered, then as an afterthought, "I wonder where Cornelia's family's ranch is? But, she's so young . . . twentyish, maybe? Lucky me I've blown one marriage. And what use is a potato grower to a rancher? But, boy, does she have spunk!" Should he get pointers from Paul and his new friends?

81

Nothing like the holidays to make the pot boil over! Monday morning when Lily arrived, there was Bernice barreling down the corridor to her cubicle.

Hugging their morning coffee mugs, Brad and his friends stepped aside to let Bernice pass, then they snickered behind her back.

As long as Bernice was unaware of their behavior, Lily held her peace.

"Don't talk to me," Bernice growled at her.

"Okay. I woke up this morning, brushed my teeth and made myself decent for work, where did I go wrong?" She tried to deadpan.

"What's so funny?" Bernice growled again.

"Nothing."

"Sure? You're staring. I demand to know!"

"Well," she hesitated.

"Come on, out with it."

"Well, I have heard something about . . . redheads," she mouthed, cognizant of company policy on stereotyping, still amused at Bernice's wardrobe——a red business suit, red nylons, red shoes, red ribbons holding up her pony tail, huge red and gold earrings and swinging from her arms, a bright red handbag.

Bernice burst out laughing. "I suppose I went a bit overboard."

"A bit overboard? Nah! I didn't notice."

Bernice whispered, "Red's what I felt like this morning. Alex and I had a misunderstanding last night. He's become unintelligible."

"Oh? Then I won't pry. But if you feel like a sympathetic ear?"

"Thanks. Let me mull over it." Bernice started walking back to her cubicle.

At Bernice's approaching footsteps, Brad turned to the glass pane of his cubicle and whistled at her. She ignored him and zoomed past——her best effort at being civil to him, since he recommended Aaron for a job at Denton and Terrel. Some days she was more successful than other days.

Being Brad, Lily knew Denton & Terrell would do nothing, despite the firm's policies on professional conduct. After Bernice had gone, she went to Brad's cubicle. He was perusing a magazine. In a low voice she said, "Brad, do you have a moment?"

He looked up, surprised and answered, "Sure."

"Could we meet in the conference room, please?"

Even more surprised, Brad followed her to the small glass conference room.

She closed the door and came to the point, "Thanks for agreeing to meet. I just wanted to say since this morning, your conduct has been bothering me."

"How so?" Brad asked.

"I don't think you are treating Bernice with respect." She smiled.

Brad turned tomato red. "It was just a joke. Take it easy."

She flashed her teeth again. "That is not the point. While I think it is okay to laugh with a person, I don't think it is okay to snicker at them, let alone, snicker and whistle. How would you feel, if Bernice did the same to you?"

Brad mumbled an apology. She thanked him, but asked him to consider apologizing to Bernice instead. He said he would think about it.

She returned to her cubicle, praying that Brad would keep his word.

Her Organizer caught her attention. She flipped through the list of urgent tasks to complete before the Christmas holidays and the New Year's rush. With so much to do, she worked straight through her morning break.

Since returning from Palm Springs, Brad had noticed that below Lily's soft exterior, was a woman of steel. Holy fear best described his sentiment towards her, in addition to his unrequited affection.

Through the grapevine, he had gleaned that Paul Van Clyden was a formidable rival in all the areas Lily considered vital to a lasting relationship. He accepted it, not because he couldn't compete, but because Lily treated him as a professional associate, with whom she shared office space between seven and four o'clock and not beyond.

For months he had tried to become abstemious, even as he abandoned all pretexts of seeking redemption. Oh yes, finally he understood that the godly were neither wimps, nor delusional after all, but he did not have the fortitude to take that step.

Because Lily——the one person who could sway him——had requested it, he dragged his feet to Bernice's cubicle. For the same reason, he had helped Aaron get a summer job at Denton & Terrell, to impress her.

At lunch time, Bernice stuck her head over Lily's cubicle. "Okay. I've mulled it over. I'm ready for a sympathetic ear."

Lily closed her files.

"I cleared with the Boss to take a slightly longer lunch. Sorry I didn't check with you first. Is it okay?" Bernice said.

She would have preferred a shorter lunch, since their annual Christmas lunch was coming up but she said, "Of course. Let me check with Mr. Chancey, just in case." She phoned Mr. Chancey and asked him about a longer lunch. He said okay.

Bernice thanked her, relieved.

Nearby was a Tex-Mex restaurant. Inside were themes of raw art of self-taught folk artists. Hispanic holiday music blared over the loudspeakers.

Lily asked for a private booth near a window, the loud festive crowd helped.

The waiter brought them fresh corn chips and their house-made salsa. She ordered cheese relleno quesadilla; Bernice ordered beef enchilada.

Bernice waited as she said grace, and selected a tortilla chip, her face in knots, then she beamed. "Oh, I've got to tell you this, Brad apologized to me. I just about fell off my chair! I never thought I would live to see the day. I wish I could've bottled that moment. Priceless! Someone bigger's up there." She pointed up.

"That was nice of him," she deadpanned, wiped her mouth and gave Bernice her rapt attention, then she steered the conversation back to Alex.

"Well, to begin with, Alex and I are a mismatch. You knew that. Right?" Bernice leveled her green eyes at her.

"Yes." She nodded.

"Having said that, what's a 'mismatch'?"

Again, she maintained a straight face, she had been waiting for this question. "When a believer marries a non-believer."

"What's the basis for your belief? Does the Bible actually say that?"

"Yes."

"Where?" Bernice pressed on.

"Second Corinthians. The verse is also used to caution against doing business with people whose moral persuasions are . . . shady."

Bernice crunched another chip, her gaze lowered to her plate, then she said, "Well, he's been getting on to me to become more serious."

Sensing that this was a crucial moment for Bernice, she held her peace.

"Oh, you know, I attend church occasionally, more regularly now than before, but still not religiously. I'm really not dedicated at all."

She smiled. "I know."

"So now, he's getting on to me to define my position. To be honest, he was really upset. And he issued an ultimatum——either I state clearly where I stand, or he's moving on. Either way, if I don't commit, he's walking."

"May be he is finally getting serious about you."

Bernice paused, a chip mid-air. "You think so?"

"Mhmm."

Bernice sighed, more exhausted than before. "But he knew from the beginning that I'm not religious and I don't pretend to be. Okay, so I allowed him to set the standard, you know . . . things like just dating platonic and stuff . . . that was fine with me. I'm like my Mum and Grandma, so I liked that he's a gentleman. But I made no promises, so why's he starting now?"

She crunched a chip, eye-balling her. "Why did you encourage him?"

"I did?"

"I assume. I mean, you allowed him to treat you as a virtuous lady, that must have given him some hope. How many women do you know today, who choose to date on just a platonic base? Even within the church, some struggle, yet the LORD's unchanging nature remains holy."

Bernice locked her hands under her chin, and leaned in. "Do you recommend that . . . you know, um . . . going platonic?" she whispered.

"Absolutely! Adamantly, yes!" Lily smiled.

"Great! So do I. I think the less baggage I carry into the next relationship if Alex and I broke up, the better."

"Well, since you made that stand, I think you raised Alex's hope."

Bernice leaned back. "In what way does that alone demonstrate a future?"

"Well, this may offend you. I'm not sure I agree with his approach. In fact I don't."

"Thank you," Bernice said, with a hint of sarcasm, though smiling.

"You're welcome!" she shot back, "He was probably hoping you would change sooner. It appears he loves you enough to gamble on your soul."

"I never thought of it that way. But it's a gamble he may lose."

"Bernice, I would not be a friend, if I was not honest with you."

"Go ahead."

She waited for the waiter to serve their food, sizzling hot from the oven, then she said, "As I was saying, you should know the price, if Alex takes that next step."

"I know."

"In addition, even if you stayed married, Alex would worry about where you stand and feel responsible for your soul. And should you go before him——may the Lord keep you healthy——without letting him know where you stood, he would torture himself wondering whether you made your peace at the last moment."

To Lily, a mismatch always resulted in either the couple divorcing, or if they remained married, a void would remain. They might get along, but they would never communicate at the deepest spiritual level, or share the most important thing——the knitting of their souls into one spiritual whole.

"Only those who believe can fathom Spiritual matters," she murmured.

"What's that?" Bernice cocked her ears above the music.

"Discerning Godly things requires the Spirit of God. First Corinthians two."

"Meaning?"

"We need help from above to understand spiritual truth. Only the Lord can reveal His mind, that is why a husband and wife may have problems communicating, if they launch from different platforms, even though they love each other."

Bernice thought for a while, then she lit up. "Well, so we don't talk about spiritual things," she shrugged. "He could always pray for my soul if I died first, right?"

"I don't think it works that way, Bernice. True, Christ preached to the dead, but since then we are responsible for our choices this side of heaven."

Bernice shrugged. "Fine. So I won't make any decision at all."

"Isn't that the same? It is like someone who knows she needs insurance, but chooses to do nothing, then gets into an accident. No one can reverse her decision."

Bernice dug into her enchilada.

"And if you had children," Lily continued, "even if you allowed your husband to teach them, your family would be polarized——your children would be torn between your position, and their dad's. Would that be fair?"

Bernice placed her fork down and stared out of the window. She appeared to be thinking of a past, long ago. "Like me and Jake."

"Right. Would you like to know your choices influenced your children? What if the Bible is true? I believe it is," she said gently.

"I don't know where to start." Bernice shredded her enchilada. "So much baggage. As you know Dad never liked the faith thing, but he wanted a good wife, the best he could find. So where did he go? Church. Mum was impressionable——reacted with her heart, initially, not prayer. Not that anything's wrong with letting the heart lead; but in Mum's case, it wasn't a good move. She later changed. After fifteen years of plodding along, they divorced. That really hurt; I tried not to show it. Mum never returned to church, but I know she prays a lot behind closed doors. I guess my reaction to Mum's ordeal is to date men like Alex."

Lily wondered about that. Could it be that——though Bernice was still incalcitrant——the Lord was listening to her mother's prayers?

On the other hand, was Alex more subconsciously attracted to Bernice's physical beauty, than he admitted? If Alex assumed that Bernice would change just because he wished it, he was gambling with his future. Bernice might change, but like father, like daughter, she might not. Had he considered that possibility?

Her ardent wish was for Bernice to believe. In that vein, she saw Bernice's friendship with Alex as a small overture in the right direction. But, if Bernice did not, she also prayed that she would not break up with Alex and get married to another man on the rebound——a worse fate.

"Bernice, I know you may not like this, but it sounds as though you're following in your parents' footsteps. How do you expect to develop a lasting relationship with Alex, without taking his God seriously?"

Bernice massaged her forehead. "I guess I could start by committing to church more often. But I still have so much cleaning-up to do."

She smiled to hide her disappointment. Bernice considered attending church twice a month a noble sacrifice, thus betraying her hidden desire to prevaricate and run her life as she pleased.

"Why don't you bring the baggage to Him. Let Him do the cleaning for you?"

"I could? I guess I could. Alex's pastor always says that."

She realized she had misjudged her and told her, gently, "Yes. You can."

Once again, Bernice dug into the enchilada. "We'd better eat or the food will get cold. These enchiladas are good. Mmm. How's your quesadilla?"

"Good. Thank you. I like the sauce." She took a bite of her quesadilla.

"I think I need more salsa." Bernice waved at the waiter.

She smiled and dug into her quesadilla. As in the past, Bernice was still skittish. It was wise not to press her any further. Only Bernice could open up to the Lord, not even Alex could make that decision for her.

Bernice had as good as admitted that Alex had broken up with her. Alex would make a solid mate for any compatible woman. She would try to help her.

Bernice chatted on about Jake and her mother and her pets when she was young, before she outgrew them. Now, she preferred a pet-free house like her mum.

Lily listened.

After the waiter had served their hot drinks and brought the bill, Bernice alternated between sipping her coffee and hugging her cup, her face cloudy. Finally, she said, "I don't want to make the same mistakes. I love my parents dearly, but I wish their marriage hadn't been. In a way, I understand Mum. We'd very few divorces before them, but what excuse would I have?"

For the first time, Lily saw the raw pain of Bernice's youth written on her face. This could be a good sign.

The waiter had been hovering in the background. After checking on their table for the third time, she was tempted to ask him for another cup of tea just to stall, but at the entrance, clusters of customers waited. She took the hint. Signaling Bernice, she nodded that they should leave.

Bernice also noticed the crowd. "I get the point."

On their way back to Denton & Terrell, Lily prayed in her heart for another opportunity soon to finish their discussion.

As they were parking, Bernice checked her watch and muttered, "Time sure flies when we need it to slow down."

She seized the moment. "How about Wednesday next week?"

"Wednesday sound's good, gives the boss one more week to smile at what a dedicated worker I am." Bernice beamed.

"I know we had intended to party, but why not?"

"You don't mind having a serious discussion over Christmas lunch?"

"I think in-person is more personal than a phone call. Tell you what, let's ask the bosses for an afternoon off, so we could leave about one o'clock, eat, and then go to the park——I don't think Mr. Chancey would mind, if I give him a heads-up."

Bernice was so relieved, that she returned to her cubicle radiant.

Hoping that she would celebrate Bernice's new life by Christmas, reminded Lily about Saturday. Praise be she would be too busy studying to fret.

82

The white slopes of Mount Alegria loomed into view as mermaids rise out of the sea. Behind the wheel, Paul played with a Christmas theme, "It was the last Saturday before Christmas, not a date to be found." A deck of his favorite carols filled the car with Christmas, but not his heart.

Lily drifted off into her own world, but halfway up the mountain, she stirred and caught him studying her face. He blushed and refocused on the winding road ahead. He found it soothing to watch her enjoy the natural scenery. If he did not love the outdoors, he would, just by watching her.

As with his trip to East Africa, she challenged his preconceived notion of her people. He had always enjoyed the beautiful outdoors and the secluded beachfronts within the social boundaries of his coterie. He still preferred quiet beaches, to crowded ones, but only with her beside him.

At their restaurant, he jumped out and escorted her inside.

Dale was at the counter, chatting to his customers. He did not seem surprised to see them both. At Paul's silent behest, he led them to a window table. Paul's date fitted well in the environment, dressed in blue denims suit, that complemented his white polo neck, black leather jacket and denims pants.

The same waitress breezed in with a smile so warm, it could melt a pile of snow, looking quite comfortable serving the tilted mix of customers.

Lily risked the iffy fish, chips and a cup of very hot tea. Paul ordered a burger and chips, sprite——without ice,——and salad to share with her.

After the waitress had served their meal, they toyed with their food, extending their tête-à-tête for as long as possible.

Lily took a sip of her tea, glanced at the door and took a deep breath.

"Lightning doesn't always strike twice in the same place," Paul said.

"Pardon me? Oh no, you are not trying to read my mind, are you?"

Paul leaned forward, until he could see the pupils of her eyes and smell her soft perfume. "Why not? Isn't that what you were thinking the last time we were here?"

"I will neither confirm, nor deny."

"In other words, I'm right. Relax. They won't bother you again.""

"Absolutely no comment!"

He continued flirting with her. She allowed him to play the game for a few safe minutes, then she studied the children playing in the snow.

He searched the direction of her eyes, until he spotted the children and joined her in watching them.

"Cute kids," she said.

"Mhmm," he agreed.

As her comment escaped her, she started. *How many times have friends warned you to never hint at children on a date?*

She lowered her gaze.

Paul drawled, "I'm not like that at all."

"Excuse me?"

"Try me."

"Paul, do I need to wear x-ray resistant helmet with you around?"

Paul threw back his head and chuckled, drawing curious glances.

She watched him, shaking her head. "Paul, you're full of surprises. Were you always this naughty when you were young?"

"May be."

The waitress brought their bill. As a gentleman, Paul had paid all the bills so far and the menus were not cheap.

He paid and guided her outside. "Come on, let's take a swing at the snow, get some fresh air."

They lingered in the lower slopes, then moved on to one of the beaten treks, but still remained close to the other hikers, limiting their exploration to occasional brave winter plants that crossed their paths.

"You said you used to get grounded a lot." Her eyes teased him.

"Lots. Speeding tickets and other innocent foibles. I didn't do drugs or anything, but I just about drove my Mum crazy."

"You, drove your Mum crazy? Nah!"

"Yes. I did. By grace alone I didn't get into any accident. My parents weren't always committed. Dad had an unconventional wisdom of drilling home his point. The first time I got a ticket; I looked at my Dad and went to my room. The second time, I looked at him and went to my room. The third time, I sat down on the couch and faced him. Then he said, 'Got another one?' and I answered, 'Yes sir,' and he said, 'How fast?' I said, 'Fifty miles, in a – – – mile zone,' and he said, 'I could've beaten you easy——not that I encourage you to emulate my youthful sins. You're paying this time?' I said, 'Yes sir.' He said, 'Good. What you need is a racing school. Get all that speed out of your system.' 'Yes sir,' I replied and went to my room."

Lily controlled her stitches. "What did your Mum say?"

"Oh, she just about scalped his head. 'You knucklehead! You're gonna send him where? You're out of your mind. You boys can take care of yourselves; I'm moving in with my mother-in-law. She's the only Van Clyden with any sense in the whole Van Clyden clan!' she yelled at him."

Lily clapped her mouth.

"She wouldn't budge. So Dad persuaded her it was for our own good and to save lives, etc., etc. Then she said, 'Promise you'll not become a race-car driver!' I said, 'I promise Ma'am, I'll not become a race car driver.' 'And you'll wear your helmet.' I said, 'Yes, Ma'am. I'll wear my helmet.' 'And you're going to college.' I said, 'Yes, Ma'am. That I will do.' 'And you're going to be a doctor,' she yelled. I said, 'No, Ma'am, but I promise to be the best I can.'"

Lily was in stitches. "So what did your Mum say?"

"She said, 'I suppose so. If you're determined to be as stubborn as your father. But you're still going to college.' I said, 'Yes, Ma'am.' So, Jonathan and I went to racing school, where we zoomed around at unmentionable speed, then they bundled us off to a Christian Camp. I shudder to think what could've happened. I wouldn't advise any teenager to follow in my footsteps."

"I would hope not."

"Camp was the best thing that happened to me."

"Praise be!"

"Amen." He nodded.

They trekked in silence for a while, then she said, "How is Shane?"

"Excuse me?" he replied, surprised.

"You had asked me to pray for an associate of yours? How is he doing?"

"Of course! I can see the difference already. He's considering returning to church." He rubbed his nose. "That's putting it mildly. Recently, I was blown away. The Lord sure works in His own way. Thank you for praying."

He continued gazing at her and seemed elated that she had asked.

"We all start with baby steps," she said.

He agreed and asked her to continue praying for him.

Two hours later, he got two steaming cups of chocolate for the road, from the restaurant, gave her a loaded look and turned on the engine.

He stopped at turn-outs with scenic views. At the last spot, he sat on the hood, and swung his legs, seemingly content. Lily joined him, enjoying the twinkling lights coming alive in the cities below. That he loved nature was no secret, but here, he was more relaxed.

Suddenly, he moved a short distance away and prayed under his breath. He had one shot at locking in the Christmas holidays. Whatever happened, his rival will have not a split second with her. If he failed, "It's Christmas in town for you, buddy," he muttered under his breath.

"I'm sorry, did you say something?" Lily asked.

"I was thinking it's time to head down for the concert." He stretched and yawned, thankful for the dusk that camouflaged his red face.

Lily returned to the car and buckled up.

Relieved, he slumped into the driver's seat, but instead of starting the car, he paused to study the setting night. A moment later, he collected himself, and pulled away from the turn-out, back to the road.

Lily sensed a change in his mood. She was at a loss. She had tossed all night, expecting Paul to cancel their trip and was relieved that he had not, defying her determination to distrust him. Now this!

He pulled up in her driveway just before five o'clock. "Is six-thirty okay?"

"Would that give you enough time? We could go a little bit later."

He assured her that six-thirty would give him plenty of time.

Her porch light was on, so instead of escorting her to the door, he waited until she had entered and turned on the inside lights, then he left.

Disturbed by the change in Paul's mood, Lily prayed——her lips moved silently, her head bowed.

83

Lily dabbed her nose, grabbed her evening clutch and winter coat and ran downstairs to answer the doorbell. A small whiff of aftershave lotion escaped and waltzed around her.

Paul looked fresh in matching gray slacks and polo neck. His eyes sailed up from her woolen slacks to her black and winter-white cashmere sweater, then up to her long neck, emphasized by her hair combed back into a pony tail. A faint trail of Dior tantalized his nose.

He bowed and kissed her hand. "Perfect! Shall we?"

The playful, teasing Paul was back. Lily sent a silent 'thank you' to heaven and grabbed her coat and purse.

At church, the parking lot attendants glowed like huge glow worms, directing guests to the remaining spaces on the grassy area.

Paul parked in his assigned space and opened the door for her. As they joined the crowd streaming into the sanctuary, he took her hand in a firm grip and held his head up high, sending a tremor through her.

At the entrance, he stood erect and surveyed the crowd——a man in control of his destiny——oblivious to the curious stares.

From the middle of the sanctuary came Sharon's cheerful voice. As if they could miss her distinctive voice, Jonathan stood up and waved.

Heads turned as he led Lily down the aisle, some looking quite pleased, others, not too happy.

"Hi Paul! Hi Lily!" came a jubilant voice from a nearby pew.

They turned just in time to avoid trampling Marc.

Marjorie gave Lily a big, bear hug; Paul and Matt grinned in approval.

A distinguished-looking African American couple sat next to the

Jonesons. They were new to ENC. Matt introduced them, and their two teenagers, as their guests and close neighbors.

The handsome young man was Jumaine, a pre-med student at Princeton University, and the pretty girl was Tanicia, Jumaine's sister, a junior in Melody's school. He explained that Jumaine had been MJ's classmate and basketball team-mate.

From the corners of her eye, Lily watched Marc slip out.

True to form, Marc rushed to the back where Melody and the other cast members were waiting, to apprise her of the happening in the sanctuary.

MJ, also backstage, welcomed the excuse to help with the props, especially, since Viviana was part of the team. Marc whispered in his ear. For his effort, Marc earned himself a playful punch and hair ruffling.

As Paul and Lily passed by, Kelly watched, buried in the crowd. For weeks she had been wrestling with Matthew 6:33, *"But seek first the kingdom of God and His righteousness, and all these things shall be added to you."* Whatever passages had not sunk in, this one had. Now, as she watched Lily, she wished she had heeded it. Her cruise with her aunt and uncle did not achieve the happiness she had hoped for, though she met some nice people on board.

Amazingly, she felt no animosity towards Lily. Lily was in no way responsible for her break–up with Paul. She had Paul at the altar, and she blew it. She had permitted her parents' philosophies to influence her choices, over the wisdom of mentors who had encouraged her to follow the straight and narrow path. Had Paul succumbed to her charm, she would have destroyed him too, and added him——impenitent——to her trophies for her prowess and power over men.

Not everybody in the congregation was exuberant. Those who assumed that Paul and Kelly were as good as married, wished Lily would go to a church more suitable for the likes of her. Why did Lily choose Evangelical Neighborhood Church as her home church? As one woman put it bluntly, "Why don't the Ethiopians go to churches in their own neighborhoods?"

What a pickle that the Lord had not consulted with them first! No doubt they had already planned how God should divvy up heaven.

To Lily, the change in Paul's behavior was balm on the wound that he had inflicted. Might it be grace that had orchestrated for her to linger at ENC?

From the comfort of Paul's arm placed protectively behind her seat, she remembered a bitter poem she had read a year before. Given a choice, it was probable that her opponents would opt for two heavens——one for them and one for the Ethiopians, as they loved to put it——albeit, it was the Lord who shed His blood to draw all who repented into His Father's kingdom.

On cue, the lights dimmed, the orchestra settled down in the pit and the Christmas Pageant began.

First, the director and the choir led the congregation in singing favorite Christmas hymns like: *"Joy to the World," "Once in David's Royal City," "Hark, the Herald Angels Sing," "O Little Town of Bethlehem."* Then the congregation stomped their feet to traditional carols, interspersed with storytelling.

After the intermission, the choir opened with the English version of *"Adeste, Fideles"* aka *"O Come, All Ye Faithful,"* then *"O Come, O Come Emmanuel,"* and finally, the evangelical Christmas musical performance. Rather than concentrating on Christ the baby, the performance highlighted the life of Christ and how He came to give eternal hope to all who repented.

Pastor Tim closed the concert with a short message, highlighting the true meaning of Christmas. "Without the Resurrection, Christmas would be just another day to commemorate the birthday of a once-upon a time child, who grew up to be an ordinary man, but Jesus was no ordinary man, nor was He just a mere historical figure or just a prophet as some claim. He is life. He is the Light. He is Hope. He is joy and peace and much, much more . . . He is Emmanuel, the God who came to dwell among us in human flesh . . ."

To end, he made an altar call for anyone who wished to start a new life. Maryann's family jumped up and walked forward, with her holding on to her father's hand.

Lily dabbed her eyes. Excluding sitting next to Paul, no better Christmas gift could have been given to her than to watch Maryann's family reunited.

Early in the year, Maryann's Dad had quit, but her Sunday school class had continued praying for the family. To the elation of the class, three months later, he had returned and was now attending church with his family and receiving family counseling. Lily noticed many children from the class were talking with more confidence about God's boundless power. True, not every story had a predictable ending, but having Maryann's father back was a boost to their young faith.

Finally, instead of the whole congregation lighting candles, a selected member lit the last candle in the candelabra at the altar, then the choir led the congregation in one last song that looked forward to Christ's return.

As the congregation dispersed, Jonathan invited them to dessert.

"Great! I wouldn't miss it," Paul replied and agreed to meet at their favorite mom and pop pie restaurant.

Paul joined the queue of cars waiting to exit. "This was probably one of the best Christmases I've ever attended," he announced.

Lily agreed.

"What did you think of the message?" he asked.

"I felt it was very fitting for this season," she replied.

"Absolutely. Too bad some people celebrate at the surface."

"I agree. For those who went forward, this will be their first real Christmas."

"Yes. I wish more would come to that realization." His hand brushed hers.

"If more people accepted the deeper meaning of the holiday, that could be remedied." She paused, then added, "I wonder where we would be today, had Christ not come? True, some places celebrated the winter solstice, but would December twenty-fifth have the global appeal it has today?"

"Probably not. Neither would the level of commercialization."

"I believe that we're partly to blame. Don't misunderstand me, nothing is wrong with having fun. I love fun——responsible fun that is——but our Christmas celebrations are so material-focused. I can understand non-believers who may not know, but what about us?"

Realizing he was having an important discourse with his date and he didn't have to apologize for it, Paul's heart pumped louder. "Perhaps we should search our souls. I wish I'd a better answer. For the others, we can keep praying and looking for opportunities to be a good example. As for us . . . maybe we should pray for the courage to stand up to our convictions."

"Even when it requires standing out?" She rolled up her window.

"Even then."

"That means no gifts or giving gifts only to those who cannot reciprocate."

"Mhmm. Or cutting down on Christmas lights?" Remembering his choppy conversation with Kelly, it was refreshing to be of one mind.

"Oh, no! That would take away so much of the festive mood. But you are right. Cutting down on the excesses may cut down on the expenses."

"And cut down on seasonal Christmas employment?" he teased.

"All right. I see where you are going. On the other hand, one could argue that the money saved could be spent in some other way, such as buying useful goods, which would create new jobs. But you know what makes me really sad?"

"What?"

"That whether or not we give gifts, as long as we are here, there is still hope for those who eschew the free help given. One day it will be too late," she referred quietly to the prophesy.

"Yup. I wish many more would realize that. Keep praying."

"Mhmm."

Silence followed, each withdrawn into their own thoughts.

Paul stirred and nudged Lily playfully. "I see I've a partner who loves to think. So, have you made any plans for Christmas?"

"Some friends have invited me."

He paused and appeared to be focusing hard on steering the car, then he murmured, "How fortunate for them."

A special note in his voice made her fumble with her purse. "Why? I'm the one who feels fortunate." She dabbed her nose with tissue paper.

"I wish there was more of you."

"That's flattering. Thank you."

"No. I am serious. My parents would love to have you for Christmas," he turned his head, though it was too dark to see her eyes.

Was he just being polite? Lily stammered, "It is very kind of them, but I would not wish to impose on them."

"You'll not be imposing on them. The Christmas spirit is to share God's love. When I was in South America, and last summer, my parents learned to appreciate what other parents experience. In East Africa, the people were very kind. I met some very neat people I'll always remember."

"Thank you. But I will be all right. Really." They appeared to have invited her out of gratitude, though they owed her nothing.

"Alternatively, I could remain in town. The beach is just a couple of hours away——less in light traffic." Paul's tone carried a hint of firmness.

"Paul! You said your parents missed you while you were gone. You should make it up to them. I'm used to being away from my family."

"I know."

"Your parents would be disappointed."

"They probably would, but they'll understand."

"Then I think you should be reasonable."

"I'm being reasonable." Paul clapped his mouth to suppress laughter.

Lily exhaled. "You are teasing me. What a relief!"

"No. I'm not. On Christmas Eve, I'll tell them I'm spending Christmas with friends."

"You wouldn't do that! Think how hurt they would be."

"They're adults. Look, I don't want to beg."

"I would not want you to. I have already accepted an invitation."

"Cancel."

"You are stubborn. I can't just cancel. Where is your sense of commitment?"

"Right here."

"Paul, be serious. I can't show up at your parents' house, just like that!"

"You're not showing up just like that. You're invited."

"Thank you. Could I take a rain check, instead?"

"When? New Year?"

"New Year! That is still Christmas break."

"All right, then that's settled." He paused, then asked, "Will you be working on Thursday, twenty second?"

"I don't know."

"I could always find out."

"How?"

"I've my ways."

"If I promised to come next year, the Lord willing, would that be okay?" Lily asked gently, hoping to appease him. The Christmas after was twelve months away, by then, if Paul had changed his mind again and patched things up with Kelly, they would be married, anyway——Kelly would see to that——and she, in turn, would have graduated and moved out-of-state and out of their lives.

On the other hand, Paul collected his prized possessions in triplets, if he did the same with his dates, would the third girl win the competition and blow dust in Kelly's face? But then again, Bernice said he could be trusted. Moreover, Sharon introduced her to his aunt and uncle, was it because they were curious to meet someone from East Africa, or was it time to trust him, totally?

Finally, her own parents——how could she manage their hopes for her?

Paul slammed on the breaks and pulled off the road. "Next year! Why, you'd be practically——I mean," he inhaled, sharply, "No!"

"Why?"

"Because that's the way it is."

"Oh?"

"Mhmm." He revved the Porsche back to life. "In fact, to show you how serious I am," he turned off the ignition again, grabbed his mobile phone and dialed a number. "Hi Mum! She said she would be delighted to join us for Christmas and the twenty second will be perfect," he said.

"Paul! Is that phone really on?" Lily whispered.

At the other end, the Van Clydens were winding down for the night, after an exhausting day hosting their annual Christmas dinner for friends.

Charlotte cupped the phone and whispered, "The Van Clydens' blood's curdling."

Igor covered his mouth with his western novel, trying hard not to be heard chuckling above Charlotte's voice.

"Paul, did you bully her into accepting our invitation?"

"Kind of, but she doesn't believe I'm talking to you," Paul replied.

"Perhaps if the invitation came straight from us, she'll understand it's our wish——no thanks to your caveman tactics. Let me talk to her."

"Just a moment." Paul pretended to be covering the mouthpiece. "She wants to talk to you."

"Who is 'she'?" Lily whispered.

"My Mum."

"Paul Truen Van Clyden, if your mother is really at the end of that phone, I'm going to skin you alive when this is over," she whispered fiercely.

"Did you hear that, Mum," he yelled into the phone, "She said she's going to break my leg when this is over."

"You tricked me, you——," Lily composed herself and took the phone.

"Hello. This is Mrs. Van Clyden," Charlotte said, formal, professional.

There was silence from the other end.

Charlotte mouthed to Igor, "She's probably threatening to turn him to pulp."

He nodded in agreement.

She uncovered the mouthpiece. "Hello? Are you there?"

"Hello," Lily answered in a soft, meek voice of a dove.

"This is Mrs. Van Clyden," Charlotte repeated.

"Good evening, Mrs. Van Clyden. This is Lily Nyaber. I'm terribly sorry about everything."

"Good evening, Lily. No need to apologize. I should be the one apologizing. Paul tells me your parents live in East Africa. It must be hard to be so far away from them. We'd be delighted to have you for Christmas. Would you forgive Paul's manners and come all the same?"

"I would hate to impose on you and Mr. Van Clyden."

"No problem. We'd be thrilled to have you. Since Paul returned from East Africa, we've been looking forward to having you visit us. We would hate for you to spend Christmas alone, with your parents so far away."

Reluctant to argue with the older lady, Lily relented, "It's very kind of you. Thank you."

"That's settled then. We're looking forward to seeing you on Thursday."

She thanked her and returned the compliment.

Mrs. Van Clyden wished her good night.

She wished her the same. "Would you like to speak to Paul?"

"Please. Thank you."

She handed the phone to Paul.

Paul suppressed his laughter, when his mother said, "Hi Darling, so that's settled. We'll be seeing whatever's left of you in a few days."

"That's right, Mum." He wished her and his father goodnight, then he pulled off the curb, his eyes focused on the road, supposedly.

Lily crossed her arms and stared at the wretch. "You know?"

"What?" He risked glancing at her.

"I was just thinking how my fingers can make a perfect circle."

"Wow, she's dangerous!"

"Dangerous is not the word going through her mind right now."

"What word then? Pretty, may be? Enchanting?"

"I'll show you what 'pretty' and 'enchanting' is!" she joked.

By the streetlights hitting the windows, he could see her fingers circled to show the size of his neck. "Jonathan and Sharon are waiting for us. I want to live to see the day Jonathan pays for my dessert," he mimicked a ventriloquist.

Charlotte picked up her devotional book. "I trust everything will go well."

"I'm sure it will. I feel good. They remind me of when we were young." Igor tried to assuage his anxiety, even as he grappled with the growing conviction that Lily and Paul would have made a perfect match, given other circumstances.

"You're right."

"Remember the time we got into a pie and water fight in your backyard and your dad walked out just in time to get the full blast on his face?"

"Oh, dear! I remember."

"That night when I got home, I fell to my knees. I thought it was over——that he would move your family across the country."

"He almost did. If you'd punched him, he'd have got over it, but wasting his favorite fresh peach pie, what more at the end of the peach picking season! You should've heard him. Mum had to talk him out of it."

Igor fell back, slapping his thighs. "Of course, if she's anything like you, we should call Jonathan tomorrow to find out where to collect the rest of Paul. I wonder whether she was going for his limbs or his neck?"

"I've a feeling she was going for his neck." Still chuckling, Charlotte pulled out her Bible, and turned to her favorite passages.

After leaving the restaurant, Paul saw Lily safely home and returned to his condo. It was empty——Jonathan was still dropping off Sharon. He walked upstairs, one step at a time, frowning, prepared for bed, then he knelt down and gave thanks for a special day. "While I believe I've come a long way," he prayed, "there's still much I don't understand. About this man, who's he? Is this the enemy trying to get me off track, or is this You, trying to help me? Please show me . . ."

He also prayed for his parents, the boys he mentored and others who came to mind. But when he went to bed, he still tossed and turned. To quell his anxiety, he recited verses he had memorized, such as, Philippians, that exhorted him not to worry about anything, but to pray, with a thankful heart. Then he listed the Lord's past faithfulness to him.

Why was he so fearful, whatever had become of his faith? Not until Lily, did he find a woman who challenged, yet strengthened him so much, driving him into the Lord's arms more. He loved her for her beauty and her deep spiritual commitment——the very same qualities that made him feel vulnerable.

With the other women, he didn't feel a finality; there were always other dates standing in the wings. Ever the perfect gentleman, he had never crossed the line with any of them, including Lily. Yet with Lily, things were different. If there were others waiting in line, he did not wish to know.

Who was the man in New York? Was he Lily's revenge? What about the hotel and presents? Was the man his serious competitor or already her fiancé——an arranged marriage? How could he compete with an arranged marriage?

Was Lily leading a double life? She seemed so innocent and her faith so genuine. She enjoyed his company too. At times, like today, he was sure she cared for him, a little. Why was she keeping secrets?

If Lily was trying to give him a taste of his own medicine, he stood chastised; but if she was leading a double life, could he forgive her? What did he really know about her background? He was dying to ask, yet the times he had ventured there, she seemed to stonewall him. If she was a fake, why did she appear so authentic? She did not pretend to be perfect, but she was natural.

Not long ago, a man like him——though a venerated gentleman——would have had the right to have his way with her. Society would have expected nothing more. But, would that have been honorable?

A righteous man will stand up for his convictions, regardless of the consequences. But had he? Was his dithering at the beginning responsible for his misery now?

A real man also accorded the woman he loved his utmost respect. He would never do anything to dishonor Lily. The same moral principle that governed the reputation of a woman, was the same moral principle that governed the reputation of a man. In the LORD's eyes, there was no double standard. So, why did he respect Lily less, initially, than he respected Kelly? He winced.

Whatever the reason for her secretive life, he would remain resolute. If she wished for tenacious competitors, he was a Van Clyden.

Van Clydens don't quit! A Van Clyden has never lost an honorable battle.

He clenched his fist.

What about his parents? Dare he apprise them? He had no clue of what was going on. What if she was already engaged? Initially, he had been afraid of fighting for her, but no more. He had begun taking it for granted that their lives would intertwine for life.

Moses married an Ethiopian; the Lord defended him against Miriam's attacks. Had Moses sinned, wouldn't the Lord have rejected him? Surely, like Moses, he too should fare okay——though he be no prophet? So sure was he, that he had made no alternative plan, except to go into self-imposed exile, if he failed.

If she dumped him, would his faith be strong enough to keep propelling him forward, or would he turn out like Shane, bitter and floundering and searching for the meaning of life? Would full time ministry heal his wounds? Paul tossed and turned all night and found himself almost hating that part of him that loved Lily so much.

84

In the early dawn of Saturday, Shane drove back home, determined to start afresh, backed by two promising prospects in Twin Falls, in case he resigned from BF&S and moved back home——basking in a great week spent with his brother's family.

Sunday morning, Paul and Jonathan were chatting with a friend——Paul half-heartedly, while searching for Lily——when lo and behold, he noticed a familiar figure hovering at the edge of the crowd. He took a deep breath and approached. "Shane, Merry Christmas and welcome to Evangelical Neighborhood Church!"

"I thought I should jump–start my new year's resolution," Shane said.

"Good for you!" Paul replied and introduced him. He did invite Shane to visit ENC. Shane said he was moving to San Gabriel Valley, supposing he chose ENC as his church, then what? Was his recent overture to turning the corner enough?

Just then, Pastor Tim appeared, as he spotted Lily talking to the McGaelics. He told Shane, "Let me introduce you to Pastor Tim, our Senior Pastor. He's the best. He has been a great mentor to me. I've found him very resourceful."

"Thanks." Shane accompanied him to Pastor Tim.

He left Shane in capable hands and joined Lily's group. On second thoughts, having Shane at ENC might work. Pastor Tim was the man——he had consulted with him when Shane was a thorn in the flesh. Who better to assume the task?

Not one to waste time, Shane made an appointment with Pastor Tim and opened up like a geyser. He dredged up his past, a penitent confessor to his priest. His dear parents were Free Methodists, ardent pursuers of the Holy God. He had thought they were too strict; in hindsight, he missed calling them. What he would give now, to have his mother raise her eyebrows at him again, when she was disappointed with him, and yet be there for him at Thanksgiving and Christmas!

He attended church as a child, more to please his parents, than to pay homage to God. As he matured, he drifted, arguing that he preferred a more open-minded approach——as though the Lord had left him that choice—— until he eventually dropped out. Ultimately, he severed the umbilical cord, rationalizing that he was an adult, who knew better than to believe in fables, albeit it broke his mother's heart.

The power of scientific facts captivated him, until he stumbled on evidence that some scientists, whom he revered, manipulated data. That did it. He disliked the pressure of conforming to data manipulated to sustain a truth that proved to be nothing but a desire to pander to unlimited peccadilloes of stretching facts.

So then he returned to exploring the spiritual. Initially, he believed that since God is love and never condemned anyone——and he was entitled to that love——God would make allowance for his foibles, though he remained impenitent. But, he could not explain the deep void inside, albeit his friends assured him self-actualization was the answer. Who could free him from his own conscience?

Pastor Tim assured him, "Only Truth can free our human conscience. We can experiment so far, but at some point, our conscience demands the truth."

For a moment, Shane mulled over this statement. "You know, I believe you might be onto something there. I'm beginning to feel there may be some value to the pursuit of truth, beyond the science lab. My conscience tells me, 'You're a man, Shane. Your parents taught you right from wrong. You can read for yourself.'

"A few weeks ago, I dusted off the old Book——their gift. I'll review it, list all the things God forbids, why He does and the consequences, then I'll make a list of things He permits us to do. And finally, I'll highlight references to His love . . . His promises to bless . . . His definition of himself as the Holy God and . . . what He expects of me as part of this human race.

Then I'll draw my own conclusions. Is God fair, or is He a severe, forbidding old man, ready to crack the whip?

"After that, I'll review my life. Is life all about pleasing myself? Is it as fair as my other colleagues imply? I see they're as capable of bigotry, not to think of their drive to get ahead at all cost. Oh, it's all cloaked in love. Believe me, no one preaches love more. Ramifications . . . what's that? We've all but rejected them. Since our action is the result of some random cosmic event——involuntary scientific incident——then we should not be held accountable for the consequences we argue. We argue further that consequence is the brainchild of the unenlightened——think positive, we urge our audiences. Yet, after all that rationalizing, we demand love——"

"You hit it over the head——the world view," Pastor Tim interjected.

"I've known those who exploit data and people to achieve goals. It's an accepted dogma that results follow action, so, I question why my friends——who insist on standing up for their ways——take umbrage when others also insist on standing up for their principle, to do what's honorable? Through recent events, I'm becoming increasingly persuaded that if I hold my end of the deal, God will hold His end of the deal. I can trust Him. He's real." He sought Pastor Tim's eyes and nodded.

Pastor Tim nodded back in agreement.

Encouraged, Shane continued, "So, after examining all the evidences, objectively, I'm confident I'll be in a pretty good position to know what *is* truth."

"Truth and truth alone can set us free," Pastor Tim repeated and prayed for him as they closed the meeting. "Listen, I'm glad you stopped by. I'm excited at the direction you're taking. I'd like to keep in touch. You mentioned that you moved . . . to what city?"

"Towards La Canada——thirty to forty minutes, depending on traffic."

"I'd like to follow up and get an update on your progress. A friend of mine pastors a great church closer to you. We've worked together for years and I would be glad to refer you to him, ultimately. Or if you don't mind the commute, ENC is a great church. Of course, you already know Paul——a wonderful young man."

"He's the best," Shane replied, relieved. At last he was mingling with those who took him seriously. They saw him; they knew he existed; he was human; he mattered and was not just a means to advance somebody's ambitions to get ahead at all cost. Thirty–minutes' drive was not so bad, unless the other church proved just as resourceful. Even more so now, he owed Paul lunch.

Pastor Tim remained inscrutable, but inside, he was exhilarated. The very notion that Shane was examining his soul, was astounding, yet not impossible. *No man is beyond redemption, who asks for help.*

As Shane's spiritual counsellor, he could not betray Shane's trust, but as Paul's friend, since Paul took the lead to help the older man, he could at least apprise him of progress in that quarter. He setup a private meeting with Paul.

After Paul had had a brief chat with Pastor Tim, he hastened to apprise Bill of the turn of events. How would BF&S react to Shane's plan, given the grand jury's finding? Ordinarily what Shane did in his spare time—— provided it did not reflect badly on the firm——was none of their business, but since Shane was in the middle of a court proceeding, it could complicate matters to be linked to him.

Caveats aside, he too was pleased, more accurately, exhilarated at the turn of events and hoped Lily would be as equally overjoyed at the good news.

85

Packing for the Beach to spend Christmas with the parents of a man you have permitted yourself to fall in love with, could be knuckle-cracking. But, packing to spend a week with parents who are not thrilled that you have fallen in love with their son, can put any brave girl to flight.

Loathed to delude herself, Lily conducted her research. Although the trend was up slightly, based on the results, 0.11% of married couples were white husband and black wife, compared to 0.34% black husband and white wife. Even less promising——from her observation——were the statistics on wealthy white men marrying black women. Barring a mighty miracle, she could not envision an upsurge in that ratio as the world approached 1995. She believed in miracles, but she was also practical.

She committed her fear into Capable Hands and got on with it. She had begun packing days ahead in case she needed to shop.

To distract her mind, she pondered what Bernice had told her. Concerned that she may have missed a great opportunity, she called Sharon and asked her to pray for the upcoming lunch. She also mentioned her trip to her. "You probably heard, I was invited to the Beach for Christmas," she said, offhand.

"Great! I'd a great time with Jonathan's family last Christmas," Sharon matched her tone.

"Instinct says conservative all the way."

"You guessed right. They're laid back, but definitely conservative." Sharon continued chitchatting, easing her anxiety.

Determined not to let Paul down, she packed two formal wear: a black evening gown and a wool flannel ivory pant suit, with a matching angora blouse. For accessories, she selected gold, a soft pastel scarf, a pair of simple black pumps and ivory evening pumps studded with a single gold ornament and another pair of black flat shoes.

For day wear, she packed two casual jump suits, a semi-formal business wear that she could dress up or down, and her sportswear. She also selected a black business suit for church and a misty blue dress of pure wool for formal outings. The dress had wide pastoral sleeves that tapered off from the elbow into a narrow straight fit at the wrists and the seamless bodice ended in a straight skirt, that hugged the hips loosely.

Finally, she added a long black winter coat, an all-purpose London Fog coat, a woolen scarf and plenty of socks.

She selected her clothes as though her mother was looking over her shoulders. Her mother's contemporaries defined a mini-skirt as anything above the knee caps. So, disregarding in vogue, she complied with their generation's taste. She would never know, until she arrived, how much grace and her mother had prepared her for life mingling with the Van Clydens' friends.

Confident that she did not have to shop at the last minute, she spent the rest of the evening on exegetical study——preparing for her Christmas lunch discussion with Bernice. The Holy Spirit did not work in a vacuum. Bernice was hungry for truth and would notice if she fudged.

Preparing ahead also freed her Tuesday evening to pick up the special Christmas gift she had ordered for Bernice from Nordstrom.

86

Lily started on the main dish in their four-course luncheon. Being the Christmas season, the popular Italian Restaurant was still full, despite the late lunch. Finally, the waitress brought their desserts and hot drinks.

Bernice wiped her mouth. "I can't wait anymore. I'm dying to see my gift." She unwrapped an elegant package, lifted up a beautiful soft blue Hermes silk scarf, and gasped. The classy scarf complemented her soft peach skin and mellowed her red hair. "Wow! Love it. And my favorite color, too!"

The simple green scarf that Lily was wearing——lovely as it was with its brown prints——was no match to the Hermes scarf that she had given her.

"I've never had anything so lovely." Bernice wiped her eyes.

"You're a kind friend, Bernice. May the Lord grant you your desires."

Lily unwrapped her gift——two Christian CD tapes of her favorite songs. One CD with her favorite songs would have been a blessing, but two! Bernice must have also placed a special order for the two CDs. "Wow! Bernice, how did you do it? They are all my favorite songs. Thank you!" She examined each label.

Bernice beamed from ear to ear. She had hoped, even stammered, "Dear Lord, I wish Lily would like her gift, in Your Name. Amen."

They finished their dessert and drove, in separate cars, to a nice family park, where they could walk and talk, uninterrupted.

Bernice plunged in. "Thank you so much for letting me do this," she said again for the third time that afternoon. "Alex's still not talking."

Lily looked at her, sympathetic. Bernice seemed to be admitting she would miss Alex more than she had calculated. "How do you feel about him?"

Bernice confessed that by doubting Alex's love, she might have created the crisis, to test him, or had she really been testing herself?

That Bernice who was always so confident around men appeared uncertain and confused, was shocking. "So that should make you feel relieved, right?"

"It's not that simple. I'd a long discussion with Mum. You were right. I've been protecting myself. Too late, I realize I'm not as indifferent to Alex as I thought.

"Dad swept Mum off her feet and made all sorts of promises that he would not interfere with her life. After their wedding, Mum realized Dad was an agnostic. She'd missed all the warning signs. The moment they married, he forbade her to associate with her friends. Soon, me and my brother . . . I mean I and my brother . . . or my brother and I, as you prefer to say, came along."

Lily rubbed her lip to hide a smile.

Bernice continued, "It became obvious they were incompatible. Dad wanted a virtuous wife, but how could Mum continue to be a strong, godly wife while shut off? Worse, his lifestyle changed. Had he been committed to his family, Mum would've put up with him, but she got tired of his antics." Bernice sought her eyes.

"Bernice, I'm sorry."

"The concept of maturing in a spiritual environment was alien to Dad," Bernice dredged up her pain. "He loved hanging out with his friends and all the shenanigans. Mum's friends were too boring for him, then he wondered why his sweetheart was unhappy! Funny, whenever he was in trouble, he knew who to call. Never failed, and she let him, until I told her not to let Dad take advantage of her anymore." She stabbed the air with her fingers. "Don't get me wrong, I don't mean believers don't have fun, but it's different . . . it's clean. If I knew that Jesus would stand by me, I'd trust Him just like that." She snapped her fingers.

"Bernice, He will. He said He will never leave us."

"Then why did He allow my family to suffer? Why couldn't my parents get along?" Bernice's eyes brimmed over. She averted her face.

"I'm sorry for your pain. Do you blame God for that?"

"Yes. In a way."

Lily wished she could encourage Bernice, without breaking her. "What about the choices your dad made? If I understood you, he wanted a godly wife, without committing to her faith. He broke his promises——cut her off from her friends——then he wondered why she was unhappy. Don't you see? It was your Dad's choices."

Bernice dropped her gaze.

"And you would be doing the same, if you continued with Alex as you are. It takes two to make a marriage."

"Boy, you don't mince words do you?" Bernice snapped.

Lily was not offended. At their last lunch, Bernice had been receptive. So far, she had only summarized what Bernice had told her. By lashing at her, it seemed Bernice was nurturing a lingering hope that she would take her side against Alex. She smiled. "I was only summarizing what you said. Did I misunderstand you?"

Bernice blushed. "No. I didn't mean it that way. Of course you can say what you think."

"I'm sorry, Bernice, but as a friend, I care enough to risk telling you things you may not wish to hear. If I don't, who else will? A friend is not just someone who cares about how much fun you have together, but someone who cares about what will become of your soul after this life."

"And I apologize." Bernice fidgeted. "It's just that . . . you sound like Alex."

"How?"

"Well, he said, he would hate for his children to choose between staying home with mummy or going to church with daddy."

She started, shocked. "He said what?"

Bernice repeated what Alex had said.

"He said that? You didn't prompt him?"

"No. He just blurted it out."

"Bernice, he proposed!"

"I guess so." Bernice hung her head.

"Bernice, if he brought up the subject voluntarily, then he has already made up his mind. Which man ever discusses starting a family with a woman, unless he is thinking of marriage? He has no other girl waiting in the wings. You have been waiting for this for months, will you let him slip through your fingers?"

Bernice opened and closed her mouth, without a word.

"Of what are you afraid? Trusting God or Alex?"

"You know me. I'm not a churchy type. I can make commitments, but I'm not always consistent," Bernice said.

Lily stared at the traffic, wondering how to help Bernice. "Every morning, I choose to walk the straight and narrow. I know I can do as I please, but that would only let the Lord down and hurt my parents, and friends, and . . . me."

"How can I be sure I'll hang in there?" Bernice shifted.

"The Lord will help you. That's how I manage——I seek guidance from Him, daily. If I make a mistake, I apologize, then move on, with His help."

Bernice lifted her chin up and walked tall. "You, blow it too?"

"Oh yes! I hate that, but I strive to be honest and admit it."

"But what would others say? I mean some people are so strict."

A light went on. Why hadn't she noticed that Bernice adulated other people? Oh, to reach her today! "Bernice, we are all human. Those who are honest will admit that they, too, blow it. I'm sure you have heard it before?"

Bernice nodded. "Many times. But I guess I was so engrossed in myself, I thought I was the exception. I've so much baggage."

"Oh, Bernice, we all need forgiveness. Ultimately, it is not what others think, it's your attitude towards God that matters to Him."

Bernice's eyes lit up. "About that. At what point is a person beyond hope?"

A speeding Corvette Arctic Blast thundered past. Lily turned and stared at the trail of smoke spewing in the air. "Teenagers. Have mercy!"

Bernice chuckled. "More like forty going on to seventeen."

She continued staring at the disappearing smoke trail. "I am mystified by boys' fascination with toys. But for the saving grace, he could be Paul."

"Paul? Wonderful, upright Paul! No!" Bernice protested.

"Oh yes. Almost turned his mother's hair gray. Ironically, it was those teenage foibles that saved his parents. They were always his role-models, but they were not always ardent believers, yet by consensus, theirs was the consummate family."

Bernice was surprised. "I guess I just assumed they were perfect."

"So did I. They were forced to re-evaluate their lifestyle for the love of Paul, then they packed him and Jonathan off to camp. Paul's respect for them grew by leaps. Parents should not ask of their child what they are not willing to model."

"That's true," Bernice agreed.

"So, you see, it's never too late. The only unpardonable sin is blasphemy. I believe at that level, it is going against God, Himself."

"Anything below that level, God can forgive?"

"Yes."

"Including getting angry at Him?"

"Even that. The psalmists and the prophets were ordinary people, endowed with insight and divine power. Psalms span the gamut of emotions, with some of the most honest confessions of anger and bitterness I have ever encountered. I'm glad they were included in the canonical books. They have taught me to be real, but reverent."

"And God still forgave them and allowed them to call themselves His children?"

"Yes. He did."

Bernice studied children running across the lawn, her eyes vacant, as though she did not see them. "Have you ever been angry at God?" She searched her face again, in earnest.

"Yes. I have. On more than one occasion." Lily had sensed Bernice's probing would eventually lead there.

"And?"

"I admitted I was angry. Then I found out why, then I talked to Him about it, as I would talk to my parents or to a trusted friend——you, for instance."

Bernice stared. "And you still thought God loved you after that?"

"Yes." Lily hesitated. How much should she tell Bernice? Yet if she was not candid, would Bernice later flounder? How many new believers expected to sail along in life without storms, only to get washed away when the Lord did not respond to their petitions at the speed of lightning?

"Bernice, I don't always feel spiritual. At such times, I depend on faith and lean on the Lord. He never reneges on His promises."

Bernice nodded.

"Some people are shackled to a life of misery, because they think they have to be good first. That is not true. Talk to Him, Bernice, tell Him everything. And you don't have to confess to anybody else, unless you wish to apologize to them. As long as you keep an open door with Him, you will make it."

"Just like in any relationship?"

"Mhmm. It's open-door policy all the way. Communication is critical. That is not to say He does not know already. But it is for my sake. It helps me remember to be honest with Him——trust Him to forgive, even when I let Him down. I try not to abuse that privilege, but I'm grateful He is merciful."

"Like a loving Father," Bernice said softly.

"Like a loving Father," she echoed.

Bernice elongated her neck and straightened her back more.

She smiled, suspecting that Bernice was ready to shoot from another angle. In the three years of their friendship, this was the longest that Bernice had interrogated her on the subject of spiritual health.

"I don't mean to pry, but were you mad at Him, when things were not um . . . straight-forward between you and Paul?"

Lily adjusted her scarf and let it blow in the wind for a while. Even before she replied, she knew she would be honest. "I was not so much mad, as numbed by the thought that being a believer was not enough to qualify me to find a suitable man of the same persuasion. Before I came here, I respected American Believers——at least the ones I met——despite the history of slavery. They seemed so . . . earnest in their faith. Being subjected to so much humiliation and pain was quite shocking to me. By the way, things are still not that comfortable, yet."

"How did you get over that phase?" Bernice asked, gently.

She sensed Bernice's empathy. "When I was leaving home, I promised my parents that I would always depend on the Lord and His Word. I can't control how others treat me, but I know God's love for me supersedes all else."

Bernice was elated. "Cool, if God's love is absolute, then, I'm home scot-free. I've always believed that."

"Not so fast. I have debated myself often over that issue. In my youthful naivety, I almost failed my exams one time and ended up suffering the consequences of looking for loopholes to justify goofing around. I delegated my homework to God——after all, He knew everything and would give me the answers miraculously. Right? My wiser, mature parents told me Jesus would help me faster, if I did my homework assiduously. As a result, I had to stay up late nights to catch up with my studies. Never again, have I abused God's grace knowingly, or taken it for granted so abominably."

Bernice chortled. "Lily, you're full of surprises."

"Yup. That's youth for you! To answer your question, as I understand, God's love is only unconditional in that I could not get to heaven on my own merit. But to benefit fully from that love, I must remain within the boundaries of his protection. If I wander off like a lamb that wanders into a lion's den, He would still love me, but I would face the consequences of drifting away from His protective fortress——barring being a Daniel."

Bernice nodded with understanding. "Sort of like . . . if I rejected what was right and did my own thing?" She snapped her fingers. "The Prince and the Pauper!"

"Excuse me?"

"The 1977 movie. In a blink, the prince lost his rights when he left the palace grounds dressed like a pauper——all because he wanted to try something different! Instantly, everybody treated him like one, though inside, he was still the prince."

"Yes!" Lily jumped up, thrilled. "I remember watching the movie in high school. Yes, you are right. If we use that analogy, believers are a royal priesthood——set apart, however, unlike an earthly prince who can load it over his subjects, we emulate our Master who is kind and loving. Kind as He is, He did set a standard for us to follow . . . just like parents set parameters to protect their children."

"Yes. And a simple rule like, don't open the door to strangers . . . or be safe, watch the traffic, are meant to benefit us," Bernice said, excited.

"Exactly!"

"It always comes back to our free will, doesn't it?" Bernice tossed her hair.

"Yes. It does. How can any of us benefit from God's love and protection, if we reject him?"

Bernice walked on in silence. From the groove in her face, she appeared to be running through an old reel of film, in the archive of her mind. She stopped and said, dreamily, "Alex says I've shut God out, but I think I'm beyond reprieving."

"Bernice? That cannot be. Have you consulted with the pastor?"

Bernice cringed.

Lily kicked herself. "I didn't mean it that way. You know you can trust me."

Bernice heaved a sigh of relief. "I didn't always choose my friends wisely. When my parents divorced, I lashed out and messed up so badly, I almost didn't make it to college. I'm more careful now."

"We all make mistakes," Lily sympathized, but resisted asking Bernice to disclose the sin that had caused her so much grief, leaving it up to her. More importantly, she had encouraged Bernice to confide in the Lord.

"I never told my Mum. Unlike the Kellies of this world, we'd hit rock–bottom, with Mum toiling to save our house." Bernice locked eyes with her.

Lily returned her gaze steadily, sympathetic, with no condemnation.

"Dad was gone and broke and Mum was trying so hard. But I did confess to Alex. He accused me of pushing him away by refusing to accept God's forgiveness. But I don't know how!" Bernice wiped her eyes.

"Oh, Bernice, from the moment you felt remorse, you were forgiven. You have been carrying an albatross around your neck, though you are already freed. Accept grace and let Alex love you. You are surrounded by those who love you. Give yourself a chance."

"I guess I've punished myself enough."

She gave her a big-bear hug. "Whatever mistake you made, let it go. The most important thing is you are sorry. The Lord heard your cries. He will never reject anyone who is truly sorry. Let Him love you, Bernice, as He promised He would."

Bernice composed herself. "Okay. What do I have to do?"

She smiled. "Thank you for asking. Ask the Lord to help you." For three years, she had prayed and waited for that question.

"My Mum and I sometimes watch Billy Graham crusades——all those people walking forward," Bernice said.

She nodded. "Yes. But only if you really mean it."

"I do mean it." Bernice nodded back vigorously.

"Okay. Then ask the Lord to help you."

"I don't know the words," Bernice said, embarrassed.

"You can ask from your heart. There's no formula," Lily replied.

"But they always recite a prayer."

A light went on. "I see what you mean. Reciting the prayer alone will not change you, unless you mean it. Ask Him," she pointed to heaven, "to help you manage your life, so you will no longer try to pull yourself up by your own bootstraps."

"I don't mind you guiding me. I might jumble my words," Bernice insisted.

"I would love to." She found a bench for them to sit. "Okay. As I understand, you choose to trust voluntarily, not just another trip, until the next big thing?"

"Yes." Bernice nodded. "I've thought through everything, I believe. I know this is the right decision for me. It's time I got serious," she said firmly.

Lily smiled. "All right. Please pray after me," she said, "Father, thank you for loving me and sending Jesus to earth, so I don't have to try to earn heaven on my own strength. I know I am a sinner. I'm sorry, please forgive me. I believe that Jesus Christ died on the cross and conquered death to set me free. Lord God, of my own free will, I choose to invite Him to live in my heart and help me manage my life. Thank you for wiping away my past sins forever. I don't have to carry the burden anymore. I'm free. Father, please protect me from evil, and teach me to walk in Your way. Thank you for saving me, in Jesus' Name. Amen.'"

She hugged Bernice again, choking, "Welcome home. May the Lord help you grow in His strength!"

Bernice dabbed her cheeks. "I'll tell Alex and Mum——Jake too. I know he'll come around. Thank you for being a true friend. And I'll be praying for you and Paul, okay?"

"Thank you." Lily's eyes also misted, even as she encouraged herself about her trip to the beach. Knowing that the Van Clydens were believers helped, somewhat. Praise be that Bernice had joined forces in praying for her as she tried to gauge where her on and off friendship with Paul was leading.

87

Paul blow-dried his hair, leaving it damp enough to coax it into a rakish look. Camel slacks and a cream ribbed-knit cotton polo neck caught his eyes. He dressed, whistling happy tunes, then he read the Bible for a quick morning devotion. On his way out, he grabbed bags of gifts and his weekend bags.

Throughout the morning, Paul dashed in and out of meetings and Christmas parties——giving reports, exchanging gifts with friends——and finally, he stopped by Bill's office to drop off his gifts, and discuss urgent business that might require a manager's attention during his absence.

His excitement mounted at the rate of his nervousness, even as he prayed that this would be a pleasant Christmas for all. At two thirty, he departed BF&S for Lily's condo.

As Lily drove up, she noticed Paul parked in the guests' parking. Overhead, the clouds were overcast, as the weather forecaster had projected. Praise be she had finished packing and had dressed appropriately for the trip in a favorite outfit——a charcoal gray wool crepe pant suit and a dusty rose crew neck silk sweater——first impressions matter.

The Christmas holidays fitted perfectly with the Denton & Terrell's annual plan to close the office for a whole week. She looked forward, nervously, to a week away from fighting the morning traffic.

Her face glowed above the dusty rose sweater and her pearl earrings were the finishing touches.

She wished Paul a good afternoon. He responded likewise and devoured her with his eyes.

"What?" She raised her eyebrows.

"Nothing." He loosened his polo-neck, fetched her luggage, then loaded them into the trunk.

The moment he turned on the ignition, it started misting, though no rain had been forecast. A Christmas CD came on.

True to form, the freeway was already slowing down, though it was only after three o'clock. A senior citizen, clutching the steering wheel of her Chrysler Le Baron Coupe, waited until Paul signaled to change lanes, then she cut in front of him——forcing him to cruise at below twenty-five miles per hour. Finally, he out-maneuvered her. "Sassy lady," he muttered.

"I heard that," Lily shot back.

Soon after, they hit another slow section. "That's what you get for calling the poor lady 'sassy'," Lily said.

He gave her another crooked smile. "She was in my way. At this rate, it'll take us two to three hours, instead of the usual one-and-halfish."

"Better safe." Lily sketched a smile, then a shadow crossed her face.

"What?" he asked, concerned.

"Nothing."

"We're going to have fun, right?" He patted her hand.

"Right." She smiled back.

Despite his efforts avoiding downtown by taking the 60 Freeway, they still hit gridlock after Freeway 405 intersection.

Two drivers were standing on the neck of the road, talking. Traffic inched along for forty-five minutes and stopped. He phoned his parents.

♦ ♦ ♦

The Van Clydens had spent the late afternoon fussing——Igor arranged and rearranged magazines; Charlotte fussed with the decor pillows and the invisible dust——the cleaning lady had already dusted that morning.

All week Charlotte had assured herself that she would be natural and comfortable, after all, this was her home. She was the mistress and queen of her house! To accomplish that, she had dressed in a down-home navy blue, red and white woolen sweater, with shades of gray and a pair of gray worsted wool slacks.

Igor had also worn a holiday attire——deep red wine Christmas sweater of angora wool over a white polo neck and gray slacks of pure wool. He had gone to the office, but he left early afternoon. Charlotte's strength bolstered him.

Paul was his only son——he had no plan B to fall back on. Why couldn't the Lord have chosen some other family better equipped to handle such an assignment, even if it turned out to be nothing but a passing phase for Paul, as in his past dates?

Upon confirming the date of Lily's visit, they had committed their future into the Lord's hands. That was the easy part. Since Paul had almost as much as confirmed that he had marriage in mind, their anxiety rose with each day. Surely, the Lord would not disappoint them? He had always been faithful. After all their petitions for Him to provide the best for their son, would He let them down, now?

Igor regretted limiting members of his inner circle in the past to friends whose ancestors could be traced all the way back to some cousin of King Louis or English Marquis or the equivalent. Well, lately, he and Charlotte had gone out to lunch with a couple whom they had admired, but had kept at the periphery of their life. They had also expanded their business seminars to include more international consortiums.

He stood by the window, stroking his chin, mulling over how he had been trying to expand his business, while forgetting the basics—— canvassing was global. As an astute business man, could he afford to sleep at the helm? At the back of his mind, he must have known all along that he was slipping in the art of global networking.

Lifting his eyes to the cloudy skies, he wondered, while the business world was changing, had the social world changed as much as Paul wished him to believe?

O ye of little faith came a quiet voice from within him.

His face lit up. "Honey, I'm confident it will be alright."

Charlotte kissed his cheek. "So do I."

Just then, the phone rang.

"Hello," he boomed.

"Dad, please tell Mum we're running late."

"Where're you?"

"Between gridlock and gridlock. I'll look for alternative routes."

"Where about exactly?"

"We're inching toward La Cienega, passed La Brea. I know L.A. like the back of my hand, but I still need one of those GPS navigation gizmos at moments like this," Paul replied.

He directed Paul to take the La Cienega exit south to Venice Boulevard till he hit Lincoln Boulevard. Lincoln would meander and turn into the Pacific Coast Highway.

"I was looking for alternate routes back to the freeway," Paul said.

"If the gridlock's after the 405, it may be difficult to gauge when exactly to get back on, but if it's workable, there're some good alternatives." He snapped off a string of other alternate routes Paul could use to get back on the freeway, instead of using Venice Boulevard.

"Just a moment." Paul said to someone in the background——Lily, he assumed, "Got pen and paper?"

"Yes. I should. One moment, please," came the soft voice of a female. After a slight pause, she said, "Ready."

"Okay, Dad. Fire away," Paul said to him.

He repeated the instructions again, as Paul relayed them to Lily.

"Got it?"

"Yes, Dad."

"Okay, drive carefully now. How's Lily holding on?"

"Fine."

"Good. Now Son, don't worry about what time you get here. Be safe! Got that?" he barked.

"Yes, sir!" Paul's tone sounded as though he was saluting.

"Son, save your hand for the wheel." He chuckled.

"Dad!"

Igor hang up, amazed. He had just heard Lily's voice for the first time. "Quite a pleasant voice! Sounds musical——like a fresh river flowing along or . . . a dove."

"What?" Charlotte asked him.

"She has a very pleasant voice."

"You too noticed!"

"I hope the rest of her is as pleasant."

♦ ♦ ♦

Paul turned to Lily. She was slumped against her seat, in stitches.

"You too!"

"Don't turn on me now. I wasn't the one who saluted!"

He scratched his head. "Dad can be something else."

"Is he scary?"

"No. He's a teddy bear."

"Sure?"

"Positive. Relax, you'll be all right." He patted her hand again.

"Okay. If you say so."

"I do say so. There's a map in the back-seat."

Traffic inched forward. Lily took the map and searched for alternate routes on the map, using the overhead light. The best option was Venice Boulevard, though it was slightly off course.

At La Cienega, Paul followed the other drivers to the off ramp, where they made good their escape. Outside, it was already dark.

The shiny surface made it difficult to distinguish the lanes, but Paul maneuvered skillfully, with flashes of the Christmas before, and his jerky drive home at Thanksgiving now replaced with hope.

Finally, one-and-half hours later, they cruised along rows of increasingly opulent, gated estates. As they started up a road, after exiting the Pacific Coast Highway, it started misting again, then it turned into a light rain.

"Almost there," Paul said.

Lily smiled, remembering a favorite saying of her people, "The Lord sends rain, but when the gentle rain announces the arrival of a guest, that guest is a blessing." Sensing that her grandma's prayers were being answered, she turned to the window, and communed in her heart, "*Thank you for Grandma and for her strength. May it please You to grant her prayers and bless Paul's parents. I bless them and come in peace, bringing goodwill. Amen.*"

88

The Van Clydens' gate closed with the finality of the last sentence of the last paragraph of the last page of the last chapter of an old book. Paul drove to the garage and emerged to the beginning of the first sentence of the first paragraph of the first page of the first chapter of a new book.

From the backyard, Percy started barking, excited.

Charlotte opened the connecting door and welcomed Lily, "We apologize for the informality. I hope you had a good trip?"

Lily said they did and thanked her.

Igor hovered in the background.

"Lily, this is my Mum and Dad," Paul said.

His Mum offered Lily her cheeks and welcomed her again.

"How do you do Mrs. Van Clyden?" Lily greeted her.

"Delighted to meet you."

"My, who do we have here? When you set your heart to it, son, you do go all out, don't you?" His father stepped forward and sized up Lily.

"Easy, honey. She's just arrived," his mother nudged his father.

"Well, how do you do, Lily? I am Igor."

"How do you do, Mr. Van Clyden?" Lily answered.

"She's pretty, isn't she?" His mother seemed delighted. "Well, don't just stand there, honey. We've the whole week. She must be tired from all that driving and all. Come on in, before you get cold."

"Hi, Mum. Hi Dad. I am doing fine too," he said, in a small voice.

"And so you are! You can come in too," His father joshed with him.

"Thank you, sir. It's very kind of you," he replied.

"My pleasure, son."

His mother offered him her cheeks. "You two can go on the whole evening, but don't forget to bring in the bags."

"Yes, Ma'am," he and his father answered in chorus.

His father carried two bags upstairs to the guest room and he carried the rest. He, of course, would have his old room across the hall.

They left his mother showing Lily around, helping her feel at home.

Lily admired her room——soft colors splashed around the room and fresh sprigs of flowers, to chase away winter gloom——then she freshened up, went downstairs and surprised her hostess with fresh chapati.

"Home-made chapati. Our special East African recipe, somewhat similar to the Indian chapati, but each region makes it differently. We eat it as a snack or with meals." She handed the container to Charlotte.

"How delightful! It smells so good. I can't wait to taste them." Charlotte stored the container in the fridge. "Come and join us in the family room."

When they entered the living room, Igor was stirring the fire and Paul was lounging in a chair. His intimate smile made her heart flip.

"Have a seat." Igor gestured to an elegant Irving Leather Armchair.

He was not half as scary as she had thought.

Charlotte offered her a choice of drinks, "We've lemonade, orange juice, apple juice, or would you prefer tea or coffee?" declaring her house alcohol-free and sparing her the embarrassment of declining a drink.

"Apple juice. Thank you."

"Don't let her fool you Mum. She's an avid tea drinker. And make that piping hot," Paul interjected.

"Is that right? I'd be delighted to make you some tea," Charlotte said.

"Thank you. Perhaps later?" she replied.

"Are you sure? Don't be shy now."

"Yes. Thank you."

Charlotte served her a glass of apple juice.

She admired the Christmas decorations quietly, then said, "This place is so peaceful."

Charlotte thanked her. "It is our safe haven. We were grateful to get it. Our other house was nice too . . . we used to live in the Foothills City before we moved up here," she explained.

"Oh? The Foothills is a very nice city," Lily commented.

"Yes. It is. When Paul was young, we lived down there because of the school system, then we moved here eleven years ago? Right honey?" Charlotte turned to Igor.

"Yes. When Paul was starting freshman at USC," Igor replied.

"We decided to do something different to cope with the empty nest syndrome." Charlotte smiled at Paul.

"That must have been difficult."

"You can say that. As parents of an only child, we were not prepared at all. One moment he was here, the next, he was off to school."

"It must've been difficult for your parents too," Igor said, "with you going miles away to a strange country."

"In a way, but I went to boarding school for my high school. I think it was the distance that got to them this time."

"You attended boarding school? Oh!" Igor was a bit surprised. "And your parents, what do they do?"

"My Dad is a business man and my Mum works too," Lily replied, softly, without offering any further information.

"Your Dad's a business man, eh? What type of business?"

"He does a variety——a little bit of this and a little bit of that, mostly dealing with, um . . . trade."

"Trade's good. Most important, he can provide for his family. He seems to have done pretty well by you from what Paul tells me."

She thanked him and asked, "How is business?"

"Excellent. We've had a few things here and there, but overall, we're managing. The economists are projecting a trade deficit, but California's steel industry's strong. We're expecting California to become the largest buyer of steel. However, I'm looking to diversify——try my hand at new fields."

"Diversification is always prudent. The rapid advancement in technology is impacting every sector," Lily agreed.

"Right on!" His voice rose a notch. "Where's Africa in that?"

"Except for South Africa, and the northern regions, Africa——especially the tropics——is behind. My Dad and his contemporaries wish they would come on board technology faster."

"I agree with them absolutely."

"Well, dinner's ready," Charlotte announced and turned to Lily, "We'll continue visiting over coffee. I'm dying to ask all sorts of questions. Don't let him intimidate you. His bark's worse than his bite."

Igor furrowed his brows. "Now, now, honey, don't divulge all my secrets."

"If you continue bombarding her with questions, I just might." She said to Paul, "We were waiting for you. We thought it would be more fun having dinner together as a family."

At the word, 'family,' Lily glanced at Paul.

Paul was rocking himself in his chair, a merry twinkle in his eyes.

Charlotte headed toward the kitchen then stopped. "Oh my! I forgot to ask. Lily, would you like to shower before dinner? We're pretty laid-back."

She thanked her. "I'm pretty flexible too. Later is okay."

"Sure?"

"Yes. Thank you."

"How about you, Paul?" Charlotte addressed Paul.

"I'll take one later too. Thanks."

"All right."

"Can I help?" Lily asked.

"Thank you. But everything's ready. We were waiting for you to get here."

"Sorry we were late."

"Don't apologize. We're glad you got here in one piece." Charlotte included Paul in her smile, then she served dinner in the cozier family dinette.

This time, Igor said grace without stumbling over his words. He also prayed for Lily's family back home, making her feel at home, as they enjoyed Charlotte's dishes prepared to perfection to Lily's taste——rice, boneless, skinless chicken braised in very light herbs, and other tasty dishes and potatoes salad (for Igor). Fresh fruit for dessert served as a center piece.

Knowing that Lily had met Aaron and Michael, Charlotte asked Paul about them, to include her in the conversation. A week after Thanksgiving, Aaron and Michael had dropped by, surprising them for a visit with their favorite aunt and uncle, before the end of the year, they had said. Did Paul see them before he left? Of course, college had already closed for Christmas breaks. Were they planning on going home or surfing? They had mentioned they might go to Puerto Vallarta.

"The water's always warmer along the Mexican beaches around this time of the year," she said.

"So are the girls, I would assume," mumbled Igor.

His audience dabbed their lips to hide their smiles.

"Aaron and Michael are the marrying kind. I doubt they'll be shopping around much beyond their current girlfriends," Paul also mumbled.

Igor glanced at Lily.

Paul added that he thought Aaron and Michael preferred spending Christmas at home. When they exchanged gifts a week before, they were looking forward to seeing their parents in a few days. They would most likely postpone any plan to the Mexican beaches to spring break.

Igor interspersed their conversation with jokes, and appeared more relaxed. Surely, everything would be all right? Didn't the Lord say He would honor those who honored Him? He and Charlotte had committed to embrace His will. He helped himself to the chicken.

After supper, Paul loaded the dishwasher, then he prepared Percy's food. Once again, they would not let Lily help.

Percy, curled up in his warm kennel, yawned and whined as if to say, "About time. Why do dogs get served last?"

"I know buddy, I know. You take second place now," Paul replied, earning himself a one-eyed scrutiny from Percy. He patted Percy once more, washed his hands and returned to the living room.

His mother served hot coffee for his father and her, hot tea for him and Lily and a cherry pie.

A little while later after they had finished their dessert, and chatted, his parents retired for the night.

"When you get to be our age, it's hard to stay up late anymore. We usually take it easy. Is breakfast around nine o'clock okay with everybody?"

"Sure Mum."

"Good night." She offered them her cheeks.

Paul's father also wished them goodnight and followed her.

Paul grinned at Lily. "Would you care for a movie?"

"Please."

"Hot chocolate?"

"Sounds good. Can I help?"

"No, thank you. Relax! You'll have plenty of opportunity later."

"I'll hold you to that."

"It's a deal."

Paul searched the archives. "What would you like to see?" he asked.

"I'm not a movie buff. What do you recommend?" she replied.

He ran off a few names, then he mentioned, "Crossed Swords, otherwise known as the 1977 version of The Prince and the Pauper——"

She perked up. "That is a favorite of Bernice's. She is a believer now."

"Wonderful! Excellent! Alleluia! Give me a five! That's great!" He high-fived her. "I was hoping I would have good news about Shane, too."

"How's he doing?"

"He showed up last Sunday."

"Really? The man you introduced to Pastor Tim——was that him?"

"Mhmm."

Lily shook her head, amazed. "Miracles never cease."

"Amen. I'm still in shock." He gave her the video.

"I saw the very old version. Why do you like this version?"

He shrugged. "I don't know. It has some action."

"It would. Can I trust you?"

"It's not bad. It's about youth."

"All right," she conceded.

He queued the video in the player, then he made some hot chocolate and threw more logs on the fire.

Lily was thankful of Paul's thoughtfulness and that he did not pull anything with her, yet he made her feel special. For a moment, a fleeting thought of Kelly flashed through her mind. She dismissed it.

They reclined their heads, and watched the movie in quiet amity.

"Still awake?" Paul stretched, as the movie ended.

"Yes. It was a great movie," she answered.

"What did you think of the overall theme?"

"Besides curiosity almost killed the cat, but for grace?"

He chuckled.

"It painted a vivid picture of why it is prudent to believe people, sometimes, when they say they are who they are, though they may not look the part."

"Uh-huh. It's amazing how a simple act of curiosity——naïve as it may be——could end in unplanned outcomes, though in this case, it is the plot. I should discuss it with my youth class," he added.

"Mhmm. But the prince became more princely due to his experiences, while Tom came to appreciate his simple life without the burdens of state, except for sleeping in a clean bed, having servants and not going hungry."

He nodded. "Reversal of circumstances happens."

"Bernice saw in the prince's escaping the privileges of the palace, the risk we take when we don't think about the consequences of rebelling and wandering off. Although I believe the similarities stop there."

"Why's that?" he asked.

"First, Twain's intentions were to highlight the class differences of that period and as a subplot, the consequences of judging people by appearance. But——unlike the prince——the average believer is not as endowed with material wealth. Even if we were, we flourish best when we choose to live simply. It is when we abandon our virtuous lifestyles and espouse a worldly standard without boundaries——call it unshackled freedom——that we take the same risk as the lamb that wanders into the lions' den."

"You hit it on the head. Our secret to abundant life is anchored in the Lord. When we see the world through His eyes, we become kinder, gentler, focused and in touch with the things that are important. And, we flourish in all areas of our lives, as He promised we would, if we remain in Him." He sought her eyes.

Lily shifted, uneasy with his penetrating gaze. She had always felt uneasy at the notion of being anybody's savior.

"I guess we are in agreement," she said.

"I agree. We should continue this conversation sometime later. I feel guilty keeping you up."

"It's all right. Eleven o'clockish is usually my routine."

"Then we're off by half an hour. Not to change the subject, about tomorrow, I'm not sure what Mum and Dad have planned."

He invited her for a drive, if the weather permitted and his parents had nothing planned or they could also loaf around the house, he said.

A lover of long drives, she accepted his invitation gladly.

"Have you ever been to this part of the coastal region?" he asked.

"No," she replied.

"Good. Then we'll cruise along the coast. Mum and Dad normally help in the community. Their Christmas Eve service starts at eleven o'clock and ends about midnight." He paused, touched her arm, uncertain. Then he let his hand fall back to his side.

Lily felt electric power shoot through her body. To cover the awkward silence and plan her morning she said, "Um, I kind of have a problem."

"Yes?"

"I was thinking about going for a walk in the morning. Um, what is your routine like, generally?"

"Varied, including walks."

"Well," she hesitated.

"Do you mind if I joined you?" he came to her rescue.

"Not at all. Seven o'clock?"

"Seven o'clock it is."

She wished him goodnight.

"Goodnight, d——" he bit his tongue and said, "Lily."

As she left the room, she turned slightly and smiled at him, then he heard her steps on the stairway.

After her footsteps had faded, Paul sat on the couch she had just vacated, collected himself and fetched a bag of ice from the kitchen. When he returned, he stirred the grid and sat down to watch the flame of the remaining one log rekindled, the ice-bag clapped to his forehead.

As the flame flickered, he heard footsteps on the stairs. Shortly, his father appeared.

"Son?" he asked.

"Dad." He blushed and grinned.

His father studied him quietly and added more logs on the fire. "How about I make some sandwiches from that delicious chicken your mother prepared, while you plug in a good old western? And I think we have chocolate vanilla ice cream. What do you think?"

"Great, Dad!"

89

Lily stirred from sleep. A potpourri of scents hit her nose. Her eyes flew open. No, she was not in her bedroom. By the clock on the dresser, it was only five o'clock. Habit, she thought, groggy.

She remembered the night before. Surely, Paul must have some feelings for her, beyond his penchant for collecting toys in triplets? But why did Kelly keep waltzing in and out of his life?

On the other hand, could a man invite a woman to his parents' home, when he was engaged to marry someone else? In the old days, boys did not introduce their intended to their parents, let alone bring them home, until they were absolutely sure. But these were the modern times.

How many girls did Paul bring home in a year? It was not unusual for a man of his looks and means to date widely, and have some of those girls meet his parents too, but, why she? She drifted off to sleep.

When she stirred again, it was after six o'clock. She took her black leather–bound Bible from her bedstand and rolled down to her knees. Half an hour later, she freshened up and returned to a sunrise panoramic view of the beautiful garden outside her window, that merged into the breath-taking sea. She daydreamed about Paul back from college, running around the compound——playing ball with his cousins or at the beach, surfing.

Reluctantly, she finished dressing and left her bedroom, rubbing freesia lotion on her hands. A small whiff of the soft scent trailed her downstairs, embracing the lavish corridor right into Paul's nostrils, as he opened his door.

Her heart skipped a bit when she heard his footsteps.

"Good morning! Did you have a good night?" he greeted her.

She wished him the same. "Yes. I slept like a baby. How was yours?"

Blushing, he mumbled, "Same." If truth were told, after he and his dad had watched the movie depicting how the west was won, he had counted sheep across the hall till dawn.

From the patio, persistent moaning and scratching assailed their ears.

"Percy seems to smell us a mile away. He usually goes out with Mum and Dad . . . by the way, do you like pets?"

She thanked him for asking. "Outside of gold fish? No. I don't care for house pets, especially cats, but guard-dogs are okay——I mean outside."

"You're like Mum. She dislikes Percy messing the house. Ok, then we won't——"

"No. We can take him. It sounds like he too prefers to stick to his routine."

Paul threw her a grateful look and fetched Percy.

Cold winds nipped at their noses as they walked briskly down the avenue of trees, bundled up in their winter gear, Percy leading the way. Paul pointed out private estates, as they walked past. Once in a while, when a lonely jogger, approached them, Paul reigned in Percy.

"I like it here, so peaceful and quiet. It reminds me of home," Lily said, stopped and stammered. "I mean, it is beautiful."

"Yes, it is. I love the solitude, especially in the morning," Paul added, then in quiet camaraderie, he showed her the rest of the neighborhood.

Over an hour later, they turned into the driveway and followed the smell of bacon to the kitchen, where Charlotte was preparing breakfast. They wished her a good morning. She wished them the same, surprised they were already up.

Paul patted Percy's back out of the house. "We went for a walk."

"Isn't it rather cold for Lily to be out so early?"

"What Lily?" Paul asked, washing his hands. "She's the avid walker. No blizzard will keep her in."

"How remarkable! I wish I'd known; we could've come." She pushed two steaming cups of tea to them.

"It would have been nice. I did not know. I thought you prefer late mornings." Lily also washed her hands at the sink.

"Oh no. We're early risers. We usually walk before breakfast."

"Then we could all go out tomorrow, if it doesn't rain," Paul said.

"Go where on Christmas Eve?" A voice said from the door.

"Good morning Mr. Van Clyden. Morning, Dad," Lily and Paul chorused.

"Go out for a walk, honey. Paul says Lily's quite an avid walker. They've already been out this morning," Charlotte explained.

"She has strong blood. That's good to know. Well, if they don't mind us tagging along, I wouldn't mind joining them."

"That would be nice, Mr. Van Clyden," Lily said.

Igor raised his hands, in protest, "No formality. Call me Igor." He grabbed a stool, sat down and patted his stomach.

"Me too." Charlotte served Igor a cup of coffee. "We don't stand on ceremony around here. Charlotte's fine."

"Except for Paul, of course." Igor's face was impassive.

"I know, Dad."

"You can call me, 'My lord' any time."

"Dad!"

Lily rubbed her nose, to hide a smile.

Charlotte cracked up. "Mercy! If you two get started so early in the morning, Lily and I'll find a place to hide for the rest of the day."

"Not on Christmas weekend. No. You don't!" Igor shot back.

"Then you boys behave yourselves."

"Cross my heart, Mum."

"And me too," echoed Igor.

Charlotte waved them off. "You two just do go on." She said to Lily, "Don't mind them. Paul came off the old chip."

"I'm learning, ma'am." Lily's eyes twinkled.

"See? She has got you boys figured out!"

Igor burrowed his eyebrows. "Don't mind my family, you'll get used to it."

Lily glanced at Paul, still puzzled over hints about her being family.

She noticed Charlotte preparing to set the table. "I insist, Mrs. Van-n-, I mean Charlotte . . . May I call you Mama Paul and Baba Paul?"

"Of course, you can call us whatever makes you comfortable."

She thanked Charlotte and stretched out her hands to her.

"All right." Charlotte surrendered the plates. "The knives and forks are in the top drawer," she pointed to the cabinet.

Paul jumped off his stool. "I'll get the glasses and the napkins."

Igor locked eyes with Charlotte.

In an instant, a spread of fresh fruits, mouthwatering pancakes, toast, bacon and eggs, along with a coffee pot and a teapot covered the table.

To Lily's great pleasure, she discovered a common bond between her and Charlotte. Having acquired a taste for a good cup of tea, Charlotte boycotted lukewarm tea. Following tradition, she boiled her water until steaming hot, warmed her teapot, and then brewed the tea for five minutes before serving it. And a hot cup of tea wouldn't be hot without hot milk, so she boiled her milk too and served it in a flask.

Charlotte had the slightest English accent. Of English descent, one generation shy of the old country, she had grown up in America, except for short trips visiting relatives, a year devoted to Shakespeare studies and another in the continent. She had learnt many a habit from an old English girlfriend who had got married to an American. The marriage lasted ten years, but Charlotte's friendship with her survived. They still kept in touch, including their annual tea at an elegant restaurant.

Other mannerisms she had also acquired included calling Paul, "Darling,"——though he was now an adult——or exclaiming "Marvelous."

She surveyed the table. "Marvelous! I think we're ready."

They held hands as Igor said grace.

"Darling, what's your plan the next two days?" She passed the dishes.

"Depends . . . we're playing it by ear. Do you have any?" Paul replied.

"The usual," she replied, then to Lily, "We didn't ask you last night, Christmas Eve we help at the homeless shelter. You're welcome to join us. Of course you can spend the day sightseeing, also. We've a lot of enchanting beaches around. Today, we were planning on taking it easy."

Lily's eyes lit up. "I would love to join you. I also help downtown."

"The weather forecasters expect cloudy weather, but no rain. We could explore the local vicinity this afternoon, then we could go farther afield next week." Paul spoke to the table, but addressed Lily.

"Good. Then that's settled. Oh, by the way, Uncle Jeremy and Aunt Angela invited us for Christmas Eve dinner before the service."

"All right!" Paul cheered.

Charlotte pouted. "Is that what you think of my cooking?"

Igor covered his mouth with his napkin. Lily followed suit.

"Mum, I didn't mean it that way. 'love your cooking. You're the best!"

"Good. Because I'm cooking tonight and New Year's Eve!"

"Luv ya, Ma!"

"Luv ya too!"

When they had calmed down, Charlotte took a piece of bacon and nibbled on it, while pondering the mystery of Lily. Lily was different from Kelly. Kelly tolerated serving the underprivileged, but preferred a suburban, upscale environment. Less than twenty-four hours after meeting Lily, she was beginning to understand Paul's attraction to her.

After breakfast, the men handled the dishes. Lily watched them. No, she could not envision her stately father bent over dishes. A good father, that he was, but dishes? Nah! She smiled.

"Anything the matter?" Paul did not miss a twitch.

"No. I was thinking how nice you and your dad look, stacking dishes."

He thanked her and bowed.

"Come, Lily. Let the boys handle it." Charlotte went to the family room.

Early afternoon, Paul dusted off his vintage jeep. Not that he needed to. His father had had it polished till it shone. He took Lily for a drive to the surrounding cities around the Pacific Palisades and returned just before dinner, never slipping off the pedal of a true gentleman.

His mother had prepared beef stew to complement Lily's Chapati. He mopped his dinner plate with pleasure, helped with the dishes, then he took out a chess board and a monopoly box. "Do you play?" he asked Lily.

"Not really, but I can learn. Back home, the believers don't care for cards."

"It used to be like that here too. Some denominations still don't. We play a little, but we don't use money." Paul prepared the table.

Lily was learning the other side of the Van Clydens. More surprising was how silly they became, at the game table.

In between making his moves, Igor discussed business opportunities in East Africa. She kept herself busy, learning how to play the game.

Charlotte reminding her that they would be serving at the shelter in the morning and she was welcomed to join them.

90

Paul glanced in the rear–view mirror of his father's Jaguar, locked eyes with Lily's briefly, then he stepped on the pedal. He could not fathom what she was thinking, but it felt good to have her sitting next to his mother.

On arrival at the homeless shelter, they parked in designated areas for volunteers. The day that had begun slightly cloudy, had turned cool and breezy, but still comfortable for serving in the open air.

At the entrance gate, Igor handed over their letter of invitation. For over ten years he and Charlotte had served at the shelter, however, they never presumed on their status as regular volunteers; they always brought their invitation letter.

For one hour, they served plates filled with turkey and ham, and trimmings, and pumpkin pies. Occasionally, they stopped to chat with their guests——some cheerful and friendly, others sitting in silent solitude.

At one point, Lily disappeared. Paul searched around with his eyes, then he spotted her talking to a family and carrying their youngest. He joined them. The father explained that he had lost his job; but they were getting computer training at the shelter and were hoping to get placed in gainful employment soon——not surprising that Lily had exerted herself to learn about them. She saw them, she cared.

Unintentionally, she had stolen the show. The men were curious about her foreign accent and wanted to know, from which country was she?

Charlotte and Igor watched her, discreetly. She was a natural.

Some of the frequent volunteers succeed in masking their emotions, others did a double turn at seeing her with the Van Clydens. It was obvious Paul was favoring her. That Paul had brought a female friend to serve with the family was surprising enough, but Lily stood out like chocolate-brown orchid, amidst a field of yellow and white roses.

By the end of the hour, the next shift had already lined up to take over. With no ceremony, and no fuss, the eleven o'clock shift dispersed to their homes and their Christmases.

As Lily said goodbye, Paul was sure that she slipped the mother dollar bills during the handshake. He smiled and guided her back to the car.

"How about a beach drive, everybody?" he asked, seating her.

"Oh, that would be marvelous. Maybe we could stop for a sandwich along the way," Charlotte answered.

'Roop, roop roop,' the first drops of rain greeted them.

"Oh! It's going to be a wet drive home. I thought it's supposed to be a clear day," Charlotte announced, crestfallen.

Igor examined the skies and said, "I think it will clear off fast enough, honey. Now tomorrow may be the big one——fireside and chocolate."

"That's okay, Mum, nothing like rain to give a cozy ride," Paul consoled her and cruised along the Pacific Coast Highway, while Igor served as the tour guide. By then, the rain had passed.

They had lunch at a sandwich place, continued sightseeing, mindful of their dinner invitation to the Kaarlyles' and arrived home by three o'clock.

Charlotte recommended a nap for everybody——it would be a long evening.

Lily welcomed the opportunity to catch up with her work, tuned her bedside radio to a classical station for the backdrop, as she validated the academic sources and citations for her paper. If things continued to improve, she would tell Paul ultimately, but not yet.

Just before five o'clock, Igor and Paul came down in dark slacks topped by Christmas sweaters. They looked approvingly at Lily coming down the stairs in her semi-formal business slacks, topped with a black, crew-neck sweater and a pair of gold earrings, her red and black lamb's wool ruana wrap slung over her shoulders. She joined them waiting for Charlotte.

Charlotte finally appeared dressed in semi-casual slacks and a rust-colored angora blouse, a rust-colored silk scarf arranged casually around her neck. A single brooch of diamond and emeralds put some life on her gray car-length coat.

♦ ♦ ♦

Christmas lights swayed in the gentle breeze, twinkling, blinking——trees and shrubs alight——a huge nativity scene on the front lawn. Tourists paused to admire the scene, then drove on to the next estate.

Inside, chandeliers lighted Christmas themes of gold, red, poinsettias, bows and angels.

The Kaarlyles worked as a team. Jonathan set the table in the formal dining room; Ingrid handled the julienne vegetables; and Jeremy cleaned the silver for the nth time; while Angela finished preparing her feast——roast duck, cranberry sauce, julienne vegetables, wild rice, stuffing, cold salad and all kinds of delicacies.

For a moment, she had flirted with retaining the cook, but resisted. She loved the family atmosphere she grew up in——laid back, with no maids. She and her sisters helped their parents and grandparents prepare the Christmas feast, amidst family jokes and ribbings. She wouldn't change a thing.

At five-thirty, the doorbell rang. Like a true Kaarlyle, Jonathan threw the door open. Soon, loud voices in the entrance hall announced the Van Clydens, laden with gifts.

Again, Jeremy did a double turn when Lily appeared.

Angela hugged her, but when Lily addressed her as 'Mrs. Kaarlyle', she protested, "Call me Angela," then she introduced Jeremy, "You remember my husband, Jeremy?"

"Yes. Nice to see you again, Mr. Kaarlyle. Merry Christmas!"

"What a beautiful young lady!" boomed Jeremy. "Don't stand on ceremony. Everybody calls me Jeremy. I'm quite comfortable with that. How about you?"

"I bet you, it's Baba and Mama Jonathan," Charlotte interjected.

"Pardon?" Angela's British roots kicked in.

"In her culture, the polite thing is to call the elders by the name of their first child or their favorite child. So, I'm Mama Paul and Igor is Baba Paul," she explained to her audience.

Lily nodded. "Yes. It is a sign of respect."

"Well, I like being called Mama Jonathan." Angela beamed.

"And you can call me Baba Jonathan any time," Jeremy boomed.

Lily thanked them.

Angela finished the introductions, "You already know Jonathan, and you met my daughter Ingrid at the Thanksgiving dinner."

"Hello Ingrid. So nice to see you again." Lily extended her hand.

Ingrid surprised her with a warm hug, as though they were old friends.

Jonathan followed suit with a kiss on the cheeks, then a secret coded greeting for Paul.

Lily took in the setting at a glance. For the occasion, Angela had laid out bottles of sparkling apple cider and sparkling grape juice. Not a drop of alcohol in sight, thus explaining Jonathan——like parents like son, just like Paul.

When the last dish was set on the table, Angela admired the beautiful setting, as her husband lit the candles.

"I'll get the video." Ingrid went to the media room.

"I wish we could keep it running. It would be so much fun," Angela said.

Jonathan jumped to action. "You know, Mum. If you put that on a stand, we could all sit down and let it roll throughout dinner."

"You think so?"

"I know so. Trust me, Mum, it'll work."

Paul agreed.

Jonathan fetched the stand. Between him and Paul, they managed to set up the video to continue running throughout dinner.

At the table, Jeremy asked Igor to do the honors and bless the food.

Igor looked around the table, swallowed hard and prayed, "Father, thank you for bringing all of us to another commemoration of the birth of your Son, but more so, thank you for His in-dwelling power in each of us throughout the year. I also thank you for bringing Lily to spend this season with us. I pray that you'll make this a special time for her and bless and watch over her family across the seas."

"Yes, Lord" the whole table agreed.

"Thank you for the food we're about to eat and bless the hands that prepared it. And Father," he swallowed hard, "thank you for bringing Paul safely home to us." He paused. "May your grace and blessings continue to rest on Jeremy's family, and mine and our loved ones during this Christmas season, and always . . ."

"Amen," chorused the table. Charlotte and Angela dabbed their eyes.

Igor's butterflies had long since subsided. Lily was so different from what he had expected, that he marveled at how much he had doubted. She was soft-spoken and a bit shy, yet with the promise of mischief that he found refreshing.

After the table had complimented the cook, Paul asked, "How's business, Uncle Jeremy?"

"Try this juicy slice, Lily," Jeremy offered Lily a slice of duck.

Igor and Paul exchanged glances.

"Honey, Paul asked how's business?" Angela said.

"Great! Stock's up," Jeremy replied.

Igor dabbed his mouth and gave him a measured look.

"Anything the matter?" Angela asked.

Jeremy cut an asparagus spear. "Christmas comes around once a year. Merry Christmas! Good cheer to everyone."

"Here, here. Merry Christmas everybody. Cheers!" Igor helped himself to another slice of roast duck, after the round of toasts.

After contemplating her husband with her eyes for a few seconds, Angela asked, "Lily, how does your family celebrate Christmas?"

Lily explained that the Christmas atmosphere was not as festive as in America, for example, hardly any Christmas trees.

"No Christmas trees?" Angela was a bit surprised.

Very briefly, Lily described a typical Christmas day, growing up in her family——having a special breakfast, wearing new dresses to church . . . and sometimes having the neighbors gather for a potluck——then she brought the conversation back to how much she was enjoying her visit to the beach.

At the end of supper, the boys and the girls, snapped up the plates and stacked up all the dishes in the dishwasher, then Jonathan transferred the video camera to the family room.

To Lily's surprise, Angela sat at the piano. A violin, a viola and a cello appeared out of nowhere and voila, a trio of old Christmas favorites filled the room!

"Chamber Music! I didn't know Paul could play cello," she admired the trio. Ingrid had the violin, Jonathan had the viola, and Paul took on the cello.

Charlotte clapped her hands. "Oh, those three could go on. They each play at least three instruments. Christmas carols! Marvelous. Come on everybody, let's practice a few carols before church."

Igor and Jeremy popped out of their chairs.

Lily hung back, shy.

"Come on, Lily. Come and join us," Charlotte urged.

"I'm afraid I'm not a very good singer and some of the carols are new to me. I'm not at all good at sight-reading."

"You'll do fine," Paul assured her, with another of his intimate smiles that made her float towards the piano.

"There you go! Just do as I do, hit any note and sing louder than everybody else," Jeremy joked.

The Van Clydens and the Kaarlyles could get a recording contract, if they wished. Lily filled in the missing lady's part with her dove-like soprano voice and she didn't miss a note. Charlotte sang alto, Igor had a solid baritone voice. Jeremy's resonating bass grounded the group, especially in songs with ostinatos.

At eight thirty, they stopped for dessert, then they continued with their happy caroling, until it was time to leave for the mid-night service.

♦ ♦ ♦

Just like with the church parking lot, the sanctuary was also full. Ushers were unloading chairs for the overflow in the side aisles, amidst the clamor of the orchestra tuning in the pit.

Looking at the over-spill crowd, Paul smiled. *Faith lives on.* He strode beside Lily, realizing life as it would be, if he succeeded.

They spotted their family-friends half way up the aisles and a whole row of reserved seats came into view——thanks to his parents' foresight in asking for their help ahead.

Just before the choir entered, the Shinebonds came over to greet them, and for the first time, laid their eyes on Lily. In their eyes, Paul saw an understanding of how Lily had won, without malice towards Kelly.

After the Shinebonds had returned to their seats, he asked Lily, "Are you all right?"

"Yes. Thank you," Lily replied.

"Sure?"

"Positive," she said, then added, "This is a lovely church."

On cue, the Senior Pastor welcomed the congregation and handed the service over to the thirtyish-looking director of music to lead the program, composed of singing and selections of scripture readings.

Uncle Jeremy belted the songs above the crowd, with total abandon, the way he approached life——despite the looming future.

Fifteen minutes to the end of the service, the pastor gave a brief Christmas message. As he delved into the sermon, Paul glanced at Lily. She was engrossed in the message and seemed at peace. It felt so good to be sitting next to her in his parents' church. When he snapped back; the pastor was giving an altar call to the audience. A handful of people responded. No better ending could have topped the evening, except for Lily sitting next to him.

Just before midnight, the ushers passed candles for the traditional singing of "Silent Night, Holy Night" at the stroke of midnight. Paul lit Lily's candle, turned to the altar and mouthed, "This is it for me. Please grant it."

After the service, he was pleased, as his parents introduced Lily to their friends, instilling in him the assurance he had craved. Among his greatest wishes was for his family to remain on good terms with old friends.

Back on the road, his father asked Lily, "What did you think of the service?"

"It was inspiring and very fitting for the season," she replied.

"It's so easy to be distracted with the commercial focus," his mother said. "We Americans push Christ to the back burner and cram everything else ahead. You were saying at dinner that it's different in your country?"

"Yes. Slightly different; but getting there. Village celebrations differ somewhat, even then I think the partying tends to last longer than our memory of Christ's birth. Commercialization has permeated every country where Christmas is celebrated. Few can resist its beguiling attraction."

"How do you mean?" asked his father.

By the tone in his father's voice, Paul knew he was excited.

"For instance, we did not have a lot of the . . . accoutrements that are now considered vital to the celebrations. Our main focus was church and feasting."

"Did you exchange gifts?" his mother asked.

"No. We did not, neither did we have Santa. We had family gatherings."

"No Santa Claus?" his father seemed surprised.

"No red nose reindeer." Lily laughed.

"That explains it!" exclaimed his mother, "I was wondering how you could escape exchanging gifts, especially if Santa came to town."

"We were fortunate about that, until now. But some of the elite have adapted the western customs, complete with trees."

"Why's that?" his father asked.

"They probably associate it with becoming affluent?"

"That's been the trend, especially, elaborate gifts," his mother nodded.

"Yes." Lily hesitated. "I don't mean to criticize. I enjoy the modern amenities that improve life and I am grateful we were introduced to Christ, despite the colonialists. Where would the continent be, without the positive influence of the Lord?"

"Same with America——where would we be without Christ? Some may disagree, but we cannot downplay the tremendous contribution that believers have made to this country," his father asked.

"No," Lily concurred. "As long as the believers are present on earth, they will always make a difference. Some people take it for granted that the world will always be good and ignore the negative impact of a godless society. There is also a tacit agreement that all modern trends are superior. We tend not to question their impact on our moral value. Even when we do, few invest time to dig deeper."

"That's the same challenge we in the West face, hence the slew of disruptive trends that have been flooding our living rooms," his father spoke as one speaking to an equal, extending to Lily the same respect he accorded his close colleagues.

Lily hesitated again. "Maybe I'm too critical. I know I'm being hard. Without the grace of the Lord, where would we be?"

"Go on," prompted his father, "Don't be afraid. Every one's entitled to his or her opinion and I'm always interested in a fresh view. Santa's a touchy subject. My family's aware of it and we always welcome other points of view."

"Well. I think the insidious effect of the guy in the red suit is in every country he has been introduced. Christmas has become a season to feel good and be nice, without thinking seriously about its spiritual significance . . . and we should feel good, but also search deeper."

"Go on. Go on!" his father's voice rose up a notch.

"Focusing on Santa and substituting him for Christ, deludes one into thinking it is not necessary to confront the real reason Christ came. I believe Santa has become a pseudo-Christ. The fantasy about him, mingled with the reality that someone actually delivers gifts, makes a person feel good, temporarily, while side-stepping the need to confront the spiritual void that material gifts cannot fill. And yet without the Resurrection, plus, had Emperor Constantine not approved the twenty-fifth as the official day to commemorate the Birth, it would be just another day."

"Uh-uh. Uh-uh. Go on!"

"Or had Constantine appointed another day——say September, in Autumn——the twenty-fifth would be just another day, and some would probably haggle over the Autumn date, instead," he joked, soliciting another round of laughter.

"Say that again! Or the other mistake we make," his mother interjected, "is to insist on celebrating Christ as a little baby. He's the only baby I know who never leaves the crib to some, year after year——a two-thousand-year-old baby!"

"That calls for a giant diaper, a giant baby bottle, a tank of milk a day and a MacCrib." He solicited laughter from everybody.

"Mhmm." Lily composed herself. "As long as Christ remains a baby, why deal with the cross and the resurrection?"

"You're right. Then that brings us to the point of view that Christmas is only for children," his mother said.

Lily nodded. "The baby in the manger doctrine——if Christmas is only for children and children are innocent and all they care about is fun; then how could anyone be so mean as to deprive them of that?"

"Say that again!" his father said.

"What I see's a very concerted effort to do away with Christ and the very purpose for which He came. The world would rather celebrate Christmas without Christ. It embraces a form of godliness, but rejects the Originator of that power as the letter to Timothy says. It's sad that we go along with it," he added.

"That's the danger of conforming," his father pointed out.

His mother jumped in, "For starters, more of us should try to curtail traditions that eschew Christ. Then we should try to be creative. For example, find venues for expressing God's love that allow us to give away as God did, more than receive."

"Lily and I had the same discussion recently," he interjected.

"Yes. I think it is easier said than done," Lily agreed.

"Why's that? Tradition?" his father asked.

"Tradition, I think and conformity, as you said. Nobody wants to be Scrooge."

"Oh! Let's not go there. True, we need to have fun and be kind, so perhaps there was a basis for that, initially. However, the spirit of helping people should spring eternal. Today, I think it's an excuse, as you alluded, to favor the pseudo-spiritual, but, underneath the surface, always going for the material," his mother said.

"Mhmm. Squeezing that last dollar, doing everything to persuade the customer they can't do without that one more toy," his father observed.

"Right. Chasing the ever-elusive joy," his mother agreed.

Paul turned into the driveway. "Here we are." He had enjoyed the family discussion very much.

His father seemed to agree. "We must finish this discussion soon," he said.

91

The rain pelted the windows, bringing a wet greeting to the Christmas morn as families gathered around their trees for centuries. By the Nativity scene in the Van Clydens' home, gifts also waited patiently.

Charlotte placed the biscuits mix in the oven, then she whisked some eggs. Paul went for the bacon; Lily washed and sliced the fruits; Igor set the table and Percy yawned in his warm pen, at the smell of bacon escaping the kitchen. A silver basket stood in the corner, ready for the hot biscuits.

Soon, they were at the table, enjoying their Christmas breakfast. Lily tried not to imagine how often the Van Clydens entertained Paul's latest fling or was it Kelly who often sat in the seat that she now occupied? Did Paul habitually bring his dates home, when he had no intention of getting serious about them? Wouldn't that become disrespectful at some point? He didn't appear to be that sort of man.

What about her parents? How would they react if they saw her now? They had dreams for her and her father especially had expectations about the type of man she should marry.

She had three potential jobs so far, two of them very promising——one job interview lined up with a financial firm in Arizona on the third Friday in January for which she would be flying out of town.

"You've hardly touched your bacon. Would you like me to get you something else?" Charlotte asked, bringing her back to earth.

"No thank you. Everything is delicious." Lily added another bacon strip and a slice of Christmas melon on her plate, to hide her embarrassment.

"Have you showed Lily your horses?" Charlotte asked Paul.

"Yes. I was hoping we could ride, if the weather permits."

"Oh no. Not me! I don't ride. I just love watching horses from a distance."

Paul smiled, arched. "You'll learn. It's easy."

"The Van Clydens take to horses like ducks to water," Igor added.

As they exchanged gifts, Lily noticed the Van Clydens had selected their presents with care. Paul gave his parents leather bound classics and funny–looking knick-knacks. They gave him a golf club——their gift for the previous Christmas,——a lovely leather jacket, and unusual gadgets for him to guess.

She was glad she had also selected her gifts prayerfully. For close friends, she had given alternative gifts——such as a water well to a village—— designated in their honor. But, since she was unfamiliar with the Van Clydens, she gave them a beautiful, unique native sculpture from East Africa.

"The sculpture is from a well-known local artist," she explained.

Paul started, surprised, when he saw the elegant statue. It reminded him of something, but he could not put a finger on it. Probably just a coincidence, after all, native sculptures run gamut to their region.

Lily surprised him with an autographed hardcover Christian devotional. She had acquired the author's signature just in time for Christmas.

The Van Clydens in turn gave her very thoughtful gifts——an old classic and a silk shawl and Paul surprised her with a beautiful picture of East African sunset he had captured and had especially framed for her.

After they had appreciated their gifts, Charlotte said, "Uncle Jeremy and Aunt Angela will be here soon. We'll watch your East African videos, darling."

"Yes, Mum." Paul selected his best videos. To his regret, he had not taken any shots of the Abrafimqodeshes' family and their compound, he said. His father would have loved knowing more about his potential business partner, but he believed he had captured enough to represent the region.

Lily, on the contrary, was rather quiet. *What else did Paul video?*

The Kaarlyles arrived around twelve o'clock——merry and carrying mouth-watering lemon pies and finger food, to the welcome of hot cider.

The women helped Charlotte finish laying out the sandwiches and baked delicacies. Igor asked Jeremy to say grace, then as they enjoyed their refreshments, Paul took center stage, narrating the videos, showing his audience more pictures of the game parks from all the three East African countries and other unique footages he had excluded in prior showings.

Aerial views of the region's notable landscapes and cities——among them, Lake Victoria and Bujagali Falls——that he had taken at close range, courtesy of a friend he had met in Nairobi, revealed his other hidden talents. He explained that he had gone over to Uganda on a special sightseeing trip when they flew over Bujagali Falls. He had wanted to go to Zimbabwe to see Victoria Falls, but he couldn't arrange the trip in time.

The footage of the cities of Nairobi, Kampala and Dar-es-Salaam and other towns that he had visited, showed the different levels of development. Unlike photographers who focused on Africa's poverty, he had left out the shanty towns on purpose, to provide a more balanced view of the continent——the forgotten working middle-class. Finally, he showed the Kisumu suburb where he had spent his time assisting with building a school.

In the middle of the videos, Aaron, Michael and their parents surprised them by phoning, one after the other, having guessed that they would all be gathered at Uncle Igor's and Aunt Charlotte's home.

Occasionally during the show, Lily would tense up, then relax. Fortunately, everyone was so absorbed with the video that nobody noticed.

At the end of the video, they complimented Paul on the professional job he had done. Uncle Jeremy then announced that their next vacation would be the East African safari, with the whole clan invited. They all jumped in to plan the trip, forgetting that Lily was in the room. On the contrary, she was content to sit quietly in her corner observing everybody with a charming smile.

"Let's go to Bujagali Falls first, then Murchison Falls," Angela announced.

"The Murchison Falls are in Zimbabwe," Ingrid said.

"No. East Africa," Angela replied.

"Really? Aunt Charlotte, you were a Geography teacher."

"Your Mum's right. They're in Uganda," Charlotte assured them.

Paul nodded and explained that they were a narrow pass after Lake Kyoga and before Lake Albert, as the Nile flowed north toward Egypt and had a popular national park attached to them. Unfortunately, he couldn't make it there due to security——but friends of his had a video clip.

"Darling, get me the atlas, please," she asked Paul.

Paul fetched a big globe and an atlas from the family library.

Charlotte thanked him, made room for the maps on the coffee table and knelt down to study them. Angela and Ingrid joined her.

"I wanna see Lake Victoria first, trace the Nile up toward Egypt, then go to the game parks." She traced the Nile with her finger, then a light went on. "Oh, you know who I really want to see? The Maasai in all their regalia!"

"Yeah! The Maasai!" everybody cheered.

"The Maasai like to hunt lions, Aunt Charlotte. So if we go to the game parks, we might also see some," Ingrid informed her Aunt.

"Isn't hunting forbidden in game parks?" Jonathan asked.

"I don't like lions. Do they still roam around?" Angela sounded worried.

"Mum, that's only in books. A long time ago they used to, but now, you've to go to the game parks or the zoo, to find them. The Maasai only hunt them now when they need to protect their livestock. Africans are a lot smarter; they don't keep pet lions like some of our knuckleheads here do." Ingrid nodded confidently to her audience.

"Whatever we do, we must avoid Swaziland," Jeremy announced.

"Why?" chorused the room.

"The king collects beautiful girls. We wouldn't want to risk Lily."

"Absolutely not," shouted the room again, Paul loudest.

"We'd have to hide her or make her wear a veil," Charlotte said.

"Then he might get more curious," Ingrid cautioned.

"We could go to Botswana and look across the border," Angela remarked.

Lily clapped her mouth, struggling hard to remain a fly on the wall.

"There you go!" Jeremy interjected. "It's better that we go to the game parks, then trace the river where Humphrey Bogart shot the African Queen. We would be on safer grounds there."

"Dad, Humphrey Bogart did not set foot in East Africa," Ingrid said.

"Where do you think he shot the African Queen?"

"In a fish tank in Britain."

"No. The film was shot on location, probably the first movie to be shot on location in Africa," Jeremy sounded as confident as Ingrid.

"Somebody said the storms were shot in a fish tank. And Bogart's too gruff for my taste. I like light, clean comedies or drama. Dad likes Bogart; he was a tough icon. I like Heston better, like in the . . . Ten Commandments."

"Yeah. Because he's tall and urghh . . . gruff!" her father teased her.

"Uncle Jeremy and Ingrid are both right," Paul interjected. "If my source is correct, some of the scenes were shot on location in Uganda and

Zaire; and some of the river scenes——the rapids and the storms were shot in England, for safety reasons——again, only if my source is reliable."

"There you go. I've always known the Van Clydens and the Kaarlyles are a smart bunch, with the potential of being full of . . . trivia," Jeremy said.

"On behalf of the Van Clydens and the Kaarlyles, I protest!" Igor raised his hand. "I'd have you know a stormy fish tank in England and a smooth river in Ugandan and Zairean forests, are very critical pieces of information, especially if they garnered millions at the box office."

"Spoken like a true business man," Jeremy shot back.

"I want to see Mt. Kilimanjaro. It would be neat to see the peaks soaring up above the landscape," Jonathan shouted above the raucous.

"Folks, listen. We could see everything. First, we should decide in what order and for how long. I say camp out there for a year," Igor shouted back.

At one point in the midst of the heated brainstorming, Lily glanced at Paul and smiled. He clapped his mouth tightly to suppress his laughter.

At four o'clock, the Kaarlyles finally left, to call on friends.

After they had gone, Charlotte prepared a light supper and Lily, the salad.

After supper, Paul asked, "Well, shall we watch, um . . . Charlton Heston?"

Four hours later, Igor and Charlotte excused themselves, as the movie was ending. Lily found herself alone again with Paul, as in their first evening.

He asked, with a twinkle, "What would you like to do?"

"Do you have documentaries of the Holy Land?"

"Yes. Any one in particular?"

"No. Surprise me." She smiled.

He scratched his head, and searched her face as a little boy would, while debating whether to ask for a forbidden favor.

"What?" she asked.

"Nothing," he replied, and fished for a Bible documentary.

She understood why it was part of the Van Clydens' library. The story was well researched and the commentators, credible——knowledgeable, objective and reverent. Paul rose another notch in her estimation of a man worth knowing and keeping as a friend. No wild parties, no drinking——so far, so good! Praise be!

92

After a nice morning walk, despite the weather, Charlotte shepherded everybody in to prepare brunch, then they sat around chatting, playing the piano or calling friends to pass time before the evening concert.

An evening at the concert called for a quick nap, Charlotte said, "Or some people might be nodding by intermission."

Dinner reservation was at six o'clock, so for over an hour, the house was quiet——giving Lily sufficient time to edit her paper.

Igor came down first in a dark-gray suit, Paul followed, also in a dark suit. Their freshly shampooed hair glistened in the soft lights. Then Charlotte swished down in a wintergreen velvet gown, which complimented her red hair, that cradled her face in soft curls. On her neck was a string of emeralds, part of Igor's gifts for their twentieth wedding anniversary.

Finally, Lily came down in her black evening gown, her hair combed into a tight chignon and secured with a gold pin; matching elegantly crafted gold earrings dangled from her ears.

Igor straightened his tie, proud, as though the ladies' choices were his idea.

Paul's eyes were riveted on the slender figure gliding down the stairs.

Lily's gown fell in soft curves to the floor. The bodice, a modest V-neck, ended in gathers under her breasts, accentuated by a star-shaped brooch. Her soft deep wine lips challenged him, though he was cognizant that even if he secured her hand, he would still have to wait, as had his father and grand-father and she would be his strongest cheerleader on moral restraint.

Igor glanced at his wife, smiled, then ushered them to the garage. En route, traffic in the Topanga Valley swallowed up their extra time. They arrived at the All-American Cuisine on the dot.

Some guests seemed uncomfortable or was it just Lily's imagination? Unbeknown to her, rumors had been circulating that Paul might be off the market, but if the Van Clydens noticed anything unusual, they did not show it.

The waiter feigned being professional, while committing a crime. Ignoring their distinguished appearance, he directed them to a back corner by the kitchen. A firm glance from Igor, reversed his direction to a window seating with a nice view, and he acted wary after that.

The restaurant owner appeared and chatted cheerfully with the group. If there was anything unusual about the two couples, the proprietor did not appear to notice. He stepped back, hovered in the background, quietly directing his waiters with his eyes and hands.

Lily too had noticed the proprietor. Remembering how Igor had chastised the waiter, she dabbed her mouth.

This is the nineteen nineties, but we might as well be back in the nineteenth century. She smiled broadly.

"Are you all right?" Paul asked softly.

"Yes. Thank you," she replied.

Paul said to the table, "Merry Christmas to us all too."

"Merry Christmas!" Igor raised his glass of sparkling apple cider and gave a toast, quoting Ephesians, "To a happy, blessed future, and to Him who is able to do exceedingly abundantly above all that we ask or hope for."

The proprietor, smiled and bowed his head from a distance.

Lily marveled. For the second time, she felt a sense of conspiracy. Everything was like clockwork. Déjà vu! Like son, like father.

Igor and Paul took turns introducing topics for conversation, until Lily asked, "Who are the artists for this evening?"

Igor explained that friends had invited them to their annual private concert designed to relax their friends from the stress of Christmas.

He mentioned two classical artists to be featured. "You'll enjoy the concert, Lily. They're very committed to family, and studious in assembling the repertoire. My friend engages musicians from within a three-hours' flight, so the musicians can spend their Christmas with their families and return home in time for New Year. Now that's my kind of man."

"That's very considerate of him," she said.

"We go way back to college. He married Charlotte's college classmate, so I can safely say, we both poached girls from the same school!"

"Dad, poaching? Nah!" Paul ribbed his father.

"But, I'd to promise grandpa I would not interfere with your mother's education or I'd have never come within a mile's distance of her pretty face!"

Charlotte chuckled. "You can say that again."

The waiter avoided Lily's eyes for the rest of the evening, but was careful to be extra attentive.

Paul drove up into the hills of secluded estates. In a glance, Lily was glad that she had brought appropriate wardrobe for formal occasions.

The Van Clydens were familiar guests, but walking in with a new face deserved a second casual look. The girl was undeniably remarkable. She exuded inner radiance that distinguished her from the other girls they had seen in Paul's company, beautiful as the other girls were.

In previous concerts, when Paul appeared with a date, he was always holding her hand. He was not holding the young lady's hand, yet he might as well had been holding both her hands. More importantly, rarely had he come with his parents and date together. They sensed a proposal in the air.

An old friend diverted Paul, forcing him to leave Lily chatting with two couples. She could not help but overhear a group huddled in a corner.

"Who would've thought the great Kelly would bite the dust? To think of all the women left at the altar because of her! My cousin had just got engaged. And worse, after Kelly stole her fiancé, Kelly dumped him and he tried to get back with my cousin again!" a woman clinging to her husband said.

"My granddaughter had already booked the venue, ordered her dress, and we'd reserved them a cruise for their honeymoon, when voila, Kelly was hanging on her fiancé's arm!" an older lady cut in.

"Mhmm. Terrible! Devastated her," her husband agreed.

"But I hear Paul was very distressed dating her and as soon as Igor released him, he broke-off the engagement," the first woman said.

"Ooh, that must explain why she went on that grand cruise with her aunt around Thanksgiving," the older woman whispered loudly.

The first woman covered her mouth. "I heard there was more to it. Good thing or she could've cleaned Paul out——he being sole heir and all."

"Praise be the Van Clydens' Enterprise is solid." The older woman patted her diamond necklace.

"Not if the market tanks," her husband side-mouthed. "Even a half-a-billion revenue with a seven-billion balance sheet needs a keen eye. Igor has cause to stay on his toes——balance sheet's dropping, he has been looking to diversify. He's a very sharp fellow. Sharp mind." He tapped his head.

Lily played with her glass, embarrassed. The couples in her group also seemed discomfited. Soon, the guests started streaming into the concert room and the gossip group joined the queue, as Paul returned to claim her.

She studied the private audience, marveling that so much went on behind closed doors of the exclusive community——private galas, concerts, whatever they fancied——would she fit in?

They were seated just before the lights dimmed, and the conductor walked in for the opening overture.

She was enthralled at the repertoire, mostly classical music, among them, Handel's arias, *"The Trumpet Shall Sound"* and *"Thou Dids't Not Suffer Thy Holy One to See Corruption"* from *The Messiah*; and *"Father of Heaven,"*——a new air she had not heard before——from the oratorio *Judas Maccabeus* and a few other tastefully selected contemporary works fit for the season.

She had watched movies where the hero and heroine fell in love at a concert, always thinking that it was nothing more than screen play. Sitting next to Paul was real. Perhaps she had been too hard on him. He could handle any situation, so could his father, as they demonstrated at dinner.

She glanced at him. His earnest eyes met hers. Even in the dim light, he seemed to pierce through her thoughts and echo her faith.

Shy, she looked away. It could work, otherwise, she would bottle her experience for the memories. By letting Paul back into her life, she had taken a risk——she might get humiliated again, or she might triumph.

For a moment, she entertained fleeting thoughts about how her parents would react given their aspirations for her, then she focused her eyes on the mezzo-soprano on stage.

93

Not privy to Lily's thoughts, Paul counted the days, wishing for a harmless storm that would close the roads back to L.A for another week, but the week had flown by with no harmless storm, alas!

On the Friday before New Year's Eve, as the Van Clydens and Lily were out on their morning walk, Paul increased his stride to a brisker pace, so he and Lily could walk ahead. His parents followed behind at a slower pace. Percy chased rabbit trails and rejoined the group at his pleasure.

"Would you care for a drive later on this morning?" Paul asked Lily.

"Loved to. Thank you," Lily replied.

The four days after Christmas had been busy, in addition to the trip to the concert, friends had dropped in for a visit during the day and on one evening, they had gone out sightseeing Christmas-lit neighborhoods. The day before, Lily and Paul had lunched with Jonathan, Sharon, Ingrid, and her boyfriend, to admire the humungous diamond ring that Jonathan had plonked on Sharon's finger at Christmas.

On the evenings that the weather shut them in or they had nothing planned, they had sat and chatted about various topics, watched their favorite movies, or listened to Paul play his instruments.

"After years of taking piano lessons from Aunt Angela, Paul could've majored in music, instead, he chose business to follow in his father's footsteps. Still, during his undergraduate years, he continued to take private piano lessons, as an elective," Charlotte had explained to Lily.

It was a pleasure listening to him play, a pleasure which guests who were aware of his talents, never denied themselves. And on occasions he teamed up with Jonathan and Ingrid to give private chamber music concerts or they got three pianos and performed piano trios.

Igor and Charlotte found Lily to be sociable and conversant with a variety of topics and not afraid to debate anybody. On those occasions, Paul pretended to be concentrating on the piano while eavesdropping on his dad having an intellectual discourse with her. Occasionally, when he locked eyes with his mother, she would raise her eyebrows playfully at him.

After a leisurely breakfast on that last Friday, Paul and Lily left for a drive. They cruised along the shore to a more sheltered beach from the crisp breeze and parked. Paul steered Lily back to the sparsely crowded shopping center. A quiet beach suited their need for a peaceful day perfectly.

He guided Lily to antique shops and gift shops, lingering over quaint gifts, teasing her and drawing her out and bought her a charming native Indian turquoise bracelet trimmed with gold that she had admired.

An hour later, they returned to the jetty and watched the waves lap the shore, then observed the multitude of shore birds congregated on the sands.

Lily watched, fascinated, as a Black Skimmer flew across the waters, rapidly skimming the ocean surface with its beak, and overhead, with no less fascination, a Common Tern sailed in the wind.

"Would you care to walk?" Paul asked.

She said she would love to.

They strolled from pier to pier, peering into the horizons of parading boats coming ashore. Nearby, Western Sand Pipers, Snowy Plovers, and Marbled Godwits pecked at the sands, unfazed by their approaching feet.

Paul picked up a pebble and threw it into the water, forming a little ripple, which was soon swallowed up by another wave. Lily was staring over the ocean, her thoughts faraway.

"A penny for your thoughts," he said.

She smiled, averted her eyes and continued walking.

"What're you thinking?" he repeated several minutes later.

"Nothing," she replied.

"Sure?"

"Mhmm." She nodded.

Ahead of them, a well-groomed grandmother with glistening youthful skin——akin to Botulinum Toxin cosmetic treatment——walked out of her beach-home with a child carrying a bucket and a small rubber spade.

Lily studied them. "Wouldn't it be wonderful to have a beach home?"

"You'd like to have one?" Paul asked, pleased.

"A beach home sounds like fun. I mean, everybody dreams."

"What's life without dreams?"

"Nothing dramatic, just little things."

"Faith as small as a mustard seed. What seed have you planted?"

"It is the process. Whether they come to pass, is another story."

"But something else is bothering you," he asked, in a quiet voice.

She took a deep breath. "Um, you mentioned you believe in things that are strong, things that endure——three cords are stronger than two and you also believe in the three functions in One? The perpetual nature of the Holy One who was and is and is to come, as Revelation says——the One who was holy, is holy and shall be forever holy, as I understand that to mean?"

"Mhmm."

"What about the seven spirits?"

"What about them?"

"I have come across scholarly discussions. Isaiah mentions only six."

"Seven, actually."

"No. Six."

He chuckled. "Revelation mentions seven sent out to all the world."

"But the Lamb is still part of the three functions in One."

"Uh-huh."

"Okay. So I count three manifestations in Isaiah eleven. If I count them separately——the spirit of wisdom, understanding, counsel, might, knowledge and the fear of the LORD——then there are six." She sought his eyes.

He rubbed his upper lip. "Okay. If you put it that way."

"But there shouldn't be a contradiction," she drew out. "Since Revelation attests to seven, the only explanation I can think of is the Spirit of the LORD is the overarching Spirit. If you start there, then Isaiah also lists the seven spirits, I concede. However, the Lamb is still part of the Three in One."

"I see where you're going. The Godhead remains, but the One who completed the mission——the Lamb——has the seven spirits that are sent out."

"That appears to be the only logical conclusion."

"You're right. I can't think of any other plausible explanation. We should research further and compare notes." He was pleased. *This is the type of conversation a man should count on in his future mate.*

He slowed down. "Let's play a game. Indulge me for a moment. Okay?"

"Okay," she replied.

"Career."

"Mhmm."

"Own your own business, or become a corporate executive?"

Lily thought and replied, "Own my own business, definitely. And you?"

"Own or be an executive in the thick of influencing company direction."

"Will power, wheedle and deal, right?"

"Mhmm. Plan strategies, steer the ship. . . next, giving to charity."

"Mhmm."

"Let's say a . . . tight money situation. Would you continue to give or would you cut back until things improve?"

"Keep my love-offering current, as much as possible. It may be prudent to reduce my donation to charities, but not my faith-giving."

Paul coughed to hide a smile.

"Okay. Your turn." Lily lifted her chin up and smiled.

"I agree."

"No-o-o! That is not fair. I demand more than I agree."

"It's only a game. Okay?"

"I know. It takes two to ping-pong."

Paul rubbed his nose again. "All right. I also believe that faith-giving's important. It opens the door to the Lord's blessing."

Lily's face lit up. "You believe that——that He loves a cheerful giver and will never withhold His blessings if we give, no matter how small?"

"Yes. I do," he replied with conviction. "Next?"

"Social."

"Okay."

"Big parties, cocktails, small dinners or a quiet evening, reading?"

"Quiet evening. Occasionally, small dinners of about ten people at the most, unless it's a very special occasion like . . . graduation or . . . the Christmas party Sharon hosted," he said with meaning. "And you?"

"Mostly quiet evenings reading; occasionally, small dinners." She strolled for a while, watching the waves. "Next, credit cards."

"Okay." He kicked the sand beneath his feet.

"Pay off the balance monthly or pay the minimum required?"

"Try not to own one——pay cash. I do have one, restricted for traveling and only if the merchant doesn't accept foreign checks or travelers', and in such cases, I pay all the balance at the end of the month. And you?"

She seemed elated by his response. "Same. Preferably pay cash. But like you, I own one for travel. Okay, your turn."

Again, his lips twitched. "Okay. Books, favorite?"

"Variety——informative, self-development or light novels."

"What type of light novels?"

"Christian romance or historical, with lots of humor, clean content. You?"

He mused, then said, "Variety. Info, self-development, thrillers, sports."

"What type of sports?"

"Different kinds . . . skiing and other outdoor sports, baseball, yachting and the like." He paused. "Next, music."

"We have some good African groups like Ladysmith Black Mambazo. I also like mostly variety——classical, gospel, ballads, and the fifties."

"The fifties?"

"Yup. There is nothing like the clean, schmaltzy romance music of the fifties——beside gospel and classical."

"What do you know! Lily Nyaber likes schmaltzy music." Paul threw his head back and laughed. "You really like the music of the fifties."

"Yes. The innocent ones——and I mean real innocent. Why? Is it funny?"

"No. Not funny. Just unusual. I would've never associated you with the fifties' music. If I'd to take a quiz, I'd have flunked big time."

"Well, I do like the well written ones——teen stuff. Nothing heavy. And I prefer to listen——not dance——and get all schmaltzy."

"Mum would love to hear this."

"Your Mum too?"

"Yes. She and Dad used to go to the dances and go crazy."

"Small world! I would have never guessed it. She looks so regal."

"Looks can deceive." He chuckled.

"And you?" she asked.

"Classical mostly, but also gospel, country——"

"You like country?"

"Yeah."

"I would have flunked that one. But then good music is good music."

"Right. And country can be spiritual, not just blue. They've some great gospel numbers. And I like a bit of jazz and modern. It all depends."

"Same here. And of course, clean lyrics, done in good taste."

"Yes! There're some obscene lyrics out there. It ruins a good song." He studied her face. "See, that wasn't too bad."

"I don't know Paul. With you, I never know."

"Come on! I'm not that bad."

She stared at him, with a quaint smile.

"I know, I made some mistakes in the past, I've regretted it. It won't happen again," he said, solemnly.

"Every rose has thorns. The thorns of a yellow rose are veiled in a bed of yellow roses. But a dark, red rose must struggle to hide its thorns in a bed of yellow roses, though it be as good a rose." She bore into his soul.

"I disagree. A yellow rose in a bed of yellow roses is a bed of yellow roses, but the crowning glory of a garden is a dark, red rose in a bed of yellow roses."

They had reached a jetty. They stared at each other; echoes of nearby seabirds mingled with the swirling billows of waves lapping the jetties.

"I want to believe you." She started walking.

"Please do. It's the truth."

Slowly, she continued moving forward. He followed her; his hands buried in his pockets. In silence, they walked, each deep in thought.

Unsure of what to expect, Paul prayed and hoped that he had reached Lily——that the time with his parents had healed the wound he had inflicted on her and that she would in due time forgive him.

If she insisted on platonic friendship, he would go to Europe to heal and accept reality, not as he had imagined, but the cup he must drink with grace.

Lily in turn continued to wrestle with herself. Her faith in him had been shaken. She believed despite his parents' hospitality, and his seemingly ardent desire to commit to her, she could find herself out in the cold in a blink of an eye. Yet a part of her was knit to him. She had fasted and asked friends to pray for her. Perhaps with time, she would conquer herself and put him out of her life for good. That was a bleak thought.

Two years had passed since he first singled her out. How much longer could she go on fasting and praying before her path became clear? Finally, she understood the wisdom of socializing widely before making a commitment to one man; but she had socialized, however, that had not protected her from getting attached to one man——a man who, given other circumstances, would be her life companion.

Just what was the significance of her coming to his home? Would he play with his own parents' emotions? They adored him.

She glanced at him; he was studying her quietly.

He placed his arm around her shoulder, "You must be hungry. Lunch?"

He guided her back to the car, took the Pacific Coast Highway to a family restaurant with home-food that tasted like grandma's cooking, then they continued sightseeing, arriving home at five o'clock.

Charlotte was lighting candles in the dining room. "I thought we should have a quiet cozy evening today before our New Year's Eve party tomorrow."

After giving thanks and filling their plates, Igor cut a slice of his turkey, and said, "Business is going good, son. Business is good."

"That's good, Dad. What new deals have you made lately?" Paul added more gravy on his mashed potato.

"Did I mention your trip paid off? I got an invitation from the company."

"Great! Good for you, Dad. Do the prospects look good?"

"The boss himself will be here in a couple of months, a very trusted friend of mine assured me. I'll meet him and talk to him man to man."

"Good going, Dad!"

Lily chased a slice of turkey around her plate.

"That's enough business, honey." Charlotte passed the salad. "We don't want to give Lily the impression we never take a break from work around here. I'm still celebrating Christmas and I intend to enjoy it."

"Yes, ma'am," chorused the men.

Lily buried her nose in her plate to hide a smile.

"That's the Van Clydens' men for you. Like father, like son; but they do have kind hearts, I can assure you." Charlotte smiled warmly at her.

A few more smiles like that and I am history. Praise be, only one more day to bask in this dream, then back to reality. Lily took a sip of her juice.

94

Lily stirred and opened her eyes to a familiar environment, back to earth from a week and half at the beach. Paul fussed so much settling her back in her condo when he dropped her off, that she had felt self-conscious.

It was incredible that she was gone for only one week. She remembered their morning walks and that New Year's Eve party! No liquor was served, but no one would have guessed from the animated conversations around.

She stretched, rolled over to her stomach and cupped her hands on her chin, trying to fathom the Paul who had emerged that evening.

All Paul's friends must have been there——Matt and Marjorie; Sharon from ENC; Bill and Sheila and two friends from BF&S . . . Phil and Julian, if she remembered their names correctly and of course their dates. Everybody.

She could not remember all the guests' names. She prayed if she encountered them again, she would at least recall their faces.

Despite the full house, Paul's manners had taken flight. Instead of entertaining their guests, he had searched for every excuse to remain close to her, but not once did he misbehave, always the consummate gentleman.

Amidst her daydreaming, she remembered Thanksgiving; a crease marred her face. A few months ago, she was searching for jobs anywhere, but California, now——she sighed——now she felt drawn to listen with her soul, and look for signs that she was heading in the right direction. Did the Lord throw curve-balls at His children? Didn't that contradict His nature?

On the other hand, in her subconscious mind, had she presumed and hoped that barring Kelly, Paul would be the perfect man for her? The LORD hates the sin of presumption. She had known that for years.

Her feelings for Paul were real. She sensed Paul felt the same. But were feelings alone enough? Despite the bond developing between them, could Paul endure the pressure of knowing that others had expected a good catch like him to do better or would the pressure wear him down?

True. Love is a commitment, but honestly? Love often starts with a feeling that progresses to a strong commitment. The mushiness came and went. If Paul was willing to commit, and of course, her parents . . .

Finally, she was becoming persuaded that Kelly and Paul had broken up forever. Despite Kelly's reputation for snatching grooms at the altar, she believed that Kelly's allure was no match to the Lord's power. Paul had said nothing to her directly, but she thought Kelly had a new boyfriend and appeared more serene and settled. She prayed that Kelly would be blessed as the Lord willed.

She also prayed for Paul——perhaps he came into her life for a purpose. As with her two serious dates that had ended, each in turn, she had felt responsible to pray for the two men, until each had married. She was pleased with the commendable wife that each of them had acquired and thankful that she had not hindered them. Perhaps the need for another prayer friend could be a valid reason to continue her platonic friendship with Paul. It was possible for a man so popular to be lonely, she concluded.

All said, if she had to choose, she would rather she remained single, than got married and divorced. So, if Kelly was right for Paul, though she would lose Paul to her, she would accept it.

She disliked relationships that thrived on yelling, throwing pots, then kissing and making up afterwards, instead of treating each other with respect from the beginning. And she did not believe in the old adage, rather, she believed, 'Kiss a toad; marry a toad. Kiss a prince, marry a prince.' For this reason, she dated by the book and drew the line——no kissing, no regrets.

About her parents, she gnawed her fingertip.

After all the Van Clydens' kindness to her! Her face knotted up, then cleared. Perhaps the Van Clydens endeavored to be gracious to her, hoping that by supporting Paul, instead of fighting him, he would get over his infatuation with her faster and move on. *It is easier to catch more flies with honey than with vinegar.* That was it! They were abiding their time, waiting for Paul to grow tired of her and move on! If the rumors were true that they preferred Kelly, this would explain everything.

But the same question continued to nag her. Would the Van Clydens have introduced her to their friends if they were just humoring Paul, or had they really been nice only because she was a Christmas guest from a foreign country, or was it their habit to hold New Year Eve's parties, regardless?

There was only one way to handle her gnawing uneasiness, she reasoned——remain unassuming. If it was meant to be, it would come to pass. Better the door opened by the Lord, than one she had kicked down.

She finally stirred from her bed, knelt down and prayed. She had two hours to complete her power-walk, shower, change and meet Paul. Since returning, she had spent some time cleaning her condo, before reviewing her academic papers.

One problem, her fridge was bare——two eggs and an orange did not exactly make a meal. Without hesitation, she dialed Paul's number.

"Hello?" a male voice answered.

"Paul? Morning. It's Lily," she said, a bit shy.

"Hello, d—— I mean Lily. Good morning. What's up?"

"I was wondering, could we change our appointment?" she stammered.

"Sure. Why? Are you having second thoughts?"

Did he sound uneasy or worried? "No. I need to get some grocery. Would later on in the afternoon work?"

"I've a suggestion." He sounded more relaxed.

"Yes?"

"How about we go together? I need a couple of things."

His suggestion caught her off guard. "It doesn't matter. I could probably do my grocery shopping later," she stammered.

"Com'on. It would be no trouble at all."

Embarrassed that he might be thinking she was presuming on his friendship, she hesitated and then drew out, "I suppose it is okay."

"You don't sound so sure?"

"Well, are you sure that is what you want?"

"Of course, I'm positive. What do you mean are you sure?"

"All right. I would love to. I mean it would be nice," she capitulated.

"That's settled then," he replied, audibly relieved. "So, same time?"

"Yes. Same time."

"All right! See you soon." He sounded jubilant.

Lily stared at the phone a long time, then she placed it down, very slowly and marched out, in resolute determination.

Two hours on the dot, Paul drove up Lily's condo complex. Lily was on the look-out for him. She turned up the central heat a notch to keep the house warmer, while they were out shopping. Before he reached the door, she came out, dressed in a subdued, moderately warm winter outfit.

Paul beamed, exuding lots of energy in his classy jeans and navy–blue pullover.

"You seem rather happy." She brushed past his hands holding the door for her.

"I've every reason to be. It's a beautiful day," he announced to the skies.

She studied the gathering clouds, dubious.

"Well, I think it's a beautiful day," he insisted, following her gaze, as he plonked himself in the driver's seat.

"If you say so."

"I do say so. Okay. Where're we headed?" He stepped on the gas.

She mentioned Providence, a popular grocery chain store nearby.

He smiled. It was the same chain store where he had bought a box of tea the day he decided to break up with Kelly for good. He continued chatting away, while zooming through the traffic.

Lily was at a loss. Was this what a week at his parents' house did to him? What competition for the woman who would get married to him!

At Providence's parking lot, he opened her door before she could beat him to it. She felt rather self-conscious. She enjoyed him opening doors at functions and when on proper dates, but the grocery store was different.

Oblivious to her emotions, he loaded his cart with the ease of an old pro, going from aisle to aisle. "What? What's wrong?" he questioned her pointed stare.

"I am surprised you actually have food in your cart," she teased. "I was expecting cereals, chips, instant snack and may be frozen food and fruits."

"I can boil real peas and not burn them."

"A man who can boil peas and not burn them, is a man worth respecting."

He bowed silently.

They stood in the shortest checkout line and were out in no time, but instead of going to her condo, he headed for the freeway.

"Where are we going?" She frowned, puzzled.

"To drop off my stuff. You wouldn't want my milk to spoil, would you?"

"No. But I don't mind if you dropped me off first."

"And I don't mind dropping my things off first." He grinned.

Her heart fluttered. She retreated into silence and watched the traffic instead, all along very aware of his long piano fingers handling the wheel.

About twenty minutes into the drive, he exited on the Brea Canyon off rump and headed up the hill. A few turns brought him to Country Club Terrace Drive and shortly after, he entered an exclusive condo estate straight to a corner unit in a quiet section, surrounded by wooded areas— perfect.

"Well?"

"Well what?" she asked.

"Come in." He jumped out and opened her door. "Don't worry about the stuff. I'll take care of them later."

"I don't mind. Besides, we still have my milk, remember?"

"Touché!" he chuckled.

She tipped her head.

"We'll only be a moment," he insisted.

She collected two bags and followed him in.

When she entered, the smell of fresh clean greeted her nose. The kitchen had more than elbow room and the spacious living room was sparsely furnished, with bachelor taste that did not fool her. The sofa set alone was of excellent leather quality. She fell in love with it at first sight.

"Hello, somebody pinch me!" Jonathan dashed down the stairs. "Finally! You had me worried for a while there." He sniffed his armpits and continued, "I was beginning to think we needed stronger deodorant or something." He jumped down the last step to give her a big hug.

"On the contrary!" She thanked him for the great time she had visiting with his family and complimented him on having such a talented family.

He returned the compliment, "You made it special for all of us. Oh, the New Year's Eve party! Who could forget that fabulous party!"

"Paul's parents are amazing."

"Yes. They are. Did you enjoy the rest of your stay at the beach?"

"I'm still coming down from the clouds. Mama Paul and Baba Paul went out of their way. They are so gracious and committed. We still made it to church. I love that! Jump start the New Year on the right footing."

"That's the way. Ingrid and I consider them our second parents. Paul's a blessed guy."

He turned to Paul in silent conversation, but said out loud, "Hi, Buddy? How's it going?" then he pumped Paul's arm.

"Wonderful!"

"Paul has been having a lovely day, never mind the clouds," she teased.

"Cheerful disposition, that's a boy! A man without fear of rain's the man!" Jonathan said.

Paul gave her a tour of the condo, then he offered her a choice of drinks, ranging from hot tea, chocolate, to Pepsi.

She opted for apple juice, without ice.

Paul served the drinks——apple for her, ice tea for Jonathan, and orange juice for himself.

Lily took a sip of her drink, conscious of being inside his home. It was one thing sharing the same roof with him in her own domain or in his parents' home and another being in his condo, even though she trusted him.

On the other hand, she had never seen him so cheerful.

She noticed a round glass coffee table——a center piece similar to hers.

"I brought it from East Africa," Paul replied, following her gaze.

"Yeah, he couldn't get any zebra skin around here," Jonathan twinkled.

She concealed her surprise and chatted about the secluded complex, and was Jonathan working on any new works? Had he and Sharon set a date yet? Jonathan enthused, bringing them up to date with the plans.

After a polite twenty minutes, she finally wished Jonathan a Happy and Blessed New Year again and took her leave.

Jonathan accompanied them as far as the door, calm and gracious as a perfect host. The moment Paul pulled off the driveway, he closed the door, jumped up in the air and dove to the ground, his fist clenched in victory, "Yes!" he shouted, phoned Sharon and announced to her, "They went shopping together!"

"Finally, some progress!" Sharon cheered. "I'll tell Linda and Raya. They'll be thrilled. I couldn't have asked for a better beginning of the new year!"

♦ ♦ ♦

Paul carried the last grocery bags into Lily's condo and settled down in the living room, while she put away the grocery and prepared lunch——omelets with mushrooms and cheese filling, topped with salsa, served with steamed green peas and warm tortilla——the first time she had cooked for him.

He mopped the last drop of sauce with the warm tortilla, leaving her in a quandary. As one who was seeking a life partner, Paul fitted the mold; as one who was not blind to societal nuances, she questioned the wisdom of choosing tenacity, over common sense. And who was the third woman? Certainly not her friend Linda. She was only a decoy the night of the reunion and was happily engaged now.

She would rather lose Paul now and suffer the pain, than lose him later. Over twelve months before, he had decimated her heart and her dignity; in hindsight, she was grateful for that betrayal. It gave her the strength that she now had of standing on the sideline as a spectator, watching the reel of their relationship play past her, even as she joined in that play as a participant.

After lunch, Paul kicked his heels as a baby would, after a bottle of milk.

"Hot chocolate?" she asked.

"Please," he replied.

She served some cookies and two steaming cups of chocolate. Outside, the clouds had darkened. Soon, the first raindrops pelted the windows.

"It looks like our day's made," he said, gleefully.

"What is so cheerful about rain in the middle of a day off?"

"I love rain on a bright day or a cloudy day or any day. Just give me a beautiful companion."

If rain was on the menu, she would have been hard-pressed not to believe that he had placed a side order for it with his lunch. She changed course. "Care for video, music or game? I have rather limited options."

"All the above," he teased. "What have you got?"

"I have Bible learning games and a small collection of videos: old romance——may be not to your taste——comedy, western classics, musicals."

"Why not to my taste? You're the strict lady."

"Some of them have scenes with smoking."

"So do my collections. How about a comedy, or a musical?"

She brought him videos and two Bible learning boxes from the shelves. He selected a family comedy and plugged it in.

Outside, the rain had turned into a steady wet drizzle, promising to last the whole evening. Their hot cups of chocolate, and the soft, persistent rain, made the living room even cozier. Still she resisted lighting the fire in the grid.

They watched the two-hour movie and while Paul plugged in the next video, she prepared more hot chocolate and returned to the kitchen.

At the sound of pots, Paul asked, "What're you doing?"

"Nothing."

"That nothing wouldn't be cooking by any chance, would it?"

"Why? Don't you like my cooking?"

"I love your cooking, but it's lonely out here," he grumbled.

"I'm only in the kitchen."

"I know, that's why I'm lonely out here."

Paul's voice got closer. She turned. He was placing the cups on the counter.

"What are you doing here? Go back and enjoy the movie," she said.

"The movie can wait. What can I do?"

"You are impossible, you know that?" She seasoned some steak.

"I know."

"All right. Would you care to prepare the salad, while I marinate this? Then we can watch the movie. I will throw this in the microwave later."

She placed the steak in the fridge and rinsed the rice.

Soon, they were back watching the second movie, a musical this time. A game box stood on the coffee table——a sign he would be spending the whole day. She peeked at him. He seemed so content, relaxed . . . at home.

As the movie ended, Paul stirred. "That was nice. My kind of afternoon."

"Rain pelting the window, a movie in the player, that's good to know."

He hesitated and asked, "Do you have any big plans coming up?"

"No. Do you?"

"Not really. My parents have been invited to a big function, end of March, as an extension of Black appreciation month."

"Oh?"

"You remember the business deal Dad talked about?"

"Mhmm."

"This function's a special dinner for the VIPs, among them, the head of the Nairobi firm Dad has been trying to contact. He'll be a guest speaker at the business symposium," he explained. "The international forum was designed to bring together global business leaders with a stake in the emerging economies of Africa. The conference will culminate in a banquet. I would like you to come."

A pregnant silence followed.

She fidgeted. "I heard about the symposium. I would have loved to come, but that week-end, I already have a prior commitment."

"The banquet's in the evening."

"I made the commitment months ago. Perhaps another time?"

Scary words a girl might use when preparing to break up with a guy. Paul grinned. "It's several weeks away. Things might change."

"Perhaps."

He continued grinning.

"The symposium is so global that lots of businesses will be there. My company is sponsoring a table——marketing is working overtime. The CEO and the executive team will be there," Lily added.

"Oh? Denton and Terrell's always a welcome addition to any global event." Somehow, that piece of news had cheered him up.

She queued *The Hebrides* and Chopin's CDs in the player and left him to enjoy the music or so she thought. She was preparing to steam the rice, when she noticed Paul at the middle island, watching her, his hands stuck in his jeans' pockets.

The marinated steaks were ready to microwave——medium for him, and well done for her. As she prepared to lay the table; Paul stuck out his hands. When she surrendered the cutlery to him, his blue eyes pierced through to her heart and chipped off another chunk of her determination to remain emotionally vigilant.

95

Denton and Terrell kicked off the New Year with clients wishing to surrender the headache of the retro-acted Revenue Reconciliation Act of 1993 to the firm. Mr. Chancey called a weekly meeting of his top accountants, first thing in the morning, complete with a side table of pastries and refreshments. He wished them a Happy New Year, then launched into the meeting.

"Last year, we drilled the conundrum of the retro Clinton Tax Reform. As my Senior Accountants, you should all be well-versed with it, by now. By raising the individual top tax rates——ordinary income to 39.1% and corporate to 35%, the Act in effect reverses Reagan's TRA of 1986 which lowered the top tax rates from 50% to 28% and the corporate marginal rate from 46% to 34%," Mr. Chancey explained.

"What is the impact on Denton and Terrell?" Lily asked.

"Good question. Reaganomics boosted growth in the formation of subchapter S Corporations. Think of this, the revenue authorities reported a total of 1.9 million S Corporations in the 1993 Tax Year, compared to over 0.8 million in 1986——that is an increase of 130%. In 1993, about 48% of corporate returns were S Corporations, compared to about 24% in 1986."

"Some are converts, probably," Lily said.

"Right. Converts——to avoid double taxation. So what's the impact on Denton and Terrell? Our clients are overwhelmed and we expect more clients. That's where you, Lily and all three of you come in. As my senior staff, I'm counting on you to take the lead. You've your work cut out. Here's what I want you to do . . .," Mr. Chancey outlined his strategy.

In addition to the pass-through corporations, Mr. Chancey also assigned Lily some off-shore companies. She had a busy year ahead.

Soon after returning to her desk, Lily heard footsteps. Bernice stuck her head over her cubicle. "Happy New Year. Where were you this morning?"

She wished her the same and added, "We were in a meeting."

"Oh. Well, I'm ready for my update." Bernice made puppy faces.

She smiled. "You are getting none."

"After a silence of almost two weeks? Here I stand."

"It is busy day. We are backlogged." She couldn't think of a better excuse.

"Lunch?"

"I was planning on working through."

"Then I'm not leaving until you give me my daily gossip." Bernice balanced her chin on her hands over the cubicle.

"Gossip is a sin," she said, solemnly.

"Pastors don't gossip; they just share from the pulpit secrets revealed in private counseling sessions," Bernice replied.

"That is naughty! Some pastors do ask for permission first."

"That's the way it should be. I like it that way."

She asked with compassion, "How are you doing?"

"Great. But as you can see, I've a long way to go. I've been trying to get into the habit of daily devotion. I've also been practicing the routine you taught me. You're right, I have to try harder."

"Not in your own strength. He will help you. I was praying for you."

"Hey, keep it down there will you!" a voice protested.

"Oh, get a life Brad B——!" The old Bernice shot back, her tongue almost slipping out Brad's nickname 'Bentley.' "Mind your beeswax!"

"I am! You're intruding in my busy morning," Brad snapped back.

"Get off it, Brad! Since when have you ever had a busy day in your life? Next you'll be telling me you'll actually help with the taxes this year?"

"Happy New Year to you two!" Lily deadpanned. "How did we make it through Christmas, without the pleasure of listening to you two go on?"

Several chuckled. "Hey Brad, are you gonna let her get away with that? You've got to stand up to her, man. Bernice is always socking it to you."

Bernice ignored them. "You were supposed to call when you got back. You said you'd take a couple of days off, but I thought you'd call."

She tried to avoid Bernice's sharp eyes. "I had meant to, but I got so busy cleaning house and doing laundry, time just flew by."

"And what about yesterday?" Bernice latched on like a bulldog.

"Yesterday I did grocery. I owe you an apology. I'm sorry."

"You're blushing."

"I don't blush."

"Yes. You do. You're blushing. My eyes miss nothing. You're glowing. You look gorgeous." Bernice whispered. "Brad's ready to kick my back for having the privilege of talking to you. It's killing him."

She doubled over her desk, in stitches. "You are mean. Brad is a decent guy, when he is not being unpleasant, and you should not tease him so mercilessly. I think you should apologize to him."

"Brad's a sleazeball," Bernice started to say then bit her lips. "I see what you mean. As a new person, I shouldn't be mean to him. Or rats!"

"It is okay. We all have our days. Tell you what? How about lunch? Let us order a take-out and eat in the car. Okay with you?"

Bernice perked up and left. As she approached Brad's cubicle, her footsteps slowed down. Lily heard her say something to Brad, and Brad respond more cheerfully, then her footsteps continued down the corridor.

After Bernice's footsteps had faded, Lily wrestled with herself. How much should she tell Bernice, without really divulging anything at all? Bernice was her best friend; but she also wanted to respect her budding friendship with Paul, even if it turned out to be only platonic. She felt compelled to protect him from speculation and gossip. Concerned her tongue might slip, she rehearsed what she should tell her.

She was about to fetch Bernice for lunch, when she heard her footsteps. They got some hamburgers and found a quiet street to eat.

She need not have worried. Bernice stuffed her mouth with French fries, bit into her juicy hamburger and sucked her fingers, "Things are coming along great with Alex. He got me a gorgeous brooch for Christmas and I got him a r-r-really nice set of golf clubs. We went out twice. Oh, we had a gr-r-reat New Year's Eve party. He was r-r-really nice. He came around and helped Mum fix things around the house. Jake's beginning to like him a lot more. How could I forget? I got this r-r-really nice outfit. It's so go-o-r-geous---soft, rust, deep forest green f-l-l-lowing number that moves. I gotta show you. You're gonna love it. Alex liked it s-s-o-o-o much. He couldn't take his eyes off me. It felt s-s-s-o-o good walking beside him. He made me feel s-s-o-o-o s-s-pe-c-i-a-l . . ."

She relaxed and let Bernice carry on for as long as she wanted.

"And oh, I'd a long conversation with Mum. She's the most loving person. You were right, I needed to unload." Bernice dabbed her eyes.

"What would we do without mums?" she murmured.

Bernice finished her burger and fixed her no-nonsense green eyes on her. "Now tell me, how was your Christmas?"

Relieved that she did not have to start any rumor, she talked a little bit about Paul's parents and how much she loved the beach, once she got over her fear of them. She enjoyed, especially, getting better acquainted with Mrs. Van Clyden. She found Paul's dad a bit intimidating, though he was just as nice as his mother. And Paul showed her his horses, but she didn't ride——she was not adventurous enough and the weather, not conducive.

Bernice smiled, arcane. She admonished her not to start any rumor.

Back at the office, she found a note convening another S Corporations team meeting with Mr. Chancey. She grabbed the chance to ask for time off.

The meeting lasted all afternoon, but she managed to book her flight to Phoenix, Arizona——leaving Thursday evening and returning Friday, after the job interview. Not even Bernice was privy to her plans, yet. When the time came, she would explain that she had a commitment.

Desk locked, folders filed, she was back on the road, mulling over Paul. Was she attracted to him because of his qualities or looks?

Had she admired looks above all other attributes, she could have dated Jake or other handsome admirers out there, except Brad. For all Brad's classic looks, she could not envision herself dating him. Paul, however, had the character, the great looks and the class. He wasn't flirty, just picky. Also, he had changed. She was now convinced he could sustain a lasting relationship. But, what if by focusing solely on him, she missed other opportunities?

She had thought falling in love with Paul would be difficult. She was wrong. Falling in love with him was easy; obeying the Lord concerning her future, even if it meant surrendering Paul, was getting tougher every day.

96

Brad swaggered into his favorite hangout, threw his car key on the counter, thought better of it and stuffed it in his pocket. He had made it through the two weeks on pure grit or whatever of it he still had left. Much good had it done him, not to think of Bernice who seemed to enjoy every minute of his misery, except for Wednesday when she surprised him with an overdue apology.

Before Palm Springs, Saturday used to be his favorite day——partying and hanging out with the crowd to get his face in the pages——but with no plan for the next day, he could burn the night away and sleep in.

Since returning from Palm Springs, he had made overtures to changing from being intemperate to abstemious, to show his redemptive qualities and sincere repentance for his earlier transgressions.

Palm Springs taught him not all women enjoyed cocktails. "Gentlemen who exhibit moderation are likelier to be taken seriously," a talk-show host said. He thought he was doing well, until the Bartender refused to serve him.

He slapped his car key on the counter and chomped out, "I can do as I please. This is a free country. I'll have you know, what's good for a Van Clyden's good for me——moi! Real gentlemen drink a dry Martini, with a dash of olives. Fill it up!"

The bartender commiserated with him and volunteered to bring his car to the front. He surrendered his key, begrudgingly.

Signaling to his assistant to cover for him, the bartender slipped to the back to get the car; but he took longer than usual.

A taxi with a familiar logo pulled up. Despite his state, Brad recognized it as a cab service with whom the restaurant had a verbal agreement to get them out of predicaments. Miraculously the bartender returned, coaxed him into the cab and gave the driver instructions to take him home. However, he was not so inebriated as to forget that he had left his car at the restaurant.

Relieved to get a ride, he sprawled in the back-seat mumbling words he had carefully selected to express his sentiment toward Paul Van Clyden, in a tone he hoped the cab driver could not hear. Until Palm Springs, he knew of a rival, but not his name. In his naivety, he had assumed his rival would be tall, dark, with white teeth. The last time he saw Van Clyden, Kelly Shinebond was hanging on his arms. Was Van Clyden just another two-timer, after all?

"There's nothing like knowing who's your rival," he muttered.

According to rumors, Lily only blinked at some people, because they attended her church, otherwise, they would be no different.

The closest he had come to believing was when Grandma made all her grandchildren memorize the Ten Commandments. A man of dos, he found too many, "Thou shalt nots" for his comfort. A friend once told him if he really tried, he would find there were more, "Thou shalt dos," than, "Thou shalt not dos," in church and believers were not as boring as he thought.

Lily was gracious, dressed fashionably, was athletic, wore her makeup tastefully natural, and oh, did she smell good, in a way that didn't choke him! Her perfume was so subtle that the first time the captivating scent floated across his path, it had graced his nose like a dream, then it had disappeared, and as he was thinking he had imagined it, it had floated in again. Hoping for a lungful to store for a rainy day, he had inhaled deeply, but yet again, it had eluded him.

For days he had circled the office flirting with every girl, then finally, on ascertaining that she was the one, he had become petrified, wondering how he could say, "Hello," without anyone discovering his secret.

He had eavesdropped long enough on Bernice's conversations to know Lily attended Evangelical Neighborhood Church. It occurred to him to drop in once in a while; but that would be so obvious. He had his pride, though how long he could hang on to it was becoming debatable. Also, just when was he getting married anyway? His dad was hinting loudly. Of course, if his father wanted a stable daughter-in-law, he may have to settle for whichever girl walked in through the door of his sprawling estate.

Had Lily been a Kelly, he would have wrestled Paul to the altar. But the

Kelly he knew was not for keeps. He had no intention of becoming her lap-poodle——old money or new. It dawned on him that sooner or later, he might have to swallow his pride and crawl on his knees to some nice girl, after all.

Once again, he muttered a few choice words to express his sentiment toward Van Clyden, then yelled to the cab driver, "Wake me up when I'm home," and flopped over. In a few minutes, he was out, but not before another troubling thought about his car had assailed his mind.

The bartender returned to the bar, twirling Brad's key, congratulating himself on his astuteness, when it dawned on him that Brad's car was still in his custody. He went out to the customer parking lot along the side of the restaurant, took one look and went white. In a panic he called his boss to apprise him of the situation.

Typical of his boss, he was not one bit rattled; apparently Brad's falling off the wagon that evening was not an aberration. "It all depends on how many times he tips the bottom of the glass and what car he's driving," his boss explained, "Not without cause his associates call him Brad Benz Bentley. One shot, driving a Mercedes Benz, someone got his promotion and they're gonna hear from his Daddy. Two shots, driving a Corvette . . . some dame stood him up, but he can get another——there's plenty more from where that one came. Three shots, driving a Thunderbird, disagreed with his Daddy and can take care of himself, thank you! But, don't you get in the middle or you'll hear from the old man. A whole bottle and driving a Porsche or a Mercedes Roadster or may be a Ferrari . . . got rejected by a Junoesque. Most unlikely he would be driving a Ferrari anyway. Usually drives it to their camera-fested playgrounds. Did you say a whole bottle and some?"

"'fraid so."

"Must've proposed to some crème de la crème and got rebuffed. I hear the old man's prodding him on to the altar. Well, do the usual."

"The usual?" The bartender sounded dubious.

"Cover up the Porsche or whatever and lock the gate!" His boss sounded blase.

"I don't think you want to lock this one up, boss," the bartender whispered.

"What? I can't hear you? Did you say, 'Ferrari'? If it's a Ferrari, don't worry——only one I've seen was a second-hand he got at a moderate price from a friend . . . so he said. Still too pricy for my retirement account. Cover it up good and make sure the gate's locked, then lock up as usual. Let the other boys help you."

"It's a McLaren F1," the bartender whispered louder.

"A what!"

"A brand . . . new . . . sparkling . . . silver blue . . . McLaren F1!"

The bartender heard noises in the background, then the voice of a woman saying, "Mind your blood pressure, honey! Here, take your pill and don't forget your jacket!" followed by a male voice——his boss——mumbling, "I've got to tell the old man. Brad will hate me for this. That boy ought to marry and settle down——let his wife take the load off my hands," then back on the phone, the boss yelled, "Don't move! Make sure one of the boys chains himself to the tires and tie the keys around your neck until I get there!"

The bartender ordered two of the burly boys to chain themselves to the car. If the car got so much as a scratch on its underside, he could spend the rest of his life paying for it and still leave the balance for his children to pay!

He returned to the counter, mopping his brow and spent the next twenty minutes checking his watch every three minutes, until his boss arrived.

The boss inspected the car and returned looking as white as the bartender had turned. Trembling, he dialed a number, said something in the phone and listened. After hanging up, he reported that the Old Man was sending his chauffeur and a security guard to pick up his favorite new toy. Until the men arrived, they were to stay rooted.

Spoiled as Brad was, he had never behaved so irrationally. Why did his father permit him to test-drive the car? And what in the world had possessed him to drive such a posh car to his restaurant——a hole in the wall, by Brad's standard——into the late evening? Sure the restaurant was Brad's hang-out, but he could have carried his problems home. According to rumors, Brad's seven-figure hide-out gave him plenty of space to emote in private. He crossed himself.

97

Now into the second week since returning from the Beach, Lily had settled back into her routine, except for Paul who had become increasingly, disturbingly comfortable. She had submitted her application to graduate and was waiting for a response. Moreover, Mr. Chancey had permitted her to change her work schedule, to spare him hustling to work early. So, on Thursdays, by four thirty, she was usually home and gone again exercising, then she indulged herself in manicure and pedicure afterwards. Paul knew that and took advantage of it.

She looked forward to his visits reservedly, as she wrestled with how she should let him down gently. She was enjoying getting better acquainted with him, but she wished she could see into the future also.

She had considered making appointment at the salon, to avoid him, but dismissed it. Frequenting salons would cut into her plans to save at least forty thousand dollars for her cost of living, before attempting to start her own business. Sure, she could appeal to her parents, but that would negate her plans to be independent and responsible, with, or without, Paul.

Just how much longer would she remain his favorite? It was no use soliciting Sharon and Jonathan's help; they were in league with him and were having a great time. Did they not care about her getting hurt? It was time to tackle, again, the subject of remaining platonic friends with Paul. She had committed to as much when they were at the beach. This way, no one would have regrets.

She was filling a basin with warm water for her pedicure, when the doorbell rang. She was not surprised to see Paul standing at the door, relaxed.

"Good evening," he drawled.

"Evening Paul." She stepped aside to let him enter.

He asked whether he was intruding. She assured him he was not, wishing she could be more candid.

He threw his jacket onto a couch, selected another facing the TV, stretched out his long legs and yawned. Concluding he was staying for dinner, she offered him a cup of tea, and left him watching the evening news, while she rummaged around the kitchen for dinner, mulling over how to remind him of their commitment to platonic friendship.

Almost immediately, he was sitting at the kitchen island, hugging his mug of tea, partially listening to the evening news, partially watching her cook. Then, without warning, his body stiffened, he strolled back to the living room, staring at the screen and sat on the edge of the couch, all color drained from his face. She joined him.

The news anchor was saying, "In a developing story, the Lead Attorney for the Chicago based Matheson, Matheson & Matheson, Law Firm, in the prosecution of Bridge Eco-Friendly Corporation in a joint lawsuit brought by Clean Water Organization——a U.S. based environmental company—— and an international company based in Mexico, against the company for violation of environmental laws, has recused himself from the case, citing personal reasons. In a bizarre twist, an unnamed source informed us that Attorney Jeremy Kaarlyle, Junior, may be linked to Mr. Kaarlyle, the CEO of Bridge Eco-Friendly Corporation."

A picture of Jeremy entering his car, hustled by the press, demanding how many more wives he was hiding, flashed on the screen.

The news anchor continued, "The unnamed source indicated there may be evidence to prove that Attorney Kaarlyle may be the legitimate biological son of Mr. Kaarlyle from an earlier marriage. Although in those days mixed marriages were not allowed in southern states, apparently this marriage may've been legal, since the couple was married in a northern state and the marriage was consummated. What more, it's possible that Mr. Kaarlyle could still be legally married to his first wife. We tried to reach Mrs. Kaarlyle, Attorney Jeremy Kaarlyle's mother. She had no comment. We also tried to reach Attorney Kaarlyle himself. His office said he was not available. We'll keep you posted as this story unfolds."

Paul jumped up. "Uncle Jeremy!"

"What is going on?" Lily followed suit.

"I don't know. Whatever it is, this should have been a very private matter between my Uncle and Aunt. Uncle Jeremy's a great man, but he has some very powerful enemies who've been hounding him. They'll stop at nothing to oust him. I suspect they're behind the press hoopla and will milk it for what it's worth."

"I'll start the prayer chain going. But first, could we pray?"

"Thank you. You're an angel." He hugged her.

"Father please cover Baba Jonathan and Mama Jonathan with your grace and help them sort out what is going on to your glory . . .," she prayed holding hands, then Paul also said a short prayer. As soon as they had finished, he grabbed his jacket, gave her a peck on the cheeks and rushed out.

Still at the parking lot, he dialed a number, "Jonathan, where're you?"

"Studio."

"Get to your Mum and Dad fast."

"What's up?"

"I don't know. It's some new development with the BEFC case. I don't think I could even begin to explain. I'm on my way. Can you call Ingrid?"

"I'll try to reach her."

"Tell her to get to the Beach fast and Jonathan——"

"Yes?"

"Lily started the prayer chain going. Whatever happens, just remember, we're one family and the Lord will get us through this."

Paul headed to the freeway. The numbness was still there, but he was beginning to think perhaps it wasn't as bad as he thought, or it would taper off when the press moved on to other news, leaving Uncle Jeremy to sort out his life in peace and in private. People made mistakes.

The red lights of a big intersection came up; he phoned his father, "Dad?"

"Paul?"

"Did you watch the evening news?"

"Half the world's watching the evening news. Where're you?"

"At a red light. I just talked to Jonathan. He's on his way. And Dad?"

"Yes?"

"Don't worry about Ingrid. He's tracking her down."

"Good going! I'll tell your mother and aunt. Drive carefully."

"I will." Paul turned off his ear phone and focused on the road, determined not to speculate about his uncle's past life.

Lily switched off the rice steamer and called Pastor Tim first, then Sharon. "Have you seen the news?" she asked Sharon.

"I can't reach Jonathan. He left a message, but I can't reach him," Sharon replied, worried.

"Perhaps he is on the phone with his family or may be he is avoiding the press. He will need you now, more than ever," she encouraged Sharon.

Her words had the opposite effect. Sharon's voice broke. "I can't fathom it. Uncle Jeremy's a pillar of the community. So many questions."

"All in time, Sharon. Nothing takes the Lord by surprise. He saw this day and His plan is already in place. Paul believes the whole hoopla has to do with an ongoing lawsuit and the press has blown it out of proportion. Jonathan's dad does not appear to be the kind of man who would let such a thing happen. No matter what transpires, they will need your support as they sort things out. Since Jonathan's phone is off, we could try Paul. Though this is a private matter, I believe Jonathan could use your support. There must be a way to avoid the press. I would be glad to drive with you."

"Oh that would be great!" Sharon seemed cheered by her offer.

She sensed that Sharon needed empathy, so she listened.

By then, she was sure that Sharon would be better off with Jonathan. At a time when the Kaarlyles' family might feel judged and rejected, the best course of action was not to ask for permission to go to them, but rather show support by being there for them. Since Sharon's engagement to Jonathan, she had become practically a Kaarlyle.

"Can you get ready in the next few minutes? We will call Paul en route."

Sharon thanked her and hung up.

She returned her food to the fridge and stuffed her work clothes and vanity supplies into her overnight bag, just in case.

Paul zoomed past a few cars, mindful of the speed limit. Half way through the drive the phone rang again. "Hello?" He adjusted his headset.

"It's me, Lily" Lily said, "I talked to Sharon. We thought it would be a good idea to have her at the Beach. I think Jonathan would appreciate it."

"Definitely. Let me get to Uncle Jeremy and appraise the situation. I'll call you then."

"Well, it is a bit late."

"Are you on the road?" He asked, pleasantly shocked. "Where about?"

"Leaving Sharon's condo. Okay, I'll get off the phone. I'm driving. Sharon will call you when we are about to arrive." She handed her mobile phone over to Sharon and merged into the heavy traffic.

♦ ♦ ♦

School was back in session, Aaron and Michael had settled into their final semester, before they went out to face the big world. The day had been strange. For an unknown reason, Uncle Jeremy and Aunt Angela had been on their minds. At breakfast, they discussed going to the beach sometime soon, to visit them.

Aaron hurried across campus to the four-bedroom house that he and Michael shared with two other housemates, also both upright men, who attended the same church. One of the perks of sharing a house with such caliber of young men was that they had never had to worry about walking into unpleasant surprises in their own home and they held weekly Bible studies together. One housemate was already engaged to a nursing student who was also in her senior year. The other housemate's girlfriend, like his girl, was going to college back east.

He had been at the library doing research. By the time he arrived home, he would have barely half an hour to get back to class. His mobile phone rang.

"Where're you?" came Michael's terse voice.

"Five minutes away."

"Get here presto."

"What's up?"

"Just get here fast."

As he entered, he noticed Michael's overnight bags in the living room.

Michael and their other two housemates were seated on the couch, focused on the television.

"Get your overnight bag and any urgent assignments you'll need to work on overnight. We're going to the beach," Michael said.

"How bad is it?"

"Uncle Jeremy's in trouble. Someone's trying to oust him. Something about the environment, public health and risk mitigation, etc. As far as we know, no injury or fatality's involved, but you wouldn't know it by the press frenzy. We'll get the facts later."

He rushed around packing, his phone stuck to his ears, talking to his professors to excuse himself from class, citing family emergency.

"Did you make all the arrangements?" he asked Michael.

"Yup." Michael slung his overnight bag over his shoulder and grabbed his car keys.

"Let's hit the road," he said.

Their housemates suggested that they should pray. "Don't worry about assignments, the professors will survive."

The moment they had finished praying, he grabbed his bags and followed Michael out.

Without preamble, Michael headed for his jeep, as a courtesy to give him more time to catch his breath.

98

The Bridge Eco-Friendly Corporation was a multi-billion-dollar company with global subsidiaries. Jeremy's upper seven-digit annual salary made him a high-profile corporate CEO and a target. In his seven years as the CEO and President of the company, he had developed a reputation for being an upright, generous, family man——a penniless young man who began with nothing but a dilapidated truck, then went on to own a law firm, and become an executive in the company, onboarding as legal counsel and later promoting to top executive.

Until the press came knocking, his concern for the impending litigation had been limited to threats from competitors and from environmental activists' groups. His legal mind had suspected that the litigants had ulterior motives; but never did he think that it would get personal and acrimonious.

His was the kind of scandal the mass media lapped up as thirsty dogs lapped water after trekking through the Sahara Desert. No doubt he must tender his resignations from the church elders board and the other boards.

He tried to pray, but he could not. One question kept running through his mind, if he had been living in sin all these years, had he grieved the Spirit beyond repair? But that the Lord had remained merciful and faithful to his family, he had no doubt——he could testify to the evidence in the lives of Jonathan and Ingrid.

Upstairs, Angela remained secluded in the master bedroom. He could not face her or answer her questions.

Did he really have a son from the love of his youth, somewhere out there? Why didn't his in-laws tell him? Was that why they sent his wife away so quickly? Surely, they couldn't have known so soon? Had he known, would he have abandoned Desiree in Georgia?

And the divorce papers? His father handled everything, and gave him copies of the court papers. When he signed the documents, he was inebriated, but he remembered signing them. Later, he realized he should have appeared in court in person, but had blocked out the thought, determined to believe in the man who fathered him.

Before Angela retreated to the bedroom, she had asked him for another copy of the papers. He examined the rest of the documents that his father had given him at their reunion, when Jonathan was about seven years old and Ingrid was four. His heart sunk. He had seen these documents before and used the certificate when he married Angela, yet now, he noticed what he had avoided through the years, Desiree's signature looked almost real, but there was something strange about it. He should have obtained another copy directly from the courthouse.

His father said their situation was not legal anyway and no state would consider it a legally or morally binding relationship. He never asked him to clarify what he meant. Now he wished he had.

Angela had trusted him when he told her that he was divorced. To the best of his knowledge, he had told her the truth.

In hindsight, since his first wife had not been unfaithful to him, the divorce would have been invalid anyway, whether or not the papers were filed properly. He should have remained single, that way, he would have complied with his father's wish, without sinning.

He heard the sound of a car stopping at the gate, but ignored it.

Igor and Charlotte opened the gate using the pass code the Kaarlyles had assigned to them and drove up the garden-lit driveway to the front of the house. It was dark, except for a light in the living room.

At the door, they rang the bell and waited. No one answered——like them, the Kaarlyles did not have a live-in housekeeper.

Charlotte took out the spare house-key that Angela had given her. She was sure that the Kaarlyles were home; she had just talked to Angela's watery voice. Just then, they heard footsteps approaching. Jeremy opened the door.

Without a word, they walked over and gave him a big, bear-hug.

He searched their faces. "Please go to her," his eyes implored Charlotte. "She needs you. I can't help her." He lifted his eyes upstairs.

"We'll get through this somehow," Charlotte squeezed his hands, turned slowly following the direction of his eyes and went upstairs.

Jeremy watched her, until she had disappeared, then he said to Igor, "What a mess! I never meant to hurt her. I thought everything was behind."

Igor patted his shoulders gently. "How could you have known, Jeremy? It all happened before you met Angela. But for the press, this should be a very private matter," Igor said, unaware that he was echoing Paul. "We'll get through this, by grace. We're a strong family. His mercy is sufficient."

He turned on more lights and waited for Jeremy to initiate conversations.

"I don't regret what I did," Jeremy opened his mouth and began to speak in a low tone, as though he in another world. "If I'd to do it again, given the times and the circumstances, I would. It was the summer of 1960, you know. Only this time, I would be much stronger——move up north right away."

Angela's face flashed through his mind, he veiled his eyes; but Jeremy read his thoughts and added hastily, "Oh, don't get me wrong. I love my family. I'd have it no other way. I love Angela and I've never stepped out on her from the very first day I met her. But Desiree was my first love, the wife of my youth. I could never forget that."

Jeremy got up and paced the room, emptying the treasures of his soul. "She was a pretty thing, a real lady. They lived across the street from us, one of only two of their kind allowed on our street. Father was a college professor, just the nicest man anyone could know; mother was a secretary. An only daughter, a southern belle, a real lady. When she dressed up for church on Sunday, Igor," he blew his cheeks, "Her copper tone skin glowed like gold amidst a bed of peach roses."

"They attended your church?"

"No. They worshipped at another . . . Baptist . . . sticking with their own. But I wished we could've invited her to church with us."

"What did your parents think?"

Jeremy stopped pacing and averted his eyes. "My mother loved my father, she always did. My father," he sighed and started pacing again. "At first I thought my father had missed his calling. I believed everything he taught me. My older brothers hinted . . . Our families were cordial . . . I used to dream about growing up to be just like Dad——member of the city council . . . elder in the church . . . community leader——so spiritual!"

"Oh Jeremy!"

"Desiree and I used to sit under the tulip tree in front of my house, talking for hours, planning, dreaming about beds of roses——without the thorns of course." He chuckled, bitterly. "She was going to college to help other people and I was going to be a lawyer, to bring justice to the world. Oh, we were so young and idealistic! It was the times. We saw every problem as surmountable . . ."

"So you went forward?"

"We executed phase one on her nineteenth birthday, just before she started college. I told my parents I was going to visit some friends and she told hers she was going to visit some relatives. One-bedroom apartments were reasonable back then. What more could two kids starting out need? I'd just completed my second year at the university——saved a bit of money . . . thought I was a man."

He swallowed hard. "Never did I ever take advantage of her, Igor." His eyes pleaded. "Like Paul, I never crossed that line. She was my lady. We went up north . . . found a real man of the frock through a friend. In hindsight, it was crazy, the pastor was even more daring. How we pulled it off? Incredible." Jeremy shook his head, reliving the experience. "It was the times you see, and I was prouder than a peacock. Then we returned home.

"I swaggered into my house, expecting if not a rousing welcome, at least some expressions of joy," Jeremy paused and rubbed his lips. "Dad took one look . . . his face . . . can you imagine, having your bride torn away from your arms . . . after just a few days . . . by your own father whom you respect? His last words to me for over ten years were, 'Why don't you get yourself a pretty blonde like all good boys – – do?'

"In hindsight now, I should've asked for permission from him and her parents. I doubt it would've made a difference. Just the thought. Our families were on very civil terms, you see. Her parents, professional and genteel——values my father had instilled in us. We'd conducted ourselves with the utmost decorum that would make any parent proud. We honestly believed they would get out the champagne glasses."

"What did you do?"

"I staggered across the street and handed my bewildered bride to her no less bewildered parents, then I hit the town, as Dad had ordered."

Jeremy stopped in the middle of the room and composed himself. "After I ran out of money, I should've appealed to my family, but I figured Dad was everywhere. They were nice, but . . . At first the businesses accommodated me, until news got around. They threw me out——nowhere to go . . . far from the Lord and bleeding inside. Couldn't find a job in the city, the old man had seen to that." He turned and stared out.

"Someone recognized me and told my in-laws. They fished me out by night, kept me at their house for three days, then drove me at night to one of their trusted relatives' house in the next town, where they hid me and nursed me back to my feet. They also re-instilled in me the value of trusting the Lord, in and out of season."

"How did your wife take it?"

Jeremy shook his head. "Gone up north to visit her aunt, they said. When I was strong enough, Mom and Papa scraped together their savings, enough for me to buy an old truck and have some change. They put together sacks of food and two boxes of supplies for the road and then they sent me to California to start over. The last words Momma told me were, 'Jeremy, after you've suffered for a little while, the Lord will strengthen you. And after He has strengthened you, strengthen your brethren. And always remember Papa and I will never cease praying for you. Be strong, no matter what! Be strong!'"

"Jeremy, forgive me. I had no idea," Igor said.

"It's all right. I thought I'd moved on. I was determined. . ." Again, Jeremy stared at his lighted pristine lawn flanked by sculptured terraces. "Angela's a good woman. I've two wonderful children, an excellent nest built. I can't complain."

"And Desiree?"

Jeremy thought for a while. "When I arrived in California, for six months, it was my truck and me and a little paraffin stove and canned beans, until I saved enough for a small apartment. For variety, I rationed the corn beef, tuna and sardines Mom had packed and occasional soup I could afford, after pay day. I'd also saved the balance of their gift for a rainy day. So, you see, I wasn't poor."

"Jeremy!"

"I worked for a construction company for a year. My two years of college put me in good standing with my bosses. They paid me well and I scraped together enough savings to hire a private detective."

"You tried to find her?" Igor asked, surprised, but then again this was Jeremy——the all, or nothing, man.

"Mhmm." Jeremy laughed, bitter. "At first, I wrote letters; they were all returned——no forwarding address. Then I hired a private eye. The naivety of youth. He couldn't find her or her family——so he said——social security numbers and all. Only years later did a trusted friend tip me off that the despicable swindler . . . the stinking, slimy skunk, never left California. Lived it up at the beach with my hard-earned cash! By grace, I've forgiven him." He lowered his big frame on the couch.

Soon after, Jonathan arrived, Ingrid and the boys right behind. They had connected through their mobile phones and coordinated their arrivals.

Jeremy raised his head when they entered. Lumbering, he approached Jonathan and Ingrid. "What've I done?"

"We love you Dad," they both said in harmony.

He let them hug him, but reciprocated limply. Then every few minutes, he would ask, "How far away is Paul?"

Jonathan assured him Paul should be arriving any moment.

Michael and Aaron commiserated with him.

As soon as was appropriate, Ingrid went upstairs to her mother.

Jonathan kept glancing upstairs longingly and seemed unsure of what to do. A few minutes later, the doorbell rang. He got up, hoping it was Paul. Already, the vultures were congregating at the gate.

To his relief, Paul stood there looking calm. He stepped aside, to let him in. Instead, Paul closed the door firmly behind them and gripped him by the elbow.

His father approached. Paul, and Paul alone, could understand.

He, Paul and Uncle Igor took charge, urging his father to lie low, until things calmed down. They asked the men to brainstorm a plan for the near future. First, his father phoned his attorney, Thomas Zachary. Zachary had been expecting his call and would arrive within the hour. Next, they searched for a spokesperson from a reputable public relations firm. In the interim, Igor assumed the role. Third, his pastor's counsel would be most welcomed. The pastor also promised to arrive within the hour.

The phone started ringing incessantly, with reporters begging for the first exclusive interview. Aaron and Michael put all the phone lines to a pre-recorded message. Then Igor assigned them the task of handling uninvited guests, ensuring that the gate was locked and no one was hanging around the family grounds, while they waited for security guards to arrive.

Paul's phone rang again. Lily and Sharon had arrived. He alerted the boys and the security that had finally arrived, but he did not tell Jonathan. When Lily and Sharon entered, Jonathan's jaw dropped. Jeremy seemed surprised too, but with the surprise was a light in his eyes akin to hope.

Lily was right, their appearance gave Jeremy the assurance that those who loved him would remain steadfast. At that moment, regardless of what the future held for her and Paul, or Jeremy and Angela, she became family.

Paul too sensed that his father was pleased that Lily had taken the initiative to support them at such an important time, even more so, knowing that she had volunteered to drive Sharon.

Finally, they reviewed the whole story. Foremost in everybody's mind was one question——how could Jeremy and Angela have married without a valid certificate of divorce from Jeremy's first marriage?

Jeremy recounted his story, excluding the unpleasant parts, until he came to the event that day. "As I told Igor, I signed the divorce papers that my father gave me. I believed in him implicitly, though it was unusual that a judge would allow him to substitute for me. Later, he gave me a copy of the purported certificate of dissolution. When I applied for a new marriage license, nobody questioned it."

"That settles it," Jonathan said, triumphant. "It's just media hoopla. Truth will prevail when you produce the original."

"Not necessarily," Jeremy replied, gloomy.

"Whatever the technicalities, Jeremy, time should support the legality of everything," Igor added.

Jeremy shook his head. "No. I've racked my brain. Whichever way you slice it——whether divorce by dissolution or by consent or by default, it all boils down to one thing, had I appeared in person, my wife's signature would've been unnecessary."

"Jeremy, if you're what I think, that's preposterous!" Igor said.

"The trusting son believes and hopes; naivety seals the deal. Underneath, I must've had an inkling. Instead, I clung to the last vestige of hope——some measure of integrity. Dad had always been my hero. Hard to believe his predisposition will affect so many innocent lives."

"We don't know that for certain, until we conduct more research," Paul spoke up. "When Zachary gets here, we can decide who should accompany him to Chicago. Though he is your legal counsel, I believe it is more prudent to get a family member involved——put a human face to it, so to speak—— since the other parties are as much victims as you are."

Others nodded in agreement.

"What I want to know is who made the connection? How did they tie you to Attorney Kaarlyle, after so many years?" Igor asked, after a decent pause.

"Who else knew about the marriage?" Michael added.

"Friend, enemy, acquaintance, the press?" Aaron echoed.

Jeremy shook his head. "Only my friend who helped me with the marriage arrangement. I know he would never do such a thing. Family members——I don't believe they would betray me either."

"And your father's friends?" Paul asked.

"None of them knew," Jeremy said, then a light dawned, "except the one fellow, father probably hired him to trail me. He was one of them, cold and ambitious . . . ten years younger, but more zealous than them all. I wouldn't dismiss him. Though why he would want to hurt my family, beats me."

His audience held their peace, and prayed silently in their hearts.

Finally, Jeremy raised his head. "The world may scoff and ask, 'What's the big deal?' I say, 'No man who's ever been to hell and back, would ever return to hell again.' I blew one marriage; how could I blow another? How could I let my Lord down again, and hurt so many innocent lives when I promised I'd try harder, with His help? No use shunning my duties."

Igor exhorted and comforted him, then he led them in prayer.

Believing they had done all they could for the evening, they chatted, trying to lighten the mood, as they waited for the attorney and the pastor.

Soon after, the pastor and Mr. Zachary arrived on each other's heels. First, they met with Jeremy in the study room. Later, they called in Igor, Jonathan and Paul.

Charlotte and Ingrid remained upstairs, encouraging Angela, letting her talk. Charlotte's mobile phone rang continually. First, the assistant leader for the women's prayer group, then her other friends offered to help. She asked them to pray, and promised to update them as needed.

As soon as she hung up, Marjorie and Matt called, also offering to help. They had heard the news first on the air, then through Lily's prayer chain request. Charlotte told them the same thing, to keep vigilance praying.

Ingrid reminded her aunt that supper was overdue. They excused themselves and returned downstairs to organize dinner, to be pleasantly surprised by Lily and Sharon, chatting with the boys.

When the pastor asked to speak privately with Angela, Jonathan knew it was time to face his mother.

Jonathan trudged upstairs, praying with each step, as he contemplated what he would do. At the door, he paused, and tapped gently. When his mother told him to enter, he opened the door and took a few steps in.

Except for a bedside lamp, it was dark inside. He spotted her sitting in a chair by the window; beside her, on a small table, a full glass of water and a half empty box of tissue paper, with the rest strewn on the floor.

They looked at each other, into the depth of their unspoken words. She saw in his eyes compassion, but no condemnation. He saw in her a mother torn with guilt.

He longed to hug her, instead, he said, "The pastor wants to talk to you."

"Jon," she said in a soft voice, using her favorite name for him while he was little, "I'd no intention of hurting you or Ingrid. I would not hurt you knowingly. You believe that, don't you?"

"Mum, the Lord has never let us down. We don't know how He'll pull us through, but He will. Remember when we had that scare with Grandma fifteen years ago? We prayed and prayed and when the doctors wheeled her to the operating room, they searched and found nothing. And another time when Ingrid and her friends got lost in the mountains and a light guided them to a ranger's station, miles from where they'd parked. Remember?"

She nodded, with a faint smile. A tear trickled down her cheeks, another followed and another. He crossed the threshold in two strides, grabbed her in his strong hands and held her tightly.

"It's okay. Mum, it's going to be okay. Everything will be okay. I love you, Mum," he murmured in her ears, as she rocked gently.

After calming down, she washed her face and freshened up.

Reluctant to intrude any further into her pain, he started to leave.

"Tell him, I'll meet him in the upstairs living room," she said, in a firm mature voice of a woman deeply loved.

He turned and went downstairs.

Charlotte and the girls popped a frozen pizza in the oven and an extra dish of lasagna in the microwave and whipped up a quick salad to supplement the dish that the maid had already prepared. For privacy, they had released her early.

They all paused when Jonathan entered the kitchen.

"She'll see him upstairs," he said.

"Thanks be!" Charlotte replied.

Jonathan returned to the living room to relay the message.

When the pastor went to the upstairs living room, Mr. Zachary discussed legal matters further with Jeremy in the downstairs study.

About half an hour later, the pastor returned to the family room and was soon joined by Mr. Zachary and Jeremy. Angela finally emerged. Like a reluctant bride, she walked downstairs, one slow step at a time. Her eyes saw everything, but Jeremy's face.

When she stepped on to the threshold, several people moved, vacating a space beside Jeremy. She hesitated, before sitting gingerly at a corner, leaving a generous space between him and her.

Uneasy silence followed.

The pastor cleared his voice and encouraged the family, speaking in a tone devoid of any condemnation, smiling often to lighten the mood, and drawing on passages from the Bible.

At the end of the meeting, Charlotte told Angela that supper was ready.

Angela perked up a little and said, "You must all be hungry. Won't you join us for dinner?" and led everybody to the dining room, where they had a subdued meal, made easier by the presence of their guests.

The last dishes were in the dishwasher, the kitchen counter spotlessly clean, when the clock struck midnight. Paul and Lily would stay at his parents' so Paul could plan for the trip. Sharon and the boys would remain in the Kaarlyles' home. The boys would use the guest house.

The next day, Paul, Attorney Zachary and a junior attorney from the law firm would leave for Georgia, to track down the certificate of divorce, before heading to Chicago, to meet with Attorney Kaarlyle, Jr.

Uncle Jeremy would lie low, until the truth was known, while Igor and Jonathan helped him squelch the fires. In the meantime, he would submit his resignations to all the boards of directors where he had been a trusted member——to make things easier for those Boards.

Aaron and Michael would have loved to have stayed longer, but school beckoned, so they would return to school by the beginning of the week, but remain on standby as needed.

Ingrid took great comfort in knowing that her aunt was practical, but very considerate. Already, she had buoyed her mother and encouraged her to develop a temporary plan, although her mother was still unclear about life with her father.

The rest of the close relatives would be updated, as necessary. But, since Angela was most likely not legally married to Jeremy, she could not remain under the same roof. She planned on renting a hotel room or move in with Ingrid, until she could find a more suitable accommodation to rent, but Igor and Charlotte protested and offered her interim accommodations. In the meantime, she would move to a spare bedroom for the night.

Earlier in the evening, Paul had called Bill to ask for vacation to attend to family business. Bill granted him the leave. He too had been following the news.

Even in the midst of the crisis, Lily remembered she had a job interview a week Friday. Things were improving between her and Paul, but she did not bank on it. As providence had it, having him otherwise occupied, would liberate her of the need to disclose her trip to him.

99

"What's gonna happen to Jonathan now?" Marc fixed his eyes on his father.

"What will, not what's gonna," Matt interrupted.

"Where will Jonathan spend his Thanksgiving and Christmas and stuff?"

"Will he spend them at his grandma's?" Melanie looked soulfully at her dad.

Matt studied his children. They stared back at him, waiting for a miracle that would wipe away the nightmare of the last three hours, since Lily phoned to start the prayer chain, disrupting dinner and the Jonesons' well-orchestrated household.

"Everybody, come here and sit down." He motioned to his family.

Melody, Marc and Melanie trooped to the family room.

Marjorie joined him on the couch and held on tightly to his hands.

"First and foremost, your mother is my first and only wife and I intend to keep it that way." Matt looked at each child in the eye, making sure he reached them individually. "Second, your mother and I have no intention of ever abandoning you, our children. We're believing the Lord for that. We intend to stay together, as the Lord's our strength and helper. You're stuck with us. No switching parents. Okay?"

There was an audible sigh of relief all around.

"We knew that," nervously, Marc said, on behalf of his siblings.

"Thank you for having faith in us. We're relieved to know you trust us. Now about Jonathan, first, what happened was neither his fault, nor Ingrid's, nor their mother's, nor even their father's. We don't know the details yet, so we wait. Second, let's pray for them. We talked to Paul's parents. Jeremy had no intention of divorcing his first wife, but Jeremy's dad was opposed to the marriage. Jeremy was very upset. His dad was a powerful man and carried a lot of clout."

"Did his first wife do something bad?" Melanie asked.

"No, honey," Marjorie replied.

"Did she um, dishonor God?" Marc asked.

"No. She is a very decent, godly woman. She loves the Lord as much as we do. The mistake Jeremy made was in assuming a surprise wedding would be fun and their families would laugh and throw a wedding party later. Back then those marriages were difficult. His dad was not amused and his dad offered to file the papers. That's all we know and we should trust them to sort it out." Matt omitted the speculative parts, to protect his children from gossiping.

"Oh, what a relief!" Melody's face brightened. "So, when the press is told the truth, then everything will be all right."

"That's what we're praying for," Matt said.

Marjorie squeezed his hand.

He responded by patting her hand, then he continued, "God does not forbid marriage between a man and a woman, He only forbids immoral relationships. And He forbids us from separating a husband and his wife. He's the holy God as Pastor Tim has said so many times and we've read during family time. He does not tempt anyone to dishonor Him. Jeremy's an upright man. He even tried to find his first wife, but the detective he hired lied."

"That's horrible! How could he get away with something so despicable?" Melody asked.

"Yes. How could Jeremy not have known that the detective was lying?" Marc echoed.

"Easy. The detective said Jeremy's wife had vanished. Jeremy was trusting and young. He wanted to believe in somebody, especially after his father had let him down. The detective was supposed to be a professional," Matt assured the children. "Of course, Jeremy will be resigning from the church board and all the other boards of directors. Integrity 's a requirement for such positions. Unfortunate, but inevitable, given the circumstances."

"The important thing you need to remember, is that your dad and I are here for you, and we need to pray very hard for Jonathan, Ingrid and their parents," Marjorie added.

"Yes. That's very important and that's another reason why I called this meeting. Your Mum and I offered our support and promised to pray. But please remember Jonathan's family would appreciate it very much if we don't discuss this with anybody. Don't volunteer any information. Okay? If anyone discusses the news around you, move on or get busy doing something——blow a bubble gum or zip your mouth."

"What if they ask?" Marc said.

"Tell them you don't know the facts and you don't watch too much TV. You're waiting for the truth like everybody else."

Melody, Marc and Melanie nodded in agreement.

"Promise?"

"We promise, Dad," the three chorused, solemnly, their hands placed across their hearts.

As soon as Matt had finished praying, he phoned MJ. College student, or not, MJ was still at heart, just another boy who needed the assurance that his world was still stable and on the Rock.

Relieved that the foundation of their stable home was still intact, the Jonesons' children resumed business as usual, chasing each other up and down the stairs and around the dining room and the living room and any space where they could work off their pent-up energy from the shock of knowing, as they approached the end of the twentieth century, no family was guaranteed a life of living happily ever after, without God's grace and hard work at keeping the family together.

Next, Matt sought out his wife and assured her that he had meant every word he had told the children. "No ghosts in the closet. You're stuck with me, as long as we both shall live." He kissed her.

100

Zachary's legal team boarded their return flight from Chicago to Los Angeles, bearing one fruit from their trip——a meeting with Jeremy, Jr. The team perused Georgia's archival records in vain, searching in every county that was recommended to them. As they had suspected, no evidence emerged to prove that Jeremy's divorce papers were ever filed.

JJ was working temporarily at another location. When they arrived, they were ushered into the firm's conference room. A tall, athletic, young man that resembled Jeremy keenly, but with a tan, strode in. After introductions, he boomed, like his father, "How's my father? Will he live?"

"He's holding on. He'll be pleased to know you're all right," Paul replied.

"I'll survive. I've much to be grateful for. I was worried about him."

"He'll rally around. He's resilient. I'm glad you're looking fine."

Paul took immediate liking to his step-cousin. Shortly after, the other senior attorneys entered to brief Team Zachary.

As a courtesy to Attorney Jeremy Jr., Matheson, Matheson & Matheson, Law Firm was in the process of handing over the Bridge Eco-Friendly Corporation case to another skilled attorney from Fields, Forrest & Flowers, LLP, who would assume the lead role. Fields, Forrest & Flowers——a reciprocal law firm for Matheson, Matheson & Matheson in conflict-of-interest cases——would work with their co-partners, Lyttle & Bergeron, experts in international law, in suing the Bridge Eco-Friendly Corporation, hitherto known as the BEF Corporation.

Also, as a courtesy to Jeremy, Sr. and JJ, both legal sides were eager to avoid litigation and were in negotiation to go to arbitration instead. If negotiations failed, they would return the case to court.

BEF Corporation was confident that they would win, as they were becoming increasingly suspicious that the case was initiated by a coalition of certain social groups who were using Clean Water Organization as a front to advance their social goals. They were also investigating the private detective whom Jeremy had hired to find Desiree. What was his connection to Georgia, and the family friend who had orchestrated the fake divorce? Also, was he acquainted with Clean Water Organization?

The company was anxious to protect Jeremy and the firm from being dragged through mud, but the authorities would still check into the social groups' activities. How low would they sink? Were insiders at BEF Corporation involved? If so, heads would roll.

Meanwhile, Jeremy had submitted his retirement to the members of the board. Most of them protested, but they had agreed to release him from his contract and pay his eight-digit severance package.

Upon Mr. Zachary's return, Jeremy would announce his resignation, citing the need to spend more time with his family, and so forth, then he would take a vacation to heal and plan his future. More pressing, he and Angela were at least talking again.

Finally, the boards of directors of the other four organizations, including a Christian university board of regents, had also accepted his resignations. They were thankful for his humility and integrity in moving so fast, but regretted the circumstances that had necessitated the resignations.

101

Jeremy parked in an empty spot, took out a document from his brief case and placed it in his inner coat pocket. A stranger, hiding behind dark glasses, yet he still felt exposed. The short walk across the lot to the hotel lobby seemed eternal.

At the lobby, he dialed a number using a new mobile phone, and sunk down on a seat facing the stairway.

At Desiree's insistence, no attorneys would be present. After all the media distortion, they had taken every precaution to keep the meeting secret, including shunning all existing telecom devices, lest a nosy reporter had wiretapped them. He had also avoided discussing his plan with anyone——family, friend, or foe——via email. For this meeting, a trusted source had provided him an unlisted mobile phone.

Would she come down the stairs or would she use the elevators? After over thirty-four years, what did she look like?

He watched guests meandering up and down the stairway. Two groups came out of the elevator, she was not among them.

Too weighed down with guilt to pray, he relied on his years of counseling others to will to pray. How often had he advised those people to lean on God's forgiving grace? It was his turn, could he do the same? Much as he loved his father, it was difficult to believe that he was his offspring. Guileless was the Lord, guileless he too had endeavored to be.

"I should've tried harder," he prayed in his heart, "I'm sorry for letting You, and her, and our son down. It was not her fault. I'm to blame, but now I've another family. They too are innocent. I messed up. I love my family. Though she was my first love, I must let go."

He sensed her presence and raised his head. Casually, he searched the lobby with his eyes, until he saw her standing near the elevator, studying him. His heart skipped a beat.

She had blossomed into a woman, making her more captivating than ever. Her skin glowed with middle age and she looked stunning in her new hair style——cropped to give more fullness to the front, tapering off toward the side and back. Her physique was sculptured like one who exercised at the gym.

She stood tall, looking every inch the wife of a CEO with a seven-digit annual income, nothing in her deportment would leave anyone in doubt. He took his briefcase and rose up slowly from his seat, mesmerized.

A smile curved the corners of her lips, the way it used to, when she was excited to see him. She strode forward. "Maynard!" she called him by his middle name, as she used to, years ago. "It's so good to see you." Her voice, now deepened, resonated and filled not just the space between them, but also the chasm and barrenness of those painful years.

"Desiree," he croaked.

Desiree held on to her dignity, glad that she had chosen to meet Jeremy at the Respirare E Vivere Hotel, instead of at a local restaurant. Based on the lobby, she guessed the hotel's restaurant would be just as crowded.

His haggard face exposed his struggles——a man built of steel, yet a man ready to crumble, not from any weakness, but from the weight of the albatross he had lugged along since they were separated. He had always been a strong and devout man. When her father-in-law forced her husband to break his vow, no father could have dealt his son a heavier blow.

She approached the concierge. "I'd reserved a conference room?"

"Of course. We were able to get a room for you. If you go to the Business Center, they will help you," the concierge replied.

She disappeared around the corner and returned shortly. "Their meeting rooms are for groups, but they offered us a smaller room. Do you mind if we use that, instead of the restaurant?" she asked.

"Not at all," he replied. It appeared she was trying to save him from making a fool of himself in public, which he was sure he would do if he remained in the lobby a minute longer.

She led him to a room that could accommodate ten people.

He sunk into a seat. "Desiree," he breathed her name.

"Jeremy, how're you?" she asked.

"Can't complain," he mumbled.

"You look good. California agrees with you."

"How's my boy?" he asked in a stronger voice.

"Holding on. He has your sense of humor."

His lower lips trembled. "Do you have a picture?"

She took out a small photo album from her purse and handed it to him. He studied each photo, pausing often. "Was it bad?"

"Mom and Pop were there and Aunt and Uncle and my cousins."

"How long?"

She stepped away. "Long enough. The last four were the hardest."

He faced the wall. "What was his favorite cereal?"

She smiled, sad. "Puffs . . . cocoa puffs, orange juice and bananas."

He sketched a smile. "He would. You raised him well."

"We'd a vision, remember? I followed the script. Mom and Pop helped."

He cleaned his nose with a handkerchief. "Is it too much to ask? No sensible man believes everything in the press."

She told her story, leaving out details such as the nights she clung to JJ running a fever, not knowing whether he would make it to dawn, or the day JJ cried so hard because all his friends' dads attended their birthdays and he wanted his dad home for at least one birthday.

He listened with his heart, then he talked about his family, especially Jonathan and Ingrid. Still longing to know about the missing years, he delved deeper. "After college, what did you do?"

"Teach . . . college. After graduate school, I had a teaching position in Washington D.C, before moving to Chicago."

He seemed awed. "You followed in Pop's shoes."

"Isn't that true, most of the time?"

"I couldn't get Jonathan into law. I tried, but he takes after Angela." He stopped, his face a picture. "Of course, we've a lawyer in the family!"

She lowered her eyes, demure.

"Upon my word! With no heir to pass to, I sold my practice ten years ago to my current legal counsel and moved to corporate."

Desiree remained silent, sensing his need to talk.

"Angela and I did pray about it, before I made the move. I thought becoming a CEO was a good move. It permitted me to see things from a broad perspective and sometimes delve into the nitty-gritty. Perhaps with all this, I could return into private practice, couldn't I?" He sought her face.

She nodded in agreement.

"It would be good to have a son to talk shop with."

She smiled. As during their secret engagement, he could go on and on, talking, planning their future again.

She studied Jeremy's face. Deep contours——evidence of the agony, the anguish and something that resembled despair——lined his face. This was the second time in her life that she had seen that look on his face. The first time was the night his father told him to put her away.

He hunched his shoulders. "What've I done? I've lain awake nights. Was it hubris? Will the Lord ever forgive me?"

"Maynard." Her heart bled.

"Is pure love as God has intended, hubris? I was not trying to change the world; I was in love with the woman of my dreams. Never, for one moment, have I ever doubted my heart. In any other circumstance, would we be here?" He looked around the room. "No. We would be at the Riviera, strolling along the beach. If I could roll back the clock!"

"Maynard, it was not hubris. The you I know has never been guilty of hubris. It was the times. Neither you, nor I, did anything wrong. We were two young people in love . . . idealistically in love."

"Oh, to roll back the clock!" he sighed.

"This is the only time I'll use that deplorable excuse——we were victims of the prevailing times . . . a society that craved two separate heavens. We observed all the principles——Old Testament and New. We even had a real pastor officiate." She laughed, bitter. "Only the Lord has that right."

"I was so trusting. How can I talk about virtue, purity . . . sacredness." Jeremy's voice cracked.

"Forgiveness? Grace?"

"Just as well I did not go into ministry. I know now why the board screens pastoral candidates."

"Those were extenuating circumstances that neither you, nor I, had any control over. You did everything right. How could you have known that the detective was such a vile creature? True, my family moved——things had become unbearable——but, we never changed our social security numbers."

She blew her nose. "That's not important anymore. What's important is that you tried to find us. The thought that you, my husband, tried to find us, is the greatest gift you could've given JJ and me."

Jeremy sketched a smile, swallowed and rubbed his eyes.

"JJ's like a new man now. Before, he had the confidence that we'd instilled in him. Grandpa and Grandma and all my family have always assured him that we love him and more importantly, the Lord loves him; but when he walks now, he holds his head up higher, knowing he has a daddy, who is a man. You've given him back all the birthdays you were never there."

The veins on Jeremy's temples stood at attention.

"Jeremy, I don't condemn you. I never have. Angela's a beautiful woman, and your children, they're all victims too. I'll sign the papers and pray that Heaven would never hold what happened against you. Go home to Angela and may the Lord bless Jonathan and Ingrid and all of you."

He opened and closed his mouth, numb, then he cradled his head.

She waited, as she had waited through the years in silence. When JJ was upset, she waited; when he was hurting, she waited; when he felt lost and alone, she waited. Now here she sat again, waiting.

Finally, Jeremy placed the papers on the table. "How's Pop and Mom?"

She smiled faintly. "Holding on. They never stopped loving you. Papa refused to go. He swore he'd never go, until he has seen you again. He's looking forward to playing golf with you. He and Mama pray for you every day, Jeremy. You're their son. They've never forgotten that."

The room had no windows, giving them privacy. Jeremy placed his head on her lap. She cradled it, knowing it was time to release him.

After he had collected himself, they gazed at each other. There was so much pain in his eyes, she struggled to control hers. She must be strong. She had promised herself she would not cry in front of him——buckets had flowed, buckets would flow, but not in front of him. She wanted him to remember her as the strong woman he had fallen in love with; the woman who had raised their son alone, the woman who had overcome.

In Jeremy Junior, she had fulfilled their dreams——plans that they had fantasized about sitting under the family tulip tree.

"May I pray with you?" she asked.

He nodded. "Of course."

"Lord, thank you for bringing my husband back. Thank you for keeping him safe all these years. I'm sorry for what happened. I don't blame him, but I'm sorry for all the lives it affected. Release him of all guilt and don't hold any sin against him, I pray. My father-in-law's gone, I hold no grudge against him, I forgave him a long time ago. Bless Jonathan and Ingrid and their mother, Angela. Strengthen them through this difficult period and keep them united as a family. Bless their future generations, and do not hold it against them. They're innocent. And Lord, I pray, please bless JJ also. He's so dear to us. Continue to make him a strong man who honors You, and bless our future generations through him, I pray . . ."

Jeremy strengthened himself, opened his mouth and prayed one more prayer with his wife, drawing deep down from years of discipline, and the knowledge that he had long since been forgiven for the sins of his father. He thanked the Lord for having given him such godly in-laws, then he prayed for Desiree, giving thanks for her strength and love and kindness. Finally, drawing from Israel's blessings, he blessed JJ as his oldest son:

"Father, JJ is my oldest son. Bless him and make him fruitful and multiply for generations, until the Lord's return. You promised to bless generations of those who honor You, bless JJ and all my descendants through him and protect them from all evil. May you prosper him wherever you lead him and enlarge his borders and let him continue to be a joy to his mother and me. May all my generations through him prosper and honor You . . ."

Desiree gazed into her husband's heart once more, then she signed the divorce papers. Smiling bravely, she released them to him and with them, the small photo album she had brought.

Jeremy took a deep breath, placed the album inside the inner coat pocket closest to his heart and stuffed the divorce papers in the brief case.

Next, she slipped off——from her ring finger——the Marquise Diamond wedding set he had given her at their wedding and held them out to him.

He closed her fist around them and said, "They came from my heart."

She rubbed her eyes. "Maynard, when you walk out of this room, don't look back. Your life lies ahead of you. You have a family to take care of. Be happy. Be very, very happy Jeremy Maynard Kaarlyle, Senior."

He swallowed hard. "Will I get to see Mom and Pop?"

"Of course!" Desiree smiled, uncertain, then seeing the earnest look on his face, she broke into a broad smile. This was the Jeremy Maynard Kaarlyle to whom she had got married. She scribbled an address and a phone number on the hotel writing pad and gave it to him.

He looked at the information, folded the piece of paper and put it together with the album, away from the divorce papers, then he got his briefcase, held himself erect and took the first step out of her life for the last time as her husband. When he reached the door, he paused.

"No Maynard," she said. "Turn the doorknob and continue walking. You're doing this as much for me, as for you and Angela. Be strong."

Jeremy walked into the cool afternoon with a knife slicing through his heart. Was there no end to his pain? If he thought surrendering his bride after his brief honeymoon was tough, walking away forever was like dying.

He had always known that love was color blind; he was living proof and could attest to how a man could die from such a broken heart, but for the grace that willed him to live. No one should ever tell a man to get over his love just because she did not blush the same shade as he did.

Desiree returned the key to the Business Center on her way to her room, clutching her wedding ring set. She walked up the two flights of stairs, put a 'Do not disturb' sign on her door, threw herself on her bed and wept.

Hours later her phone rang.

"Mum, I know you told me to stay out of it. I'm coming to take you home," Jeremy Kaarlyle Junior said in a firm, yet gentle and loving voice of a son who knew how much his mother had suffered through the years and shielded him from pain.

He spoke as a son and a man speaking to the woman who had withstood the test of time and modeled to him true virtue——the woman who had brought so much dignity to him that he could never pay her back in his lifetime. She had persistently and consistently refused to date or remarry and she had never stopped wearing her wedding ring. Now he understood why.

102

Life goes in cycles, even taxes sometimes get discounted; the only constancy for eternity remains the LORD. Paul's life too had followed the same pattern and left him leaning on grace.

While Uncle Jeremy and Aunt Angela's marriage floundered, Paul clung to the Lord, hoping to continue drawing closer to Lily. He wished that his rival would prove to be nothing more than just that——a rival. Needless to say Valentine was subdued. He had looked forward to giving Lily a dozen red roses, and a box of chocolate strawberries, instead, he had to compete with the shadow of the unknown rival and of the Kaarlyles' marriage that never was. Yet even in the midst of the uncertainty, a beacon of hope had shone when Jeremy returned from his trip, with Desiree's blessings. Desiree's kindness, despite the injustice dealt her, boosted everybody's faith.

◆ ◆ ◆

It was late-morning, the weather promised to cooperate with the wedding couple. The atmosphere was more relaxed than it had been for weeks. In the Van Clydens' estate, the family had finished brunch. Some guests had already dressed up and the wedding party was preparing to leave for church.

Jonathan looked stunning with his new haircut. Sharon stepped forward and dusted off a speck from his jacket.

He examined his frame in the hallway mirror and straightened his tie. "I've always fantasized about attending my parents' wedding."

"Jonathan!" Sharon said, softly.

"Cheer up Mum. Just think——"

"Jonathan!" Sharon said, sternly.

Angela blushed a deep red.

"How could you!" Ingrid's glared at him.

"No comment." Sharon tried to smile as one who knew Jonathan's confidence had been shaken, and he needed her love, not judgment.

The other family members chuckled, sheepishly.

Jeremy tried to join in, but he could not meet his wife's eyes. "And to think all my life, I strove to honor the Lord. That's okay son, you can joke all you want."

Jonathan blushed every shade of God's planet earth. "I didn't mean it that way, Mum, Dad." He hugged his mother. "I love you, Mum."

"I know. But I'd rather have you joke about it, son, than have you hide in a dark corner. I didn't say it would be easy, but the Lord's merciful. We've never received so many expressions of support," Jeremy said.

Charlotte's eyes softened. She hugged her niece and nephew as her own children. "His grace and his grace alone. You're pure, because you've entrusted yourself to His protection. You're covered. He died for you long before you were born. And since you've submitted to Him, you belong to Him. He sees you as His own. Trust in His grace. Look up to Him. His grace and His grace alone is sufficient for you," she whispered in their ears.

After Paul had returned from the trip, he had invited Ingrid for a sleepover——never had she and Jonathan felt more like siblings to him. He had laughed and prayed with them and encouraged them, knowing, ultimately, none of them was to blame for the debacle of their grandfather. Those hours had paid off. When Jonathan started cracking jokes, he knew Jonathan was ready to forgive his grandfather.

◆ ◆ ◆

Over thirty years ago, a train of seven bridesmaids and their groom attendants marched down the aisle to the organ pipes pumping Bach's "Jesu, Joy of Man's Desire;" on this beautiful early spring day, five bridesmaids and their groom attendants again stood at the altar, after marching to the same tune.

Charlotte and Igor flanked the bride and groom, next to them, the other bridesmaids——more like matrons of honor——and the groom's attendants.

All Angela's sisters had hinted loudly that they would like to be bridesmaids. They would not let their sister walk down that aisle a second time to marry the same man, and face the wedding guests alone!

Over three hundred guests had attended the first wedding; on this day, over one hundred guests were in attendance.

Apart from relatives who fell neatly into the groom's or bride's side, guests were seated on either side of the pew indiscriminately. Paul, his cousins, Lily and Sharon spread out in the first pew, making it difficult to differentiate to which side of the family they belonged.

Angela had wrestled with inviting about fifty guests, which would have ruled out just about everybody, except the immediate family members and a handful of very close friends; but after so many friends had extended their support to them, they could not exclude them from the wedding.

The Jonesons had proven true to their mettle——inviting Jonathan home for dinner, singling him out at church, dropping by the beach to visit and taking the Kaarlyles out to dinner and a show——the Kaarlyles could not ignore such love.

After burning the midnight candle to complete their college papers so they could relax and enjoy the wedding, MJ and his girlfriend, Viviana, drove straight from Pursue Holy Life University to the wedding and sat behind Paul's row.

With Lily at his side, Paul sat still, stunned at the turn of events. Now he understood what she had been trying to tell him these last two years and why she had been so resistant to his courtship. In his naivety, he had failed to grasp the full import of her dilemma when he tried to return to her, after he had broken up with her so thoughtlessly.

Seeing Aunt Angela broken, knowing this disaster could have been avoided, wrenched him. But then, had Jeremy's first marriage succeeded, there would be no Jonathan or Ingrid or Uncle Jeremy. What a pickle!

Security vetted occupants of limousines, Jaguars, Bentleys, Mercedes and the likes as they filed through the gate of the Van Clydens' estate, for a private party, where they danced deep into the evening. Security around the estate was so tight, not a fly was allowed to buzz over a trellis!

◆ ◆ ◆

What's a wedding without a honeymoon, especially after waiting for over thirty years? Jeremy took Angela as far away from the provoking crowd as he could for their first real honeymoon——a week in Israel, the Holy land, and two weeks in the islands, drinking coconut juice and falling in love all over. If he spent some nights lying awake, thinking about his first wife and his oldest son, he never let it show to his new bride.

To clear the air before the wedding, he had discussed with Angela his future relationship with JJ. With BEF Corporation behind him, he had explained to her his need to keep busy. Volunteering at a non-profit organization was an option, but the Bridge case had rekindled his passion for justice. Starting a legal firm that would also offer pro bono work, would fulfill those passions.

He expressed his desire to invite JJ to become his partner. She gave him her blessings. JJ responded with alacrity and promised to begin preparing for the California Bar examinations. Once cleared, he should be available after giving his notice to Matheson, Matheson & Matheson.

Another loud confirmation of grace at work was when Mr. Zachary hinted that he was considering retiring and would much rather sell back the law firm to him than to a stranger and, had also offered to remain on board part-time to help with pro bono work for as long as possible. In other words, since Zachary was only sixty-four years old, Zachary was offering to sell back his law firm to him and manage the pro-bono work for him.

When Zachary bought the firm, he was a religious man, but not passionate about faith. Since then, he had matured into a man of strong faith. Apart from JJ, Jeremy could think of no better partner.

103

In two months, Paul had learnt more about the history of America than he had learnt all his life. No amount of college work could have taught him the valuable lessons that the fiasco of Uncle Jeremy and Desiree's marriage taught him, not to think of all the unplanned consequences!

He was more conscious of subtle manners that he used to dismiss and as a result, had become more protective of Lily than before. With open eyes, he now moved forward, determined to succeed.

He rung Lily's door bell, then turned and watched a sparrow perched on a fence. A minute later, he rang the bell again.

A groggy Lily stuck her head out. "What are you doing here so early in the morning?" she scowled. The flower delivery, now wiser, usually arrived later.

"Good morning to you too. Are you always this grumpy in the morning?"

"I bite off heads. Are you hiding any Witnesses behind you? Where are the tracts? I believe Jesus is the Son of God."

"What? So do I."

"Are you distributing tracts . . . pamphlets?"

He twirled around and emptied his pockets. "U-u-uh, no. Do they come this early?"

"Sometimes. I suppose I can let you in." She opened the door wider. "To what do I owe this bright-eyed and bushy-tailed visit?" She still sounded a bit grouchy.

He told her to wear a casual outfit and sturdy shoes.

She went upstairs to freshen up, still grumpy.

A few minutes later, he drove her to a local mom and pop restaurant, where the food reminded him of home cooking——pancakes and fresh strawberries for her; the same for him but with bacon and eggs.

Despite his cheery disposition earlier on, he became very pensive during the meal, studying her, and seemed to be debating with himself.

"Would you care to join me for a quick walk?" he asked as they were finishing breakfast.

She accepted graciously, though surprised.

He drove to Be Still Lake and guided her up a hill, along a beaten trail.

"My uncle seems happier than I've ever seen him in all the years and my aunt's coming along too." He negotiated a rough patch. "She's much stronger than before, basking in the support she received from family and friends. She loves JJ too, though she regrets all the pain he was subjected to——however, knowing that Desiree had a loving, supportive family and a great job that made her financially secure, brought her some comfort. So, all's well that ends well."

"I am glad. They are such great people."

"I'm glad too. I learnt a lot these last two months. I'd taken a lot for granted."

At the apex of the highest hill, they studied the surrounding cities.

His mood became subdued. "I came here many months ago, when I realized I was falling in love, and all I could do was pray," he addressed the valley.

I hope he is not going to propose. Lily prayed that he would do no such thing, while externally remaining calm. Since their reconciliation, she had only asked for a stable friendship and nothing more. Moreover, if he proposed, it could be a rebound from the Kaarlyles' recent debacle——far worse than not proposing.

He looked at her, "Lily, it's possible for a woman to hold so much power over a man. I've never permitted that."

She returned his gaze steadily. In the depth of his soul, she saw and comprehended his vulnerability and her power over him; but, she resented that he would think her capable of deliberately hurting him.

Whatever she might be, she would never try to catch a man just for the pleasure of discarding him as a toy that had fallen out of favor. Yet, she realized that any woman could hurt a man who loved her. The notion that she had power over Paul, perhaps more than any woman had ever had, including Kelly, terrified her.

There was so much he was taking for granted. Perhaps she should not have allowed him to persuade her to go to the beach for Christmas, after all, even if it had meant being ungracious to his mother. Had she known that he would invite her to his parents' home, she would have bought a plane ticket and taken off early to visit friends. He wouldn't have argued with a plane ticket, would he?

She loved Paul too much to abuse his trust——an act that could create a greater chasm than the dip of the valleys below.

"Ever since I was a child, I have never been good at collecting toys, Paul. But I also have things beyond my control." She echoed the familiar phrase he used a year ago when he tried to explain why he wished to reconcile with her, after having broken-up with her abruptly.

He started. "All I ask is, don't hurt me."

She pondered Paul's behavior. It might be beyond her power to avoid hurting him. She had not yet told him about her trip to Arizona. It was easy to leave town without disclosing her destination, since he was in Georgia. The interview was successful and the financial firm had offered her a job, as soon as she graduated. All her other options were also out of state.

104

Since her scrape with the law, Kelly's family and friends began noticing a difference in her. Her parents especially, noticed that she had become quiet and thoughtful. She preferred spending weekends at home, to spending them with her friends. Whenever she socialized, she was known to steer her friends away from excesses.

Moreover, her mix of friends had changed——fewer party socialites and more low-key friends who preferred quiet dinners and reading the likes of Tolstoy, C.S. Lewis and Dietrich Bonhoeffer.

Tonic water had become her preferred drink. Believing that was not enough, she was also attending alcohol anonymous meetings at church.

At church, she observed Lily, furtively. She wished she could chat with her, but refrained——though Lily had never rebuffed her——afraid her motives might be misconstrued. After all, all her life, she had made friends for destructive reasons. Had Paul surrendered, he would have been another victim of her love——a priced achievement, no less than an Army General felled in battle and she would have earned herself a diamond tiara among her fans for conquering such a great General. But, she had not counted on his God being so powerful.

The new Kelly dressed more modestly, was more sociable, spent time in the patio mingling with ordinary people during coffee time and tried hard not to cuss or use profanity, even when with her old friends. They found her rather dull, though she laughed hard at clean jokes.

A friend was overheard saying, "Kelly's become a bore! What's with the 'becoming temperate' business? Good grief! She's acting like a bluestocking!"

"Com'on! You never say good things about anyone," another friend said.

"Just an observation. She really has become a bore."

"Give it a rest! I like the new Kelly. She's fun and caring."

The Shinebonds too were brought to heel. Seeing how much they had wrecked their daughter's life, they searched their own souls.

The break–up shocked them and their friends. In breaking-up with Kelly, Paul had sent a strong message about his sentiment towards affluence. His missionary trip to East Africa put any residue of doubt to flight.

In due time, an admirer approached Kelly expecting to be rebuffed. He was pleasantly surprised, even more so, when Mr. Shinebond granted him permission to date her, contrary to all the horror stories he had heard.

Ron came from very modest means. As a potential suitor for their dear Kelly, the old Shinebonds would never have let him within a mile of their threshold, unless as a simple guest——for charitable reasons——as long as he stayed away from their daughter. The new Shinebonds had seen the Light. A good man was worth the keeping. Ron seemed as upright as Paul, what more, he had a good education and a solid career. Stable men like them, could detect an impostor in a snap——though she came bedecked in diamonds.

Tom and Trish realized that Kelly had a second chance at getting a decent match and they determined to change. Some of their old friends warned them not to become fanatics. Among the groups were those who confessed they used to be believers, but had moved on and those who had rebelled outright, saying faith no longer satisfied their longing for a higher realization. But was it true that Christ did not satisfy? There were many Jesuses even during Christ's time. Which Jesus had not satisfied their longing to become better people?

The couple admitted that no tepid response could serve justice to their need for the Jesus of the Cross and the Resurrection.

As husband-and-wife, they experienced their best times when they were unselfish to each other. Their change began with admitting that they were not self-sufficient gods. What would it hurt to follow their new script? So, they set out by faith. They had tried a few of their friends' recommended solutions, even as they continued attending church. None of their friends' gods had provided them the internal peace they longed for. Moreover, they had other children to worry about——Kyrk, Alison, and Justin——whose lives they had no desire to see wrecked on the Los Angeles freeways.

Worried that they might be judged for their failure as parents, but determined to make a fresh start, the Shinebonds sought help. Trish joined Charlotte's Bible study group and Tom joined the men's group.

They need not have worried. Neither the Van Clydens, nor their other friends judged them. Like them, some of these couples also struggled with family problems——wayward children, some who had left home, on a self-destruction course——they too desired support. For the first time, Tom and Trish found themselves with a new set of friends where they felt safe. Their fear of being judged as imperfect, vanished. They also joined alcohol anonymous' meetings at their church. Soon, the absence of hard liquor at their parties reflected their permanent reform.

To Tom, this was a new phenomenon——that he could be successful, without being afraid. If he lost everything, he would still have the LORD, his family, and his trusted friends who would help him rebuild his life. And he had no doubt that he would recover.

Moreover, he no longer identified himself with his possessions. He had become a new man who related to himself not as a man confined, but a man freed of collecting toys. He could see the evidence in his wife's eyes. Her adoring eyes were that of a woman who was settled, and confident and secure. That some of their old friends were surprised at how Trish was now treating him, was flattery enough.

He never thought he would live to see the day that he thanked the Lord for losing what he craved. In losing Paul and almost ruining her life, Kelly may have saved her family. If Lily had not been around, would Paul have forced himself to marry Kelly? He knew some friends in that dilemma now——marriages of convenience, where the children had persuaded themselves to believe they were compatible.

In his own way, he developed an interest in Paul's quest for a marriageable girl and prayed that Paul would succeed. After all, he was really a very nice young man——a good catch for a son-in-law.

105

Mid-afternoon on Friday, Paul listened gravely to the caller on his mobile, hung up, and reversed with screeching wheels out of BF&S' parking garage. He had options, a minor consolation——he could sit with the Jonesons and the Daelvins, or should he sit with Phil and Julian at the BF&S table? He should have informed his father, but what would Bill and Sheila think? They were especially invited to sit at his family table.

Alone is alone, whichever way you slice it.

The moment he entered, his father blurted out, "Where's Lily?"

Looking for a place to crawl, he replied, "She had prior commitment."

His mother looked at him sympathetically. "Of course they're not yet married, honey. We don't have much time. Traffic will be backed up."

He averted his eyes, kissed her on the cheeks, and ran upstairs to shower. She must know. Inside the wardrobe was his freshly dry-cleaned black tie, "Thanks Mum."

When he returned, his father was sitting in the living room, flipping through news channels. Soon, his mother swept downstairs in a lovely long black velvet gown, that brought a twinkle to his father's eyes.

His father patted his tie and mumbled, "Too bad Lily isn't here."

"I heard that. We're not going to discuss that tonight." His mother swept to the garage to her favorite seat where she was happy to drive from the back to Malibu, while his father navigated from the front passenger seat.

At the valet parking, a figure stepped out of the crowd. Paul excused himself, "I need to say a quick hello to a friend, before it gets too busy."

If his parents thought this was odd, they didn't say so, instead, they told him, "Take your time," and turned to admire the city view.

Paul approached the stranger.

"She's here with him," the stranger said.

"Impossible! She said she'd a commitment." He adjusted his collar, hot.

"I followed them here from her condo."

He blew his cheeks. "Of all the nights!"

"Sorry. I wish I'd better news," the stranger commiserated.

"No need to apologize."

"One more thing. I took the liberty to inquire about other customs."

"Mhmm."

"According to a reliable source, it's a common practice among some international students to leave their spouses, or betrothed, back in their home countries. I hope it's not the case, in your situation."

"I hope so too. Good job. I'll get in touch with you this coming week."

The stranger tipped his head and melted into the night.

Remembering the recent surprising twist to the Kaarlyles' marriage, Paul composed himself, before rejoining his parents.

"Son?" His father asked.

"I'm ready." Again, he avoiding their eyes.

In tandem, his parents flanked him and swept him forward with their power. He had never felt so loved, yet so alone, as then. Within minutes, he would be coming face to face with his rival. "I've never been good at collecting toys, Paul. But, like you, I also have things beyond my control," she had told him.

What he had called 'faith' a year ago was just the routine of going through the motions, without depending on the Lord for his social life.

Paul winced. Months ago, he had promised to trust the Lord alone, but had permitted doubt to creep in and had reneged on his commitment. Where did it get him? To a night of disgrace! In a few minutes, he would be humiliated before his parents, his dear friends and the world. What worst fate could befall a man?

Humbly, he repented and surrendered to whatever awaited him behind the banquet doors. When he raised his head, they were entering the hall and Uncle Jeremy and Aunt Angela were right at their heels.

Suddenly, there was Lily, standing awfully close to a young man or appeared to be. He froze. Her black and winter white gown and cascades of onyx and diamonds dangling from her ears, sparkled. Her hair . . . he sighed. Did her unknown friend purchase her that outfit at Thanksgiving? She had never looked this beautiful for him!

Before him was a formidable foe indeed——at least six feet two inches tall, with a chiseled body that resembled an Olympian. As if that was not enough, his facial features were enough to land him a leading role in a major movie. His fingers were as long and as elegant as Lily's. Worse, he had strong, perfect, white teeth that lit up his face when he smiled——which he did often, seeming to enjoy everything that Lily was saying. No wonder Lily was hanging on every syllable that fell from his rival's lips!

He sensed his parents had seen Lily too. A shadow crossed his father's face. He blushed. Fifteen months flashed by. Was this a reprisal for how his family initially treated Lily?

Looking at Paul's face, Igor realized nothing in the world was more important to him than Paul's happiness. All his ambitions to expand his business vanished. Had he known what would transpire, he would have sent his regrets and arranged to meet with Abrafimqodesh later. He marched forward with his wife, exuding the confidence of the CEO of The Van Clyden Enterprises as they mingled.

"You don't say!" Uncle Jeremy's voice rang out. Since the wedding, he had regained his confidence and jauntiness.

Right then, Lily tossed her head back and laughed and another familiar voice also rang out. Paul recognized Bernice's voice. There she was with Alex. Who else was there to witness his public humiliation?

All that remained to complete the scene were the Shinebonds, after all, they too were likely to attend such an international function. Sure enough, there they were towering over the head of a couple dressed in Chinese costume. The reformed Kelly was hanging on to Ron's arms, her new date——the man who would have never stood a chance with her. She appeared quite happy and very sober.

Just then, Kelly turned her head and saw him. Their eyes locked. Was that sympathy he saw in her eyes? He yearned for a place to hide.

"A-a-h, Igor, I'm so glad you could make it," a voice nearby said.

Paul turned and saw the conference benefactor and his wife. When his father introduced him to them, he shook their hands vigorously, as befitting an up and coming executive and heir to the Van Clyden Enterprises.

"Come, I must introduce you to Moses and his beautiful wife, Milcah, before it gets too busy." The host led the way.

The Van Clydens and the benefactor negotiated their way through the crowd, stopping, chatting with friends or familiar guests, Lily ubiquitous. From the sides, Jonathan, Sharon, Ingrid and her date acknowledged them. Finally, they spotted Mr. Abrafimqodesh and his stunning wife, amidst a small group.

Abrafimqodeshes turned and saw them. Mr. Abrafimqodesh recognized Paul first, stepped forward to give him a warm handshake. "Ah, young Paul Van Clyden, it is so nice to see you again."

"Nice to see you too, sir," he replied, spirited.

Mrs. Abrafimqodesh extended her hand. He bowed and shook it, as he had seen polite East African men do. He was rewarded with a dazzling smile.

The host led the introductions, "Moses and Milcah, this is Igor and Charlotte Van Clyden. Charlotte is a former high school teacher and now works with various charitable organizations. Igor is the head of the Van Clyden Enterprises I'd mentioned. He's mostly in steel business, but is looking to diversify."

He introduced the Abrafimqodeshes, "Dr. Abrafimqodesh is the head of Mungu Huponya Pediatric Hospital in Nairobi. She has been instrumental in implementing positive changes to children's health. And Moses, as you may know, is the head of the Abrafimqodesh Enterprises, dealing in import and export. He and I've worked on various improvement projects——such as solar energy——targeting East Africa. He's currently exploring fiber-optics."

Paul commented that Mr. and Mrs. Abrafimqodesh had graciously invited him for a party at their home, then he introduced his Aunt and Uncle, mentioning that Aunt Angela was an excellent concert pianist and Uncle Jeremy had returned to private practice, including pro bono work, after years in the corporate world.

The Abrafimqodeshes' warmth, alleviated somewhat his humiliation, though his pain was raw like a fresh wound, soaking through swabs and swabs.

However much he was imploding, his father had waited long to meet the elusive mogul. It was imperative that they gave the Abrafimqodeshes a positive first impression. Looks and wealth meant nothing to them, character and family did.

Paul woke up from his reverie. Mr. Abrafimqodesh was addressing his father. "You have a fine son. We were very impressed with him. You should be very proud of him."

His father thanked him. "He's the apple of my eye."

"Well, I was hoping I would introduce some very special people too." Mr. Abrafimqodesh searched the crowd.

His hostess craned her neck. "I think they're over there." She walked over to a group of people partly camouflaged by curtains.

The Abrafimqodeshes chatted on, until they spotted the hostess returning.

"Oh, there you are," Mr. Abrafimqodesh said to someone, then to his audience, "May I introduce my daughter? She actually lives here in your neck of the woods."

A young woman emerged from the shadows.

"This is my daughter, Lily," Mr. Abrafimqodesh gestured to her. "Mr. and Mrs. Van Clyden, their son Paul, and his uncle and aunt Mr. and Mrs. Kaarlyle."

An audible gasp greeted his announcement, before everybody hastened to conceal their emotions with their cordial demeanor.

"Hello. We've already met. Mr. and Mrs. Van Clyden were very kind to invite me for Christmas. They were the family I mentioned. Mr. and Mrs. Kaarlyle hosted Christmas dinner, and Jonathan and Ingrid and Paul have become dear friends," Lily told her parents.

"Ah! I am very pleased to meet you finally. My daughter was very impressed with your families. We owe you a debt of gratitude. We must visit sometime soon," Mr. Abrafimqodesh shook their hands again, warmly, then continued, "And my director and right-hand man is also here somewhere. He has been quite an asset to me, I don't know how I would run my business without him. He does most of the travelling. Very sharp. I think you will like him." He surveyed the room again.

"Oh, here we are." He beamed, as a young man emerged from behind a couple who had blocked him from view. "This is my brother, Shadrack," he said, then he explained to Shadrack that Lily spent her Christmas with Mr. and Mrs. Van Clyden and Mr. and Mrs. Kaarlyle. He explained further Igor's connection to the Van Clyden Enterprises.

A low murmur followed. Charlotte and Angela gawked at each other.

"Your brother?" Paul gasped. "Lily's um . . . uncle?" The concept of Mr. Abrafimqodesh having a brother seemed unfathomable. In his blind jealousy, he had overlooked other plausible explanations for the alliance.

Mr. Abrafimqodesh chortled. "You look puzzled. I know he looks too young to be her uncle."

Paul, blushed. "I'm sorry, sir."

"No need to be sorry. Most people are puzzled. We come from big families. My mother has twelve children, so my youngest siblings are about the same age as my children. Milcah and I raised Shadrack to help my parents. So Lily and Shadrack grew up together. He is like her oldest brother. He takes very good care of her. I was telling her she should exert herself to mingle with the other guests. But they have always been very close, since they were young. You see one, you see the other."

"Sir, she doesn't need to mingle," Paul blurted out. "I mean, it's perfectly all right for her to visit with her uncle." He turned beetroot red.

"You are right, but they have been visiting since Thanksgiving."

"Thanksgiving! That's great." Again, he parroted Mr. Abrafimqodesh. He had been taught a very expensive lesson, worse, he had yet to pay his private investigator for the three months of service he had provided. He congratulated himself for having locked down a fixed contract with the private eye.

"We spent a nice time together at Thanksgiving, since she could not join us for Christmas. They went shopping; their mother and I stayed warm in the hotel, except for dinner. We liked it that way," Mr. Abrafimqodesh explained.

Paul stared at Lily standing, looking as docile as a dove!

Mr. Abrafimqodesh's smile had become inscrutable. The fear that had paralyzed Paul when he realized he was in love with Lily, gripped him again. Knowing now that his opponent was a phantom of his own making, he wondered how the Abrafimqodeshes would react, if they knew the truth. What else did she tell them? That for cause, she had insisted on platonic friendship, he now understood.

Would they retaliate? And if they did, would he pass the test? On the scale of one to ten, how would he measure on being treated as an object with no feelings? Would he conduct himself with as much dignity, as Lily had?

His palms dripped with sweat. It had never occurred to him that he would run into any obstacle, once he had secured Lily's affection.

"Sir, I'd no idea," he stammered.

"Well, how could you have known?" Mr. Abrafimqodesh replied.

Dark brown eyes matched wits with sea-blue eyes. Paul scratched his head. Just how much did the Abrafimqodeshes know?

"Wow!" Uncle Jeremy said.

"We live in a small world." Mr. Abrafimqodesh and his wife laughed.

A light came on, taking Paul back to the estate. When he first saw Dr. Abrafimqodesh, his heart had skipped a beat. The regal look of the docile creature beside them was a combination of mother and father, more of mum. Curly ringlets that fell over her shoulders were definitely from her father. No wonder he had felt such a strong pull from the moment he first laid eyes on them.

How elusive she had been. "My father is a businessman, my mum works too," she had told his father. 'Mum works too,' had thrown his Dad off the scent. And to think his father had been jumping through hoops to meet the formidable Mr. Abrafimqodesh, when all he had to do was to . . . he prayed for grace.

For once, his father too was thunderstruck.

"Upon my word!" Uncle Jeremy spoke for all of them.

When Paul dared to look at Shadrack, he was observing him, his face also inscrutable. He wondered how much he was in on the joke.

Someone had once warned him that Africans had a tremendous hidden sense of humor. If they chose to, they could be the worst teasers in the world, and mess with your brain. Ironically, he did not dislike Shadrack for it. Now that Shadrack was not a rival, he actually admired him. He already liked him. Looking at Lily, it didn't matter anymore, anyway.

He gave Shadrack a warm handshake. Shadrack reciprocated. Could he count on that as the promise of friendship? Were the Abrafimqodeshes more benevolent than his own parents had been, initially?

He had come face to face with grace. Throughout the roller coaster months of emotions, heaven had remained faithful, even as he vacillated. But he was not so naive as to suppose that there would be no challenges. During the same months, he had also experienced vicissitude spanning the gamut, from those who opposed him, to the support of true friends and family——the regenerated ones.

The rest of the evening passed in a blur. Paul spent most of the banquet, scratching his head at the woman who had outwitted him.

At one point, Jonathan whispered, "We've a lot of bridges to mend."

"Tell me about it," he had replied.

His dad took him outside, placed his hands on his shoulders, and said, "Son, I'm not usually at a loss for words, but she got me. For now, relax and enjoy the banquet. We'll figure this out later."

"At the earliest opportunity, I intend to declare my intentions properly to the Abrafimqodeshes and seek their consent, as is the appropriate thing to do. I regret that had not been possible earlier."

"Good idea!" His dad had agreed. "You helped set up BF&S' branch office in Nairobi and I plan to pursue the business end of things. An opportunity is bound to come up to redeem the situation."

He had learnt a valuable lesson about the folly of presumption and jumping to conclusions based on perceptions.

Not without cause does the Holy Book say the Lord hates the sin of presumption; but the Lord is also gracious, willing to forgive those who repent. And repented he had.

Never before had he felt so naked and vulnerable, but also so hopeful and amazed at the wonder of the grace that had kept him walking the straight and narrow path, even when he had nothing more to offer.

106

The doorbell rang. Lily took one last look in the mirror and opened the door. Paul stood on the threshold, dressed in a dark gray suit with a starchy white shirt and a distinguished looking tie. Lights danced from his hair. His pair of oxfords looked so slick, she could use it for putting on her makeup. A small whiff of a new cologne floated in the soft breeze. French, she thought.

He had managed to set a dinner date with her at the banquet. So here he stood now, staring at her in the soft light of spring, clasping a bouquet of red roses. His eyes spoke volumes as he stared at her winter-white gown, overlaid with gold sequins and her hair held up with a tortoise gold comb.

She invited him in, rescued the roses from his hands and went to the kitchen. When she returned, she had arranged them in a beautiful spiral of an open fan, deserving of the central theme on her coffee table.

He did a double turn.

"Anything the matter?" she asked.

"Very nice!" he said.

"Thank you." She smiled and offered him a choice of soft drinks.

"Would tea be too much trouble?"

"Not at all."

In no time, she brought two steaming cups of tea. "I had the water boiling," she responded to his raised eyebrows.

"A companion that reads my mind. Mmm."

"I'm learning."

He had drained his cup. "That hit the spot." He got up. "Shall we?"

Traffic on the 60 Freeway, Los Angeles bound was surprisingly flowing for an early Saturday evening.

Lily relaxed, content to listen to the music, trying to gauge his mood. Sooner or later, he would expect a thorough explanation, she knew.

Paul accelerated past the downtown gridlock to Freeway 405 and exited on Santa Monica Boulevard. A few turns brought him to L'Amore Prevale Restaurant, a family-owned private dining, suitable for the occasion.

Yes, he was expecting an explanation; but his guilt weighed heavily on him. Should he confess his five-grand foolishness——that he had lost his faith, momentarily? If he did not, would it affect their trust for each other?

And, what about Lily's family? Had he proven himself enough to be accepted into the Abrafimqodeshes' threshold, or would they exact their pound of flesh?

He sensed Lily was avoiding talking about her family, so he had waited. He took her hand and escorted her inside the restaurant.

Lily's trust arose with Paul's firm grip and by the welcoming ambience of the restaurant, whatever insecurities she still had, dissipated.

They were ushered into a private dining room.

Lily chose a light appetizer and soup, but hesitated about the main course. "How about you?" she asked him.

"Appetizer sounds good——antipasto L'Amore Prevale. For Risotto e Pasta, I'll have rice, lobster in burrata cream; and for secondi, I'll have roasted lamb chops," he rubbed his nose to hide a smile, "baked potatoes and roasted vegetables."

She studied the menu again and selected arborio rice with asparagus and for second course, grilled salmon, fregola and heirloom tomatoes. "Their salmon is grilled; I assume it will be well-done. I hope we can ask without offending the chef?"

"Sure, we can. You don't like sushi?" he flirted with her.

"What's so funny?"

"Nothing," he replied, but he continued looking at her.

She lifted her chin. "Mr. Van Clyden, are you going to trick me?"

"No. Absolutely not."

"Your word of honor?"

"My word of honor. Promise!"

She contemplated his face, but before she could reply, the waitress appeared. "Saved by the waitress," she muttered.

"I heard that," he shot back.

"Ready to order?" The waitress placed a goblet of apple juice and an elegant glass of mineral water on the table.

Paul ran off the orders, his eyes still focused on Lily. Would this be one of a life time of evenings of dinner together after a long week at work? He prayed so.

From their appetizers through the main course, they made small talk, more often communicating with their eyes. She asked him about work. He replied that Bill had hinted at a promotion——most likely Assistant Director of Finance. BF&S was very pleased with his bailing them out and saving the project, and how he handled two employees——Shane being one.

"About time. You deserve it." She took a sip of her water. "So Shane found a church closer?"

"Yes. He did. Pastor Tim recommended a friend's church. I'd given up, at the end of my wits. Every time I saw that man, I wanted to punch something!"

She chuckled. "Isn't it like the Lord to bring people into our lives to help us grow! It's a good thing you obeyed."

"Yes. I grew a lot." He dabbed his mouth.

She looked at the pictures on the wall. "This is a very nice restaurant. I like the ambience."

"So do I. It's family owned. The husband immigrated from Italy, where he met his wife who was working on her M.A in Food Studies and Culture. The wife's paternal grandparents immigrated from French Guiana, but it's not obvious. Her mother is German-American."

"That's interesting," she murmured.

"And, she's a former novice . . . spent two years in a novitiate in Rome, studying to be a nun."

"Really?"

"Mhmm. She'd already taken her temporary vows of poverty, chastity and obedience, when she decided she could keep her vows just as well by upholding the marriage vow." He took a sip of his apple juice.

"I admire her honest courage. I believe those who take vows so young should be permitted to revisit them. The world would be better off for it."

"I agree. Celibacy for life's not for everyone, considering the Lord has given each of us the freedom to marry or remain single," he observed.

She admitted that she had heard about nuns leaving their vows, but had never actually met one. "Do you know them?"

"Yes. Through Bill. They've a boy and girl——five and three. Bill and Sheila stood in as some sort of Godparents when they dedicated their son. Needless to say, they now attend a more evangelical congregation."

"Amazing what the Lord will do when we trust Him."

"True." He took a slice of his lamb chops. "Has Bernice and Alex set the date?"

"Yes. In early autumn, when the weather is cooler."

"Jonathan and Sharon are shooting for a hot August wedding, 'when the girls can wear straps to church legally,' to quote Jonathan."

"And shock the grandmas!"

"Not past Sharon. Jonathan's a decent fellow, but he does put his foot in it, sometimes. He got rapped for that. Sharon said, 'Not on your life! No thin straps and no décolleté. I'll measure each strap personally——nothing less than three inches wide. I'm having no wardrobe malfunction at my wedding!'" he mimicked Sharon.

"Those two need help. They need prayers," she said in stitches.

"More like lay hands on them," he chuckled.

Finally, they finished their main course. The waitress brought them the dessert menu. As they were reviewing the menu, he said with a gleam in his eyes, "I think today deserves a dessert, don't you?"

She smiled. "You have a sweet tooth."

"Hershey kisses."

"Chocolate cake."

"With a dash of cream?" He grinned.

"All right. I will split it with you."

He signaled the waitress, "Two Cuore di Cioccolato, with a dash of gelato alla vaniglia and two piping hot cups of tea."

Assured that he could always depend on her to back his effort to be a gentleman in the true sense, he pondered how long it would be prudent to wait before he proposed to her. Would she rebuff him?

If she accepted him, he was cognizant of the challenge of a long engagement.

Jonathan and the other upright men he admired, admitted how tough it was to walk the line. According to Jonathan, a wise man selects a fiancée who is as committed to virtue as he is. As Sharon was that woman to Jonathan, so Lily was to him.

The waitress served their dessert and left.

He took a bite of his chocolate cake, then he placed his fork down. "So, would you like to start from the beginning?"

"What beginning?"

"Let's start with, 'My Dad is a businessman and my Mum works too.'" He mimicked her soft accent.

"That's true." She wiped her mouth a bit longer than a dot of chocolate cake and ice cream warranted.

"How did you remain anonymous for so long? For crying out loud, I met your parents in Nairobi. I felt drawn to them, but little did I know how important they would become to me." He pinned her with his eyes. "Why's your last name different?"

"Each child is given a name at birth, just like here. Western names were a misunderstanding of our culture. The missionaries meant well——probably to distinguish between those who are baptized and those who are not."

"Why did your parents call you Nyaber? Does it have a special meaning?"

"Daughter of the beautiful one or it could also be an abbreviation for 'nyako aber', which means a beautiful girl."

"Very befitting. So, your full name is Lily Nyaber Abrafimqodesh?"

"Yes."

"Do you sometimes use Abrafimqodesh?"

"Sometimes."

"Except in the church roster."

"Mhmm."

The waiter brought the bill.

He thanked her, waited until she had left, while weighing what Lily had said. "Your parents——are professional people."

"My Dad was a college professor, hence his nickname Mwalimu. He is now an adjunct professor and a full-time businessman. My mother is a pediatrician."

"Quite a good one, from what I hear."

"By grace."

"Your entire family, are they all believers?"

"Getting there," she scooped her ice cream. "My parents were already believers when they married. My Mum's side are Luo——Grandpa is a Lango from Uganda, and Grandma is a Kenyan Luo. Dad was a non-practicing Muslim, even so, Mum resisted him. He was a rebel . . . dropped out of school, and . . . she had issues with trusting him."

"That makes sense." He nodded.

"Dad was very headstrong. Initially, he tried to please his parents, but the older he got, the more he searched for peace. To my grandparents' chagrin, he argued, made excuses and showed up only at wedding receptions. He was searching, but none of the answers helped him, so he stopped practicing, then he met my Mum. She was at peace with her life, but she did not like him at first."

"He seemed so agreeable now."

"He has mellowed."

He nodded, reliving his teenage years. "How did your grandparents take it? It must've been difficult." He took another bite of his dessert.

"At first, my grandparents were upset."

"I can imagine."

"Thanks to Mum, he changed and went to college. To my grandparents' surprise, he became the son they had wished for. My Mum speaks softly, but she is very firm. My grandparents would much rather a son who respected them, than one who didn't. What more they knew he would no longer be exposed to some of the scary ideologies out there or worse, disappear." She sought his eyes.

"Mhmm. I wish more parents would realize that."

"It was gradual. Once Mum realized he was serious, she told her parents and they gave their consent. So, as we children came along, we made our commitment each in turn, once we understood the message. We are blessed in that my paternal grandparents, finally moved over."

"Praise be! It's always a blessing when everybody comes on board. That's a miracle right there that your grandparents realized their need and did something about it. I suppose they experienced challenges?"

"Unfortunately. Some of their friends felt betrayed——that hurt them very deeply." A cloud marred her face.

"I'm sorry."

"Thank you. But, there were also those who saw the wisdom of their decision, especially after witnessing the remarkable change in Dad. More importantly, they gained new friends."

He said he was even more relieved that they were on board. "The Lord always takes care of the details. And, Shadrack's your Dad's right-hand man?"

"Yes. He travels mostly between Europe and home. He went to Oxford, so he feels comfortable in that world."

He had to be, remembering how Shadrack had so much poise.

Lily dropped her eyes and added in a monotone, "Mr. Odhiambo, our cousin, helps with the local business."

Paul narrowly missed spewing his tea across the table. "I knew it!" He reached across and kissed her hand. "You dear! You had me staked out. Where was Shadrack during the party? Com'on, time to confess."

Lily dimpled. "Upstairs watching you arrive. It was his job to make sure you were treated well. He came down later but kept fleeting in and out of the party to stay out of your way. But his fiancée was on the floor."

"He's engaged!" Paul chuckled.

"Mhmm. His fiancée and her friends were mingling, guarding you from being snatched up! She told me she noticed several international female VIPs gobbling you up with their eyes."

"You naughty girl!" He chuckled loudly.

Finally, after he had settled the bill and the waitress had withdrawn, he took a deep breath like a diver preparing to jump into a deep river, hoping to swim across to the other side in one piece. "I'm afraid I've not always had strong faith. I wish I could roll back the clock!"

"Paul we are all human——in the process of maturing, but still human. I have made my mistakes too and will. I wish I could be like Him and please Him all the time," Lily said softly.

"Yes, but some of the mistakes I made were foolish," he insisted.

"So foolish that the Lord couldn't forgive them?"

Taken aback, he stared into her soul and appeared to see her for the first time. Bereft of speech, he took a sip of his tea.

"You know Paul, the Lord is not such a hard task-master as to punish a man for hiring a private detective in a moment of doubt. A costly mistake perhaps, but not beyond His forgiveness." She lifted her cup to her lips.

He choked and asked in between coughing, "You knew?"

"I had an inkling."

She is having a ball——impish girl. May heaven forgive me!

"As you very well know, Mr. Van Clyden, restraint is the mark of a gentleman," she teased him.

"I wouldn't count on it, Ms. Abrafimqodesh." He emptied his cup and helped her out of her seat.

107

"How did you know I had you followed?" Paul queued a CD and pulled off L'Amore Prevale's valet parking.

"Instinct. Your investigator was good, but not necessarily discreet. You can't follow a person around without being detected," Lily replied.

"I'm sorry. Hadn't I been so blinded, I wouldn't have done it."

"That is all right." She had pondered his actions many times and wondered about his motive, even as she prayed that he would confess. By him owning up to a moment of weakness, her prayers had been answered.

At first, she had felt betrayed. His distrust of her had stung like alcohol on a fresh wound. She had rationalized that he was human; but she could not ignore the added insult to her dignity——hiring a detective to chase a woman he had jilted so callously, was not the best way to reclaim her favor.

As quickly as the anger came, as quickly she had challenged herself to forgive him, even before she had understood his logic for taking such a drastic——if not foolish——step. Forgiveness was more than platitudes.

"Those who forgive to make their enemies angry, have not learnt forgiveness, let alone love," she had told herself often.

The sooner she released her anger, the easier it became to forgive her offender and begin healing and loving again.

She was not spineless, neither did she diminish the pain that Paul had caused her; but she was convinced that she should forgive him, if for no other reason, than because of the Lamb. Forgiveness was the only road to freedom, yet she still struggled to vocalize it. But, if she remained silent, how would he know that she had forgiven him? Intuition? Had they connected that deeply on a spiritual level? She could take that easy road and assume that he already knew. Not for one moment did she believe that the Lord would buy that excuse.

If she did not train herself to voice her forgiveness on those occasions that he might hurt her, how could their relationship ever mature? She desired spiritual bonding above all things, that inseparable oneness——feeling his pain, celebrating his joy——a true friend he could depend on. For hours she had prayed that he would confess his blunder. He had. Now what was restraining her from forgiving him?

"Paul," she patted his hand, "It is all right, really. I understand."

Paul thanked her and squeezed her hand. In the two years that he had known her, this was the first physical affection she had initiated towards him——the first real affirmation that she cared. He kissed her hand.

In the silence that followed, he glanced at her periodically and she could make out his free hand fidgeting with his tie. To ease his discomfort, she said, "That's a nice selection you have. You mixed the CD yourself?"

"Special order, courtesy of Jonathan and Sharon for my birthday."

"That was nice of them. When was it?"

"July."

Last July, when all she could think about was getting a one-way ticket out of California. Last July when Kelly flaunted her sense of entitlement to him. Last July when the last thing on her mind was that one day, his birthday would become her right to celebrate and the phantom of Kelly would be laid to rest.

More silence followed.

"So," he finally said, "Did your parents know?"

"They had an inkling."

"And…?"

"Well," she measured her next words carefully, "they were a bit concerned, quite rightly so, all factors considered."

"All factors considered?" He drummed the steering wheel.

"Yes. They hinted at the impact of decisions we make. I suspect your parents had the same reservations?" she turned the table on him.

"Kind of." He loosened his tie.

"I guess when it comes to such issues, all parents feel concerned."

He stopped drumming. "They were so warm at the banquet."

"Parental instincts span the gamut."

Paul took a deep breath. "I respect you, Lily, more than I have ever respected any woman before."

"I respect you too," she replied.

He put the car on cruise. That seemed the only thing to do to fill the silence.

They were cruising past Rosemead when she opened her mouth again. "I'm grateful for my parents' commitment to grow. They spent a lot of time praying and combing through the scriptures. As each of us was born, they committed to seek wisdom in raising us and teaching us godly principles, and to support us in whatever decision we make as adults."

He exhaled.

She continued. "My parents believe children are gifts from the Lord and He decides each child's course. They also believe that He would never lead any child astray, if that child walks in obedience to Him. By faith, they have done their best to keep their promise."

"I stand chastised."

She did not respond. It was not necessary, but she needed answers for his silent months. "If I may ask? You collect your valuables in three."

"Ok."

"I know about the cufflinks, and the guitars and the horses . . ."

"Mhmm."

"Who is the third girl?"

He burst out laughing. "Lily! There's no end to you."

"Seriously."

"I value people. I don't consider them toys. But, if you must know, my mother——I wouldn't trade her for another; my cousin, Ingrid——she's like a sister to me; and——you! And not necessarily in that order."

For a moment, she was rendered speechless. After she had recovered, she ploughed on. "Why did you start dating Kelly?"

He answered right away as though he had been anticipating that question. "My parents. At first, they were concerned, as you guessed, but in the end, it came down to trust."

"It is nice when parents allow the Word to guide them."

"Yes." He seemed relieved that she had given him a chance to explain. "But, as I tried to explain before, it was over before I tried to rekindle our relationship. Kelly and I are not compatible."

"She appears to have changed. I think Ron is good for her. He looks like the kind of man who will take good care of a girl."

"Don't get any ideas now," he teased.

"Just checking," she ribbed him.

"May I not boast, but if Kelly and I hadn't broken up, I'd have armed her with more ammunition to pursue her own vice. As things turned out, her pain propelled her to get help. She hit rock-bottom and took a hard look at her life. I'm glad she's on the mend."

"Was that what you were trying to tell me the night you came over?" She sounded subdued.

"Yes."

"I am sorry," she said, softly. The magnitude of the pain she caused him astonished her. She marveled that she had so much power over one man, but more so, she marveled at the grace that had bolstered her to stay, when she had planned to move on.

"No. It was my fault. I should've been a man from the beginning. Lily, I value you. Can you forgive me?"

"I already have," she replied.

As if by miracle, George Strait's voice started crooning, *"I Cross My Heart."* Wouldn't you know it!

As the last note died, Paul's chains fell off, freeing him from societal expectations and leaving him only one obligation——to live by grace, supported by Lily's love.

He drove past her exit to Hollenvine Hills and stopped at the top of the hill. The street lights above glowed and together with the nearby new middle-class homes that once used to be coyote playground, provided that feeling of security.

They sat in silence for seemingly long, but it was only minutes, really.

"This is my lair," he said. "I often come here when I feel alone. I get the impression that some people believe I'm this awful philanderer——always out looking for reckless fun, but this is my retreat. Ever since I became a follower, I've tried to honor the Lord as best I can, with His help. It's not easy to be an only child. Here, I can hear the coyotes, and gaze at the stars and converse with the Lord, alone."

"It is beautiful."

He thanked her.

They permitted their silent camaraderie to bind them, as they enjoyed the view. Finally, he said, "We've come full circle, haven't we?"

"I believe we have," she replied.

"Lily, I'm not perfect, as you already know. I deeply regret walking away so insensibly. At least, I should've given you the courtesy of an explanation that day and I'd have preferred to have introduced myself to your family first. I've regretted it deeply. If this is of any comfort, I learnt a lot as a result and I believe I've a better grasp of commitment. Your choosing the Lord over me, forced me to re-evaluate my priorities. I promise to do the best I can, with the Lord's help and if you'll give me another chance?"

"And you promise not to put me on a pedestal? I'm also not perfect."

"None of us is. I still love you!" he said, adamant.

"I too depend on grace. Without the Lord, where would I be? At first, it was hard and I was uncertain about the future, but I decided to trust Him, and complete my PhD."

He started. "You did what?"

"I'm afraid I did."

"You amaze me. Congratulations! I'm proud of you."

She thanked him. "I was waiting for your engagement to be announced."

"Engagement?" he scoffed. "What else aren't you telling me, Lily?"

"That's it. Everybody assumed you had chosen Kelly and you were engaged, I respected that and I thought it was time to move on. I had planned to relocate after graduating, so I was surprised and scared when you started singling me out again. I thought you were toying with me."

"I can't believe I was going to lose you based on rumors! Kelly meant nothing to me, outside of being one of God's children. And, I could never toy with you. From the onset, I never thought of you as someone to toy with. I was afraid. You caught me off guard, but very pleasantly so."

"Please forgive me for clamming up and not releasing my pain sooner."

"I have. I know you were reacting to how I'd treated you."

"You are right. Promise you will give me room to grow."

He placed her hands on his heart. "I promise."

For a moment, Paul struggled with the memory of the agony of the months past, then he rallied and drove Lily back to her condo. He did not linger after seeing her safely inside, instead, he asked her out for a drive to the beach on Sunday afternoon.

"My parents are holding their annual spring party. I thought you might enjoy it."

"I would love to come. Thank you."

"And, thank you! Good night." He kissed her hand. "Until tomorrow."

♦ ♦ ♦

Paul drove up Country Club Terrace Drive. His worries of many months had melted. Somehow, he knew all would be well. Lily was worth all the pain and the waiting that he had been through. Was he worthy of her love?

Instinctively, he knew——he did not need to be worthy; but true. Being true meant he should have faith that should he fail, she would forgive him. She was that kind of woman——she understood him and knew his weaknesses, yet, she still loved him.

He went straight to his balcony and faced the direction of Lily's condo. Months of his pent-up emotions dissolved, as his despair gave way to hope——the hope of a man who had experienced the Lord's restorative grace. He was free to love Lily and in learning to love her, had learnt abiding love.

He took out a twenty-four-karat gold box from his inner coat pocket and opened it. A classic solitaire diamond engagement ring glittered back at him. He had already arranged to travel to East Africa to ask Mr. Abrafimqodesh's permission to marry Lily. "Lord, grant me favor," he prayed.

In the distance, the howling of a lone coyote——lone wolf——faded, and nearby, a nightingale serenaded the night.

Paul gazed at the same city lights with the eyes of a new man who had sought and found the Light. "Wherever I go, wherever I make my home, I'll always walk in the Light, never alone again!"

I J E Okello was born in Lango District, Uganda. She studied Commerce (Business) at Makerere University, Uganda and liberal arts at Azusa Pacific University, California. She later got an MBA from California Polytechnic University and went on to work as an analyst. She continues to live in the United States of America.

www.ingramcontent.com/pod-product-compliance
Lightning Source LLC
Chambersburg PA
CBHW070149310726
48976CB00001B/38